GALICIA DIVISION

THE WAFFEN-SS 14TH GRENADIER DIVISION 1943-1945

GALICIA DIVISION

THE WAFFEN-SS 14TH GRENADIER DIVISION 1943-1945

Michael O. Logusz

Schiffer Military History
Atglen, PA

Note: Throughout the text and notes an asterix* refers to the use of a pseudonym.

Book Design by Robert Biondi.

We are interested in hearing from authors with book ideas on related topics.

Published by Schiffer Publishing Ltd.
4880 Lower Valley Road
Atglen, PA 19310
Phone: (610) 593-1777
FAX: (610) 593-2002
E-mail: Schifferbk@aol.com.
Please write for a free catalog.
This book may be purchased from the publisher.
Please include $3.95 postage.
Try your bookstore first.

CONTENTS

Introduction

10 May 1945

"Just moments ago, I laid my rifle down. For a true soldier, this is not an easy task. I now truly understand the sadness my father experienced when his battered but proud and undefeated Galician Army surrendered. But orders are orders! And as I part with my rifle, I part with a true friend. We first met at Heidelager. Both of us were new to the army. Since then, we have gone through an ordeal that only those who have attempted it would understand. Together, we laughed and cried. We trained, ducked live bullets, bombs and shells and we marched many hundreds of miles through heat, snow, mountains and plateaus. Indeed, we experienced life as few will ever know. And although I am saddened to leave you, I am glad that your master is dead. I know the Americans are a decent lot of Christian men. We hope they will treat us well.

I hear a whistle. I must fall in for formation. Soon, we will march down the road into American hands. My next entry will be from captivity."

With these words, the young Ukrainian soldier unwittingly made the final entry in his diary. Although he probably would have written more, upon entering American captivity he was searched. As a prisoner-of-war, his diary was confiscated by his captors.

Undoubtedly, the American soldier who returned home following the deactivation of his unit had no real understanding of whom he had taken prisoner and what he stood for. But it doesn't matter. Placed into a duffel bag, the diary traveled half-way around the world and ended up the American Midwest. There, it was placed into an air-tight trunk, which ended up in the attic of a veteran's home.

Years and decades passed. In 1985, the trunk was opened and its contents were placed upon a table at a garage sale. For the next several days, the diary lay on the table waiting for a buyer to come along.

Driving his van through the small mid western town's main street, a Texas gun dealer spotted the sale. He probably would have continued to drive on, but when by chance he noted a table with some World War II artifacts, he pulled over. Spotting the diary, he picked it up but was unable to read it. Because the American veteran who had originally brought the diary had passed away several years earlier, and neither his wife nor daughter had any knowledge of its contents, they were unable to assist him.

The dealer might have just left it behind. But a well-preserved photograph taped to the well-preserved manuscript inside cover caught the dealer's eyes. Of exceptional quality possibly taken by a private photographer sometime in the latter part of 1943 in the Eastern Galician capital city of Lviv, the photo revealed a handsome young man posing in a crisp, new uniform. Because every detail was immaculately clear, the Texan must have also noted the soldier's Divisional patch with its lion and three crowns displayed on both his collar and uniform sleeve. Deciding to purchase the diary, he handed the ladies a $5.00 bill and drove away.

Upon returning to Texas, the dealer placed the diary in a glass display case. In the ensuing months, various sportsmen, gun collectors, World War II memorabilists, and other dealers thumbed through it. No one knew what it was. But one day, an Arkansas dealer came by. A collector of souvenirs and memorabilia of the Third Reich's foreign units, he purchased the diary from the dealer.

At first, his intention was to take the diary to a local university's language department where, he hoped, someone would be able to translate it. In the meantime, someone told him it probably came from a "Russian Vlasovite." Satisfied for the moment with such an answer and preparing for an upcoming knife and gun show, the dealer packed the diary into his truck, and drove to Columbus, Georgia.

As a U.S. Army Special Forces (Green Beret) friend and I slowly made our way through a noisy crowd within a coliseum packed with hundreds of tables exhibiting a wide range of collectibles, I noted a table with some books on Hitler's foreign legions. None were in depth, but while glancing through one of author Andrew Mollo's insignia books, my Special Forces friend turned to me and said "Over there. Look at that!" He pointed to several authentic Latvian sleeve shields within a plastic envelope. Next to the Latvian sleeve shields, other foreign sleeve shields were exhibited, as well as various helmets, an authentic Muslim 'fez' cap from the 13th Waffen-SS 'Handschar' Division, and other foreign artifacts. It was then that I spotted the diary.

Opening its hard cover, I noted the photograph on the inside cover. Beautifully maintained with every detail in order, the diaries pages were also in good condition. From the soldier's handwriting, I concluded that the diary was that of an educated person. My observation proved correct when I soon learned that prior to his enlistment into the Division, he had studied engineering for two years.

For the next two hours, I simply read. The information and detail were awesome. "Yesiree. He sure kept a good log!" exclaimed the collector in his western drawl. Meticulously dated, the diary was divided into various chapters: the recruitment phase, training at Heidelager and Neuhammer, Brody, Czechoslovakia and Austria. Although it appears he did not participate with Kampfgruppe "Beyersdorff" in late February and March 1944, references were made to these actions. Unfortunately, I do not remember the soldier's name. But his account began several days before his departure on 20 July 1943 to Heidelager. (If I recall correctly, the date was 15 July 1943). He wrote about six pages on life in Lviv under the Soviet and Nazi occupations, and his reason for enlistment. Officially, he started his log on 20 July on the train enroute to Heidelager.

Indeed, it was a truly moving tale. As I carefully read the diary, I noted that it was not only written in an interesting style but likewise, well documented with dates. And as I read the Division's history I experienced moments of laughter, sorrow and, on several occasions, I was almost moved to tears. From beginning to end, the diary captivates the reader.

Looking up, I again asked the collector "how much?" In his slow drawl, he replied "young man, as I have already told you, things like that are not sold!" Though I offered top dollar, the dealer refused to sell but inquired as to why the interest in the diary.

I told the dealer that this soldier was not a "Russian Vlasovite." While explaining who the soldier had been, I reached for a book on the various foreign units found in the armies of the Third Reich. Opening to the page which showed the various divisional patches, I compared the soldier's lion collar patch as well as the "Galicia" Division's lion sleeve shield with its three crowns displayed on his uniform to that of the Divisional lion patch exhibited in the book. "Well, I'll be damned!" was the collector's reply.

So who was this young soldier? What did he represent? Why did he enlist?

Following the collapse of Nazi Germany, the Waffen-SS, an army independent of Germany's Wehrmacht but always under the Wehrmacht's command at the front when committed into combat, was immediately investigated by Allied authorities. Well before the basic investigations had even been concluded, it became evident that a very high percentage of the Waffen-SS – no less than fifty percent – were composed of foreign personnel.

While, of course, many reasons may be cited as to why so many non-Germans served within the Waffen-SS, for the greater part these non-Germans fought not to protect Hitler's national-socialism but rather, served only to defend their loved ones and homelands from Soviet Russia's communist domination, which trailed a history of brutalities. In addition, a number of foreign personnel entered German service to improve their position under Nazi occupation. For some, enlistment was the only way to resist and counter Nazi rule.

Regardless, to write on any aspect of the Waffen-SS was, and still is, a complex task. Professor George Stein's work *Hitler's Elite Guard: the Waffen-SS*, is testament to that. Stein's book, regarded by many as one of the first true objective studies of the Waffen-SS in the English language, was published twenty years after World War II. Unfortunately, Professor Stein (along with the other authors of that period), who attempted to portray the Waffen-SS objectively, did not have – nor could they have had at that time – much of the accurate information which is currently available on this subject. As a result, much fascinating information was never presented and a number of mistakes were made. However, these earlier authors must be highly complimented for their noble attempts to portray objectively such a highly controversial topic with limited resources.

In this book, I have attempted to capture one such military force – the 14th "Galicia" Division, known also in the concluding months of the war as the "1st Ukrainian Division of the Ukrainian National Army."[1] But I also felt that in order to fully understand why such a force evolved, it is important to understand the events – but especially the tragic events – which contributed to the rise of the Ukrainian "Galicia" Division. As a result a brief, but somewhat detailed history of European and world events, is presented.

When I began this project, I received some support, assistance and sympathy from various people; simultaneously, there were also a number of those (including some very close to me), who denounced my efforts and encouraged me to stop. As a result, I did. For a period of no less than six months, I didn't write a thing. Papers, manuscripts, and copies of archival World War II orders and documents were given away, lost, or thrown away. During those six months, I did do some writing, but mostly on a fictitious ex-Army Ranger turned mercenary and anti-drug enforcer by the name of Michael Louis Brycker. After all – trash does sell.

Introduction

But one day, as I browsed through a book store underneath one of the twin towers in the lower part of Manhattan, I entered its military history section. As I fumbled through books and military magazines, I noted the objectivity of the current writers as they wrote about World War II battles, and even credited certain German and Japanese units, such as General Heilmann's 5th Paratroop Division in the Ardennes during the Battle of the Bulge in late 1944 and early 1945, for their bravery and stamina under adverse conditions.

Not one writer (such as the late U.S. Army General S.L. Marshall, a former World War II European combat veteran), presented anything from a pro-Nazi or Fascist point of view. On the contrary, everything was presented in an objective manner. As I thumbed through various topics, including a couple of works on the Waffen-SS, I began to wonder "Why can't I do the same?"

Days later, I dropped into the main Central Research Library on 5th Avenue and 42nd Street. As I sat in the Slavic division reading room, I noticed an older man enter. In his trembling hands, he held a blue colored book. I noted its yellow title – "UPA."[2] Because I was sitting close to the reception desk, I could not help but to overhear the conversation.

In broken English, the man asked, nay, pleaded, for the librarian to place the book into its system. "Perhaps, someday, someone will benefit from it." Kindly informed by the librarian that she would enter it into the system the elder man thanked her and stepped out into the hallway. I returned to my reading.

My curiosity piqued, I stood up and stepped out into the hallway. Attracting his attention by a simple "excuse me," I then asked him what this book was all about.

The man told me that he had brought in the book so that someone could possibly learn something about Ukraine, its people and its history. It is important, he declared, to spread our history and traditions among all people "so that those who died in its struggle will not have perished in vain."

"Why?" I asked. "And what do you mean?" His eyes clouding over with sadness, he told me how his one and only older brother had died in Volyn in the spring of 1943 while conducting a raid on a Nazi police center. His brother, along with some other guerrillas, had made a failed but desperate attempt to free those imprisoned and marked for execution by Nazi rule.

At this time, I told him that I had once published an article in a magazine about the UPA. He then asked me if I had ever written anything else. I replied that I once started some writings on the "Galicia" Division, but had stopped. He remarked that the Division had a fascinating history but it is virtually untold and someday, someone must present it. He encouraged me to finish it.

Returning home, I could not forget the older man, nor his words. As I sat by

11

my desk, rereading parts of Brycker's anti-drug exploits in Queens, N.Y., I could not forget my conversation with the older man. Folding up the papers, I put Brycker away, and began to recover what papers, military orders, documents, etc., that I had. I knew that he was right. If other writers are currently delving into the history of World War II in a manner that at one time was unthinkable, and even unpermissable, why can't I? Besides, someone needed to reveal at last the ordeals of that young soldier found in the diary.

My project began well over 40 years after the conclusion of the Second World War, and my suspicions that this undertaking would be no easy task proved to be correct. Written and factual information is available but for the most part it is scattered about in bits and pieces, frequently in foreign languages, and largely unpublished. National and regional borders have changed. Cities, towns, and villages that existed at one time, along with whole regions, either disappeared or were amalgamated into other states. With the re-emergence of the search for suspected war criminals residing in the west, such an activity also makes it difficult for anyone to conduct any research in a free manner. As a result, a number of the Division's veterans were hesitant or unresponsive to any requests for assistance, including even those who had conflicts with Nazi authorities and witnessed the destruction of family members by the Gestapo, Police SS and other Nazi agencies. Most of my writing was done prior to the collapse of the Soviet Union. It was still easy to falsely accuse individuals, men or women, of alleged "war crimes" in Eastern Europe and, along with state supplied "eyewitnesses" and "evidence," commence procedures. Therefore, I can understand war veterans reasons for any hesitancy to speak openly about the past.

In order to accomplish any kind of mission, one needs the advice, assistance and knowledge of others. This is especially true in undertaking a project such as this one.

Former Divisional staff officer Yuriy Krokhmaliuk provided me with much valuable information. I first met Yuriy in October 1987. As we conversed, I wondered how he felt about my project. I would soon find out.

On the following morning, Krokhmaliuk's wife told me that after our discussion, Yuriy was up until 2 a.m. assembling numerous papers, military orders and archival documents found in his collection. When I entered Yuriy's study, he immediately proclaimed that "yesterday, you asked me questions that should have been asked thirty years ago." I had my answer.

For the next two days, we talked incessantly. Nothing was left uncovered. With tremendous patience and true professionalism, Yuriy answered all of my questions, as well as translating a number of documents and military orders. We also discussed in extensive detail the issue of war crimes, and the numerous allegations made against the Division. At no time was I afraid to ask sensitive questions nor did Yuriy refuse to discuss any matter in depth.

From Yuriy, I also obtained numerous copies of military orders, documents and letters. Yuriy had been obtaining these materials from archival sources located in Western Germany. As mentioned earlier, he did make an effort to translate, but because there was so much material everything could not be handled. Later, others would also provide me with additional orders and documents. Soon, I was more than swamped.

Yuriy Krokhmaliuk's brother, Roman, also assisted me. Although he was never in the Division, Roman was a member of its Military Board. Along with Yuriy, he filled me in on the role and mission of the Military Board, its relation to the Division, and the problems and difficulties the Military Board encountered. Roman also provided me with photographs and negatives which, to the best of my knowledge, are seen here for the first time.

Besides the Krokhmaliuk brothers, there were others. Among them is William "Bill" Nasi. A first-rate historian, Bill possesses some of the most clever skills of researching and obtaining information on historical matters. This is especially true when he deals with matters pertaining to espionage, intelligence/counter-intelligence, and the combat factors which affect everything. Bill is the type of person who can tell you many things about various Allied and Axis World War II leaders. He offered fascinating insights into 20th century European events, as well as the events which occurred in Berlin, Moscow, and within the inner strata of the NKVD, Gestapo, SS, SD and so forth. On more than one occasion I would call Bill and ask "who is so-and-so." If he did not have the answer immediately, he would have it within a few hours. "Thanks Bill."

Retired Colonel Harold "Harry" Belil also assisted me. A former jump-qualified Marine corporal who participated in the successful breakout of the 1st Marine Division in the frozen mountains of North Korea's Chosin Reservoir, Colonel Belil at one time also edited and published *New Breed* magazine. In the 1980s, he kindly published some of my articles on Airborne, desert combat training, and a detailed article on the Ukrainian UPA insurgency. A first rate military historian, Belil provided me with books and information on the Second World War, the Waffen-SS, and much positive guidance. Colonel Belil, thank you, "Airborne All the Way, Semper Fidelis and forever, Shalom!"

Another former Marine veteran, Anthony "Tony" Munoz, provided me with much information on Germany's foreign legions. Also a first-rate military historian, Munoz especially specializes in the complex pre-World War II and World

War II events which led to the rise of the many foreign legions found later within Nazi Germany's military. Tony's book, *The Forgotten Legions: Obscure Formations of the Waffen-SS, 1943-45*, is a classic. "Thanks, Tony, Airborne All the Way and Semper Fidelis!"

Noted historian Hugh Page Taylor provided me with much guidance, factual information and assistance. Author of the series *Uniforms, Organization, and History of the Waffen-SS*, Mr. Taylor kindly contributed much of his time to read parts of my writings and to offer constructive comments. Through his lengthy letters, Mr. Taylor assisted me tremendously and opened new trails for research and knowledge.

In Ft. Benning, Georgia, the U.S. Army's Infantry Center, with its phenomenal military library in Building No. 4, provided me with tremendous assistance and information which simply, is not yet available in any other location. Virtually unknown is the fact that during World War II, Germany's Waffen-SS and its foreign units were extensively studied by the U.S. Army's intelligence service. And by no means was the "Galicia" Division excluded. With the kind and professional assistance of Ft. Benning's library staff, I was able to obtain and present information which no longer is classified and is available to the general public. Retired 1st Sergeant Richard Cunningham, a former Vietnam combat engineer and one of the curators of the library, was of exceptional help. Mr. Cunningham copied pages of fascinating information and helped me to locate much material. To him and the rest, I owe many thanks and my sincerest appreciation.

The U.S. Army's Armor School Library and Professional Center, located in Harris Hall (Bldg. 2368), Fort Knox, Kentucky, also harbors a wealth of information. Among its numerous books and military documents, I found valuable information. The library's curator, Mr. William Hanson, is assisted with a highly professional and dedicated staff. Amongst them are Ms. Janice Kendall and Ms. Gladys Burton. Both were of exceptional assistance. When Ms. Kendall was informed of my research topic, she came up with information that was buried for decades. And I will never forget the site of Ms. Burton sitting at the computer searching to locate for me the whereabouts of a particular book, military document, or journal. In the following chapters, one will note the numerous Soviet combat accounts. Ms. Burton played an instrumental role in locating these accounts among the various civilian libraries, military academies, and the U.S. Army and Air Force bases. To these kind-hearted individuals and Ft. Knox, I express my deepest gratitude.

Colonel (Retired) David M. Glantz, former Director of the U.S. Army's Soviet Army Studies Office located in Ft. Leavenworth, Kansas, was of exceptional help. An expert on the Soviet military and the German-Soviet War of 1941-1945,

Introduction

Colonel Glantz offered me much valuable assistance. His book, "The Soviet Conduct of Tactical Maneuver: Spearhead of the Offensive" is a classic and explains in depth the evolution of Soviet forward detachments and their role in both the defense and offense such as in the period of World War II. When I informed Colonel Glantz that I planned to write a highly detailed book on the Ukrainian "Galicia" Division, Colonel Glantz' immediate response was "Captain, it's about time! Do it! And if you need any help, give me a call!"

I did. And whenever I called or wrote to Colonel Glantz, his response was immediate. Colonel Glantz gave me information on what transpired on the eastern front, especially in the area of the Western Ukraine in the years 1943-1944; his kind assistance enabled me to firmly grasp the critical sequence of events occurring in the summer of 1944 on the eastern front. Consequently, I developed a more comprehensive – and clearer – understanding of the major and minor circle of events evolving around the Ukrainian "Galicia" Division during its period of combat in July 1944. Sir, thank you, and the best to you, especially in your future writings.

Former Divisional soldier, Mr. Vasyl Veryha, is a first rate Divisional historian and one of the defenders of the Division during the war crimes allegations raised against it. He painstakingly read my writings and provided me with much encouragement. In addition to being fluent in the English language, Mr. Veryha is also proficient in German and several Slavic languages. These language skills assist him tremendously in his on-going research and writings pertaining to the Division. Mr. Veryha also closely monitors current events in Eastern Europe. But most importantly, through his persistent research and usage of original archival sources and facts, he has successfully countered the many false accusations perpetrated against the Division. Thank you, Mr. Veryha.

And Mr. Roman Kolisnyk, who also served in the Division, was of exceptional help. After reading my final draft, Mr. Kolisnyk provided me a considerable amount of additional information. But most importantly, Mr. Kolisnyk provided me the names of some former Divisional soldiers who had excellent non-published war-time accounts. After establishing contact with these former Divisional soldiers, I was able to obtain information which is not only fascinating but enabled me to analyze and understand certain Divisional events in a clearer manner. I am deeply grateful to Mr. Kolisnyk.

My dear friend, Luba, read, edited, and improved my original manuscripts. A certified Slavic translator, Luba carefully translated more than one Slavic account. Totally devoted to the publication of this work, Luba put many hours of labor into this project and she encouraged me immensely. "Thanks, Luba!"

Galicia Division

Lastly, I thank my publisher Robert Biondi and Schiffer Publishing Ltd. for accepting my manuscript. Since this is also my first book, I am very grateful to Mr. Biondi for his kind patience and concerns.

In my travels with the elite Rapid Deployment Force, I had the opportunity to meet some very interesting – and truly fascinating – individuals. One such person was Oleh Dir.*[3], a former Divisional infantry/UPA fighter who has since retired from a western military service. Dir and I met by chance. How we met doesn't matter but behind Dir's piercing blue eyes lay a story untold for over 40 years. Had I not been the officer-in-charge of an Army pistol, rifle, and machine gun competition team, and had I not been a military man, Dir would have never spoken to me. As he stated "it's difficult and useless to talk to those who haven't been there." I fully agree.

At his residence in a very rural area, we spoke for the first five or six hours about various Army tournaments, new methods of firing, shooting teams and other pertinent subjects. But after his wife turned in for the night, Dir remarked to me "earlier, you mentioned to me that you might possibly be doing some writings on exotic and little known military topics." It was then that he told me that he had served in the "Galicia" Division, and he wanted me to take down his story for possible usage in any future writings.

Stepping out to my Bronco truck to obtain a yellow note pad, I felt slightly drowsy. Although it was approximately 10 p.m., I reasoned that within an hour or so, I would wrap this up. Stepping back into the house, I noted Dir was making coffee and sandwiches. Clearly, he had something to say.

Within minutes, I was fully awake. Dir told me things that fascinated me. He showed me a journal which only his wife had seen previously. Until 4 a.m., I listened and took down careful notes. Retiring for the remainder of the night, at first I could not even sleep as I was so overwhelmed with his story.

Rising at noon, I came downstairs and sat in the kitchen. As I drank the coffee provided by Dir's kind wife, I watched Dir through a patio window. Swinging an ax, he was chopping firewood. He had already been up since 8 a.m. His wife stated "he doesn't require much sleep." As we sipped our coffee and watched him, she also remarked "you know, I sometimes wonder what goes on in his mind." So do I. For Dir and his uncle, I have told their remarkable stories.

In my book, I have also examined the "Galicia" Division through a source never utilized before – the UPA. It is virtually unknown that within the UPA's intelligence, there existed a section which monitored the Division. Organized in April 1943, this section was headed by Ostap Vashchenko.*

Introduction

Born in Lviv in 1910, Vashchenko experienced life under various occupants and regimes. By the time he was a teenager, Vashchenko knew (as he himself stated), "how to keep your eyes open, your ears open, how to quickly analyze a situation, and how to keep your mouth shut!" Proficient in eight languages – among them German, English and Hebrew, Vashchenko was educated in Galicia and Austria. After completing his education, Vashchenko travelled throughout Europe. Upon his return to Lviv in late 1938, he joined the Polish Army. Following recruit training, Vashchenko was transferred to the field of intelligence; thus becoming one of the limited number of Ukrainians to serve in that nation's intelligence.

With the destruction of his unit in the 1939 German blitzkrieg, Vashchenko made his way to Cracow, Poland. There, an OUN (Organization of Ukrainian Nationalists) confident offered him a change of clothes, a new identity, and safe passage to Lviv, a city then under Soviet occupation.

In Lviv, Vashchenko never resided at home. "After all, it was too dangerous!" Shortly after the Nazi arrival and the birth of the UPA, Vashchenko entered its intelligence cell. Along with the UPA's expansion, Vashchenko quickly rose in rank and stature. He served in the UPA's upper echelons, and frequently briefed the UPA's top commanding officer, General (alias Taras Chuprynka) Shukhevych. And Vashchenko was one of those who encouraged Shukhevych to utilize the "Galicia" Division for the UPA's needs.

From this former intelligence officer, I learned what I had always suspected – that the UPA had totally infiltrated the Division; indeed, the operation was so secretive that none of the UPA's "plants" ever knew each other's identity. At the very most, a fellow infiltrator knew the identity of only one or two others (and even that was an exception). As Vashchenko himself stated "there was a military reason for this. We knew the SD and Gestapo was monitoring the Division. Had one of our individual's been captured or, for some reason switched sides knowing the identity of the others, he would have revealed that we had thoroughly infiltrated the Division from its independent companies right up to Divisional staff. In their anger, the Germans might have even disbanded the Division. And if this had happened, we would have lost our access to conventional training, intelligence, and critically needed arms and equipment. Therefore, we had to be constantly on guard."

In the 1944 Battle of Brody, Vashchenko lost some of his best operatives; yet, information continued to pour in. Even when the Division was interned in Italy and England in the postwar period, accurate information came in. The UPA's operatives not only observed and monitored the Division, but also the Gestapo agents whose mission was to counter any insurgent activities within the Division. Psychological warfare was waged at its best. When from Cracow the UPA learned that a certain Gestapo officer's wife was cheating on her husband, Vashchenko ordered that one of her letters be intercepted. Afterward, the UPA's counter-intelligence duplicated a false letter. Utilizing the woman's style of writing, color of ink, paper and envelope size, the forged letter, through Gestapo channels, was forwarded to her husband. So overwhelmed was the Gestapo agent by his "wife's words" that he immediately requested an emergency leave. He never returned.

Although in his seventies, Vashchenko's mind is still clear. One immediately senses that his eyes and mind analytically penetrate not only a question but like-wise, those with whom he speaks. I met him through a former Divisional soldier who at one time served as one of Vashchenko's operatives. Because Vashchenko arranged his "death" and Soviet authorities believe he was killed in Ukraine in 1952, the former guerrilla intelligence officer has always kept his identity a secret. For many years even his wife was unaware of his activities in the UPA. But now, in his latter years, Vashchenko feels he must reveal the UPA's role within the Division. With utmost respect, I am including the Division's history as seen through the eyes of the UPA.

During my research, a number of people assisted me with advice, information, translations, World War II letters, orders, documents, and various types of pertinent material. None of these people have ever advocated, believed in, or es-poused any form of Nazism or Fascism. In a number of cases, they have not only lost family members but were themselves victims of Nazi rule. Others, born in the years following World War II, never had a chance to know a certain grandfather, grandmother, uncle, aunt, brother or sister as a result of Nazi rule. But for personal and professional reasons, most have requested anonymity. I understand their concerns and respect their desires. But I shall always remain grateful.

In my writings, I have also tried to capture the human factor. I felt that as of date, no one has ever adequately portrayed the "Galicia" Division's human side. Contrary to what the Division's critics claim, Divisional soldiers also had feelings. They were subjected to arrests, brutalities, torture, and death; they witnessed the destruction of family, loved ones and friends at the hands of both the Soviets and Nazis. They experienced fear, sorrow, grief, hunger and thirst. In a number of cases, Divisional soldiers not only had fathers, mothers, brothers, sisters and loved ones taken away and destroyed by either the Soviet NKVD or Hitler's Gestapo or SS, but they themselves experienced periods of incarceration. In combat, Divisional soldiers experienced the terrifying sounds of incoming bombs and shells. They witnessed brothers, cousins, and close comrades loved no more or less than a family member torn apart by bullets, shrapnel, bomb bursts or enemy bayonets. They saw fellow soldiers being executed for infractions that were simply overlooked in other armies, and they experienced the loneliness, boredom, fear and anxiety of post-war imprisonment. Simply put, each and every Divisional soldier had his share of tragedies.

Combat, but especially close-in combat, is brutal. In the following pages, a reader will find a number of combat accounts. These accounts were obtained from former Divisional soldiers, from the currently published Ukrainian military journal "Visti Kombatanta," and from interviews conducted with some of the Divisional soldiers by American Army authorities who, in the immediate aftermath of World War II, began to intensively study the German-Soviet conflict and Eastern Front experience in the event of a possible conflict with Red Russia (as perceived at that time prior to the termination of the Cold War).

Some of the accounts might be difficult to believe; others might question the necessity of including them. But because I wanted to capture the full human spectrum, I felt it was necessary to insert these accounts. In the following pages, readers will finally witness what every Divisional soldier experienced decades before.

In my writings, I did not cover the Division's prisoner-of-war history, which initially was my intent. I chose not to include a chapter on this subject because the topic merits a separate book in its own right.

I had no desire or intention to write a chapter on the issue of war crimes. But because I was asked for some research assistance in this matter, and because I felt that as of date no one has adequately examined this issue in relation to the Division, I began to do so. Ultimately, I realized the necessity of including such a chapter was to protect myself. Now no one can imply or accuse me of deliberately avoiding the topic or of unearthing pertinent evidence and for whatever reason, deliberately excluding it.

With regard to war crimes, I want to make it absolutely clear that had I uncovered any crimes, or what may be perceived as such, I assure my readers that I would have inserted it without a moment's hesitation. In my discussions with Messers Yuriy Krokhmaliuk and Veryha, I informed them that in the event I came across anything, it would be presented. "Go right ahead," were their replies.

In the very end, nearly half of my research time and energies were devoted alone to this issue. Through a friend of mine who holds a senior position within an American police agency, I established contact with a high ranking officer within the Royal Canadian Mounted Police (RCMP) and made a special trip to Canada. I have no regrets that I did so.

Galicia Division

However, as I continued to work on this chapter, I came across so much information and material that I began to realize that even a condensed chapter would easily turn into a very sizable one. Indeed, as the information accumulated and I began to add more and more, I began to realize that even one large chapter would fail to properly cover the issue of war crimes pertaining to the Division. Factually speaking, to properly examine the various accusations, numerous pages would be required.

So I decided to do this: instead of writing a very lengthy chapter, detailed references would be made regarding the various accusations. For the greater part, these references were inserted in footnotes.

As for the future, I plan to produce a work which will examine not only the allegations made against the Division, but what really lies behind the accusations; how certain nations benefitted (or continue to benefit) from "war crimes;" what Canada's various ethnic communities experienced during this time, and so forth. Along with these accusations, a detailed examination of the World War II European holocaust, especially in relation to Ukraine, Galicia, and Eastern Europe, will be presented.

In the following pages, readers will note a number of photgraphs. Among the photographs, a number of personnel are seen. In some of these photographs, the clearly visible slanted "SS" (the lightning bolt designation for the "SS"), is seen. It is important to point out that among the non-German (foreign) personnel, it was exclusively forbidden for them to wear the "SS" runes. In the place of the "SS" runes, foreign personnel could only wear their national insignia – in the case of the "Galicia" Division, the golden lion encompassed with three crowns, which was the traditional coat of arms of the Galician principality.

Yet in a number of photographs, the "SS" runes are clearly visible. Readers must understand that within the foreign units of the Wehrmacht and Waffen-SS, German personnel – both cadre and attached advisors – were found. And by no means was the "Galicia" Division an exception. Therefore, readers must keep in mind that those soldiers pictured wearing the "SS" runes (a symbol, incidentally, despised by most Ukrainians), were either German personnel who were posted into the "Galicia" Division from other Waffen-SS formations or, they were non-Divisional Waffen-SS personnel who just happened to be at a particular place among Divisional soldiers when a particular photograph was taken. With regard to rank, the Division's non-German personnel were not authorized to use the "SS" title preceding a rank. For example – a German Waffen-SS officer, who held a rank comparable to that of a 1st Lieutenant in the Wehrmacht, was titled and addressed as an "SS-Obersturmführer." But in the case of the non-German personnel, "Waffen-

Introduction

Obersturmführer" (or simply "Obersturmführer"), was only authorized.

It is important to note that amongst themselves, the Division's Ukrainian personnel strictly utilized their own native titles when addressing one another. While, of course, on occasion there were exceptions to this (if, for example, higher ranking German personnel were amongst them or during an official ceremony, etc.), excluding such moments, native ranks and titles were exclusively used.

In the following pages, readers will also note that I used the non-German rank structure from the period of approximately mid-1943 until April 1945. From April to May 1945, I strictly used rank titles as those found in western terminology.

The reason for this is that until virtually the conclusion of the war, non-German Waffen-SS titles were officially used within the Division on various orders, documents, etc. So for purposes of both accuracy and clarity, I kept the rank titles as they were used. But readers will also note that in the final pages of the book, non-Waffen-SS rank titles are exclusively used. The reason for this is that in the concluding weeks of the war, the Division ceased to be a Waffen-SS formation; therefore, its Waffen-SS titles were immediately – and officially – dropped and Ukrainian Army ranks were instead incorporated. While I could have used transliterated Ukrainian military ranks and titles, for purposes of clarity, I simply substituted western rank titles comparable to the Ukrainian ones. (For example, "Lieutenant" for "Poruchnyk").

I did, however, make one exception. With regard to Divisional General Fritz Freitag's rank and title, reader's will note that I just utilized "general." The reason for this is that within the entire Waffen-SS most soldiers (both officer and enlisted), used (against Himmler's explicit orders), the term "general" instead of "SS-Brigadeführer" or whatever other SS title indicated a particular general's rank. Whenever the Division's soldiers addressed Freitag, the term "general" was usually used. So once again, for historical reasons and purposes of clarity, I simply went along with "general."

In the following pages, readers will note various spelling styles and transliterations made in regards to certain cities and regions. When I commenced my writing, on the international level spellings such as "Galicia," "Lvov" and "Kharkov" were still being utilized. With the re-establishment of an independent Ukrainian state in 1991, the traditional Ukrainian spellings of "Halychyna (for Galicia), "Lviv" and "Kharkiv" are slowly being incorporated into western terminology.

So I decided to do this. Although certain spellings such as "Galicia" and "Kiev" will remain for simplicity and clarity, I will only utilize the now internationally recognized spellings. These new spellings are also utilized by such respected journals and newspapers as the *National Geographic* and the *New York Times*. Hereafter, Ukrainian spellings will be mostly utilized.

Readers must understand that a number of the original German documents and orders have already been translated; therefore, I used them in their exact form. Not one word, or letter, was changed. But there were many other documents, letters, military orders, award/promotion certificates, etc., which I needed to have translated.

Regarding such translations, I acknowledge that they were conducted in an informal manner. However, I requested the services only of those who are totally proficient in the given language. I especially sought the services of language specialists and those with an expertise in World War II German military terminology. Frequently, I would sit alongside such persons as they translated. If I saw, or suspected in the least that anyone had difficulties or was not as proficient in a specific language as he or she claimed, I immediately ceased the translating and sought others. As well, everything that was translated was cross-translated by others to ensure accuracy. But one must keep in mind that until official certified translations are made, unofficial translations must be utilized.

At this time, I must thank my dear mother, Zenobia Logusz, for her constant inspirations. "Thanks, Mom!"

Finally, the words found in the following pages are exclusively my own. Although it remains for the reader to reach a final subjective conclusion in regards to the "Galicia" Division, ultimately, readers must understand that history itself – and not the Division's critics – will pass the final judgement upon the "Galicia" Division.

C'est la Guerre!

1

Hitler Attacks Russia!

SUNDAY. 22 June 1941. 0315 hours. **"FEUER!"**
Instantly, with the shout of this one-word command, the stillness of the hot summer night was shattered as thousands of artillery and rocket batteries unleashed their deadly salvos and rained shell after shell on Soviet Russia's forward positions. As exploding shells ripped men, fortifications and units' into pieces, the thunderous roar announced to the world the invasion of Soviet Russia and with it, the largest military land invasion in history.

Operation "Barbarossa," the code name of Nazi Germany's invasion of Soviet Russia, was the final result of much of Hitler's personal thinking. The Soviet state had to be invaded so that Communism could be destroyed (for Hitler considered it a threat to National-Socialism), and so that the German race could obtain the necessary "lebensraum" – or living space – in the east, together with its enormous potential in foodstuffs, industrial raw material and oil.

Barbarossa's plan called for a major drive into Western Russia with three major army groups. From the south, commencing with Southern Poland and Rumania, Field Marshall Gerd von Rundstedt's Army Group 'South' (or Army Group 'Ukraine'), was to advance through Ukraine, destroy all Soviet forces in its path and occupy Ukraine. From the center, starting with central and northern Poland, Field Marshall Fedor von Bock's Army Group 'Center' was to advance on Moscow, the administrative capital of the communist world. From East Prussia, Field Marshall Ritter von Leeb's Army Group 'North' was to strike through the Baltic States and link up with Baron Field Marshall Carl Mannerheim's Finnish forces.

Pushing southward into Russia from Finland, the combined force was to seize Leningrad. And from central and northern Finland, General Nikolaus von Falkenhorst's combined Finnish and German mountain troops were to strike eastward to cut Russia's vital Murmansk railway line. Altogether, a total of 162 German and satellite divisions were deployed for the invasion.[1]

Because none of the ground armies were completely armored or motorized, the panzer and motorized divisions were formed into four compact panzer units known as "panzergroups." The mission of these panzergroups was to race for their main objectives as rapidly as possible. Any bypassed, mauled and unengaged Soviet units were to be mopped-up by the slower advancing infantry and cavalry units. In as much as Germany's military could only deploy twelve panzergrenadier (mechanized) and nineteen panzer divisions,[2] five of which belonged to the Waffen-SS,[3] both the Wehrmacht's and Waffen-SS' armored and mechanized forces were called upon to perform a crucial military mission.

On the day of the invasion, the combined troop strength of Germany's 'Feldheer' was 3,800,000.[4] Of this figure, 160,405 represented the total strength of the Waffen-SS.[5] Of the combined forces, nearly 3,200,000 soldiers were used for Barbarossa[6] including almost the entire Waffen-SS.

The Waffen-SS

Historically, the organization of the Waffen-SS can be traced to the post-World War I period. For his personal protection and to drive his automobile, Hitler relied on a handful of thugs known as the "Chauffeureska." Realizing that a larger and stronger group would be required for the upcoming Munich Putsch of 9 November 1923, a new group – called "Stosstruppe Hitler" or "Shock Troop Hitler" – was organized. (The name of this group was derived from Germany's elite assault divisions which, in March 1918, had spearheaded Operation "Michael," Imperial Germany's last desperate military offensive). During the aborted Munich Putsch, "Stosstruppe Hitler" actually did very little other than ransack the offices of the social-democratic newspaper 'The Munich Post.'

After his failed attempt to seize power, Hitler was almost immediately imprisoned and "Stosstruppe Hitler" fell apart. A year after he was released from prison in December 1924, Hitler reformed and renamed the "Stosstruppe" into the "Schutz Staffeln" (Protective Squads) and, thus, the SS was officially established. Because the SS served to protect Hitler and Nazi Party speakers at public meetings, there was no need to maintain a large strength.[7] In January 1929, its strength did not exceed 280 men and no effort was undertaken to expand this tiny force.[8]

Chapter 1: Hitler Attacks Russia!

In April 1929, Hitler decided the SS needed bolder leadership. He relieved Konrad Heiden as commander of the organization and assigned an ex-chicken farmer named Heinrich Himmler[9] to head the SS. Under Himmler, the SS organization expanded rapidly. By January 1933, it exceeded 50,000 men.[10]

Soon, the SS outgrew its original function of serving solely as a bodyguard to Hitler. While, of course, much can be written about the various branches of the SS, the Waffen (Armed) SS was born on 17 March 1933 when Hitler's old comrade and former bodyguard, SS Gruppenführer Josef 'Sepp' Dietrich, formed the SS-Stabswache (Headquarters Security) Guard. Composed of 120 handpicked men,[11] this small elite paramilitary force became the Führer's personal bodyguard. In due time, it developed into the SS-Verfugungstruppen and the Waffen-SS. On 2 September 1933, Hitler publicly announced that the name of this unit would be the "Leibstandarte SS-Adolf Hitler."[12]

In the years between 1933 and 1939, armed sections of the SS gradually began appearing throughout Germany. Known as "Politische Bereitschaften" (politically prepared troops), these paramilitary units were initially the direct forerunners of the "SS-Verfugungstruppen" (SS-VT) or armed reserve troops. As such, they quickly developed into a secondary – and politically active – army. Units of the SS-VT participated in the occupation of Austria and the Sudetenland and by their actions, strengthened their position in Hitler's military.

Because the Wehrmacht, and not the Waffen-SS, was to be Nazi Germany's sole bearer of arms, Hitler never developed (nor intended to develop) the Waffen-SS into the armed strength that it would later achieve.[13] With Blitzkreig warfare rapidly overrunning Europe with few German casualties, there was no need to expand the small Waffen-SS. However, Hitler's eastern struggle would soon change everything.

Germany's Stalemate In Russia

Despite Soviet Russia's huge losses in men, material, tanks, aircraft and weapons, the Soviets not only managed to survive the initial Nazi attack but, on 6 December 1941, successfully launched a massive counteroffensive against Hitler's forces on the Moscow front. In a desperate attempt to rectify the collapsing tactical front line situation, Hitler's generals requested permission to retreat.[14]

Excluding some partial withdrawals, Hitler forbade any large scale retreats. The Führer argued that a retreat under winter conditions would finish off the armies. to reestablish and hold the front, self-contained "kampfgruppes" (battlegroups) would be used along with reserve, police, and other forces. But the front would be held! On Hitler's insistence many front line units, especially those of the Waffen-SS, held their positions through the cruel winter of 1941-42. By the spring of

1942, the fighting ability of the armed SS was not only clearly recognized by Germany's High Command but even by the Soviets. Determined to employ additional such units in upcoming eastern-front campaigns, Hitler began to expand the Waffen-SS.[15]

By the conclusion of 1941, Germans were no longer the only nationals serving within the Waffen-SS. For years, Heinrich Himmler and Gottlob Berger, Chief of the SS Main Office and the man in charge of Waffen-SS recruiting, had shown enthusiasm for foreign SS units. Soon, from the occupied countries, Danes, Dutch, Belgians; northern Europeans such as Finns, Swedes, and Norwegians, began to volunteer for Waffen-SS service. These volunteers were incorporated into special legions bearing their countries' names, as for example 'Flandern,' 'Niederlande,' and 'Norwegen.'

At first, Himmler only permitted "Nordics" to volunteer. While some foreign volunteers could be recruited from certain occupied nations, the numbers were truly insufficient to build the foreign units to divisional strength. The legions, which were meant to serve in action, made slow progress in completing their preparations. They hovered well below the minimum necessary for combat efficiency. The 5th SS "Wiking," a division to be formed from western Europeans and Scandinavians, is a prime example. At the outbreak of war with Russia, "Wiking" was so deficient in Scandinavian manpower that the bulk of that division had to be raised from Germans. Therefore, by the end of 1942, the SS leadership was forced to admit that the so-called "Nordic Alliance" was nothing but a failure. Yet manpower was needed not only to mobilize new SS divisions but also bring the existing ones, which had suffered heavy casualties, back up to their original strengths. Originally, the Waffen-SS was to be a small military elite detachment with strict German and northern European racial and physical requirements. But critical military needs, combined with the establishment of the 13th Yugoslavian "Handschar" Division in the spring of 1943, forced the Waffen-SS at last to disregard its "Nordic" theories.[16]

Germany's Plan For Galicia
Initially, the Hitler and Stalin Pact of 23 August 1939 had divided Eastern Europe and the Baltic States into German and Soviet spheres of influence. As for Galicia, Hitler and his foreign minister, Joachim von Ribbentrop, permitted that region to be annexed by the Soviet Union. Shortly afterwards, on 17 September 1939, Galicia was "liberated" by the Soviet army. On 4 December, the Soviets divided Eastern Galicia into four "oblasts": Lviv (Lemberg), Drohobych, Stanyslaviv, and Ternopil.

Chapter 1: Hitler Attacks Russia!

Prior to the Nazi invasion of the Soviet state, Germany's Minister for Eastern European Affairs, Alfred Rosenberg,[17] personally submitted to Adolf Hitler on 2 April 1941,[18] a plan which was to make Galicia the seed for a new Ukrainian state.[19] In his plan, Rosenberg outlined separate states for Ukraine, Byelorussia, the Cossack lands, Caucasia's Region and even, Turkestan. Such a move, claimed Rosenberg, would ensure that Germany would maintain a balance of power in the event that the destroyed Russian communist state should ever regain its strength. On 20 April 1941, Rosenberg was instructed by Hitler to produce a more detailed plan for the Reichskomissariats.[20] The following month, on 9 May, Rosenberg once again met with Hitler to present his plans. Rosenberg specifically based his views for creating separate states on a Soviet stature, Article 17 (enacted in the Soviet constitution of 5 December 1936), which provided (but in reality never permitted) the Soviet Union's sixteen republics the right to secede if they so desired. Rosenberg believed his plan to be ingenious, but instead of obtaining a sympathetic ear from Hitler, saw that Hitler was no longer interested in any separate states. Instead, the soon-to-be conquered eastern territories were now to be regarded as nothing but temporary territories pending future German colonization.[21] And on 16 July 1941, Hitler officially announced at the Angerburg Conference that "the former Austrian part of Galicia will become Reich territory!"[22]

Rosenberg, however, continued to urge some degree of freedom for Ukraine and even requested that Kiev be its capital.[23] But that same day on 16 July, Hermann Goering, Nazi Germany's Luftwaffe commander who also headed Germany's Four-Year Plan regarding the economic exploitation of occupied Eastern Europe (and in all sense wielded power over Rosenberg), proposed that Erich Koch be appointed Reich Commissioner over either the Baltic States or Ukraine. Although Rosenberg strongly protested Koch's appointment on the grounds that Koch earlier had stated that he would not obey any of Rosenberg's directives, Rosenberg was unable to influence Hitler. Regardless, that same month, Hitler established two Reich Commissariats: "Ostland" – to encompass Byelorussia and the Baltic States of Lithuania, Latvia and Estonia under Heinrich Lohse and "Ukraine," under Erich Koch.[24] In turn, the Reich Commissariats were subdivided into various regions and districts.[25] Although the Reich Commissariats were supervised by Berlin's Ministry for Occupied Territories, with regard to who actually governed what, the Reich commissar would be the supreme ruler.[26]

On 29 September 1941, Hitler informed Rosenberg of a "policy by postponement."[27] As for Ukraine, there was to be no Ukrainian state[28] and with regard to the "Galizien Land," Eastern Galicia would be temporarily incorporated into Poland's General Government[29] until it would officially become Reich territory.[30] Prior to this announcement of 29 September, Generalleutnant Franz von Roques[31] had already, on 1 August, transferred Eastern Galicia into Hans Frank's[32] General Government as "Distrikt Galizien." SS Brigadeführer Dr. Otto Wachter was appointed Galicia's governor.[33]

Recalling how Galicia was secured as Austria's "Kronland" (Crown Land) in 1772 with slight border adjustments in 1814, Hitler believed that Galicia had benefitted heavily from German and Central European culture. Germans had settled Galicia during the reign of Casimir the Great in the early and mid-14th century. At that time, they had inhabited the Lviv, Sambir, Striy and Drohobych areas of Eastern Galicia. When Galicia officially became a part of the Austro-Hungarian Empire in 1772, Empress Maria Theresa, in 1774, began the first planned colonization of Germans throughout Galicia. After her death in 1780, her son, Emperor Joseph II, commenced a second colonization on 17 September 1781. That year, Germans and Austrians began to settle throughout the whole of Galicia and remained there until the Second World War. As a result, Eastern Galicia was greatly influenced by Germany and its capital Lviv[34] was named "Lemberg." The city was also known as the "Little Vienna of the East."[35] In 1939, approximately 55,000 Germans were living in Eastern Galicia.[36]

Because of such widespread German settlement, the "Galician" inhabitants of Eastern Galicia were considered by Nazi racial theorists to be partly Germanic in blood and, hence, racially superior. While, undoubtedly, throughout the centuries some intermarriage did take place, Hitler's "Galicians" viewed themselves strictly as oppressed Ukrainians seeking some form of self-determination.

To properly understand the Ukrainian situation in Galicia at the outset of the Nazi invasion of 1941, it is important to understand Galicia, its people, how they felt under various occupiers, and what role they played in the rise of Ukraine's national revival while attempting to establish an independent Ukrainian nation.

2

Ukraine's National Revival

The Ukrainian national revival started to flare up in the mid-19th century. But the Polish uprising of 1863 gave the reactionary voices within Imperial Russia's Government an opportunity to attack the Ukrainians. After the Polish uprising, they claimed the Ukrainians would be next if the Tsarist government failed to take firm precautions. Some even claimed that the Ukrainian national movement was a product of the "Polish intrigue" and was created by the Poles to weaken Russia.[1] To counter this revival, a heavy campaign of persecution was planned, organized, and directed by Imperial Russia against the Ukrainian movement, its schools, and literature. In 1875, Tsar Alexander II ordered the creation of a special commission of ministers to "consider means of combatting the Ukrainophile danger."[2] The commission concluded that if Ukrainian literature was tolerated, it would give permanent footing to the possibility in the distant future of the separation of Ukraine from Russia. Therefore, on 18 May 1876, Tsar Alexander secretly signed the Ems 'Ukaz' (Directive) which prohibited the existence of Ukrainian arts, language and books and, in fact, renounced everything Ukrainian.[3]

Repressive measures were also taken against key individuals.[4] Besides repudiating the existence of a Ukrainian nationality, the commission decided to give regular financial support to the Russophile movement in Galicia, secretly sending subsidies to combat the Ukrainian national movement in Galicia. Although the 'Ukaz' of 1876 did not destroy Ukrainian patriotism, nor Ukrainian literature, it did have a negative impact on the Ukrainian movement for its national revival. The activities of several Ukrainian societies declined significantly. Because such unfavorable conditions existed in Russia, Eastern Ukrainian patriots were forced to turn their eyes to the Ukrainian territory of Eastern Galicia, under Austrian rule, where a Galician Ukrainian revival had also been under way for some time.

Austria's Galicia

Despite acute economic and social problems, despite the exhaustive and bitter national struggle with the Poles, by the turn of the 19th century the Ukrainian national movement in Galicia had attained a higher degree of maturity and universality than in Eastern Ukraine. Austria's relatively liberal political atmosphere provided extensive legal means for the advancement of the Ukrainian society. It offered education in the native language and it facilitated the political enlightenment of the masses. All of these conditions made the materially poor Ukrainian Galician peasants more nationally and politically conscious than the inhabitants of the Eastern (Russian) Ukraine. By the time the First World War erupted, the intelligentsia was most receptive to a national revival and the numbers that joined the national movement grew steadily.

With the collapse of Imperial Russia in November 1917, Ukrainians proclaimed, on 22 January 1918, an independent republic in Eastern Ukraine. With the collapse of the Austro-Hungarian Empire in November 1918, that same month Galicia's Ukrainians also proclaimed independence. On 22 January 1919, the two united together into the Ukrainian National Republic. But internal and external strife, foreign invasions, and the successful Soviet offensive of 1920[5] subjected this short-lived republic once again to foreign rule. As for the Ukrainians in Galicia, they also failed in their bid for Eastern Galicia to be a part of an independent Ukrainian republic. By 1923, Eastern Galicia had become a part of the newly created postwar Polish state. Because the Galician issue arose on the international scene, it therefore requires some study.

The Eastern Galician Issue

Throughout the 19th century, Poland attempted to liberate itself through a series of armed rebellions. But caught between the powers of Russia, Austria and Prussia, Poland's efforts were always suppressed. Imperial Prussia and Russia were especially united in their commitment to prevent Poland's restoration. Because of Poland's geopolitical location, little help could be expected from the west. With France's defeat in the Franco-Prussian War of 1871, any hope of securing outside support had vanished. So until the 20th century, the Polish question was considered of minor significance on the international scene.

Chapter 2: Ukraine's National Revival

On 8 January 1918, President Woodrow Wilson, addressing the United States Congress, announced America's war aims. These aims, simply stated in fourteen paragraphs, became universally known as Wilson's "Fourteen Points." Translated into virtually every language, Wilson's Fourteen Points were widely acclaimed and were accepted worldwide as a viable foundation to end foreign domination wherever it might be found and to establish independent states.

Wilson's thirteenth point stated "that an independent Polish state should be erected which should include the territories inhabited by indisputably Polish populations, which should be assured a free and secure access to the sea, and whose political and economic independence and territorial integrity should be guaranteed by international covenant." To ensure the success of Wilson's declaration for a just peace, the allied powers called for a series of discussions to be held in Paris, France. With the conclusion of World War I on 11 November 1918 the discussions, termed as the "Paris Peace Conference," were set to begin on 18 January 1919. In December 1918, President Wilson, who headed America's delegations, sailed to France.

The Paris Peace Conference was convened not only to make treaties among former enemies but, hopefully, in the ensuing discussions, to establish a foundation for a just and lasting European peace. While the Fourteen Points and the subsequent discussions were widely accepted as a basis of peace for the many different nations, their individual aspirations and needs, desires and demands, the discussions would be no easy matter. Furthermore, age-old animosities and hatreds would resurface and add to the confusion.

In regard to Poland, there were a great number of details which had to be resolved. Wilson's promise for an independent Polish state would "include the territories inhabited by indisputably Polish populations." But exactly where the "indisputably Polish populations" were located soon developed into an ugly problem. Well before the war concluded, the Americans realized that establishing Poland's borders would pose to be a problem. When Roman Dmowski, a fiery nationalistic Pole who headed the "Komitet Narodowy Polski"[6] (Polish National Committee or KNP which, prior to the emergence of a Polish state was based in Paris and was considered by many as Poland's official representative party in exile) heard about the upcoming discussions regarding Polish statehood, he personally sailed in August 1918 to the United States to discuss the matter with America's leaders. Along with Dmowski sailed Ignacy Paderewski, a prominent Polish pianist who frequently took advantage of his fame and charm to elicit support. On 8 October, both men met with the American president. When asked by Wilson what boundaries they had in mind for the proposed Polish state, Dmowski produced a map which outlined Poland's vast 1772 pre-partition frontiers, including Upper

Silesia and much of East Prussia. Flabbergasted, Wilson later remarked that "they presented me with a map which claimed half the world!"[7]

But with Imperial Germany and the Austro-Hungarian Empire rapidly collapsing in October and November of 1918, events in Eastern Europe moved quickly. In Lemberg (Lviv), on 1 November, the Ukrainian National Council proclaimed an independent Western Ukrainian National Republic. That same day, a Polish committee arrived to transfer power from Austria's administration into its own. Shots were exchanged. Within a matter of days, a serious conflict had arisen between the newly established Polish and Western Ukrainian National republics.[8]

Logically, the only way to have properly resolved such a matter would have been to establish national borders along areas which contained a majority.[9] As for any minorities residing within a majority (i.e. Poles, Jews, Germans within the Ukrainian East Galicia), the minorities would be afforded the same rights and privileges as those granted to the majority. Because Wilson's Tenth Point emphasized "independence for those within the Austro-Hungarian Empire," in addition to the emergence of a Polish state, a number of new states would also arise within central and southeastern Europe. As for borders, it was hoped by the Paris delegates that they would be established along ethnic lines.[10]

But it soon became apparent that this would not be the case. With regard to the Polish border, Dmowski presented the issue on very broad lines. He totally rejected historical, ethnic, and linguistical criteria. Dmowski demanded all of Galicia, half of Czechoslovakia's Teschen region, the "Kingdom of Poland" (known as "Congress Poland" from 1815),[11] the Russian provinces of Rivne, Vilnius, Grodno, Volyn, parts of Belorussia's (White Russia's) Minsk province, and the German provinces of Posen, West Prussia, Upper Silesia and much of East Prussia.[12] Prior to his personal visit to the United States and the total collapse of the Austro-Hungarian Empire, Dmowski theorized on the maturity of the various nations when on 27 and 28 February 1918 KNP members addressed the frontier issue.[13] As for the Poles and Czechs within the former Austrian Empire, Dmowski felt they were mature enough for independence. But those within the borders of the Russian Empire, such as Ukrainians, Lithuanians, and Byelorussians, were not.[14] Dmowski strongly opposed the idea of an independent Ukraine and felt that a Ukrainian state was not in the best interests of Poland and her allies. Therefore, he proposed that both Lithuania and Ukraine be placed under Polish and Russian influence instead of achieving independence.[15] Dmowski also regarded the Ukrainians as an unprofessional ethnic mixture to be either assimilated or dominated by the Poles.[16] He reasoned that if an independent Ukrainian state was created, Poland would lose East Galicia.[17]

Chapter 2: Ukraine's National Revival

As for Eastern Galicia, an area strongly disputed between the Poles and Ukrainians, the Galician issue would prove to be one of the most difficult issues to resolve. On 10 January 1919, Lt. Stephen Bonsal, a U.S. Army officer who served as a linguist/translator for the American delegation in Paris, stated "that the Ukrainian problem is the most complicated of the many with which the Conference is confronted. There are probably 45 million of these vigorous and interesting people, all hitherto held in leash, indeed often under the lash, by half a dozen alien rulers."[18]

Since 1772, East Galicia[19] encompassed the northeastern corner of the Austro-Hungarian Empire. In the west, East Galicia bordered on the San River (which roughly bisected Galicia), the Zbruch River in the east, the Russian Empire to the north, and the Hungarian Kingdom in the south. Within this area of approximately 55,700 square kilometers, Ukrainians constituted the majority. In an Austrian census conducted in 1910, the population of Eastern Galicia was set at 5,336,000. Of this figure, 3,291,000 (62%) were Greek Catholic (Uniate) Ukrainians; 1,351,000 (25%) were Roman Catholic (including a small number of Roman Catholic Ukrainians); and 660,000 (12%) were Jewish.[20]

Another observer noted that Eastern Galicia encompassed an area of slightly under 50,000 square kilometers with a population of slightly over 4.5 million. By using religion as a census, just under 3,000,000 (63%) were Ruthenian; more than 1,000,000 (23%) were Poles and slightly over 500,000 (12%) were Jewish.[21] Additionally, the Ruthenians cited that the Polish figure was greatly exaggerated and that in reality, there were only some 500,000 to 600,000 Poles.[22] Regardless, the Poles constituted less than a quarter of the entire population, of which nearly two-thirds was composed of Ruthenians.[23] Worldwide, there were many who expressed such opinions. In October 1918, two American journalists, Frank Cobb (editor of the *New York World*) and Walter Lippman, on a request from Colonel House, prepared a commentary report on Wilson's Fourteen Points. Regarding Wilson's Tenth Point which called for the "freest opportunity of autonomous development" for the peoples of Austro-Hungary, Cobb-Lippman concluded that "Western Galicia is clearly Polish. But Eastern Galicia is in large measure Ukrainian (or Ruthenian) and does not of right belong to Poland."[24]

With such figures and observations, it was unequivocally clear that while Western Galicia rightfully belonged to Poland, Eastern Galicia in turn should have remained Ukrainian. Because Dmowski and his compatriots could not explain away their numerical inferiority and, as a mater of fact, even conceded that Eastern Galicia's population was mostly non-Polish, they, in turn, based their arguments on Poland's "cultural superiority" and the "fact" that the Ukrainians should be united to Poland because they had "not yet reached the stage of nationhood."[25]

Such was the case on 29 January 1919 in Paris, France. In front of numerous Paris Peace conference representatives from various nations, including President Wilson, Dmowski argued (in regards to Poland's eastern frontiers), "that the Ukrainian state at present was really organized anarchy and the Ukrainians were not so far advanced on the road to nationality." Dmowski insisted "the great need in Eastern Europe was to have established governments, able to assure order and to express their will in foreign and in internal policy. It was too early to think of Lithuania or Ukraine as independent states." As for Eastern Galicia, Dmowski also insisted that its inhabitants "were unable to create a separate state;" hence, his argument for controlling such regions.[26]

Yet, within Poland, there were those who differed. Among them was Marshal Josef Pilsudski. In mid-December 1918, Pilsudski wrote: "I do not wish to take all of East Galicia, they (Dmowski and the KNP), want the whole of East Galicia."[27] In an attempt to establish cooperation between Poland and the Ukrainians against Red Russia, Pilsudski advocated that Poland support an independent Ukrainian state and part with Eastern Galicia.[28] And when Pilsudski stated that Eastern Galicia is a "Ruthenian (Ukrainian) land" many Poles, including the peasant leader Wincenty Witos, were shocked."[29]

Pilsudski did, however, strongly insist on Polish control of Eastern Galicia's capital city of Lviv and the oil-rich area of Drohobych.[30] He based his argument on the fact that Lviv's population was largely Polish and that Poland would need oil. Regardless, his argument had no justification because the historical fact remains that Lviv was founded in approximately 1250 by King Danylo (Daniel) the Lion Hearted, the Ukrainian King of Galicia, who named the city after his son Lev.[31] (In Ukrainian 'lev' means lion, hence the Ukrainian name of Lviv). Danylo built many towns throughout Eastern Galicia. He developed a reputation as a town builder and it was Danylo who introduced the lion emblem for the Eastern Galician principality. Additionally, arguments that Lviv's population contained a large Polish element and therefore, that city belonged to them, were misleading because until well into the 20th century, Ukrainians were predominantly a rural and village people who resided mostly outside of the Ukraine's cities.[32] Throughout the whole Ukraine (including its capital city of Kiev), every major and secondary Ukrainian city had a very large non-Ukrainian populace. As late as 1926, 86 percent of the Ukrainians were farmers, and 94 percent lived in communities of less than 20,000.[33]

Allied Views Regarding Eastern Galicia
Among the allied negotiators, there was a considerable amount of uncertainty, debate, and difference of opinion regarding the Galician issue.[34] To properly un-

derstand the Principle Allied Associated Powers viewpoints, it is important to understand the various allied views regarding Galicia:

England: Briefly, under Prime Minister Lloyd George, England supported the Ukrainians. Along with Arthur Balfour, Britain's Secretary of State for Foreign Affairs, Lloyd George opposed Poland's claims to Eastern Galicia.[35] The Prime Minister insisted the Ukraine should have the province "unless very cogent reasons to the contrary existed."[36] And Louis Namier, a British civil servant who worked tirelessly to examine the issue in depth, frequently wrote papers repudiating Polish untruths concerning Ukrainian, Lithuanian and Byelorussian matters. Namier, until the very end, criticized Dmowski and the KNP.[37]

At the same time, however, England was also committed to establishing a Polish state. And during this time, England's leadership was immensely pressured by its military (among them General Sir Henry Wilson), to grant Polish control over Eastern Galicia so that Poland could utilize that region as a buffer zone against Red Russia.

France: Having maintained the closest relationship with Poland, France was extremely sympathetic to the Polish cause. France's Prime Minister, Georges Clemenceau, not only advocated the restoration of Poland but also (as did the military) the creation of a ring of strong states around Russia. Therefore, the French encouraged the incorporation of Eastern Galicia into Poland.[38]

Italy: Although sympathetic to Poland, with regard to its eastern demands, the Italian delegation did not earnestly support Poland's desires.

Japan: Regarding the Eastern Galician issue, Japan stayed out of this dispute.

United States: President Wilson and the American delegation, although very friendly and sympathetic towards Poland, viewed its problems from the general principles involved. America basically took the position as one Pole remarked, "that Poland should get neither too much, nor too little, but just what belonged to her."[39]

But while the discussions were under way in Paris, critical military events in distant eastern Europe were rapidly deciding the issue. Russia's Civil War of 1918-

21 was largely fought in Ukraine. In turn, this conflict placed a heavy strain on the Ukrainian National Government and its army, the UNRA. (Ukrainian National Republic's Army). Because the UNRA never evolved into a well organized and powerful force, it could not effectively engage and destroy Russia's Red Armies, the various roving anarchist bands and the numerous foreign interventionist forces operating within Ukraine. In desperation, the Ukrainian National Government would occasionally request the services of the more elite Ukrainian Galician Army[40] (whose core was composed of former members of Austria's army) to assist the UNRA in battles outside of Eastern Galicia. Such was the case, when from 16-19 July 1919, Galicia's 100,000 troops marched eastward into central Ukraine. Coordinating their actions with the remnants of the UNRA, the combined forces repulsed Red Russia's forces and by 31 August, had recaptured Kiev. But such temporary victories only prolonged the inevitable defeat. Needless to say, once the Ukrainian Galician Army moved the bulk of its strength eastward, Poland's army encountered lesser resistance.

Overwhelmed by superior Russian, Polish and foreign forces, shattered by internal strife and receiving very little foreign assistance, the Ukrainian government (to include the one in Eastern Galicia), began to collapse. In late 1919 Simon Petliura, who continued to head the Ukrainian National Republic, fled to Poland proper. In desperation, in April 1920, he negotiated a joint Polish-Ukrainian treaty with Pilsudski to wage war on Soviet Russia.[41] Many Ukrainians, especially the Galician Ukrainians, were unhappy with such a move but, for the moment, Petliura had no choice. On 25 April 1920, Pilsudski, with the support of anti-Bolshevik Ukrainians, launched an offensive.[42] On 7 May, the combined forces captured Kiev.[43] Although Poland's military had grown in quantity and quality, Pilsudski's plan was too ambitious and his army lacked effective logistical backup. That same month, reinforced Red Army forces under Mikhail Tukhachevsky and Semen Budenny began to repel Poland's forces. By 25 July, Pilsudski had retreated to Poland proper. For the Poles, the situation looked bleak.

As Red Russia's armies poised to take Warsaw and overrun the rest of Poland, Pilsudski's resistance stiffened. At this critical moment, France tremendously assisted Poland by dispatching French advisors under General Weygand with massive amounts of military aid. On 16 August 1920, Pilsudski's and Weygand's forces struck the Bolsheviks both north and south of Warsaw. As the combined forces shattered the Red front, Tukhachevsky's forces fell back. Rapidly exploiting their initial breakout, the Poles quickly advanced eastward.

On 12 October 1920, a ceasefire was proclaimed. On 18 March 1921, as a result of Poland's successful war with Soviet Russia, the Treaty of Riga, concluded between Red Russia and Poland, conceded to Poland many of the lands it coveted. By virtue of this treaty, Ukraine was divided between Poland and Russia. A large part of western Ukraine, 132,000 square kilometers with a population in excess of 8 million, of which at least 6 million were Ukrainians, was allocated to Poland.[44]

It must be noted, however, that before the Treaty of Riga was signed, the Council of the League of Nations declared in Paris on 23 February 1921 that "the territory of Eastern Galicia, although under temporary Polish military control, still officially lay outside of Poland and therefore, the Poles have no legal mandate for any permanent administration of Eastern Galicia."[45] On 10 September 1919, by the Treaty of St. Germain, the Ukrainian territory of Bukovyna was ceded to Rumania. This was done despite previous American efforts at the Paris Conference to attach the former Austro-Hungarian area of Bukovyna, which was home to 85,000 Ukrainians and approximately 300 Rumanians, to the disputed East Galician territory.[46]

Ukrainians, as a people and a nation, were never officially permitted to participate in the Parisian discussions. Although a Ukrainian delegation arrived in Paris[47] to present its cause (and on occasion did succeed in meeting certain representatives), Ukrainians were, as a rule, excluded from the discussions.

By 1921, Poland had secured a tremendously large number of minorities. In its first official census of 1921, 69.2 percent of the population cited their nationality as Polish; but some have claimed that this figure was too high;[48] 10 years later, on 9 December 1931, a strict Polish census revealed that of 31,916,000 inhabitants, 21,993,400 were ethnic Poles and nearly 10,000,000 million were non-Poles.[49] Clearly, Poland was composed of minorities. These minorities, including a large proportion of the Jewish population, regarded themselves as separate nationalities apart from Poland. While of course other censuses would provide slightly different figures, basically the figures indicated that over 30 to nearly 40 percent of Poland's population was non-Polish. To be sure, there was danger in this and a number of observers and historians of that era did note Poland's perilous position: "The Poles have taken on as enemies all their neighbors ... the state they have formed contains so many alien elements in geographical juxtaposition to "brothers of blood" that it is bound to be seriously affected when irredentist movements get under way."[50] "By concluding the Treaty of Riga, Poland had "condemned herself and, in fact, insisted on signing an advance copy of her own death-warrant."[51]

With America's withdrawal from European affairs, President Wilson's principal of 'self-determination' fell into disruption. Because the Paris Peace Conference could not find a solution to the difficult Galician issue, they handed the problem over to the League of Nations. In the meantime, throughout 1921, the Polish government, in the face of mounting international criticism of its Ukrainian (and other minorities) policies, publicly proclaimed its position on minority rights. On 26 September 1922, Poland's 'Sejm' (parliament) even passed a law granting autonomy to Eastern Galicia's three provinces of Lviv (Lemberg), Stanyslaviv and Ternopil.[52] Since the League and its Council of Ambassadors (consisting of Britain, France, Italy, and Japan), were impressed by Poland's assurance of autonomous status for Eastern Galicia's inhabitants, on 14 March 1923, they recognized that part of West Ukraine as a part of Eastern Poland.[53]

This decision of the Council of Ambassadors compelled the Ukrainians of Eastern Galicia to accept the fact that they would have to remain within Poland's borders until the next major European upheaval. And that upheaval would be the Second World War which for Eastern Galicia would begin under Soviet occupation.

3

September, 1939

With the outbreak of the Second World War and Soviet Russia's thrust into Eastern Poland, the Red Army occupied Eastern Galicia and publicly proclaimed the "liberation" of those under Polish rule.

At that time, the total population of Eastern Galicia was 5,824,100. Of this number 3,727,000 were Ukrainian (64.1 percent); 76,000 or 0.3 percent were Polish speaking Ukrainians; 874,700 or 15 percent were Poles; 73,200 or 1.2 percent were Polish colonists who had settled in the region after 1923; 514,000 or 8.8 percent were Latynnycky;[1] 569,000 or 9.8 percent were Jewish; and about 49,999 or 0.8 percent belonged to other nationality groups, in this case mostly German.[2]

By December 1939, the Soviet administration – with its laws and courts – had replaced the previous Polish ones. Soon, Red Russia's party officials, employing the highly dreaded NKVD secret police, began a systematic liquidation of Ukrainian political, national, and religious leaders.[3] The Ukrainian intelligentsia was especially targeted. Mass arrests, murders, and deportations occurred routinely. Because it did not require much to be classified as an "enemy of the people" or as a "capitalist exploiter" any person, regardless of class, educational, social, or economic status, was a potential victim of NKVD terror.

The deportations which took place in Eastern Galicia throughout the period of 1939-41 (as well as those which occurred in Poland proper, the Baltic States and other areas subjected to Soviet "liberation"), in addition to being very brutal and inhumane, are also very instructive for anyone interested in NKVD deportation methods.

Often, the names of individuals selected for arrest and liquidation were secretly drawn up well before a given area was even occupied.[4] Awakened in the early morning hours by squads of NKVD police personnel who often were assisted by local communist militiamen, its victims, for the greater part, were totally unprepared for the terror that awaited them.

Permitted no more than two hours to assemble themselves and to pack no more than two suitcases or bags, the deportees were then either driven to the deportation centers on the back of a truck or force marched. There, husbands were frequently separated from their wives and children. By no means were even infants and children excluded from such deportations. According to estimates by Poland's authorities, of more than 1.2 million persons deported to the interior of the Soviet Union from Poland's southeastern regions during the first two years of the war,[5] some 220,000 to 250,000 of the deportees were children under 14 years of age.[6]

Once the deportees were packed into crowded cattle cars, a long journey awaited them. In winter time, the deportees froze in the unheated cars and in the summer, they suffocated in the heat. In the overcrowded, filthy, cold, and sweltering cattle cars where starvation, thirst, and disease were constant companions, men, women, and children died by the masses. How many perished on such journeys has never been established, and probably never will be.

Yet at the end of such a hellish journey, the deportees were awaited by another hell. It made little difference whether a deportee ended up in a Siberian concentration camp or a place of exile. Relentless hunger, disease, hard labor and brutality at the hands of sadistic drug and vodka-consuming guards extracted a heavy toll on the deportees.[7]

But Hitler's 1941 eastward advance brought a rapid end to Soviet rule and, for Eastern Galicia, another period of occupation under a different occupier.

Hitler Strikes Russia!

When Germany's armies advanced eastward, many people of various nationalities greeted the Germans as true liberators.[8] In Ukraine, this was also true, especially by those western Ukrainians who had just experienced communism in practice. Advancing into Eastern Galicia, they encountered a society drastically altered by two years of Red terror.

Galicia's leadership, whether Ukrainian, Polish, or Jewish was shattered.[9] The constant arrests, confiscations, exploitations, terror, propaganda and ethnic agitations had thoroughly exhausted the region both physically and emotionally. Consequently, such brutal excesses made the German army seem like the proverbial savior.

Chapter 3: September, 1939

But the initial joy of German liberation soon evaporated. Although there were those Germans within the higher circles of the Third Reich who were cordial and sympathetic to Eastern Europeans and Ukrainians, their arguments for utilizing the communist-exploited nations to the advantage of Germany's position fell on deaf ears. Nazi policy immediately demonstrated that it came only to rule and exploit the newly conquered areas. And by no means was Eastern Galicia an exception.[10]

Hostile relations between Ukrainians, especially the Organization of Ukrainian Nationalists (OUN),[11] and the Nazis officially began on 30 June 1941.[12] On that day, when Ukrainian personnel serving with Germany's armed forces[13] took over a radio station in Eastern Galicia's capital city of Lviv and announced the proclamation of an independent Ukrainian republic,[14] they were immediately suppressed and arrested. On 12 July, Prime Minister Yaroslav Stetsko, of the short-lived Ukrainian Provisional government, was arrested.[15] Shortly afterwards Stepan Bandera,[16] a key individual in the Ukrainian movement, was also arrested. Another Ukrainian government established further to the east in the Ukrainian capital of Kiev under the leadership of Andreas Melnyk fared no better than the one previously established in Lviv.[17] And by no means were the arrests just limited to these Ukrainians. Throughout the whole Ukraine in the summer and fall of 1941, Germany's Gestapo and SS police viciously attacked the OUN, members of the Ukrainian intelligentsia who had survived the communist occupation, anyone who refused (or was suspected of refusing) labor deportation orders to work within Germany, or those who harbored OUN, Jews, and others marked for arrest. Directives and orders on dealing with Ukrainian patriots were issued, such as the one issued from the Service Command of the Security Police and Security Service on 25 November 1941:[18]

> Service Command of the
> Security Police and of
> the Security Service S/5
> Command Log-Book No. 12432/41
>
> Headquarters
> November 25, 1941
>
> To: the advanced posts of
> Kyiv, Dnipropetrovsk,
> Rivne, Mykolaiv,
> Zhytomyr, Vinnytsia.

Subject: OUN (Bandera Movement).

It has been ascertained that the Bandera Movement is preparing a revolt in the Reichs Commissariats which has as its ultimate aim the establishment of an independent Ukraine. All functionaries of the Bandera movement must be arrested at once and, after thorough interrogation, are to be liquidated as secretly as marauders.

Records of such interrogations must be forwarded to the Service Command C/5.

Heads of commands must destroy these instructions on having made a due note of them.

(Signature – illegible)
SS-Obersturmbannführer

Needless to say, such attitudes and policies adopted by the Nazi leadership complicated matters for those trying to establish a strong bond between Germany and the eastern regions. As a result of such negative behavior, in late 1941 elements of the "Nachtigall" battalion mutinied in places as far east as Vinnytsia and Tiraspol in central Ukraine.[19]

Recognizing a dangerous situation, German officials immediately disarmed and arrested a number of the units' leaders and shortly afterwards, dispatched a number of them to Sachsenhausen Concentration Camp. As for the survivors of the so-called "Ukrainian Legion" who did not desert or who were not initially imprisoned, they were transferred back to Germany and stationed at Frankfurt-on-the-Oder. There, the two units were reorganized into one military battalion: "Roland-Nachtigall;"[20] in turn, "Roland-Nachtigall" was simply redesignated Schuma-Battalion 201.[21] In March 1942, the battalion was redeployed to Byelorussia's vast Polotsk-Vitebsk forest and swamp region to protect German communications and railways. However, the battalion proved to be unreliable. When its soldiers refused to take an oath of loyalty to Hitler and renew their contract, Schuma Bn. 201 was disarmed and disbanded.[22] Its commander, Major Evhen Pobihushchyj-Ren, was arrested.[23]

On 5 December 1942, under a heavily armed police escort, the German command began to transport the Legion's personnel in small groups to Galicia's capital city of Lviv and once there, its members were imprisoned.[24] Some, however, were moved shortly afterwards to various Nazi concentration camps such as

Sachsenhausen. By 14 January 1943, with its leaders dead, imprisoned, or scattered, the Legion ceased to exist.[25]

But by no means were all of the surviving legionnaires imprisoned. Some fled to Ukraine's forests and swamps. Establishing contact with the numerous individuals fleeing Nazi excesses, they quickly organized themselves into various small guerrilla bands. In due time, these bands evolved into the Ukrainian Povstans'ka (Insurgent) Army or simply, the UPA.

4

The UPA

In the annals of modern warfare, very few guerrilla forces have ever undertaken such a unique and difficult mission as that undertaken by the Ukrainian Insurgent Army. This is especially true when one takes into consideration the length of the conflict, the numerous enemies encountered, regions of combat, severity of fighting, the brutality experienced by UPA's personnel upon capture, and the fact that the UPA received no external military, political, or moral support.

It is now a matter of historical fact that the UPA arose out of the need to resist Nazi Germany's repressive "Ost" policies.[1] But within a few months, the UPA would not only be engaging Hitler's Nazism, but also those European fascist powers allied to Hitler's Germany as well as Ukraine's traditional enemy – Russia.

In order to escape Nazi arrests, executions, and "volunteer" labor programs, by the end of 1941 sizable numbers of Ukrainian men and women had sought refuge in Ukraine's forests and swamps. In March 1942, in Northwestern Ukraine's Polissia region, the various bands merged into a "Polissia Sich."[2] (The word "Sich" denoted a band or group). But under advice from the OUN, a new reorganization took place. On 14 October 1942, the Polissia's and Ukraine's various guerrilla groups merged into one army, under one command, and under one name: the Ukrainian Povstans'ka (Insurgent) Army, or UPA.[3]

Commanded by General Roman Shukhevych,[4] an ex-Roland officer who had escaped from German police authorities while enroute from Byelorussia to a prison cell in Galicia, the UPA quickly developed into an effective fighting force. For purposes of tactical efficiency and control, the UPA organized itself into four territorial regions: *UPA-North*: This comprised Northwestern Ukraine and the south-western/southcentral region of Belorussia (White Russia); *UPA-South*: consisted of Bukovina, the southeastern Carpathian region, and Vinnytsia's province; *UPA-East*: encompassed the Ukraine's capital city of Kiev and its surrounding area, and *UPA-West*: comprised the whole of Galicia, most of the Carpathian region, and parts of Southeastern Poland.[5]

Bold raids and ambushes, reinforced with a strong anti-Nazi propaganda campaign, strengthened UPA's ranks and hindered Nazi efforts to fully exploit Ukraine.[6] In April 1943, a number of Nazi police posts, such as those at Horokhiv, Tsuman, Olyka and Ivanova-Dolyna were attacked and destroyed. Ivanova-Dolyna was especially targeted. In a subsequent Nazi casualty report, hundreds of German and Polish policemen were reported killed and wounded.[7] And in May 1943, on the Brest-Litovsk highway, UPA guerrillas, under the command of Colonel Vovchak, ambushed and killed one of Erich Koch's closest collaborators, SA General Victor Lutze.[8]

To neutralize the Ukrainian underground, Nazi Germany dispatched its leading guerrilla hunter, SS-Obergruppenführer Erich von dem Bach-Zalewski, to destroy the UPA. Through a series of heavy anti-UPA operations termed Operation "BB" and conducted through the months of May, June, and July 1943, Zalewski's forces engaged the Ukrainian guerrillas with massive strength.[9] UPA-North was specifically targeted because Zalewski reasoned that once UPA-North was shattered, the rest of the UPA would collapse.

Zalewski struck hard. Day after day, week after week, the sound of clanking armor and the high-pitched screams of diving Stuka aircraft pierced the air as Nazi tanks, artillery, and dive bombers pulverized much of Polissia and Volyn. And as the "diving death" aircraft unleashed their bombs, whole villages disappeared amid explosions of red and orange flames.

Zalewski's tactics were undertaken not only to eliminate the guerrillas, but to terrorize the local Ukrainian populace into submission. However, ultimately, the Nazi's terror tactics not only failed, but actually propelled many more into the UPA's (and the OUN's) ranks, thus further strengthening the Ukrainian liberation movement. Noteworthy of the UPA is the fact that throughout this period UPA's guerrillas not only fought defensively, but also offensively. During this period in 1943, primarily in Polissia and Volyn, the UPA recorded no less than 178 engagements (excluding skirmishes) with German forces.[10] Numerous raids and ambushes were launched against Gestapo headquarters, deportation centers, fixed garrisons, and against regular Wehrmacht and Police SS units.[11] What is especially interesting is that in a number of these operations, UPA's guerrillas frequently encountered and engaged Polish personnel serving in Germany's military and police.[12]

Simultaneously, as the UPA battled the Germans, it also fought Red Russia's guerrillas. The best example of this is the case of Sidor Kovpak, a communist guerrilla commander. Stavka, the Soviet Military's Supreme Command, approved in April 1943 a plan for Kovpak to conduct a deep raid into Galicia and the Carpathian region to strike at Galicia's communications, roads, railways and oil facilities. Additionally, such a raid would demonstrate German military-political weaknesses within German occupied Galicia.[13]

Commencing on 12 June 1943 from Mulashevychi (north of the Pripyat River), a total of 2,000 hand-picked fighters accompanied Kovpak southwestward. Because UPA's intelligence had successfully infiltrated the red organization, the moment Kovpak moved, UPA's leadership was notified of the Red commander's strengths, dispositions, and intents.

At first, the UPA totally avoided the Red guerrillas' southwest advance. But once Kovpak entered Galicia's Carpathian region, his force was attacked and hounded to the point of almost complete annihilation.[14]

For arms and supplies, the UPA resorted to materiel primarily captured or secured from defectors fleeing into UPA's ranks.[15] At no time did Nazi Germany (or for that matter any other power), assist the UPA. While it is true that in 1944 certain German military officers (such as Otto Skorzeny, Nazi Germany's commando leader) attempted to co-ordinate a combined German-UPA campaign against Soviet Russia, UPA's leadership officially rejected all Nazi appeals for any concerted and combined effort. Furthermore, it ordered its commanders to avoid all such negotiations. In a few cases, the UPA executed several of its commanders who disobeyed this order.[16]

UPA's commander-in-chief was assisted not only with an operations staff but with intelligence/counterintelligence, medical, communications, supply, security, propaganda/counter-propaganda and psychological warfare sections. In addition, military training schools were established. Deep, underground bunkers (such as those later found in use by North Vietnam's guerrillas) with interlocking tunnels, were constructed. Numerous agents and spies were infiltrated into the German armies (including the 14th Waffen-SS "Galicia" Division), the German police, the various Soviet Army fronts, the Rumanian and Hungarian armies, the NKVD police, Poland's underground and even, it is alleged, into the higher circles of Soviet Russia's military and political leadership. Nazi Germany's and Soviet Russia's movements and activities throughout Ukraine were constantly monitored, and a very effective "Avengers" assassination group curbed the activities of the Gestapo and NKVD.

Chapter 4: The UPA

An exact accounting of UPA's strength has never been established. Figures were difficult to compile. The insurgents moved from region to region, and large numbers of fighters did not serve in the "regular" UPA units but served within UPA's numerous self-defense village detachments, propaganda, sabotage, "Avenger" and espionage services. Additionally, it was difficult to account for many of those who had been serving in Europe's various armies and undergrounds and, from 1945, in UPA's underground "railway" which ran from Ukraine into Germany and Austria. Through this underground, manned by a number of sympathetic Czechoslovakian, Hungarian, and German civilians, the UPA successfully evacuated thousands of Ukrainians and non-Ukrainians.

Professor Lev Shankowsky, a former UPA soldier and historian, cites a strength of 60,000.[17] Bilinsky provides a figure of approximately 20,000 fighters in Galicia,[18] but undoubtedly, Bilinsky is referring to Galicia's "regulars" and not to the Galician UPA's militias, agents, spies, and others. Mirchuk cites 60,000 "active" armed fighters,[19] but Codo provides a figure of 300,000.[20] German wartime intelligence estimated UPA's strength in late 1943 as between 40,000 to 50,000,[21] but in late 1944, it raised its estimation to 100,000.[22] The Ukrainian journal "Visti Kombatanta," cited a strength of approximately 40,000,[23] and Ukrainian emigres claimed a strength of more than 200,000.[24] But Vashchenko stated that at its height the UPA had no less than 100,000 armed regular and militia fighters bolstered with another 100,000 in direct support. However, on occasion, direct support personnel were transferred to combat units. As for deriving the number of agents, spies, and "eyes-and-ears," that figure will never be established because, as Vashchenko stated "that would include much of the entire Ukraine's populace, and large numbers of non-Ukrainians."[25] Yet Yona Liron, a former NKVD police officer who defected from the former Soviet Union, cited a strength of 300,000 fighters and direct sympathizers.[26]

Regardless of the true figures, by mid-1943 the UPA was a formidable force composed not only of Ukrainians, but also of non-Ukrainians. UPA's foreign strength was acquired through raids and ambushes conducted against enemy convoys, railway systems, deportation centers, Gestapo, SS and NKVD police systems; from foreign military deserters; and in some cases, from captured soldiers who requested asylum.

By the end of 1943, thousands of Russian, Georgian, Armenian, German, Italian and others were found serving in the UPA.[27] Sizable numbers of Jewish personnel also served in the UPA. According to Dr. Friedman, a number of Eastern European Jews (in some cases whole families) were saved by the UPA and, at the conclusion of the war, were able to emigrate to Israel and various parts of the world.[28] Lev Shankowsky wrote to Friedman that almost every UPA unit had Jewish support personnel.[29] Precisely how many Jewish personnel served in the ranks of the UPA has never been established, and probably will never be established because regional commanders often classified all personnel as "Ukrainian." Furthermore, with the end of World War II, the majority of UPA's Jewish personnel emigrated worldwide. Among the more famous Jewish personnel recorded in UPA's history, the following stand out: Dr. Margosh (pseudonym Dr. Havrysh), who headed UPA-West's medical service; Dr. Marksymovych, Chief Physician of the UPA Officers' School; and Doctor Abraham Kum, who directed an underground hospital in the Carpathians.[30] All three received military decorations but Dr. Kum (who was killed in February 1946 while defending his hospital against an NKVD onslaught) was posthumously awarded UPA's highest award for valor, the Golden Cross of Merit.

On 29 February 1944, the Commander of the 1st Ukrainian Front, Marshal Nikolai Vatutin, accompanied by an armed escort, set forth to visit General Chernyakhovski's 60th Army Headquarters for a briefing on an upcoming offensive. As Vatutin's force travelled through the peaceful snow covered countryside, a sudden burst of automatic small-arms fire shattered his car while a well-placed anti-tank round ripped the Soviet commander's truck escort to pieces. Immediately, from all sides, a force of approximately 100 UPA soldiers descended upon Vatutin. But as the UPA moved in, machine-gun fire from the survivors forced the insurgents back. The UPA, however, did not totally disengage itself and in the ensuing struggle, Vatutin was wounded. Though rescued and removed to a field hospital and shortly afterwards to a military hospital in Kiev, the Marshal died on 15 April.[31]

In response, General Marchenko, who commanded Ukraine's Internal NKVD troops, immediately dispatched strong NKVD forces into UPA-North's eastern region. On 2 April 1944, the NKVD commenced its operations. Historically, 2 April may be cited as the date when UPA's struggle shifted from a major anti-Nazi into that of a major anti-Soviet struggle.[32]

From then until well into the 1950s, UPA's forces were increasingly embroiled with Soviet Russia, with Soviet Russia's Polish puppet state[33] and on occasion with the Hungarian, Rumanian, and Czechoslovakian regimes.[34] Viciously, the whole eastern block struck the UPA and massive battles were fought throughout Ukraine but especially in its northern and western regions. These battles actually covered vast regions and involved hundreds of thousands of troops. Such was the case on 23 September 1944, when 30,000 Soviet troops (primarily from the NKVD) encircled a force of 5,000 insurgents in UPA's Carpathian Western Region's Black Forest.[35] To assist those surrounded, UPA's leadership immediately dispatched sizable numbers of insurgents from its various regions into UPA-West. Loaded down with supplies frequently exceeding 60 pounds, UPA's reinforcements conducted forced tactical marches to reach the battle area. And so it went. Until the Korean Conflict of 1950, UPA's personnel, without any respite, continued the battle in hopes that sooner or later, a major strife would erupt between the Soviets and the West, and with this conflict, the UPA would be able to play a role in ensuring the demise of Soviet communism.

Pursued, harassed and constantly engaged by superior forces, with massive amounts of forest acreage deliberately burned, with units shattered or weakened and driven deeper into Ukraine's forests and swamps, with hunger and disease extracting its toll, UPA's situation, by the beginning of 1950, appeared bleak. And it only worsened when on 5 March 1950, near the town of Bilohorshka, near Lviv, in UPA's Western Region, UPA's Commander-in-Chief, General Roman Shukhevych, was killed as he lay in an underground hospital recovering from an illness.[36]

With the general's death and the realization that a Soviet-Western conflict would not occur, the battered UPA was forced to change its tactics. By no means did their resistance cease. Rather, different methods were adopted. UPA abolished its remaining guerrilla groups and went further underground. Open, pitched combat ceased and raids and ambushes decreased. A number of UPA's guerrillas fled westward, some penetrated deeper into remote areas, while others returned to civilian life in hopes of reestablishing a peaceful life.

Minor armed conflicts, sabotage and assassinations were reported as late as 1956. Officially, UPA's last military engagement occurred in October, 1956. That month, some of UPA's survivors fought valiantly on the Hungarian border region to assist the Hungarian anti-communist uprising.[37]

5

Germany's Foreign Troops

"It must always remain a cast-iron principle that none but Germans shall be allowed to bear arms. Only the German must be permitted to bear arms, not the Slav, not the Czech, nor the Cossack, nor the Ukrainian."[1]

So uttered Adolf Hitler on 16 July 1941 during the opening phase of Operation Barbarossa. Hitler's words were especially directed against those who proposed to recruit foreign contingencies from regions previously suppressed by Stalin. While in the first few weeks of the Russian campaign it seemed as if Hitler's 'blitzkrieg' would indeed shatter Stalin's empire, and thus would not require any Eastern European assistance, military events within the next few months would quickly prove otherwise. With Germany's 'feldheer' sinking deeper and deeper into Russia's mud and snow and with its casualties steadily rising, by the conclusion of 1941 the policy of not recruiting former Soviet soldiers and citizens was quickly being reconsidered. Increasingly, more and more German front-line divisional and corps commanders, desperately seeking additional manpower, began to halt the practice of deporting all Soviet prisoners westward, and instead began to utilize Soviet prisoners-of-war for their needs.[2]

At first the Slavs and Balts, whether captured or recruited, were primarily used for work purposes and for security measures. Many, especially those who were employed as labor troops, initially were not even permitted to bear arms. As Germany's front-line situation continued to deteriorate and its eastern armies encountered a phenomenal partisan and guerrilla activity, Germany's work and security troops found themselves increasingly employed as combat troops. For purposes of efficiency and to overcome native language difficulties, the foreign troops were organized into small sections and detachments.[3] Originally, these small units had predominantly German leadership. But as the situation continuously worsened throughout 1942, and as manpower needs hit the critical level, company and battalion sized units with foreign leadership began to appear. By late 1942, some of the battalions were merged together into brigades and, in turn, these units were subordinated into Germany's eastern front armies.

By early 1943, Germany's eastern front venture had extracted from that nation – and its allies such as Italy and Rumania – a huge toll of human lives. With the German surrender at Stalingrad on 31 January 1943, the threat of total defeat struck the Third Reich harshly. Desperate now more than ever in its search for fresh manpower, Germany began to abandon many of its racial and political considerations. And those who had much earlier strongly opposed using Ukrainian manpower for the eastern front, were now quickly reversing their position. However, the recruitment of Ukrainians for Germany's military was a difficult and risky venture, especially when trying to recruit those within the Reichskommissariat under Koch's brutal rule. Yet there was one region where certain German officials had for some time been trying to organize a Ukrainian force on an anti-communist theme. True, promoting such an armed Ukrainian formation could – on one hand – renew a strong spark in Ukrainian patriotism (especially within the OUN) and thus, only intensify the OUN-Nazi struggle. However, on the other hand, it could have its advantages for certain German officials firmly believed that if the region's Ukrainian youth were organized into a distinct military formation, they would not only provide Germany its desperately needed manpower but, simultaneously, this plan would enable German authorities to maintain a stronger grip on the region's youth which was growing increasingly receptive to the OUN-UPA underground and, thus, could be easily swayed into anti-German activities.[4]

To be sure, there were dangers in such a venture. But for the moment the dangers had to be chanced, for victory on the disastrous eastern front was now Germany's main priority. Because, at last, a decision had to be made and action needed to be taken, it was. And it was this action which laid the foundation for the rise of a Ukrainian Division in East Galicia.

Dr. Otto Gustav Wachter, Galicia's General-Governor, initiated the establishment of the Ukrainian Division.[5] Austrian born, Wachter had been in Galicia since his appointment in August 1941. Unlike many other Nazi officials, Wachter had a much better understanding of the Ukrainian people, their needs and aspirations. In general, Wachter was sympathetic to Eastern Europeans who had suffered under

Galicia Division

Stalin's rule and he sought to establish a better relationship between them and Germany.

Although a non-military man, Wachter was closely observing Germany's eastern-front campaign and by the spring of 1943, had concluded that it was in serious trouble. Knowing that Germany would need additional manpower, Wachter reasoned now was the time to try to persuade Germany's leadership to take advantage of Galicia's manpower in the war against Soviet communism. Wachter also reasoned that if his proposal was accepted, eventually those in Germany who strongly opposed the Ukrainians would perceive the situation differently. Perhaps this would even lead to a different type of Ukrainian policy which eventually, might reduce tensions and benefit both sides. But, for the moment, at least it would secure the desperately needed manpower.

On 1 March 1943, in the Third Reich's capital city of Berlin, Wachter personally discussed the matter with Reichsführer Heinrich Himmler.[6] Under normal conditions, Himmler would have unconditionally vetoed such an idea. But manpower was desperately needed.[7] Because earlier Himmler had authorized the establishment of a Yugoslavian Moslem Mountain Division, very little now stood in the way of recruiting similar foreign formations.[8]

Upon his return to Galicia, Wachter immediately wrote a letter on 4 March, presenting Himmler a draft of an appeal that he (Wachter) proposed to present to Galicia's people.[9] After studying the draft, Himmler presented Wachter's proposal directly to Hitler. Both men discussed the matter and agreed that the Division would be recruited in Galicia, financed by Galicia, and would be titled "Galicia" rather than "Ukrainian."[10] And on 28 March 1943, Himmler personally replied to Galicia's governor to proceed with his plans.[11]

In his reply, the Reichsführer also emphasized the significance of the upcoming spring planting season (for he realized the need of a good harvest), and the importance of securing manpower capable for military needs. Himmler also recognized and emphasized that the unit would not be a police division but rather, would be a grenadier (infantry) division.[12] Its transport would rely on horses,[13] and all necessary horses, clothing and certain equipment were to be provided by Galicia's inhabitants. As for organizing and training the Division, Himmler preferred this to be carried out within the Reich's troop training areas rather than in Galicia. Himmler also urged Wachter to discuss further the above matter with Walter Friedrich-Wilhelm Kruger, the police chief and state secretary for the security in the General Government of Poland, and with Berger. As for establishing locations where volunteers could be physically screened and registered, Himmler stated that this matter would still have to be discussed, but added that at the proper time, a military commission would be sent from Germany to assist in this matter. The Reichsführer concluded his letter by informing Wachter that he was aware of his appeal to Galicia's people and that he favored the idea of a proclamation.

With permission secured, Wachter proceeded with much enthusiasm and devotion. But to raise any kind of military force, especially at divisional strength, is no easy matter. Wachter expected that problems would be encountered and to best prevent them, Wachter held a series of meetings with various German and Ukrainian officials.

On 4 April 1943,[14] he discussed the entire matter with Walter Kruger. Two days later, on 6 April, Galicia's governor met with Gottlob Berger, who headed Waffen-SS recruiting as well as the Policy Department of the Reich's Ministry for Eastern Territories.[15] And as Wachter was discussing the "Galicia" venture with various officials, Colonel Alfred Bisanz,[16] a former Galician Army officer, was surveying the sentiments of Galicia's former military men toward the idea of raising a sizable Galician military force.[17] Bisanz reported to Wachter that he had encountered considerable sympathy and support for such a project.[18]

Ignoring a warning from Himmler's secretary, SS-Obersturmbannführer Dr. Rudolf Brandt, to proceed with caution,[19] Wachter held a conference on Monday, 12 April 1943.[20] Attending this conference were various SS, police and party officials.[21] During the discussions, some details were worked out regarding the soon-to-be established Division; these propositions were then laid down for approval by the Reichsführer:[22]

1. *The Name*: Governor Wachter proposes these names for the Division: "SS-Freiwilligen Division Galizien" or the "Freiwilligen Division Galizien." The word "police" must be avoided in the name for political and psychological reasons. In accordance with the Division's name, the lowest rank of a soldier shall be that of "Grenadier," as the Division shall be a grenadier (infantry) Division.

2. *Uniforms*: Suggested uniforms are those of the police division prior to the "SS" designation or badge (field-gray, with a guard-type border). These uniforms are attractive to look at and they are in adequate supply. An acceptable badge might be that of the "Polizei-Hoheitszeichen." As with other volunteer European units, the division's own badge shall be sewn onto the right arm sleeve – a shield with the specific Galician emblem (Sonderabzeichen), which belongs to this country's tradition, but is not, however, a particular symbol of Ukrainian nationalist (grossukrainischen) aspirations.

3. *Arms*: Uniforms, same as in #2. The soldiers shall be armed according to the norms of a grenadier division. Horses, conveyance vehicles and harnesses could ostensibly be provided by the country, but as we know, the German and Soviet armies have requisitioned a large number of horses, while those that remain are fit to transport only lightweight vehicles. Two or three thousand horses is the maximum number that can be counted upon. The people can sew the harnesses if the Wehrmacht is willing to supply the necessary leather. Because Ukrainians are music lovers, the creation of an orchestra (or music section) is desirable.

4. *Quarters*: It is necessary to differentiate between quarters for the Division, itself, and its training camp versus barracks for reserve sections which can be assigned to surrounding cities. It would be an advantage if the Division could be quartered in Galicia. In that case, an adequate training site must be constructed. Barracks in surrounding cities would also have to be built.

5. *Funds*: All costs pertaining to personnel and materials shall be covered by the Ordnungspolizei. These costs will only cover those that are related to military service. Prearrangements, recruitment, enlistment, and transport, however, shall be financed out of a discreet budget.

6. *Training Period*: A longer period of time must be provided than for German formations, since here a singular human material is being dealt with.

7. *The Officer Corps*: It appears that a large number of officers and non-commissioned posts can soon be filled by Ukrainians. According to preliminary estimates, we have available:

a) Approximately 300 officers of Ukrainian nationality from the former Austrian Army;
b) Approximately 300 officers of Ukrainian nationality from the former Polish Army;
c) At the moment, the number of the Ukrainian intelligentsia who served in an army – especially the Polish Army – is unknown; however, they were denied officer status for political reasons. It is advisable that following a three-month stint of frontline service, they should be sent to a four-month officer's training course at an officer's training facility.
d) Officers from the former Ukrainian Army, for the greater part, served in the former Austrian Army. But due to their age, most former officers of the

Austrian army are unsuitable for service at the front; therefore, it has been suggested that they be attached to reserve units, because for political reasons, we should not withdraw them from this particular constituency and halt their active participation. Officers for the frontline sections will have to be supplemented. The ranks held by officers in former armies should be restored to them. This also refers to those ranks which were elevated in the Ukrainian Army during the liberation wars, provided adequate documents can verify this. It can be expected that some of them will prove incapable of performing their duties adequately or fulfilling the obligations required of their rank. In that case, they shall be released from service. Nevertheless, lowering ranks should be avoided. Initially, approximately 600 officers, 50 physicians, and 20 veterinarians are necessary. Age limits for officers shall not yet be established.

8. *Non-Commissioned Officers (NCOs)*: Around 2,000 NCOs are required. NCOs trained in the Polish Army outnumber the officers. It will not be difficult to supplement them from the ranks of the soldiers. The positions of the so-called [Ukrainian] "bunchuzhny" (standard-bearers: chief or head of the administrative and personnel functions of a company and a position comparable to the rank of a senior NCO) must be filled by older NCOs from the Austrian Army because they are conversant in both languages as well as experienced in the internal procedures, of military service.

9. *Cadres (Stammpersonal)*: Major Degener has disclosed that he can provide the following for the cadres: 300 NCOs from Holland and 300 NCOs from Orienburg, while a battalion cadre presently enroute to Lublin shall be available for the proposed police regiment "Galicia." For transport purposes and delivery of provisions, an auto-column or convoy can be formed out of 62 wagons.

10. *Composition of Privates*: Recruitment must be conducted on a grand scale. On account of the average low class of human material, especially from the racial aspect, individuals from racial groups III and IV shall also be accepted.[23] Minimum height 165 cm's (approx. 5'5"). Those born between 1908-1925, inclusively, shall be accepted for enlistment, and those who have previously served in the military – 1901, inclusively. The same shall apply for NCOs. Wages for the soldiers and the members of their families shall be equal to those of the Germans. Specific information concerning this shall be announced during the recruitment procedures.

Galicia Division

11. *The Oath*: The oath shall remain the same as has been up to the present for all volunteer formations.

12. *Religious Guidance*: Because of the deeply religious character of Ukrainians in Galicia, as well as their particular attachment to the Greek Catholic Church, it is advisable to provide the Division with field clergy.

13. *Recruitment and Deadlines*: Means of recruitment action:

a) Appeal. An appeal already has been sent to the Reichsführer for approval.

b) Colored posters.

c) Announcements with specific information about wages, insurance, and the Division's task.

d) The Military Board. It shall be composed primarily of former officers of the Austrian Army and the Ukrainian Army as well as representatives of the Ukrainian Central Committee. Its primary function is the recruitment effort. It shall maintain authorized representatives at the Kraishauptmans and Landkommissars who shall, in a coordinated operation, conduct the recruitment effort in their regions and districts (counties).

e) Obviously, all possible methods of propaganda shall be utilized, such as the media's press and radio.

In order to facilitate the work of the committees to enlist the SS and police, recruitment shall be divided into the so-called "Vormusterung" (pre-selection recruiting) and "Musterung" (selection recruiting). The branch or organ known as the "recruitment committee" ("Wehrbekommission") shall be headed by the Vormusterung, whose composition shall include a Kreishauptmann or Landkommissar, a police officer and an authorized representative of the Military Board. The police officer shall have the right to decide who shall receive the so-called "Vorlaufigen Annameschein" (temporary certificate of summons), which requires the volunteer to report to the recruitment committee (Annamekomission), which shall then conduct the actual review. These two phases should occur within 6 to 8 days. The purpose of a "temporary certificate" is to avoid having officials assign a given individual to a different service. The approximate plan of action is as follows:

28 April: Festive proclamation in Lviv. The following must be encouraged to attend: Kreishauptmanns, Landkommissars, representatives of the Wehrmacht, the Police, other government officials in the district, the Military

Board, the Ukrainian Central Committee and representatives of the Greek Catholic Church. By then, Colonel Bisanz will have organized the Military Board and its subordinate sections.

29 April: Each Kreishauptmann shall convene the appropriate officials and begin the recruitment action. Propaganda material from Lemberg (Lviv) shall be distributed simultaneously.

1 May: From this day, the work of the recruitment commission can begin. Within a week, the other committees can begin. The projected number of committees that will work simultaneously is six.

15 May: Lt. Gen. Pfeffer-Wildenbrunch claims that a cadre will be prepared to accept the first volunteers. With the aim of reaching a wider populace, it is advisable to conduct a special recruitment effort among those called to "Service for the Fatherland" (Baudienstangehorigen). In principle, the promise of volunteerism should be adhered to.

14. In order to regulate organizational matters which shall arise in connection with the creation of this Division, it is necessary to subordinate the working staff to the Führer of the SS and the police in the district of Galicia (SS-und Polizeiführer). Later, he will be replaced by a "Kommandeur der Erganzungseinheiten" (Commander of Supplemental Sections). Special attention must be paid to these sections from the very beginning, because that is where various difficulties may arise – as previous experience has shown – and which may later lead to dire consequences.

Signed:
Dr. Wachter

As the initial preparations were being undertaken Gottlob Berger, undoubtedly to see just how favorably Galicia's populace would react to the formation of a combat division, began a prerecruitment drive to seek volunteers for a so-called "Galician Police Rifle Regiment." (Polizei-Schutzen Regiment "Galizien"[24]). On 24 March 1943, Berger noted no less than 12,000 volunteers had stepped forward.[25]

Satisfied that enough volunteers could be found for a new Waffen-SS division, Wachter proceeded with the many necessary tasks required to establish a military formation. But as the originators of the "Galicia" Division continued with their planning, on 16 April, a telegram arrived from Himmler's adjutant, SS-Hauptsturmführer Werner Grothmann. Signed by Grothmann, the telegram informed Wachter that at the moment Himmler was unable to speak further to Wachter in regards to the Division and to wait for further instructions.[26] Needless to say, Wachter was very displeased with the 16 April directive, and he feared Himmler was possibly changing his mind. Therefore, he asked Berger for assistance in convincing Himmler to keep the "Galicia" infantry division in motion. And on 19 April 1943, Wachter personally wrote to Himmler's adjutant asking Grothmann to encourage Himmler about the previous agreement designating 28 April as the day of the proclamation.[27]

In the very end, only Himmler's final approval would determine whether the inauguration would actually be carried out or not. Informed by Berger and Wachter that preparations for the "Galicia" Division were nearing completion, that Galicia's populace was awaiting the official announcement, and fully aware of the demands posed by the Russian front, Himmler gave in and approved the proclamation of 28 April.[28]

During the same period of time that Galicia's governor was conferring with Himmler and other high-ranking Germans within the General-Government in regards to the "Galicia" Division, he also held a series of meetings with Galicia's Ukrainian leaders in the General Government, as well as with members of the Ukrainian Central Committee (UCC). Overall, the idea was supported by many Ukrainians and by the Chairman of the Ukrainian Central Committee, Professor Dr. Volodymyr Kubiyovych.[29]

In order to understand why so many Ukrainians supported such a venture, especially after so many of them had suffered at the hands of the Nazi's, it is important to understand what the Ukrainian Central Committee represented, who Kubiyovych was, what role he played in this committee, how Galicia's Ukrainian leaders viewed upcoming world events in the spring of 1943, and what they strove for.

6

The UCC and Its Role in the
Creation of the "Galicia" Division

Following the Nazi-Soviet destruction of Poland, a small part of the Western Ukraine was incorporated into the General-Government. Under Nazi Germany's occupation, all Ukrainian parties and organizations were dissolved. But because of widespread communist brutalities occurring throughout Soviet-occupied Western Ukrainian regions and Poland proper, large numbers of people, including approximately 30,000 Ukrainians,[1] fled into the German zones of occupation.

Faced with a huge refugee problem and seeking ways to ease the problem, German authorities permitted the establishment of a non-political Ukrainian coordinating committee in April 1940. This was done strictly for administrative purposes.[2] As a result, the Ukrainian Central Committee was formed.[3] Throughout the war, this Ukrainian body was the only organization permitted by Nazi authorities to exist in the General-Government.[4] And in August 1941, when the rest of Eastern Galicia was incorporated into the General-Government, the Ukrainian Central Committee's work was extended to this area as well.

The Ukrainian Central Committee organized and conducted as much humanitarian and cultural work as it could within the limits established by Nazi authorities. The committee especially involved itself in social welfare, coordinating its activities through the International Red Cross. It provided food, medical assistance, and shelter to numerous wartime refugees; ran orphanages, soup lines, and clothing centers; and reorganized the various professionals among the many refugees to reestablish as best as possible educational, vocational and technical training. The committee also revived the shattered Ukrainian churches and promoted religious instruction.

Under the Nazi occupation, Ukrainians were exposed to much ruthlessness. Forced labor conscriptions, arrests, concentration camps and firing squads characterized the daily lives of Galicia's inhabitants. As a responsible social-service agency, the Ukrainian Central Committee frequently appealed on behalf of many individuals and, on occasion, actually succeeded in saving human lives.

Because someone was needed to direct the Ukrainian Central Committee, Volodymyr Kubiyovych, an internationally-established scholar but a political novice, was appointed as its director. Although apolitical, Kubiyovych was also fluent in a number of languages. Thus, he was acceptable to all Ukrainians as well as to the German occupiers. And from the outset, Kubiyovych demonstrated exceptional abilities as a leader, organizer and, in every sense, a statesman.

As head of the Ukrainian Central Committee, Kubiyovych frequently protested to German authorities about Nazi brutalities inflicted upon the Ukrainian population, both orally and in writing. Following the collapse of Hitler's Germany, some of Kybiyovych's letters were found among the German documents and placed in the archives of the Nuremberg courts.[5] On several occasions, Nazi police forces not only threatened Kubiyovych with arrest, but even threatened to dissolve the Ukrainian Central Committee.[6] Kubiyovych felt that the only reason this threat was never carried out was because from the autumn of 1941, the German military and political situation continued to deteriorate on a daily basis.[7]

In the spring of 1943, many Ukrainian leaders were carefully reevaluating the current situation to gain an understanding of what might happen in the near future. Although they feared, hated and opposed Nazism, the Ukrainian's also feared, hated and opposed Soviet communism. They fully realized that the chances of a German victory, especially after Stalingrad, were slim. What many Ukrainian leaders now hoped to see was a protracted struggle which would weaken both Nazi Germany and Soviet Russia to the point that both totalitarian powers would be forced to abandon their designs of controlling Eastern European lands. Many also believed that the United States and Great Britain, in accordance with the Atlantic Charter,[8] or out of concern for the balance of power resulting from Soviet Russia's expansionism, would not allow the Soviets to control Eastern Europe once Hitler's Germany was defeated. Galicia's leaders also recalled the "Four Freedoms" address delivered on 6 January 1941 by President Franklin Roosevelt to America's congress which advocated a "just and peaceful world order."[9]

Some Ukrainian leaders believed that once Germany was defeated, a break would immediately occur between the Soviets and the Western Allies.[10] Galicia's national leaders also knew that a military formation could be used politically as well as militarily. With the collapse of one totalitarian power (inevitably Nazi Germany) and the withdrawal of Soviet Russia, the Ukrainian leaders anticipated a period of uncertainty in the region, much like that witnessed after the First World War when both Imperial Russia and the Austro-Hungarian empires collapsed.[11] And the Ukrainians knew that one of the main reasons (if not the reason) why the Ukrainian National Republic collapsed was due to military weaknesses. Fully aware of the fact that the only nations which arose after World War I were those which possessed a strong military, Galicia's leaders realized that in order to reassert themselves in the near future, the Ukrainian nation would-need to possess an efficient and skilled military.

Some Ukrainians felt that the UPA guerrilla army could fill this need. But others considered the UPA's military value (especially from a conventional military point of view) to be negligible. Because unconventional guerrilla groups are frequently difficult to control – both militarily and politically – for such reason the need for a conventional military force was emphasized. Since it was also argued that thousands of Ukrainians had already been conscripted for labor, and some were already incorporated into Germany's military, it would therefore be more advantageous to the Ukrainian cause to have their manpower concentrated in a distinct Ukrainian formation rather than scattered throughout various non-Ukrainian units.

Regardless of the many arguments for or against the establishment of such a military formation, in the end, most Ukrainian leaders and the UCC did concur that Galicia's Ukrainian movement had to seize the chance to organize a professional military force for immediate and near future needs. And once organized, a sizable, armed Ukrainian force could be used against any opponent and even, if necessary, against the Germans who originally had sponsored the project.[12]

It should be pointed out that had Kubiyovych or the UCC opposed this project, neither Kubiyovych nor any other opposing Ukrainian organization or group would have been able to stop this project.[13] European events were moving swiftly and German authorities would always have found a sufficient number of anti-communist males to recruit for a division. Fully realizing this, Kubiyovych therefore went along with the project and, through it, attempted to improve the Ukrainian position.[14] In his autobiography, "Meni 70" ("I Am 70"), Kubiyovych claims he felt the forming of such a volunteer formation could possibly have resulted in a German change of policy toward Ukraine. It was even speculated that Hitler might reconsider his racist policy toward the Ukrainians and, perhaps, would even accept a form of Ukrainian statehood or, at least, curb the excesses of his police.[15] Additionally, because Ukrainian leaders had learned in early 1943 that Governor-General Frank, in close cooperation with the Gestapo and SS, planned to conduct a mass deportation of the Ukrainian populace from many areas of Western Ukraine in the summer of 1943 to make room for German colonists,[16] Ukrainian leaders reasoned a military force in divisional strength would thwart any such plans.[17]

With these observations and thoughts in mind, the UCC's leaders brought the matter up to other Galician leaders for discussion. But the idea of a German-sponsored division, as well as the enthusiasm shown for it, caused much confusion and uncertainty within the underground Bandera and the Melnyk factions of the Organization of Ukrainian Nationalists, within the ranks of the UPA guerrilla army, and amongst a number of former Galician military men. Hearing of Wachter's plans for organizing a division, and the UCC's support for it, the Ukrainian underground found itself forced into a crossroads situation. Needless to say, the various groups ran into a serious problem and whether they wanted to or not, they were forced to take a stand on this matter.

OUN-B/OUN-M/UPA Views Regarding the "Galicia" Division
Strong opposition to the formation of the "Galicia" Division (or for that matter any kind of Ukrainian-German co-operation), immediately came from Bandera's OUN-B faction.[18] In an underground bulletin published in May 1943, Bandera's followers denounced the "Galicia" Division venture by submitting an article titled "Around the SS Division "Galicia.""[19] This article strongly criticized the idea of forming a Division under German auspices and claimed that the Germans were forming it in order to "deprive (the Ukrainian movement) of its active element" by "throwing it away as cannon fodder." Emphasizing that "this is a typical colonial element, somewhat comparable to the British Army's Indian or New Zealand Divisions," it also warned that "the creation of the so-called 'Galicia' Division will, in the long run, result in a loss of prestige for the idea of a Ukrainian state altogether."[20] In conclusion, the article stated, "today, we have no doubts that not a Ukrainian, but a German colonial element is forming. The attitude of the Ukrainian nation to it is, as it was to all previous German experiments – negative."[21]

Bandera's faction also argued that from the German side there is not only no discussion about creating an independent Ukraine but no recognition about any kind of Ukrainian political leadership.[22] Therefore, many Ukrainians pondered and asked "how can the patriotic Ukrainian youth even be called up to sacrifice their lives for the Hitlerites who have savagely destroyed millions of Ukrainians and are not even renouncing their plans of depopulating the whole Ukraine and turning it into an area for German settlement." As proof, the Division's opponents cited the destruction of the Ukrainian 30 June 1941 government and the fact that German authorities would not even permit "the Division to use its proper title – Ukrainian."[23]

Throughout Galicia, Bandera's faction strongly agitated against the Division.[24] Bandera's followers insisted that Nazi Germany could not be trusted, and that supporting such an idea would in the long run only harm the Ukrainians. Repeatedly, they warned that such a project would be totally fruitless because if somehow the Germans should win, then "this would be the end of the Ukrainians." But if they lost, "Ukrainian participation in German formations would only smear the whole Ukrainian nation." Therefore, they posed this question: "and just what exactly are the Ukrainians to fight for within the ranks of the German army?"[25]

Along with the OUN-B, a number of Galician military men also voiced their opposition. One of the strongest critics and opponents was Colonel Roman Dashkovych. Years later, General Mykola Kapustians'kyi, a former Galician Army leader, would recall how:

> "Governor Wachter never covered the political strategic views set forth by the OUN...Wachter's act of 28 April 1943 was strictly one of a military character, and one without a political program. This complicated our viewpoints towards enlistment into the Division. As a result, our military elite could not take an active participation neither in the negotiations, and neither in the creation of the Division."[26]

As for Kubiyovych, the Ukrainian leader never discussed the Division's matters with any representative of the OUN-B, OUN-M, or, with any other Ukrainian party or organization.[27]

Because Nazi authorities forced Bandera's OUN-B faction to operate underground, at no time did Bandera's faction, or Bandera himself, participate in any negotiations or efforts to establish the Division.[28] Furthermore, in as much as during this time Bandera was incarcerated in a Nazi concentration camp, he had very little information about the Division, had no control over the forming of the Division, and throughout the period of its active existence, Bandera had absolutely nothing to do with the Division.[29]

In the very end, Bandera's followers could not reach a compromise on the issue. But the last thing the OUN-B faction wanted to do (or could afford to do), was to oppose the proponents of the Division by assassination or sabotage, which would only further weaken the Ukrainian position. Therefore, the OUN-B officially announced that although their battle would continue against Nazism and communism, they would remain neutral regarding the issue of the "Galicia" Division.[30]

Galicia Division

Unlike Bandera's OUN-B, a number of Andreas Melnyk's OUN-M faction did favor the creation of the "Galicia" Division.[31] As early as 1941 and prior to being arrested, Melnyk had petitioned German authorities for permission to establish Ukrainian military formations in order to assist Germany in its eastern campaign.[32] But Melnyk received no reply and shortly afterwards, when Himmler's police began to arrest Ukrainian members of the OUN factions, Melnyk, in a desperate attempt to preserve the OUN-M, repeated his offer in a personal letter to Hitler. Once again, Nazi authorities stubbornly refused Melnyk's proposal and because Hitler himself insisted that "only Germans may bear arms," nothing ever became of this.

By 1943, Melnyk, himself, was incarcerated and many of his followers were dead or incarcerated. Melnyk's faction was largely shattered and those of his followers who were not arrested or shot were conducting underground activities. Yet, a number of Melnyk's survivors were receptive to the project on the grounds that the "Galicia" Division could be used as a future nucleus for the establishment of an independent Ukrainian Army. Although there were those within Melnyk's faction which opposed the Division[33] (one of the strongest protests came from Deputy Leader Oleh Olshych who headed the OUN-M's underground faction) in general, Melnyk's survivors favored the Division. Melnyk's survivors reasoned (as did the UCC) that once organized, the "Galicia" Division could be utilized not only against Soviet Russia but also against Hitler's Germany. Solely for this reason, a number of OUN-M survivors supported the project.[34]

General Roman Shukhevych's Ukrainian Insurgent Army (UPA), which in 1943 was actively engaged in combat against Nazi Germany and its fascist allies, immediately denounced and opposed the "Galicia" Division.[35] Discouraging Galicia's youth from entering the Division with such slogans as "Flee into the forests!", the UPA simultaneously encouraged them to join the guerrilla ranks.[36]

But such a stand, although seemingly correct, only created problems for the UPA and, in desperation, the UPA's leadership was forced to reexamine the situation.

To begin with, problems and confusion developed when a lack of ideological agreement and coordinated actions among the various Ukrainian groups arose at this crucial moment. Within the Ukrainian community, certain Ukrainian leaders supported the idea of organizing a division, while others strongly opposed and propagandized against it. But, realistically speaking, in the end, the Ukrainians realized that they, themselves, would suffer most from such squabbles. And when the UPA encouraged young men to flee into the forests with no more than the clothes on their backs, it found itself inundated with large numbers of young males who not only had to be fed, clothed and sheltered, but at the same time needed to be armed, disciplined, trained and toughened to a guerrilla's way of life. Under such conditions, the UPA was faced with tremendous demands and, as with any other newly-founded guerrilla movement, in 1943 the UPA still lacked sufficient resources to take on any kind of major expansion. Thus, after carefully reevaluating UPA's position, Shukhevych and his followers were forced to reach a compromise with their fellow Ukrainians who supported the establishment of the "Galicia" Division.[37]

To best resolve the differences, a secret meeting was held between the UPA guerrilla general and Roman Krokhmaliuk, a member of the Galician Military Board.[38] Through underground channels, a pre-designated location was established, and the rendezvous was held late one night in early October 1943 in a widow's house on a side street on the outskirts of Lviv.[39] Because Shukhevych was a "most" wanted figure for Nazi authorities, such a meeting was not only dangerous personally for the guerrilla commander, but also for anyone attending it. Therefore, to best protect Shukhevych and the others, few knew of the event and the differences were discussed and resolved only by Shukhevych and Krokhmaliuk.

The last time that Krokhmaliuk had seen Shukhevych was in 1937, during a skiing competition in the Carpathian Mountains. So after a quick exchange of greetings, both men got down to business.

The meeting lasted no more than thirty minutes. But in that short period of time matters regarding the Division's mission, the UPA's mission, Shukhevych's needs, the underground's propaganda effort against the Division and how the UPA could use the Division for its needs were discussed. The guerrilla commander emphasized that his goal was to organize and train elite units for the Ukrainian underground but, as Shukhevych conceded: "the underground has recently been receiving much unqualified personnel."[40] Realizing the importance of possessing both strong guerrilla and conventional forces, Shukhevych informed Krokhmaliuk that he now planned to use the proposed "Galicia" Division to his advantage. From the ranks of the Division's volunteers, Shukhevych would eventually organize strong cadres.[41] Pretending to volunteer, a number of UPA men would enlist into the Division, receive first-rate training, gather as much intelligence, weaponry and equipment as possible, and then desert into the ranks of the UPA. To accomplish this, Shukhevych promised that the UPA would no longer hinder or threaten the Division and that all of those who had previously volunteered for the formation but had then soon fled into the ranks of the UPA, would be released so that they could report back to the Division.[42] Shukhevych also told Krokhmaliuk that he respected its volunteers and considered them true Ukrainian patriots.[43] The meeting ended in an atmosphere of agreement and cooperation, and before they slipped away into the dark night, both men established a password. This password would only be known to themselves in the event that some important or personal meeting would again need to be set up at a future date.[44]

Forced at last to face the fact that the Division would become a reality – with or without the formal approval or support of the OUN-B, OUN-M, or the UPA – the various factions either had to render support to the project or, if still opposed to it, remain completely neutral.

Ukrainian Proposals For the Division
In early 1943, Volodymyr Kubiyovych held a series of meetings with General-Governor Wachter to establish some basic rules and needs for the Galicia Division.[45] After extensive discussions, the Ukrainian Central Committee presented a number of demands, of which the most important were:[46]

1) The Division is to be used only against Communist forces on the Eastern front;[47]

2) The officer corps is to be Ukrainian;[48]

3) The name and patch of the Division is to be Ukrainian;[49]

4) Members of the Division are to be assured spiritual-religious rights;

5) All Ukrainians held in prisons and concentration camps, including the imprisoned officers of "Nachtigall" and "Roland" are to be released immediately;[50]

6) The Division will become a part of the Ukrainian Army which shall arise in due time;

7) The Division is only to be a part of the Wehrmacht;[51]

8) The soldiers' families are to be provided with security;

9) In the territory of Galicia, a Military Board is to be formed to help tend to military matters and to look into the interests of the soldiers and their families.[52]

After these demands had been presented, discussed, and largely met, the first steps for forming the Division had been taken. Now the idea had to be proclaimed to Galicia's citizenry and volunteers had to be sought.

The Proclamation
Wednesday, 28 April 1943. From an old palace located on Charnetsky Street in the Galician capital of Lviv, where Galicia's ancient rulers had presided at one time, Wachter's proclamation was officially made public.[53] Announced throughout the

66

whole of Galicia, the Galician governors' proclamation of 28 April may be cited as the Division's official date of birth.[54] With this proclamation, a number of main points were announced and these points were as follows:[55]

1) ... Now and then, the Ukrainian Galician population had expressed the desire to participate, with arms at hand, in the armed struggle of the German state. The Führer, acknowledging Galicia's stand, acceded to this wish to take part in the battle and so permitted the creation of the SS Division "Galicia."

2) Every soldier of this Division shall obtain full military equipment, pay, meals and benefits for his family on the same scale as soldiers of the German army. Spiritual guidance for the volunteers shall rest within the hands of your clergy.

3) The Division's volunteers shall wear their regional insignia. When enlisting into the Division's ranks, those volunteers whose fathers fought valiantly in the ranks of the old Austrian army shall be given top priority.

4) Ukrainian-Galician youth! You have earned the right to battle your mortal enemy, the Bolshevik, for your faith and fatherland, for your families and for the beloved fields of your land, and for a just new order in a victorious new Europe...

For Wachter, the issue was critical: he knew that, in essence, the success or failure of the entire operation depended on the number of registered volunteers; as well, the future of Wachter's career was probably also contingent upon it. So after taking into consideration Galicia's population, Wachter established a goal to raise one division of approximately 20,000 volunteers.

In his orders issued to the Germans on 28 April 1943, Wachter emphasized the need to refrain from the use of force in attaining this number stating:

"The application of any methods of coercion, including any sort of moral/ psychological pressure must be excluded – otherwise, the entire enterprise will lose its political significance."[56]

That same day, Wachter appealed to Galicia's youth to enlist into the "Galicia" Division to fight communism, and to defend their families, their homeland and Europe.[57] And on 6 May 1943, professor Kubiyovych appealed to Galicia's youth. In a highly moving appeal, Kubiyovych stated:[58]

Galicia Division

"The long-awaited moment has arrived when the Ukrainian people will again have the opportunity to come out with gun in hand to do battle against its most grievous foe – Bolshevism. The Führer of the Greater German Reich has agreed to the formation of a separate Ukrainian volunteer military unit under the name SS Riflemen's Division "Halychyna.""

Thus we must take advantage of this historic opportunity; we must take up arms because our national honor, our national interest, demand it.

Veterans of the struggles for independence, officers and men of the Ukrainian Galician Army! Twenty-two years ago you parted with your weapons when all strength to resist had ebbed. The blood of your comrades-in-arms who fell on the Fields of Glory calls you to finish the deed already begun, to fulfill the oath you swore in 1918. You must stand shoulder to shoulder with the invincible German army and destroy, once and for all, the Bolshevik beast, which insatiably gorges itself on the blood of our people and strives with all its barbarity to arrive at our total ruination.

You must avenge the innocent blood of your brothers tortured to death in the Solovets Islands camps, in Siberia, in Kazakhstan, the millions of brothers starved to extinction on our bountiful fields by the Bolshevik collectivizers.

You, who followed the thorny but heroic path of the Ukrainian Galician Army, understand more than anyone what it is to fight in the face of uneven odds. You realize that one can only face an enemy such as Red Moscow shoulder to shoulder with an army capable of destroying the Red monster.

The failures of the anti-Bolshevik forces of the European Entente in the years 1918 to 1920 testify irrevocably that there is only one nation capable of conquering the USSR – Germany. For twenty-two years you waited with sacred patience for the holy war against the barbarous Red hordes menacing Europe.

It goes without saying that, in this titanic struggle, the fate of the Ukrainian people is also being decided. Thus, we must fully realize the importance of this moment and play a military role in this struggle. Now the battle is not uneven, it is not hopeless. Now, the greatest military power in the world stands opposed to our eternal foe.

Now or never!

Youth of Ukraine!

I turn to you with particular attention and call upon you to join the SS Riflemen's Division "Halychyna." You were born at the dawn of the great age, when the new history of Ukraine began to be written in crimson Blood and golden Glory.

Chapter 6: The UCC

When your fathers and elder brothers, first and alone in all of Europe, took up arms against the most fearful enemy of Ukraine and of all humanity;

When your brothers, inflamed as you are now, first wrote into history the peerless heroic deeds at the Battle of Kruty;[59]

When your brothers covered themselves with the glory of the first Winter Campaigns against the Bolshevik monster;

When they, in the midst of a newly "peaceful" Europe, were the first to go forth against the Bolshevik invader in the second Winter Campaign, writing into history the heroic deeds of the Battle of Bazar;

It was then that You, our Youth, were born, and as You grew, across the whole of Ukraine revolts rose up against the Bolshevik invader, who by ruin, famine, exile, torture, and murder strove to wipe our nation from the face of the earth. Then you, our Ukrainian Youth, laid your colossal sacred sacrifices on the altar of your Fatherland. You burned with the sacred fire of love for it, hardened your spirit for it, readied yourself for the right moment of reckoning by arms. With longing in your heart, with glowing embers in Your soul, You waited for this moment.

And now this moment has come.

Dear Youth, I believe that your patriotism, your selflessness, your readiness for armed deeds, are not mere hollow words, that these are your deep set feelings and convictions. I believe that You suffered deeply and understood the painful experiences of the past struggles for independence, and that You culled from them a clear sense of political realism, a thorough understanding of the national interest and a hardy readiness for the greatest of sacrifices for it. I believe in You, dear Youth, I believe that You will not idle while the Great Moment passes by, that you will prove to the whole world who you are, what you are worth, and what you are capable of.

Ukrainian Citizens!

I call upon you for great vigilance. The enemy does not sleep. In the memorable years of 1917-19, enemy propaganda lulled our people with lofty words about eternal peace, about the brotherhood of nations. Now this propaganda aims to tear weapons from our hands once again, and disseminates among us countless absurd slogans, groundless conjectures, febrile dreams. You know where this propaganda originates. You know its purpose. Counter it decisively, even when it comes forth under a Ukrainian guise, guilefully exploiting the uninformed and confused among the Ukrainian people. You know the value of arms, and thus I believe that, with God's assistance, You will worthily pass the test of political maturity history has put to you.

Ukrainian Citizens!

The time of waiting, the time of debilitation and suffering has come to an end. Now, the great moment of armed deeds has also come for our people. Side by side with the heroic army of Greater Germany and the volunteers of other European peoples, we too come forth to battle our greatest national foe and threat to all civilization. The cause is sacred and great and therefore it demands of us great efforts and sacrifices.

I believe that these efforts and sacrifices are the hard but certain road to our Glorious Future.

> Dr. Volodymyr Kubiyovych
> President
> Ukrainian Central Committee

Shortly after Kubiyovych's appeal, the aged ex-Austrian soldier and former commander of the Ukrainian Galician Army, General Kurmanovych, spoke on radio Lviv in support of the Division. With the final details at last worked out, with Wachter's and Kubiyovych's appeals presented, the Division officially entered its recruitment phase.

The Recruitment Phase

It should be noted that in the opening phases of recruitment, the number of potential volunteers for the Division was not that significant and, as a matter of fact, Wachter even feared that his plan might end up a fiasco.[60] Wachter needed 20,000 men[61] but at first he came no where close to finding that number.[62]

What caused the low enthusiasm is attributable to several factors. To begin with, the quarrel which developed among Ukrainian leaders (especially within the OUN-B, OUN-M, and the UPA) on whether to support or oppose the Division created an air of confusion and uncertainty for much of Galicia's youth. But to make matters worse, Wachter's proclamation indirectly announced to Galicia's people what many had already been suspecting for quite some time: that Germany's position was progressively deteriorating, the Soviets were advancing and that Galicia would be forced into the conflict.

Unfortunately, this situation no longer allowed Galicia's inhabitants to remain neutral. Those who had earlier hoped that Nazi Germany could be defeated without a Soviet reoccupation were forced to admit the fact that German defeat would only result in a Soviet reoccupation and with it, a renewal of the 1939-41 communist atrocities. So the question was no longer whether to "go or not to go" into military service but rather, the question was "whose service?"

Chapter 6: The UCC

Under such chaotic circumstances, many in Galicia were forced to make a decision on what course of action would be best for themselves, their families and their homeland. While several various options were available to an individual caught in these wartime circumstances, unfortunately, none was better than the others and yet, from one of the options a decision had to be made.

The first option was the UPA. But living, fighting, and simply surviving in any kind of guerrilla force is no easy task. To make matters worse, Shukhevych's guerrillas, in mid-1943, were in no position to take on an immediate major expansion. Furthermore, Shukhevych was now very supportive of the "Galicia" Division, and he planned to exploit the Division to the underground's advantage. So even if a man wanted to join the UPA, his possibilities of being accepted into guerrilla ranks were questionable.

The second option was to try to evade the Division, and any kind of military service, by hiding at home, or in the home of a relative or an acquaintance. However, in the long run, if sufficient numbers of volunteers were not recruited, there was always the possibility that manpower for the "Galicia" Division would be secured by conscription.[63] Still, even if someone would have managed to avoid a German draft (or another German "volunteer work recruitment" program), in the event of a communist reoccupation of Galicia, the Soviets would immediately impose their own military conscription. Of course, a Soviet draft would be far harsher than anything the Germans would ever impose. By the time a Russian conscription was concluded, virtually every male (and even many females) from the ages of 15 to 60 was swept up.[64] And to serve Stalin's state as "cannon fodder" was not an appealing idea. Therefore, a man living in Galicia had to take into consideration the survival factor, and determine if his chances of surviving the war would be better in the German or Soviet army.

The third option would be to enlist into the Division. Because it was a recognized fact that a strong and well-armed force could benefit Galicia (and eventually the remainder of Ukraine), for the moment, service within the "Galicia" Division could prove to have its advantages. And it did offer a young men residing in Galicia a much better alternative than service within a guerrilla or Soviet force.

By mid-1943, a number of those Ukrainians who were still not very fond of the idea finally consented to the fact that for the moment there was nothing else available to them and therefore, they stopped agitating against the Division and remained neutral. Others, (especially those within the UPA), concluded that perhaps the Division could somehow benefit the Ukrainian cause; therefore, they also reversed their position and now supported the venture.

With the arguments set aside, with influential Ukrainians sponsoring and encouraging men to volunteer for the Division, with a number of former Galician military men supporting the project and with the threat of a possible Soviet reoccupation of Galicia imminent, the number of men now willing to volunteer increased dramatically.[65]

"YOUTH OF GALICIA! ALL GREAT DEEDS BEGIN WITH SMALL ACTS! NOW OR NEVER! WITH A STEEL WALL, BAR THE EASTERN ENEMY! YOUTH OF GALICIA! NOW OR NEVER! NOW OR NEVER!"

Such slogans, heralded in a number of rallies and demonstrations throughout Galicia's many towns and cities, brought home the true seriousness of the present and upcoming situation. As a result, the recruiting campaign which followed produced a higher number of volunteers.

So why did large numbers of men willingly volunteer for the "Galicia" Division? Who were they? What, exactly, motivated a man to volunteer for a division under German auspices, especially after so many Ukrainians had suffered under Nazi rule? Undoubtedly, there were various complex reasons, and for a more thorough understanding, they must be examined in depth.

To begin with, many Galicians were idealistic and patriotic. Seeking ways to improve Galicia's and Ukraine's position, they were willing to undergo military training so that they could fight both Stalin's Russia and Hitler's Germany. Within Galicia (as previously in some other European nations), out-right enemies of Nazism and the SS volunteered only to preserve their nation and to better their national position against any external threat, including Nazism.[66] Although they fully realized that initially they would have to cooperate with Germany, they longed for the day when Galicia would be free of any foreign rule.[67]

Undoubtedly, some of Galicia's youths who volunteered had little or no understanding of the historical and political implications of the moment. Misinformed, misguided, bombarded with various propaganda, caught up in rapidly moving events, they believed that the creation of the "Galicia" Division (and even a "Ukrainian Army") was (or soon would be), the beginning of a major German political change toward Galicia and, in general, toward Ukraine.[68] As many other European volunteers, they were willing to volunteer into the Waffen-SS because of Berger's promise of independence for their states if they served for a while in Germany's military.[69] These volunteers were especially encouraged when in April and May of 1943, they witnessed the release of a number of imprisoned Ukrainians from various German jails and concentration camps.[70] And once released, some of the leaders themselves volunteered for service in the "Galicia" Division.[71]

In many cases, UPA guerrillas and its sympathizers joined the Division in order to infiltrate the formation and to obtain arms, equipment and training. Approximately how many of Shukhevych's fighters penetrated the Division has never been established, but it is known that a number of UPA fighters did enlist into the Division.[72]

Fear and hatred of communist Russia compelled many to volunteer for a formation destined for eastern front combat.[73]

Some joined because they feared that if enough volunteers were not recruited, manpower would be secured by conscription; therefore, to possibly secure a better position within the Division, it was advantageous to volunteer.[74]

As in any nation, there are always some whose quest for action, adventure and excitement – coupled with a desire to soldier – drives them to volunteer with little or no regard for a particular cause; and, as in other European nations, undoubtedly a small number who volunteered did so out of a sympathy for the Nazi concept of a "New Europe."[75]

But, the vast majority of those who volunteered did so out of a love for Ukraine and a sincere hatred for all forms of totalitarianism. At that time, most felt that this was the only path to self-liberation. Most had little regard for Nazi Germany and did not espouse its cause; their willingness to serve in a German-controlled formation was only surpassed by their desire to improve the Ukrainian position.[76]

Most of the recruits who volunteered for the Division were between the ages of 18 and 30.[77] Though there were those who attempted to enlist at 15, and a few were as old as 70.[78] Almost all were inexperienced recruits, most were from Galicia and very few had seen any previous military or police service.[79] A high percentage of the men came from professional or skilled families, but a number also hailed from agricultural backgrounds. The vast majority could read and write, and a percentage were college graduates (some of whom even possessed advanced degrees), or had been university or high school students at the time of enlistment.[80] A high percentage of the men were proficient in two or three languages, but others were proficient in more languages. They loved Galicia, Ukraine, its people, and because the vast majority possessed a high level of national consciousness, such virtues compelled them to volunteer.[81]

How many were willing to volunteer, and how many were in fact accepted, is difficult to establish. Often, the numbers varied tremendously, and propagandists boosted various (and unusually high) figures. In a number of cases, volunteers, themselves, inflated the figures. When a number of volunteers were rejected for military service, they attempted to enlist elsewhere; simultaneously, there were those who, in an attempt to avoid service, registered in several locations to cause confusion. The fact that the volunteers were not immediately accepted upon completing their physicals and were sent back home to await a call-up period also created some confusion when afterwards an attempt was made to properly recruit – and once again record – enlistment numbers. Regardless of the various discrepancies, it is important to determine as accurately as possible the true figures.

The Enlistment Figures
On 20 March 1943, Berger stated that at least 12,000 volunteers had stepped forward for the so-called "Galician Police Rifle Regiment."[82] But this figure was said to have increased to 20,000 once a strong anti-communist Russian theme was accepted.[83] It seems apparent, however, that the figures of 12,000 and 20,000 are approximate and in both cases were undoubtedly rounded out to the closest higher figure. If, for example, it had been known for a fact that 21,400 men had sought entrance, the organizers – but especially the German propagandists of the "Galician Rifle Regiment" – would undoubtedly have increased the figure to 22,000. Whatever the factual or exaggerated figures were, it may be stated correctly that enough volunteers for a regimental-sized unit could have easily been secured had the "Galician Rifle Regiment" been actually formed.

From 1 May to 8 May 1943, close to 32,000 had been registered for the Division.[84] On 11 May 1943, Kruger turned to Berger for further guidance[85] and on 1 June, a German broadcast announced 60,000 volunteers.[86] According to former Divisional staff officer, Major Wolf Dietrich-Heike, during May 1943 nearly 80,000 volunteered for service.[87] By 21 June 1943, a figure of 26,436 was announced for the Division.[88] Because these 26,436 were from the 1 June figure of 60,000, it is not known whether all of the 26,436 were properly processed and officially inducted into the Division. With so many candidates available, it is doubtful that all of the potential recruits were interviewed, classified, and physically examined by 21 June. Regardless, at the end of June, Berger again wrote Himmler and in his letter stated that around 80,000 volunteers had been found for the "Free-Volunteer Legion Galizien."[89] Of these 80,000 volunteers, 50,000 had been tentatively accepted and of the latter figure, 13,000 were in the process of being examined.[90] On 2 July 1943, in another letter to Himmler, Berger informed the Reichsführer that a strength of 28,000 had been reached.[91]

According to Kubiyovych, around 15,000 were called up out of 80,000 who sought to enlist;[92] Doroshenko cites that over 80,000 registered, 27,000 were found acceptable for military service and 19,000 were actually enlisted;[93] and Roman Krokhmaliuk, a former member of the Galician Military Board, states in his memoirs that from 28 April to 2 June 1943, a total of 81,999 men sought to volunteer.[94]

Some sources cite the number of volunteers as high as nearly 100,000 but of this figure, fewer than 30,000 were accepted.[95] As late as 29 March 1944, a British

Office Research Department Memorandum on "Liberated Ukraine," in analyzing
Ukrainian-Russian Relations and the Ukrainian Resistance Movement, erroneously
stated that four Waffen-SS divisions had been created in Galicia.[96] But the highest
(and most inaccurate) figure ever provided was in 1985 when a Polish source cited
"some 150,000 men."[97]

Needless to say, such reports and figures – whether actual or exaggerated –
were indeed truly impressive and Nazi propagandists had a heyday with the figures. Though the figure of "approximately 80,000" was indeed impressive, the
fact remains that the numbers would soon drop to a far lower range. To better
understand why this happened, it is important to understand what took place.

In order to determine a true figure of volunteers, and to have a better control
over the number of volunteers, Galicia's Military Board established this sequence
for the volunteering process:

1) All volunteers born between 1920 and 1925 would report to the recruiting centers;

2) All former soldiers, born between 1900 and 1920; and

3) All former officers and non-commissioned officers, who served in any
kind of army, should report to the reception centers regardless of age.[98]

Once established, the above recruiting criteria were very effective in formulating a more precise system of keeping tabs. Such control immediately provided a
more accurate and realistic figure of 53,000 volunteers.[99] From this strength, a
total of 42,000 volunteers were called up during the "Galicia" Division's first recruitment phase which lasted from 11 May to the end of June 1943.[100] From these
42,000 volunteers, 27,000 were found fit for military service,[101] but of the latter
figure only 13,000 were initially recruited.[102]

While, of course, approximately 13,000 eligible men were more than adequate
to create a division, it is clearly evident that many more were not accepted from
the initial approximate figures of 80,000 and 53,000. So the question remains,
what happened to the rest?

To begin with, a high percentage of the men who sought to enlist were either
too old, too young, ill, deformed, or physically/mentally unfit. Strict height restrictions also weeded out many.[103] Others were found to be politically unreliable,
and because it was suspected that such individuals could pose a direct threat to
Germany (and possibly even the Division), such volunteers were not permitted to
enlist.[104] Homosexuals (or those suspected of homosexuality) were also excluded.
In some cases there were those who wanted to enlist and actually signed up but

family matters prevented them from enlisting. And, finally, there were many who were sympathetic to the cause, signed up, and even passed their physicals. But when the 11th hour came, they lacked the courage and moral strength to go. Years later, these individuals would cite various excuses for their ineptness, with the most popular one being "I knew that in the end it would not amount to anything!"[105]

Yet at the same time Galicia's manpower was being sought, processed, and inducted, a number of leaders from within the higher circles of the Third Reich, as well as from the Allied world, began to oppose the Division.

German, Soviet, and Polish Opposition to the "Galicia" Division
For a number of SS leaders, it was difficult to acknowledge the fact that a Waffen-SS formation was being created from "subhumans."[106] In a letter addressed to Lt. General Winkelmann in Berlin, SS-Oberst-Gruppenführer Kurt Daluege[107] was one of the first high-ranking Nazi officials to voice warning signals on creating such a Division. What is especially interesting about Daluege's letter is that in his opening paragraph, Daluege claimed that Himmler had no knowledge of a "Polizei-Schutzen Division" (Police Rifle Division), nor was he aware of its designation and the formation's present status.[108] As a result, Daluege issued the following directive on 14 April 1943:[109]

> "A front-line division will be raised for the Waffen-SS and formed by the Waffen-SS. It will consist of Greek-Catholic Ukrainians and will be titled the "Galicia" Division because these Ukrainians hail from Galicia. The other Ukrainians in the General Government, including those in the Lublin area, are Greek-Orthodox. From these will be formed police regiments, which will possess a German (leadership) cadre; these Ukrainian regiments will not consist of more than 3 battalions. Entirely excluded from participation will be the Ukrainian intelligentsia which is nationalistically minded, including Bandera. The Reichsführer SS categorically prohibits such individuals because he fully recalls the war period years of 1917-1918, when German agents attempted to form an independent Ukraine. Yet when the moment arose, the Ukrainian leadership, to whom belonged a majority of Bandera's people, thanked and praised the Germans [for their assistance] by opening fire on German officers and soldiers. I also desire that SS-Gruppenführer Berger establish as soon as possible the strength of the two Ukrainian [OUN] groups, as well as the [religious] Greek Catholic groups (in Galicia) and those of the Greek Orthodox (in Lublin)."

Of course, both Himmler and Daluege were incorrect in blaming Bandera and his followers for the 1917-1918 situation because in those years, Bandera was a boy of no more than eight or nine years of age. However, both men were correct in projecting a possible threat because it was a matter of historical fact that patriotically-inclined, German-trained Ukrainians did stage a violent revolt against the Kaiser's forces and on 30 July 1918, killed Field-Marshall Erich von Eichorn, Imperial Germany's Commander of Ukraine. Prior to this revolt, many Ukrainians had been recruited and armed by the Kaiser's generals in an attempt to secure manpower against Imperial Russia. Fearing a potential repetition of such a negative historical event, Himmler sought to keep hard-core Ukrainian patriots out of the "Galicia" Division.[110]

From the Reichssicherheitshauptamt (Central Security Department – RSHA), a shadowy organization which existed strictly for internal security, voices of opposition also arose. Months later, Karl Wolfe, one of the highest ranking SS officials within the RSHA, himself verified the RSHA's dissatisfaction when he stated:

"We, within the RSHA, were against the forming of the Division. We did not believe in Ukrainian loyalties in regard to any cooperation with Germany. To us, it was apparent that we would only train our enemies which, sooner or later, will defect to the UPA."[111]

And from the city of Horokhiv, where 'Gebeitskommissar' Harter's Headquarters for the provinces of Volyn and Podolia was located, 'Gebietskommissar' Harter sent no less than two notes of protest through party channels to his superior in the city of Lutsk, Volyn province.[112] As had Daluege, Harter emphasized the events of 1918 and voiced a strong opinion on "how arms meant for the Ukrainians in the Galicia Division would be utilized against the Germans." In turn, on 30 June, Lutsk's SS and Police commander endorsed Harter's protests to SS commander Erich, who was the Higher SS and Police Führer (HSSPF) of Southern Russia, and whose main headquarters operated from the Ukrainian capital city of Kiev.[113] In a short but expressive note of concern and warning, Lutsk's police commander stated:

"There is the memory of what happened in 1918. In a moment of opportunity, they'll turn their [German] provided arms against Germans."

Faced with such a grave matter, on 8 July 1943, "Southern Russia's" Police Führer addressed the matter directly to Himmler:

Galicia Division

"I would be grateful, if the Reichsführer-SS would issue a directive, in which it would be explained, that the "Galicia" Division is limited to the territory of Galicia, and categorically would bar Ukrainians."[114]

Although, earlier, he had granted permission for Himmler's proposal to raise a volunteer force in Galicia, Hitler continued to distrust Eastern Europeans. Hitler's negative viewpoints were clearly expressed during a military conference held on 8 June 1943 when he was shown a copy of a leaflet proposed by Colonel General Reinhard Gehlen, Germany's eastern fronts intelligence director, to be dropped over Soviet lines. Although nothing in the leaflet mentioned anything about Andrei Vlasov (a former Soviet general who sought to topple Stalin), it did contain such phrases as "liberation army" and, to make matters worse, Hitler was also informed that many of his eastern front commanders, including Field Marshal Kluge, were supportive of such an army.

Angered by such ideas, Hitler went off on a long monologue. Condemning any talk of a "liberation army," he declared:

"...I can tell Kluge and all those other officers just one thing: I will never build up a Russian army. That is a first-class fantasy. I don't want anybody harboring the notion that all we have to do is to establish a Ukrainian state and everything will be all right, it will give us a million soldiers. We won't get anything, not a single man. But we would be committing an act of sheer madness. We would throw away our war aim, which has nothing to do with a Ukrainian republic!"[115]

Erich Koch, Ukraine's Reichskommissar, also strongly denounced the idea of raising the "Galicia" Division. Virulently opposed to Ukrainian autonomy or statehood in any degree or form, Koch and his cohorts in Ukraine, upon learning of plans to create the "Galicia" Division, immediately began to agitate against the formation.[116] Koch especially feared that perhaps this would be the beginning of a new German change of policy towards Ukraine.

At first, Koch's criticisms were largely ignored. But Koch's criticisms finally reached such a high-pitched tempo that Berger, on 10 December 1943, wrote a protest directly to Reichsführer Himmler and Berlin's Reichsminister of Internal Affairs about Koch's outrage. Berger wrote:[117]

"Reichsführer!
Some time ago the Reichskommissar of the Ukraine, in his unprecedented

letter, took a stand against the "Galicia" Division. It contained distortion after distortion and many falsehoods.

Contrary to my proposal, Reich Leader Rosenberg demanded answers to that report from the Governor-General [Frank] which would precisely and heavily charge Reichskommissar Koch in exact terms.

Now, weeks later, the enclosed reply has arrived. As usually is the case with Gauleiter Koch, Koch's reply contains half-truths, half-lies, and again, involves the Reichsführer-SS. Unheard of rudeness!

Today, Rosenberg gave me that [Koch's] report with an ironical smile. As the enclosure manifests itself, I have taken a clear stand. I do not intend to quarrel with Gauleiter Koch. But, please, I would like you to understand that I must denounce such improprieties.

Whenever I officially inform someone of some matter, and if I have to write it down so that it corresponds with facts, at least I take the pain to observe the highest principle of the Schutzstaffel [which is] – to be truthful, and to accomplish it in an exemplary manner."

(Signed) Berger
SS-Obergruppenführer

To satisfy the Division's critics, Himmler strongly reiterated the point that the Division would not consist of "Ukrainians" but rather, would be composed of "Galicians."[118] And to combat Ukrainian patriotism within the Division (or at least curb it), as early as 30 June, Himmler ordered that only the word "Galicia," rather than "Ukrainian," was to be used; furthermore, its volunteers were to be referred to as "Galicians."[119] On 14 July, Himmler reiterated his previous order with another decree addressed to all 'Hauptamtschefs.' Very briefly written, the order simply stated:

"In reference to the Galician Division, I forbid any talk about a Ukrainian Division or Ukrainian nation."[120]

To say the least, such orders created many bad feelings and conflicts between those like the Governor of Galicia who defended – and those like Himmler – who opposed the establishment of a Ukrainian state.

Desperate to change Himmler's thinking, Wachter responded to Himmler's viewpoints with a detailed six-page report. In this report of 30 July, Wachter tried to persuade Himmler to change his views in a matter perceived by Wachter as dangerous to both Galicia's people and the Division. In nine short but straightforward points, Wachter emphasized such matters to the Reichsführer:[121]

1. Galicia is a state/territorial concept, rather than a national one (Volkstumbegriff). Our immediate task should not include the assimilation of Ukrainians and Poles into one entity – that of 'Galicians.'

2. Within the General Government, the Germans have verified and officially acknowledged the titles of "Ukrainian" organizations, such as the "Ukrainian Central Committee" and others.

3. Within the Reich, there is a wealth of literature concerning Ukrainians in Galicia.

4. If there are no Ukrainians as such, but only "Galicians," then how is one to differentiate between Ukrainians and Poles when addressing them directly? Who is to be enlisting into the Division?

5. At the present it is impossible to introduce a new designation for Ukrainians in Galicia. Should we revert back to using the term "Ruthenians?" The latter went out of common usage in 1918; also, it is synonymous with the concept of "Russophile" (Russlandfreund).

6. Incorporation of the terms "Galicia" and "Galician" into the Division is misleading from a political consideration for such a practice explicitly implies that the Germans intend to denationalize these people."

7. The Germans have managed to elicit the sympathy of Galicia's inhabitants – from the Poles and even more so from the Ukrainians – because their treatment of these people is more favorable than in the other occupied territories of Eastern Europe. Because they are nationally conscious, Ukrainians reject Red Moscow. These Ukrainian tendencies must be taken advantage of and "steered" toward an anti-bolshevik track. Simultaneously, if their efforts are strengthened, than it benefits the Reich.

In conclusion, Wachter appealed to Himmler to reconsider his orders, and added:

"With regard to the situation in which the Reich is presently in, and taking into consideration my beliefs that the key to our victory – or defeat – is hidden, as in the past, in the politics which the Reich conducts in the east..."

Wachter then awaited and hoped for a more positive response from Himmler.

But how did the Reichsführer respond to Wachter's letter? In a sharp refutal dated 11 August, Himmler chastised Wachter for his views and stressed how the words "Galicia" and "Galician" prolong the traditions of the Austrian Crown Land. Himmler persisted on banning the usage of the words "Ukraine" and "Ukrainian." Mistrustful of the Ukrainian intelligentsia, Himmler charged how the Ukrainians:

"When permitted to attend Lemberg's University, this intelligentsia, to cite as an example of ingratitude and worthlessness which is attributable only to Slavs, sent their emissaries to the Russian Ukraine to conduct activities of consciousness."[122]

Yet it is interesting to note that at the end of his reply, Himmler (possibly to appease Wachter or perhaps to resolve the matter) stated that "those Galicians who call themselves "Ukrainian" will not be punished." Himmler's reply not only demonstrated, once again, the fact that he abhorred Slavs, but, specifically, his anti-Ukrainian sentiment. This was especially evident when the Reichsführer charged that the Ukrainian intelligentsia from Galicia was behind the anti-German activities in both Galicia and Ukraine.[123]

Angered by Himmler's charges, Wachter again replied on 4 September.[124] Although admitting that a whole new generation had been brought up on Ukrainian patriotism, Wachter also tried to clear the Galician intelligentsia of any infractions in Ukraine. Informing Himmler that he had personally investigated the allegations, Wachter also insisted that the charges had originated in the District Commissariat of Dubno and that such slander was unjustifiable because although there was some unrest in Volyn's region, Galicia's Ukrainian intelligentsia had remained relatively peaceful. In conclusion, Wachter requested from the Reichsführer a personal meeting so that both men could discuss the matter on a personal level.

Himmler, however, refused to discuss the matter any further. The fast approaching battle front, the intensified guerrilla activity and the evacuation from Galicia overshadowed for the moment the dispute over the Division's name; thus, the Division was officially denied its true national identity until November, 1944. By then, the issue was irrelevant because by the end of that year the entire Ukraine, including Galicia, had been reoccupied by Soviet forces.[125]

Galicia Division

Soviet Russia and its military high command, Stavka, immediately took a strong interest in the Division. In an attempt to hinder recruitment, Stavka dispatched Soviet guerrilla general Sidor Kovpak on a long-range mission into Galicia in late June and early July 1943. Kovpak's mission was twofold: to inflict military/economic damage and to demonstrate to Galicia's populace German weaknesses. Once accomplished, it was hoped that Galicia's inhabitants, witnessing German weaknesses, would reject German proposals of cooperation and would withdraw support from the "Galicia" Division. However, as a result of Kovpak's failure, proving for the moment that such raids were ineffective, the Soviets could only resort to propaganda.

In order to establish a closer bond with Ukraine (and possibly even Galicia), Soviet propagandists increasingly began to use the word "Ukrainian." They also began to resurrect the names of many former Ukrainian military leaders in Soviet issued awards, decorations, and honors. On 10 October 1943, the Soviet Supreme Presidium issued a high-ranking award for valor[126] named after the legendary Ukrainian Zaporozhian Cossack leader Bohdan Khmelnytsky.[127] Two months later, in December, several Soviet units were officially redesignated as "Ukrainian."[128]

In late 1943, Yaroslav Gallan, a leading Soviet propadandist, directly attacked the Division. Critical of Erich Koch, but especially of Galicia's Governor Otto Wachter, Gallan stated:

"...the same Wachter who earlier a dog wouldn't bark about, all of a sudden became a very popular person within the German Information Bureau."

Gallan attempted to discredit Wachter by claiming such high-pitched broadcasts were heralded triumphantly throughout the summer of 1943 by Germany's Eastern Information Bureau in an effort to secure recruits: "Wachter is recruiting eastern volunteers," "Governor Wachter is mobilizing 70,000 volunteers," "Galicia's Black Division" (the word "black" here denotes something very sinister, terrifying and fascist in nature), "Wachter prepares to overcome the Eastern front," and "Governor Wachter accepts many Galician SS men."

"But just how triumphant was Wachter?" asked Gallan. According to the Soviet propagandist:

"Wachter, from the bottom of the depths, pulled out the old Austrian General Kurmanovych who hurriedly and unsuccessfully mobilized only several thousands of supporters from Greek-Catholic believers; therefore, he instructed his police to begin a manhunt for "volunteers." And once it seemed that all was ready, the Governor travelled to Kolomyia. There, in a market square,

Chapter 6: The UCC

Wachter reviewed a group of 'Hutzul's' [Carpathian mountain people] who were pressed into service from various regions and who were supposed to rescue Hitler's Germany from disaster. For the sake of amplified sound effects, Wachter used stage techniques and blared music from the opera "Aida" [undoubtedly when Gallan mentioned Verdi's opera "Aida" he was referring to its famous "Military March" theme], during which his poor "SS" was forced to march for two hours, thereby creating the effect of a whole legion. But before Wachter could even enroll the newly recruited "Eastern Tyroleans," it became evident that some of them, along with their arms, successfully fled into the forests. The rest simply went home.

It would have been risky for Wachter to personally meet with any of them, because they might have done the same thing to Wachter that Wachter had done to many of their fathers and brothers – they would have hung Wachter from a street lamppost! As a result of all of this, Wachter's fame became clouded."

In conclusion, Gallan posed the question: "And what ever became of this "Black" Division?" Himself, he replied:

"Its life was short-lived, as was the career of its instigator. After mobilizing a limited number of men, they were dispatched to conduct a "new order" in, of all places, Norway.[129] As for the rest, Wachter secretly dispatched them for German penal service and the demoralized "commander" of this division was put away with the moths."[130]

Eventually, however, Soviet propagandists began to realize that such public statements, in addition to being highly fictitious and untruthful, would also expose the fact that within the Soviet empire there were many who were actively opposing Stalin and communist rule. Fearing danger in this, Soviet propagandists greatly curbed their broadcasts and publications in regard to such German-sponsored foreign units.[131]

Poland's London-based government-in-exile learned about the "Galicia" Division through German propagandists and the Polish underground. Initially, the exilists were baffled by such a formation and could not fully realize the scope of its meaning. But seeing that a Waffen-SS Division was in the process of being raised from a fiery and patriotically minded minority in Eastern Galicia, the Poles began to take the matter seriously.

83

Poland's leaders fully realized that although the Division was being formed for combat against Soviet Russia, a well-armed, trained, equipped and combat-experienced force could eventually pose a serious threat to any future Polish plans to reoccupy Eastern Galicia. And the last thing Poland could afford, especially in the event of a repeat of the 1918-1923 era, was for its minorities to possess a strong military force. Knowing that there was no way of militarily preventing the mobilization of such a formation, Poland's foreign-based authorities campaigned vigorously against it through its underground.

What especially compounded Poland's problem was the fact that its exiled government encountered a situation which plagued few other nations: the fact that Poland was simultaneously at war with both Nazi Germany and Soviet Russia. This, in turn, intensified the difficulty faced by Poland's London-based government in constantly keeping alive Poland's aspirations and its needs. And one of these passionate aspirations was not only to restore a Polish state at the conclusion of the war but, simultaneously, to ensure that its borders remain within the 1921 Treaty of Riga.[132]

Premier Stanislaw Mikolajczyk was especially adamant about this issue.[133] Poland's London based government also knew that it was totally powerless without massive American and British support. Furthermore, the exiled government feared that its Western allies would remain impartial to Poland's needs or worse, would significantly alter the course of Poland's post-war development by appeasing and acquiescing to their mighty eastern ally (and Poland's enemy), Soviet Russia.[134]

So once again, as it had two decades earlier, the 1921 Polish-Soviet Treaty of Riga raised concerns about its pre-1939 territory and the complex issue of an independent Polish state.[135]

Stalin, however, had made up his mind. Accusing the Poles of refusing Ukrainians and Byelorussians their "historical rights" of national unity, Stalin demanded that the Poles return to the previously proposed 1919 Curzon Line. But the Poles were not content with such a compromise because they feared losing approximately 46 percent of their pre-1939 territory.[136] "Every Pole must consider it his duty to fight for the inviolability of our eastern areas!" uttered Edinburg's renowned Polish professor, Wladyslaw Wielhorski. This sentiment was widely echoed by Poland's exiled leaders. But a simple overview of a number of personal, as well as top secret letters, messages and telegrams exchanged between Churchill, Roosevelt and Stalin, clearly indicated that by mid-1944, the Allies were leaning strongly in favor of the Curzon line.[137]

Much of Poland's troubled past laid in the eastern territories where a strong anti-Polish sentiment existed. Therefore, Poland's exiled government was not only forced to closely monitor the Allied powers' views and plans regarding its border issue and eastern region, but also the activities of all non-Poles now under German occupation.[138] In regards to such people, it was hoped that none of Eastern Galicia's inhabitants would take advantage of the chaos and attempt to establish national independence.

To counter such attempts, thousands of leaflets, addressed to Galicia's inhabitants in various languages, appeared in the beginning of May, 1943. One such leaflet, published on one side in the Polish language and on the other in Ukrainian, was signed by the "Regional Political Representation." Specifically addressed "To the Ukrainian People" it stated:

"The war is concluding. The triumphant righteousness over rape and force is nearby. Oceans of blood spilled by millions in defense of freedom and righteousness will not be wasted. Poland, whose contribution in this war was tremendous, and whose sacrifice and suffering was colossal, will emerge from this conflict a victor and along with the allies, will participate in the development of a new and better world.

Sadly, the Ukrainian community, under the guise of enemy propaganda and disorientated by those who regard themselves as leaders and spokesmen for freedom of the Ukrainian nation, took a different road than the Poles: the road of collaboration with the occupants. Yet already in the first months of the war, it became apparent that "collaboration" meant blind servitude and help for the occupant in his battle with the Polish nation and its people.

With blood, the Ukrainian people pay for this naive political service. In the end, all illusions of political independence, even in its most minute form, result in forced labor in favor of the war machine in Germany, and hard economic exploitation in the homeland which ultimately achieved only the "privilege to shed blood" in the auxiliary German army – here are the dividends of four years of Ukrainian-German cooperation.

The Ukrainian people well remember their "cooperation" with the Soviet occupier. Those two years of Bolshevik rule left ugly recollections. Arrests, mass deportation and, in the final phases, executions. With such methods, the Bolsheviks aspired to benefit themselves through "liberation from Polish tyranny" the Ukrainian population.

At the same time, the Western Ukrainian population was introduced to the same Soviet rule that had been entrenched for 25 years in Soviet Ukraine; a rule which was characterized by destruction of the most conscious elements of the Ukrainian nation: destruction by proletarian assimilation and in the end, by mass liquidation of Ukrainians. It would seem that such a breaking dawn should remind the Ukrainian people to perhaps review their present position. The beginnings of such reminders are already visible throughout much of the Ukrainian nation. But acts of further cooperation with the Germans, acts of ruin and rape, which lately were conducted by Ukrainians against Polish settlements in eastern lands and are carried out by the encouragement of the occupiers, and sometimes on personal initiatives, continue to prolong the split between the Polish and Ukrainian people and, simultaneously, digs a grave for any dreams of a Ukrainian nation.

At this hour here is dawning a great historic moment – at last a time of justice. He who does not anticipate it, will draw judgement upon himself. We, Representatives of the Polish nation, call on you at this historical moment to:

Return from the mistaken road;

Break away from your dependence on the occupier;

Condemn the cannibalistic mass murder of Volyn's Polish people who perish at the hands of Ukrainians incited by the Nazis and Bolsheviks;

Immediately stop all aggressive Ukrainian activities against the Polish people and nation;

Condemn the recruitment to the Ukrainian Division[139] and oppose it;

Organize with us a solid self-defense against the destructive deeds of the occupant and, by yourself, actively reveal that the Ukrainian nation is hostile toward the Germans.

We have mutual enemies, therefore, stand up and help us do battle with them. Only by a mutual spillage of blood with the common enemy – which consists not only of the Germans pillaging both our nations, but also Russia, which already is spreading its greedy hands on our lands, inhabited by Poles and Ukrainians – she [Russia] could close this split which today divides both nations, and form a base for further cooperation between Poles and Ukrainians in the name of such a motto: "for your and our freedom!"

We understand and duly appreciate the aspirations of the Ukrainian people to form an independent Ukraine. Simultaneously, we declare that we will not resign from the eastern lands common in the southern parts where Poles and Ukrainians lived from time immemorial; which through centuries the Polish nation offered great cultural and economic contributions. But these lands should without doubt become the territory of brotherhood, living together as two nations. We guarantee on these lands the FULL AND FREE development of life on fundamental principles of freedom and equality based on human laws and obligations. On this road the Ukrainian nation will find full understanding and support from the Polish nation along with a willingness to forget all former grievances and wounds."[140]

Chapter 6: The UCC

How much Poland's so-called "Regional Political Representation" had discussed the above matter regarding the Ukrainian issue with Poland's exiled government is difficult to assess and probably will never be known. Undoubtedly, some discussion must have taken place.

Poland's Regional Representatives had to be credited for recognizing both Nazi Germany and Soviet Russia as the enemies of both the Poles and Ukrainians. Although they emphasized a spirit of mutual cooperation and "brotherhood" among both people and a "willingness to forget all former grievances and wounds," admitting their "understanding" of the Ukrainian people's quest for the establishment of an independent Ukraine by claiming... "we guarantee on these lands full and free development of [Ukrainian] life on fundamental freedoms and equality based on human laws and obligations," at the same time the Regional Political Representatives made it clear that "we will not resign from the eastern lands." Thus, it was still evident that Poland still considered it its historical prerogative to return Eastern Galicia's inhabitants to the same status they had previously been in, namely minorities within Polish boundaries.

For Galicia's Ukrainians, such false rhetoric and promises were nothing new. They had heard similar sentiments expressed previously in the post-World War I period by expansionist Poles (such as Dmowski) who dreamed of a Polish empire. Eastern Galicia's inhabitants remembered how Poland's delegation had deceived the Allied powers into believing that Poland would "guarantee full equality" and "rights" in areas dominated by a non-Polish majority. To demonstrate that its intentions were honest and just, Poland even legislated "a minority bill" meant to impress (and delude) the allied powers; yet, the moment the Allies gave in and allowed Poland regional control of Eastern Galicia, Poland's government ruled with an iron hand. As for attempting to "understand the aspirations of the Ukrainian people to form an independent Ukraine," throughout the interwar period Polish authorities imposed a chauvinistic rule over Eastern Galicia's minorities, granting them only limited rights. To make matters worse, Poland's guerrillas demonstrated no efforts to resolve any past or current grievances. Divided into various factions, they basically shared the views of Poland's London-based governments regarding the eastern regions. To demonstrate their intentions, on occasion they would viciously attack Ukrainian villages or private citizens in an attempt to impose terror on the region's non-Polish inhabitants, thus facilitating Poland's post-war plans to reoccupy and readminister the eastern regions. Fully aware that the Poles had no true intention of establishing a "just rule and valid peace with full rights" for its minorities, Eastern Galicia's inhabitants paid little heed to Poland's underground propagandists.[141]

Another group of propagandists the Ukrainians refused to heed, and strongly resisted, were those Nazis who opposed religion.[142] Countering Himmler's atheism, the Ukrainians demanded – and received – the right to freely practice religion; as a result, the 14th Waffen-SS Division was one of the few fighting SS formations permitted free religious practice.

The Role of Religion In the "Galicia" Division
One of the key points raised and emphasized by the Ukrainian Central Committee was the right to religious freedom and worship. And once granted this right, the Ukrainian advocates were able to secure the support of both the Ukrainian Autocephalous Orthodox Church and the Greek Catholic Church headed by Metropolitan Andrei Sheptytsky.[143]

In June 1941, Galicia's Metropolitan Andrei Sheptytsky had greeted the advancing German army as a protector and liberator of Eastern Europe from communist tyranny. A strong opponent of communism for many years, as early as 24 June 1933, the Metropolitan, along with a number of Ukrainian and European bishops, openly condemned Stalin and the Soviets for abusing religion and for engineering a deliberate famine which was then devastating large regions of the Eastern Ukraine and parts of Soviet Russia.[144] Sheptytsky's protest was endorsed by Pope Pious II.

But Galicia's Metropolitan quickly discovered that the leaders of Germany's Wehrmacht (with whom he had established a cordial relationship), were not responsible for Germany's policies regarding Galicia, Ukraine, and, in general, the whole of Eastern Europe. To make matters worse, the brutality displayed by Germany's police toward Ukrainian leaders, the OUN, the Ukrainian intelligentsia which survived the Soviet terror, Galicia's Jews and others caused the Metropolitan to radically change his attitude toward German rule.[145]

Aged, partially paralyzed and confined to a wheelchair, Sheptytsky continued to denounce and condemn Nazi atrocities. What especially revolted the Metropolitan was the way Nazi policy (as the communists had previously) agitated Galicia's various nationalities against one another, and the methods by which the Nazi police recruited and used some Ukrainians and members of the Ukrainian auxiliary police for assistance.[146] In protest, Sheptytsky personally wrote in February 1942 a letter to Reichsführer Himmler. Condemning the Nazi excesses, Sheptytsky also demanded an immediate end to such criminal practice.[147]

Angered by this letter, Himmler immediately informed Lviv's German Security Service of Sheptytsky's protest, submitting the letter as proof.[148] In turn, the Security Service then retaliated against Sheptytsky. While fully realizing that strong papal and world condemnation would result in the event that Sheptytsky was ever arrested or harmed in any way, the Security Service decided to leave the Metropolitan alone but, in turn, it closed down Lviv's National Council Agency, whose honorary chairman was Sheptytsky.[149]

In August 1943, a secret report on the Metropolitan was prepared by a "Dr. Frederic." A Frenchman and a student of Eastern European affairs, "Dr. Frederic" was a Nazi collaborator who worked for the Germans in Eastern Europe. After managing to establish a meeting with Sheptytsky, the Frenchman submitted a report to his German superiors on the Metropolitan. This report provided conclusive evidence that Metropolitan Sheptytski was not only opposed to Nazism[150] but that he had even come to regard Nazism as a greater evil and menace than Soviet communism.[151]

By no means did Sheptytsky's opposition simply consist of verbal assaults on the Germans and their collaborators. From the outset of the atrocities, Sheptytsky's moral indignation compelled him to shelter and conceal many Galician Jews. In the Galician capital alone, the Metropolitan concealed a number of Jews seeking refuge.[152] Among them was Rabbi Dr. David Kahane, a prominent Rabbi and teacher in Lviv prior to the war. Rabbi Kahane, along with Rabbi Chameides, personally appealed to Sheptytsky in mid-August 1942 for assistance in concealing the 'Scrolls of the Law' from Nazi destruction.[153] That same night, Sheptytskyi not only took in the Hebrew Scrolls, but also both rabbis and their families. Years later, as Chief Chaplain of the Israeli Army, Kahane would recall Sheptytsky's letter to Himmler and the Reichsführer's rude reply.[154]

In one instance, Sheptytsky, along with his brother Father Superior Clement Sheptytsky and Sister Josepha, Mother Superior of Galicia's nunneries, together offered haven to around 150 Jews, most of whom were children.[155] By admitting and concealing them in various monasteries, the clerics saved their lives for they all survived the war. Additionally, the Metropolitan appointed the Reverend Marko Stek to conduct a rescue operation to assist those seeking refuge from Nazi terror. Through Stek's efforts, many more Jewish lives were saved.[156] Eventually, approximately 550 priests, nuns, monks, religious students and various assistants throughout Galicia became involved in this underground rescue operation. What is noteworthy is that not one of them ever revealed the operation, nor any of the concealed individuals, to German authorities.[157]

Because German authorities allowed the establishment of a Chaplain's section and abolished any Nazi indoctrination of the Division's personnel, the unit became acceptable to Galicia's Church leaders.[158] Sheptytsky, although still abhorring Nazism, supported the project solely for security reasons. As a former military man, the Metropolitan, by mid-1943, had sensed that German defeat and withdrawal was probable. At the same time, he was deeply concerned about the increasing violence directed against Galicia's populace by both extremist Polish elements and Soviet guerrillas. Sheptytsky also knew that once the Germans withdrew, the possibility of a total collapse, followed by an extremist takeover and slaughter of many people, was probable. Realizing that only a military (or at least a paramilitary) force could prevent such bloodshed and maintain order, solely for such reasons did the Metropolitan support the project.[159] To ensure that religious freedom was observed and to ensure that a chaplain's corps was properly established and maintained, Sheptytsky dispatched one of his chief clerics (and a former military chaplain), Dr. Vasyl Laba, to head the Division's chaplains.[160] According to one source, the Division had nine chaplains,[161] but in a memo from Berger to Himmler, Berger cited twelve priests and added that their military training would commence from 20 August to 3 October, 1943, in Zennheim, Alsace.[162] In Ren's memoirs, twelve chaplains are also cited and they are identified as such: Julian Gabrusevych, Dr. Ivan Durbak, Emanuel Korduba, Danylo Kovaliuk, Dr. Osyp Karpins'kyi, Dr. Vasyl Laba, Dr. Josef Kladochnyi, Vasyl Leshchyshyn, Bohdan Levyts'kyi, Izydor Sydir Nahayewsky, Liubomyr Syven'kyi and Dr. Volodymyr Stetsiuk.[163] But in a post-war account submitted from Canada in 1952 by Reverend Laba, the former Divisional chaplain identified a total of nineteen chaplain's as having served. In addition to the chaplain's cited by Ren, Reverend Laba also cited such chaplain's: Roman Lobodych, Myhailo Levenets', Ivan Holoida, Oleksander Babij, Oleksander Markevych, Ivan Tomashivs'kyi and Myhailo Ratushyns'kyi.[164]

Regardless of the precise figure, the 14th Waffen-SS Division has gone down in history as a unit which encouraged and promoted religion, and its dedicated chaplains corps endured all of the Division's ordeals.

7

The Building of the "Galicia" Division

"Military leadership is a process by which a soldier influences others to accomplish the mission. A soldier carries out this process by applying his leadership attributes (beliefs, values, ethics, character, knowledge, and skills), to obtain obedience, confidence, respect, and loyalty to execute combat operations and missions."[1]

For any type of military formation to exist, function, survive and succeed, whether in peacetime or combat, it is critical for it to possess a solid inner core of officers and non-commissioned officers. Leadership, along with maneuver, protection and firepower, comprises one of the four key elements of combat power.

Although Galicia's leaders demanded that the proposed Division be officered by Ukrainian personnel and Wachter's 12 April conference established a figure of 600 officers,[2] a problem immediately arose in securing enough qualified officers for the new formation.

Some Ukrainians have accused the Germans of deliberately denying officer positions to Ukrainian personnel so that they could maintain a complete control over the Division; some, such as the Division's former Army Major Wolf-Dietrich Heike, have substantiated that claim by stating that a number of the officers and non-commissioned personnel provided for the Division consisted not only of Germans, but largely of unreliable personnel rejected by other formations.[3] In turn, these officers and NCO's, lacking an adequate understanding (and undoubtedly in some cases not caring to understand) the Ukrainians and their political stance, only further complicated and aggravated relationships between both groups;[4] some, (such as, again, Heike), have also accused Divisional General Fritz Freitag of never specifically addressing this issue and, thus, failing to provide the proper guidance to narrow this rift.

Since World War II, various discussions, accusations, and counter-accusations have been made. To this day, it has never been properly explained whether Ukrainians were deliberately denied officer and NCO positions and what, if anything, was ever done to remedy the situation. In order to understand this situation, and to finally resolve the matter, it is important to fully understand the Ukrainian situation, Germany's miliary situation in mid-1943, and the Division's miliary needs.

One of the largest (and undoubtedly most important) problems faced by the Military Board was to find enough qualified personnel for the creation of an officers corps. After their first attempts to do so, it quickly became evident that few were qualified enough to meet the numbers and quality needed.[5]

In fact, it was not possible in mid-1943 for the Division to be fully led by Ukrainian officers and non-commissioned officers. Although a number of inefficient, overage Ukrainians could have been quickly scraped up to form a hastily organized officer and NCO corps, such a move would have never produced a sufficient number of qualified personnel and, in the long run, would have actually been detrimental to the Division. Quality, and not quantity, was of the essence. Quality leadership would not only establish a solid inner corps for the Division but would also enable it to expand its knowledge and expertise in eventually organizing an army corps and, in the long run, an army. But for the moment at least, a solid inner core was the essential component necessary for the Division.

Finding this leadership core was not an easy task. It has already been established that most of the volunteers were simply raw recruits with no prior miliary experience. Prior to the forming of the Division in 1943, Hitler's policy forbade the recruitment of Ukrainian personnel. As a result, from 1941 (the year of the German occupation) until 1943, most of Eastern Galicia's inhabitants had not been directly involved in the war. By staying out, there was no easy way of acquiring any military knowledge and experience. During the Soviet occupation of Galicia from 1939-41, some men were drafted into the Red Army, but their training was pitiful. Primarily employed as labor troops, few, if any, served in any type of leadership position. Although some Ukrainians had served in Poland's army prior to 1939, the Polish military system (especially by 1939) was highly outdated, its training (because of no strong efforts to modernize it) was questionable, and a number of Ukrainian men who were inducted into Poland's army were denied officer and NCO positions because of suspected ties to various self-liberation organizations such as the OUN. In some cases, Ukrainian men were even relieved of duty when accused (or simply suspected), of such activities. Needless to say, negative anti-Ukrainian sentiments and dismissals prevented a number of Ukrainians from furthering their knowledge and expertise. But in all fairness, it must be noted, that once a man was accepted into Poland's officer corps, he was afforded the best training that Poland could at that time provide.

Of all central and eastern European nations (excluding Germany), Czechoslovakia alone had an elite army. Composed largely of volunteers, the Czech pre-1939 army was indeed a formidable force to be reckoned with. Sympathetic to the plight of the Ukrainians, its army accepted any Ukrainian who sought to volunteer. But because few Ukrainians volunteered, what training, knowledge and expertise that could have been acquired was never sought.

To a large extent, Ukrainians themselves created this problem. As a people, Ukrainians in general have never viewed military service as a noble profession. Prior to the First World War, when Austria ruled Galicia, Ukrainians were permitted to enlist into Austria's service and to take advantage of any opportunities its service could offer. While a number of Poles and many Germans did take advantage of this, few Ukrainians responded. Military service was viewed by Ukrainians as an unworthy profession, as a haven for losers, and a way of life for those too lazy to accomplish anything productive in life. If drafted, most men served. But once their mandatory time expired, very few extended their time of service.

Yet Ukrainian men could make fine soldiers, as illustrated during World War I. When drafted and retained in Austria's service, Ukrainian men adjusted very well within the system and a number succeeded in achieving non-commissioned and officer positions. As a result, by 1918, a sufficient number of men were available for the Galician Army raised that year.

Among those who had previously served in the Austrian Army and Galician Army, a number did attempt to enlist into the Division. But the majority of the former officers were now too old and most had not served for at least twenty years. Because few had stayed abreast of military developments and changes between the interwar period, few were in any position to reenter the military and benefit the Division. Although many former Galician military men thought otherwise, realistically speaking, the new type of war with its modernized tactics was not known and fully understood by them. Additionally, some former officers undoubtedly sought to enlist out of a need to succeed, since civilian life had proven to be unproductive. Regardless of the real motives for enlisting, the fact remains that while a limited number of ex-officers could be utilized, most of Galicia's former military men were unsuitable for any type of military service.[6]

Thus, an officers corps had to be built from scratch. Because only a limited number of Ukrainians were initially available, for the time being Germany's personnel would need to be utilized. But finding effective German leadership in mid-1943 was a complicated matter, especially in lieu of the fact that by mid-1943, Germany's officer and NCO corps was in decline.[7] Whereas only several years earlier Germany could boast of an elite corps of leaders, such a claim was no longer valid by the conclusion of 1942. Now, it was becoming increasingly difficult for Germany to obtain skilled leaders for its rebuilt and newly forming units.[8] And as the more established formations obtained the first pick of officer and NCO material, the newly organized divisions found themselves scraping the bottom of the barrel for their leadership needs. Simply put, the "Galicia" Division was not the only formation desperately seeking leadership material.

So what kind of men were needed to fulfill an officer's position? In addition to being a volunteer, a man had to be both physically and mentally tough, and possess enough confidence and capability to accomplish an assignment or mission; he had to be tactically and technically proficient; he had to be tactful, placing himself ahead of his men, assisting them in their personal, economic, and family affairs; he had to be mission-minded, aggressive, and in combat, fully devoted and determined to succeed.

Along with the Division's officers corps, an NCO corps was also needed. The backbone of any military force, a solid NCO corps ensures success. NCOs not only advise and assist officers with their duties and responsibilities, but also train soldiers, officers, officer candidates/cadets, and NCO candidates. If a unit does not have a sufficient number of officers, senior NCOs take their place. In combat, if an officer should become a casualty, an NCO assumes the officers' responsibilities. For any unit to succeed, its NCO corps must be just as solid as its officer corps.

But as in the case of the "Galicia" Division's officer corps, a problem also arose in finding a suitable number of men to fit the Division's NCO slots. Basically, the problems which faced the officer corps also faced to NCO corps. So along with the Division's officer corps, an NCO corps had to be developed from scratch.[9]

Allegations have been made that in May 1943 Nachtigall's and Roland's officers were integrated into the "Galicia" Division. Along with these charges, some have alleged that a number (or all) of the former battalion officers had committed or participated in "war-crimes" previously in 1941 and prior to volunteering for the Division; therefore, with their entry into the Division, "war criminals" entered

Chapter 7: The Building of the "Galicia" Division

the formation. Since these allegations have been made, they must be examined.

Ukrainian sources do concede the fact that some ex-Nachtigall and Roland personnel did enter the Division.[10] But most do not provide a figure. From such Ukraininan and non-Ukrainian sources various historians and journalists, such as Alti Rodal and Paul Lungen, have alleged that a number of "imprisoned officers of Nachtigall and Roland, who were released to join the Division," did so.[11] While both Rodal and Lundgen factually cited that both units "were formed with German officers but an unofficial Ukrainian staff," neither provide any figures about the number of Nachtigall and Roland officers "who, in May, 1943, were integrated into the Galician Division."[12] But what are the facts? How many ex-Nachtigall/ Roland officers actually entered the "Galicia" Division?

According to Roman Bojcun, an ex-officer of the Legion, the total number of Ukrainian officers found in the "Ukrainian Legion of Nationalists" (which comprised both the "Nachtigall" and "Roland" units), comprised a strength of exactly 22.[13] Of these 22 Ukrainian officers, one was a medical officer and one, a chaplain.[14] As for unit Nachtigall, the bulk of its leadership was composed of German officers.[15]

In his memoirs, Colonel Evhen Ren, an ex-Roland soldier, has provided the names of the Ukrainian officers (and the positions they held), found in the beginning of 1942 within "Roland's" headquarters and its four infantry line companies. A close examination reveals no more than 18 officers.[16] On 5 January 1943, when the Legion of Ukrainian Nationalists (or Schuma Bn. 201 as the Legion was now classified by the Germans) was de-activated, Ren placed its strength at approximately 650 soldiers and 22 officers.[17]

Of these officers, only a limited number actually entered the Division. Bojcun cites a figure of 9,[18] but Ren cites no more than 6.[19] Regardless of the exact figures, the historical fact remains that the so-called Nachtigall and Roland battalions (which in a short time evolved into one standard-sized battalion) barely had enough Ukrainian officers for their own needs. When one takes into consideration those who deserted to the UPA, officers killed in action or wounded and incapacitated, and those who refused to associate themselves with the Division when released from imprisonment, there remains only a handful of officers (and for that matter ex-Nachtigall and Roland soldiers and NCO's), who entered the Division.[20]

On 5 July 1943, Reichsführer Heinrich Himmler ordered the first call-up of the Division's volunteers.[21] The Division's volunteers would finally begin their training. Twelve days later, on 17 July, the Division's first group of departing volunteers began to assemble in Galicia's capital city of Lviv. On the following day, Sunday, 18 July, in a large square adjacent to Lviv's Opera Theater, a crowd of

95

over 50,000 Ukrainians attended an outdoor Mass which commenced at 7:30 A.M. to bid farewell to the first group of departing volunteers.[22] Attending this Mass were a host of Ukranian, German and foreign dignitaries: Kubiyovych from the Ukrainian Central Committee, Colonel Bisanz from the Military Board, Galicia's Governor General Wachter and a host of other officials; Bishop Mykyta Budka and the Chief Field Chaplain of the formation, Reverend Vasyl Laba, performed the ceremonial Mass.[23] Afterwards, a number of speakers, to include Wachter, Bisanz, Pankiwsky, and the youngest representative from the departing groups volunteers, 16-year-old Yuriy Ferencevych, spoke on behalf of the departing volunteers.[24] That same day, in mid-afternoon, the first troop transport set out for Brno, Czechoslovakia, where, in Wehrkreis (military district) Bohemia and Moravia,[25] a non-commissioned officers academy was located. Along with the first group of departing recruits was a handful of chaplains departing for Zennheim.[26] Two days later, on 20 July, the first transports set out to Heidelager, a troop training area near Dembica in Wehrkreis General Government.[27] Because at this stage the Division was in its preparatory phases and its departing volunteers were simply raw recruits heading directly to their training areas, at no time could two "Russian-speaking Galician SS men" threaten the Pole Wladyslaw Razmowski with execution.[28]

During these two days, a total of 300 men (including medical doctors) were dispatched to various officer schools. The 2,000 NCO candidates (including some ex-NCO's, mostly from the recent pre-September 1939 Polish Army), were sent to Brno's NCO school. From Brno, many were sent to other NCO academies. As for the 2,000 recruits, most were dispatched straight to Heidelager but some also arrived at Heidelager via Brno. According to renowned Waffen-SS historian Dr. Klietmann, 300 officer candidates and 48 medical doctors were dispatched to officer training; 1,300 NCO's and 800 NCO candidates to various NCO schools, and 2,000 recruits to Heidelager.[29]

However, within parts of Galicia certain oblasts (or counties) showed less enthusiasm than did others. A prime example is that of Berezhany County. Although mass appeals and cries of "ALL GREAT DEEDS BEGIN WITH SMALL ACTS!" were heralded during the initial recruitment phase, few in that county responded favorably. Disgusted with Berezhany's negative response and hoping to induce more positive recruitment, Berezhany's Ukrainian Committee condemned its youth and reissued a strong appeal. Published on posters and displayed throughout Berezhany, the poster denounced Berezhany's youth for "its lack of military spirit and youthful enthusiasm." The poster cited a low figure of only 439 enlistees "whereas neighboring Pidhayetski provided 1,400." While acknowledging that the Division had sufficient volunteers and "could go without Berezhany," the poster also warned that "in future years Berezhany's district will be remembered for its apathy and cowardice," and cited "how fingers will be pointed at Berezhany for having been so unworthy of its ancestors." In conclusion, the poster stated "that the Ukrainian Committee in Berezhany does not believe that its youth would allow such a situation to exist..." and urged men "to enlist into the Galicia Division." How much of an influence the committee's appeal and criticism had, and whether it induced more enthusiasm, has never been established.

As the volunteers boarded the trains, huge crowds of well wishers bade them farewell; but once the trains pulled out, each man fell into his own thoughts.

For Vasyl Sirs'kyi, enlistment into the "Galicia" Division served as an escape route from the hands of the Gestapo. Along with Ukrainian publisher Colonel Dmytro Honta, Sirs'kyi was implicated by the Gestapo in July 1943 for alledged anti-German activities. Unlike Honta, who had managed to escape, Sirs'kyi was arrested. But as the Gestapo prepared to interrogate him, Sirs'kyi displayed a card which cited membership with a departure date set for Sunday, 18 July. Seeing this, the Gestapo immediately released him.

Karpiak, a well-known Galician actor and opera singer, was on the first train bound for Heidelager. Although Karpiak had enlisted as a rifleman, little did the 35-year-old opera singer realize that simply singing a song inside an army barracks would launch him into a new career as a singer at various soldiers functions.

For Bohan Semenyk, this was his second military service. Drafted into the Red Army in 1939 when Eastern Galicia was under Soviet occupation, Semenyk was captured by German troops in 1941. Placed into captivity in Rumania, the moment the Soviet prisoner heard of the Division, he successfully pressed his captors to be released. Shortly after returning home, Semenyk left for Heidelager.

54-year-old Dmytro Hamoniv was one of the oldest volunteers. Pretending to be in his early 40s, the Ukrainian patriot, who was born in Kiev on 26 October 1888, had seen service in the Imperial Russian Army, the Ukrainian National Army, the Galician Army and in the winter of 1920-21, he participated in the winter expedition against Red forces in Ukraine. Wounded in the head, legs, and right eye, Hamoniv, along with a number of other Ukrainian patriots, was captured. Forced to dig a ditch, the Ukrainian raiders were then lined up, one row at a time alongside it, to face a Chekist firing squad. As the executed men plummeted into the ditch, another row of captured men was lined up. And so it went, until Hamoniv's row came up. Standing in the cold and bloody snow beside a ditch filled with bodies, Hamoniv closed his eyes as the Reds raised their rifles.

Suddenly, the crack of the Communists' Mosin Nagant rifles shattered the air. As men fell forward, Hamoniv, realizing that he had not been hit, plunged forward into the muddy, bloody and gory ditch. Lying still, Hamoniv escaped detection from the inspecting Chekists because of his bleeding head wound. By the time the shooting had ceased, it was dark and a heavy snow was falling. Too lazy to fill in the ditch, the Chekists just left the scene. Later that night, Hamoniv crawled out from underneath the snow-covered corpses and found shelter. Returning to Galicia, he recuperated, reentered the Galician Army, and remained with it until its surrender. Following a brief period of Polish captivity, he resided both in Warsaw and Eastern Galicia. Hamoniv survived the Red terror of 1939-41, but as a Ukrainian activist, he was arrested by the Gestapo and held for 99 days. Shortly after his release, he joined the Division. Now on the train, he thought about the upcoming events. Little did he realize on that July day that not only would he fully endure the Division's ordeals, but far into the future, he would participate in the Division's various veterans functions.

Myhailo Solomko was scared like hell, but eager to go. He wondered what lay ahead, and what his parents would think once they learned he had enlisted. But by then it would not matter because he would be miles away. Myhailo reasoned that once he got to Heidelager, he would sit down and write his parents a letter. The fact that he had lied his way into the Division at the age of 16 did not bother him; but the fact that he had lied to his father, a priest, did.

Dmytro Sachkivsky reflected on his own life. As he sat inside the railway car and began to nod off to sleep, the sudden burst of a Soviet manufactured Ppsh 41 submachinegun and the screams of men inside a crowded jail awakened him. Dmytro, because of his affiliation with the OUN, was classified by the occupying Soviets as an "enemy of the people" and for this, was arrested. Placed inside a crowded jail cell in Lviv, he barely survived the June 1941 "Lviv massacre."

And Vasyl Rudnyk, who had just turned 17, momentarily thought about the woman who had bade farewell to her son. Up until the time her son had boarded, the woman remained strong. But the moment the train pulled away, she broke down and cried. "God," thought Rudnyk, "I hope my mother can take it."

Soon a silence, vaguely shattered by the clanking wheels of the train, pervaded in the cars. And as the silence absorbed each and every man, there was not one who was not thinking about the upcoming journey – a journey which most would never again experience.

8

Heidelager: 1943

To properly understand the type of training the "Galicia" Division's soldiers received, it is important to understand Germany's training system – its organization, and how it adapted and changed to meet Germany's needs and demands during the war years of 1939-1945.

Nazi Germany's military evolved around a Wehrkreis – or military – district. Originating in 1919 in Germany's post World War I Weimar Republic, the Wehrkreis system remained under Hitler as the force responsible for recruiting, inducting, training, organizing, and replacing the German Army's manpower needs. These military districts were at first located in certain areas within Germany, but as the continuing war demanded more and more manpower, the number of Wehrkreis' increased and some were even established outside of Germany's 1939 borders. By mid-1943, a total of 20 numerical Wehrkreis' (numbered 1-20 but excluding number 19, and two in name (General Government and Bohemia/Moravia), for a total of 21, were established.[1]

To assist the Wehrkreis military districts, a Replacement Army (Erzatzheer) was also established. Organized in 1938 by Berlin, the Replacement Army was to supervise, direct, but most importantly, coordinate the training of the numerous military districts.[2] While of course Germany's various Field Armies (Feldheers) also conducted unit and officer/NCO training between battles and campaigns, it was the Replacement Army found within the Wehrkreis districts which conducted recruit basic training and the training of potential officers, NCO's, and specialists.

The Replacement Army also conducted refresher courses for incoming soldiers, re-drafted personnel and for those who had been wounded or injured and after a brief period of convalescent leave, were re-entering the army.

In the fall of 1942, the Replacement Army's training was severely reorganized. Until then, there was no need to change the system because Germany's losses prior to Russia and North Africa were not heavy and thus, the training organization proved adequate. But in late 1941, as manpower demands grew tremendously, and new weapons, concepts and ideas were being introduced, it became clear that training in the Replacement Army would require more attention, coordination and stricter control.

The first step in establishing any kind of centralized and coordinated training was to provide leadership for it. A new post, designated as Chief of Training in the Replacement Army, appeared in the fall of 1942. Through the study of inspection, combat, field, and monthly situation reports, the Chief of Training began to incorporate actual battle experiences into the training. This post was also to establish a stronger control over officer/NCO training, and ensure that military training was uniform throughout the various military districts.

Another problem which arose in 1942 was how to obtain enough weapons, ammunition and equipment for the Replacement Army. Contrary to popular belief, Hitler did not revive Germany's pre-war 1939 economy by placing it on a massive war-footing. While of course, an expansion did occur, the German Army, well before Russia, was known to have suffered severe ammunition and other shortages following a campaign. (Such as in the case of the 1939 Polish campaign). And prior to the commencement of Operation "Yellow" (the 1940 German attack on the west), Hitler was repeatedly warned by his generals that Germany's military, even with current production, would face grave ammunition shortages if stalemated as in World War I.[3] Simply stated, the Reich's factories, from 1939 until 1942, were not producing what Germany's military forces: army, air force, navy, submarine, and paratroop forces, needed to effectively sustain its needs.[4] Because Germany's front line needs seriously curtailed weapons, ammunition, and equipment desperately needed by the Replacement Army for its training, one of the main functions of the Chief of Training was to develop, organize, and advise the Replacement Army on how to conduct its training with simulators, "mock-up's," and various improvisations in as much of a realistic scenario as possible; additionally, the training was also revised.

In general, a recruit's training lasted 12-16 weeks. At the conclusion of this training, if a trained soldier was not immediately sent to a front line unit or placed into a newly forming division, he was provided further training until needed. All unnecessary training, such as rifle drill exercises, goose-stepping, heel snapping, and so forth, was prohibited by the Replacement Army starting in 1942. In contrast to the policy of many nations (including the United States), once a recruit entered the Replacement Army, he was assigned a branch. Once within a certain branch, he was immediately introduced to his weapons system. For example, an artillery recruit was immediately introduced to the artillery piece. If he was also designated to serve as a radio man within his battery, he then received all necessary radio training. Because a battery could come under a direct attack, throughout this 12-16 week period, a recruit learned how to be proficient with a rifle, handgun, or even a machinegun. The end result was to create not only an independent warrior, but one that would be an efficient member of a gun battery, an infantry squad/platoon, radio section, tank crew, etc. Such a method of instruction proved more than favorable and time efficient because it enabled a recruit to become fully acquainted from the very beginning with the weapons and equipment he would later use in combat.

Waffen-SS Training

Waffen-SS training was also conducted within the Replacement Army. In general, Waffen-SS divisions were organized along the lines of Army divisions and Waffen-SS recruits and soldiers trained in the Wehrkreis military districts.

But insofar as training installations, weapons, ammunition, and equipment needs were concerned, the Waffen-SS, versus the Wehrmacht, received preferential treatment; additionally, whereas in the beginning of the war the Waffen-SS relied primarily on army schools for specialized training, by mid-1943 the Waffen-SS had established the necessary schools, training courses and training areas required by a complete and well operated military organization. It should be noted, however, that in certain areas, such as chemical warfare, the Waffen-SS continued to resort to Army schools.[5]

By 1943, military materiel shortages were encountered by the Replacement Army. In turn, these shortages forced the Replacement Army to adopt various simulation devices and new methods of instruction for the training of regular army recruits. But this was not so in the case of the Waffen-SS. Waffen-SS training units were not only stockpiled with weapons and material but, in fact, had the newest models of material and many of the finest officer and NCO instructors, both from the Wehrmacht and Waffen-SS, as instructors. The amount of live ammunition fired, the numbers of live grenades thrown, anti-tank rounds fired, etc., far exceeded that of regular army trainees. To be sure, regular army troops did receive the best training which could be afforded to them, but because the Waffen-SS had the first priority, their recruits were able to experience more realistic, effective and superior training. And as Galicia's recruits arrived for training, they fell into the hands of first-rate instructors.

Galicia's volunteers (excluding those who were sent to the officer and NCO academies), were dispatched to the "Heidelager" training area located in Wehrkreis General Government.[6] Shortly afterwards, they were joined by those (excluding those who remained in Wehrkreis Bohemia-Moravia's officer and NCO schools) who came via Brno.

Officially constituted 1 November 1943, this military district was established in late 1939 in central and southern Poland[7] but, in 1941, it was extended southeastwardly to incorporate Eastern Galicia. Within this military district – which encompassed a total area of 142,207 square kilometers with an estimated population of 17,957,000 people comprised mostly of Poles but in the southeast primarily of Ukrainians[8] – were located a number of training areas, such as SS-Truppenubungsplatz "Heidelager." Established east of Debica approximately 65 east of Cracow and 125 miles northwest of Lviv, in June 1940, "Heidelager" was first known as "SS-Truppenubungsplatz 'Debica.'" But on 15 March 1943, it was renamed as "SS-Truppenubungsplatz 'Heidelager.'"[9] According to a U.S. Military Intelligence report, the main headquarters of Wehrkreis General Government was in Cracow and its commander was 64-year-old General of Cavalry Freiherr von Gienanth.[10] One year later, in 1944, 66-year-old Infantry General Siegfried Haenicke was identified as the Wehrkreis' commander.[11]

When a young man steps into a training camp, he enters into a whole new world. Arriving with no more than the clothes on his back and possibly a few possessions, he must be sheltered, fed, clothed, possibly medically reexamined, equipped, armed, and trained. To maintain healthy morale, and to ensure proper training, all of the above must be conducted in a proper manner. When one takes into consideration that one volunteer alone requires two or three pairs of boots and shoes, socks, underwear, a uniform for dress, a minimum of two or three pairs of fatigue shirts and pants for training, a jacket, a trenchcoat, scarf, gloves, one or two caps or hats, a helmet, personal gear such as canteens with carriers, first aid/ ammunition pouches, an entrenching tool such as a shovel with case, mess kit with utensils, flashlight, bedroll with one or two blankets, poncho, rain gear, tent, rucksack, knife/bayonet, a kit with soap, toothpaste, toothbrush, bandages, shaving gear, and two or three towels for training and field use and a cot/bed, mattress, locker, storage area, tables with chairs for studying/reading, etc. for garrison living and training, one can see that just one incoming recruit requires a tremendous amount. Multiply that recruit by at least 2,000 incoming recruits, and it becomes obvious that it requires an exceptionally well established, organized, efficient and knowledgeable staff of instructors and training support personnel to effectively deal with an influx of incoming recruits or otherwise, chaos will only prevail and the training mission will not be accomplished.

To train native men is one matter. But to train, live, and work with foreign personnel is a more complex endeavor. For trainers, it is critically important to understand their foreign trainees. The more one knows their language, arts, culture, and heritage, their way of life, history, national aspirations and goals; what they eat, drink, enjoy and so forth, the easier it will be to adjust, work with, and effectively train the foreign troops.

It is important to note that as Galicia's recruits trained at Heidelager (as later at Neuhammer) in the hands of first rate instructors, simultaneously, a Divisional leadership cadre was being prepared for the Division. Unfortunately, a number of those who were selected for the Division's cadre were, unlike the German trainers found in the training areas, totally indifferent to the Division's needs.

Some have criticized the Division's inserted German personnel of being unsympathetic, unreceptive and, at times, harsh with the Ukrainian volunteers. One problem stemmed from the fact that a sizable number of the assigned German officers and NCO's, especially those from the Reich proper, never fully understood (and, tragically, in some cases did not care to understand) the Ukrainian volunteers' national aspirations, needs, and concerns. Compound the problem with a German officer and NCO who was unwillingly placed on a foreign assignment, or who might have possessed an anti-Slav mentality, and the end result was – more problems.[12] Because the Division was at this time commanded by General Walter Schimana, who was more of an administrator than a military commander, it appears Schimana never properly addressed this problem. So until the Division obtained more receptive German personnel, but more importantly its own Ukrainian officers, NCO's, and specialists, this problem could not be properly dealt with. However, it must be noted that there were those Germans who were correct in their attitude and behavior towards the Ukrainian volunteers, always displaying true military professionalism.

So what kind of training did the recruits receive? As mentioned earlier, depending often upon their special skills, abilities, knowledge, education, and previous military training, they were placed into various branches such as artillery, infantry, etc. As more recruits arrived, additional infantry, artillery, anti-aircraft, panzer-jäger (anti-tank), and other companies were formed which commenced their training. Slowly, but surely, the Division began to develop into a cohesive force.[13]

Galicia Division

The training Galicia's infantry volunteers received conformed to the training changes established in late 1942. Basically, these consisted of three categories: combat training, rifle training, and heavy weapons training.

Combat Training: Special attention was given in the following subjects: positional warfare in both the offense (attack) and defense; reconnaissance and combat patrolling; close combat/anti-tank combat; construction of positions and obstacles; security deception and diversions; squad assault tactics; protection against chemical attack; foxhole construction; and related subjects.

Rifle training: "Gentlemen, every fired round that goes downrange must have someone's name on it. Every round must strike home!" With these words, heavy emphasis was placed on rifle marksmanship. In order to produce qualified shooters and to improve firing results, only the best NCO weapon instructors were utilized for training.

Various positions were demonstrated but the prone position was primarily stressed. The kneeling position was totally omitted. Rapid firing (Schnellschuss) in the standing position required in close combat, was also stressed. But this training did not commence until the recruits were thoroughly proficient with their weapons. Once a rifleman could shoot well, he was elevated into a higher category – either into the sharpshooter class or the highest, the expert. The latter group's best riflemen (no more than 5 percent of the experts) were trained with telescopic sights for preliminary sniper/countersniper training. In addition to rifle training, each recruit also learned how to fire a pistol and the MG34 and MG42 machine gun. Many also learned how to fire the BRNO Czechoslovakian machine gun. To provide the Division with well-trained machinegunners, approximately 30 percent of the recruits were designated to become specialists with machineguns.

Heavy weapons training: In addition to throwing a number of live handgrenades, each infantry recruit learned how to handle and fire anti-tank weaponry, set anti-tank/personnel mines, light mortars and rifle grenades; additionally, certain men were taught how to utilize a portable flamethrower.

From the first day, training was conducted as though the enemy were present. Divided into a 12-16 week period, the recruit training was conducted as follows:

1st week: Cover and concealment by taking advantage of the terrain; field orientation; arm and hand signals; advancing under fire by cover – walking, crouching, creeping and crawling; observation exercises in connection with target designation and range estimation; and rifle training. During the fist week the recruits learned the mechanics (functioning) of the Kar 98 Gewehr Rifle: the weapons sights, aiming and aiming defects, how to adjust the rifle on the sandbag and standing position, aiming exercises, at targets which at first were no more than 10 meters out, methods of grasping, breathing, inhaling, exhaling, and squeezing the trigger; how to estimate target range, and at the end of the week, rifle firing with live ammunition at targets usually no more than 100 meters away was conducted. Because the Waffen-SS were masters of camouflage, proper camouflage techniques were stressed. From the first week until the very end "what can be seen can be hit! And what can be hit, can be killed! So if you can be seen, you can be hit. And if you can be hit, you can be killed!" constantly reverberated through the recruits ears.

2nd week: Squad tactics: taking advantage of cover against enemy high-angle and flat trajectory-fire; advancing in bounds; pushing forward and looking for new cover or a new position. "When under fire you move. You don't have time to think. You stop to think, you're dead! Remember the golden rule. If under fire, and you can't get to cover in less than five seconds, stay where you're at. You are safe there. No more than five seconds!" The use of entrenching tools in the attack along with further rifle training (mostly from the prone position), continued. During the second week, the recruits were introduced to the machine gun and night training, with an emphasis on the proper usage of clothing and equipment for noiseless movement.

3rd week: Going into position and rifle firing in open terrain with emphasis on camouflage. Use of gas masks in combat, ten mile route marches in full field packs. During these marches, march security, scout activities, and anti-aircraft defense tactics were taught. Night training with an emphasis on listening, observation, and ranges estimation continued along with rifle firing – with the gas mask – and machine gun training.

4th week: Preparing the squad for attack and offensive actions. Utilizing the light machine gun for support. Attacking with supporting fire of heavy weapons. Constructing entrenchments. Camouflage discipline. How to react, protect and properly disperse if under artillery fire. Night training. Close combat training with the hand grenade; bayonet training in the attack and defense. More rifle training/firing. Firing at moving targets under combat conditions. Emphasis on 200 meters. Machinegun firing at moving targets. Rapidly changing the barrel and bolt under attack. 12 mile tactical marches through a wooded environment with combat equipment were undertaken.

<u>5th week</u>: Attack, support of riflemen in the advance; changing or abandoning positions; assaulting, obscuring, securing, reducing obstacles/fixed positions; field orientation with maps and compasses. Light mortar teams received extensive training. Close combat training to include assaulting/defending fortified buildings. In this training, men learned how to throw grenades into windows, while behind cover, through open doors, out of shell holes, trenches, rooms, etc. Rifle, pistol, machinegun training continued.

<u>6th week</u>: Continuation of squad, day, night training, rifle, machinegun, grenade throwing, attacking fortified positions such as a farmhouse; chemical decontamination; shooting from the hip with subsequent bayonet thrusts along with rifle firing continued.

<u>7th week</u>: Repeat of much of the previous training.

<u>8th – 14th week</u>: Combat training with emphasis on attacking enemy tanks; identifying tank strengths and weaknesses; Soviet weaponry – how to identify it and use it; more squad/platoon and company offensive/defensive tactics; anti-guerrilla warfare; countering, reducing and destroying enemy river assault crossings; how to engage low flying aircraft with rifles/ machineguns; security measures; disengaging under enemy pressure; escape and evasion methods; first aid; recognizing enemy armor and aircraft; and infantry marches exceeding 30 miles were conducted both day and night.

Galicia's volunteers trained hard. Very hard. Frequently, the training commenced at 5 a.m. in the morning and went well into the night hours. To toughen the recruits, approximately half of the training was conducted in the field.

Whether in heat or cold, through rain or sleet, the training never ceased. In the morning a man could be lying on a warm, dry ground, but that afternoon, he could be lying in the mud with a downpour soaking him to the bones. Yet the recruit would continue to seek targets, through the rain and mist, with his rifle or machinegun.

Men learned things about themselves. The Division's volunteers experienced sights, smells and tastes; and experienced life in such a way which few had experienced before.

To march 10, 12, 15, 20 miles or more was no longer an ordeal or something to fear; to run two or three miles with a rucksack, gear, weapon, ammunition, and machinegun was considered just another thing. Men began to move swiftly and efficiently, and to react without a thought. As the days went by, proficiency levels reached the point were weapons could be stripped and assembled within seconds; almost instantly, a recruit could spot a target, sight in on it, engage and hit it. Certain recruits, to demonstrate their proficiency, would allow themselves to be blindfolded and then, with pride, disassemble and assemble an MG34 or MG42 machinegun in under two minutes. Because few of Galicia's recruits had ever fired a weapon prior to entering the Division, and had not developed any poor shooting habits, this enabled the weapons instructors to proficiently train the men right from the beginning. And many months later at Brody, such mastered shooting skills not only enabled the Division to break out, but actually saved many a life.

Physically, the recruits changed. Overweight men lost weight, yet gained strength; weaker men gained weight and strength. Some even grew taller. All stood straight, and could snap to a perfect position of attention within a second. As more than one man recalled years later – "I went in there dragging my feet. By the time I left, I was swifter than an arrow!"[14]

Yet despite the arduous training, the men found each other. Every company had their story tellers, comedians, and jokesters; among themselves, the men laughed and joked. Someone would begin to sing or play an instrument and within seconds, many voices joined in.

Men lived, worked, ate, and trained together. If someone needed assistance, many helped out. "Come on Roman, you've got it!" "Let's move Myhailo, you're almost there" and other words of encouragement and support were repeatedly expressed.

Home was no longer Ternopil, Stanyslaviv, Peremysl, Pokuttya, Buchach, Kolomyia, Lviv, or any other place; rather, home was the barracks, a place to return to from field training. There, a man would find in its spartan conditions a true luxury. A letter from home was appreciated more than ever before. A family was no longer mother, father, brothers, sisters; aunt, uncle and other loved ones. Rather, it was the squad, platoon, company, battery, section, or whatever other unit a man found himself in. True, the family was still loved, but the brotherhood and camaraderie that a man now experienced was something never felt or known before in high school, the university, at work, in a youth organization or any civilian place. And that camaraderie developed into unity. Men no longer moved individually but rather, as a team. They shared everything. A package from home containing 50-60 or more cookies made the rounds in minutes; a sausage disappeared; a half-empty canteen was still shared by a thirsty soldier. If for some reason someone had to leave to return home because of an emergency, illness or accident, his loss was mourned by all. With each passing day, as the men got better, they developed a pride known and felt only amongst themselves.[15] And they especially resented those thousands who earlier had flocked to the recruiting centers but when the time came to go, sought various excuses to escape entry.

None of this, of course, went unnoticed among the Germans and those Ukrainians who previously had served in the Polish, Soviet or Rumanian forces. The latter knew that the current training which they were receiving was far superior to anything they had previously undertaken. The German instructors, for their part, noted the enthusiasm displayed by most of Galicia's volunteers, their eagerness to succeed and their high morale and spirit of unity. In Heidelager (as shortly afterward at Newhammer), Ukrainian volunteers met, and on occasion exceeded, the standards of other German and foreign training personnel. In rifle marksmanship, artillery drills, camouflage, marching and unit cohesiveness, "der Galizianer" volunteers were standing out.

Although much of the Division's forming and initial training was conducted in Heidelager and later in Neuhamer in Silesia, different military bases and training centers throughout Europe specialized in various types of selected training. Personnel for such training were sent to these various centers before being placed into the Division, or immediately after recruit training. This training was conducted in the following locations:[16]

> Outside Prague in Czechoslovakia there was an officers' and non-commissioned officers' school and on 30 October 1943, 93 officers and NCO's arrived from here to the Division.[17]
>
> In Amsterdam, Holland, there was a course for the commanding personnel of the Division.
>
> At Radolfzell, there was an NCO academy.
>
> In Warsaw, Poland, a veterinarians's horse care and training center.
>
> In Holland, in various coastal locations, anti-aircraft training was carried out.
>
> In France, but especially throughout the various Wehrkreis' located throughout Germany, infantry anti-tank training was provided.
>
> Maerchingen, Alsace. Radio and communications training.
>
> Pikowitz, Bohemia. Sapper/combat engineering training.
>
> Porschitz, Bohemia. Officer artillery training.
>
> Dachau, Germany. Military administrative training for NCO's was provided.
>
> Arolsehn, Germany. Military administrative training for officers was provided.
>
> Munich, Germany. Anti-aircraft training.

Chapter 8: Heidelager: 1943

Berlin, Germany. The care and maintenance of horse and animal equipment.

Lauenburg, Pommerania. NCO's leadership school.

Posen-Treskau (near Poznan, Poland). Officers school.[18]

Zenheim, Alsace – Chaplain's training.

Those who were sent to the various schools and training centers were afforded the opportunity to travel throughout Europe. As in any military school, free time is always allowed; such time enabled a soldier to explore new places, cultures, and life outside his native Galicia.

While attending an officer's school in Treskau, Poland (then Reich territory), Volodymyr Motyka had the opportunity to experience a true adventure. As part of a group of 27 Standartenjunkers (of whom 3 were Galician Ukrainians) sent to Danzig (present day Gdansk), a port city in Northern Poland on the Baltic Sea, to participate in a sporting event, Motyka experienced something far more exciting – a submarine trip.

Near Danzig was located a submariner's training school. For infantry officer candidates touring the U-boat school was fascinating enough but soon, the men actually descended into a submarine. The moment the men climbed inside, the main hatch was shut behind them, and the boat submerged. As the men toured the craft, they were awed by its various machinery, its numerous compartments, engine and torpedo rooms. Heading out into the Baltic, each officer candidate viewed the coastline and the port city through the craft's periscope. Resurfacing, the craft returned to port, and the school's commander bade the infantry candidates success in all future endeavors. For Motyka and his friend Yuriy Skarupa (who shortly afterwards graduated at the head of the class with an officers rank), the trip was indeed a memorable one.

Years later, Roman Prypkhan would laugh about the hilarious – but at that time not so hilarious – affair: a lost rifle.

As a recruit at Heidelager, Prypkhan learned from his NCO instructor "how from now on the rifle will be your best friend. He will replace your father, mother, sister, brother, and your girl. He will remain with you at all times. You must care for him, as you care for the eyes in your head. Remember, without your rifle, you are nothing. Only the rifle makes you a true soldier." Remembering these words, Pyrpkhan always took exceptional care of his weapon.

Shortly after the conclusion of his recruit training, Prypkhan was sent to an NCO school in Streep, approximately 16 miles northeast of Lauenburg, Pommerania. And it was there that his not-so-hilarious adventure took place.

One morning, at the conclusion of a night compass course and a brief period of rest and sleep, the men assembled for the march back to the barracks. As the NCO candidates marched down the road, Prypkhan reached for the rifle strap over his shoulder. He froze. He felt around. Nothing. Thoughts of severe punishment, dismissal from school, a firing squad and so forth raced through his mind. Immediately informing his NCO instructor about what had happened, Prypkhan was told to retrieve his weapon. With another Galician NCO candidate, Prypkhan ran back nearly two miles. And how he ran. Had someone timed him, a new Olympic record might have been set. Arriving to the spot where he had last seen his rifle, Prypkhan found it lying in wait. The NCO candidate was overwhelmed with delight. But realizing that the longer his NCO instructor waited, the angrier he would be, Prypkhan raced back. Ordered to fall back into place, the group continued to march down the road.

Prypkhan, however, knew that the matter was not yet closed; surely, some form of punishment would be meted out. But he was never summoned. Days later, Prypkhan learned the incident was never reported. Had it been, not only would Prypkhan pay for it, but possibly his NCO instructor would have lost his training duty and would have been dispatched to the front. Regardless, Prypkhan never again lost his rifle.

In November 1943, shortly after recruit training, as Vasyl Sirs'kyi stood in an early morning formation at Heidelager, he heard his name announced for the translators school. Sirs'kyi, along with a group of others, was to report to the "Dolmetscher – Schule der Waffen-SS" at Oranienburg, near Berlin, located in Wehrkreis III.

Sirs'kyi's train trip was very comfortable. But on the following day, as the train pulled into a Berlin station, American medium bombers suddenly swooped in. As they flew at rooftop level, strafing and bombing the railway station, Sirs'kyi and his friends piled out of the train with the rest of its civilians and soldiers. Running down the platform towards a bomb shelter with crowds of civilians and soldiers, Sirs'kyi could hear the "whumps" of the exploding bombs and anti-aircraft fire. Smelling the fire and smoke, he realized at last what war was like.

In the following five months at Oranienburg, Sirs'kyi witnessed many more "Berlin raids." Nightly, from Oranienburg, Sirs'kyi would watch as the night sky over Berlin would suddenly be lit up with thousands of parachuting night flares, only to be followed by the numerous beams of search lights and anti-aircraft fire. Nightly, he would hear the distant "thumps" of exploding bombs in the distance and occasionally, he would catch a glimpse of a rapidly descending aircraft wrapped in orange reddish flames. Sirs'kyi always felt sorrow for the craft's crew and wondered if its young pilot and airmen managed to parachute out of the plane, or if they were entombed in the fiery hell; he also felt sorrow for the many innocent Berliners that perished daily during such raids. As he viewed the bombings from safe distance, Sirs'kyi frequently wondered "what madness ever created this?"

Noting the underfed Polish workers who were housed nearby and brought in daily to clean and repair the barracks, Sirs'kyi and his friends would wrap pieces of bread, small cans of meat, sardines, and fruit among trash items which daily were deposited into the trash bins for disposal. Of course, there was danger in this, but the Poles who came in daily to empty the trash found the extra food. "We thank you, friend" was quietly expressed to Sirs'kyi when no German was around.

Riding in the back of a German Opel "Blitz" 3-ton army truck from a day of training not far from the town of Arnhem in the Netherlands, NCO candidate Ostap Veryn heard the sound of an incoming aircraft engines. Although there was nothing unusual about this because in the spring of 1944 many an Allied aircraft flew in the vicinity, Veryn noted the sputtering sound of the aircraft's engines. Turning around in the truck, he saw the aircraft's plume of black smoke. To Veryn, it seemed as if its pilot was making an attempt to land his battered plane on a field.

Stopping the truck, the men watched as the American bomber came in. Landing on its belly, the craft slid forward until it stopped; encompassed in smoke, it was evident that the burning plane posed a danger for those inside.

Jumping out of the truck, the NCO candidates raced toward the plane. As Veryn ran, he spotted flames rising upward from underneath the plane; from the rear, a door opened, a man tumbled out, stood up, and attempted to pull another man out. Within seconds, a few of the Germans reached him and began to assist the American airman but Veryn, along with another candidate, jumped up on the aircraft's wing. Clambering aboard the craft above its bullet riddled cockpit and nose, Veryn looked inside.

The bomber's nose gunner was lying on his back, his stomach nothing but a bloody red mass. Pieces of his stomach actually hung out; yet the man was still alive. Inside sat the pilot. He looked alive, but his co-pilot seemed dead. Quickly un-shouldering his Kar 98 rifle, Veryn shattered the craft's top window panel, threw his rifle to the ground, and reached inside the cockpit. As he worked the pilot's shoulder and chest seat belts, Veryn could feel the heat of the approaching flames.

Shouting for assistance, Veryn began to lift the body straight upwards. Passing the pilot to a couple of men beside him, Veryn shouted "I'm going in to pull the others out!" Jumping down on the pilot's seat, Veryn shook the co-pilot. Seeing that the man was dead, Veryn climbed into the aircraft's nose compartment to retrieve the craft's nose gunner. As he pulled the unconscious airman backwards, flames began to absorb the cockpit. After passing the airman to the top, Veryn pulled himself up, jumped down to the ground, retrieved his weapon and with his free hand, assisted the stretcher-bearer team. As they ran back to the truck, a massive explosion ripped the plane apart.

Quickly pulling up to a nearby hospital, Veryn helped to rush the airman inside. But as they placed the stretcher on the floor for the hospital doctor to assist the wounded man, the airman suddenly opened his eyes, smiled, and said "Danke." Closing his eyes, he never reopened them.

Only at this point did Veryn realize the pain on his lower legs. Looking down, he saw his shredded pants. Escorted to an adjoining room, he awaited treatment. Soon, a doctor and nurse entered and began to treat his burns. As they bandaged him, a high-ranking German officer entered the room. He informed Veryn that the pilot would survive, and that he had expressed his gratitude. Shaking Veryn's hand, the Colonel stated "a true warrior is one that helps his enemy when he is down. Today, you have demonstrated not only bravery, but that you are a true warrior!" Years later, as an American citizen, Veryn would journey to the Smithsonian Institute in Washington, D.C., to view the type of plane the airmen were heroically rescued from.

After boarding his train in Lviv, Chaplain Ivan Nahayewsky and a number of other chaplains journeyed to Zennheim, Alsace, via Peremysl, Sanik, Cracow, Breslau (Worslaw) and Berlin. Upon arrival to Zennheim, Chaplain Nahayewsky noted thousands of officers and volunteers from various European countries. In private and personal discussions with the Frenchmen and others, the chaplain noted their enlistment was much the same as those who entered the "Galicia" Division – defense of the homeland and to obtain training which could eventually be utilized against Nazi Germany.

All of the Divisions' chaplains were housed in a separate barracks, two in a room. They were issued helmets, gas masks, military clothing for training and physical exercises, and other material required by soldiers. However, the chaplains were issued no weapons.

Along with the other soldiers, the chaplains learned military drill, exercised (an emphasis was placed on distance running and it was not uncommon for the chaplains to run several miles each morning), ran obstacle courses, and crawled through barb wire fences. Because it was common knowledge that in a field training or combat environment a battalion or regimental chaplain would have to cover sizable terrain areas, a strong emphasis was also placed on map/compass and terrain orientation. Weapons identification, both allied and German but especially Soviet, was taught along with soldier psychology. Zennheim's instructors were amazed at how much the Ukrainian chaplains knew about Soviet soldiers, their strengths and weaknesses.

Chapter 8: Heidelager: 1943

Nahayewsky benefitted from the training. Although there were moments of ugliness such as on 26 July 1943 when Italy's "Duce," Benito Mussolini, was removed from power and arrested, and the camp's commander assembled the troops and condemned Pope Pius XII for instigating the overthrow and breaking the alliance with Germany, such few negative moments were over-shadowed with the time spent with the region's French and German citizens. Alsace's Frenchmen especially loved the Ukrainian songs and whenever possible, Nahayewski and the other chaplains always informed the region's citizens of their goals and aspirations to achieve their freedom.

On 1 August 1943, the SS-Freiwilligen Division "Galizien" was ordered to be organized into an "Infantry Division New Type." (Infanteriedivision n.a.)[19] Compared to an "Infantry Division Old Type,"[20] the "new type" was organized as follows:

> The basis of such a division was still centered around three infantry regiments, but each regiment was to have two battalions of ingantry rather than the three traditional battalions. Although the battalions maintained their authorized strengths of 4 companies per battalion with 4 platoons per company, now each platoon was reduced from 4 squads of approximately 10 men per squad to 3 squads of approximately 9 men per squad; however, since the caliber of mortars, submachine guns and anti-tank hand fired weapons and other armaments increased, the platoon's firepower (which before required more men), was not decreased. Within such a division other changes were made: the Reconnaissance Battalion was replaced by a Fusilier Battalion (which participated more in combat whereas the Reconnaissance Battalion was involved more in probing and searching for enemy activity) and at least 10 percent of the "new type" divisions' signal, anti-tank, engineer and supply support personnel were reduced; however, in some "new type" divisions it was much more. (I.e.: the signal battalion could be no more than 1 company). Additional manpower savings were done in staff, communications and other sections. Whereas the "old type" (pre-1943) infantry division had a strength of approximately 17,000 men, the "new type" (1943-45) had a strength of approximately 12,500 soldiers.[21]

It is important to note that although the order of 1 August specified that the SS-Freiwilligen Division "Galizien" was to be a "new type," compared to most "new type" Divisions, the "Galizien" Division was in actuality a cross between an "old type" and a "new type." This was demonstrated by the fact that from the beginning, three infantry battalions per regiment were planned.

As the Division's volunteers trained at Heidelager and in Europe's various schools, the Division gradually began to emerge into a fighting machine. By the end of September 1943, the Divisions' Headquarters Staff, commanded by 50-year-old Walter Schimana,[22] was established. A Divisional staff section came into being, and was organized as such:

IA: Planning, training, and operations. This section prepared and supervised the Division's training, its tactical operations; it updated and refined all necessary training and recommended courses of action for training, operations during combat, movements, and similar related areas.
IB: Weapons, ammunition, construction of barriers, transportation.
IC: Intelligence/counterintelligence, control and interrogation of prisoners, political control and matters, censorship of mail if necessary.
IIA/IIB: Updated personnel records and controlled the Divisions' officers, non-commissioned officers and soldiers' movements (i.e.: leaves, school leaves, passes and during combat, the Division's losses through deaths, wounds/injuries, desertions, missing-in-action, etc.). This section also updated the Division's overall and sectional strengths.
III: Field court-martial (trials) of soldiers who committed criminal acts against fellow soldiers, prisoners-of-war, and civilians.[23]
IVA: Uniforms, footgear, clothing, food, and rations.
IVB: Medical/sanitation.
IVC: Veterinarian.
IVD: Dental.
V: Vehicle and mechanical company.
VI: Morale. Religious observation and practice; press; theater; radio; reading/recreational needs, sporting events, etc.

In addition to be above, the Divisions' staff had at its disposal a quartermaster, military field police platoon and its own medical staff section.[24]

In September 1943, the Division's three infantry regiments also fell into place.[25] The following month, October 1943, an order to renumber all Waffen-SS divisions and their infantry regiments into a numerical sequence was issued; therefore, in October 1943, the SS-Freiwilligen Grenadier Regiment 1 was redesignated into SS-Freiwilligen Grenadier Regiment 29 and SS- Freiwilligen Grenadier Regiment

Chapter 8: Heidelager: 1943

2 was redesignated into SS-Freiwilligen Grenadier Regiment 30. Additionally, the Divisions title was redesignated from the "SS-Freiwilligen Division "Galizien" into the "14. Galizische SS-Freiwilligen Division."[26]

What is interesting is that the order of 22 October 1943 only covered (in addition to the numerical and title designator), the Division's first two infantry regiments. Whether this occurred because someone in the higher channels interpreted the 14th Division to be a "two-regiment new type" infantry, or because a mistake had been made is not known but regardless, on 12 November 1943, another order was issued which updated the order of 22 October, which reclassified SS-Freiwilligen Regiment 3 into the SS-Freiwilligen Grenadier Regiment 31.[27]

In addition to the three infantry regiments, a host of various other units – from company to regimental strength – also arose. Although at this stage these units (to include the infantry regiments) were not yet in full strength, they nevertheless began to appear on the Divisions organizational charts. By the latter part of 1943, such units were found within the Division:

Infantry: Worldwide, the backbone of any army is its infantry, "the Queen of Battle!" While, of course, tanks, artillery, airpower, and combat support play a critical role, it is the infantryman – with his personal weapon, knife and bayonet – who decides the issue.

Artillery: The Division's "King of Battle," artillery, began to form in August, 1943. However, it was not until the latter part of 1943 that selected incoming recruits were immediately placed into the first organized battery's and provided training. The training they received included: the handling, caring, and firing of the 105mm and the heavy 150mm artillery piece and its various ammunition during day and night; target acquisition, actions to take against counter battery fire; firing on the move; selection of targets; how to handle firing communications equipment and methods of communication; the caring of horses, small arms firing, camouflage and other related topics were taught.

Commanded by SS-Standartenführer Friedrich Beyersdorff (born 9 August 1892, SS-Nr. 405,820/Party No. 1,738,054),[28] and a holder of the Iron Cross 1st and 2nd Classes along with an Iron Cross 1st Class won in World War I, Beyersdorff was the epitome of a professional artillery man. His key officers included SS-Sturmbannführer Alfred Schutetzenhofer (born on 16 July 1898, SS-Nr. 58,056/Party No. 1,451,051) who commanded the regiments 2nd Artillery Battalion and who was a two time holder of the Iron Cross 1st Class; SS-Hauptsturmführer (Captain) Hans Wagner (born on 5 August 1916, SS-Nr. 422,126/Party No. unknown) who commanded the 3rd Artillery Battalion and Waffen-Sturmbannführer (Major)

Mykola Palienko, [29] who commanded the 4th "heavy" Artillery Battalion. [30]

During the late summer, fall, and early winter of 1943, the artillery regiment's four artillery battalions, although organized, were not yet fully built. With the arrival of additional recruits, and the return of artillery and communications personnel from Europe's various schools, the artillery regiment began to quickly shape into a formidable force. By the conclusion of 1943, it was virtually formed.

Beyersdorff's artillery crews trained hard. Men learned how to move, unlimber an artillery piece from its horses or vehicles, setup, adjust sights, fire, readjust, reload, and reengage to the point where all crew drills were automatic. "Too slow, let's do it again!" "Enemy, 900 meters, target...Report!" "Gun one, up ... gun two, up..." FIRE! "VAROOOOOOOM!" "Hit, good." And so the drills went, both day and night.

Beyersdorff demanded perfection. His batteries drilled to the point were Galician's artillerymen were quickly earning a first rate reputation.

Anti-aircraft: The Division's anti-aircraft "Flak" unit of battalion strength began to form in late August, 1943. In due time, it would be commanded by SS-Hauptsturmführer Serge von Kuester (born on 12 December 1896, SS-Nr. 313,013/non-party member). The anti-aircraft unit consisted of an array of single barrelled and four barrelled 20mm and 37mm guns. In addition to these two weapons, the "Galicia" Division also received a weapons system highly coveted by all German and foreign built divisions, and highly dreaded by all allied nations – the 88.

Classified by mid-1943 in Maryland's Aberdeen Proving Grounds by world-renowned artillery specialists as "the finest artillery piece ever made," the 88 was a weapons system well ahead of its time. With its automatic rammer and electrical firing mechanism, the weapon had a firing rate of 15-20 rounds per minute. Although initially designed only as an anti-aircraft weapon, it soon became apparent that it could be used effectively against tanks, sea-targets, and massively constructed positions. Whether mounted on a truck, or pulled by horses or a vehicle (if mounted on a wheel carriage) the 88, with its traversing ability of 360 degrees, was a weapon which could be fired, traversed (and reloaded at the same time as it was turning) towards another target at any front, side and rear position and angle within a matter of seconds. Its hydraulic system also enabled the weapon to be quickly suspended onto its four pods.

Found within the Division's anti-aircraft was one battery containing a total of four 88 guns.

Anti-tank: Soviet tactics are based on tank tactics. Because of Red Russia's armored strength and a lack of German armor and weapons to effectively counter this Soviet might, Axis soldiers, frequently under tank attacks, were forced to develop methods of countering armored threats. And what they developed by the conclusion of 1942 by trial and error was quickly being incorporated into a very popular and skilled art on the Eastern front – tank hunting.

Tank hunters – panzerjägers – were noted for their patience, courage, resourcefulness, and calmness under extraordinary conditions. Whether operating with a team or individually, tank hunters played a critical role in repelling an armored thrust.

By September 1943, almost every German division had one anti-tank unit of battalion (or comparable) strength. A similar strength was found in the "Galicia" Division. With an array of 37mm anti-tank guns, 44mm panzerfausts (panzerfists), the 88mm Raketenpanzerbuchse 54 (known also as the 'Ofenrohr' [Stove-pipe] and 'Panzerschreck'[Tank Terror], the weapon being similar to the 2.36 inch American rocket 'Bazooka' launcher), the hollow charged "Panzerwerfmine I' anti-armor hand-grenade and various 'Teller' anti-tank mines, a well-trained and disciplined anti-tank unit did pose a threat to enemy armor. Additional training was also provided on how to properly construct and hurl a Molotov "cocktail" gasoline bomb; where to place a log or block of wood in a tanks' track and suspension system to disable a tank from moving; camouflage; how to approach and stalk enemy armor and a tank's strengths and weaknesses.

SS-Hauptsturmführer Hermann Kaschner (born 7 November 1914, SS. No. 317,675) commanded the Division's tank-hunters. An experienced Eastern front "tank-ace" and the recipient of a number of tank-destroyer badges, Kaschner's unit was formed in August 1943. In the late fall of 1943, as graduating recruits united with those who had returned from their specialized anti-armor training, Galicia's 'panzer-jäger's' began to train in earnest. Virtually unknown is the fact that the panzer-jägers were actually placed into captured Soviet-made T-34 tanks and other armored vehicles, driven around, and from the gunner's seat and a tank's sighting system, tank-hunters viewed what a tank-gunner sees – and cannot see – outside an armored vehicle.

Pioneer (Engineer): For any unit to succeed, it must have a strong engineer force to effectively conduct mobility, counter-mobility, and survivability operations.

Organized in September 1943 with a staff section and three companies, the battalion was augmented in January 1944 with a weapons staff. At first, it was commanded by SS-Sturmbannführer Sepp Syr (born 18 October 1903, SS-No. 283,029/non-party member, and a recipient of the Iron Cross, 1st Class) but in March 1944, SS-Sturmbannführer Josef Remberger (born 9 June 1903, SS-No.

267,977/Party No. 1,929,332, also a recipient of the Iron Cross 1st Class) assumed command. Remberger's adjutant was SS-Hauptsturmführer Krause; Waffen Hauptsturmführer Rembalovych was the assistant commander.

The Division's engineer battalion was finally organized in March 1944 when it was bolstered by personnel who had completed recruit training. The battalion's 3rd Company was known as the "speed company" for it was within this company that the battalion's bridge laying platoon, entirely mechanized with three "schwimmwagen's" (river crossing vehicles) and trucks, as well as the battalion's motorized heavy weapons platoon and mess section, was found. The remainder of the company travelled with bicycles or motorcycles.

The Division's engineers played a critical role. During combat it included: deception activities; placing and removing minefields; securing and reducing (if necessary by assault) bridges, obstacles, barriers, and fortifications; constructing fighting positions; and identifying bypass routes and cleared lanes around obstacles and mine fields. The removal or destruction of any unexploded and threatening explosives and construction/reinforcement of bridges, roads, airfields during an advance or retreat was also of essence. To simplify their mission, engineers provide critical support for all operations – from small unit actions to full divisional operations. During periods of peacetime, engineers help train troops in the usage and handling of explosives, conduct construction projects, ensure base maintenance, and frequently assist civilians in their construction needs and civil affairs programs.

Within the German army, engineer battalions were classified as 'combat engineers' and frequently, suffered higher combat casualties than even the infantry battalions.[31]

Signals (Communications): Formed in September 1943, the Division's signal battalion, with its two signals companies, played a critical role in maintaining proper communications, which ultimately determines success.

At all times, leaders must know what is going on, receive and convey instructions, request support, and base their decisions on a proper knowledge of the situation. This can only be accomplished and maintained through good communications. Without communications or in the event of its loss, any unit – from platoon to divisional level – begins to die. Every unit's communications equipment must be simple, mobile, flexible, and very reliable. In addition, hand, arm, visual, flag, and sound methods were taught and utilized.

Under the command of SS-Hauptsturmführer Wolfgang Wuttig (born 22 October 1915, SS-No. 423,132), the Division's communications personnel, equipped with the latest and newest equipment, were found throughout the whole Division.

Chapter 8: Heidelager: 1943

<u>Bicycle Battalion:</u> Formed in September, 1943, this unit was officially disbanded on 2 June 1944. Well before June, its men began to be incorporated into other Divisional units, such as the Fusilier Battalion.

<u>Fusilier Battalion:</u> Allied intelligence, by early 1944, was aware of the fact that within Germany's infantry divisions a battalion, described variously as "Divisions-Battalion," "Jäger-Battalion," or "Fusilier-Battalion," came into being.[32]

To reinforce a division's infantry battalions (especially if the division only possessed six infantry battalions), reserve battalions were utilized. One reserve involved the field-replacement battalion (long a part of any German division) but the other consisted of the newly organized Fusilier Batallion. Subordinated strictly to divisional command,[33] fusiliers contributed an added element of flexibility and strength to any organization spread too thin. Besides serving as reconnaissance troops, fusiliers were also utilized as "shock-troops" at any critical point during the battle.

The original German plan for the formation of a fusilier battalion called for drawing a division's various elements into one battalion-sized unit. But this was not always the case. In Italy, for example, during 1943, some divisional reconnaissance units were converted into fusilier battalions. But the "Galicia" Division's fusilier battalion was raised in January, 1944, from trained infantry, anti-tank, and mortar personnel originally intended for the 29th Regiment's 3rd Battalion.[34]

Initially, the Division's fusilier battalion was commanded by SS-Sturmbannführer Sepp Syr (born 18 October 1903, SS-No. 283,029/non-party member and a holder of the Iron Cross 1st Class). Syr was later transferred to the 23 Yugoslavian Muslim "Kama" Division where he served as a fusilier and later, as a regimental commander. His last assignment was with the 31st Freiwilligen German/Central European Panzer Division "Bohmen-Mahren."

With Syr's transfer, SS-Hauptsturmführer Karl Bristot, an Austrian, assumed command. A true professional and a first rate leader, Bristot, in order to establish a closer bond with his soldiers, even replaced the slanted "SS" runes on his collar patch for the Galician lion patch. According to Allied intelligence, a fusilier battalion consisted of a Headquarters section, 3 well armed and trained line companies, 1 heavy company and a battalion supply train. In turn, each line company – with three platoons – was exceptionally well armed with faustpatronen and panzerfausts; the heavy company had 3 machine gun platoons (each with 4 heavy MG42 machine guns) and 2 infantry gun platoons (each with 2 75mm light infantry guns for a total of 4) and a battalion supply/support train to supply the fusiliers. Within the line companies, besides the three platoons, each company had a mortar section with 2 81mm mortars and a tank-destroyer section. These two sections were, in every sense, a company's 4th platoon and were sometimes referred to as a "heavy" platoon.

According to Stefan Shuhan, a former officer in the fusilier battalion, the "Galicia" Division's fusilier battalion consisted of a headquarters staff section, 3 line companies, 1 heavy weapons company, and 1 motorized supply and support section.[35] The companies, including the heavy company, were numerically numbered from Company 1 to Company 4. A total of three platoons were found in each line company. Each platoon, in turn, consisted of 4 squads with 12 men per squad. Because of a lack of officers, all of the platoons were commanded by non-commissioned officers. With 12 men per 4 squads and one platoon NCO commander with his assistant, a total of 50 men were found per platoon. With 3 such platoons per company, a total of 150 soldiers (minus 1 or 2 officers per company) were found per line company. Within the "heavy" or 4th Company, a strength of 250-300 soldiers was found. The 4th Company was organized into 4 platoons. Within this company were found 4 truck-towed two-wheeled heavy 105mm mortars, and 4 two-wheeled Pak 75mm light infantry guns. Within the battalion, a total of 16 light 81 mm mortars were also found. Each squad had 1 MG34 or MG42 machine gun and 1 grenadier who fired an assortment of high explosive, anti-tank, illumination and, even, propaganda leaflet rifle grenades. Every soldier was armed with a Walther 9mm pistol, and a disproportionate number of men were armed with the 9mm Schmeisser MP ('Maschinenpistole') 38/40 submachine gun or the light Czechoslovakian BRNO machinegun. Every fusilier, excluding those armed with panzerschrek bazookas, carried two anti-tank panzerfausts and a handful of stick or "egg" hand-grenades.

In addition to the approximately 700 soldiers found within the four combat companies, a headquarters staff of almost 100 soldiers assisted the battalion commander and ran the battalion's supply/support train which ensured the battalions' supply, direct support, immediate repair, medical and transportation needs. Including these 100, a total strength of approximately 800 was found.[36]

Bristot's adjutant was SS-Untersturmführer Karl Strasser, a Slovakian German. Two other German and one Ukrainian staff officer, Waffen Hauptsturmführer Evhen Pobihushchyj-Ren,[37] rounded out the battalions staff. One German officer took care of administrative matters while the other, a supply transport officer, ensured the battalion's supply, ammunition and transport needs.[38] According to Shuhan, excluding the 1st Company which had two Ukrainian officers, each of the other three companies were commanded by one Ukrainian officer assisted with a number of German and Ukrainian NCO's.

For mobility, bicycles were used. These bicycles were obtained from the deactivated bicycle battalion. Battalion trucks moved the heavy mortar section and ensured a quick delivery of essential items.

Medical/Sanitation: To ensure proper health, morale, and physical/psychological strength, and to provide adequate care of soldiers' needs, it is critical for every military organization to have a solid medical corps. But obtaining a sufficient staff of medical personnel proved to be one of the most difficult problems encountered within the Division until the conclusion of the war.

The problem actually began well before World War II. Because it was difficult for Ukrainians to achieve a higher education, only a limited number studied medicine. The problem was so acute that at the outbreak of World War II, there were only abut 360 Ukrainian doctors in the whole of East Galicia.[39] To make matters worse, in the 1939-41 period, this figure was reduced when a number of these professionals were deported to Siberian slave labor camps, or murdered by the NKVD; and from 1941-43, some of the Ukrainian doctors who survived the Red terror became in turn victims of Nazi terror.[40] And in order to survive, some fled into the ranks of the UPA.

Of the surviving doctors, by June 1943, a total of 161 doctors had volunteered for the Division.[41] But some doctors (especially those from Lviv) opposed the Division and did not volunteer.[42] (Realistically speaking, they, along with many other Galician doctors, were unfit for military service).[43] Eventually, almost 60 were found suitable, but when called up, only 33 showed up.[44] Of these 33, one was soon released.[45] By 19 November this figure was increased by 2 dentists, 6 dental technicians and 2 opticians, but the Division was still in need of skilled medical personnel.[46]

The Division's doctors and medical personnel were at first under the guidance of Doctor Volodymyr Bilozor. A Galician of mixed German-Ukrainian extraction, Bilozor was a 1915 graduate of Czechoslovakia's Medical Institute. That same year, he began his practice in a Ukrainian unit found within the Austrian Army. In 1918, he joined the Galician Army. With the Galician Army's thrust into Ukraine, he directed a military hospital in Vinnitsa, Ukraine. Following the Army's 1921 surrender, Bilozor practiced in Lviv and Kolomyia, where he established a medical clinic. Together with his wife, Marianna, he spend many hours assisting those in need.

Accused in 1938 by Polish authorities of pro-Ukrainian sympathies, Bilozor resigned his position in Poland's National Health Agency, yet he continued to administered to all who sought his services. Under the Nazi German occupation, Bilozor frequently used his connections and "by taking care of matters," succeeded in saving many Ukrainians and even, in some cases, Poles. Secretly, he provided medical advice to the UPA and in trips to Lviv, assisted Metropolitan Sheptytskyi's "children" with their medical needs.

Despite Bilozor's efforts to find a sufficient number of doctors for the Division, there was still a shortage; therefore, on 8 March 1944, Dr. Bilozor proposed to the Ukrainian Military Board "that all doctors under the age of 35 be mobilized."[47] To add to this, Makarushka, a member of the Board, proposed a decree be issued throughout the whole of Galicia placing "all doctors, Ukrainian and Polish, for two years under the direction of the authorities. Afterwards, the Ukrainians, if willing, would enter the "Galicia" Division, whereas the Poles would return to their medical practice.[48]

Seeing that a problem existed, the Germans appointed SS-Obersturmbannführer Dr. Maximillian Specht (born 8 November 1898, SS-No. 118,403/Party No. 2,725,210), to the Division. Posted to the Divisional staff, Specht served as the Division's Chief Medical Officer and Divisional Surgeon. Specht arrived with SS-Sturmbannführer's Dr. Gerhard Striddle (born 26 December 1893, SS-No. 187,591-Party No. 4,206,368) and Dr. Helmut Schmitt (born 19 May 1910, SS-No. 28,967/Party No. 661,338), a former medical officer for an SS Combat Engineer School and holder of the Iron Cross, 2nd Class.

Along with the Ukrainian doctors, the Division's medical staff constantly strove, frequently under adverse conditions, to improve the Division's medical services. It must be noted, however, that although improvements were made, the Division was short of trained doctors throughout its existence.[49]

Veterinarian: Excluding panzer, mechanized infantry, and paratroop divisions, an average German division had 3,000 to 6,000 horses and mules.[50] To ensure proper care of a division's critical animal strength, every division had one or two veterinarian companies.[51]

Galicia's Division had one veterinarian company. Headed by Waffen-Untersturmführer Dr. Volodymyr Kischko, Kischko was the epitome of a true horseman. Born in Drohobych on 14 January 1906, Kischko graduated from both an Austrian and German veterinarian school. As a youth, he participated in equestrian events and later served as a veterinarian officer in Poland's Army Reserve. During the 1936 World Olympic Games held in Berlin, the doctor participated as a veterinary advisor to Poland's equestrian team.

Established 29 September 1943, the veterinarian company had, by 19 November 1943, 9 veterinarians who had volunteered for service.[52] Until the end of the war, the company was headed by Dr. Kischko.

Chapter 8: Heidelager: 1943

Supply: Every army organization requires an efficient, effective, and expeditious combat supply and service support. Without food, fuel, ammunition and other essentials, the best troops in the world will succumb to defeat.

The German system of supply during World War II was based on simplicity and flexibility. In the field, supplies were delivered from army to division to battalion. Army motor columns delivered supplies to a division's supply trains, which in turn shuttled the supplies to a regiment. Each regiment had one supply train which in turn was subdivided into sections. In turn, each battalion had its own combat rations and supply sections. Normally, supply sections were found within a battalion's headquarters.[53] Generally, one supply company took care of a Division's needs. This was true also within the "Galicia" Division.[54]

Napoleon was correct when he stated that "an army marches on its stomach." Within the Division, a bakery company, meat/butcher company, ration (food) company also came into existence. To ensure proper morale and to inform the general public of the Division's activities and deeds, a Field Post Office, Financial/Pension, Administrative and Reporter/Public Relations platoons were established. To ensure a proper, efficient and quick delivery of supplies, ammunition, fuel, rations, mail, clothing, equipment and other items to the Division's regiments and battalions, the "Galicia" Division was provided with a motorized transport comprising 2 light truck columns and 1 heavy truck column. A Divisional Maintenance and Truck repair company serviced and repaired the Division's light and heavy supply trucks.

The commander of the Division's supply troops was SS-Obersturmbannführer Franz Magill (born 22 August 1900, SS-Nr. 132,620/Party Nr. 4,137,171, and a holder of the Iron Cross, 2nd Class). SS-Sturmbannführer Otto Sulzbach (born 18 May 1901, SS-Nr. 1,364/Party Nr. 61,317) served on the Division's staff as the Division's Maintenance Officer and Waffen Hauptsturmführer Leopid Martyniuk commanded the Division's Maintenance and Repair Company.

29 September 1943 is the date cited for the formation of the Division's supply, morale, bakery, butcher, ration, and financial units as well as a post office, two motor ambulance platoons, and the vehicle repair company.

Military Field Police Troops: A military police unit's responsibilities are manifold. Security control; prisoner control; protection of restricted areas (such as ammunition depots, Divisional/Brigade Headquarter's); traffic control; supply escort through hostile guerrilla/partisan areas; assisting units in an advance or retreat; establishing and controlling civilian areas; conducting anti-subversive/sabotage and sniper operations; assist local (native) police forces in patrolling and maintaining order in occupied regions; anti-looter security measures and crime investigations are just some of the assignments police personnel frequently perform. During combat, military police personnel frequently serve as combat troops.

The Division's military field 'feld-gendarmerie-trupp' was established 29 September 1943. Initially, it was organized with 2 platoons, but with the Division's expansion, it possibly reached the strength of a company with 4 platoons.

Training and Replacement Regiment: A Training and Replacement Regiment was also organized. This non-front line regiment was established to assist in the training of recruits. Under the leadership of SS-Obersturmbannführer (Lieutenant-Colonel) Karl Marks (also spelled as Marx, SS-Nr. 257,785/Party Nr. 3,601,899), the regiment trained rigorously. Marks, the holder of the Iron Cross, 1st Class, and a soldier who had previously commanded a mixed German, racial German, and Italian Waffen-SS Mountain Brigade (designated later as the 24th Gebirgs "Karstjäger" Mountain Division), and who had experience working with foreign troops, was a perfectionist. From his troops, Marks demanded – and received – the best.[55]

Field Replacement (Reserve) Battalion: Not to be confused with the Training and Replacement Regiment, a field replacement battalion (found years before World War II in every German division), was, by mid-1943, undertaking a far more important role in replacing manpower deficiencies.

The "Galicia" Division's field replacement reserve battalion, with a strength of approximately 800 soldiers,[56] provided replacements for all divisional units, and it had at least one weapon of each type found within the Division. This unit was organized with a headquarters staff, 3 rifle companies, a heavy company, a division training section (referred to as a 'school' which provided advanced and refresher training on equipment and weapons from a handgun right up to artillery weapons), and a supply company.

Commanded by SS-Hauptsturmführer Johannes Kleinow (born 10 February 1901, SS-Nr. 28,740), the Division's reserve battalion provided critically needed officers, NCO's, and soldiers for the Division's various units. Upon arrival into such a battalion, a trained soldier continued to train, assisted others with training, or was sent to a specialized training course or school prior to being placed within a permanent Divisional unit.

Chaplain's Corps: In the middle of October 1943, the Chaplains completed their training. But some chaplains, among them chaplain Ivan Halibei, were released from service as a result of age or an inability to complete the training. Chaplain Severyn Saprun, who developed an injury during the training, "gutted" his pains, prayed to the Lord for help, and continued to train; he succeeded in completing his training.

Following a brief period of leave, excluding chaplains Danylo Kovaliuk, Ivan Holoida, and Osyp Karpins'kyi who immediately returned to France to serve with one of the independent rifle regiments, the remaining chaplains entered the Division in Heidelager in November 1943.

Within Neuhammer, Chaplain Josef Kladochnyi was posted to the 30th Regiment; Chaplain Emanuel Korduba was posted to the 29th Regiment; and Chaplain Severyn Sapryn, following a brief period of recuperation and leave, was posted to the anti-aircraft battalion.[57] In successive months, as the other chaplains arrived from France, they were incorporated into other Divisional elements. Upon entry into the Division, Chaplain Nahayewsky served as Laba's assistant. He was posted, by a Divisional order, to the Divisional staff section.[58]

Divisional Band: By November 1943, a Divisional band came into existence. Although civilian bands had played in July 1943 in the Galician capital as the recruits departed, the Divisional band was finally formed in November 1943. This band was formed from recruits who arrived to training with musical instruments and upon the completion of recruit training, auditioned in Heidelager for the band.

At first, the band was directed by Andrei Krushelnyts'kyi and later, by a Galician German, Johann Thiessen. The band specialized in marches, Ukrainian songs, and opera music. A Divisional choir was also established and was headed by Vasyl Ostashevs'kyi. Both the band and choir played at various functions and frequently toured Galicia.

Around such organizations was built the "Galicia" Division.[59] The Division was provided with the required training, weapons, and equipment needed for combat success and to be administratively, tactically and technically self-sufficient from squad to Divisional level. The "Galicia" Division was organized to be a powerful, self-contained tactical force capable of operating either in combat teams, battle groups (kampfgruppe's), or in its entirety. And once enough capable and aggressive leadership was found, the "Galicia" Division was to be a very flexible and destructive combat force.

On 30 October 1943, Lviv's Military Board issued its final report for the recruitment campaign. Extensively detailed, this report covered the period of 1 May – 30 October 1943, and cited the following figures:[60]

- Total volunteers for the Division: 82,000;[61]
- Assigned for examination: 53,000;[62]
- Showed up for examination: 42,000;[63]
- Examined: 27,000;[64]
- Reclaimed: 1,400;[65]
- Summoned for call-up: 25,600;[66]
- Summoned: 19,047;[67]
- Actual enlistees: 13,245;[68]
- Permanently released from military training as a result of injury, illness, family problems, etc.: 1,487;[69]
- Currently on military training: 11,578;[70]
- Recruits to be summoned in the period of 1 – 13 November 1943: 6,150.[71]

9

General Fritz Freitag

On 20 November 1943, SS-Oberführer Fritz Freitag (SS-Nr. 393,266/Party No. 3,052,501 and promoted to SS-Brigadeführer und General Major der Waffen-SS und Polizei on 20 April 1944), replaced SS-Brigadeführer und General Major der Waffen-SS Walter Schimana.[1] Schimana needed to be replaced by a commander more knowledgeable in military affairs.[2]

Born in Allenstein, East Prussia, on 28 April 1894, Freitag was the product of a military family. During World War I, he served in the trenches. Although at the conclusion of the war Germany's army was restricted in size by the Versailles Treaty, Freitag remained in its service. He served in both the infantry and cavalry.

With the eruption of World War II, Freitag participated in the Polish and Western European campaigns. In France, he served briefly as a police commander before assuming in late 1941 a regimental command in the 4th SS "Polizei" Division. On 5 February 1942, he was awarded the Iron Cross 2nd Class and then the following month, 6 March, the Iron Cross 1st Class. On 30 April 1943, Freitag was awarded the German Cross in Gold for valor on the eastern front. During 15 February 1943 until 20 April 1943 Freitag, in the rank of SS-Standartenführer (Colonel), temporarily commanded the 8th SS Cavalry "Florian Geyer" Division when its commander, SS-Brigadeführer und Generalmajor der Waffen-SS Wilhelm ("Willi") Bittrich, left the "Florian Geyer" to command the 9th SS "Hohenstauffen" Division. With the appointment of SS-Brigadeführer und Generalmajor der Waffen-SS Herman Fegelein on 20 April to command the "Florian Geyer," Freitag went back into the replacement pool. On 20 November 1943, he assumed command of the "14. Galizische SS Freiwilligen Division."

Galicia Division

According to former 1st General Staff Officer Major Heike,[3] General Freitag "was driven by an almost pathological ambition to succeed," and "strove for advancement to the higher posts, and coveted recognition and awards." As a result, claims Heike, Freitag "was suspicious of most people and made life unpleasant not only for his colleagues but also for himself." Additionally, Heike claims "he [Freitag] was not accepted among either the Ukrainian or German cadres of the Division." As a result, Heike has written in his memoirs that "one of the greatest tragedies of the Division was the appointment of such a man as its commander."[4]

Yet Heike does admit the fact that "Freitag was respected for his military knowledge, diligence, and good intentions," and "on the whole, Freitag was a diligent and consistent man, knowledgeable about military tactics, and their application in battle." But Heike continues to criticize Freitag and especially faults Freitag who "could not understand the psychology of Ukrainians and attempted to force upon them the Prussian spirit." As a result, he "never developed amicable relations with either the Ukrainians of the Division or his closest German colleagues."[5] Certain ex-Ukrainian officers, such as Colonel Ren, corroborate Heike's appraisal with their own accusations. As Ren wrote "Freitag, upon arrival to our Division, cared little about his officer leadership personnel," and claimed (as did Heike), that Freitag "filled all important posts in the Division with Germans."[6] Angrily, Ren cites how one day shortly after Freitag's arrival, when Ren returned to his 29th Regiment he was immediately informed by some of his NCO's that some newly arrived regimental commander, SS-Standartenführer Friedrich Dern (born 5 March 1896, SS-Nr. 38,707/Party Nr. 1,202,729 and holder of both the Iron Cross 1st Class and Iron Cross 2nd Class), was going around and inspecting the various companies. Although Dern was slightly higher in rank, Dern undoubtedly had been informed that Ren was commanding (if only temporarily) the 29th Regiment. Under the circumstances, prior to any inspections, the incoming officer should have made an appearance at Ren's headquarters office, informally introduced himself, and spoken with Ren. If the incoming regimental commander did show up at Ren's office and Ren was not there, than a message should have been sent to Ren. After an informal and informative meeting, an agreement should have been reached among the two on how to inspect the regiment, and the various battalions and companies notified that Ren and an incoming regimental commander would shortly be meeting with the various battalion and company officers and NCO's. Then, with Ren escorting the incoming commander and making introductions, a proper and smooth transition would have occurred. Such a transition would have ensured an easy changeover with no misunderstandings or bad feelings and would have earned Dern respect. Since Dern had acted abusively, Ren went to see General Fritz Freitag.

Chapter 9: General Fritz Freitag

Ren immediately informed Freitag that some officer had arrived to his regiment of whom he had no knowledge, and that the colonel had refused to introduce himself. Freitag, although surprised by such behavior, immediately informed Ren that Dern was assuming command of the 29th Regiment. When Ren asked "so why was I demoted?" Freitag replied that he had no knowledge of any degradations, but that because of an order by Hitler, all staff posts "must be reserved for Germans." But to please Ren (and undoubtedly calm the situation), Freitag also informed Ren that he was being transferred to another regiment and soon, would be scheduled to attend a regimental officers course in Antwerp, Belgium.

Ren knew that he would lose his regiment. But Ren, who knew for a fact that Hitler had never issued such an order, was furious with Freitag for his inability to properly explain the situation, and for offering Ren nothing but an untruthful alibi; Ren did, however, attend the course in Antwerp and by his own admission, did benefit from its training.

Needless to say, such behavior infuriated many individuals. Amongst Ukrainians and others, much has been said and written about Freitag. Some accounts have been harsh, a few sympathetic, and others were undoubtedly written from a biased point of view. Yet to this day, no objective and clear cut account has been presented about Freitag; therefore, an objective study must be revealed.

Freitag, shortly before assuming command, had achieved the rank of general. For Freitag, a respected regimental commander who briefly commanded the "Florian Geyer" Division, such a promotion was regarded – rightfully – as deserving. Undoubtedly seeking to make a mark in military annals, he knew that success as a Divisional commander was especially critical; conversely, as every high-ranking officer knows, failure of any kind could prove deadly for career development.

To prove himself, Freitag wanted to command a Division. But what he wanted to command was a German division, and not a foreign division. To command a native division is a challenge in itself, but to command a foreign division with its numerous demands, needs – and dangers – is a far higher challenge and if unsuccessful, would tarnish a man's career. Fully realizing this, Freitag strove to avoid such an assignment.

But an order was an order. Since Freitag could not escape from his orders, he arrived to command the Division. Undoubtedly, he initially did not know how to approach his command and assignment. What complicated the problem was the fact that there was a lack of solid leadership, something which every newly assigned commander needs in order to create and maintain an effective force. Therefore, one of the first major undertakings of Fritz Freitag was to create solid leadership. In all fairness, it should be noted that prior to the arrival of Freitag in late

November 1943, a number of the German officers had already preceded him and in the following weeks, more would arrive. Fully aware of the fact (or he soon would realize) that many of them were poorly qualified, Freitag was initially hampered with a largely ineffective leadership corps.

Regarding allegations that Freitag "reserved all important positions for Germans," it must be also noted that Freitag, who wanted to establish a crack outfit, had realized as early as 19 November 1943, while in Lviv, that a leadership problem was present. During a meeting attended by Freitag, Wachter, and members of the Galician Military Board, the Division's needs were stressed. Various matters were addressed but Makarushka, during his twenty minute referendum on the committee members' various responsibilities, also issued a report on the Division's cadre personnel. Following Makarushka's words, Freitag stated that "within the Division are over 1,100 graduates [of secondary schools] which are good. There are 540 NCO's, therefore, there is enough. The biggest problem lies with the officers. Among them there is no inclination about new methods [of warfare], but although they do learn quickly, many fall out because they are older people. Therefore, at the beginning, German officers must come in and [as admitted Freitag], this poses difficulties. Immediately, we must hasten to seek fifty young officers. Many companies have only one officer.[7] Himmler was begged to provide German officers, because only one from among many Ukrainians may be a regimental commander."[8]

During this visit to Lviv, Freitag also noted that within the Military Board, there were a number of young members. From among them Yuriy Krokhmaliuk and Liubomyr Makarushka entered the Division.[9]

Stronger efforts were renewed to obtain Ukrainian officer personnel. Although in Galicia some 200 Ukrainian ex-Polish Army officers were still available, as of 22 January 1944, none entered the Division.[10] The situation became especially acute when an attempt was made to recruit at least 50 officers that were critically needed,[11] but nothing became of this. So desperate was the Military Board that a draft of ex-officers (or at least some of them), was even considered.

On 22 November 1943, Khronoviat announced "that of these 50, among them are younger men, but some are older, born in 1894." Khronoviat also acknowledged the fact that calling them up would create an outburst, yet realizing the situation's necessity, proposed "that tomorrow all must be sent a notice that because of a shortage of officers within the Division, they will be called up and that will be done on 1 December of this year."[12] Khronoviat especially voiced his opinion on a report submitted earlier that day by Divisional officer Dmytro Paliiv that: "our Division does not have good officers. It does not have the number of good officers that are needed and because of this, this is a Division which is [a military force], but is not."[13] As a result of Paliiv's criticism, Khronoviat once again returned to his previous proposal to draft officers. "If 50 are unable to lead, then up to 40 officers, which we urgently need, we will secure. How many of these 40 officers will be regimental, troop, company commanders – is not known [at this time]."[14]

In the end, however, it became apparent that little to no support would be gained from the ex-Polish Army officers. The Military Board gave up on the idea of a draft and began to search for officers elsewhere. Discussions began with the Slovak Army to determine whether it held any Ukrainian officers, and the Germans were asked to release some Ukrainian officers if any were available within the Wehrmacht. Additionally, some Ukrainians, primarily former students who were hiding out within the community for patriotic activities but who possessed language abilities, were found. Following promises that they would not be harmed, approximately fifty were secured as translators for the Division.[15]

Fully realizing the dire situation and seeing that the sincere efforts of the Military Board were not fruitful, Freitag then proceeded to raise a professional and solid officer corps from German personnel. Needless to say many Ukrainians, as well as Governor Wachter, opposed this move. But realistically speaking, Freitag had seen that since May 1943, little had been done. Therefore, he moved quickly to obtain – one way or another – a solid officers corps.[16]

At no time did Fritz Freitag ever openly loathe Ukrainians, or refer to his Division as a force composed of "untermenschen." Not once did he ever stand in front of the soldiers and mock their nationality, nor did he ever display contempt or a careless attitude towards the "Galicia" Division. On the contrary, as attested by Heike, "everything that Freitag considered necessary for the Ukrainian Division he carried out with vigor and consistency," although, as acknowledged Heike, "without special consideration or adjustment and with a rigid adherence to the rules and regulations he had learned."

Unfortunately, Heike does not explain his latter remark in detail. In all fairness, it must be noted that Freitag had no previous experience working and serving with non-Germans and probably was never ever given a thorough briefing or even the least kind of instruction, on what to expect. Because every leader has his personal leadership style, his own beliefs, methods, concerns, rules and regulations, Freitag probably felt that the best approach would be from a Prussian point-of-view, with strict discipline. It must be noted, however, that Freitag himself realized that many of the German officers within the Division were poorly qualified to lead and needed to "shape-up" and set a proper example to the Ukrainians. As a result (as verified by Heike), Freitag "was led to treat Germans more harshly than Ukrainians."[17]

Undoubtedly, under Shimana's command, a state of laxness had developed during the time Galicia's recruits trained under the replacement army's experts. As the German cadre within the "Galicia" Division awaited for the recruits to end their training, there was not much to do. For those assigned to the Division (especially in the Division's early months), assignment to the Division was probably comparable to that of duty in Paris, France. Fully realizing this, Freitag came down hard.

According to former Divisional staff officer Yuriy Krokhmaliuk, Freitag had achieved a high position in the Nazi Party. He acknowledged the party's ideology, preferred to surround himself with those who accepted its ideology, and strove to adopt it in his positions.

At first, Freitag presented the party's viewpoints within the Division. But in due time, he perceived that the Ukrainian soldiers in the Division were honorable soldiers, and they were not "sub-humans" as Nazi racial theorists had classified Eastern Europeans. Expressing no interest whatsoever in Nazi ideology, the Ukrainians volunteered only in order to defend and preserve their own heritage, values and ideals. Realizing this, Freitag ceased promoting Nazi ideology and worked only to create an elite force.

Freitag established high standards for the Divisions officers – whether German or Ukrainian. Krokhmaliuk, in his study of General Freitag, states that "Freitag never presented himself in any negative or abusive way towards the Ukrainians on his Divisional staff and, as a matter of fact, Freitag never raised his voice to the Ukrainians as he did on occasion to German officers."[18] When it came to disciplinary measures, Freitag's wrath frequently fell harder on the Germans than on the Division's Ukrainian volunteers."[19]

Regarding the common soldier, there were times when Freitag was more than fair. Years later, Krokhmaliuk would recall how a certain German SS-Hauptsturmführer, who was abusive towards some of the Division's Ukrainian soldiers on a parade ground in Neuhammer, suffered from Freitag's wrath. In this particular case, part of the misunderstanding arose from the fact that some of the Galician volunteers did not understand the German language. To shout at soldiers under any circumstances is not only incorrect, but unprofessional. But when the German officer began to use vulgar language, racial epithets and yelled at the volunteers "why can't you learn our language!" Krokhmaliuk, who had had enough, went directly to Freitag.

Although the general was in a meeting, he still came out to see Krokhmaliuk. Despite his anger, Krokhmaliuk maintained his composure and professionalism.

Chapter 9: General Fritz Freitag

Politely, but firmly, he informed General Freitag that it was bad enough for the officer to shout at the troops, but to use such foul words was worse. In conclusion, Krokhmaliuk forcefully stated "let me remind you, General, that we all bleed the same color! And as far as learning the language, let me also remind you that many more of our men speak your language than your men speak our language. So why don't some of you Germans learn Ukrainian!"

Freitag only stared at Krokhmaliuk. After a long pause, the General quietly replied "You are correct" and returned to his meeting. That evening, the abusive German officer was packing his bags. He never reentered the Division.[20]

Shortly after returning from his regimental course, Waffen Sturmbannführer Ren, Paliiv, Krokhmaliuk, as well as the rest of the Division's Ukrainian and German officers, were ordered to immediately report to Divisional headquarters. After assembling his officers, Freitag, very sternly, asked "why did a military doctor find on one soldier two lice bugs?" And without waiting for a reply Freitag (who undoubtedly was concerned about the soldiers and disease) scolded the officers, accused the Division's soldiers of negligence, and in conclusion shouted "that in my regiment even after two months on the front line lice were never found!"

Silence only prevailed. Not one officer dared to say anything. But then Paliiv's voice was heard when he calmly replied "Sir, I cannot believe, that no one had any lice after being on the front for two months." Without waiting for a reply he asked "General, do you know the soap ration per family in Galicia?"

The Division's officers were awed by Paliiv's approach. All anticipated that Freitag would verbally assail Paliiv. But the opposite only occurred. Freitag calmed down, quickly finished his lecture, and dismissed the group. But as the officers left, he asked Ren and Paliiv to stay behind, and calmly spoke with both men.

After the two officers briefed the General on their past front-line personal experiences with hygiene, they slowly convinced Freitag that undoubtedly his soldiers had also encountered lice during front line service. Politely, they also informed the General about the chronic soap shortages faced by Galicia's citizenry. Following this incident, Freitag behaved more rationally and a stronger emphasis was placed on troop hygiene.

On 5 January 1944, during the Ukrainian Christmas, the Ukrainian officers held their traditional dinner. Members of the German cadre, as well as Freitag, were invited. Accepting their invitation, Freitag attended. That evening, during the ceremonial dinner held in a very informal atmosphere, a closer bond of trust and camaraderie was attained.

In the following days, as Germany's situation turned darker, more and more Nazi officials and leaders, both within the Party and SS, began to realize the fallacy of Nazi ideology and they sought ways of making new changes. And Freitag was no exception. As his dreams of establishing a career on the basis of any previous doctrines, ideologies, and racial policies collapsed, Freitag changed; and as talk of forming a Ukrainian army corps arose, Freitag envisioned the possibility of heading its leadership. He fully realized that such a corps would represent a solid unity and would be much stronger than any one German Waffen-SS division. As time went by, Krokhmaliuk and others observed a change in Freitag's approach to the Ukrainians; increasingly, Freitag himself used the term "Ukrainian" Division, or the "1st Ukrainian" Division, well before the "Ukrainian" title became official; as well, he began to give more credit to the Division's Ukrainian personnel. To be sure, problems and moments of ugliness would occur. But in general, Freitag developed a stronger sympathy and respect for the Ukrainian soldier and his cause.[21]

10

The Continuing Training of the "Galicia" Division and the Division's Training and Replacement Regiment

On 30 October 1943, the "Galicia" Division received 11 Ukrainian Waffen-Hauptsturmführers (Captains), 53 Waffen-Obersturmführer's (1st Lieutenants), and 29 Waffen-Untersturmführer's (2nd Lieutenant's).[1] That same day, Wachter informed Himmler of the Division's progress and even invited the Reichsführer to visit the Division sometime in November.[2]

By November 1943 the Division, which until now had existed mostly on paper, began to acquire some semblance of reality. Its strength was estimated at 6,000,[3] but this figure rose daily as more and more trained recruits arrived following their initial training within the Replacement Army. At last, the various Divisional units began to train together.

As mentioned earlier, one of the first units organized around the Division was the reserve Training and Replacement Regiment.[4] Because there was a lack of space at Heidelager, the Division's Training and Replacement Regiment was stationed at Wandern (near Frankfurt-on-the-Oder), Germany. At first, because of a limited number of recruits, it was able to train somewhat effectively but soon, the training standards depreciated tremendously when the Training and Replacement Regiment found itself swamped with manpower.

According to Heike, "4,000 to 5,000 recruits, all raw civilians without any form of military preparation,"[5] were found within Wandern. But this figure would soon rise significantly. According to Roman Krokhmaliuk "by early 1944, about 10,000 men were found at Wandern."[6] And the greater percentage of this manpower came from Ukrainian slave labor deported to Germany not only from Galicia, but from various parts of Ukraine.[7]

As the deportees heard about the "Galicia" Division and its Training and Replacement Regiment, many soon began to volunteer for service.[8] Such was the case of Vasyl Hnativ who, in 1941, was deported to work in Germany. In January 1944, he enlisted into the Division while working as a coal-miner in Leipzig, Germany. Along with 13 others, he enlisted into the Division.[9] In a number of cases, the Ukrainian Central Committee secured volunteers. Thus, the Division's manpower was no longer solely secured from Galician volunteers but also, from manpower within Germany.

However, this manpower created some problems. To begin with, a high percentage of the men who "volunteered" from within Central Europe did so only to be with their own kind and to find an alternative to factory, mine, or farm labor. They had no strong desires to serve within a military unit, and many were not patriotically motivated. Some, in fact, even possessed leftist sympathies and regarded Galicia's volunteers as a "bourgeois" element. A number came from such simple backgrounds and were so illiterate that before they could even begin any kind of military training, they first had to learn how to read and write. As with many others who would later arrive (but especially after January 1945), service within the "Galicia" Division was only sought as a means of escape.[10]

The following factors especially compounded the problem: besides the fact that many were illiterate, the militarily inexperienced men were herded into overcrowded conditions. With only about 40 to 50 German and Ukrainian instructors of questionable quality and a lack of modern equipment and weaponry, no solid training was being conducted. The remainder of the Division, stationed at Heidelager, could not provide any trained manpower because it barely had enough of its own skilled personnel to effectively conduct Divisional training. Needless to say, such conditions at Wandern (as also within several of the independent rifle regiments) caused a considerable amount of grievances and complaints. In turn, these grievances and complaints circulated as far east as Galicia proper, angered many within Galicia, and further reinforced the false civilian rumor that all of Galicia's volunteers were faced with "insufficient arms, training, morale, and living conditions."

By the conclusion of 1943, America's Military Intelligence was fully aware of the evolution of the 14th Waffen-SS Division. In a report titled "Development of the Waffen-SS," the "Galicia" Division was identified under part B, titled "Germanic and Foreign Elements in the Waffen-SS." Section B reads:

Chapter 10: The Continuing Training of the "Galicia" Division

"Since 1940, assiduous attempts have been made to recruit SS legions from among the "Germanic" populations of Scandinavia, Western Europe and the Baltic States. This process of incorporating non-German elements in the Waffen-SS had gone a stage further in 1943 by the recruitment of the SS Division Galicia, SS Croatian Mountain Division, and Baltic and Walloon divisions or brigades."

But what is interesting about section B is that it acknowledges that the Waffen-SS is beginning to develop into a multi-lingual army. "How this is reconciled with the original conception of the SS as the racial elite of Aryan Germany is difficult to see," and the report emphasizes that: "this in turn has an obvious bearing on the important question of the value of the Waffen-SS as an instrument of internal security."

Under section D's "Conclusion," the report accurately concluded that: "the Waffen-SS on the whole presents the picture of an institution which is still developing." However, it is important to note that the intelligence report does make it clear that its (Waffen-SS') expansion could possibly prove negative for Germany. "Whether this accretion of numbers represents in every case an access to strength for Hitler, Himmler and the Party Organization is less certain."[11]

Enlistment into the "Galicia" Division, however, was by no means guaranteed even to those in Galicia who earlier had been screened and accepted. Such was the tragic case of Johann Lutschyn, who was born on 12 June 1917 and was to report on 30 July 1943.

On 11 November 1943, the Commander of the Security and Service Police in Lviv received a letter from Galicia's Bureau of People's Concerns and Welfare regarding Auschwitz prisoner Johann Lutschyn.[12] The letter stated:

"Prior to his arrest on 29 July 1943, Lutschyn's wife received a visit from the 'Burgenmeister' of the village of Kamyanka-Sturmilova. The Burgenmeister, who was with some unidentified male, begged the woman to let the unidentified man stay overnight. Lutschyn's wife objected and pointed out that her husband was not home. But because the Burgenmeister insisted and guaranteed that the man was reliable, the man stayed overnight. On the following day, the man who had stayed overnight was arrested.

Johann Lutschyn, who returned home on the same morning, went to the local town market to make some purchases because he was to report to the SS Freiwilligen Division "Galizien." But there, he was arrested along with the Burgenmeister and the unknown man. Although the Burgenmeister attested that Johann did not know the unknown man, and was not at home during the night, Lutschyn was not freed and currently, it is believed he is in Auschwitz. We request that action be taken for Lytschyn in order [for him] to report to the Division."

On 2 December 1943, Lutschyn's wife, Mrs. Paraskewia Lutschyn, once again personally wrote to Colonel Bisanz who was in Lviv. Desperate for information on her husband's fate, Mrs. Lutschyn wrote:

"I am Mrs. Paraskewia Lutschyn from Kamyanka-Sturmilova, and beg you to provide me information about my husband Johann Lutschyn who, on 29 July 1943, was arrested by the Gendarmerie in Kamyanka-Sturmilova. I have sent three appeals requesting information as to what happened to him. I have received only information that he is in Oswiencim."[13] [Continuing with her letter, Mrs. Lutschyn made it clear that] "he was the first man in Kamyanka-Sturmilova to volunteer for the SS Division Galicia and therefore, I ask you kindly to release my husband from incarceration so that he may report to the Galicia Division."[14]

On 21 December 1943, Alfred Bisanz sent a short but strong message to the Security and Service Police regarding "the arrested Johann Lutschyn in Auschwitz." The letter stated:[15]

"I demand your answer and immediate action on my letter dated 11/11/43 regarding the person mentioned above."

On 19 January 1944, Mrs. Lutschyn wrote to the Leader of the Family Welfare Organization for Members of the "Galicia" Division. As in previous letters, she again explained the dates and circumstances of her husband's arrest, and appealed for assistance. Her letter was strongly endorsed by Myhailo Kul'chuts'kyi, a member of the Divisional Family Committee who also verified that Johann Lutschyn was to enter the Rifle Division "Galicia" on 30 July 1943.[16]

But on 31 January 1944, Galicia's Security and Service Police responded directly to Galicia's People's Concerns and Welfare Bureau's main office located in Lviv. Titled: "Reference Johann Lutschyn, born 12.6.17," and "Action Taken on the Letter of 11/11/43 Inn. IV 702-02," the letter was brief, succinct, but tragic. It read:

"Johann Lutschyn was arrested because he was active in the political organization OUN. During his interrogation, he acknowledged that he was active in the OUN and that he was a county leader; therefore, he cannot be released from incarceration in the near future."[17]

Johann Lutschyn (whose activities were undoubtedly monitored by the Nazi police), never entered the "Galicia" Division. To this day, his fate at Auschwitz remains unknown. Because no one ever saw or heard of him after the war, it may be safely assumed that Lutschyn probably perished at Auschwitz. Lutschyn's fate, however, serves as a prime example of Nazi fears and actions against the OUN as late as 1944, and their efforts to prevent OUN members from entering the "Galicia" Division.

11

The "Galicia" Division's Periodicals

On 21 November 1943, the first issue of "To Victory" was published. A weekly newspaper dedicated to the Divisions soldiers, "To Victory" was published by the Military Board.

Initially, the Military Board had planned to publish the first issue months before. But because of tight press censorship and opposition from certain Nazi officials, for these reasons the publication was delayed.[1]

Chief editor Myhailo Ostroverkha was assisted with assistant editors V. Dzis' and Artym Orel. Maria Kobryns'ka was the chief secretary. Colonel Bartolomei Evtymovych, Iar Slavutych, M. Sytnyk, Leonid Lyman, P. Karpenko-Krynytsia, E. Kozak and L. Perfets'kyi rounded-out the editorial staff.

Within its four pages, information was provided on military-political events, commentaries on various national and international issues; and articles on history, literature, and international sporting events. Various cartoons and humorous articles to bolster morale were also inserted. Initially published in Lviv, the press later worked out of Cracow. Exactly 51 issues were published with approximately 10,000 newspapers in each issue. Issue No. 51 was last published on 7 January 1945.[2] These issues were distributed amongst the Divisions soldiers and Galicia's people.

With the transfer of the Military Board to Vienna in late January 1945, the Military Board commenced a new publication. Titled "To Arms," basically, it was the same newspaper as "To Victory." This publication, however, was short-lived and it ceased to exist sometime in March 1945. Very few (if any) of its issues ever reached the "Galicia" Divisions soldiers.

For the greater part, throughout the Divisions existence, its soldiers read whatever European newspapers and publications they could come across.

12

Kampfgruppe "Beyersdorff"

On 31 December 1943, the strength of the "14. Galizische SS-Freiwilligen Division" consisted of exactly 256 officers, 449 NCO's, and 11,929 enlisted for a total of 12,634.[1] This strength included those training in Heidelager and Europe's various schools, those found within the remaining Divisional independent rifle regiments, and men on convalescent, emergency, and family leave. This figure did not include the nearly 10,000 found at Wandern in the Training and Replacement Regiment.

Beginning in January 1944, additional manpower for the Division was derived from the disbanded independent rifle regiments and from those who earlier had volunteered in Galicia but had not yet been called up. These volunteers, as those who had preceded them, immediately fell into the Replacement Army; there, they were organized into training companies, and were provided a thorough 12-16 week period of training prior to entering the Division.

On 10 January 1944, Major Wolf-Dietrich Heike entered the Division.[2] Posted to the Division's IA as a senior general staff officer, Heike remained in that position until the end of the war.

Major Heike was born on 27 June 1913, in Graudenz, West Prussia to Rosemary (nee Von Wedel) and Richard Heike. His mother was of Prussian aristocracy, and his father a career army officer who retired as a Major. Heike completed his formal education in Uckermark, Prussia, and passed his final school examination in Wenigerode (Harz) in 1934. That same year, 21-year-old Heike began his military career by enlisting as an officer-cadet in the 2nd Prussian Artillery School in Schwerin, Germany. Shortly afterwards, he attended Munich's Military Academy and upon graduation, was commissioned as a 2nd Lieutenant. Assigned to an artillery garrison in Schleswig-Holstein, Northern Germany, he rose to captain and Battery Commander. While stationed there, he married in 1939.

At that time, Heike was serving in the 30th Infantry Division, which was composed of soldiers recruited primarily from Schleswig-Holstein. With the 30th, he saw action in Poland[3] and western Europe but, in early 1941, was transferred to the 110th Infantry Division as a battery commander.

As an artillery commander with the 110th, he participated in the Russian campaign, fought offensively at Bialystock, Minsk, Smolensk and advanced to the Northern Volga River near Moscow. Repulsed in the December 1941 counteroffensive, the 110th fought defensively at Welyki Luki in the central sector. During this time, Heike became 1st aide-de-camp on its divisional staff.

From 1 September 1942 until 3 March 1943, Heike first attended general staff training provided by the 5th Panzer Division in Russia (and actually on the front), and that spring and summer, he attended Berlin's Academy of War Studies. Transferred back to the Eastern front, in the second half of 1943, he served as a 2nd General Staff officer (IB) with the 122nd Infantry Division in Northern Russia. (Vicinity of Southern Finland). On 1 August 1943, Heike attained the rank of major; his orders also specified he was to serve as a general staff officer. Five months later, Heike was posted to the "Galicia" Division. An experienced Eastern Front combat officer and the recipient of the Iron Cross 2nd and 1st Class as well as the Close Combat Assault Badge, Heike brought much needed expertise and knowledge.[4]

Several weeks after Heike's arrival, General Fritz Freitag left to attend a special four week divisional commanders' training course in Hirschberg, Silesia. Previously, this course was conducted in Berlin, but because of daily raids on Germany's capital by Allied bombers, the course was transferred from Berlin to Hirschberg. With Freitag's departure, Divisional command fell to SS-Standartenführer Friedrich Beyersdorff, who headed the Division's artillery. And it was during Freitag's absence that the Division was ordered into combat for the first time.

In the early days of February 1944, a critical situation arose when a guerrilla group from Kovpak's 1st Ukrainian Guerrilla Division, under the command of Lieutenant-Colonel Petr Vershyhora,[5] struck rapidly westward from Byelorussias's vast swamp and forest region into the current border region of Eastern Poland, Northwest Ukraine, and Southwest Byelorussia.[6] Vershyhora's mission has never been clearly defined, but undoubtedly it was conducted to maintain pressure on

Germany's hard pressed Wehrmacht and security forces, destroy certain targets, update Stavka's intelligence information on the region and its population prior to any occupation by regular Soviet forces and to terrorize certain individuals. But as the Red guerrilla force moved into the region, they also encroached upon a territory claimed by a host of other guerrilla forces, such as the UPA and the Polish guerrillas from both the AK and communist factions.[7]

As a result of the intensified Soviet guerrilla activity, the Division received, in mid-February 1944, an order from Cracow's Higher SS and Police Leader, Wilhelm Koppe. The order read:

> "The Division is to immediately form a battle group to combat Kovpak's Soviet partisan formations that have penetrated into the territories of the General-Gouvernment. This strength of the task force is to be one infantry regiment, one detachment of light artillery, and detachments of sappers and anti-tank grenadiers. The task force is to be placed under the jurisdiction of the SS and police leader of the General government."[8]

One or two days later, on 15 February 1944, another directive was received which reiterated the previous order that the battlegroup was to be in regimental strength. But this order also specified that the battlegroup was to be ready within 48 hours.[9]

In response, SS-Standartenführer Beyersdorff immediately informed the Higher SS and Police that the Division was in no position to establish a battlegroup in regimental strength for battle efficiency, and Beyersdorff insisted that he could not be held responsible for any failure. Simply stated, Beyersdorff replied that the Division was in no position to undertake such a mission.[10] But since the order had arrived from the Higher SS and Police Leader in cracow,[11] thus assuming that it most likely had Himmler's full approval, it was not easy to rescind it.[12] As a result, a battlegroup was quickly formed.

The success of a German battlegroup lay in the fact that although they usually evolved in the chaos of a battle, the groups were always self-contained. They varied in size from one platoon to many thousands of men. For the Germans, a "Kampfgruppe" was a military force composed of the necessary arms and services under one designated commander to accomplish a single specified mission.

Although the Division's leadership stated that it "was not in a position to hand over a battle unit the size of a regiment,"[13] a regimental sized force was actually formed. According to Roman Krokhmaliuk, the group consisted of a command

Chapter 12: Kampfgruppe "Beyersdorff"

(headquarters) section under SS-Sturmbannführer Kleinhoff; the 1st and 2nd Infantry Battalions under Waffen-Hauptsturmführer Karl Bristot and Waffen-Obersturmbannführer Ivan Rembalovych; a 105mm horse artillery battery under Waffen-Sturmbannführer Mykola Palienko; a 15 horse scout/reconnaissance section under Waffen Obersturmführer Roman Dolynsky; a communications position under Waffen-Untersturmführer Adrian Demchuk and a supply/support section under Waffen-Obersturmführer Myhailo Polakiv.[14] Other Ukrainian and German officers served as company commanders.[15] To ensure that the battlegroup was properly utilized, Beyersdorff not only led the group, but personally supervised its construction, providing the finest personnel (including some instructors) and equipment.

At first, it actually seemed as though the "Kampfgruppe" would not be deployed,[16] but in the end it deployed with a total strength of 2,000 soldiers.[17] Who commanded the Division in Bayersdorff's absence is not known; possibly, Beyersdorff designated no one in particular.

Contrary to popular myth as well as wartime propaganda, Soviet Russia's guerrillas were not indestructible. By early 1944, Germany had developed special units and solid anti-guerrilla tactics to effectively counter the various insurgencies found within the Soviet Union and Eastern Europe. But until a victory was achieved over Soviet Russia's frontline forces, no major action could be undertaken to eliminate totally the numerous and various insurgencies; yet, some pressure had to be maintained. To achieve at least some degree of success, various divisional elements were on occasion formed and utilized against the Soviet guerrillas. And that is one of the reasons why Kampfgruppe "Beyersdorff" was dispatched.[18]

Kampfgruppe "Beyersdorff" conducted its operations in the Pidliashia, Polissia, and Volyn regions from the border city of Liubachiv (approximately 50 miles northwest of Lviv, 25 miles northeast of Yaroslav and almost 30 miles directly north of Peremysl). In addition, the Kampfgruppe also operated towards the vicinity of Kholm (presently a city in Poland adjacent to the Ukrainian and Bylorussian border and approximately 100 miles directly northwest of Lviv and 110 miles northeast of Peremysl) and Volodymyr-Volynski, located 75 miles directly north of Lviv.

Terrain has always played a critical factor in the conduct of military operations. On occasion, it was actually the decisive factor between victory and defeat. In the vicinity of Peremysl and Yaroslav (north of the Carpathian Mountains but virtually at the base of the mountains, the terrain, at an average elevation of 200-500 meters, is characterized as rolling, wooded, and hilly. But as one advances northward to the vicinity of Kholm, the terrain slopes downward to the Northern Lowlands plateau. This plateau comprises much of central and Northern Poland and extends through the whole of northern (and much of the Central Ukraine) into

Byelorussia and Russia proper. It also encompasses most of the Byelorussian Republic.

From the base of the Carpathian Mountains to the region of Kholm, patches of forest abound the terrain. Numerous year round flowing rivers, creeks and streams (along with seasonal intermittent streams) abound within the region. A number of swamps are also found. But as one approaches Kholm, (and the region of Northwestern Ukraine), the wooded areas of mixed trees (especially birch, beech, fir and alder), is largely characterized by mixed brush, swamps, and forests which overlap into Poland from Byelorussia's and Northern Ukraine's vast Pripyat forest and swamp region. Here also, are found many ponds and lakes.[19] Cultivated farm land and pastures along with towns and cities containing sizable populations also characterize the region. Unlike regions further to the east, more hard paved roads were found.

Critical road networks (such as Zamosc in Eastern Poland; Stanyslaviv and Rava-Russkaya in the Northwestern Ukraine and Volodymyr-Volynski south of the Byelorussian border) crisscross the region. These road networks, providing essential communication systems, are critical for military/civilian movement and for the delivery of supplies and materiel into Europe, Ukraine, Russia and the Baltic States.

Large wooded, swamp areas provide an abundance of concealment for guerrilla forces. From these areas of concealment, frequently armed with information provided by village, town, and city inhabitants,the various guerrilla factions launched raids and strikes against military, communication and economic centers; they terrorized into submission those trying to remain neutral and disrupted ordinary life.

But such forested areas could not only be utilized by local partisans and by guerrillas arriving into the region from distant regions (such as those of Vershyhora's group), but also by regular conventional military forces. The wooded areas not only provide an abundance of cover for the movement of military units conducting offensive and/or defensive operations, but the forested swamps may be utilized for blocking or channelizing enemy advances, and as staging areas for launching diversionary attacks or raids upon an aggressor's flanks and rear.

Undoubtedly, in the early weeks of 1944, Germany's high command also reasoned that in the event the Soviets should succeed in advancing further westward, the region would play a critical role in halting any further Soviet advances into Poland and Central Europe. The Germans also knew that to defend a region containing a sizable insurgency was not only difficult, but could prove to be impossible. So for the moment, if the guerrillas could not be fully destroyed, it was at least as critical to keep the local insurgency (but especially any newly inserted guerrillas) at bay. Because previous German experiences proved that mid-winter is the best time of the year to successfully conduct any kind of offensive anti-guerrilla/insurgency operations, this factor played a major role in formulating a plan to conduct another anti-guerrilla operation which resulted in orders for the Division to dispatch a battlegroup into that region.

Departing from Heidelager on 16 February 1944, Kampfgruppe "Beyersdorff" moved eastward in three echelons.[20] A lack of sufficient motorization did not enable the battlegroup to be transported eastward via truck convoy; therefore, the railway system was utilized.

Kampfgruppe "Beyersdorff" was organized into two subgroups: "A" and "B."[21] After passing through Yaroslav and Peremysl, both subgroups proceeded to an assembly area in Liubachiv, a border town located 20 miles northeast of Yaroslav and 30 miles northeast of Peremysl. Sizable elements of the battlegroup, however, were sent to Lviv, almost 60 miles east of Peremysl.[22] After a brief stay in the Galician capital for only several days, the group moved northwest and rejoined the bulk of Beyersdorff's group in Liubachiv.

To this day, it has never been explained why a large part of Beyersdorff's group was diverted to Lviv. Since communist guerrillas were known to have been operating north and northwest of Lviv, it is possible that initially a plan existed to use Lviv as an assembly area for the anti-guerrilla operations. Perhaps a two-pronged thrust, one from Lviv and one from Liubachiv, was initially planned but then abandoned. Other possible motives could have been for propaganda; possibly the destruction of certain railway systems by guerrilla activity forced a diversion first further eastward to Lviv and then northwest to Liubachiv or else, someone simply just forgot to stop the trains where the troops were to unload and they ended up in Lviv.[23]

For those who ended up in Lviv, Lviv turned out to be a good deal. As the troops hung around the railway depot waiting for the next northwest bound trains, townspeople showed up with goods, family and close friends appeared, and some soldiers even snuck away with them to visit favorite cafes.[24] Years later, Ostap Veryn would humorously recall how his parents appeared – while his father graciously handed out cigarettes and tea to the troops, his mother repeatedly created embarrassing situations for him as she produced items of clothing from a bag and lectured him. "Now, son, when it gets cold, I want you to wear this sweater," and "don't forget to change your socks,"and "why don't you write more often!" etc., etc. Months later, Veryn would hear such motherly replays from his friends: "now, son, don't forget to wear your sweater," and "write more often!"

The moment the first troop train approached Liubachiv, Beyersdorff's troops encountered a destroyed railway bridge approximately five miles south of that town on the Liubachiv River. Until the bridge could be repaired, nothing could move across it. Forced to disembark from the train, Beyersdorff's leading elements would have to find a suitable river crossing site, and march on foot into town. Years later, Veryn would recall how he leaned against the horses and its blankets to escape the severe harshness of the winters nightwind.

After entering Liubachiv, the soldiers occupied a school. They immediately set up security, a mess facility, and rested. Beyersdorff himself established his headquarters in the school house and, for the greater part of the operations, remained with Subgroup "B." But the troops did not stay long in Liubachiv.

On 28 February 1944, Kampfgruppe "Beyersdorff" commenced its anti-guerrilla operations. These did not cease until 27 March 1944.[25] Throughout this period, the Kampfgruppe's two battle groups moved from one area to another. Not once was a permanent base of operations established. Whenever a group moved, everything rolled with it, including its supply and mess sections. All repairs, feeding, medical and veterinarian needs were taken care of in the field. Contact with the enemy, however, was very minimal. As the troops patrolled and searched for the enemy and their caches, they encountered mixed sympathies. Within this border region was found a heavy Ukrainian, and Polish populace, although some Byelorussians also resided there. In general, the Ukrainian population looked upon the battlegroup as saviors not only from the terrorist activities of Soviet guerrillas, but also from the Polish insurgency which was known to conduct acts of terrorism against Ukrainian inhabitants in order to drive away as many non-Poles as possible to facilitate Polish re-occupation of the region upon the war's end. On their part, the Poles looked upon the battlegroup with suspicion; some doubted that the Germans would allow a Slavic Waffen-SS unit to even come into existence. The Byelorussians remained neutral, although some were sympathetic to the Ukrainian battlegroup because Soviet (and on occasion communist Polish) guerrillas were known to create hardships for them.[26] It must be noted, however, that most people, whether Ukrainian, Polish or Byelorussian, simply tried to survive as best as they could under very adverse, unpredictable and terrifying circumstances. Harboring no hatred or animosities, they only sought to live in peace and avoid any conflicts with all military/insurgent personnel.

As Subgroup "A" advanced north towards Frampol, 10 miles north of Bilhorad, the quiet of the peaceful snowy countryside was suddenly shattered with bursts of automatic small arms fire and explosions. As men dropped into eternal silence or to seek cover, Russian shouts of "BROTHER AGAINST BROTHER!" were heard. Against such firepower the troops could only fall back, and the solders withdrew south; tragically, there was no opportunity to remove the wounded as the enemy, clad in white winter camouflage, surged forward.[27]

But the soldiers did not retreat far. Within minutes, the swept ranks fell into a semblance of order. The horse artillery galloped in, and although this was their first engagement, the gunners, well-trained through hours of drill, moved with speed and efficiency. "Let's go, gentlemen, let's go. We're fighting a war." "BAT-TERY, REPORT!" "GUN ONE, UP!" "GUN TWO, UP!" "GUN THREE, UP!" "FIRE!" "FIRE AT WILL!" As the 105mm gunners unleashed a number of high explosive anti-personnel rounds, they especially concentrated their fire toward the wooded line from where the enemy struck – and to where they undoubtedly would retreat.[28]

"SMOKE, SMOKE!" The gunners lobbed in smoke rounds. Within seconds, highly condensed and thick plumes of white and grey colored smoke rose in the background; automatically, the gunners reloaded high-explosive rounds. For the moment, their task was over; now, the subgroup's infantry would take over.

Cautiously, with a series of bounding movements, the infantry advanced. Moving quickly through the fog and smoke, they secured the wood line, cleared it, checked the road for mines and explosives, and posted sentries in the event of a renewed Soviet guerrilla attack.[29]

Along the wood line, the troops came across bodies of dead guerrillas. A few lay minus their heads, arms and legs. In some cases, faces were so destroyed that any recognition was impossible. The fact that intact and smashed weapons, mortars and equipment laid around the dead indicated that the enemy had sought to withdraw in haste from where they had attacked, and had underestimated the subgroup's ability to react against a surprise attack.[30] But after the troops secured the area, they also recovered the bodies of 25 of their comrades lying on the road and snow-covered fields adjacent to it.[31] Most of the dead lay within a small area, but it was clearly evident that when the Soviet guerrillas had moved in to finish off any remaining troops and to secure their weapons, equipment, and personal items, they stumbled across some wounded. Quickly, these were dispatched. But in one case, two individuals were stripped and repeatedly bayoneted. This also explains why moments before the artillery had fired, their screams were heard by some of those who had withdrawn. As the soldiers looked down upon the bodies, they realized the fate that one could suffer if captured by communist terrorists.[32]

The Division's engagement at Frampol may be classified as a draw. The enemy was bloodied, but so also was subgroup "A." Yet the fact remains that although the subgroup's members did not flee in panic, reacted effectively under enemy fire, and successfully repulsed the enemy ambush, 25 members were lost. So the question remains – what happened?

Whenever a significant strength of troops perish in an ambush, it is a clear indicator that something went wrong. How and why did the leading element just stumble into an ambush? A look at the map reveals potential danger in a northward advance with a river flowing southward and to the immediate right of the advancing troops. In the event of a massive enemy strike from the west, south, and north, the river would prevent an effective withdrawal. Even if it was frozen, running across an open frozen river would expose the men to enemy fire and natural dangers. Why, then, did the advance group virtually walk into an ambush?

A number of factors may be addressed, starting with intelligence. Did the Kampfgruppe receive proper intelligence and updated reports on Soviet guerrilla movements, strengths, and capabilities?[33] Possible ambush sites? In addition to intelligence, were scout/reconnaissance teams utilized? If so, were the scouts mounted on horses and thus, possibly moving forward too fast to observe the enemy? If foot scout teams were utilized, they clearly failed to locate the well-concealed and camouflaged guerrillas, or at least identify a potential ambush sight. Of course the possibility does exist that the guerrilla force occupied the ambush site after the scouts reconnoitered the area, but if that was the case, why did the scouts reconnaissance teams operate so far ahead of the main body? In military operations in insurgency-infested regions, especially where civilians are found who supply information to guerrillas, it is not permissible for scouts/reconnaissance teams to operate far ahead of a moving force. Also, was flank security conducted? In difficult terrain, the importance of reconnaissance and all around security is especially important. Any commander who fails to provide proper front, flank, and rear security, especially in forest and swamp areas, has only to blame himself if his troops are caught up in a surprise attack or an ambush site is not identified in time. Possibly one or more of the above factors played a role in the loss of 25 soldiers.

Critical lessons, however, were learned. More so than in other areas, weather conditions dominated the eastern struggle. Russia's winter warfare called for specific knowledge and skills far beyond the usual norm. The importance of a proper diet and the need to drink plenty of fluids, even in winter, was especially realized by the men. Soldiers learned how to keep their ammunition cold, for ammunition which sweated after being stored in warm rooms tended to jam; and not to touch weapons with bare hands or otherwise human flesh was left on the surface. Very little or no oil was placed on weapons. Wood handled hand grenade sticks (more accurate for throwing) proved to be more effective than the ice-cold metallic egg-shaped grenades. Soldiers realized that in winter, reliable, well-clad, adequately fed and spirited sentries (especially at night) were critical. In a howling snow-storm, or in foggy conditions, a cold, hungry and miserable sentry could easily be eliminated in seconds.

Because the battlegroup moved on foot, men learned what type of footwear, clothing and equipment was of essence. Camouflage lessons, previously stressed at Heidelager, were improved upon; as well as the proper care and handling of horses and heavy artillery in winter and sub-zero temperatures. Such lessons, in turn, were later taught to other members of the Division and much of what was learned was also later utilized in the high-altitude snow-covered mountain regions of central Europe.

Kampfgruppe "Beyersdorff's" personnel had strict orders to behave properly and with respect for all Polish and other non-Ukrainian civilians.[34] Simultaneously, however, its soldiers were constantly approached by Polish – and to an extent Ukrainian agitators – who attempted to spread defeatism, demoralization and desertion. Some desertions were recorded, but most who deserted entered the ranks of the UPA.[35]

Simultaneously, as the Ukrainian battlegroup conducted its operations against the marauding communist bands, certain regular German Wehrmacht and Police units were also undertaking operations within the same region. As in any anti-insurgency operation, certain actions frequently arise which later can be interpreted as excessive, possibly even falling under a war crimes category. If any excesses did occur, and if committed by German forces, various ways would be sought to avoid responsibility and subsequent punishment. One of the easiest ways for a unit to avoid prosecution was to place the blame on other units but, better still, on any foreign troops – in this case, on the "Galicia" Division's Kampfgruppe. According to Major Heike, this is exactly what happened.[36] Unfortunately, it would not be the first and last time.[37]

On 27 March, Kampfgruppe "Beyersdorff" ceased its operations.[38] Several days later, the battlegroup rejoined the rest of the Division at its new location, Neuhammer.[39]

13

The Further Building of the Division

On 9 February 1944, Governor Wachter's assistant, Otto Bayer,[1] was assassinated. Along with Bayer, Dr. Heinrich Schneider, another member of Wachter's staff, died also. Both men were assassinated on Poniatovski Street in the Galician capital by Mykola Kyznetsov, a terrorist assassin dispatched by Colonel Medvedev, who headed Stavka's Special Operations Bureau.

Since Bayer's funeral was to be held in Lviv, a delegation was dispatched from Heidelager to Lviv to serve as an honor guard for the funeral. In the strength of a company and accompanied by the Divisional band, the soldiers were issued new uniforms and winter garments. According to Myron Mackyi, a member of the honor guard, the delegation (excluding the band and possibly a few others), was composed primarily from the 5th Infantry Company.[2] The delegation travelled eastward through Peremysl to Lviv.

On 13 February, the soldiers marched down Lviv's main avenue. During the procession, thousands showed up and gave the troops a very friendly welcome. Following the funeral, the honor guard was released until 10 p.m. on the following day. During their free time, they visited family and friends.

Upon returning to Heidelager, 5th Company was immediately assigned a new task – to reinforce Kampfgruppe "Beyersdorff." Its departure was scheduled for early morning. "That's right, gentlemen, you had plenty of time to rest and sleep on the train. So let's get ready." Through the whole night, men drew ammunition, loaded and tied down equipment onto flat bed cars, harnessed horses into cattle cars, painted their helmets white, drew white camouflage parkas and packed personal items.

Chapter 13: The Further Building of the Division

At daybreak, an eastward bound train showed up. After hitching up the flat bed and cattle cars, the troops set out. Initially, their destination was Rava-Russka, but because the bridge on the Rata River in Rava-Russka was blown up by the guerrillas, a lengthy delay transpired at Peremysl.Eventually, the train was diverted to the beloved city of Lviv. Thus, once again, in a matter of a few days, the men saw Lviv. But this time, they did not stay; within hours, the 5th Company was enroute northwestward towards Liubachiv where the soldiers stayed overnight in the same school house occupied one or two days earlier by elements of Kampfgruppe "Bayersdorff."

On the following morning, the 5th Company, in a defensive travelling mode, marched northwards to link up with the rest of the Kampfgruppe. Warm receptions and many expressions of gratitude greeted the company as it travelled through Ukrainian villages and towns previously terrorized by Soviet and other guerrillas. Never would Mackyi forget this moving experience.

By the beginning of the new year, Galicia's communities began to feel the Division's impact. Members of the Division, whether on leave or pass, were seen and heard. In general, Galicia's populace was sympathetic to its soldiers, but there were some who continued to loathe those in uniform.[3]

As in any community, soldiers present an impact – both positive and negative. And Galicia was no exception. Investigations arose regarding sporadic incidents of fighting between returning Galician troops and Polish railway workers; troop commanders and the Military Board received written complaints about soldiers seen with local women into the wee hours; the local bully-boy (usually the same one who earlier had volunteered but when the time came to go lacked the inner strength to go), now decided to prove his toughness by picking a fight with a well trained and conditioned volunteer – in the process – bully-boy got beat up; and stories of gambling and drinking also surfaced. But overall, the troops behaved, and many men were received cordially and sympathetically into the homes of total strangers.

But on more than one occasion, as the soldiers returned to Galicia, they carried their personal sidearms and weapons with them. And whenever a group of volunteers noted a civilian in trouble with Gestapo or SS police authorities, they had a habit of stepping in, and freeing their victim. As a result, by the spring of 1944, the activities of the Gestapo and Police SS, especially around railway depots and major cities, began to decrease.[4]

In mid-February 1944, Galicia's Nazi administration issued a decree proclaiming that a forced mobilization of the regions Ukrainian population into its army, as well as various para-military organizations, would take place. This decree was in response to Germany's critical military needs, and it stipulated that all males from 21 to 35 years of age would be subject to mobilization.[5]

On 8 March 1944, Galicia's Military Board held a special meeting to discuss the matter. A heated debate ensued among those attending concerning the validity of such a decree, and how to respond to it in the event that an attempt should be made to carry it out. A discussion arose specifically about the German demand that the Military Board prepare regional lists of all males within Galicia's various districts. That same day, the Military Board decided not to conform to the demand. But fully realizing that the Nazi administration would have the final say, the Military Board decided that in the event the decree would be carried out, the committee would have its members present to prevent abuse and to ensure that anyone conscripted would be afforded the option of entering the "Galicia" Division if they so desired.[6]

But rapidly moving events, the Military Board's resistance to the order, the upcoming spring planting season and the German realization that for the moment it would be impossible to handle a mass of draftees precluded any such mobilization. Temporarily postponed, the conscription never materialized.[7]

By April 1944, America's Military Intelligence Service not only positively identified the "Schutzen" (Rifle) or "Grenadier" (Infantry) "Galizien" Division, but its components. The Divisions commander, its composition and depot were not yet positively identified, but the report was accurate in identifying its Ancillary Number as 14. The Division was also identified as being the first infantry division in the order of the Waffen-SS organized around three Schutzen (rifle) or Grenadier regiments correctly identified as 29, 30 and 31.

The report emphasized that the unit is in Divisional strength and is not a "legion." (Undoubtedly, America's intelligence service looked into Berger's earlier [and erroneous] remark describing the unit as a "legion"). The report also correctly concluded that "the Division was formed in Poland in summer of 1943." However, the report slightly erred when it also included Poles in its observation that the Division was raised "from Polish and Ukrainian volunteers."[8]

That same spring, an incident arose which actually proved that even Ukrainian members of the Military Board were not totally exempt from the wrath of Nazi police authorities.[9]

The arrest in Lviv of Stepan Hryhortsiv, a long-time friend and assistant to Roman Krokhmaliuk, serves as an example. Prior to 1943, Hryhortsiv, by profession an engineer, had resided in Poznan, Poland. Fluent in German, he was posted to the Military Board and worked alongside Krokhmaliuk; frequently, especially in Krokhmaliuk's absence, Hryhortsiv took care of the latter's assignments and other matters.

Returning to his office one early morning, Krokhmaliuk was immediately informed by a waiting messenger boy that Gestapo authorities had arrested Hryhortsiv the previous night. Unfortunately, Governor Wachter had left several days earlier for Vienna, so Krokhmaliuk immediately went to Dr. Alfred von der Laens, one of Wachter's chief assistants.

In turn, Laens immediately went to the "Galizia" Districts Gestapo headquarters located in Lviv. There, the Gestapo confirmed that Hryhortsiv had been arrested following a lengthy investigation. According to the Gestapo, a native Volksdeutscher, who had been posing as a Ukrainian and who had obtained Hryhortsiv's trust, had informed German authorities that Hryhortsiv, along with members of the Ukrainian underground, had secretly buried weapons in a cemetery outside of Lviv. To accomplish this, Hryhortsiv had even used the grave of his deceased father-in-law, the Reverend Hnatkivs'kyi. As proof, the Gestapo cited that at the time of arrest, a search of his apartment produced a revolver.

To this, Laens replied that he saw no connection between the charges and the fact that a revolver was found was insignificant since it was common knowledge that members of the Military Board and their assistants were permitted to carry firearms for personal protection against assassins and guerrillas. Dr. Laens' answer immediately created a heated argument; Laens was also informed that his own intervention in this matter would proof to be detrimental for Hryhortsiv, since the Gestapo categorically refused to release him.

Two days later, Krokhmaliuk received a note from Hryhortsiv. Pleading for help, the note revealed Hryhortsiv was enroute to Auschwitz. (To ensure that Krokhmaliuk received the note, Hryhortsiv added that he had given his gold wedding ring as a bribe to one of the German guards transporting him).

Subsequently, Governor Wachter intervened in the matter. But Hryhortsiv never reappeared. Wachter was informed that the detainee, while enroute to Auschwitz, "had suffered a massive heart attack and died." Needless to say, no one believed the gestapo's claim. In his angry condemnation of the gestapo, Wachter himself shouted "DAS IST ABER EINE BAND!"[10]("THEY ARE RABBLE'S!").

In the spring of 1944, the "Erganzungsstelle Warthe" appeared in Galicia.[11] Headquartered in Lviv on Baloviy St. under the command of SS-Hauptsturmführer Doctor Karl Schultze and SS-Obersturmführer Schmukershlag (a former Vienna lawyer), the above organization took over from the Military Board its most critical function – the recruitment and summoning of sufficient, skilled, volunteers for the

Division. This organization was strictly a German one, and, excluding the part-time services of Dr. Stepan Molodavetz, was composed entirely of a German staff of approximately ten.[12] To this day, it has never been fully explained why this branch was established in the Galician capital. Most likely, it arose as a result of German disillusionment about the manner in which the Military Board was handling its recruitment, as well as fears that the Board's recruitment efforts would break down in future months when men would have to be sought to replace front-line casualties.

Although months earlier Nazi propagandists had a heyday with the huge volunteer figures, and some actually were predicting enough manpower would be available for two, three or more divisions, in reality, barely enough men were found to outfit a single division. Compounding the massive decline in manpower was a lack of sufficient leadership; therefore, one can see that it would have been impossible to raise another (second) division. Even an attempt to raise an independent 3,000 to 5,000-man brigade would have proved to be impossible.[13]

14

Further Training

By the conclusion of March 1944, with a strength of 12,901,[1] the "14 Galizische SS Freiwilligen Division" was assembled in entirety within Wehrkreis VIII in Neuhammer. Established in 1935, Wehrkreis VIII was initially located in Upper Silesia (Oberschlesien) and included almost the whole of Lower Silesia (Niederschlesien). In 1938, it was extended to include a part of the Sudeten area of Czechoslovakia and in 1939, a portion of Poland's Eastern Upper Silesia (Ost-Oberschlesien) and the Teschen area. Comprising a total area of 56,091 square kilometers,[2] with a population estimated at 8,441,000, the Wehrkreis headquarters, commanded by 58-year-old Cavalry General Rudolph Koch-Erpach, was located in Breslau.[3]

The Wehrkreis' region was characterized mainly by flat terrain in its northern and central areas; rolling hills culminating in mountainous terrain characterized its southern portion. Within Wehrkreis VIII, three major training areas were established: Hohenelbe, Lamsdorf, and Neuhammer.[4]

In the final weeks of 1944, Germany's High Command decided to transfer the Division from Heidelager to Neuhammer. Although such a move would place the Division further away from Galicia, Neuhammer did offer the Division a more modernized training environment.[5] The move was completed in February 1944, requiring a minimum of 30 troop trains. Transporting any kind of military force, especially one of sizable strength, is a feat in itself; successfully accomplished, the procedure provided the Division's movements personnel with an excellent opportunity to gain experience and additional training in the area of movements.

Once assembled, the Division continued its training. At Neuhammer, strong emphasis was placed on specialist training and unit training. Fresh recruits continued to arrive from Galicia. As previously at Heidelager, these incoming recruits were not immediately placed into the Division but were first organized into companies or batteries and provided recruit training by the Replacement Army's Wehrmacht and Waffen-SS. Upon the completion of their training, the trained soldiers entered the Division.

Neuhammer's camp commandant was very receptive to the Division. Assisting the Division with its needs, he ensured ample amounts of clothing, supplies, equipment, horses, some vehicles but most importantly – arms and ammunition. Regarding the latter, at Neuhammer (as earlier at Heidelager), the Waffen-SS' supply distribution ensured the Division's arms and ammunition needs.

At Neuhammer, the Division began to acquire more Ukrainian leadership. As Ukrainian officer graduates and non-commissioned officers arrived, the Division's leadership gradually began to transform itself from German into Ukrainian. It should be noted that for the greater part, these incoming Ukrainian graduates assumed leadership positions at lower levels and seldom beyond a company command; for the greater part, most officers from the rank of Hauptsturmführer (captain) and Sturmbannführer (major) were German. Senior Ukrainian officers were desperately needed to command units from battalion strength and higher.[6]

With the arrival of well-trained Ukrainian leadership and Freitag's policy of "shape-up or ship-out," changes began to occur. Incompetent, irresponsible, and inept leaders were being replaced by competent incoming Galician officers and NCO's who achieved leadership positions in squad, platoon, and company levels. Uncaring, incompetent and irresponsible German leaders, initially brought into the Division as a result of a lack of Ukrainian leaders, either submitted requests to leave or in some cases, were dismissed outright. As a number of such German squad, platoon, and company commanders left, incoming Ukrainian leaders filled their positions. For the greater part, the newly arrived Ukrainian leaders adjusted well with their compatriots and many of the previously encountered problems began to subside. Although at this stage the higher positions were still primarily held by German leadership, everyone now knew that it was just a matter of time before the lower ranking Galician Ukrainian officers and NCO's would rise in rank and replace those in higher positions.

At Neuhammer, the emphasis was placed on completing the building of the Division,[7] conducting specialist training, and fully training the Division through a series of Divisional maneuvers. To accomplish this, much time was spent in the field, and all training was carefully critiqued by both Wehrmacht and Waffen-SS instructors. Overall, the training went very well, with Galicia's volunteers displaying a tremendous willingness to learn. They continually exhibited a strong motivation and desire to master various skills.[8] They also demonstrated an interest in mastering technical matters, quickly grasping the skills and knowledge required for the communication, artillery and anti-aircraft fields. As previously at Heidelager, Galicia's artillerymen excelled in Neuhammer. The 88 crews, composed primarily of former college students who had majored in mathematics and technical subjects, especially demonstrated remarkable skills. Within each gun crew were members who mastered the 1-meter, 1.5-meter, and 4-meter 'Entfernungsmesser' range finder scopes, a very complex system of range finders. Such rangefinders, in the hands of skilled observers, enabled crew members to accurately judge the distance and speed of ground and aerial targets. Once taken, the readings were quickly provided to the 88 crews resulting in numerous hits.

In field training, the Ukrainian volunteers demonstrated toughness and endurance; quickly, they acquired the necessary knowledge to soldier well. This knowledge, in turn, created confidence and internal strength, as demonstrated one evening when a German staff officer, hurrying to his quarters in a downpour, was suddenly challenged by a Galician sentry on guard duty.

Well-versed and trained in the critical responsibilities of sentry duty, the sentry shouted "HALT! OR I'LL FIRE!" and denied the officer further passage. Seeing that the guard meant business, the officer froze. "PASSWORD!" Because the officer had failed to learn that day's password (which changes daily), he explained his predicament after identifying himself, and stated he should be permitted to enter the official area without having to reveal the code.

Undaunted, the volunteer slammed his weapons bolt forward and shouted in German "HINLEGEN!" ("GET DOWN!"). Forcing the senior ranking officer into the mud, the sentry continued his vigilance until an NCO appeared and took the half-frozen officer into an office where his identity was confirmed. On the following day, while Freitag dined with some of his staff, the General spoke approvingly of the dutiful sentry's actions. Praising the latter, Freitag proudly exclaimed "these Ukrainians will yet make fine soldiers."[9]

Simultaneously, however, Fritz Freitag's leadership could waiver between that of a compassionate leader supposedly beginning to understand his troops, to that of an inept general with little concern for proper troop welfare. Such was the dual character Freitag displayed when forced to intervene in the case of a soldier sentenced for execution – grenadier Evhen Burlak.

Galicia Division

Unknown to Burlak and his friends, who had just arrived at Neuhammer from the Replacement Army, soldiers were required to stand at the position of attention beside their beds whenever a fully attired and helmeted NCO or grenadier would enter the barracks for a night inspection. Any NCO or soldier as such was regarded as the Charge of Quarters and, for the night, was assuming responsibility in the name of a unit's company commander and even, the Divisional commander; therefore, such an inspection was considered a serious matter. But Burlak, never properly informed of his responsibilities, decided to play a joke one night.

As the charge-of-quarters proceeded down the center aisle of the barracks, he encountered a volunteer standing at attention but covered with a blanket. Stopping in front of the volunteer, the inspector just stared at the covered figure. Suddenly, laughter erupted within the barracks.

Ripping the blanket off the volunteer, the charge-of- quarters undoubtedly would have just dismissed the matter. But unfortunately for Burlak, precisely at that moment a German NCO happened to be passing by the barracks. Hearing the laughter, he came charging into the barracks just in time to witness the incident. Immediately, he placed Burlak under arrest. Burlak's allegedly disrespectful conduct was then brought up to the high command.

On the following day, a military court-martial sentenced Burlak to death. An execution was set for the following morning. Needless to say, Freitag had the final say and the general could have swayed the execution or administered another form of punishment; nevertheless, Freitag upheld the court's decision. Throughout that day and night, repeated appeals by various Ukrainian and German Divisional members to terminate the execution fell on deaf ears; Freitag was determined to carry out the sentence.

For Chaplain Nahayewsky, the ordeal proved to be exceptionally difficult. Throughout the night, as he tried to comfort Burlak in his prison cell, Nahayewsky hoped – and prayed – for a last minute reprieve. Totally devastated, the young volunteer trembled all night, and pleaded for assistance. Only in the late morning hours did Burlak fall asleep.

Awakening shortly before dawn, the volunteer told Chaplain Nahayewsky "I wanted to fight for Ukraine, but my friends dared me to play a joke. This German who recently arrived here – on account of him, I now have to die. Dear Chaplain, please write to my parents, and tell them the truth." Minutes before the execution time of 7 a.m., the chaplain received the young volunteer's last confession and administered Holy Communion.

With the arrival of the military police, Nahayewsky escorted Burlak into a small drill field where representatives of the various regiments and separate units were waiting to witness the execution. As the youth was led toward the wall from which he would face a firing squad, miles away Yuriy Krokhmaliuk and Paliiv were having a showdown with Freitag. So furious was the encounter that years later Krokhmaliuk was still amazed that Freitag did not have them arrested and shot.[10]

Facing the firing squad, Burlak refused a blindfold. With trembling lips, he repeated over and over "Jesus, Mary and Joseph, be with me in my last moments!" As Chaplain Nahayewsky administered the youth his last rites, the chaplain himself prayed for a last minute cancellation. But as it turned out, Burlak's fate was sealed.

"READY, AIM" ... with the shout of "AIM!" Burlak suddenly pressed forward his body and with tremendous defiance shouted "SLAVA UKRAINI!" The crack of 7.92mm fire forever silenced the 18-year-old.

Yet in the final analysis, the executed Burlak struck the final blow. Following his death, the Division's morale plummeted, taking days to improve. Freitag himself felt the impact and probably wondered if perhaps he had dealt too harshly. And when several weeks later the German NCO who initially had arrested Burlak was found on the outskirts of Neuhammer one night, lying dead from a knife wound, Freitag did not dare call for an investigation for he fully realized that the entire affair would come to the attention of his superiors and disclose certain inept leadership as well as other problems within the Division. In order to save face, protect his rank, and avert possible dismissal, Freitag deliberately kept the matter under lid while the NCO's death was attributed to a "training" accident.[11]

Throughout the Division, the NCO's death was perceived in such a fashion – the Ukrainian soldier had already been pushed too far and would no longer tolerate unnecessary abuse. Those Germans who acted sympathetically remarked "you see, I knew that something like this would happen." Those who felt that they could be next began to modify their behavior while others, under various pretexts, requested to be transferred out of the Division. With their departure, more leadership positions became available for the incoming Ukrainian leaders who, by March and April 1944, were arriving weekly to Neuhammer from various European officer, NCO and specialist schools. As these Ukrainians acquired positions, unit training improved, morale rose, and stronger units developed. Ultimately, grenadier Burlak emerged as a hero and a highly-respected soldier.

On 3 May 1944, Governor Wachter wrote to Reichsführer Himmler in regard to the "Galicia" Division. In his report, the governor criticized the mistreatment of Galicia's volunteers, and admitted that he had certain doubts about the Division; however, Wachter did indicate that it was all beneficial because the Division did recruit some Ukrainians who probably would have ended up in the Ukrainian (OUN/ UPA) underground.[12]

According to certain western writers, highly unsatisfactory conditions (such as a lack of Ukrainian leadership, a resentment of General Freitag, and a lack of good German instructors, arms, training and living conditions), continued to exist at Neuhammer which precluded the Division's progress.[13] To be sure, while problems did arise, the above allegations must be examined and a clearer understanding of what took place at Neuhammer must be presented.

By the time the "Galicia" Division had arrived to Neuhammer, much progress had been made in the area of developing a solid core of Ukrainian officers and NCO leadership. This largely arose as a result of Paliiv's insistence and Freitag's own realization that a number of the German officers and NCO's assigned to the Division were of low-quality and needed to be replaced by solid leadership. Only then could the Division progress into a formidable force; thus, efforts were undertaken to develop Ukrainian leadership. By the time the Division deployed eastward from Neuhammer at the end of June 1944, approximately 600 officer candidates and 2,000 NCO and specialist candidates had successfully completed, or were in the process of undertaking officer, NCO and specialist training.[14] As graduating candidates arrived at Neuhammer, they immediately began to occupy leadership positions. As attested to by Heike in his memoirs, Ukrainian specialists and NCO's, upon arrival at Neuhammer, immediately began to seek opportunities for advancement.[15] According to Veryha, most of the soldiers who achieved officer, NCO, and specialist leadership positions in Neuhammer had, in addition to completing their respective schools, also completed recruit training at Heidelager.[16] Therefore, these leaders were well trained. Although, of course, additional leaders were still required, compared to Heidelager, the situation at Neuhammer showed significant progress; weekly, incoming Ukrainian leadership testified to this.

Freitag's approval of the execution of 18-year-old Burlak proved that the general still had not fully grasped the nature of his role as commander of a non-German force. Yet Burlak, Krokhmaliuk, Heike, Paliiv, Bisanz and others were nevertheless exerting an influence upon Freitag. At Neuhammer, the Ukrainians increasingly began to assert themselves. When soldiers of 2nd Company, 1st Battalion, 29th Regiment created in front of their barracks a large garden-bed of flowers with their national symbol, the "Truzyb" trident, in its center, upon seeing it, their company commander, SS-Obersturmführer Bauff, was so infuriated that he jumped upon the flower-bed trident and with his boots, totally destroyed it.

Bauff's barbaric action so infuriated the entire 2nd Company that grenadier Kushniruk, the company's standard bearer, immediately brought the matter up to

Chapter 14: Further Training

Paliiv. Shortly afterward Paliiv, accompanied by Heike, appeared in Bauff's office. To this day it is not known what was said in the office. Bauff was, however, ordered to apologize to his company. Prior to confronting Bauff, the matter was brought up to Freitag, who, seeking a way to raise morale and restore his prestige following Burlak's execution, agreed that some action needed to be taken.

Assembling the 2nd Company, Bauff apologized. Trying to save face, he justified his actions by saying that "I did not know that the trident was the symbol of the Ukrainian nation, but thought it was some type of communist symbol." Needless to say, no one believed Bauff because everyone throughout the Division – and even many of Neuhammer's non-Divisional personnel – knew what the trident stood for. It was obvious that Bauff's apology was not sincere and it was only a weak attempt to redress a grievous error.

For Bauff, however, the worst was yet to come. Because news of his actions and apology spread throughout the Division, everyone now knew that Bauff, in addition to being a brute, was also a liar. Realizing thi, himself, and knowing how he stood in the eyes of both his superiors and subordinates, Bauff requested a transfer. After it was granted, command of the company fell to a recently promoted Ukrainian, Waffen-Untersturmführer Herman-Orlyk.[17]

According to Heike, Veryha, Krokhmaliuk, and many others, Neuhammer's camp and its facilities were far better than Heidelager's.[18] Neuhammer's commander was much more receptive towards the Division, working very closely with the Division's staff and supply sections to ensure that ample amounts of arms, equipment, horses, and vehicles were delivered.[19] At Neuhammer, what Divisional elements remained to be formed were completed. Such was the case with the Division's anti-aircraft battalion; the anti-aircraft received its 88 weapons system and its crews were thoroughly trained in its usage.[20] It is important to note that the 88 was a weapons system highly coveted by all; yet, at this stage of the war many German divisions (because of a lack of 88's) were not even provided the system, while the "Galicia" Division was.

Yuriy Krokhmaliuk would recall years later that prior to the Division's departure from Neuhammer to Galicia, the Division exchanged much of its weaponry for the newest models. The Division actually received certain materiel, such as hand weapons which, when uncrated, were still lubricated with fresh factory oil. Excluding the test firing conducted at the factory, most of the MG34's and MG-42's had never been fired by any soldiers.[21] To ensure the machine guns were properly sighted for combat, many thousands of rounds of ammunition were allocated for test firing.[22]

Galicia Division

Allegations that the "Galicia" Division was nothing but a "cannon-fodder" outfit prove to be completely unfounded.[23] The Division was never meant to be such an outfit.[24] In addition to the fact that the Division was well-trained throughout Europe, it was also equipped with the most advanced modern arms, equipment, camouflaged clothing, and materiel of its era.[25] As Ren stated: "Its soldiers went into combat as some of the best trained in the world. Our soldiers needed to master hand-held weaponry, pistols, anti-armor weapons, light machine guns, various types of rockets, mines, hand-grenades, anti-armor/aircraft tactics, chemical defense, and various forms of assault tactics; obviously, the combat training of the soldier in World War II was greater and more extensive than that undertaken by those during World War I."[26]

Ren did, however, feel that the Division could have benefitted with more training time and feels (as did Heike) that the Division did not begin its training in earnest until March 1944.[27] Although Ren is correct in his observations that additional training time would have benefitted the Division, it must be remembered many of the Division's personnel did train for a year. Even those who entered the Division from January 1944 through March 1944 and who accompanied the Division to Galicia, were exposed to intense training. "The Ukrainian Division – this was an excellent military formation which underwent at Neuhammer the severest military training ever previously undertaken by any existing Ukrainian armed formations."[28] Comparing the Galician soldier to the average German drafted into the Wehrmacht in 1943 and 1944, Galicia's volunteers had much more training and even, a higher quality of training.[29] Indeed, their training even surpassed that received by many Allied soldiers (including American and British).[30]

On 15 May 1944,[31] Reichsführer Heinrich Himmler, who possessed a strong interest in foreign volunteers and who closely monitored the progression of the "Galicia" Division, visited the formation as he toured Neuhammer. Himmler was accompanied by Governor Wachter, Fritz Freitag, and other dignitaries. The fact that Himmler spent nearly two full days with the Division indicates that the Reichsführer had a strong interest in the formation's development. During those two days, Himmler inspected every unit. He spoke with the German and Ukrainian officers, as well as the enlisted men, and listened to their comments and opinions. Himmler even shook hands with many of the troops. Although many knew that the Reichsführer was scheduled to visit, for some it came as a surprise. As Myhailo Tomash* searched downrange for targets through the sights of his MG-42, he heard a number of voices behind him. Continuing to scan, Myhailo heard the voices grow closer, and sensed that a group was standing slightly to his rear. Assuming it was just another group of soldiers, Myhailo paid no attention.

Chapter 14: Further Training

Spotting his targets, he quickly unleashed a series of short – but well placed – bursts into each target. "Hit!" "Hit!" "Hit!" heralded the observing instructor. From behind Myhailo, comments of "excellent shooting," "he shoots well," "Sir, he' s one of our best" and so forth were expressed. Aware that the comments were directed towards him, Myhailo thought to himself "you haven't seen anything yet!" Figuring it was the press, Myhailo quickly opened the weapons-feed cover tray, checked its interior, inserted another 200 round belt of ammunition, and scanned for targets.

The crack of the MG42 split the air as Myhailo rapidly ripped volley after volley into each target. As the last round exited the barrel, Myhailo quickly lifted the weapons-feed tray, dropped the weapons barrel, and inserted a new one. "After all," reasoned Myhailo, "press people always like to see a show."

"Gentlemen, you may now step forward." As he continued to lie on the ground, Myhailo saw a pair of highly polished boots. At that moment, he knew that someone "big" was standing beside him. Looking up, he got the shock of his life.

Myhailo sprang to the position of attention. The order of "at ease, grenadier!" placed him at ease. Surrounded by Freitag, Himmler, Wachter, Neuhammer's Camp Commandant and others, Myhailo wondered what was the occasion.

Himmler spoke first. He praised the young grenadier for his excellent performance. Firmly grasping Myhailo's hand, the Reichsführer continued to speak. At this moment (and to Myhailo's relief), stepped up Paliiv. After all, Myhailo was not proficient in German. For the next half hour or so, Myhailo explained to the group the mechanics of the MG-34 and MG-42, how they operate, and various ways of firing. At one point, he got down to demonstrate the proper way of holding the weapon when in a prone position. Myhailo also fielded many questions, and toward the end was queried on what he thought of the training, his origins, his family and so forth. Repeatedly complimented, Myhailo particularly noted Freitag's smile. Usually Freitag's fat face and frosty stare exhibited the demeanor of one emerging from a funeral parlor but today, Freitag cracked a broad grin from ear-to-ear. Again shaking Myhailo's hand, Himmler thanked him and encouraged him to continue his efforts. Replying "Jawohl, Reichsführer!" Myhailo snapped to attention as the group turned to depart.

On 16 May, Himmler concluded his two-day visit with a reception in the officer's mess hall.[32] Attending the reception were primarily the higher-ranking German and Ukrainian officers. Because the Division only had a limited number of higher-ranking Galician Ukrainian officers, Himmler addressed an officer's corps consisting primarily of Germans; nevertheless, the fact that some Ukrainians were present forced Himmler to address the Ukrainians as he spoke about his impressions regarding the Division.

In his speech, Himmler attacked the communists but, unlike previously, did not denounce the Slavs. Undoubtedly trying to appease the Ukrainians, he admitted that the "Galician's" were actually Ukrainians and cited that the Division should have been titled "Ukrainian" rather than "Galicia."[33] Himmler also appealed for a strong unity amongst both groups. He instructed the Germans to "get along [with the Ukrainians] as if you were born with them," encouraged the Germans to continue to spread their knowledge and stated "I require from you, my German officers, that you rescue in battle the wounded Galician Ukrainian comrades as if they were your own brothers."

But, fully realizing the Ukrainians were dissatisfied with their current status in the Division, Himmler also stated "I know, with the way things are, that you Ukrainians are not fully satisfied. I also know, that if I would issue you the order to slaughter the Poles, you would be so grateful that you would carry me in your arms. But I, as a national leader, cannot issue such an order because I am responsible for my deeds not only to the Führer, but also to history."[34]

Following Himmler's words, Paliiv approached the Reichsführer and, in the presence of the Divisional commander, the Division's senior officers and Himmler's entourage, stated: "Let it be permissible in your presence, Herr Reichsführer, for me to declare, that we Ukrainians are not preparing to slaughter the Poles and that is not why we voluntarily enlisted into the Division Galicia. But after observing German policies in Eastern Europe, we cannot fail to cite how you Germans continue to incite us against the Poles, and the Poles against us. Unfortunately, I feel that it is necessary to inform you that your politics in Eastern Europe are not correct and lead to nothing good. Forgive me for such an unpleasant rebuttal, but that is the way it is."[35]

Total silence reigned in the room. Among the Ukrainians, only one thought went through each and every mind – "and what will become of Paliiv now?" But nothing happened. Himmler instead spoke about other matters, and shortly afterwards, left the reception. Paliiv's words, however, were not totally forgotten. Following the reception, a senior-ranking German officer approached Paliiv, extended his arm in a friendly manner to shake Paliiv's hand and stated "Waffen-Hauptsturmführer Paliw – Ich gratuliere Ihnen!" ("I congratulate you!").[36]

Following Himmler's inspection, the Reichsführer accompanied Wachter to Lviv. Satisfied with what he had seen, and convinced the Division was combat ready, Himmler and Wachter met with the commander of Army Group North

Chapter 14: Further Training

Ukraine, Fieldmarshal Walther Model. A gifted tactician who was especially noted for his ability to create sufficient reserves out of nothing, 51-year-old Model had earlier replaced Field Marshal Erich Manstein as front commander on 30 March 1944.[37] Together, the men conferred about the possibility of utilizing the Division on the eastern front.

Himmler's inspection did not conclude the Division's training. As discussions were under way in Lviv, the Division continued to train. Divisional maneuvers with live-fire training continued, and night training was intensified.[38] In mid-June, members of the Ukrainian Central Committee, accompanied by a number of civilians, visited the Division. Headed by Kubiyovych and Colonel Bisanz, the civilians examined the soldier's living quarters, viewed various arms and displays, and observed some exercises. Those who had sons serving in the Division were allowed to spend some time with them. For a number of soldiers, fathers, and families, this free time would be the last meeting between loved ones.

At Neuhammer, the Division suffered some training casualties. If not checked, a disproportionate number of accidents indicate that soldiers are not being properly trained and supervised. Excessive training accidents hinder training, eliminate qualified personnel, waste valuable resources, and lower morale. Although safety measures are always implemented, whenever large amounts of live ammunition are handled, especially under stressful conditions, casualties do, unfortunately, occur. Within the Waffen-SS, German SS units tolerated training casualties of up to 5 percent; amongst foreign units, five percent was also tolerated. Exactly how many Divisional training deaths and injuries were suffered is not known; however, it is known that some were lost due to live-fire training accidents or illness. In addition to those who were discharged from service as a result of injuries, Volodymyr Pakoch, Myhailo Machnyk, Pavlo Voloshyn, Ivan Vynnychuk, Volodymyr Vivchars'kyi, Bohdan Ivachiv, Bohdan Yakiemovych and Oleksa Shelerkiv were among those who perished in Neuhammer as a result of training accidents.

On 17 May 1944, Galicia's Military Board received notification about another recruit who was barred entry into the Division as a result of an arrest attributable to OUN activities.

Addressed to the Board's Recruitment and Replacement Section, the notification covered the case of volunteer Myhailo Shupian. According to the notification, a district overseer, named Tremyak, had shortly before notified his superiors that Shupian was no longer in solitary confinement; once released Shupian (who had volunteered for the Division prior to his arrest), sought to enter the Division on the

30 April 1944 call-up. Because the 30 April call-up was postponed to 15 May, Shupian was told to wait.

In the meantime, Germany's SD Security (which continued to monitor Shupian) informed Shupian that he was unable to enter the Division; likewise, they confiscated his call-up card. Desperately seeking to enter the Division, Shupian personally appealed to Tremyak. But as verified by Tremyak, without the SD's approval, Shupian could not enter the Division.

The 17 May notification did not cite for what reasons Shupian was denied entry. Undoubtedly, Nazi authorities still suspected Shupian was involved in some OUN/UPA activities. Regardless, the fact remains that although the Soviet front was now in Galicia proper and manpower was still being sought on an anti-communist theme, men such as Shupian were still regarded as a threat and were barred entry into the Division.[39]

In mid-June 1944, Germany's Eastern front intelligence service again began a propaganda campaign, code-named "Operation Scorpion," inducing Soviet soldiers to desert and join the German side. The Division was also required to dispatch individuals to assist in this propaganda war.[40] According to Heike, the Division did dispatch some men, but because within a matter of days it deployed eastward, nothing was heard about their deeds.[41]

In mid-June 1944, General Freitag received a telegram inviting him to a military conference regarding the Division.[42] According to Heike, it was Galicia's Governor Wachter who suggested this meeting.[43] Arriving by aircraft, a quick meeting was first held in Lviv with Wachter about certain organizational and possible political problems within the Division.[44] Following this meeting Freitag, Heike, Wachter and some others travelled to Model's field headquarter's near Stanyslaviv where they discussed the Division's strengths, weaknesses, and combat capabilities. Agreeing with Freitag's proposal for the Division to be stationed in a peaceful area where it could conduct field training and achieve some combat experience prior to entering, if necessary, heavy combat, Model posted the Division to the region of Stanyslaviv. At this time, Stanyslaviv's region was defended by General der Panzertruppen Erhard Raus, Commander of the 1st German Panzer Army. Shortly afterwards, Model also dispatched ten Wehrmacht officers and NCO's to familiarize the Division's cadre on the region's terrain and current frontline situation.

On 25 June 1944, the "Galicia" Division's executive corps left Neuhammer for Galicia.[45] On the following day, 26 June, other members of the Divisional staff, including Major Heike, departed for the eastern front. But moments before Heike flew east in the Division's Fieseler Storch aircraft, Divisional command received a copy of a telegram message from Germany's Oberkommando des Heeres (Army High Command – OKH) . Initially addressed to Army Group "Nordukraine," the message revealed that a strong Soviet concentration was observed east of Lviv. Warning that a possible enemy thrust would be launched directly towards the Galician capital, OKH's message resulted in a change of the Division' s original deployment mission. Now, the "Galicia" Division would occupy a secondary defensive position within the 'Prinz Eugen' defensive belt.[46]

On 27 June, as the Division prepared to deploy eastward, it was re-designated as the 14.Waffen-Grenadier-Division der SS (Galizische Nr. 1).[47] This new title would be the final one using any form of the word "Galicia." The order for this change, however, possibly did not reach the Division until 8 August 1944. By then, the Division had already returned from the Eastern front. As to when the above change officially took place, various dates have been cited.

What is especially interesting about this order is that the Division's official title was now preceded by the word "Waffen." This word, minus its "SS," was used to signify that the Division was not a German or "Nordic" formation but rather, was composed of soldiers of another nationality.[48]

On 28 June 1944, the Division's first echelons departed from Neuhammer.[49] For nearly a week afterwards, Neuhammer bustled with activity as the bulk of the Division loaded itself onto railway cars. Daily, under "Movement tempo 4," no less than four railway transports rumbled out of Neuhammer. Their destination – the Eastern front.[50]

Despite the order of 22 January 1944 from Cracow's Higher SS and Police leader ordering the incorporation of "Schutzmannschafts" Battalion 204 to the Galizische SS- Freiwilligen Division,[51] this was not accomplished until the end of June 1944. Organized in the beginning of 1942 from Ukrainian volunteers who volunteered for eastern front combat, the battalion was instead sent west to Neuhammer to perform security duties.[52] According to Mark Zuk, a former rifleman and NCO of Battalion 204, the reason the unit was never dispatched to the eastern front was because at first its personnel were never properly trained but later (following the revolt of the 201st battalion), of German fears that Battalion 204 would also revolt and its soldiers would desert and disappear into the ranks of the UPA as did the 201st (formerly Roland-Nachtigall) Battalion.

In mid-1943, the battalion's personnel requested to be reassigned into the proposed "Galicia " Division. For no confirmed reason, the battalion was not permitted to enter the Division. With the "Galicia" Division's arrival at Neuhammer, repeated requests for the release of the 204th Battalion were always rejected by

Galicia Division

Germany's Higher SS and Police. So as the Division trained, the 204th continued its security mission.

Possibly, Himmler's visit to Neuhammer was connected with the battalion's release to the Division. But once disbanded, its personnel were not immediately incorporated into the Division; rather (excluding those sent to NCO and specialist schools), the majority were incorporated into the replacement system to undertake military training. As for the battalion's German cadre, none entered the "Galicia" Division.

Along with other incoming recruits from Galicia, the ex-security soldiers were trained by Neuhammer's Replacement Army. Few, if any, ex-members of the 204th saw action at Brody.

On 30 June 1944, Myhailo Khronoviat, who continued to head recruitment, submitted one of the last reports (in letter form) from the Galician capital. Addressed directly to Colonel Bisanz, the letter covered recruitment difficulties, improper conduct and even, corruption. Along with Khronoviat's letter were attached five examples of some of the problems the recruitment had to deal with. Khronoviat wrote:

> Report of Observations For Colonel A. Bisanz, Leader of the Military Board – Galitsia. Lemberg. (Lviv).
>
> Recently, within the Recruiting and Reserve Office, matters have arisen which make my work difficult, if not impossible. Already, I had an opportunity to report to you that designating personnel "essential for war effort" could be damaging.
>
> In many cases, when notified recruits would like to be exempted from service and cannot obtain exemption from this Board, they either go directly to you, Colonel, or to the Recruitment Office, where they are released from service. Previously, I asked you, Colonel, as well as Dr. Schulze, to contact us of such cases. But as of date, this has not been done.
>
> 1. Recently, I submitted to you a copy of a letter from a Recruiting Office by which a Johann Antoniak, a merchant in Peremysl, was declared as "essential for war effort." The above office noted Antoniak was called up many times but he had always managed to avoid service. His last postponement was signed by Oberscharführer Mitscke. Til present, Antoniak continues to reside in Peremysl; it is rumored that he bought the postponement from the Military Board because he is a rich man!

Chapter 14: Further Training

2. Enclosed is a copy of a letter (enclosure No. 1) in which Dr. Volodymyr Pretorius, born 1907, from Nizankowice, county of Peremysl, was also declared as "essential for war effort." Yet, at this time, it is said that the Division urgently needs veterinarians. These are just two cases which appeared by chance but regretfully, we did not learn of these cases from the Recruiting Office but rather, from our representative.

3. During our last conference and in your presence, I appealed to all of our representatives to be firm. This is especially important if we are to organize the second division. The majority of the representatives understand this.

Subsequently, however, many of those called [for military duty] arrive in Lemberg and exert all possible pressure to seek ways out of military service. On 9/29/44, in front of me appeared a Mr. H. Chanyk from Dobromyl (again the county of Peremysl), and he requested to be declared "essential for war effort." Shortly before his arrival, we received a telephone call from our representative in Peremysl who told us that in the event Chanyk received an exemption, other volunteers called up would fail to report and our efforts would be ruined. Our Peremysl delegate even threatened to resign from his post. (Enclosure 2).

When Chanyk failed to accomplish anything with me, he turned to the Military Board and then finally to you, Colonel. Directly from you, he requested a postponement for one month. You gave him a postponement for two months without even notifying me.

4. On 30 May, you also issued a postponement to Roman Skorobohatyi, a merchant from Sanok, who is eligible for immediate military service. Again, this was done without me being informed. (Enclosure 3).

5. On the basis of the [call-up] circular, some young men from Drohobych were called. Two of them, former Polish Army officers Theodore Zahalak (1902) and Osyp Horodyskyi (1907), presented to the delegate a written postponement from the recruiting office for a number of months. As a result of this, other former officers now refuse to obey their call. (Enclosure 4).

Such procedures have a demoralizing effect not only upon those who are to be called but simultaneously, it affects those currently in service awaiting for the others to join them. And this also makes our representatives work impossible. For all of this, the Military Board is blamed and I, especially, who controls the entire effort. In the countryside, people are already saying: "if you cannot succeed with a representative [to avoid military service] in your area, than go to Lemberg where success is very easy to achieve."

As for all of those who fail to achieve anything with us but then achieve positive results with the German offices, they deride us openly.[53]

So where is our authority?

Are we necessary at all?

6. Another problem is the fact that the 8,000 volunteers for the Division were attached to the Wehrmacht.[54]

Under such circumstances, it is impossible for me to continue my work because I do not intend to be blamed by my compatriots.[55]

[Signed]
Khronoviat [56]

At the same time the "Galicia" Division was deploying to the eastern front, approximately 200 Divisional soldiers, previously classified as "aspirant" for officer candidate training, departed to the Posen-Treskau "SS und Waffen-Junkerschule 'Braunschweig,'" located in the vicinity of the present day Polish city of Poznan.[57]

Most of the Ukrainian candidates were graduates of a secondary school with some college. A small number, however, were university graduates. Organized into five platoons of approximately 40 per platoon, upon arrival to the officer school, the platoons were merged together into one Ukrainian student company. With the arrival of the Ukrainians, the number of officer candidates rose from approximately 440 to 640.[58]

Posen-Treskau's academy was commanded by SS-Brigadeführer und Generalmajor der Waffen-SS Ballauf. The 16th class of instruction, the course was to be held from 15 July to 15 December 1944.

Each of the 640 candidates was a graduate of an NCO school. Most of the German candidates had combat experience whereas most of the Ukrainians (excluding those who served in Kampfgruppe "Beyersdorff" or fought in the Polish or French Army in 1939-40 against the Nazis) had none. But this did not discourage the Ukrainians – in spirit, the Ukrainians possessed an exceptionally strong willingness to master the art of modern warfare.

Along with the German candidates, the Ukrainian candidates who previously had completed an NCO school but had not yet attained an NCOs' rank were promoted to the rank of "Junker."[59] But because the Ukrainians were not permitted to carry the "SS" title, the word "Waffen" preceded "Junker." From then on, the Ukrainians were referred to as "Waffen-Junkers" whereas the Germans were titled "SS-Junkers."

The training was very intense. Subjects included: tactics, the role of the various combat arms, military unit organizational strengths from company to regimental level, administration, combat engineering, weapons training, and even how to ride a horse. Physical training was emphasized and each candidate, with rifle, ammunition and rucksack weighing no less than 40 pounds, had to complete a 10 kilometer (6.2 mile) cross country/road distance forced march under 50 minutes. Each candidate was also required to jump blindfolded off a diving board in boots and fatigues. Once in the water, a candidate could remove the blindfold. But than he had to swim in deep water for no less than 15 minutes.

Needless to say, such arduous training takes its toll. Despite the efforts of a first class training cadre, candidates continued to be dismissed. By the time the course reached its mid-way point, a sizable number of German – and approximately 120 Ukrainian candidates – were discharged.[60] These men returned to their respective units. As for the Ukrainians who remained, they were promoted to the rank of "Waffen-Standarten-Junker" ("SS-Standarten-Junker" for the Germans) and they continued to train.

15

The Eastern Front: January 1943 - July 1944

In order to properly understand what the Division "Galicia" was facing in the summer of 1944, it is important to follow the sequence of events which arose on the eastern front from early 1943 to July 1944.

On 31 January 1943, when newly promoted Field Marshal Friedrich Paulus emerged from the basement ruins of a Stalingrad department store serving as his headquarters to surrender what remained of the battered 6th and part of the 4th Panzer Armies, Nazi Germany was facing a disaster which had seldom been experienced by any nation. Continuing to advance rapidly, Soviet forces recaptured Rostov and further north, began to approach the Eastern Ukrainian city of Kharkiv. To hold Kharkiv, Hitler personally ordered General Hubert Lanz, Commander of Armeeabteilung Lanz, to the Führer headquarters in Rastenburg, Prussia.

Fully aware that if Kharkiv fell Ukraine would be lost – along with its agricultural and mineral wealth – and determined to keep the conflict within Russia proper, Hitler personally ordered the general to "hold Kharkiv to the last man!"

Although determined to carry out the Führer's explicit orders, Lanz' forces were limited in strength. What further complicated Lanz' mission was that he had no control over the elite 'Leibstandarte SS Adolf Hitler,' 'Das Reich,' and 'Totenkopf' tank divisions promised to him by Hitler. Commanded by SS-Obergruppenführer Paul "Papa" Hausser, the SS divisions were to help defend Kharkiv. But Hausser, noting a dangerous situation, withdrew on 15-16 February to the south and southwest of Kharkiv in defiance of Lanz' and Hitler's orders.

Chapter 15: The Eastern Front: January 1943 - July 1944

Determined to regain control Hitler, on 17 February, flew to Army Group South's temporary headquarters located in the town of Zaporozhye (approximately 45 miles south of Dnipropetrovsk), on the Dnieper River. Such a frontline visit by the Führer was rare. But because Hitler needed a face-to-face conference with his generals to fully grasp the situation, a quick meeting was held in an airport hangar.

Prior to his arrival at Zaporozhye, Hitler was furious. But perhaps the lengthy flight and sub-zero weather calmed him, because at Zaporozhye, Hitler immediately learned that Soviet spearhead forces were approximately 35 miles away. To make matters worse, no front stood between Zaporozhye and the enemy. On 18 February, Manstein outlined his plan to repulse the Soviets and recapture Kharkiv. Initially, Hitler had planned to dismiss Manstein, but because he needed a victory to attract world attention, the Führer only listened.

On 19 February, Manstein struck. That same day, as Hitler flew back to Berlin with a bomb underneath his plane which failed to activate as a result of a frozen mechanism, Manstein's forces moved rapidly. By 18 March, against odds of at least one against ten, Manstein's brilliant counter-offensive was carried out. In a counter-offensive now regarded as one of the finest in military history, Manstein not only successfully restored the Eastern front's southern front line to its previous June 1942 position, but simultaneously, retook Kharkiv.

In a desperate effort to bolster the German forces and their faltering allies with the hope that victory could yet be attained, Hitler launched Operation "Zitadell" (Citadel). Aiming to strike fear into Stalin's state, repeatedly postponed, by the time it was launched on 5 July 1943, the Soviets had ample knowledge of it and by 13 July, had exhausted Hitler's forces. Besides some recaptured territory, nothing positive was gained by this offensive.

Massively reinforcing their forces, the Soviets immediately went on the counteroffensive, pushing towards Kharkiv. On 3 August, they officially commenced the "Fourth Battle of Kharkiv." As before, Hitler demanded the city to be held, but so drained were Hitler's forces after Zitadell that on 23 August 1943, Kharkiv was yielded to the troops of the Voronezh, Steppe and Southwest fronts. As Germany's battered forces pulled out, its hardliners knew that while after Stalingrad there was still some chance, with Kharkiv's fall the beginning of the Third Reich's end was imminent.

Kiev fell on 6 November 1943. By January 1944, the Dnieper was successfully forged both north and south of Kiev. In the north, Soviet forces thrusted towards the Baltic states while Finland began to seek a way out of the war; south of Kiev, at Cherkassy-Korsun, a successful breakout was achieved. But in the Crimea, poor evacuation plans, combined with a lack of aggressive leadership in the German Navy's Black Sea Fleet, resulted in an unsuccessful evacuation of Sevastopol and the Crimean Peninsula.

By March 1944, Soviet forces began to strike deeper into the Western Ukraine which, prior to 1939, was under Polish rule. Like the Finn's, the Rumanians and Bulgarians also began to seek a way out of the war. Excluding the Byelorussian front which jolted into Soviet Russia, Stalin's forces had recaptured a tremendous amount of territory.

Desperate now more than ever to reestablish and solidify the Eastern front, and angered by the loss of the cities of Nevel and Rivne, on 8 March 1944, Hitler issued Führer Order II.[1] This new order was designed to turn certain towns and cities with road, rail, and communication lines into "fortresses." These fortresses were to be amply stocked with arms, food, and ammunition. Although advancing Soviet forces would initially bypass such "fortresses," their critical locations would soon force the Soviets to contest the occupants. Once contested, much Soviet manpower and material would need to be diverted to secure such a location, and by the time it was secured (if at all) and any damage repaired, a "fortress" would slow an advance. Altogether, twenty six towns and cities were designated as "fortresses,"[2] among which were Ternopil, Kovel, and Brody.

In March 1944, the advancing Soviets encircled the German 1st Panzer Army in Southwest Ukraine. On 25 March, Fieldmarshall Manstein met with Hitler at Berchtesgaden, Bavaria. Throughout the afternoon, they quarrelled about the fate of Hube's surrounded 1st Panzer, and how to counter the Soviet thrust nearing southeast Galicia.

Manstein proposed to extradite Hube's army in the vicinity of Kamenets-Podilsky (southeast of Ternopil and Buchach). Hitler agreed to it, but refused to release any additional troops to assist the panzer army's breakout. But at a second conference held after midnight, Hitler authorized the movement of the 2nd Waffen-SS Panzer Corps, comprising the "Hohenstaufen" and "Frundsberg" tank divisions, from Northern France to Galicia.

On 2 April, Soviet Fieldmarshal Zhukov issued a brutal surrender offer to the 1st Panzer Army. Zhukov warned that if the army failed to surrender, it would be destroyed and every captured officer would be executed in front of his men. But on 5 April, the 2nd SS Panzer Corps and the 100th Light (Jaeger) Infantry Division ripped into the Soviet front, retook Buchach, and dashed towards Hube's Army; simultaneously, Hube struck to the southwest towards Khotin but then veered northwest towards Buchach. Close Luftwaffe air support and reinforcement (seldom seen in 1944), ensured a successful breakout. By 10 April, nearly twenty divisions, with much of their materiel, had made their way to safety. By operating behind the Soviet lines, Hube's army severely hampered the Soviet supply and communications lines, tied down innumerable numbers of Soviet forces, and during its breakout, had successfully destroyed sizable Soviet forces. In the end, the breakout had actually helped to stabilize the front. On 17 April, the 1st Ukrainian Front received an order to go on the defensive.[3] Until mid-July 1944, it remained that way.[4]

The Soviet Army
Despite its heavy losses, by the beginning of 1943 the Soviet Army's strength actually rose.[1] At the time of the Battle of Kursk in July 1943, Germany's eastern front intelligence estimated that Soviet Russia's military strength stood at 5,755,000.[2] But on 1 January 1944, Germany's intelligence placed the Soviet strength at 5.5 million.[3] Russia, however, classified its front line strength at 5,568,000 with a further 419,000 in the Stavka reserve.[4] Together, the combined strength totalled over 6,000,000. To make matters worse, Germany's eastern front intelligence estimated that while its own strength (even with expansion) would be declining, the Soviet strength (including casualties) would not only maintain itself, but would actually rise. This was attributable to the fact that Soviet Russia's population was considerably higher in 1941 than initially estimated at the outset of Barbarossa, and more eligible men reaching the 17-18 year age mark were found in the Soviet Union than in Germany. Additionally, manpower was also being secured from the far reaches of Siberia and Mongolia, and from regions previously occupied by German forces.[5]

In addition to its increased personnel strength, by the close of 1942, the Soviet Army had begun to massively increase its front line fire power. Its rocket launcher brigades (first established in its inventory at the close of 1942), were not only expanded by the conclusion of 1943, but were also reinforced with 26 independently formed artillery divisions.[6] Further expansions were also made in the armored and aircraft field. This was attributable to the fact that between July and November 1941, 1,360 industrial sites were disassembled and shifted deeper into Siberia and Central Asia, along with much of its the management and workers.[7] In spite of the fact that for a period of time Soviet Russia's western territories and Ukraine, with its agricultural and mineral wealth were occupied, the Soviet Union not only continued its industrial production but even surpassed that of Hitler. By the conclusion of the war, Stalin was more than correct when he boasted that he had won his so-called "battle of machines." Nearly 80,000 tanks, 16,000 self-propelled guns, and 98,000 artillery pieces were produced along with mass numbers of small arms.[8]

Lend-lease assistance, mostly from America, also bolstered Russia's war effort. Between 22 June 1941 and 20 September 1945, the Soviet Union acquired no less than 409,526 trucks and jeeps (mostly the "Studebaker" truck); 12,161 armored vehicles; 325,784 tons of explosives; 13,041 locomotives/railway cars; approximately 1,798,609 tons of foodstuffs,[9] and vast amounts of tires, steel, fuel, aviation fuel, and high-grade machine tools were provided. All totalled, Soviet Russia received nearly 10.2 billion dollars worth of war goods.[10]

In organization and tactics, the Soviets progressed continually. Whereas before tanks were relegated to the infantry, by 1943 compact groups of tanks and mechanized infantry – organized into corps and armies – began to appear.[11] These tank and mechanized forces enabled Soviet armies to move rapidly, strike decisively, and exploit any breakouts with tremendous firepower and speed.[12] Close air support was increasingly developed and improved upon. While of course it would not reach the level of America's strength, Soviet airpower in 1944 posed a far higher threat than it had just one year earlier. In 1944, every Soviet front had at least one air army for support.

The average strength of an infantry (rifle) division stood at 9,000-10,000; a guard infantry division had a strength of 10,000-12,000. But all the way down to company level, an increase in automatic, semi-automatic, mortar and hand-held anti-armored weapons enabled a company to possess stronger fire power than that possessed by a German company. With regard to quality, however, Soviet infantry was still inferior. Frequently in the midst of a battle, Soviet armies acquired much "infantry" through forced conscription. Untrained, poorly armed and equipped, these "soldiers" were forced to quickly master the art of combat and survival. Needless to say, many perished. But many survived. In due time, the survivors were afforded proper training, arms, equipment and were incorporated into regular or guard rifle, mechanized, or even airborne units. Regardless of how elite a Soviet infantry division was or was not, if one takes into consideration that by 1944 many German divisions were no longer in full divisional strength,[13] leadership and soldier qualities were degraded, and arms, ammunition and equipment supplies were low – a haphazardly organized Soviet infantry division, reinforced at the last moment with untrained men, could still pose a threat to any weak German force. This is especially true if the Soviet division was bolstered with additional armor, air and artillery support.

In the opening months of the war, "Generalissmo" Stalin (who achieved every military order except the wound badge), had a nasty habit of interfering in military affairs and turning everything into a disaster. However, Stalin eventually admitted that he was no military genius and began to grant his generals freedom in strategic planning. Excluding rare appearances, such as in August 1943 when he threatened his general staff if they failed to secure Kharkiv, Stalin stayed out of military matters.

In the area of leadership, the Soviet armies tremendously improved their tactical abilities. This was largely due to the purges of the 1930s and to the high military losses initially incurred in 1941 and 1942. With positions opening up in the higher levels, a number of exceptionally gifted leaders, many under the age of forty, who were less politically motivated but had a better understanding of newer concepts in modern warfare, assumed positions of leadership.[14]

The First Ukrainian Front

On 15 May 1944, Marshal Ivan Stepanovych Konev assumed command of the 1st Ukrainian Front.[1] Originally, the 1st Ukrainian Front was known as the Voronezh Front and Steppe Front. But on 20 October 1943, shortly after entering Ukraine, the two fronts were merged together and redesignated as the 1st Ukrainian Front.[2]

In the summer of 1944, Konev's 1st Ukrainian Front was assigned the mission of breaching the German defense in Galicia, overrunning Western Ukraine, routing the main forces of Army Group North Ukraine's 1st and 4th Panzer Armies, and pressing into Poland and Rumania proper.[3]

Army Group North Ukraine

Army Group North Ukraine (AGNU) was created on 5 April 1944.[1] Its mission was to defend the Northwestern Ukraine, Eastern Galicia, and the northern central Carpathian region. At first, it was commanded by Field Marshal Walter Model, but in late June 1944, Colonel-General Joseph Harpe assumed command. Army Group North Ukraine's front stretched from the base of the Pripyat Marshes in the vicinity of Kovel, to a point just south of Kuty in the Carpathian Mountains. Its strength consisted of 35 German infantry and field security divisions, 10 Hungarian divisions (primarily concentrated in the 1st Hungarian Army),[2] 8 panzer and 1 motorized division.[3] Although this strength might seem impressive, if one takes into consideration that very few of the German infantry divisions exceeded a strength of 10,000,[4] none of AGNU's panzer divisions were in full strength; the Luftwaffe's air support was negligible at best; and the Hungarians were far to the rear seeking a way to extricate themselves out of the war, clearly, AGNU faced a difficult mission. What especially compounded the situation was that the elite 2nd SS Panzer Corps, refitted within Army Group North Ukraine in anticipation of another summer offensive, was ordered by Hitler on 11 June to return to Normandy.[5] With its return to the west, a large and effective armored force was lost by AGNU.

Yet, Army Group North Ukraine's mission was of essence. It was to defend what was left of Ukraine, protect Lviv's critical road, air and rail center, protect the vital oil region of Drohobych and Borislav, and ensure the Soviet forces did not advance into Czechoslovakia and the plains of Southern and Central Poland towards Silesia.[6] Any further German defeats and withdrawals from the remainder of Ukraine and Galicia would result in severe military, political, economic and psychological setbacks for Nazi Germany.

Galicia lies on a central plateau and upland belt which, in elevation (excluding the Carpathian and Crimean Mountains), is higher than most of Ukraine. A series of major rivers, such as the Buh, Dniester, San, Zbruch, Seret, Strypa, and Styr, along with numerous streams and tributaries, bisect the whole of Galicia. The land is characterized by rolling, hilly terrain with patches of forested areas and wooded ridges rising up to 600 feet. Swamps, and deep ravines, with occasional high hills (suitable for observation), are also found. Galicia's roads frequently cross the tops of dams and dikes, and heavy rains often swell streams and creeks, turning roads and adjacent fields into quagmire. Realizing the importance of Galicia, and determined to hold the rapidly moving Soviet juggernaut from advancing into the European plateau and Poland proper, the Germans established a strong defense.

From the Polissian swampland to the Carpathian Mountains and around a series of rivers such as the Buh, Strypa, and Styr, the Germans constructed a defensive zone of fortifications extending (from east to west) three lines in depth. As always, terrain played a major factor in determining the depth of this defense, but its depth averaged 25 to 30 miles. Much of this defense hinged on the so-called "Prinz Eugen Stellung" (Prinz Eugen Position), which stretched southeastward from the vicinity of Kholm into the region of Ternopil. Within this defense zone, a series of designated forces were instructed to hold the forward two defensive lines and "fortified" centers, while the armored forces were kept in reserve approximately 10 miles behind.[7] In the event of a Soviet attack, these armored forces would only be committed to bolster an area or position threatened to be overrun or to counterattack any Soviet armored forces weakened in their attempt to break through the German defense. Along with the armor, any forward infantry companies or battalions not being attacked could contribute to the defense by marching rapidly into a designated location and assisting its defenders. The German defense of Galicia was centered (as always is the case) on four strict defensive characteristics: preparation, concentration, disruption and flexibility.

Theoretically speaking, the plan was excellent. If properly administered and executed, it could have yielded results. But as with any plan, weaknesses may be found.

Chapter 15: The Eastern Front: January 1943 - July 1944

Following Hitler's dismissal of Manstein on 30 March 1944,[8] Field Marshal Model took over. A soldier of great drive, ability and power, Model undoubtedly did not have enough time to properly acquaint himself with the situation; as with any new commander, Model would undoubtedly propose changes and additions to the defense plan. Unfortunately, once such changes begin to reach the lower units (especially battalion and company levels), and training changes must be made to meet the new defense missions, confusion and problems frequently arise. And if sufficient time is not allowed to resolve any difficulties, unpreparedness in warfare equals disaster!

According to former Wehrmacht General Frederich von Mellenthin, former Chief of Staff of the 4th German Panzer Army, General Model "was prone to interfere in matters of detail, and to tell his corps and army commanders exactly where they should dispose their troops."[9] Certain commanders found this very irritating. Complicating the situation was this order issued by Model: "Forward lines are to be held at all costs, artillery and armor are to be disposed in rear along a defensive line showing no gaps; if the enemy breaks through, he must be met with obstacles everywhere."[10]

But a number of commanders, such as Panzer General Hermann Balck, deferred. Balck, whose 48th Panzer Corps was to operate in the vital Lviv-Ternopil sector (and the scene of major battles in 1914 and 1916), argued that the forward line should be thinly manned in a series of outposts; as for the main defensive line, it should be far to the rear. Such a positioning would keep the brunt of the infantry out of the range, and massive firepower, of the Soviet artillery. Mellenthin, Balck, and others also felt that the order requiring the forward lines to be fully manned through the night, with the majority of the troops at daybreak retiring to the main position, had to be changed. This procedure was only wearing out the troops and could possibly expose them to dangers when on the move. To increase firepower, Balck also believed it was better to concentrate the artillery and anti-tank guns in compact groups and to establish independent assault and anti-tank gun detachments as mobile reserves instead of just deploying the guns in long defensive lines.

At first, Model refused to accept these proposals, but eventually gave in. Although the infantry was disposed in the new manner, at the time of Konev's offensive, the accepted regrouping of artillery and anti-tank guns was not yet accomplished.[11]

To complete its defense, Army Group North Ukraine was to be reinforced. As was always the case, reinforcement was no easy matter. What especially compounded the problem was that on 6 June 1944, the western allies had landed in France and that same month on 22 June, the Soviets launched Operation

"Bagration," a major offensive in Byelorussia.[12] Striking an overextended and thinly held bulge protruding far to the east, Stalin's armies advanced rapidly. Disgusted with Field-Marshal Ernst Busch's defense of Byelorussia, Hitler relieved Busch on 28 June and ordered Model to take over the defense of Army Group Central. Model would still retain his position as commander of AGNU; however, with his transfer to the central sector on 29 June, Colonel-General Josef Harpe, commander of the 4th Panzer Army and Model's deputy, assumed command of AGNU in Model's absence. With the temporary transfer of Model to the central sector, AGNU lost a very capable commander; likewise, it would be difficult for Harpe to direct both his army and the entire AGNU at the time when Konev struck.

To halt the threatening Soviet advance into Central and Northern Poland, Lithuania, and East Prussia, AGNU was ordered to dispatch six divisions (three armored),[13] north to the Central front; likewise, because of the Soviet offensive in Byelorussia, no German units would be able to be diverted south to assist AGNU in its operations against the 1st Ukrainian Front.[14] As was always the case, whenever a front gave up any of its forces, frequently many weeks – or months – (if ever in many cases) passed before the forces were returned or replaced. Therefore, at the time of the Soviet offensive, AGNU did not man its defense with a strength of "40 divisions, two brigades and other units totalling 600,000 men, 900 tanks and assault artillery, 6,300 cannon and mortars, and 700 aircraft" as attested in the 1980s by Soviet Colonel Panov;[15] rather, when the 1st Ukrainian Front struck, AGNU's strength consisted of thirty-four infantry divisions, five panzer and one motorized divisions, and two brigades.[16] Virtually all were under strength.

On paper, a German infantry division of 6 infantry battalions was authorized a strength of 12,000; a division of 9 infantry battalions was authorized approximately 15,000.[17] But in reality, by the end of 1943, many infantry divisions were operating on unauthorized strengths.[18] Excluding certain Waffen-SS and Wehrmacht divisions, for the greater part German generals operated with understrength divisions and brigades.

In addition to the fact that most of the infantry divisions were understrength, AGNU's 1st and 4th Panzer Armies were "panzer" in name only. In 1944, a panzer division was authorized up to 125 tanks.[19] But (excluding certain Waffen-SS and a few Wehrmacht panzer divisions), most panzer divisions had tremendous difficulties in maintaining their authorized tank strengths, and along with combat losses, frequently had fewer than 100 tanks.

On 22 June 1944, the corps composition of 4th Panzer Army stood as such: 13th Corps, 42nd Corps, 56th Panzer Corps, and a Rear Reserve (numerically unidentified) corps consisting of the 213th Field Security Division; the 1st Panzer Army's corps composition consisted of the 24th Panzer Corps, 46th Panzer Corps,

48th Panzer Corps, and 59th Corps. To these two armies, OKH designated the 3rd Panzer Corps as a reserve which contained the 20th Panzergrenadier and 5th Waffen-SS "Wiking" Divisions.[20]

Minor changes, however, occurred between 8 and 15 July and on the eve of Konev's thrust, the composition of the 4th Panzer Army stood as such: 8th Corps (a battered corps diverted from the 2nd Army which previously was holding a front in the southwestern part of Byelorussia within the bulge of Army Group Center); 56th Panzer Corps, 46th Panzer Corps (brought over from the 1st Panzer Army), 42nd Corps, and Rear Reserve Corps. As for the 1st Panzer Army, it was commanded by Colonel-General Erhard Raus and its corps composition stood as follows: 13th Corps (previously with 4th Panzer Army); 48th Panzer Corps; 24th Panzer Corps; 59th Corps and AGNU's 3rd Panzer Reserve Corps transferred to the 1st Panzer Army by OKH. Again, it is noteworthy to mention that although both armies were classified as "panzer," in truth neither of the two armies was even close to being a true panzer army. Although a number of the corps' were also designated as "panzer," in actuality they existed as infantry corps'. Excluding the 16th and 17th Panzer Divisions within the 4th Panzer Army's 46th Panzer Corps and the 1st and 8th Panzer Divisions within the 1st Panzer Army's 3rd Panzer Reserve Corps (shortly afterwards these two panzer divisions were diverted to the 1st Panzer Army's 48th Panzer Corps headed by General Hermann Balck), no additional panzer divisions or brigades were found.[21] As for tank strengths, 16th Panzer Division listed a strength of 22 tanks and 17th Panzer Division 21+;[22] simultaneously, within the 1st Panzer Division, there existed 34 Mark IV's and 27 Mark V "Panther" tanks.[23] The 8th Panzer Division was regarded as the strongest with 9 Mark IV's and 68 Panthers.[24] All four panzer divisions did possess some mechanized (self-propelled) anti-tank guns, but these were limited. For the greater part, the 4th and 1st "Panzer" Armies infantry and panzer corps consisted of a number of jaeger (hunter) and understrength infantry divisions. Except for the 1st Panzer Divisions "1" rating,[25] the remainder of the 4th and 1st Panzer Armies divisions fell into a "2" to "4" rating. And with such forces, AGNU was to stop the Soviet thrust.

Konev's Plan
Unlike Stalin who advocated Zhukov's previous proposal to advance in Lviv's direction with one single massive thrust, Konev and his Chief-of-Staff, General Vasiliy D. Sokolovskiy,[1] proposed a double thrust – one from an assembly area in the vicinity of Lutsk and Dubno towards Rava-Russka/Yaroslav and the other from an assembly area in Ternopil towards the Galician capital of Lviv.[2] Both Konev and Sokolovskiy feared that a single thrust, even if massively supported, could be

repulsed by AGNU. Therefore, Sokolovskiy, a first-rate military historian, hatched a plan based on a military event which occurred from 23 August-2 September 1914 in Galicia.

In the summer of 1914, General Nikolai Ivanov's southwestern Russian Front (comprising the 3rd, 4th, 5th and 8th Imperial Russian Armies), advanced towards Lemberg from the east and northeast. On 23-24 August, Austria's 1st Army repulsed the 4th Russian Imperial Army northeast of Lemberg. Several days later, Austria's 4th Army repulsed the 5th Russian Army. But on the southern flank (east/southeast of Lemberg), the Austrian 3rd Army (with elements of Austria's 2nd Army), was repulsed towards Lemberg by Russia's 3rd and 8th Armies. Falling back on Lemberg, the Austrian's were unable to re-establish a front because northeast of Lemberg, the 5th Russian Army (under renewed leadership) suddenly penetrated itself between Austria's 1st and 4th Armies. Abandoning Lemberg, the Austrians retreated west in hopes of establishing a new front. Because General Ivanov's southwestern front maintained a rapid advance, Austria's armies were unable to re-establish the Galician front. With such a two-thrusted envelopment, Imperial Russia, had, by mid-September, secured the whole of Galicia. Recalling how such a two-thrusted blow had rapidly overrun Galicia before, both Konev and Sokolovskiy began to incorporate Ivanov's successful strategy into the Soviet basic principle of land warfare which advocated violent, sustained, and deep offensive actions hinging on three major areas: a) seizure of the initiative at the outset of hostilities; b) penetration; and c) to drive deeply and decisively into an enemy's rear.

But in order to achieve tactical success, both Konev and Sokolovskiy knew that a breakthrough of the first and second defensive zones would have to be rapidly achieved in order to begin a massive disruption of the German defense system. This, in turn, would create an advantageous condition for committing the reserve (or second echelon) armored and mechanized forces into battle to develop the initial tactical breakouts into an operational one. Afterwards, continuous, non-stop troop movements would seize river crossings, defeat enemy reserves, and overrun fuel, supply, and communication points; thus achieving important objectives. Once such massive forces were injected into the German rear, it was anticipated a collapse would ensue. But for such a high-rate of advance to be achieved, everything hinged on a rapidly executed breakthrough. And that is why a two thrusted blow was advocated.

Half-heartedly, Stalin gave in to Konev's proposal for a two pronged Galician thrust[3] – one towards Rava-Russka and the other, towards Lviv. Because this was the only time during the entire Soviet-German conflict that one entire Soviet army front was assigned the mission to destroy an enemy army group, to ensure that Konev would be able to rapidly overrun Galicia and at long last carry the war into Europe proper, STAVKA massively reinforced Konev's 1st Ukrainian Front.[4] By 13 July 1944, Konev's front had approximately 1,200,000 officers and men, nearly 2,200 tanks and self-propelled guns, some 14,000 guns and mortars, and well over 3,000 aircraft.[5] According to Konev's own calculations years after World War II, the 1st Ukrainian Front had 80 rifle (infantry) and cavalry divisions; 10 tank and mechanized corps; approximately 16,000 artillery and mortar pieces; about 2,000 tanks and self-propelled guns; and 3,250 combat aircraft.[6] In troop strength, the 1st Ukrainian Front accounted for 1,110,000 personnel.[7] Retired British Army Colonel Albert Seaton cited 1st Ukrainian Front's strength as consisting of no less than 840,000 troops, 14,000 guns, 1,600 tanks and self-propelled artillery pieces, and 2,800 aircraft organized around 80 infantry divisions, 10 tank or mechanized corps, and a number of brigades.[8] And Lt. Colonel Myhailo Lishchyns'kyi, a former Divisional officer, cited that Konev had 80 divisions, 6 cavalry divisions, 10 tank and mechanized corps, 4 specialized tank brigades, and 1 corps of Czech communists. As well, over 1,600 tanks and over 13,900 artillery and mortar pieces exceeding 76mm were found.[9] To this, 10 partisan formations and no less than 53 specialized detachments and a number of highly-trained snipers were inserted to cause havoc. Totalling no less than 9,000 men and women,[10] these forces bolstered the regions communist insurgency in the late spring of 1944 to no less than 12,000 fighters found within 11 guerrilla groups and 40 independent detachments.[11] Their mission was to support the front's thrust by striking communication, supply, rail centers, roads and key personnel.[12] In the end, a total of seven infantry armies (1st Guards,[13] 3rd Guards, 5th Guards, 13th, 18th, 38th and 60th); three tank armies (1st Guards Tank, 3rd Guards Tank,[14] and 4th Tank[15]), and two independent mechanized cavalry groups "Baranov" (consisting of the 1st Guards Cavalry Corps and 25th Tank Corps), and "Sokolov" (6th Guards Cavalry Corps and 31st Independent Tank Corps), were found within Konev's 1st Ukrainian Front.

In addition to the strong armored concentrations, a number of "artillery" divisions were also dispatched to Konev's front. Such divisions, which contained their own permanent planning, fire direction, reconnaissance, forward fire support observers, intelligence and liaison personnel, were centered around approximately 210 artillery pieces utilized especially for offensive operations. Such artillery divisions were provided to the following armies: 1st Guards Breakthrough Artillery Division – 13th Army; 3rd Breakthrough Artillery Division – 5th Guards Army; 3rd Guards Rocket Barrage Division – 1st Ukrainian Front; 13th Breakthrough Artillery Division – 1st Ukrainian Front; and the 17th Breakthrough Artillery Division operated with both the 5th Guards and 60th Armies.

To ensure success along the "Rava-Russka" Axis Konev authorized (in the vicinity of the town of Lutsk) the establishment of the "Lutsk Assault Group." This group encompassed Gordov's 3rd Guards Army, Putkov's 13th Army, Katukov's 1st Guards Tank Army, and General "Baranov's" mechanized cavalry group. A combined strength of 14 rifle divisions, one tank army, a mechanized corps, a cavalry corps and two artillery divisions were supported by Col. General Krasovskiy's 2nd Air Army; to ensure success along the "Lviv" Axis Konev assembled (north of Ternopil) the "Lviv Assault Group." This encompassed Moskalenko's 38th Army, Kurochkin's 60th Army, Rybalko's 3rd Guards Tank Army, Lelyshenko's 4th Tank Army, and "Sokolov's" Mechanized Cavalry Group. From amongst the 3rd Guards, 13th, 38th and 60th armies, 32 specially formed "shock assault storm" battalions were formed to penetrate AGNU's front.[16] Air support was provided by the 2nd Air Army as well as elements of the 8th Air Army.[17] And on Konev's left flank (facing westward), Colonel-General Grechko's 1st Guards and Lt. General Zhuravlev's 18th Army were established. These two armies had the mission of covering "Lviv Assault Group's" left flank or, on order, reinforce any breakthroughs by the "Lviv" group or, push southwest towards the city of Stanyslaviv (currently Ivano-Frankivsk). As for Zdanov's 5th Guards Army, along with the 47th Independent Rifle Corps (with a strength of six rifle divisions), these forces served as the 1st Ukrainian Fronts reserve.[18]

According to Colonel Panov "nearly half of the infantry divisions, three tank armies, as well as artillery, engineer and various special units, were transferred into the Lutsk-Ternopil [assembly area] sectors in the period of 24 June to 7 July 1944. As a result, this massing of manpower and equipment and the deep operational formation gave the 1st Ukrainian Front considerable superiority over the enemy in the sector of the break-through and ensured favorable opportunities for following up the operation."[19]

Colonel Panov was correct in his observations that the 1st Ukrainian Front had developed a "considerable superiority" over the German enemy. And his estimates of "five-fold in manpower, six-fold in artillery, and four-fold in tanks" are also correct.[20] Realistically speaking, especially in the breakout sectors, Konev's forces had very high superiority ratios.

To conceal his plans, Marshal Konev imposed strict secrecy. All movement and staging orders were coded, all couriers were closely escorted by NKVD agents and combat police and deception was extensively utilized.[21] Front movements were also carried out to fool German observers and intelligence into believing that the main thrust was going to evolve from the vicinity of the 1st Guards and 18th Armies. It was hoped that such movements would develop a false impression that not two,

Chapter 15: The Eastern Front: January 1943 - July 1944

but rather four (two infantry and two tank) armies, along with an independent tank corps would be staging northeast of Stanislaviv. Galicia's forested and swamp areas were utilized extensively to conceal approach's and assembly areas. To cite an example, the extensive forests east of Lviv were utilized in June 1944 for the purposes of concealment in establishing the assembly areas. In areas where swamp and marshy terrain was found, Soviet engineers laid corduroy roads.[22]

On 7 July 1944, Konev's attack plans were flown from his 1st Ukrainian Front headquarters to Moscow's Stavka for final inspection. Two air supported blows – separately orchestrated but massively inflicted – would be launched no more than 45 miles apart. Once the German front was shattered, its defenders would be denied the ability to effectively deal with an onslaught of men and materiel moving rapidly on two axis'. To ensure the breakout would occur, the 1st Ukrainian Front assembled 56 of its 84 infantry rifle divisions, over 90 percent of its armor and up to 65 percent of its "God of War" (artillery) into the two assembly areas.[23] Although the 1st Ukrainian Front held a frontage of 440 km's, both axis' were to strike at a combined front of no more than 26 km's (16-17 miles). Per kilometer, no less than 200-300 guns were emplaced.[24] And once a breakout was achieved, Soviet planners hoped to achieve a depth of 220-240 kilometers.[25]

None of the front's tank armies or mechanized cavalry groups would be committed in the initial breakthrough; rather, a full twenty-four hours would elapse before any armor was committed; this would only occur after the infantry penetrated the front and achieved operational depth. Konev's date of attack was set for 14 July 1944. To ensure his troops received a good rest, all preparations were to cease by 12 July.

On 10 July 1944, Stavka approved Konev's plan.

187

16

Brody!

Wednesday, 28 June – Wednesday, 5 July 1944

As the "Galicia" Division's soldiers boarded the trains, most believed they were bound for Stanislaviv. Although the initial intention was for the Division to be posted to Stanislaviv, Germany's Eastern Front intelligence began to detect the Soviet buildup northeast of Brody.[1] To reinforce the Brody front, the Division was diverted from the OKH's 3rd Panzer's Reserve Rear Corps,[2] and instead posted to Arthur Hauffe's 13th Army Corps.[3]

An infantry corps within the 4th Panzer Army, Hauffe's corps was holding the Brody front. Although disgruntled voices within the Division tried to rescind the order. it was to no avail; the Division was headed for Brody.

Meeting with Hauffe and his Chief of Staff, Colonel Kurt von Hammerstein, the Division's advance party (including Heike), were told the Division would occupy a reserve secondary position behind the 13th Corps' front line divisions. Until the 13th Corps commander and von Hammerstein actually met the Division's representatives, neither had ever heard anything of such a foreign Division. Because the Division's effectiveness status was rated with a "?" mark beside it, Hauffe did not know what to make of it. Nevertheless, he was more than glad to have it assigned to him because Hauffe's corps at the time consisted of General Oscar Lasch's 349th Infantry Division,[4] General George Lindemann's 361st Infantry Division,[5] Major General J. Netwig's 454th Field Security Division,[6] and Lt. General Walter Lange's 'Corps Abteilung C' (Corps Formation C) consisting of the

183rd, 217th and 339th Infantry Divisions much reduced by casualties.[7] Altogether, 13 Corps was holding a front of 50 miles.[8] Although impressive on paper, 13th Corps actual strength stood at approximately 25,000. Reinforced with the "Galicia" Division, 13th Corps strength rose to approximately 35,000.[9]

Upon returning to Galicia, the Division simultaneously reentered UPA territory.[10] Always closely monitored by the Ukrainian insurgency, the Division was now a target for the Ukrainian insurgency which was desperately hoping to recruit the Division's manpower with their arms and equipment for its underground army. The UPA planned to accomplish this by establishing contact with Divisional members as well as by taking in deserters.

Yet, there were few deserters. Although the vast majority of the Division's personnel were receptive to and supportive of the UPA, they were not interested in furthering their cause by serving as guerrillas. However, constant contact was maintained between both forces. By utilizing the UPA's intelligence service, the Division was able to obtain much information on Soviet strengths, dispositions, and activities in regions occupied by Red Army forces.

There were also fears that upon, reentry into Galicia, large-scale desertions could occur by soldiers seeking a way to visit, or assist, their families. This justifiable concern was especially raised by the ominous fact that the Soviet front line was now in Galicia proper and the evacuation of East Galicia was underway; under such conditions, soldiers could very well respond to a strong urge to leave behind their units to assist families in need. And yet, it soon became apparent that this fear was unjustified for very few fled to their families; of those who did, the majority returned after a brief visit and an assurance that all was well. To alleviate unnecessary anxieties, provisions were made to permit the Division's members brief visitation periods. A number of soldiers who resided locally were granted permission for daily or overnight visits. Overall, in Galicia the problem of desertion never reached a dangerous level; undoubtedly, this was attributable to unit cohesion, pride and unity.

After travelling through Yaroslav, Peremysl, Horodok, Lviv, and Busk, the Division arrived at Ozhydiv, a town located about 43 miles northeast of Lviv and 22 miles southwest of Brody. Because the Division arrived at various times of the day, unloading was done around the clock and conducted on the outskirts of the railway town. Arriving on 1 July, Liubko Zmak,* a member of the 31st Infantry Regiment, marched no more than 2 miles from Ozhydiv when Soviet Ilyushin aircraft suddenly appeared to strafe and rocket the troops; Leo Smerenko*, upon arrival late one night, took no more than several steps from the train when suddenly, descending parachute flares, followed immediately by the piercing screams of falling bombs, turned night into day and peace into hell. As the infantry soldiers raced for the safety of a nearby forest, the massive sounds of exploding bombs shook the entire area.

In anticipation of possible Soviet air attacks, the Division had installed some of its anti-aircraft to protect Ozhydiv's railway. The moment Soviet aircraft came flying in, they encountered intense ground fire. And Markian Fesolovych, a member of a 20mm gun crew serving within the Division's 88mm gun battery, along with the other 20mm gun crewmen, was more than ready. Since their departure from Neuhammer, Markian and the others stood a constant guard over the two railway flatbeds carrying the Divisions indispensable 88s. At Ozhydiv, as the men unloaded the 88s, "Ilyushin" aircraft once again flew in; yet, effective small arms and anti-aircraft fire kept the aircraft from destroying the guns.[11]

In desperation, Soviet pilots sometimes dropped their bombs from high altitudes; for the greater part, the bombs just exploded and dropped debris upon the troops. But for most, it was also their first combat experience.

Following one such air raid, an unexploded bomb was discovered inside a railway car. Because the device lay inside a car full of small-arms ammunition and mortar rounds which stood inside a railway depot, it was impossible to detonate the device without destroying the valuable contents as well as most of the railway station; therefore, the Division's bomb and explosive experts, headed by Bohdan Tyr*, were called in to handle the matter.

Carefully sliding the partially opened railway car door a couple of feet, Bohdan entered the car. Aiming his flashlight into the dimly lit car, he noted the scattered boxes within the center and the loose rounds of ammunition lying around. Cautiously approaching the center, he detected the bomb's tail, and a beam of light entering a hole in the roof. From its size, Bohdan knew that a sizable bomb, possibly a 1,000 pounder, had entered the car. "Oh well," thought Bohdan, as the old saying goes "the bigger they are, the better they are." Needing room to work, for the next couple of hours Bohdan and his assistant carefully removed the ammunition boxes around the bomb. But as they cleared the area, they noticed the bomb's markings. It was American made. For Bohdan, this was bad news, for he knew that the unexploded device was not only more destructive than a Soviet bomb but worse, Bohdan had not received much training on how to deactivate and dismantle an American made bomb.

Painstakingly, barely breathing, Bohdan disassembled the device. His fingers moved with the ease of a feather, his eyes observed everything; constantly, he listened for any unusual internal noises. Throughout the whole ordeal, not once did Bohdan ever panic, flinch or give up. As he commented to his assistant – "a bomb is just like a woman. Treat her right and she won't explode in your face." After 12 hours of intense labor, Bohdan succeeded in deactivating the device.[12]

Thursday, 6 July – Tuesday, 11 July:
As it moved into the line, the Division's mission was to occupy a secondary position behind the Styr River within the Prince Eugene defense system to bolster the 13th Corps front. It was also hoped the Division would continue its training.

Spanning from north to south to the southeast, the Division manned a position nearly 22 miles in length[1] and occupied the following area: <u>Northern Sector</u>: From Stanyslavchyk to the main Lviv-Brody highway south on Razhniv stood the 31st Infantry Regiment. Its regimental headquarters was established at Turie. The Division's 3rd Artillery Battalion reinforced the regiment. Chaplain Bohdan Levyts'kyi served as regimental chaplain. <u>Central Sector</u>: The 30th Infantry Regiment was established from Zabolottsi to Sukhodoly. The 30th Infantry Regiment occupied a position between the Lviv-Brody highway's southern shoulder and the northern shoulder of a secondary highway which ran north/northeast from Sasiv and Pidhirtsi past Sukhodoly to Brody. Regimental headquarters was established east of Chekhy. Artillery Battalion 2 reinforced the regiment. Chaplain Josef Kladochnyi served as regimental chaplain. <u>Southern Sector</u>: Held by the 29th Infantry Regiment, its line ran from the vicinity of Sukhodoly to the Seret River. Regimental headquarters was located southeast of Yaseniv; the regiment was reinforced with the 1st Artillery Battalion. Chaplain Myhailo Levenets' served as regimental chaplain. Divisional headquarters was located north of the main highway but south of Sokolivka. To maintain control of the Divisions 4th Heavy Artillery Battalion, Divisional headquarter's posted the 4th in the vicinity of Kadovbytsi. Chaplain Vasyl' Leshchyshyn served in the artillery and Chaplain Volodymyr Stetsiuk served on Divisional staff.

The Division's supply trains were located north of Ozhydiv and the main highway, and the Fusilier Battalion was positioned east of the 29th Regiment, across the Styr River. The Field Replacement Battalion was located west of Ozhydiv in Busk's vicinity, approximately 13 miles west of the front line. Unlike the brunt of the Division which detrained at Ozhydiv, the Field Replacement Battalion arrived, by rail, to the village of Krasne, on 7 July 1944,[2] thus being one of the last units to arrive. The Division's strength, as of 30 June 1944, stood at 346 officers, 1,131 NCO's, and 13,822 men for a total of 15,299.[3] Of this strength, 10,400 deployed eastward as cited by Yuriy Krokhmaliuk.[4] Various Ukrainian sources quote figures of at least 10,000 to 10,300, but rarely over 11,000[5] while Heike estimated a strength of "around 11,000 men."[6] But the figure of "20,000 trained soldiers defending its freedom in front of the approaching hordes and external enemy"[7] is inaccurate. Leadership-wise, the brunt of the senior ranking officers from battalion command and higher were German; however, the majority of the platoon and company commanders were Ukrainian.[8] Approximately 150 Ukrainian officers deployed with the Division.[9]

As for its command structure, the Division's command was centered around such senior ranking personnel:[10]

<u>Divisional Commander</u>: General Fritz Freitag; adjutants - SS-Sturmbannführer Georgi and SS-Hauptsturmführer Finder;
<u>Section 1A</u>: Major Heike;[11] adjutant – SS-Obersturmführer Mikhel;
<u>Section 1B</u>: SS-Hauptsturmführer Shaaf;[12]
<u>Section 1C</u>: SS-Hauptsturmführer's Nerman, Wiens[13];Waffen-Hauptsturmführer Ferkuniak; and SS-Obersturmführer Shenker;
<u>SectionIIA/IIB</u>: Waffen-Hauptsturmführer Paliiv; SS-Obersturmführer Steingorst;
<u>Section III</u>: SS-Sturmbannführer Ziegler; SS-Haupsturmführer Herman; Waffen-Obersturmführer Stadnyk.
<u>Section IVA</u>: SS-Sturmbannführer Zultsbach; SS-Obersturmführer Mayer;
<u>Section IVB</u>: SS-Obersturmbannführer Dr. Spech V;
<u>Section IVC</u>: SS-Obersturmbannführer Dr. Kogen;
<u>Section IVD</u>: SS-Obersturmführer Meier;
<u>Section V</u>: SS-Sturmbannführer Berns;
<u>Section VI</u>: SS-Sturmbannführer Zoglawer; SS-Obersturmführer Lenard,[14] Waffen-Hauptsturmführer Uhryn Bezrishnyi and Chaplain Stetsiuk.[15]

The moment the Division occupied its sector within the Prinz Eugene defensive system, UPA's regional leadership immediately warned certain Ukrainian Divisional officers that, whether the Germans realized it or not, AGNU had placed the Division into a "sack." UPA's intelligence was fully aware of the two major Soviet assembly areas located to the northeast and southeast of Brody. The UPA stated that Brody would not be an objective but rather, commencing in mid-July, two main blows would be simultaneously directed along two axis' – one from the north towards Busk and the other from the east towards Zolochiv. The UPA also warned that Konev's front possessed approximately 1,800 tanks and armored vehicles and no less than 1,000 attack aircraft, of which most were found in the two assembly areas. UPA's intelligence also concluded that in the event the Soviets succeeded in rupturing the front, "the Division could be engulfed in an ocean swarm-

Two Waffen-SS officers with members of the Ukrainian Military Board. Because the slanted "SS" runes were not permitted to be worn by non-German personnel serving within the Waffen-SS, the two pictured individuals are German personnel. This photograph was taken in Neuhammer. Both leaders are also adorned with the wound badge tucked into their uniforms.

The Ukrainian "Tryzub" National symbol along with Galicia's ancient national lion symbol. These symbols were erected by Galicia's volunteers adjacent to their barracks and training facilities within the Neuhammer training camp.

A Ukrainian Waffen-Rottenführer with a bicycle. Note the Galician silver-piped lion patch on a black background worn on the collar. He is wearing the ordinary 1944 army pattern field gray/green uniform. This uniform tunic, with plain collar and plain unpleased pockets, was actually first introduced in 1943 and was worn by the Wehrmacht. With the expansion of the Waffen-SS and a shortage of Waffen-SS field uniforms, the standard army (Wehrmacht) uniform was adopted. However, various insignias were worn differently to distinguish Waffen-SS troops from the other branches of service. In addition to the collar patch which indicates the rank of corporal, the shoulder straps adorned on his field grey uniform also indicates the rank of corporal. But the most distinctive feature which indicated membership in the Waffen-SS was the way the "hoheitsabzeichen" (eagle with swastika and the German Army national emblem) was worn. Whereas in the other armed forces the eagle was worn on the right breast of the uniform, in the Waffen-SS both German and foreign soldiers wore the eagle insignia on the upper left arm sleeve of their dress uniforms, coats and, on occasion, on camouflaged jackets and smocks as can be seen in this photo. The eagle was sewn either in silver or gray on a dark green background. The belt worn around his waist is the typical black leather belt normally issued to enlisted soldiers. This belt was always worn with a steel buckle. According to Allied intelligence reports, the Waffen-SS buckle bore an eagle with outstretched wings extended across the upper part of the buckle with such an inscription: "Meine Ehre heisst Treue" (My Honor Is Loyalty!). Possibly, this NCO has such an inscription on his buckle. For headgear, a 1940 forage cap with the eagle and death's head (skull with crossbones) is worn. As for the strap cord hanging from his pocket into his uniform, it probably holds a whistle tucked into the right breast pocket. The Ukrainian Waffen-Sturmmann pictured facing a civilian member from Galicia's Military Board has such insignias on his left arm sleeve: (from top to bottom) the National eagle emblem of the Waffen-SS, the Galician Lion patch which here appears to be in yellow on a blue background and under the lion patch is the white "V" on a black shield. The "V" patch indicates the rank of a Private who previously had served either in the army or in combat. Possibly, this individual had witnessed combat with Kampfgruppe "Beyersdorff" or with one of the independent rifle regiments (disbanded totally by June 1944). The possibility also exists that he could have served in combat with some German Wehrmacht unit prior to transferring into the Division "Galicia."   .

Assembled soldiers at a parade ground in Heidelager. (It is believed that they are from the 29th Infantry Regiment).

A young volunteer receiving instructions prior to his military physical. Note the recruiting posters in the background.

A member of the Military Board conferring with two Ukrainian soldiers. Neuhammer, June 1944. Note, however, the contrast in uniforms. Whereas the soldier in the left wears an earlier 'earth grey' uniform with the dark collar, the one in the center (with the cigarette in his mouth) is wearing the latter 1944 uniform.

These soldiers, from the 4th Heavy Company (Battalion and Regiment unknown), were designated to serve as an honor guard for Bayer's funeral. The second and fourth soldiers pictured from the right are armed with the Czech 7.92mm ZB 26/30 "Zbrojovka" (BRNO) Light Machine Gun. Produced by the Czech arms industry before World War II, the BRNO was regarded as one of the finest light machine guns ever produced. During World War II, it was widely utilized by the German Army. A number were issued to the "Galicia" Division and the weapon was utilized on the squad level. This photograph was taken in the Galician capitol city of Lviv in February 1944.

Members of the 4th Heavy Company. Because the soldiers are surrounded by civilians on both sides, are not in military step, and several appear to be speaking to the civilians, they are either enroute to their assembly area from where they will proceed to march to Bayer's funeral or they are returning from Bayer's funeral. Because the three SS-Scharführer's and the SS-Rottenführer pictured in back of the NCO (seen only partially in the front right of the photograph) are wearing the "SS" runes on their collar tabs whereas the other soldiers are wearing only the Galician Lion Patch, undoubtedly, the pictured NCO's are German personnel. The NCO's, however, are also wearing the Galician Lion patch on their lower right sleeve which was the norm.

Mounted on a horse, a section leader leads his troops in Lviv during Bayer's funeral.

Members of Kampfgruppe "Beyersdorff" in Lviv, February 1944. These soldiers are waiting to move out. The pictured rifles are the Kar 98 7.92mm rifles. The rifles, in excellent condition, appear to be new and undoubtedly, were of first issue. The soldier pictured thumbing through the newspaper "L 'vivs'ki Visti" (as well as some of the others) is also carrying an anti-chemical warfare canister. Within this canister was found the GM 30 or GM 38 Gas Mask, each equipped with either an FE 41 or FE 42 anti-gas device which simply was screwed into the bottom part of the GM 30 or 38 Gas Mask. Because the G 38 began to replace the GM 30 in 1938, undoubtedly the G 38 Gas Mask was found within the pictured canisters. As seen, the standard carrier is a corrugated cylindrical metal case with a hinged cover and cotton carrier straps. The canister was usually painted a drab, field gray, or blue gray color. A small booklet with instructions was also inserted into each canister. Of interest to note is the M1935 steel helmet with its swastika decal found on the right side of the helmet. In actuality (excluding a few premier German Waffen-SS units which wore the swastika on the right side of the helmet at the outset of the war), by 1943 the entire Waffen-SS was not authorized to wear the swastika symbol. How these soldiers obtained this type of helmet has never been explained. Former members of Kampfgruppe "Beyersdorff" stated that this helmet was actually issued to them in Heidelager upon their arrival for recruit training. If that is the case, than it shows that the German military system was not thorough – or at the moment there was a lack of helmets – because Galicia's volunteers should never have been issued any helmets with swastika patches.

Civilian volunteers issuing a lunch sack to a departing volunteer.

Civilian volunteers issuing food parcels and other items to members of Kampfgruppe "Beyersdorff." It is believed that the woman walking adjacent the railroad car and momentarily looking downward is Mrs. Ivanna Gardetzka, one of the directors of the Women s Auxiliary Board, a branch found in Galicia's Military Board.

A member of the Military Board conferring with an officer from Kampfgruppe "Beyersdorff." Because the SS runes are worn on the right collar, the SS-Untersturmführer is undoubtedly a German. Of interest is that the officer in the background is wearing a pair of cavalry boots with both the strap and cavalry spurs. Officially, such boots were unauthorized in a non-cavalry unit. But as Nazi Germany's military situation worsened uniformity – always emphasized by military units – began to decline.

Sack lunches, home baked goods, cigarettes, and reading materiel being distributed to the departing soldiers.

Members of the Military Board with an officer and NCO from Kampfgruppe "Beyersdorff." Note the wound badge, Iron Cross, and the Galician Lion Patch worn by the officer.

A civilian volunteer preparing to give out newspapers.

Members of Kampfgruppe "Beyersdorff" outside of Lviv. Note the anoraks and heavy parkas issued to be worn in severe weather. Wool or fur lined, these field grey or tan colored garments were designed with a reversible white camouflage. Some of the soldiers are also wearing heavy wool trousers. Such clothing refutes any charges that Kampfgruppe "Beyersdorff" deployed with insufficient winter clothing.

Divisional Chaplain (Major) Severyn Saprun preparing services for the troops in the town of Am Himmel in the vicinity of the city of Linz, Germany. Note the Luftwaffe officers dress hat. Because there was no official field and dress uniform for the chaplains, the chaplains generally wore the field grey or olive green uniform issued to the troops. However, the "Galicia" Division's chaplains refused to wear the Waffen-SS officers dress hat with its "death's head" (skull and crossbones) insignia. Therefore, in the field, they usually wore the camouflaged battle cap minus its "death's head" insignia. For dress and official functions, a regular Wehrmacht or Luftwaffe dress cap was utilized.

Members of Kampfgruppe "Beyersdorff" on a railway car. The weapon pictured appears to be a German MG 08 Maxim 7.92mm machinegun which was widely utilized in World War I by both ground, naval and air forces. By its position and the standup anti- aircraft rear sight, the weapon was undoubtedly positioned for anti- aircraft usage; however, it could be utilized very effectively in a ground role. Note the hay bundles positioned to the left and right of the machine gun as well as what appears to be woolen blankets lying adjacent to the hay bundle. These items were positioned to protect and comfort those assigned to man the machinegun while enroute to their area-of-operation. The hay was positioned to provide protection both against enemy bullets and the cold wind, and the extra blankets bundled up any soldiers assigned to the position. Later on the hay bundles were utilized for the battlegroup's horses and mules.

OPPOSITE TOP: Members of a local choir performing during a recruitment drive. This photograph, taken in the summer of 1943, was taken outside of Lviv. It is believed to have been taken in the town of Kolomei.

OPPOSITE BOTTOM: Governor Wachter conducting a recruitment drive in the town of Kolomei, Galicia district in early May 1943.

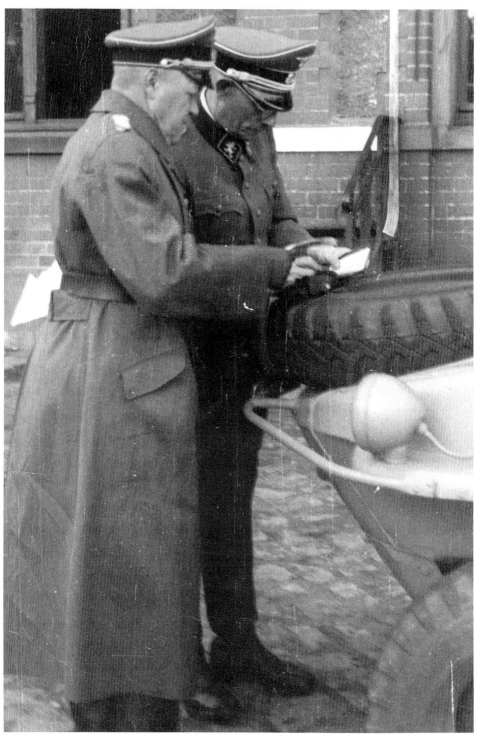

Captain A. Honcharenko (left side) discussing military matters with Captain D. Paliiv (right side) in the spring of 1944 in Neuhammer. Both men are adorned with the high-peaked officers cap and Honcharenko is wearing the olive green field greatcoat. Note the Galician Lion patch on Paliiv's right collar.

Chapter 16: Brody!

ing with armor."[16] Knowing this, the UPA decided to officially warn the Division and even, the 13th Corps. It is not known, however, if 13th Corps Headquarters was warned. But as attested by Ren, UPA's intelligence proved to be totally accurate.

Although the Division was in a secondary position and 6-8 miles behind the main front line, this did not necessarily indicate that it was totally exempt from danger. Aerial attacks, long-range rocket and artillery fires, as well as infiltrators, snipers, saboteurs and enemy agents, all posed a threat. On 9 July, SS-Hauptsturmführer Hans Wagner, who commanded the Artillery Regiments 3rd Battalion, was killed in action. (KIA). It appears SS-Hauptsturmführer Guenther Sparsam assumed command. To ensure the Division was properly dug in, Divisional engineers supervised and assisted the various units with the construction of bunkers, trenches, and communications. The Division's fusiliers were positioned ahead of the Divisions front line east of the Styr River with the mission of screening the Division's front and right flank. And its personnel were so close to the main front that they were the first to actually make contact with the enemy by encountering its patrols and infiltrators.[17]

Exhaustion completely engulfed fusilier Stefan Huk*. Awake for nearly 48 hours, his body screamed for rest. Positioned hours before to occupy an observation post several hundred meters in front of his unit, Stefan was to warn his company by telephone, small arm's fire, or a green night flare of any possible enemy activities to his front, sides and rear.

Stefan had no objections about his assignment and, as a matter of fact, looked forward to it. But when posted, he was told that anywhere between 11 p.m. and midnight, he would be relieved by one or two members of his squad. After being relieved, Stefan would retire to his unit, grab something warm to drink, and catch a good night's sleep. Looking at his watch, Stefan noted it was 3 a.m.; angrily, he swore mentally and wondered for the 1,000th time what had happened to his relief. Feeling a chill, Stefan covered himself with his camouflaged poncho.

Suddenly, the sound of a snapping twig brought Stefan to his full senses. Straining his ears, he listened hard. His eyes searched ahead. Momentarily looking upwards, Stefan noted through the opening of the trees the myriad of stars. He wondered if his mind was playing tricks.

After several minutes, Stefan concluded that probably an animal had caused the noise, and he began to settle down. But there was another sudden scuffle of brush and Stefan instinctively knew that only a two-legged animal could cause this particular sound. He wondered if possibly someone from the Division or fusiliers was ahead. Of course no one was to be out there but then, out here, anything could happen. Continuing to strain his ears, he heard a barely audible voice. Clearly, it was a human voice. Stefan could not make out the language but whoever it was, Stefan hoped they were his comrades.

The sound of a Russian exclamation proved Stefan wrong. Continuing to lie still, Stefan hoped that they would just crawl past him, and pose no problem. But another split-second scuffle directly in front of him verified Stefan's fear that hostile company was heading his way.

Stefan knew they were probers. And one of their duties was to capture someone on guard or in the rear and bring the captive back for interrogation. From a captured man, even a low-ranking soldier, NKVD interrogators could extract much information. They always had methods. Stefan knew that stories of NKVD officers placing a revolver against the side of a man's kneecap and firing a bullet to blow off the kneecap were true. As the screaming man would curl up in agony on the ground among his friends, the NKVD interrogator would turn to the rest and calmly say "Now, I believe you are willing to talk!" And talk they would. Stefan also knew that if he survived such an ordeal, the chance of a later execution or worse, a 20 or 30 year sentence in a Siberian slave labor camp, was virtually guaranteed. Stefan was not going to let them take him. Realizing they were too close for him to just turn around and run, Stefan knew that he would have to take them on by himself. "This is really great," thought Stefan, "the whole Division is in back of me and I've got to do this by myself!"

Estimating that they were no more than fifteen to twenty feet in front, Stefan decided to let them come in, for about five more feet; then, he would throw forward a potato masher stick grenade, spray everything with his MP 38-40, and get the hell out.

Again, he heard a barely audible sound. He almost ceased to breathe as his hands slowly uncapped the aluminum cap of the hollow stick grenade; he felt for his close combat knife and wondered how ironic it was that here the Division had such modern weaponry and, yet, the engagement could end up in a primitive caveman type of struggle. Removing the cap, he slowly pulled its ring, extended his arm to the rear and chucked forward the grenade. The moment he threw it, he covered his helmet with his hands and awaited the blast.

The last thing he heard before the massive blast which seemed to rock the whole world was the Russian shout of "GRENADE!"; within split seconds of the blast, Stefan unleashed a deadly spray of 9mm fire to his front, left and right sides, and again to his front. Emptying the MP's magazine, Stefan leaped to his knees, pulled out his handgun, and emptied that. Grabbing his flare with trembling hands, he fired it also. Then he raced back.

Chapter 16: Brody!

Stefan ran like hell. Flares exploded above him, and another massive explosion was heard to his rear. Fearing that someone on his side might fire and kill him as he ran in, Stefan filled the night air with screams of "DON'T SHOOT! THIS IS STEFAN! I'M COMING IN! DON'T SHOOT, YOU BASTARDS! I'M COMING IN!" Suddenly, a pair of hands grabbed Stefan. Immediately, he saw that it was his officer and NCO. So overwhelmed was Stefan that when he opened his mouth, he could not even talk. Assisted to the rear, Stefan regained his composure.

At the crack of dawn, three dead NKVD police troops and one Soviet regular, who undoubtedly was a scout assisting the NKVD, were found lying to the front and left of where Stefan had laid hours before.

Wednesday, 12 July 1944:
By 12 July, the Division was established in line. Because of a slight reorganization by Army Group North Ukraine, on 8 July, the 13th Corps was transferred to the 1st Panzer Army.[1] Now, the Division was a part of the 1st Panzer Army. Excluding those left behind in Neuhammer and in Europe's various schools, the Division was in place with a strength of 10,400.[2] The Division's three infantry regiments, however, were not in full strength in the sense that each one of the regiments 3rd battalion was left behind in Neuhammer.[3] But in contrast to the other infantry divisions within the 13th Corps (or for that matter within the 1st Panzer Army), the "Galicia" Division was equal and, compared to some of the other 1st Panzer Army and AGNU divisions, actually surpassed their strengths. But when it came to arms and equipment, as General Lange himself noted "the Galician Ukrainians were well armed and equipped."[4]

12 July was spent as the other days – further digging in and training as best as possible. But as the night sky engulfed the Division, and its men settled dawn for rest, the following day would begin a new chapter in the Divisions history.

Thursday, 13 July:
Initially, Konev had planned to strike on 14 July in the direction of Rava-Russka. But because Hitler allowed the 4th Panzer Army's 42nd Corps to retire from a minor bulge jutting towards Torchyn (a town approximately 52 miles north of Brody), to shorten the front line, Konev, when informed of the German move, immediately moved to exploit the situation.[1]

Hoping to shatter the German withdrawal and thus create an opening for the 1st Ukrainian Front's tank armies, Konev ordered Gordov's 3rd Guards Army to pursue, strike, and overrun the withdrawing force to achieve a massive disruption.

But because Gordov's army moved inefficiently, the 42nd Corps was able to halt in place and repulse the 3rd Guards thrust.

Yet, 3rd Guards continued to press forward. By mid-day, a small sector of the 42nd Corps' front line began to collapse, and the 46th Panzer Corps 291st "Elk" Infantry Division, defending a sector adjacent to the 42nd Corps right (southern) flank, was massively struck.[2] By mid-day, a small sector of the 42nd and 46th Corps' front line began to collapse.

To rescue the situation, the 16th and 17th Panzer Divisions moved immediately in counterattack. But heavy Soviet air attacks slowed all movement. From their secondary positions, the Division's troops could hear the distant battle and they noted the intensified enemy air activity as Soviet aircraft flew over their positions to and from their missions; throughout the day, 48-year-old Waffen-Obersturmführer Julian Temnyk, who served as the anti-aircraft battalion's Chief Battery Officer, along with the Division's anti-aircraft gunners, repeatedly engaged the aerial threat. Sensing an upcoming danger, Myhailo Tomash field stripped and thoroughly lubricated his own MG42 and an MG 34 which Stepan Kolko* had requisitioned earlier at Ozhydiv.

But as Myhailo worked on his two machine guns, at that very moment in the darkening late evening hours of 13 July, elements of the 336th and 322nd Rifle Divisions from within the 15th Soviet Rifle Corps, 60th Army, began to quietly occupy their pre-designated attack positions in preparation for a major thrust.[3] And approximately 1.5 to 2 miles behind them, the 1st Ukrainian Front's tanks and independent artillery units began to occupy attack positions in preparation for their attack.

Friday, 14 July:
Taking a risk, Konev moved Putkov's 13th Army into the weak spot and immediately, 13th Army began to exploit the 3rd Guard's initial minor gain. Following a bitter fight, by the end of the day the town of Horokhiv (north of Brody and within the first German line of defense), fell to Putkov; yet, the 13th Army, on account of tough resistance and counterattacks, was not able to move rapidly into the second line of defense.

Determined to break out towards Rava-Russka, and to possibly relieve some of the pressure against the attacking Soviet forces north of Brody, the Soviet 38th and 60th Armies began to press forward that same morning south of Brody in the early hours of approximately 4 to 5 a.m.[1] But their attempt was quickly terminated by a heavy night rain and thick fog which tremendously reduced visibility. Unable to operate in such conditions, the offensive south of Brody was halted for the moment. Excluding minor activities on the part of several units, all other movement was halted as well.

Simultaneously, that same morning, as the 38th and 60th Armies pressed forward, the Division's 30th Infantry Regiment was ordered to advance southward toward the vicinity of Pidhirtsi, an area west of the Soviet 60th Army.[2] To this day, it has never been officially explained why the 30th Regiment alone was dispatched, or what was the logic behind this. But undoubtedly, the 30th's relocation was a result of the early morning Soviet activities, along with German needs to reinforce their front south of Brody.[3]

North of Brody, the 4th Panzer Army's right wing began to collapse. As verified by Soviet chronicles, the 291st "Elk" Division was so massively struck by Putkov's 13th, by elements of the 3rd Guards and by air attacks, that, "established on the edge of the defense, [the 291st] was unsuccessful in extraditing itself from its first positions and was completely routed."[4]

Following the lifting of the rain and fog, Konev immediately resumed the offensive previously canceled south of Brody as a result of the inclement weather. After a massive artillery and air attack, which commenced at approximately 2:30 p.m.,[5] Moskalenko's 38th and Kurochkin's 60th Armies attacked at 4 p.m. The two armies advanced on a front of almost 10 miles and simultaneously attacked the 48th Panzer Corps' northern sector. 48th Panzer Corps' northern sector, and the 13th Corps' southern sector. 48th Panzer Corps' 357th Infantry Division (with a number "3" rating), and the 13th Corps' 349th Infantry Division (with a number "2" rating), were especially hard pressed.[6] Continuing to press forward in the face of stiff resistance, by the end of the day, across a front of approximately 10 miles, they achieved minor – but critical – penetrations from 1 to 5 miles. To counter the 38th and 60th Armies' advances, and to bolster AGNU's front south of Brody, the 1st Panzer Army committed its tactical reserve. This reserve consisted of the 1st and 8th Panzer Divisions (now within the 48th Panzer Corps), and the 14th "Galizien" Division.[7] All three divisions were to counterattack.

Although the "Galicia" Division was notified in the late hours of 14 July, its 30th Infantry Regiment was already on the move. By now, its mission was defined: it was to advance southward from Kadlubytsi towards Pidhirtsi's heights and to a point approximately 6 miles east of Sasiv. Once south of Sasiv and the Buh River, the regiment would immediately strike southeastward toward Koltiw to seal the 60th Army's penetration.

Galicia Division

Commanded by SS-Obersturmbannführer Forstreuter, the 30th Infantry Regiment consisted of a regimental staff, Klokker's 1st and Wittenmayer's 2nd Battalion and the 3rd Battalions Heavy 13th Company.[8] Accompanied by the 2nd Artillery Battalion and supported by various signal, engineer, anti-aircraft and support personnel, its entire strength (along with the attaches), stood at 1903.[9] Excluding the regimental staff of 12 officers (6 of whom were Ukrainian), the Battalion staffs with 4 officers (3 of whom were German), and the 13th Company's 3 officers (one of whom was a German), each of the line companies only had one or two officers. The lower ranking officers were primarily Ukrainians from Galicia.[10] A total of 34 officers (14 German) and 116 NCOs (35 German], were found within the regiment.[11]

Leading the way was the regiment's 2nd Battalion. Utilizing the region's secondary roads, the battalion's soldiers passed through villages and farms and encountered friendly civilians. Because 14 July was an exceptionally hot day, with the sun blazing upon the heavily laden soldiers, the cool water and milk offered by a supportive populace refreshed the regiment's soldiers both physically and spiritually. Until now, all had gone well. By mid-day, the 30th had reached Pidhirtsi. Except for the distant rumbling of the war's battles, it actually seemed as if the 30th was on an outing. But not for long.

As it departed from Pidhirtsi and advanced in a southeasterly direction enroute to Sasiv, the 30th Regiment encountered a stream of disorganized and demoralized German troops retreating westward. As Galicia's volunteers marched alongside the retreating mass, it seemed as though the once mighty and proud Wehrmacht was now on its deathbed.

Here and there, men carried stretchers loaded with the wounded; others walked with bandages around their heads. Many no longer carried weapons. Amongst the masses, lone trucks and motorcycles ambled slowly. As the retreating mass surged westward in hopes of escaping the Soviet onslaught, their naked eyes clearly betrayed the weary stare of defeat and amongst them voices exclaimed "Alles ist kaput!"[12]

From the moment the Galician troops encountered the retreating Germans, it was immediately apparent that the Division's troops were far more superbly armed and equipped than those of the Wehrmacht. As Peter Lehmann, a Galician of German ancestry, pressed forward alongside the retreating troops, he noted not only that the Germans lacked the superb camouflage gear worn by "Galicia's" troops, but that the Division's arms and equipment was of a higher quality than those possessed by the Wehrmacht. Lehmann even noted the anti-aircraft fold-down sight

Chapter 16: Brody!

on his MG42, something which none of the retreating German machinegunners possessed on their MG42s.

Continuing to advance southeast, the Division's troops encountered the leading vanguard of the Soviet thrust. It has never been properly established whether the 30th's leading vanguards encountered the Soviet front's Combat Reconnaissance Patrols, their Forward Security, or what. But because it is known that contact was minimal and the Soviet force, consisting of only a handful of tanks and mechanized troops, was repulsed, the 30th undoubtedly encountered Konev's 1st Ukrainian Front's scout/reconnaissance. Knowing that the enemy thrust needed to be repulsed, and that with each passing moment the enemy was gaining in strength, the 30th Regiment hastened preparations for its attack. As the regiment's soldiers marched forward and readied for action, they, as well as all those within the Division, would soon experience the true meaning of the word Armageddon.

Flying in at tree-top level, Ilyushin aircraft bombed, strafed, and rocketed the columns of the 30th Regiment. Years later, Ostap Veryn would recall how a perfectly intact head, with its helmet strapped firmly in place, flew past him like a soccer hall. Another casualty, minus both legs, sat calmly in the middle of a road as if nothing had happened. When a medic ran up, the wounded man refused his assistance, picked up his MP 38/40, placed its barrel into his mouth, and pulled the trigger.

Again, at tree-top level, Ilyushins flew in. But this time, as the planes surged in, they were met by a fusillade of small-arms and machinegun fire. A four-barrelled 20mm anti-aircraft gun swung into action, its red-hot barrels filling the sky with tracer rounds as the weapon unleashed hundreds of rounds of ammunition.

The noise was overwhelming. The shouts of orders, the screams of men, the piercing mechanical shrieks of incoming aircraft engines combined with the constant chatter of machineguns, small-arms fire and explosions created a scene reminiscent of Dante's Inferno. Within this hellish inferno, vehicles and wagons burned, terrified horses galloped past the dead and dying, and explosions shook the ground. Yet, amidst this carnage, soldiers stood with MG34's, MG42's, submachine guns and rifles. Aiming their weapons at the incoming "flying tanks," Galicia's Iron Lions struck back. Another explosion ripped one of the 1st Battalion's light ammunition trucks into pieces. As thousands of sparks flew skyward, the devastating explosion vaporized its driver. With deep sorrow, regimental Chaplain Josef Kladochnyi administered the last rites to the dying.

In the evening hours of 14 July, the 2nd Battalion reached the so-called 'Dark Forest' between the villages of Lukavets', Kryhiv and Koltiw, where, the battalion encountered a small group of Wehrmacht soldiers led by an officer. Whether this was a coordinated link-up or just happened to be a chance encounter has never been explained and will probably never be known. But in response to inquiries of "where is the Bolshevik?" the 2nd Battalion's soldiers received the reply: "Everywhere!" Needless to say, such a response brought home the reality of the situation. To ensure that he was ready for instant action, Lehmann once again lifted the feed tray of his MG42 upwards to ensure that no sand or debris was within the chamber to cause the weapon to jam. Because the 30th Infantry Regiment's 2nd Battalion became the Division's first unit to reach the damaged front near Koltiw, the 2nd has rightfully gone down as being the first unit to reach the front.

From the vicinity of Koltiw to a point slightly northeastward towards Lukavets' the 2nd Battalion's companies occupied such an area: Waffen-Obersturmführer Myroslav Malets'kyi's 7th company, closest to Kryhiv, covered the battalion's right flank; Waffen-Obersturmführer Iuryniak's 5th Company covered the center; Waffen- Obersturmführer Petro Sumarokiv's 6th Company covered the left flank and the road which ran from Lukavets' to Peniaky; and Waffen-Obersturmführer Myhailo Makarevych's 8th Company, with its heavy weapons systems, centered itself in the rear between the 7th and 5th Company's.[13]

For the moment, the 2nd Battalion's left (northern) flank was not covered. But ahead of the battalion stood a force of 40 Wehrmacht soldiers commanded by a 1st Lieutenant. Shortly after 6th Company occupied its position at daybreak, this group of German soldiers, headed by their lieutenant, decided to abandon their positions and retire westward. Stumbling into the 6th Company, the officer informed Sumarokiv that approximately two miles in front of his company, a sizable Soviet force, supported with three T-34's, was cautiously approaching his position.

To this day, it has never been properly explained whether the 2nd Battalion occupied a defensive position or what possibly could have been an assault position prior to an attack on Koltiw. Undoubtedly, in the period of 13-15 July, some confusion did exist and possibly neither the 2nd Battalion's leadership, nor Divisional headquarters, nor 13th Corps, nor even AGNU knew what was fully transpiring in Koltiw's vicinity. Because on 14 July the soon to be known "Koltiw Corridor" was still in the process of being expanded by Soviet forces, 13th Corps or AGNU could have ordered a series of defensive positions constructed in the vicinity of Koltiw to contain and prevent Soviet forces from expanding the "corridor" into a major breakout. And once sufficient firepower could have been brought down into the "corridor," a massive destruction of enemy armor and personnel would have ensued. But if the 2nd Battalion was momentarily utilizing the area as an assault position prior to counterattacking into the corridor, cover from ground and aerial observation was of essence. This explains why a wooded area was chosen.

Chapter 16: Brody!

Saturday, 15 July:

Between the hours of 5 and 7 a.m., the 30th Regiment's 1st Battalion appeared; immediately, 1st Battalion occupied an area east of Sasiv facing Koltiw almost adjacent (but slightly south), of the 2nd Battalion's right flank. As previously experienced by the 2nd Battalion, the 1st Battalion found few pre-established Wehrmacht defensive positions; however, several German NCOs and one officer did officially hand over the area to be defended to the 1st Battalion's command.

1st Battalion established itself in the following manner: Waffen-Obersturmführer's Bohdan Pidhainy's 3rd Company, located to the left of Koltiw, covered the battalion's left flank and the road which ran from Koltiw to Sasiv; Waffen-Obersturmführer Berezovs'kyi's 2nd Company, as well as the battalion's 1st Company, commanded by Waffen-Obersturmführer Rozanetz, occupied positions extending towards the 2nd Battalion. The battalion's 4th "Heavy" Company, commanded by Waffen-Obersturmführer Pospilovs'kyi, provided one platoon to each of the 1st Battalion's three line companies. To ensure proper control, Pidhainy positioned himself in Bohdan Tarnawsky's 1st Platoon which commanded the best view. Amongst the Ukrainians were also found a handful of surviving Wehrmacht personnel left over from the previous day's battle. And directly ahead of 1st Battalion stood the village of Koltiw, now occupied by Soviet armor accompanying the 60th Army's 15th Rifle Corps.

What especially made the situation difficult for the 30th's troops was that there was very little knowledge about enemy strengths, dispositions, and possible intents; as well, neither Heike, nor the regimental commander, had any time to conduct a proper route reconnaissance and terrain study. And enroute to Koltiw's vicinity the 30th Regiment (already understrength to begin with), suffered some casualties from enemy air. But there would be no time to lament these circumstances.

Following the penetration of the 349th German Infantry Division's right and the 357th Infantry Division's left wings, the 15th Rifle Corps moved the bulk of its strength forward to continue a strong momentum. After a short but intense artillery preparation, at approximately 8:30 a.m., the 60th Army's entire 15th Rifle Corps, commanded by Major-General Petr Bakulovich Tert'ishni, attacked.[1] And as Tert'ishni's rifle corps surged forward, its 336th Rifle Division suddenly encountered the "Galicia" Division's 30th Infantry Regiment in the vicinity of Kryhiv and Lia Oshovishcha adjacent to Koltiw.[2]

Commanded by Colonel Mikhail A. Ignachev, the 336th Rifle Division was a battle experienced division in full strength. Prior to the 336th's advance, Colonel Ignachev conferred with his divisional Chief of Staff, Lieutenant-Colonel Andrei D.

Nikitan, about the critical importance of a successful attack. To ensure success, it was agreed that in the upcoming attack, in addition to utilizing all three of the 336th's Division's 1128th, 1130th, 1132nd Infantry Regiments, and the 336th's entire 909th Artillery Regiment, armor support from Rybalko's 3rd Guards Tank Army, as well as additional firepower from the 1st Ukrainian Front's independent artillery, rocket, and air units, would support the 336th Division's attack. In all, the 336th possessed a total of 373 artillery pieces and heavy mortars.[3]

Because on the previous day, the Soviets had only created a gap in the German line, and they were fully aware that speed and power was of essence to achieve a successful breakout both north and south of Brody, the Soviets struck hard.

"HURRAH!!! POBEDA!!! HURRAH!!!" Ripping into the 2nd Battalion, the 336th's regiments were determined to expand the gap. Malets'kyi's 7th Company was especially hard pressed. To assist the 7th, Makarevych ordered his 8th Company's PAK and mortar gunners to engage those Soviets advancing toward the 7th Company. Totally disregarding the explosions of numerous hand grenades, gunfire, and even their own artillery and mortar fire, the Soviets continued to surge forward. Determined to hold, Malets'kyi did the unexpected – he counterattacked! Despite the heavier odds, 7th Company was not only holding its own but actually began to repulse the attacking Soviets.

Realizing that their attack was not faring well, the Soviets shifted the focus of their effort upon the 5th and 8th Companies. 7th Company continued to be engaged, but by late morning, both the 5th and 8th Companies were under tremendous pressure as well.

But Soviet efforts to overrun the two companies proved unproductive. Skillfully directing the 8th's weapon systems to its maximum, Makarevych continued to inflict grave losses upon the advancing foe.

Despite their losses, the red mass continued to surge forward. Observing that the advancing Soviets had begun to surge through and approach the 8th Company's position, and realizing that if his company was overrun, then the entire battalion's critical weapons systems would be lost, Makarevych grabbed an MG42 and charged forward. Singlehandedly, he mowed down large numbers of the attackers. Exhausting his ammunition, the giant warrior stood up and swung his machinegun like a club. Only when he was repeatedly shot and bayonetted did Makarevych go down.

During this time, Petro Sumarokiv's 6th Company remained unengaged. Excluding some personnel dispensed to assist the other companies, the 6th had not fought. But this was not to be the case for long.

Chapter 16: Brody!

In an attempt to secure the main road and possibly outflank the 2nd Battalion from the left, the Soviets cautiously probed their way forward. Utilizing the several T-34 tanks previously reported, a small Soviet infantry force approached the 6th Company. But they failed to spot the company's well-camouflaged and concealed positions. Detaching itself from the probing force, one of the three tanks moved slightly forward, stopped, and began to observe.

Undoubtedly, its crew felt no pain as the 6th grenadiers turned the steel hulk into a ragging inferno. Well-placed rifle shots dropped Soviet infantrymen and from a well-concealed position, Lehmann unleashed short, but deadly, bursts of machinegun-fire. Although the communist force withdrew, they soon returned in full strength. By mid-day, the entire 2nd (and 1st Battalions) were fully engaged, and more enemy tanks appeared.

With smoke protruding from the rear of its engine compartment, the T34 slowed to a crawl. But not for long. As it crawled, the explosion of a hand-thrown grenade blew away a section of the tank's front right track and immediately, the disabled tank halted sideways in front of the men. Suddenly, the turret's hatch popped open, and from within, emerged a helmeted, bearded trooper with a Ppsh 41 submachinegun in hand. Exposed from the waist up, he shouted "SMERT FASHISTAM!" and unleashed a long fusillade of 7.62mm rounds. As he sprayed, the other turret's hatch flung open, and a dark-skinned Asiatic tanker popped out, flinging a grenade as far as he could. Its explosion immediately ripped the life out of two Galician troopers lying on the ground. Miraculously, a third trooper, standing upright, survived the blast. Firing his MP 38/40 from waist-high level, the Ukrainian NCO attempted to silence the turret's tankers. But before he could raise his 9mm fire further upwards, the Ppsh 41 gunner released a salvo of hot rounds which terminated the NCO's life.

"HURRAH! STALIN!" "RATATATATATA!!!" Another burst. And another dead Ukrainian NCO. "HURRAH!" "RATATATATATA!!!" A long burst silenced two more. Running out of ammunition, the Red gunner threw down his Ppsh into the turret and accepted from someone inside the tank a previously captured German MP 38/40. Raising the weapon to his shoulder, the Red tanker took aim and sprayed 16-year-old Ihor Borak who, with an anti-armor hand grenade, had disregarded his German NCO's shouts to stay under cover and had raced forward to get closer to the tank. The son of parents slaughtered by NKVD terrorists in 1941, Ihor left behind a 5-year-old sister, Marichka, in Lviv's orphanage.

Ihor's NCO swore. "GODDAMN IT! GODDAMN IT! WHY DIDN'T HE LISTEN TO ORDERS?" To ensure that no one else would attempt such a feat, he immediately shouted "NOW! EVERYONE! STAY DOWN! STAY CALM!" Russian shouts of "YOU GALICIAN BOURGEOISE PIGS!" intermingled with the gunfire. Standing on the commander's seat inside the tank with the rest of his body lying on the turret, the tanker had good vision and was difficult to engage; his counterpart, who was now behind the turret, only popped up now and then to fire a handgun or fling a hand grenade.

"VAROOOM!" Another explosion. Men cried out for help. Others screamed. As the constant chatter of machinegun fire and the screams of "HURRAH! STALIN! HURRAH! DEATH! DEATH! DEATH!!!" filled the air, a trooper, who could take no more, stood up; instantly, hot slugs cut him down. "GODDAMN IT!" shouted the German NCO "STAY DOWN!" "EVERYONE!" "NOW!" Someone shouted "GOD!" PLEASE, HELP US!" But to these words the NCO only replied "HE WON'T HELP YOU! NO SON-OF-A-BITCH WILL HELP YOU! SO STAY DOWN! STAY DOWN!" Russian shouts of "DEATH! DEATH! YOU GALICIAN DOGS!" again intermingled with gunfire.

Ivan Wosniak could take no more. Crawling rapidly to the rear for at least 100 meters, he then stood up and circled wide. As he approached the edge of the clearing, he crawled again. Reaching the clearing, Wosniak slightly parted the brush and surveyed the scene.

He saw the front of the tank, and its two gunners. One was lying partly on top of the turret, while the other was squatted behind it. Wosniak realized, however, that they were some distance away. Taking aim, he carefully sighted.

Observing the rules for a long shot, Wosniak first aimed at the one firing from the top of the turret. Exhaling half of his breath, he slowly squeezed. "CRAACK!" Wosniak's KAR 98 rifle recoiled into his shoulder. Without thinking, he ejected the spent round, slammed in a fresh one, took aim at the Asiatic and fired. Slamming in another round, Wosniak saw the commander standing fully upright, his hands clutching his face. Taking a quick but careful aim at his heart-and-lung-area, Wosniak, who himself was now standing fully upright, squeezed the trigger. The commander collapsed into the interior of the tank. Squatting back down, Wosniak removed his remaining rounds and inserted a fresh five-round clip into his rifle. As he reloaded, he noted an eerie silence.

But not for long. As the smoldering fire turned into a blazing inferno, an internal explosion tore the tank's rear deck apart. As flames began to consume the iron monster, a lone figure suddenly emerged from within. Shouting "COMRADES! BROTHERS! TAKE ME!" the man stood on the tank's turret with his arms extended upwards. He pleaded for mercy.

Standing up, Wosniak placed his rifles sights on the tanker's heart and lungs. "God? Can I do it?" As he pondered, the German NCO's shouts of "KILL HIM! KILL HIM! NOW! KILL THE BASTARD! NOW!" filled the air. Wosniak held

Chapter 16: Brody!

his breath, and his aim. "COMRADES! PLEASE!" "KILL HIM!" "COMRADES! PLEASE!" "KILL HIM!" "COMRADES! PLEASE!" "NOW! GODDAMN IT! KILL HIM! KILL THAT BASTARD! NOW! NOW! NOW!"

Madness reigned in the air. Sweat poured out of every pore. Wosniak felt hot...cold...sick...angry...sorry...resentful...and hurt. As the insane screams of "KILL! KILL!" combined with "COMRADES! PLEASE! PLEASE!" filled the air, Wosniak did not know what to do.

But he did not have to wait long. Within seconds, another internal explosion rocked the tank, shot a sheet of flame upward, and engulfed the tanker in a ball of flame. Hearing his screams – and imagining his pain – Wosniak fired. Lowering his rifle, Wosniak looked upon the carnage. A burning tank, its Asiatic crewman lying dead beside it. Here and there, lay dead Galician troops. Disgusted, Wosniak threw down his rifle. He thought of his dead friends. And he thought of what he had just done. Putting his face in his hands, he broke down and wept.

As the Division's two battalions fought to hold their positions, the 4th Panzer Army's right wing began to collapse. So massively was the 291st "Elk" Infantry struck by Putkov's 13th, elements of the 3rd Guards Army and air attacks, that its fighting effectiveness ceased to exist. The situation became especially acute when earlier on the 15th, Konev committed the bulk of the 1st Guards Tank Army to further exploit the initial gains and thus achieve a breakout. To ensure success, north of Horokhiv, in the vicinity of Volodymyr-Volynski, one of the 1st Guards Tank Army's brigades – the 1st Guards Tank Brigade – conducted a successful diversion. After drawing the bulk of the 16th and 17th Panzer Divisions into its sector, the brunt of the 1st Guards Tank Army immediately attacked further south and penetrated the front between Horokhiv and the northern perimeter of the 13th Corps.[4] By now, it was apparent that a major Soviet breakout was in the process of developing north of Brody.

On the 15th, General Hermann Balck's 1st and 8th Panzer Divisions counter-attacked south of Brody.[5] Ripping into Moskalenko's 38th Army, assault groups from both the 1st Panzer and elements of the 8th Panzer not only halted the Soviet thrust in the vicinity of Oliiv (approximately 20 miles northwest of Ternopil), but actually began to repulse the 38th.[6] North of Oliiv, however, the brunt of the 8th Panzer failed to obey its movement orders to move directly through a forest on a pre-established and rehearsed route. Totally disregarding Balck's specific orders forbidding any mass troop movements on any road outside of a forested area, the 8th's divisional commander decided to save time by moving in the open. Observed in the open, the 8th Panzer was immediately pounced on by Krasovskiy's air force.[7]

Galicia Division

By the end of the day, nearly 2,000 sorties were directed against the 8th Panzer.[8] As Balck raged in fury, the 8th went up in flames, while Kurochkin's 60th Army's 15th Rifle Corps, supported by tanks, artillery and air strikes, created a small "corridor" (approximately 18 miles south of Brody) up to 10.5 miles in depth (18 km's) and about 2.5 to 3.5 miles (4-6 km's) in width in the vicinity of Koltiw and Trostianets'.[9]

But unlike the breach created north of Brody, the Soviet "corridor" created in Koltiw was the only one which had breached the second German defensive line. Sensing a major breakout could possibly be achieved in Koltiw's vicinity, Konev personally re-established himself in Kurochkin's advanced command post, located in what was now referred to as the "Koltiw corridor."[10] Though a brave move, Konev's decision was a risky one because artillery and mortar shells rained all around Kurochkin's forward command post.

Under tremendous pressure, the 48th Panzer Corps' northern sector (or left flank, if facing eastward), began to collapse. If not contained, the Soviet breakthrough would not only achieve operational depth but simultaneously, could endanger the 13th Corps by encirclement. Realizing this, 13th Corps understood that it was now largely up to them to make a strong effort to halt the Soviet thrust. Since 13 Corps could not remove any of its front line forces, and its right flank was already embroiled in the conflict, the Corps' effort would have to be undertaken by its only reserve – the 14th Waffen-SS.[11]

As the Soviets were attempting to break through the German defense, and Balck's panzer divisions were counter-attacking, and the "Galicia" Division (minus its 30th Regiment) was moving towards the "Koltiw corridor,' Konev concluded that although some success had been achieved, overall, his frontal attacks were faring badly.[12] To rectify the situation and achieve the desired breakthrough, Konev needed an immediate exploitation. Realizing the keys to a successful exploitation are speed, pressure, and audacity, Konev, in the evening hours of 15 July,[13] decided to commit both the 3rd Guards Tank and 4th Tank Armies into Koltiw's "corridor" during the same time the "corridor's" flanks were being pressured by AGNU's counterattacking reserve forces. Konev's decision to achieve operational depth by conducting this action is interesting because this was the only time throughout the entire German-Soviet War of 1941-45 that such a move was made.[14]

In retrospect, however, Konev's decision was sound. Although it involved a tremendous amount of risk, in every sense the decision ideally met the situation. Because AGNU had committed the bulk of its reserves against the Soviet forces threatening to break through both north and south of Brody (but especially in the

Chapter 16: Brody!

area of the Koltiw "corridor"), the Germans lacked sufficient forces to defend their depth. Konev also knew that the German panzer divisions had minimal armored strengths. When informed that the 8th Panzer was massively struck, the 1st Ukrainian Front's commander concluded that overwhelming odds moving rapidly could barrel their way through. With Konev's decision to commit armor into the "corridor" to achieve a breakthrough, the beginning of the end of AGNU was ensured.

Indeed, Konev's decision was risky. To begin with, Kurochkin's 60th Army had only partially succeeded in creating a breakout. Against a number of disorganized weak German units and the "Galicia" Division's two battalions with its minimal attached support, the 60th had encountered very stiff resistance, so fierce that years later, General Lashchenko would recall how "inserted fresh forces from the enemy's depth organized a strong defense against the breakout forces."[15] Continuing on, the former 322nd Divisional Staff officer also recalled how "the enemy was retaining [holding on to] his position in the vicinity of Koltiw. The German enemy established a threat and menaced the flanks of the 3rd Guards' Tank Army and our 15th Rifle Corps."[16]

Although Lashchenko does not cite specifically which enemy forces were offering stiff resistance and threatening the flanks, one of the key units participating in this action was the Division's 30th Regiment.

By the evening hours of 15 July, Koltiw was fully ablaze. Throughout the entire night, flames rose hundreds of feet upward, creating a massive eerie glow which lit up the countryside for miles around. Not one building remained intact. Among the crackle of burning wood and collapsing fiery walls lay Koltiw's civilians who earlier, had failed to flee. Yet the battle was far from over. Throughout the night, Soviet shouts of "HURRAH!!!" constantly intermingled with Ukrainian screams of "SLAVA!!!" along with the constant deafening roar of incoming shells, explosions, gunfire and clanking sounds of armor.

Sunday, 16 July:
3 a.m. Meeting with Konev, Rybalko personally requested from Konev authorization to commit his 3rd Guards Tank Army into the corridor.[1] Although Kurochkin's 60th Army and a small part of the 3rd Guards Tank Army were still battling to expand the corridor's penetration, and the corridor itself was not wide enough for a massive thrust, Konev authorized the remainder of the 3rd Guards Tank to advance forward. To ensure success, that same morning Konev also ordered Baranov's cavalry-mechanized group to advance through Putkov's 13th Army. Once achieved, Baranov's force was to strike southwest towards Derevliany, a town approximately 30 miles west of Brody. If successfully accomplished, Baranov's group would not

only further disrupt the German defense but most importantly, would deny AGNU commanders the ability to reinforce the Brody front. And in the event of a German withdrawal, Baranov's group would bar the way.

Driving through the corridor in a single column, leading elements of Rybalko's armored strength began to exit out into open terrain. Clearly, it was becoming apparent that if this corridor adjacent to the 13th Corps southern sector was not sealed, and the breach developing in the 46th Panzer Corps (north and adjacent to the 13 Corps where earlier Konev had inserted the 1st Guards Tank Army and Baranov's cavalry-mechanized group) was not plugged, massive Soviet forces would pour through and encircle the 13th Corps from behind. To avert such a threat, and to prevent further Soviet advances, AGNU's high command, fully aware of the fact that it was in no position at this time to conduct a major withdrawal, renewed its attempts to seal the corridors, but especially the one south of Brody. If successful, a renewed attempt would stop the 1st Ukrainian Front's advances, isolate Rybalko's tankers, upset Konev's plan, and buy time for the German defense.

The moment the 30th Infantry Regiment moved on 14 July, the remainder of the Division was placed on full alert. On the 16th, the Division's 29th and 31st Infantry Regiments received orders to link up and assist the 30th.[2]

To seal the corridor once and for all, German forces would strike the corridor at its southern sector. Simultaneously, the "Galicia" Division's main mission was to strike the corridor's northern boundary, penetrate it, and establish a blocking position east and southeast of Sasiv to deny the enemy further access into the Sasiv Valley and AGNU's rear. To accomplish this, piece-meal regimental attacks would no longer be carried out; rather, the entire Division would be utilized. And as the Division advanced forward to counter the Soviet attack, it advanced against "a mass phalanx of [Soviet] tanks, attack aircraft and dive bombers."[3]

From the north, the 31st Regiment began to conduct a forced tactical march of approximately 15 miles southeastward through Turie, Sokolivka, and Oles'ko into quickly designated assembly areas south of Pidhirtsi. The 29th Regiment[4] was to move rapidly from Yaseniv to an area west of Maidan. Along with the regiments, all of the Division's units would advance southeastward. Because the remainder of the 13th Corps was on the line and could not move, the effort to penetrate into the expanding corridor from the north to seal it would be accomplished primarily by the Division. Air support was again promised, but everyone knew that the Luftwaffe could not be counted upon.

The moment the Division moved, Soviet aircraft again pounced upon the regiments.[5] Simultaneously, the 29th Regiment, enroute to Maidan, encountered enemy tanks for the first time. In response, the Division's anti-aircraft units poured massive amounts of firepower into the skies. On this day, anti-aircraft batteries 3 and 7, under Waffen-Sturmbannführer Myhailo Freithariv, a former participant in Ukraine's 1918-21 War of Liberation, recorded their first kills. As flaming aircraft and dead parachutists plummeted downward, other ground troops were drawn into a battle with Soviet armor.[6] Never would Yaroslav Smyl* forget the terrifying noise of clanking armor, and the clang of metal against metal as fired rounds from PAK anti-tank guns and panzerfausts slammed into the 6th and 7th Guards Tank Corps' and the 9th Mechanized Corps found in Rybalko's 3rd Guards Tank Army. And Waffen-Hauptsturmführer Ostap Chuchkevych, who commanded the Division's Independent 14th Anti-Tank Company attached to the 29th Regiment, displayed exceptionally strong, and courageous, leadership. Repeatedly, Chuchkevych hurled himself into tough situations and under his personal guidance, enemy armor began to burn. For his gallantry, he was later awarded the Iron Cross 1st Class.

Under such adverse conditions, and steadily taking casualties, the men arrived into their assembly areas. Between 6 and 7 p.m., in a heavy downpour which for the moment quieted the front, the 29th and 31st Infantry Regiments prepared for their attack. As for the 30th Regiment, hours earlier Freitag ordered Forstreuter's battered 30th to withdraw approximately 3 miles to the northwest of Koltiw, behind the Buh River's northern bank in the vicinity of Ruda-Koltivskaia for immediate reorganizational and resupply purposes.[7] Outnumbered at least 5 to 1, and against superior firepower, the 30th's attempts to contain the Soviet thrust and seal the enemy corridor had failed. It is important to note, however, that certain individual companies did succeed in containing – and delaying – 15th Rifle Corps' attack. But attempts to totally contain the Soviet thrust failed as the 30th Regiments artillery and communication support diminished, and German air support was unavailable.[8]

As the 30th withdrew, retiring from the battle, the regiment left a number of its dead behind. From its leadership, such losses were recorded – 1st Battalion: Rozanetz (1st Co.), killed; Berezovs'kyi (2nd Co.), killed; Pospilovs'kyi (4th Co.), killed; Pidhanyi, who commanded the 3rd Company, as well as his executive and assistant commander, NCO Bohdan Tarnawsky, were both wounded. From the 2nd Battalion, such losses were noted: Iuryniak (5th Co.), missing; Sumarokiv, (6th Co.), who, wounded in the arm, refused evacuation and following first-aid treatment, continued to lead; Malets'kyi, (7th Co.), along with his senior German NCO, Rehn, were both wounded and evacuated; and Makarevych (8th Co.), was wounded and captured.[9] But by no means would the 30th's time in hell be over. Once reconstituted to a desired level of combat effectiveness, the 30th would go in again. But for now, it would serve as a Divisional "reserve."[10]

His MG42 red hot, with its belt containing no more then 20 rounds of 7.92mm ammunition, Peter Lehmann raced uphill to the remains of what had once been a building. Reaching the ruins of a wall heavily pockmarked with holes from tank, artillery, and heavy machine-gun fire, Lehmann stopped besides its smoldering wall. He immediately noted the dead lying around. Exhausted and covered with sweat, the grenadier knelt down to rest. This way, he would pose much less of a target.

But the moment he looked downrange, he spotted Red troops pouring into the ruins of the once flourishing town of Koltiw. "Shit!" thought Lehmann, "it's like an army of ants!" The sole survivor of what was once a proud platoon in the 30th Infantry Regiment's 2nd Battalion's 6th Company, Lehmann knew he had to move. Although the 30th Regiment was supposedly in the process of withdrawing across the Buh between Sasiv and Koltiw for reorganizational purposes, nothing here resembled what was perceived earlier by many as to be an easy withdrawal. Since the terrible morning of 15 July when the 30th had advanced into the Soviet thrust, or perhaps when the Soviets had advanced into the Galician thrust – or both had thrust into each other – "Shit!" thought Lehmann "what difference did it really make?" Lehmann was fighting.

Running along the side of the blazing building toward what remained of its rear, Lehmann turned and immediately came face-to-face with an exceptionally well-armed and equipped three man Soviet mortar team. Lehmann dropped all three. But he took no more than one step forward when he spotted a very young Komsomolyk trooper with a Ppsh 41 lying on the ground behind a few rocks several meters away. Apparently, the three had left the youth to cover their rear.

Rolling on his back, the Komsomolyk attempted to raise his weapon upward to blast Lehmann. Instantly realizing that if he ran backwards he would perish, Lehmann instead screamed and charged forward. Kicking the Ppsh out of his hands, Lehmann also smashed his left boot into the youth's stomach. Utilizing his MG42 as a club, Lehmann brought it straight down onto the youth's head. Lehmann struck hard. So hard that he actually shattered the youth's helmet. Continuing to scream, he repeatedly raised the MG upwards to strike the Komsomolyk. Only until he shattered the MG in half did Lehmann cease to strike. Looking down, Lehmann saw no head or face, only a shattered mass covered in blood, blotches of which splattered the nearby rocks.

Noting the dead youth's water flask suspended from his belt, Lehmann removed it and gulped down its contents. Throwing the flask aside, he picked up the Komsomolyk's weapon and ran to his next engagement.

Chapter 16: Brody!

That evening, the 31st Infantry Regiment, and elements of the battered 30th, attacked eastward towards Kruhiv (a village located southeast of Koltiw), and Lukavets' (a town located almost 6 miles east of Koltiw). Simultaneously, the 29th Infantry Regiment attacked towards such villages and towns as Holubytsia (on the northern bank of the Seret River), Peniaky (on the Serets southern bank), Huta Peniats'ka, and Huta Verkhobuzhka.

If one takes into consideration that the regiments launched their attacks immediately following a forced infantry march (particularly the 31st Regiment, which force-marched no less than 20 miles), during which they had encountered heavy aerial and ground attacks, then their attacks demonstrated that the Division's personnel possessed a true "winning spirit." This may also serve as an example to dispute any postwar accounts of "low-morale."

Fighting the entire night of 16-17 July, the Division did achieve some measure of success. Throughout the night, the Division's artillery, including its "heavy" 4th Battalion and 88 battery, rained numerous shells in support of its infantry, fusiliers, and engineers. As blackened, burned hands slammed shell after shell into hot breach blocks, Myhailo Lobach was amazed at how the numerous nightflares, parachute flares and star clusters, along with the flash of the guns, could turn night into day. So bright was the countryside that on more than one occasion objects and men could actually be seen hundreds of meters away. By attacking and shelling the corridor, the Division did delay – and possibly momentarily halted – the advance of certain Soviet units.

As tough as the situation was for AGNU and the newly-inserted "Galicia" Division, Konev' s 1st Ukrainian Front was also experiencing its share of hardships. In a desperate effort to break through both north and south of Brody, Konev had committed the brunt of his front's strength, yet, advances were limited in depth and gains were measured in yards. And as Konev's casualties rose, the need for an immediate breakout rose urgently. Regardless of its impressive strength, the fact remains that no military force can sustain a lengthy struggle with heavy losses. Realizing this himself, Konev pressed his commanders to achieve a breakout.

But in order to achieve a breakout, more information was needed. This was especially true pertaining to enemy units, strengths, and dispositions. Sensing that a newly inserted force was holding up the advance, the 52nd Rifle Corps – a Soviet Army corps within the 38th Army operating south of Brody and adjacent to the 60th Army – ordered its divisions to send forward reconnaissance/scout troops in pursuit of such information.

One of those assigned the mission of gathering information was Senior Lieutenant Baskakov. As a scout platoon leader within the 52nd Rifle Corps 117th

Guards Rifle Division, Baskakov was also given this specific order: "Podat' Iazyka!" ("Give us a speaker!" or simply, produce a prisoner from whom information could be extracted).

As recalled years afterwards by Gregory Krivokhizhin, a scout/reconnaissance soldier within Baskakov's platoon, since the crossing of the Dnieper River, all had gone well. Soviet forces had advanced rapidly, most of Ukraine was secured, and a rapid thrust and takeover of Poland was anticipated. But south of Brody all of that changed when the 1st Ukrainian Front's advance was halted by a newly inserted force.

Repeatedly, Baskakov's efforts to secure a prisoner ended in failure. After four attempts, not only was no prisoner secured but to make matters worse, eight reconnaissance scout soldiers were killed. For the scout platoon these were indeed heavy losses and, in addition to the physical loss, it was also a very demoralizing one.

Realizing the critical importance of securing vital information, Baskakov's men decided to make one more attempt. Spotting what appeared to be an officer accompanied by two soldiers near a farm house, the reconnaissance troops opened fire and charged forward. Grabbing the officer, they withdrew under heavy counterfire directed against them from those within the farm house.

But as they ran back, the officer suddenly died. Baskakov returned empty handed. Regardless, on the following day, the Soviet command received the following vital information: 117th Guards had encountered elements of the combat SS.

Krivokhizhin does not specify exactly which Waffen-SS formation was encountered. But because at that time the "Galicia" Division was the only Waffen-SS formation operating south of Brody (or, for that matter, the only Waffen-SS division on that entire front), against the 1st Ukrainian Front, it is obvious that Baskakov's troops had encountered the "Galicia" Division and with it, tough resistance and heavy losses.[11]

In the concluding hours of 16 July, the situation was as follows: the Division was still attacking the "Koltiw corridor" from the north, German forces were attacking it from the south, and General Wolfgang von Kluge's 357th (48th Panzer Corps), was fighting to hold a front east of Trostianets' Malyi adjacent to the corridor.

Monday, 17 July:
Dawn. As heavy fighting continued to rage both north and south of Brody, Konev moved in additional fresh tank and mechanized forces. To the north, the 1st Guards

Chapter 16: Brody!

Tank Army (with orders to strike towards Rava-Russka), would further breach the efforts of the 13th Army and Baranov's Cavalry Mechanized Group while simultaneously, south of Brody in Koltiw's vicinity, Lelyshenko's 4th Tank Army would reinforce the 3rd Guards Tank Army. Konev's actions not only placed more pressure on the front but as well, made it increasingly difficult for the counterattacking forces to "plug-up" the two now rapidly expanding breaches.

By mid-morning, heavy concentrations of enemy infantry and armor, spearheaded by a criminal penal battalion, began to surge forward. From an observation point atop Hill 416 near Volokh, at approximately 10:30 a.m., the 29th's Regimental commander, SS-Obersturmbannführer Dern, personally visited Myhailo Dlaboha, who was observing the countryside.

Immediately, Dlaboha informed Dern that the enemy was renewing its effort, but that the 29th was unaware of fresh concentrations developing on its front. Although the enemy was shrouded in a late morning mist, Dlaboha further informed Dern that the 29th was not yet fully positioned defensively, and that he was going to open fire to disrupt the enemy, thus warning the 29th of an upcoming action. Without waiting for any orders or guidance, Dlaboha called for one artillery round.

"Mister, have you gone mad? What the hell are you doing?" demanded Dern. "Ivan's come. I have to fire!" replied Dlaboha. An argument ensued. Dern threatened Dlaboha with death, but as Dlaboha adjusted his batteries, as well as the artillery regiment's 1st battalion's artillery fire, the 29th's commander finally realized that Dlaboha was not firing on either the Wehrmacht or the "Galicia" Division but rather, on Soviet forces.

Well-placed artillery rounds decimated the advancing communist penal unit. At first, the criminal unit maintained its momentum, but as more incoming rounds shattered those who pressed forward to kill and pillage, their momentum suddenly broke and they fell back.

But efforts to escape proved fruitless as NKVD police troops commenced fire on those who reeled back. Adjusting his sights, Dlaboha carefully plotted the NKVD's location. Again notifying his battery, Dlaboha called for one round; within seconds, he heard its flight hundreds of feet above him. Exploding within meters of where Dlaboha estimated the NKVD stood, he shouted only one word – "FIRE!"

The battery rocked. Outgoing rounds pierced the air. Exploding shells tore enemy trucks into pieces. As Dlaboha viewed flames rising upwards amidst pieces of trucks flying hundreds of meters in every direction, the artillery officer knew that his men were ripping the life out of the NKVD. "That's right, boys, pour it on!" Outgoing rounds continued to rain death and destruction.

With his decision to insert another tank army into Koltiw's vicinity in order to expand the corridor and achieve a breakout and operational depth, Konev also created some serious problems for the "Galicia" Division. But the worst was yet to come. That same day, he also committed the 1st Ukrainian Front's strategic reserve into combat. From this combination of armored and reserve strength, certain units were immediately brought up against the Division. As the Division began to face additional fresh forces with superior odds, firepower and combat experience, the estimated initial ratio of odds of at least 1 against 3 now rose to even higher levels. It has never been ascertained, nor will it ever be, what odds the Division faced from 17 July. But realistically speaking, odds of at least 1 against 5 to 6 may be considered accurate, although some claim that even this figure is too low. In addition, if one takes into consideration the massive aerial and ground firepower the Soviets possessed, the odds tremendously favored the attackers.

That same day, the 357th German Infantry Division collapsed, while the "Galicia" Division was forced strictly over to the defensive. Again, it is important to note that certain individual companies did succeed in outflanking the corridor and striking into it. But attempts to seal the gap failed as the Division's artillery and communication support diminished, while German air support was unavailable.[1] So until AGNU could somehow dispatch immediate reinforcement to establish blocking positions, nothing else could be done.

But the battle was far from over. As previously it had been critical to seal the corridor, now it was equally imperative to hold it in order to prevent Soviet forces from expanding it.

Occupying a hilltop position northeast of Kryhiv, Myhailo Tomash and his two assistants quickly dug two foxhole fighting positions. Myhailo's position, which held him and his assistant gunner Stepan Kolko, along with their two machine guns, an MG34 and MG42, was slightly larger than the position situated about 100 feet to Myhailo's right and occupied by Pavlo Budka. Lack of time prevented the threesome from constructing overhead cover for their positions, but the dug-out positions were tightly packed in the front and sides by some sandbags.

From his vantage point, Myhailo had an excellent view. Directly to his front and left, the ground sloped downward into a slight valley, and then rose upward to a series of small hills. Except for a handful of trees, the terrain was open. To his front and right, approximately 300 meters away, stood a sizable wooded knoll. This wooded area could provide cover, but once anyone emerged from it, they would have to advance downward and then uphill through open terrain. But before anyone could occupy Myhailo's hilltop position, they would first be forced to encounter Myhailo, Stepan, and Pavlo. Myhailo held an ideal position. From it he could cover hundreds of meters of terrain. After establishing their positions, the three were personally visited by Myhailo's company commander. The 4th heavy Company leader had a reputation throughout the entire infantry battalion for taking care of his soldiers. Upon arrival, he not only brought some cans of food and water, but seeing that extra ammunition could be needed, he immediately ordered more. An incredible supply of 20,000 rounds showed up. As Stepan unrolled strap after strap, he jokingly remarked "I think we've got enough to stop an army!" Myhailo just laughed at his friend's remark, but deep down, he hoped Stepan was wrong.

Indeed, it was Stepan who proved right. It didn't matter that further to the left and right other Galician machine-gunners had established positions. The might of the 99th Rifle Division was coming their way, and it was Myhailo's machine-gun team which barred their way.

"HURRAH! HURRAH!" From the woods to his right, and from across the hill to his front, Myhailo saw the brown-clad figures surge forward, totally intoxicated with the idea of overrunning the hill. "OH GOD!" shouted Stepan," it looks like a whole regiment's coming at us!"

Myhailo remained calm. Firmly grasping the MG42 in both hands, he decided to first engage the group coming out of the wooded area. But before opening up, he would permit them to advance for about another 50 meters. After engaging them, he would deal with those to his front. Glancing momentarily at Stepan, Myhailo exclaimed "Get ready!" and peered through the sight of the MG42. His plan was to fire a Z pattern at the first group. Such a pattern, fired from the right to the left, and then upwards at an angle to the right and again to the left, would not only drop the first row, but some of the attackers in the center and rear. Once this was accomplished, Myhailo would then fire a reverse Z, move the weapon a couple of feet to his left, and use the same pattern on the other group.

He sighted carefully. With his left hand, he released the weapon's safety and with his right, he released the weapon's bolt forward. Quickly resighting, he slowly squeezed the trigger.

The weapon thundered. As the red hot 7.92mm rounds ripped into the body of a charging soldier and shoved him backwards, Myhailo slowly swept the group with a Z pattern. As the cries of "HURRAH!" subsided, the group's survivors, stunned by what they had just experienced, immediately retreated, in total chaos, to the safety of the woods.

"God," thought Myhailo, "how beautifully that worked." He raised the weapon upward, placed it approximately two feet to his left, sighted, and repeated his maneuver of a few moments ago. Within seconds, he noted that the second group's survivors were also quickly retiring uphill to seek cover over the hilltop.

But there was no time to savor any victories. Within seconds, the first group's disorganized survivors, linking up with newly arrived reinforcements, charged out of the woods. Shouting "HURRAH! "POBEDA!" "HURRAH!" they pressed forward in renewed strength and determination. Aiming at them, Myhailo fired and began another Z pattern. But before he could totally sweep over the group, his weapon fell silent. "Ammo!" realized Myhailo. "Need to reload! Pass it down! Grab the MG 34!" Shouting "GUN ONE, DOWN!" from Stefan he heard "GUN TWO, UP!" As Myhailo reached for the second machinegun, he also heard the shouts of "HURRAH!" rising over the crest of the hill. "Shit!" thought Myhailo. "Gotta work faster. The other group's coming in!" Sighting on a group, he heard the quick staccato shots of Pavlo's KAR 98 rifle and the bolt's action. "Not bad, Pavlo. Not bad at all!"

Myhailo aimed. He fired. He fired again. And again. And again. He ripped both groups into pieces. As he fired, the crack of enemy small-arms fire filled the air, mortar and artillery rounds dropped all around and chunks of earth rained down. The weapon's hot slugs acted as an invisible wall. Men dropped singly, in two's and three's and on occasion, in clusters; yet, the living continued to press forward, jumping over the dead and dying, until a 7.92 round or burst silenced them in turn. "HURRAH! HURRAH! POBEDA!" "Easy," thought Myhailo. "Easy. Let them come in. Easy. NOW!" He squeezed the trigger. Nothing. Instantly, Myhailo pulled on the bolt, and squeezed. Again, nothing. Shouting "JAMMAGE!" Myhailo was about to pass the weapon to Stepan but before he could do anything, Pavlo's shout of "LET ME CLEAR IT!" was heard. Jumping out of his position, Pavlo raced towards Myhailo. Myhailo saw the folly in this. But before he could stop him the boy was on his knees beside the weapon lifting its feed tray cover. But that was as far as he got. Within a second, a rifle bullet struck Pavlo squarely on the right side of his head. Collapsing over the weapon, several more rounds ripped into his body. Pulling Pavlo's body and the jammed weapon into the position, Myhailo ducked down just in time as more enemy bullets flew over. Another mortar round came screaming in. Chunks of debris and dirt rained down. "My God!" cried Stepan. "HE'S DEAD!" But Stepan had no time to ponder his friend's death. Reaching for the jammed weapon, he began to extract the jammed round with a knife. Myhailo could not fail to notice Stepan's burned and bleeding hands; pieces of flesh actually hung here and there. As Stepan worked, cursing the jammage, Myhailo picked up Pavlo's body and, as much as he hated to do it, lay it in front of the position. This way, Pavlo's body would provide some extra protection.

Turning around, Myhailo saw six Red Army soldiers charging in from behind. "STEPAN! SIX COMING IN FROM BEHIND!" Replying "STAY DOWN!"

Chapter 16: Brody!

Stepan quickly pulled the pin out of an egg-type grenade, and tossed it no more than several feet outside the hole. The explosion rained more debris into the hole. But immediately following the blast, both men stood up – Myhailo with an MG and Stepan with a P-38 pistol. And before the attackers were silenced for eternity, the last thing they saw was two men pop up and spray lead.

Squatting back into the fighting position, Myhailo asked "How do you think they got behind?" "WHO THE HELL KNOWS! WHO THE HELL CARES!" screamed Stepan as he worked to unjam the weapon. "WEAPONS UP!" More incoming rounds tore up the ground. As Myhailo and Stepan lay in the foxhole, hands covering their ears and heads, their bodies rolling with the blasts and convulsions, both men knew that unless a direct shell exploded within, neither would die.

"HURRAH! POBEDA! HURRAH!" Myhailo wondered how much more he could take. Removing the weapons bipod, he placed the red hot barrel on Pavlo's body. The weapon's firing pin had shattered hours before, but the chamber was so hot that as rounds entered it, a combination of heat and exploding rounds set the bullets off.

Myhailo sighted. Again, he wondered how much more of this he could take. His body was covered with sweat, his face blackened by grime, sweat, and burned powder, his mouth felt hot and dry and his burned hands ached while his head and ears rang from the constant noise and exploding shells. Yet, he maintained his self-control, and through the entire day and night, continued to engage the attacking mass.

Throughout the hot day of 17 July, tough defensive battles were fought. Fierce battles especially raged for the villages and towns of Holubytsia, Peniaky, Huta Peniats'ka, Huta Verkhobuzhka, Maidan, Kryhiv, Sukhodoly, Koltiw, Opaky, Lukavets' and a host of other places as Soviet forces repeatedly thrust forward and the Division was determined to hold; throughout the countryside, farms and settlements burned and the smoke and crackle of burning wood could be seen and heard well into the night. Charging towards Huta Peniats'ka, Chaplain Volodymyr Stetsiuk saw a grenadier fall. Rushing to his aid, the chaplain attempted to assist him. Suddenly, a German NCO rushed up, and told the chaplain to move. Refusing to leave the dying grenadier, the chaplain was shot dead by the NCO. Because this incident was witnessed by a number of soldiers, the NCO was later "killed-in-action."[2]

By way of information extracted from prisoners of war, intercepted radio messages, and unit identification markings on vehicles, the following units (in part or completion), were identified as operating against the "Galicia" Division: the

68th Guards Rifle Division;[3] the 99th Rifle Division;[4] the 117th Guards Rifle Division,[5] the 336th,[6] 322nd,[7] and 148th Rifle Divisions[8] which comprised the 15th Rifle Corps;[9] and the 6th Guards Tank Corps,[10] 7th Guards Tank Corps,[11] and the 9th Mechanized Corps.[12] The 23rd Independent Rifle Corps,[13] as well as elements of the 52nd Rifle Corps[14] along with a part of the 102nd Rifle Corps[15] and the 17th Guards Rifle Corps,[16] also fought the 13th Corps, and its elements saw action against the Division. "Sokolov's" cavalry-mechanized group[17] (comprising the 31st Independent Tank Corps[18] and the 6th Guards Cavalry Corps[19]) also fought the Division. These various divisions and corps belonged to the 3rd Guards Tank Army[20]; 13th Army;[21] 38th Army:[22] 60th Army[23] and the 1st Ukrainian Front's Strategic Reserve.

In several instances, elements of the Division were taking on entire Soviet divisions. By 17 July, the 29th Infantry Regiment was battling the entire 68th Guards Rifle Division reinforced with artillery, armor and air, and the 31st Infantry Regiment fought the entire 99th and no less than half of the 336th Rifle Divisions, also massively reinforced. For reinforcements, the two regiments utilized the Division's fusiliers, engineers, the independent anti-tank company, and as much of the Division's artillery as possible. But when one takes into consideration that none of the Division's regiments were in full regimental strength, and no air support was available, what reinforcement became available could not even come close to equalling the Soviets' strength.

In addition to the artillery regiments found within each Soviet rifle and tank division, a number of independent rocket and artillery divisions were utilized by the 1st Ukrainian Front. Such units were: the 7th Breakthrough Artillery Corps[24] (comprising the 1st Guards Breakthrough Artillery Division[25] and the 3rd Guards Rocket Barrage Division[26]), found within the 13th Army; the 13th Breakthrough Artillery Division;[27] and the 17th Breakthrough Artillery Division.[28]

Besides battling the regular infantry, artillery, rocket,armored, mechanized and cavalry units committed by the Soviets,the Division also fought "booty" Ukrainians forcefully pressed into service as "reinforcements,"[29] NKVD police troops, penal battalions,[30] and specialized troops.[31]

Bombarded with overwhelming firepower, repeatedly strafed, bombed and rocketed by low and high flying aircraft, massively struck by enemy armor reinforced with mechanized, criminal penal battalions and NKVD troops, the Division began to fold. What especially saddened the soldiers was to encounter untrained men and boys, some as young as 15, who were gathered up by the communists in Galicia's regions and, with no training whatsoever, were pressed into "volunteer" battalions. Brutalized and terrorized to the level of being no more than beasts of burdens, such "volunteers" began to make a regular appearance on the battlefield and frequently, spearheaded Soviet attacks. Eventually, members of the Division actually encountered family members among such "volunteers."[32]

"HURRAH!" Looking up, Myron Baran* saw a Red Army soldier, with a bayonet protruding from the tip of his Tokarev rifle, charging towards him; instantly, Myron knew that he would have to go one-on-one with the charging threat.

Rising up from his prone position, Myron faked to his right, moved to his left, and with his KAR 98 rifle, thwarted the thrust of the Tokarev. Simultaneously, he raised his right leg to ankle height and tripped forward the incoming trooper. The moment the Soviet trooper fell forward to the ground, Myron turned, fired, pulled back the rifle's bolt, slammed in another round and fired again. The fact that Myron had just killed his first human being was bad enough, but the worst was yet to come.

Staring at the lying corpse, Myron noticed the man's wallet lying approximately ten inches from his upper right side; apparently, as the man felt forward, his wallet had slipped out of an inside coat pocket. Placing his rifle down, Myron picked up the wallet. Inside, he saw the man's photograph, his membership in the 23rd Guards stamped with an official seal, and a folded letter. Opening it, he saw it contained a photograph. Tears welled up in his eyes.

"MY GOD!" cried out Myron. "WHAT HAVE I DONE? WHAT HAVE I DONE?" As he read the letter, Myron noted that it was addressed by a woman to Ivan Hopenko, a Ukrainian who hailed from the Kharkiv region. Its opening lines read: "My dear husband. It has been over half a year since we have last seen each other, but very recently, we had our second child. For months, although you have been away, you have waited with me. At last, our child has arrived. It is a baby girl, two months old, beautiful and healthy. I am enclosing a photograph of her with me, and our little Markian." As tears continued to run down his cheeks, Myron looked at the photo of the Ukrainian woman sitting with a baby in her lap and little Markian standing at her side. Squatting beside the dead man, Myron carefully reinserted the letter with the photo back into the wallet. Muttering "Tovarysh, please forgive me!" he pushed it back underneath the deceased man's coat. Myron not only felt the tremendous burden of having killed a fellow Ukrainian, but also sorrow that his action had inadvertently resulted in a new widow and two fatherless children.[33]

On 17 July, the Division's front line, which was initially established on 15 July slightly southwest from Litovytsi over the Seret River past Peniaky, Lukavets', Kruhiv and to the outskirts of Nushche on a front of approximately 6 miles – began to fall back under severe pressure. And with the collapse of the 357th German Infantry Division and the insertion of additional Soviet forces into the corridor, the Division was not only pressed from the front, but was now forced to establish and defend a line on its right flank west of Koltiw towards the town of Sasiv located south of the Buh River. Again, the 30th Infantry Regiment found itself heavily engaged on the front line. But continuing enemy pressure, and the incorporation of fresh divisions, such as the 359th Soviet Rifle Division[34] west of Koltiw to strike northwards, forced the Division to move its line further westward. By midnight, the Division's front line faced eastward from the vicinity of Sasiv to Pidhirtsi to the north of Zahirtsi at a distance of approximately 7-8 miles. Under the best conditions, no division should ever hold such a lengthy sector. But neither 13th Corps nor the Division had any choice.

Tuesday, 18 July:
On the morning of the 18th, the Division's 14th Field Replacement Battalion was forced to withdraw. Positioned slightly north of Busk on the Buh River, until that morning the Battalion had only trained. On one or two occasions enemy aircraft did make brief appearances but excluding that, nothing had occurred.

As the battalion's soldiers queued for breakfast, the rattle of machine-gun fire was suddenly heard. "Wehrmacht's already training" muttered a German NCO as he munched on his cereal. But suddenly, the thunder of a tank's cannon and the abrupt appearance of enemy armor exiting out of the forest's treeline announced a very grim situation to the men. All scrambled for cover. Those who earlier had cursed their misfortune for being assigned to a unit which had remained inactive while the Division was in combat, now cursed the enemy appearance and wished that the Soviets had never arrived. Although armed, many of the soldiers lacked ammunition for their weapons and only a few had any anti-armor weaponry.

Fortunately for the field replacement battalion, the Soviets were not interested in a fight and as quickly as they had arrived, they moved on. Immediately, the field replacement battalion notified Divisional headquarters (now located almost 2 miles west of Pidhirtsi) by radio of its encounter and, along with its commander, Kleinhoff, and some rear area German units, the battalion quickly withdrew westward.[1]

When Rybalko's tankers linked up with Baranov's mechanized corps in the vicinity of the railway town of Krasne and Busk (approximately 30 miles east of Lviv and 40 miles southwest of Brody), in addition to achieving a successful breakout, its commanders, whether they realized it or not, were ahead of an army corps that not only was being battered, but one that was now encircled.[2]

Chapter 16: Brody!

One of the simple, golden rules of warfare is "don't get yourself surrounded." But if a unit should find itself in that unfortunate position, its options are either to remain in its current location until relieved and rescued or, conduct an immediate breakout from encirclement. Needless to say, a decision must be made immediately.

In the case of the "Galicia " Division, as well as the remainder of the 13th Corps, a breakout was the only option available. This was especially true in view of the fact that both the 1st and 4th Panzer Armies were beginning to fall back. While the 1st Panzer would certainly assist the Corps in its breakout attempt, realistically speaking, the brunt of the effort had to he conducted by the encircled corps.

A breakout is strictly an offensive operation undertaken by those surrounded in order to escape. A force is considered totally encircled only when its supply, reinforcement and ground evacuation routes are completely severed by an advancing enemy. The purpose of conducting a breakout is to allow the encircled forces to re-establish contact with their respective armies, to avoid destruction and capture, to regain freedom of movement, and to survive for future operations. Realistically speaking, survival was of the essence for the "Galicia" Division, more so than for the remainder of the corps.

When a force is initially surrounded, this does not mean that it is necessarily surrounded by a vastly superior enemy strength, nor that it will be immediately struck. Because Soviet military doctrine stresses momentum, speed, and deep penetration, its advancing forces frequently bypass a surrounded force and leave it behind to be dealt with by the secondary, or "mopping-up," forces. Yet in order to breakout, a surrounded force must deceive the enemy as regards its composition, strength, and intent; conduct a successful reconnaissance; organize breakout, support, flank, and rearguard forces; organize a security force which can be rushed to any critical sectors; and concentrate sufficient combat firepower at its breakout points. Speed is of the essence, and all of the above must be accomplished with no wasted time.

At the time of its encirclement, the "Brody Pocket" covered a sizable distance. An oval shaped area, from the northwest to the southeast it covered an area of about 25 miles, and from its southern center at Bilyi Kamin to the north at Turie, approximately 14 miles with an average distance (from east to west) of about the same.[3] According to Soviet sources, eight divisions were encircled,[4] but others cite differently.[5] Inside the Brody Pocket, General Hauffe's 13th Corps was made up of these units: General Oscar Lasch's 349th Infantry Division; General Georg Lindemann's 361st Infantry Division; Major General Johann Netwig's 454th Field

Security Division; General Fritz Freitag's 14th SS "Galicia" Division and General Wolfgang Lange's Corps Abteilung C (Formation C), consisting of the 182nd, 217th and 339th Infantry Divisions. If one takes into consideration that the whole of Formation C equalled a strength of no more than one division, then Veryha's estimate of four German divisions and one Ukrainian ("Galicia") Division is correct. Various sources have cited the 13th Corps' strength from no less than 32,000 to 40,000[6] but at the time of encirclement, its strength was already reduced.

Regardless of the exact strength, on 18 July, about 7,000 of these soldiers were from the "Galicia" Division,[7] the majority of whom were holding and defending the southeastern sector of the pocket. Within this area, heavy defensive fighting continued for Koltiw, Sasiv, Bilyi Kamin, and the overlooking heights of Pidhirtsi. A town located on higher terrain with distant views, Pidhirtsi held the key to either victory or defeat. If held in enemy hands, Soviet forces would not only be able to have a vantage point from which to direct heavy firepower down upon the Division but for that matter, upon the entire 13th Corps. Concurrently, this higher terrain could (and was) utilized by the Division for target acquisition and flank security for its own defense as well as that of the 13th Corps. As a result, for a couple of days, Pidhirtsi repeatedly changed hands.[8]

Apart from the town, an old castle also stood on the hill. Built by Galicia's ancient rulers to repulse Mongol and Tatar invasions, for centuries the castle was contested by many defenders and attackers. Charging up the slope toward the castle with an explosive packet in his left hand and an MP 38/40 in his right hand, combat engineer Vasyl Soroka* was amazed that no one ever seemed to learn anything from centuries of warfare. Rushing to a wall of concertina wire, Vasyl dropped to his knees, lay flat on the ground, carefully placed the packet into the wire, and set its fuse. Observing several huge boulders to his right, Vasyl first rolled towards them; and then leaped behind for cover.

A massive explosion rocked the wire. Removing his last remaining smoke grenade, Vasyl popped its fuse, and hurtled it as far as he could beyond the wire. Then, he sprayed 9mm slugs into a huge hole in the castle's wall. Lifting his weapon upwards, he emptied the remainder of the magazine into the upper part of the ancient structure.

Thick clouds of dense smoke heralded to the grenadiers that the wire was breached. "SLAVA!" Charging over the crest of the hill, the grenadiers scrambled through the gap. To cover them as best as possible, Vasyl quickly inserted another 9mm magazine into his MP and sprayed a Soviet soldier who was attempting to hurtle a hand grenade downward from the upper part of the castle. Falling backward into the castle, his grenade exploded inside. "Hopefully, thought Vasyl, "the blast took out a few more."

Chapter 16: Brody!

"SLAVA! SLAVA!" Reaching the solid five-foot thick wall at the base of the castle, grenadiers hurtled several grenades inside. Following the blasts, the grenadiers immediately rushed in. Now, the battle for the castle would be concluded with close-in combat. And such hand-to-hand combat, between Soviet paratroopers, guardsmen and NKVD personnel versus the 14th Waffen-SS, frequently took a turn for the worse. Weapons were handled as clubs; handguns were fired at point-blank range; and knives, daggers, bayonets, as well as bare hands, frequently decided an outcome.

Throughout the whole ordeal, the Division's communications, engineer, supply, support, veterinarian and medical units worked long hours under tremendous pressure. Waffen-Untersturmführer Doctor Volodymyr Kischko, along with other members of his veterinarian company, constantly went up and down from one column to another inspecting, treating, and tending to the Division's horses and mules. In addition, Dr. Kischko and Stepan Balko, the company's medic and a former veterinary student, eased many soldiers' psychological strain. Losing a beloved animal is always painful, but to lose an animal in combat is all the more so. On more than one occasion, both Kischko and Balko had to console a grieving soldier as a pistol or rifle was aimed to end the suffering of a wounded or injured horse or mule.

The Division's communications personnel constantly strove to establish, re-establish, and repair communications. Constantly on the move, they laid many miles of wire, repaired radios, and directed communications by various means. Especially compounding the problem was the fact that at first, numerous artillery and bomb blasts blew sections of wire, which needed to be repaired or replaced immediately. But with the disappearance of the communications commander, Wolfgang Wuttig, and increased enemy pressure along with Soviet infiltrators and guerrillas who began to cut wires and destroy communications, the situation only worsened. At Brody, on more than one occasion, as a communications soldier "walked" the wire to find a break, he would come face-to-face with enemy personnel. The Division's communications, however, had begun to break down before encirclement.

The Division's engineers worked around the clock under tough conditions, performing numerous offensive and defensive missions. Especially in the area of Kryhiv, Lukavets', Koltiw, Peniaky, and Huta Peniats'ka, where the 29th and 31st Regiments were withdrawing under constant enemy pressure, engineers lay many mines and some obstacles. As best as they could, they assisted friendly units in their withdrawals. As combat soldiers, Divisional engineers tore apart hastily constructed enemy positions, attacked enemy armor, and supported Divisional counteroffensives. Attacking an enemy tank with a teller anti-armor mine, engineer Ivan Koval successfully scrambled aboard the tank, placed the device underneath its turret, and rolled off the tank's rear deck. But as he stood up to dash away, the tank's turret suddenly spun in his direction and sprayed him with fire. The moment Koval fell, a blast tore the turret apart.

The Division's workshop company, under Waffen-Haupsturmführer Leonid Martyniuk and Theodore Vynnyk, repaired equipment, radios, vehicles, wagons, and artillery; frequently, this was accomplished under enemy aerial and ground attack. The fact that the workshop company was destroyed attests to the difficult conditions it encountered.

Operating along with the Division's repair company, were its food, bakery, and meat butcher sections. Never would Waffen-Untersturmführer Shuhan forget how at the end of a day, after repulsing another Soviet thrust, he would turn around and see, standing a short distance behind, a field cook, decked out in a white apron and even, a white chef's hat. Cupping his hands around his mouth, the cook loudly announced "BOYS, DINNER TIME!" As the goulash wagon was ready to serve a meal, it was apparent that while Shuhan's company was fighting, the cook had been setting up to feed the company. Until surrounded, the bakery, butcher, and food companies held their own. But they began to collapse as food supplies failed to reach the corps and its divisions. In the upcoming breakout, its personnel fought as regular infantry.

Virtually unknown is the fact that the Division's one or two 'Feldgendarmerie,' or military police platoons, were destroyed at Brody. This occurred one night while they were defending the Division's headquarters.

In World War II, on the eastern front, it was not uncommon for a divisional, corps, or even an army headquarters to come under attack. Specially designated Soviet soldiers, or guerrillas (and in some cases both), were frequently assigned the mission of destroying a headquarters and killing its personnel in order to create havoc by crippling a unit from within.[9] Throughout the night of 18/19 July, military police personnel, along with Divisional headquarters personnel, fought a battle with one such specialized force. At daybreak, approximately 30 dead enemy personnel, all armed but some in civilian attire, lay around the headquarters. Among them lay a female; it was believed she had been the group's commander.

Under the direction of medical officers such as Drs. Koldewsky, Panasiuk, Farion, Prokopovych, Karpevych, Tymchyshyn, Myhailo Hryhorchuk, Zenon Lokach, Roman Turko, Anatole Pyrozhynskyi, the Division's medical personnel worked around the clock to provide medical care to wounded and injured personnel. The fact that the Division's hospital was clearly identifiable by Red Cross symbols did not deter any attacks against it; throughout the battle, the Division's medical personnel and its ambulances were constantly fired upon. At Brody, the Division's two ambulance platoons, along with its personnel, were destroyed. To prevent total destruction, the Division's hospital was relocated to Pochapy by 18 July.[10]

Never faltering from their mission, the chaplains gave their best. Frequently, they were observed walking over a battlefield to assist those in need. And later, many a man attributed his survival to a chaplain's friendly smile, assurance and support. But as with the other units, the chaplains also paid a price. At Brody, chaplains Vasyl Leshchyshyn[11] and Volodymyr Stetsiuk were killed; Ivan Durbak was reported missing and presumed killed;[12] and Josef Kladochnyi was reported as killed but in actuality, he was wounded and captured.[13]

By the end of 18 July, the Division's 29th Regiment, with its commander wounded and its leading personnel dead or missing, ceased to exist as an effective force. In the vicinity of Pidhirtsi, the 29th's staff made a valiant stand alongside the regiment. Of a strength of 275 personnel assigned to the 29th's regimental headquarters company, only 7 were accounted for after Brody.[14] All surviving 29th personnel were incorporated into the 30th and 31st Regiments.[15]

In the early evening hours of 18 July, the OUN lost one of its most effective operatives – Oleksa Babiy. Born in the vicinity of Buchach, Babiy entered the Polish Army in 1931 where he served in its artillery. He also graduated from an NCO academy and several specialist courses. Following his discharge from the Polish Arrny, Babiy returned home. He became active in a Ukrainian cultural revival movement and joined the OUN. At first he served as an OUN courier, but later in Cracow, he began to provide the OUN's Cracow based operatives military lectures.

Threatened with arrest, Babiy fled to France; there, he obtained employment with a Ukrainian newspaper the "Ukrainian Word." (Ukrains'ke Slovo). Shortly after the outbreak of the German-Soviet War, Babiy returned to Galicia. Renewing his activity with the OUN, he was posted to an OUN cell in the Eastern Ukrainian city of Kharkiv where he conducted anti-Nazi propaganda and helped to smuggle and conceal Ukrainians sought by Nazi authorities. In the spring of 1943, he left Kharkiv for Galicia to enlist in the Division. Armed with a false identity, Babiy entered the Division under the alias of "Andriy Levchuk." Following recruit training, he was dispatched to an artillery school in Beneschau, Czechoslovakia. Returning to the Division as an honor graduate, Babiy deployed to the eastern front as an artillery observer. But on 18 July, as "Andriy Levchuk" proceeded to inspect an observation point in the vicinity of Huta Peniats'ka, a communist sniper killed him.

Galicia Division

Historically speaking, 19 July may be cited as the date of the German collapse.[1] By this date, AGNU had no chance of containing the Soviet breakout. Konev's forces were in full motion, and the entire momentum was in Soviet hands.

13th Corps immediately planned on a breakout. To accomplish this, the corps' perimeter was withdrawn closer to the Buh River, major assault groups were formed, remaining supplies quickly distributed, all unnecessary supplies and equipment were destroyed, and blocking positions were established. Simultaneously, as the corps was to move southwest, the remnants of the 8th Panzer Division, now commanded by von Mellenthin, along with elements of the 20th Panzergrenadier, were to attack northeastward.[2]

Severe problems, however, immediately set in. To begin with, communications problems not only developed within the encircled corps, but a lack of effective communications prevented General Balck from establishing proper contact with Hauffe. Von Mellenthin, meanwhile, having personally briefed the 8th Panzer's regimental commanders on the physical and psychological importance of withdrawing the 13th Corps out of the pocket, was shocked to learn that instead of advancing, certain commanders were withdrawing.[3] Von Mellenthin immediately dismissed those commanders and personally re-organized a relief. But critical time had been lost.

At the same time that AGNU and the 48th Panzer Corps was planning to extradite the 13th Corps, the Soviets were quickly reacting to the situation. When on 18 July they realized that a whole corps was surrounded, they immediately decided to destroy it. Whether this decision arose out of the fact that one of the surrounded divisions was Ukrainian, or because the 13th Corps still posed a threat to further Soviet thrusts to the west, or because of the Soviet military strategy which advocates the destruction of any sizable surrounded force, or a combination of the above reasons, Konev's front (with Stavka's full approval), moved in rapidly for the kill.[4]

Realizing this, the 13th Corps hastened its preparations. No novice to encirclement, General Lange quickly dispatched reinforced patrols west and southwest to determine breakout routes and terrain conditions, and to establish contact with friendly forces. In the meantime, the "Galicia" Division was holding the corps' northern, and part of its southeastern sector. But late that night, at approximately 10 p.m., the Division lost Pidhirtsi when Soviet troops, shouting "HURRAH!" poured into Pidhirtsi's flaming ruins on the outskirts of which the 29th Regiment's 2nd Battalion, and other Divisional units, were quickly reorganizing themselves.

With the Corps' withdrawal to the southern sector, Soviet forces crossed the

Chapter 16: Brody!

Krasne-Brody railway line north of Oles'ko, and began to strike the bulge east-ward from the vicinity of Krasne and Busk. Breaking through, they not only cre-ated chaos within the center of the corps pocket, but also reinforced those units pressing against the Division from the north. In conjunction with the ground at-tacks, Soviet air continued its relentless pressure.[5]

By now, the Division was not only exposed to the danger of military destruc-tion but also to something which every commander fears on a modern-day battle-field – fatigue. And on a modern-day battlefield, exhaustion, stress, and hunger, if not controlled, can destroy units just as quickly, if not sooner, than enemy activity. According to Heike, surviving unit commanders (who by 19 July had them-selves reached exhaustion levels), began to call in that they were unable to hold on to their positions much longer. It became apparent that a way had to be found to control fatigue, yet the volunteers continued to resist. Calling upon their deepest inner reserves, they found that extra strength needed to carry them through. Whether this was attributable to training, fear, mission awareness, or because the Division was fighting in its homeland, can only be surmised.

Linking up at Oles'ko from the north and west, Konev's armor immediately struck to overrun the town. Capturing Oles'ko would enable Soviet forces to out-flank the Division's troop battling in Pidhirtsi's vicinity, approximately 4.5 miles to the east. But hopes of a rapid capture quickly faded as Oles'ko's streets and the rolling fields adjacent to the town quickly turned into an inferno of burning armor as one enemy tank after another went up in flames. Rushing into Oles'ko with PAK guns, panzerfausts, panzerschreks, teller mines and even Molotov cocktails, the Division's fusiliers once again demonstrated more than enough tenacity and bravery against superior odds. At point-blank range, fusiliers stalked and engaged Soviet infantry and enemy armor. Frequently, their technique was as follows: well-camouflaged fusiliers would allow the enemy tanks to pass through them. Once the tanks were engaged by those further behind, the bypassed fusiliers would "hunt" the enemy's armor from behind. This anti-armor "hunting" technique, largely de-veloped and perfected by the Waffen-SS on the eastern front, proved to be very effective. Needless to say, it demanded composure, nerve, and inner strength to operate behind and amongst enemy armor. But within the Division, Bristot's fusiliers were noted for that.

Rocking on its suspension, its barrel emitting smoke, a T-34 prepared to fire another round in Shuhan's direction. "BOOM!" As another red-hot shell flew no more than three feet over his head, Shuhan could actually feel its heat but in a sense, was relieved the tank was unloading its munitions on him, and not on his men. Squeezing his body as close to the ground as possible, Shuhan braced for more. Ahead, behind, and around him, small clods of earth flew upwards as 7.62mm machinegun rounds ripped up the ground's surface. To further obscure himself from the iron monster's gunner, Shuhan removed his helmet, and pushed it several feet to his front. More hot rounds tore up the ground ahead of Shuhan or deflated upwards from his helmet.

"BOOM!" Another red-hot round flew over. As the round exploded behind Shuhan, raining more earth and debris upon him, he felt assured that his position was actually safe. Shuhan knew the T-34 could not depress its barrel anymore, while distance and angle made it difficult for its gunner to strike Shuhan.

Ceasing to fire, the tank stood in place. An eerie silence filled the air. But not for long. Revving its engine, the tank moved slowly backwards. Shuhan immediately knew that by moving back, the behemoth's gunner would at last be able to fire a round squarely into him. "O.K. Gotta move!" Shuhan's first thought was to just race across the field, and chance it. But deep down, Shuhan knew the golden rule: "if you dash for cover, no more than five seconds. If you need more than that, stay put, or look for a closer spot." And Shuhan was not going to break that rule, especially after witnessing how two soldiers had been killed by bursts of enemy fire after they had abandoned a relatively safe position in order to run a short distance.

Spotting a natural semi-depression enlarged by a heavy mortar or artillery round, Shuhan reasoned it would not take him more than three or four seconds to race for it. As well, by moving forward and actually into the tank's direction, Shuhan would once again deny the tank's gunner the ability to further depress his barrel to strike him. Tensing his body, Shuhan leaped and ran forward. As he ran, his right hand firmly gripped an anti-armor grenade and his left hand firmly gripped an MP 38/40 and the strap of a small rucksack. The moment Shuhan plopped to the ground, enemy bullets flew over. Chuckling to himself, Shuhan was delighted that the tank's crew was having such a hard time in eliminating him. Also, he knew that the tank did not dare move forward, for its crew feared that the fusilier with his grenade and possibly a teller mine inside the bag, could easily devastate them. "If I can just hang on!" thought Shuhan, "I'll beat this son-of-a- bitch yet!"

Another round screamed over Shuhan. "That's right, you Leninist whores, just keep on firing!" And so it went, for several hours; yet not once throughout the ordeal did the almost middle-aged fusilier panic, or doubt his success. Shuhan's body, acting in concert with his mind, moved as if he were still a youth, and he prided himself on the fact that due to his actions, a number of his men had escaped harm.

Chapter 16: Brody!

Shortly before dusk, Shuhan heard the roar of the behemoth's engine. Backing up several feet, the tank turned around. The moment it did, Shuhan raced to his left, seeking cover in another depression. Spying a small wooded clump he ran for it and crawled in. Shuhan's camouflaged jacket and trousers blended perfectly with the terrain. Lying still, he only listened. With darkness setting in, Shuhan pulled out his thermos bottle, sipped some coffee, and consumed an iron ration. Deciding to sleep, he instructed his mind to awaken him at 3 a.m. After placing his MP on his chest with a finger on its trigger for instant action, Shuhan fell into a deep and restful sleep.

After a quick meeting with his divisional generals and a number of high-ranking personnel, Hauffe approved a southwesterly breakout. To achieve maximum success, a slight reorganization took place. The breakout, which was to take no longer than three days, was to follow such a plan: Corps Abteilung C (now redesignated as Kampfgruppe or 'Battlegroup C' but still commanded by Lange), would also include a large part of Lindemann's 361st Infantry. Along with Lasch's 349th Infantry, Battlegroup C would strike southward to create a breakout. Once achieved, Battlegroup C would secure the town of Bilyi Kamin (adjacent to the Buh River), and overrun Hill 366. Continuing to advance south/southwest, a river-crossing site would be secured at Pochapy on the Zolochivka River; immediately afterward, Hill 257 (approximately 1.5 miles southwest of Pochapy and overlooking Kniazhe) was to be secured for flank protection.

At the same time this would be occurring, Lasch's 349th Division (adjacent to Corps Abteilung C's left flank), would take Sasiv (south of the Buh River and almost adjacent to Hill 334) and Hill's 334 and 274 (Hill 274 was immediately north of Khylchychi), between the Buh and Zolochivka Rivers to ensure flank protection and to expand the breakout corridor. Simultaneously, as the breakout assault forces were moving, Netwig's 454th Field Security would be holding the Corps' right flank and part of the rear while the "Galicia" Division would be protecting the Corps' left flank and also a part of its rear.[6]

Within the corps' inner perimeter would be assembled the supply and service units, Corps headquarters, and several battlegroups from Lindemann's 361st to be rushed to whatever critical sectors needed reinforcement. Once the breakout was achieved, Task Force C and Lasch's 349th would move first, followed by the 454th and the "Galicia" Division bringing up the rear guard. Through such a "funnel," it was hoped that by the second day, Battlegroup C and Lasch's 349th would link up with Balck's 48th Panzer Corps on the Lviv-Ternopil Highway between the towns of Lakye and Zolochiv; on the 3rd day (but hopefully still on the second), the corps' two remaining divisions, along with its supply and services, would also pass through the "funnel" and the highway into the hands of the 48th Panzer Corps.

At no time was this decision based on subsequent Ukrainian criticisms that "this was a plan to deliberately leave the Division behind in order to enable the Germans to escape." Additionally, it must be noted that those German forces conducting the breakout had a mission just as essential (and in the initial breakout phase possibly more so), as those holding the flanks and rear. Considering as well that the 13th Corps would be fighting to the southwest and the "Galicia" Division was in the pocket's eastern/southeastern sector, under such circumstances there was no possibility for the surrounded and pressured corps to conduct a major repositioning. For military reasons, it was only logical for the "Galicia" Division to fall in last. 13th Corps attack hour – 3:30 a.m., 20 July.

Thursday, 20 July:
Problems, however, arose well before the attack hour. Within the 13th Corps, communications were poor. To reach Balck's 48th, and AGNU, was almost impossible. And Generals Lange and Lasch had no knowledge of Soviet strengths, dispositions and intents. Patrols dispatched earlier returned with limited information; what was received portrayed a grim situation. A sudden, but heavy rain turned roads into mud and swelled creeks. And the corps' commander, General Hauffe, lay dead.[1]

Assuming command of the 13th Corps, Lange was aware of the continuing Soviet effort against the "Galicia" Division which was covering the corps' left flank. Therefore, he dispatched some German units, initially authorized for the breakout, to assist the Division.

Prior to this breakout, a delegation of Ukrainian insurgents appeared at Freitag's headquarters with a proposal to assist the Division. What exactly was discussed, and what the UPA proposed, is not certain. The UPA most likely wanted to save the Division, but as it turned out, Freitag declined their offer. By no means, however, did the UPA totally retreat. Well before meeting with Freitag, the UPA's guerrillas had begun infiltrating the region to gather up any Divisional personnel and as much of its arms and equipment as possible.

Following a short delay, at 5 a.m., Battlegroup C attacked. Passing through Bilyi-Kamin and over the Buh, the corps' right wing (moving south/southwest), crossed the Zolochivka River and secured Belzets'; southeast of Bilyi-Kamin, the battlegroup's left wing fought a tough battle for Hill 366. After securing the hill and a handful of Soviet anti-tank guns, the Germans quickly turned these weapons against the Red Army. By 9 a.m., the initial breakout had succeeded.

Chapter 16: Brody!

With its flanks momentarily secured, the center of Battlegroup C surged forward. North of Pochapy, a tough battle ensued with Soviet armor but very quickly, no less than 20 enemy tanks were destroyed. Rushing into Pochapy to battle the entrenched Soviets, engineers scrambled to repair and reinforce the bridge. During this time, one of the corps' first supply columns, moving up to pass through the "funnel," approached Bilyi Kamin. But immediately at dawn, at approximately 7 a.m., Soviet aircraft appeared to blast the column. The sole defenders of the column were one of the "Galicia" Division's anti-aircraft batteries assigned to protect its own vehicles. Throughout the morning, the battery shot down no less than 25 enemy aircraft. But so intense were the air attacks that the column, as well as the anti-aircraft, were totally destroyed. Never would the anti-aircraft survivors forget the screams of the wounded as they burned alive inside their ambulances, and when Waffen-Hauptsturmführer Porfirii Sylenko[2] came through Bilyi-Kamin on his way to Pochapy a couple of days later, he would never forget the twisted and burned medical column he encountered, and the awkward positions of the burned bodies lying around. In some instances, the victim slumped half-way out of a vehicle. "Rather than being called Bilyi Kamin [White Stone], this place should be called Kryvavyi Kamin [Bloody Stone]," thought Sylenko.

At approximately 12 o'clock, Lange's forces secured Pochapy and Hill 257; simultaneously, Battlegroup C's left wing was now fighting in and around Zhulychi. Satisfied so far with the breakout results, and determined to exploit the initial success, Lange ordered the battlegroup's right wing (on the hill mass of 257), to take Kniazhe, while the left wing was to push towards the village of Khylchychi (on the Zolochivka River) to capture the elevation overlooking the village and river.

But whether Lange realized it or not, the corps' breakout forces were now beginning to penetrate into the Soviet rear.[3] Such an advance would cut Soviet communications, endanger its supply system and effectively prevent Soviet reinforcements from assisting those units already beyond Busk. In the end, 13th Corps' breakout could actually help to stabilize the front. Realizing this threat, but still determined to destroy the corps, Konev's front immediately countered Lange's breakout. The end result was a massive head-to-head confrontation.[4]

To contain the breakout, the 1st Ukrainian Front's air forces flew one massive sortie after another. So vicious were the air attacks that in the annals of the German-Soviet War, seldom were such air attacks experienced. These attacks were not only directed against Corps Formation C's attacking breakout units, but were also aimed against the artillery batteries north of Bilyi Kamin supporting the breakout. Such constant and uninterrupted air attacks, combined with heavy usage of the new 80 pound shrapnel bombs compacted into bundles which exploded and hurtled shrapnel with devastating effect, destroyed men, horses, wagons and light vehicles within areas of 100 by 100 meters. Such explosions not only shattered units physically, but also morally. Because Germany's Luftwaffe was virtually invisible, Soviet airmen encountered only ground fire.

By 5 p.m., Lange's ground thrust began to die out. Although the right wing reached Kniazhe, Lange's forces encountered dug-in Soviet armor, airborne, and guardists. Difficult to extract and outflank, and lacking proper artillery and aerial support, the Germans were unable to overcome the resistance. Simultaneously, Lange's left wing and the 349th encountered heavy Soviet forces rapidly arriving from the southeast which immediately challenged Lange's forces for Zhulychi and the high ground to its north. To prevent the Soviets from recapturing Hill 366 and close the gap, certain attacking units were immediately re-directed to assist Lange's left wing and help defend critical terrain. But of course, once this happened, the main effort was weakened. Clearly, Konev's front was determined to block any further movement.

As the villages and towns of Pidhirtsi, Bilyi Kamin, Belzets', Zhulychi, Yasenivtsi, Sasiv, Pochapy, Kniazhe, and Khylchychi burned, and as massive, violent, and high-pitched battles surged back and forth around the countryside south of the Buh and Zolochivka Rivers, the situation to the north of the Buh was just as brutal for those attempting to hold the 13th Corps' flanks and rear while simultaneously, preparing to follow the breakout forces.

North of Sasiv, the 31st Regiment began to collapse. With its regimental commander dead, and much of its officer and NCO leadership eliminated, the regiment began to fall back towards Ushnia, Cheremoshnia (two towns located directly east of Bilyi Kamin), and Bilyi Kamin. As for the battered 29th, its efforts to hold the ancient town and castle of Oles'ko, from which such defenders as Roman Ostashevsky were able to view everything to the north, south, east, and west, were proving unsuccessful, Preparing to withdraw, they buried those who earlier had fallen in shallow graves: Stefan Hladij, 4th Co., 1st Bn., 29th Rgt.; Fedir Salanyk, 3rd Co., 1st Bn., 29th Rgt.; Waffen-Untersturmführer Danylyzhyn; Ivan Kopczuk; Peter Bacher, who hailed from Brody – these were just some of the names placed into eternal rest.

Throughout that day, the surviving batteries of the Division's artillery continued to assist the pocket's eastern defenders and those to the north withdrawing from Oles'ko. Repeatedly, the artillerymen plastered all approaches and intersections in the vicinity of Pidhirtsi and Oles'ko to ensure a successful withdrawal, while the fusiliers covered the withdrawal.

Chapter 16: Brody!

After his personal encounter with Soviet armor, Shuhan linked up with his troops. But Shuhan's hopes for an uninterrupted disengagement and withdrawal from Oles'ko to the south of Pidhirtsi suddenly ended with the sound of clanking tank treads. "Sons-of-bitches can't leave me alone" thought Shuhan. As the 29th's rear guard, fusiliers, and support personnel sought cover, they observed the enemy armor circling and positioning themselves for the kill.

Fear gripped the men. Looking around, Shuhan noted that very few of the men possessed anti-armor weaponry. With only their small arms, they stood no chance. The crack of tank cannons split the air. Dirt and debris rained down on the men. Hot, 7.62mm slugs tore up the ground, incoming rounds destroyed trees and tore natural cover – and men – into pieces. For Shuhan and the rest, the end seemed in sight.

Suddenly, out of the blue, a well-camouflaged light-supply truck appeared. Totally covered with brush, and driven by the fusilier battalion's German supply officer, the truck appeared just at the critical moment. Seeing earlier that the fusiliers were beginning to run out of anti-armor and small-arms ammunition, and knowing that the supply system had broken down, the German officer drove his motorcycle into the center of the pocket in a search for critically needed panzerfausts and ammunition. Jumping out of the truck, the officer shouted "BOY'S, OVER HERE! QUICKLY, LET'S UNLOAD THESE CRATES!" and ran to the rear of the truck. Immediately, two fusiliers jumped onto its rear and tossed the truck crates onto the ground while others, along with the German officer, ripped the crates apart. In some cases, the crates were not even opened; simply, rifle butts and bare hands tore them apart. Years later, Shuhan would recall the sight of fresh blood on several of the crates.

"HERE! TAKE TWO! EVERYONE! TAKE TWO!" The moment a crate's cover was opened or ripped apart, its four panzerfausts disappeared. Shuhan's machinegunner, noting an MG 34 on the back of the truck, reached for it. Quickly opening the boxes of ammunition adjacent to it, he linked the 100 round straps together and fully armed, followed Shuhan.

The moment a man had a couple of panzerfausts and some extra ammunition, he raced off to engage a tank. Within minutes of the truck's arrival, Soviet tanks began to explode into flaming pyres. Well-aimed panzerfausts struck home, and a circle of burning tanks surrounded the trapped men. Of the approximately 30 tanks which had surrounded the group, Shuhan counted no less than 16 burning hulks while the remaining tanks withdrew. Cheers of joy rose from the defenders.

Standing approximately 15 feet in back of the truck amidst a pile of broken cases, the German officer, undoubtedly aware that he had done a good job, reached into his pants pocket for a pack of cigarettes. Facing the truck and looking down the road, he never saw the T-34 which suddenly popped up in his rear.

In his attempt to warn the officer, Shuhan raised his hand, but the officer only waved back. He probably felt no pain as the T-34's red-hot tank shell ripped him in half, tore into the truck, and with a massive explosion, literally blew the blazing truck a good 200 feet down the road.[5]

Curses and screams rose from the men. Angrily, one soldier after another fired his panzerfaust at the T-34. It didn't matter that the tank was totally consumed by flames – panzerfaust rounds continued to devastate the hulk.

In a small wooded grove between Bilyi Kamin and Pochapy, Lange met with the various corp's commanders. Freitag, Heike, Beyersdorff, Sylenko, Dolynsky, and Paliiv represented the Division.[6]

Lange spoke directly to the point. Acknowledging that the breakout forces had overrun their first objectives but then had run into problems, Lange persisted in an immediate renewed effort. He firmly believed the Soviets were rapidly gaining strength. Although admitting that a night's rest would benefit the troops, he pointed out that the lost time would enable the Soviets to further gain strength by the crack of dawn; additionally, the Red Air Force would appear at the crack of dawn, Therefore, Lange opted for a night attack to reach the Lviv highway between the towns of Yasenivtsi and Liats'ke (west of Zolochiv). Everyone supported Lange.

Lange was then briefed by the other commanders on their current situation. But when his turn came, Freitag stated he was in no position to give an adequate report because "I believe the Division is no longer under my control!"; and promptly, handed in his resignation.

Freitag's abrupt reply not only demonstrated a complete lack of professionalism, but rudeness and stupidity as well. A highly embarrassed Heike could not believe what he was hearing. And Lange, who was anticipating an intelligent and realistic account, frowned in disapproval and disdain upon Freitag. At this moment, Waffen-Obersturmführer Dolynsky informed Freitag and the others that certain Divisional units were still available. Accepting Freitag's resignation, Lange posted him to the 13th Corps Headquarters, while Lindemann was given command of the Division.

Although for the moment such a move placed the Division under a more fit commander, as noted by Ren himself, Lindemann was hindered by the fact that he was unfamiliar with the Division, its commanders, and the full scope of its current situation.[7] However, Ren credits Lindemann for his efforts in withdrawing the remains of the Division out of encirclement and destruction.[8]

Chapter 16: Brody!

Besides the fact that Freitag had put his commanders in a negative light, demonstrating nothing but contempt for the Division, his accusation that the Division was uncontrollable was totally false. True, within the perimeter the Division had received a pounding, but it was far from a complete annihilation. From the beginning, shattered units were constantly reformed and pressed into other units,[9] the Division's supply and support had functioned reasonably well; no major panic had set in; no desertions to the other side were reported; fusiliers were still rushing from one sector to another and another to bolster a unit or front, and the Division's remaining anti-aircraft and artillery were still operational. Throughout the whole ordeal, not one Divisional officer had approached Freitag with a suggestion to surrender. And unlike Lange and many other high-ranking officers who, with a rifle or Schmeisser in hand, personally fought and in some cases died side by side beside their men, Freitag was seldom seen. So little, in fact, was seen of Freitag that within the pocket, a rumor emerged that Freitag had flown out of the pocket in the Division's airplane.

If Freitag harbored any doubts about the Division's ability to hold out, he should have at least consulted with Heike. If he feared his Division was collapsing, and if he were a true soldier, Freitag should have replied to Lange's inquiry in such a manner:

> "General Lange, our situation is as such: Our Division has taken a blow, but we've got units operating. Some of my commanders, assembled here, can provide you detailed reports. Although we will continue to do the best we can, I fear we may not be able to hold out. As a result, I am asking you for some additional assistance. In the meantime, I propose to break the Division into a number of kampfgruppes which will continue to assist the corps breakout, hold any necessary flanks and corridors, and then withdrew once the bulk of the corps is out. As for me, I will attach myself to one such group."

By such an honest appraisal, Freitag would have demonstrated loyalty, concern, and some measure of optimism, instilling some additional pride at a critical moment, and maintaining morale. Instead, Freitag chose to create an attitude of enmity towards himself which, months later, he possibly regretted.[10] Needless to say, Freitag's words were never forgotten. In the following days, when during the breakout Dolynsky met Lange by chance, Lange remarked "Your Division has a strange commander!"[11]

By the end of the day, the Division's 31st Regiment collapsed. SS-Obersturmbannführer Paul Herms, along with most of his staff, was killed north of Sasiv. Lying on the ground and feigning death, staff soldier Mark Tork would never forget how Soviet officers went around and administered the coup-de-grace to the wounded. Robbed as he lay feigning death, Mark prayed in silence as two Russians removed his boots, and then began to argue over who should get his pants. The argument, however, was never resolved because suddenly, the Division's fusiliers came storming in, saving Mark's life. He later recovered his wallet from a shot and bayoneted commissar. As with the 29th Regiment, the 31st's remaining personnel were incorporated into the various units. Late that day, continuing efforts to defend or retake Opaky, a town approximately 4 miles east of Sasiv, ceased.

In a pitch black forest deep in the Carpathian Mountains, Vashchenko met with UPA's general, Roman Shukhevych. Realizing that the 13th Corps' efforts in conducting a successful breakout were nil, a discussion arose on a course-of-action to assist the Division's personnel.

But efforts to assist the Division would not be easy. Aside from the fact that 13th Corps was surrounded by a ring of Soviet steel, Konev was quickly dispatching reinforcements to contain and destroy the entire corps. "It will not be easy," stated Shukhevych, "but every man, every gun, every round that we can gather up will benefit us. So let's do it, and do it now!" With' such words, UPA-West was ordered to extradite whatever Divisional personnel it could.

Friday, 21 July:
At 1 a.m., Battlegroup C's right wing, with no preparatory artillery fires, pressed forward once again. Reaching Pochapy at approximately 5 a.m., Lange quickly established a forward command post. There, he was informed that Battlegroup C's right wing had captured Kniazhe but because of a heavy Soviet counter-attack, lost the town. As for the left wing, reorganizational problems, combined with sporadic night fighting, had delayed its attack time until 4 a.m. But once reinforced with groups of soldiers from the other divisions and some assault guns, the left wing successfully advanced from its starting positions in Khylchychi's vicinity into Yasenivtsi. At last, 13th Corps reached the main highway.

Communication problems, however, prevented the assault groups from notifying Lange of what had transpired. Under orders to establish contact with the 48th Panzer Corps, and realizing the dangers of halting the advance, the left wing's commanders decided to continue to press forward, Moving directly southward, south of Yasenivtsi (and virtually adjacent to the village of Zalizya), Hill 412 was secured.

Continuing to push southward, the advancing force reached the town of Zhukiv, located approximately 8.5 miles south of Yasenivtsi and the main highway. There,

Chapter 16: Brody!

at last, 13th Corps left wing established contact with the 1st Panzer Division, while the right wing renewed another attack on Kniazhe, but again failed to secure the village. As Battlegroup C's assault soldiers fought and died around Kniazhe, other groups east of Kniazhe successfully bypassed the Soviet forces and broke through. Advancing quickly to the highway, they crossed it east of Liats'ke, bypassed Hill 412 and after a rapid southwestward march of approximately 5 miles, established contact with Balck's 8th Panzer near Holohory.

Lange, however, had no knowledge of this either. And although a breakout had been achieved, by noontime, the Soviets had immediately closed the escape corridor with heavy forces, reinforced Kniazhe, and were attempting to retake Hill 257. As for Lasch's 349th Infantry, a division again earmarked for the breakout, it once again encountered severe problems south/southeast of Zhulychi. Aside from a very limited number of its personnel who somehow ended up with Battlegroup C, the 349th, forced to a standstill, was being systematically destroyed. And excluding the limited number of personnel who had succeeded in running the gauntlet and breaking out, the bulk of Battlegroup C, the 349th, 454th and the 14th Waffen-SS was still inside a pocket that was rapidly shrinking in size.

That day, the remainder of the 454th Field Security collapsed. Never a strong division, with only two security regiments, one reconnaissance, anti-tank, engineer and signal companies, what remained of the 454th was incorporated into the various 13th Corps units. As for the remaining units within the pocket, their situation only worsened as ammunition shortages developed and constant enemy aerial, ground, artillery and rocket attacks continued to compress the pocket's size. With anti-aircraft and artillery pieces running out of ammunition or simply destroyed, it was becoming virtually impossible to counter Soviet aircraft and ground batteries. And by now, it was not even uncommon for Soviet armor to suddenly appear within the pocket, causing mayhem.

Totally disregarding the wagon filled with wounded, the heavy KV-85 rolled slowly forwards. Its machine guns fully blazing, the tank clambered upon a crowded wagon, crushed it, neutral-steered over the wreckage to ensure that everyone and everything was crushed and then, the iron behemoth continued forward.

"RATATATATA!!" "RATATATATA!!" Struck with 7.62mm rounds, two more horses whinnied, stood up on their rear legs and collapsed into a heap. Attempting to escape, the wagon driver jumped off, but the moment his feet touched the ground, 7.62mm tank bullets tore him apart. Collapsing on top of the dead horses, the man lay for no more than several seconds before the incoming KV-85 crushed the two dead animals and one human into the ground, with bursts of fresh blood actually splattering out from beneath the tank tracks.

Suddenly, the steel monster's turret swung rapidly to its left. A slight distance off the side of the road beneath a couple of trees, stood a military ambulance, with its distinct Red Cross symbol. Aiming its barrel, the KV fired a round into it. A high velocity shell tore the ambulance into pieces and silenced forever its medical crew. Spinning its turret a full 360 degrees, the tank's co-axial machinegun sprayed everything within range. Revving its engine, the KV pressed forward and continued to unleash more death and destruction.

A chaplain, who could take no more, appeared from behind a wagon. Standing directly in front of the tank, he raised and held upward his cross. Hot slugs killed him instantly. An anti-tank PAK team, swinging into action, fired at the iron monster. Striking too high, the round angled off the turret. But before the crew could re-adjust and fire again, the KV shattered the PAK and its crew with one well-placed shot. Then, someone fired a panzerfaust round at the steel behemoth, but missed. Exploding beside the tank, the round only challenged the KV crew to move again.

7.62mm slugs dropped more men and horses. A supply officer, his legs shattered from the machine-gun fire, attempted to crawl away. But he crawled no more than several feet when the incoming hulk flattened him into the ground. Another round tore into a maintenance repair truck. Its driver, or what was left of him, emerged shrouded in a circle of flame. Falling to the ground, the torched human stood up, extended his burning arms sideways, took several steps forward and collapsed in a burning heap.

For those on the road, the end seemed in sight. But suddenly, a lone figure was seen snaking his way amongst the carnage toward the steel behemoth. Clutching a satchel charge in his right hand, the figure was identifiable as a member of the Division by the "Galicia" lion patch on his camouflaged smock. Clambering aboard the tank's rear deck, he surged toward its turret. Lying on the turret's top, the grenadier hung onto a hatchet's handle as the tank's crew repeatedly spun the turret and slammed it to a stop in a vain attempt to throw him off. Failing to open the turret's hatch, the grenadier tied the satchel to the base of the turret. Removing from his boot his remaining stick grenade, the figure pulled its pin, shouted "SLAVA UKRAINI!" and leaned the grenade beside the satchel charge.

A massive explosion tore into the turret. Within seconds, the entire KV was consumed in one massive flame. Indeed, the fire was so intense that hours later, the surrounding countryside was still lit up by the burning pyre. As for the grenadier who tore the tank apart, he was never seen again.

Chapter 16: Brody!

Failing once again in another concentrated effort to break out, and fully aware that if an immediate breakout did not occur, then all would be lost, Lange insisted on another attempt. But unlike previous efforts, the upcoming breakout would be conducted by a number of independently operating battlegroups. What worried Lange and his commanders, however, was that a number of these battlegroups would be conducting what every military commander has always feared and hated since the advent of organized warfare: frontal assaults.

Readying himself and his men, Evstakhyi "Stasho" Il'nyts'kyi wondered how the breakout would go. By profession a first-rate mechanic, "Stasho" had previously served as a corporal in the Polish Army. In the closing days of the German blitzkrieg Stasho, along with elements of various battered Polish units, broke out of a series of German encirclements to retreat successfully into Rumania. In 1940, as an NCO in the reformed Polish 1st Infantry Division based in France, "Stasho" once again fought the Nazis. But as previously in Poland, the German blitzkrieg overran Western Europe. Along with a number of other Polish, Moroccan, Belgian and French Foreign Legionnaires, "Stasho" fought a successful rear guard operation at Dunkirk. It was because of soldiers such as "Stasho" that many a fellow allied soldier – Pole, English, French and others – escaped via the English Channel to England.

Unable to escape, "Stasho" was forced to surrender. But several days later, he fled from German captivity in Northern France. Knowing that there was a Ukrainian emigre organization in Paris, "Stasho" made his way to Paris. Concealing him, the Ukrainian emigres also provided him with an alias and false papers. In 1941, "Stasho" returned to Galicia and found employment as a postal worker. In 1943, the former allied soldier enlisted in the Division. Now, as a section leader, "Stasho" calmly briefed his men on what to expect during the upcoming breakout.

Since it had become apparent that an organized corps effort would no longer be feasible, time was running out, no relief force was in sight, and communications were virtually non-existent, it was now hoped that a breakout could be achieved by a series of battlegroups. Rapidly striking the enemy, certain groups would tie down the Soviet forces, while others would bypass to breakout. Because the road from Bilyi Kamin to Pochapy was devastated, blocked by columns of burned out and battered vehicles, and with massive Soviet air attacks relentlessly continuing, it was obvious that the corps would not be able to drive its remaining vehicles, heavy equipment and artillery out of the pocket. Orders were thus issued to destroy all remaining vehicles and heavy equipment.

The plan was as follows: those 13th Corps units still operating north of the Buh River would fall back to Bilyi Kamin and cross the Buh River. Once crossed, any remaining bridges would be destroyed. Such a move would shorten the line, reduce the distance to the southwest, and relieve much ground pressure against the corps from the north. Once south of the river, the battered formations would reorganize themselves into battlegroups. Discarding all unnecessary equipment, the groups would arm themselves as best as possible, rest, and prepare to break out. But in the meantime, as the Buh was to be crossed, flank and rear security around Bilyi Kamin had to be maintained.

But as the corps' northern perimeter withdrew into Bilyi Kamin to cross the Buh, Soviet forces continued their relentless attacks in an effort to secure Bilyi Kamin and trap and destroy the remaining forces north of the Buh. By evening, the battle was spilling into the burning town of Bilyi Kamin, where the Division's fusiliers, bolstered by survivors from other units, were holding out as long as possible to enable others to cross the Buh through Bilyi Kamin.

"Mama! Mama! I can't see. I can't see!" A little girl, no more than four or five years of age, stepped out of a burning cottage into the street. Her tiny hands clasping her eyes and forehead, she screamed in agony as blood ran down her cheeks.

Both sides immediately ceased to fire. Continuing to scream, the little girl walked halfway out to the center of the street, stopped, and just stood. "Mama, Mama. It hurts!"

An eerie silence prevailed. Only the crackle of Bilyi Kamin's burning and simmering wood could be heard. As the child stood in the middle of a row of flaming and smoking buildings, she once again cried out.

Suddenly, a medical Waffen-Rottenführer's voice was heard as he shouted "I'LL GET HER!" Dashing from his position of safety, he ran up to the child, swept her into his arms, and turned to run back. But his attempt to remove the child to safety was suddenly ended by the burst of an enemy submachine gun. The very same hot rounds which ripped into his back and exited his lungs, simultaneously, took the life of the little girl.[1]

Saturday, 22 July – Monday, 24 July:
Throughout the early morning hours of 22 July, within a pocket approximately 4-5 miles from north to south and about the same from east to west, the battered 13th Corps prepared for its breakout. With the last troops out of Bilyi Kamin, the town was no longer within the pocket and the pocket's northern border was on the Buh River's southern bank, where, its survivors quickly prepared for the breakout.

Realizing that he would pose a burden and a threat to the survivors of the 31st Regiment's 1st Battalion's, 1st Company, SS-Hauptsturmführer von Zalzinger, its wounded company commander, committed suicide. After hearing the shot, Leshko Zur* came over and gently covered the officer with a poncho.[1]

By now, a number of the groups were no longer composed of just soldiers from a specific unit. Excluding the fusiliers and the survivors of certain artillery batteries who remained intact, the remaining Divisional and corps' regiments and battalions began to collapse, and its survivors found themselves incorporated into mixed battlegroups. Soon, infantrymen, artillerymen with or without guns, anti-aircraft gunners, mechanics, communications personnel, cooks, and others from various Divisional units were compacted together. Additionally, a number of the "Galicia" Division's personnel found themselves mixing in with some of the German battlegroups. Such groups were either led by those who held the highest rank or, regardless of rank, exhibited an ability to lead.

Lange planned to strike at 3 a.m. But one of the problems frequently encountered by a breakout of this type is that no one would be making a concentrated effort to secure any flanks or key terrain. Communications, as well, were virtually non-existent. Simply stated, once a group began its move, it would continue until it either successfully broke out, or perished. The wounded, if not carried out on someone's shoulder or on a stretcher, were simply left behind. It is known that a number of the wounded were brought to Pochapy where, in a church located at Pochapy, a temporary, makeshift hospital was established. But when those at Pochapy realized that the only way out was by attacking through the Soviet ring, simultaneously, it was realized that, excluding a limited number of the wounded personnel which could be evacuated, the majority would have to be left behind. Those Divisional troops which passed through Pochapy would never forget the sight of the wounded and injured as they lay around Pochapy's church, awaiting to be taken inside for treatment.[2] As the brave medics and doctors treated the incapacitated, Chaplain Durbak was observed among them. Refusing to depart with any of the breakout groups, the brave chaplain was last seen assisting the wounded. To this day, his fate remains unknown.[3]

As the "Galicia" Division's troops prepared to breakout, a final effort was made by certain Divisional commanders to utilize as much as possible the Division's remaining firepower. Orders were issued to bring up any remaining artillery and heavy mortars.

After crossing the bridge at Bilyi Kamin, Dlaboha's men worked their way south towards Pochapy. Along the way, they passed columns of stranded, destroyed and smoldering vehicles and wagons. Frequently, they also encountered groups of demoralized German soldiers who sat motionless by the side of the road, or milled around, simply waiting for the enemy to gather them up. Clearly, it was now becoming evident that a large part of 13th Corps was beginning to disintegrate in defeat. Dlaboha was proud of the fact that out of the entire artillery regiment, his battery was the only one that still maintained its four artillery pieces.

Observing his soldiers pulling and pushing the artillery pieces, Dlaboha wondered what they were made of. For the last seven days, he had dragged them through hell and yet, throughout the entire ordeal, not one man had complained or faltered. "Damn," thought Dlaboha, " they were good." Tough 16 and 17-year- old kids; a former boxer; a middle-aged ex-Austrian soldier turned accountant who lied about his age to enlist; a former NKVD officer; and a UPA guerrilla fighter who, just two days earlier, had confided to Dlaboha that he had infiltrated the Division to learn about artillery and how, near Stanislaviv in April 1943, he had killed two Gestapo agents. But then, Dlaboha momentarily reflected on men such as Spyrydon Hrybenko, Vasyl Duboshchuk, Ostap Dovhan, Vasyl Zahaidachnyi, Roman Levandivsky, Boryslav Dolyk, Yuriy Kolodynskiy, Volodymyr Valiy, Ivan Vynnychuk, Yuriy Bohoniuk, Myhailo Batiuk, Chaplain Vasyl Leshchyshyn ... "Oh God," thought Dlaboha, "its endless."

As soon as Dlaboha's men set up their four 105mm guns adjacent to several other guns, Dlaboha briefed them on what was to transpire.

At dawn, another corps breakout was authorized. Prior to the forward charge of the assault groups, the remaining artillery would saturate certain designated areas in the vicinity of Kniazhe. Because of a lack of ammunition, the preparatory fire would be short but intense. Once the remaining shells were fired, the artillerymen would latch on to an assault group. By then, it was hoped that a breach in the enemy line would be achieved; if not, the artillerymen would have to fight their way through. To ensure a rapid breakout, the guns would be destroyed and all remaining horses released. Dlaboha was saddened at the prospect of destroying the guns, a weapons system which had well served his men first in Northwestern Ukraine and now, at Brody. But seeing that there was no alternative, explosive packages with timers were prepared. Realizing also that for the last five days he had not slept a wink, and had subsisted only on cigarettes and a handful of iron rations, Dlaboha lay down beside one of his guns.

At approximately 4:50 a.m., Dlaboha rose. His body trembling from sheer exhaustion and a high fever, he noted his men already standing beside their guns. "0456, 0457, 0458, 0459, FIRE!" At exactly 5 a.m., Dlaboha's gunners unleashed their remaining salvos. Within moments, distant explosions were heard.

Setting their timers, the men blew their guns. Merging with a group of German and Divisional survivors, the self-composed battlegroup surged forward. Unlike many who lost their will to fight and survive, the battlegroup struck hard. Near

Chapter 16: Brody!

Kniazhe, at point-blank range, Dlaboha sprayed a Soviet submachine gunner. Dropping the empty MP 38/40, Dlaboha instantly reached for his remaining stick grenade, pulled its pin and with his remaining strength, hurtled the device into a hastily constructed blocking position. Screams, followed by silence, told Dlaboha the grenade had struck home.

Collapsing to the ground, Dlaboha attempted to stand up. Exhaustion, however, prevented his body from doing so. The end seemed in sight for the artillery officer but suddenly, he felt his body being heaved over someone's shoulder. Carried to safety, Dlahoba survived the ordeal.

Having secured Khylchychi, the mixed battlegroups continued to surge forward toward Kniazhe. Among them was Waffen-Sturmbannführer Palienko. With a transmitter/receiver radio strapped to his back, and armed with a clipboard, map, pencil, compass, and a pair of binoculars suspended from around his neck, Palienko, adorned in a peasant cap, actually looked more like a schoolteacher on an outing rather than an artillery battalion commander charging into battle. But there was nothing timid about the soft-spoken and very patient man who seldom displayed anger. Hitting the ground hundreds of meters in front of Kniazhe, Palienko immediately searched for targets. Using a couple of the Division's artillery pieces, and two Tiger tanks, which earlier had reached the breakout forces, Palienko immediately suppressed two dug-in T-34's. Spotting another T-34 inside a building, he called for an artillery round, adjusted its impact, called in for two more rounds, and watched as the well-placed rounds tore the T-34 apart. Running another hundred meters forward, Palienko spotted a dug-in infantry position and a tank to its right. Accurately estimating its location, Palienko requested another single round and watched as it exploded in the midst of the enemy position. The moment Palienko shouted the command: "FIRE!" Galicia's gunners unleashed a handful of rounds, killing everything in Palienko's sight.

Suspecting that the stone ruins of a demolished school building could well be concealing enemy snipers, Palienko transmitted its location to the artillerymen, noted with approval the way the young voice repeated its location, and waited the artillery round's flight.

The moment the round struck, a well-concealed T-34 went up in a ball of flame. Spotting two more tanks, Palienko called in their locations. Informed by the youthful voice that only two more explosive and four smoke rounds remained, Palienko instructed the gunner to "Wait one!" Because earlier Palienko had personally established contact with the two tanks and they had been monitoring his activities, Palienko requested the tanks to suppress the enemy armor.

With no less than six tanks demolished, and at least several positions demolished, the Soviets began to withdraw from Kniazhe. Informing the two-gun battery of their deeds, Palienko requested the remaining rounds to be dropped outside of Kniazhe among the fleeing foe and the remaining smoke rounds dropped on the edge of Kniazhe. Palienko undoubtedly regretted there was no more smoke to cover the assault groups attack, but at least some smoke was better than none. Waving to the battlegroup to press forward, the artillery officer observed their thrust.

"SLAVA!" Charging forward, the primarily Ukrainian battle- group quickly dug out the remaining Soviets, retook Kniazhe and continued to surge beyond the town. Until the Soviets returned and re-occupied the town, Kniazhe no longer barred the way. As he stood up, Palienko reached underneath his camouflaged smock, and felt the stickiness of blood. As several soldiers rushed up, he ordered them to move on, and then collapsed.

Unfortunate events, however, continued to plague 13th Corps. Although another penetration had been achieved, the bulk of Balck's 48th Panzer Corps was nowhere in sight. To make matters worse, as the encircled troops broke out, they only broke into masses of Soviet forces pushing westward. Such a situation forced those who broke out to continue fighting.

Correctly assuming that a rescue effort from Balck or AGNU would not arrive in full strength, and that AGNU was probably itself withdrawing, Lange ordered the corps' remaining personnel to retreat as rapidly as possible toward the southwest. How many received the order will never be known, but undoubtedly every survivor now understood that the only way out was to fight in a southwest direction.

Approaching Yasenivtsi from the west, Waffen-Obersturmführer Karatnytsky and a number of his men set fire to a small building in order to create a smoke screen. Simultaneously, Waffen Hauptsturmführer Dmytro Ferkuniak's group, with their nine machine guns set up on a railway embankment, commenced fire on the eastern edge of Yasenivtsi in an attempt to pin down any defenders. Behind Ferkuniak a Wehrmacht officer, Major Ziegler, covered Ferkuniak's group while Waffen-Hauptsturmführer Chuchkevych provided flank protection to the east of Yasenivtsi. These four battlegroups, with a combined strength of approximately 1,000 Waffen-SS, Wehrmacht and Field Security personnel, were rapidly moving southward during the night to reach and cross the main Lviv-Zolochiv Highway. Once across, in the area of Zalesie's thicker woods and rough terrain, better natural cover and protection would be found. But at least for now, it was just as critical to break out.

Chapter 16: Brody!

Until the 1,000-strong armed force had arrived to Yasenivtsi at approximately 4 a.m., all had gone well. South of Pochapy, the escape corridor had narrowed to a distance of no more than 150-200 meters, but no problems were encountered.[4] Proceeding swiftly and quietly, the four battlegroups moved with one group forward, two in the middle and one in the rear. Carrying only personal weapons, anti-armor weaponry and as much ammunition as possible, the leading force automatically bypassed any danger the moment it encountered enemy forces. The others followed suit.

But at Yasenivtsi, a night battle ensued. In difficult hand-to-hand combat, the enemy was finally dislodged. By 7 a.m., all four groups crossed the highway and reached Zalesie and Hill 412; there, they paused to rest. But they were quickly interrupted by the appearance of one German fighter-bomber. Mistaking the soldiers for a Soviet force, it strafed and bombed the men. Following the air attack, everyone laughed when someone said "Oh, well. The high command did not lie. They said the Luftwaffe would arrive!"

At night, the groups continued to push southward. Sometime during the night of 22-23 July, in Zhukiv's vicinity, the leading group encountered a motorcycle courier who informed the men that the Germans were withdrawing from Zhukiv. For the remainder of the night, the men quickly marched westward. At last, in the morning, the groups linked up with the retreating German front and with a "Galicia" battlegroup led by Chaplain Myhailo Levenets' and consisting of 120 well-armed men. For those who broke out, it was a jubilant encounter. But from an initial strength of approximately 1,000 men within the four groups (of whom about 750 were from the "Galicia" Division), roll call revealed only 430 survivors. Most were lost either at Yasenivtsi or during the attempt to cross the highway.[5] The casualties included Waffen-Untersturmführer Pashchak who shot himself after being wounded in action.

In desperate and intense combat, the Division's soldiers, as well as those from other divisions trying to break out, continued to surge forward. Through their efforts, 13th Corps divisions constantly kept the pressing enemy at bay, re-opened escape routes, and although continuously taking casualties, simultaneously extracted a toll from the attackers. Through burning villages and towns, such as Bilyi Kamin, Belzets', Ostrivets, Skvariava, Pochapy, Kniazhe, Khylchychi, Liats'ke, Yasenivtsi, Zolochiv, Stinka, Holohory, Luni, Zhashkiv, Zhukiv, Vyshnivchyk and Plenykiv, the Division's and corps' troops ran through a gauntlet of hell.[6] In an attempt to contain the breakout, Soviet airmen flew no less than 2,340 air sorties.[7] At Zhukiv and Holohory, blocking positions were successfully established, temporarily preventing the Soviets from decisively halting the breakout and finishing off 13th Corps. Realizing that efforts to prevent a total breakout were failing, and that the Division's and corps' troops were pushing into the 1st Ukrainian Front's rear and communications, Konev stopped some of the front's units from pushing westward, instead redirecting them east into such areas as Bilyi Kamin, Krasne, Pochapy, Holohory and Zhukiv. But as the freshly committed units arrived, they only encountered determined groups of soldiers bent on breaking out. Such was the case of the 91st Independent "Proskurov" Tank Brigade. Part of Rybalko's 3rd Guards Tank Army, the 91st was stopped in its tracks and redirected back eastward. Passing south of Krasne in the vicinity of Ostrivchyk and Skvariava, the 91st, after crossing the Zolochivka River, drove headlong into Bilyi Kamin to seal the escape corridor. But there, the independent tank brigade took such a pounding that it ceased to exist. Days later, the bullet-riddled body of one of its commanders was found lying atop a devastated hulk.[8] As its armor joined the graveyard of Soviet armor throughout that region, 13th Corps and Galicia's volunteers once again demonstrated that even in defeat, they could strike a severe blow. But in such fighting, self-contained battlegroups did not only display success; on occasion, one man alone could demonstrate it.

As the battle raged in and around the ruins of Zhukiv, rifle-man-turned-sniper Oleh Dir* was not only fighting his own kind of war, but was actually in a position to alter the course of events.

Dir did not care to shoot at individual Soviet soldiers. After all, he reasoned, these guys were just like him and the rest – "Nothing but a bunch of poor bastards just caught up in this madness." But when it came to Soviet officers, and especially the hated NKVD and their commissars, Dir sought them out with a passion. Continuing to lie in the smoking ruins of what was once a school house, Dir scanned the battlefield and momentarily reflected upon the events which had brought him there.

By nature, Dir was not a violent person. He considered his upbringing a normal one and, if it hadn't been for the war, he might have continued his studies as his uncle had desired. Dir was no more than three years old when an accident had taken his father's life, yet, practically speaking, Dir was never without a father. Although Dir and his mother resided in another part of Lviv, and there was no blood relationship between him and his "uncle," the latter was always helping out. Later, when he married and had a daughter of his own, the man still continued to treat Dir as if he were his own son. Dir tremendously respected his uncle and through the years, grew exceptionally close to him.

But all of that changed in the madness of 1941. Awakened one early Saturday morning in June by the cries of his aunt, who had suddenly arrived, Dir learned that just hours before, the dreaded NKVD had arrested his uncle and that now, the woman was desperately seeking refuge for herself and her eight-year-old daughter. To make matters worse, throughout that awful month of June nothing was heard about the man's fate. Mass arrests only continued, and from day to day the family feared for their own fate.

But late one evening toward the end of June, Dir dared to leave the house and go outside. Standing in the deserted street, he thought he heard the rumble of an explosion in the distance. He wondered if this had anything to do with the German air squadron which he had momentarily spotted the day before, or with the strict Soviet curfew prohibiting anyone from leaving their homes or apartments. Regardless, on the following day, as strange-looking vehicles with black and white crosses rolled into the city's streets, Lviv's citizenry realized what they had suspected all along – that hostilities had at last erupted between Europe's two major totalitarian powers. Along with the German arrival, Lviv's inhabitants would soon learn the fate of those arrested.

Leaving the little girl behind with their neighbors, that afternoon Dir accompanied his mother and mother's sister to Lviv's Brigidky prison where, it was rumored, the prisoners were kept. As the threesome approached the center and made their way through the large crowds which had preceded them, they came upon a horrifying sight.

Inside Brigidky's courtyard, the screams and wails of Lviv's women could be heard as they walked among the rows of dead and identified their loved ones. Closely following his mother and aunt, Dir watched as they would lift a blanket, peer at a face, and gently restore the blanket over the victim's face. And so it went until they found the man they sought. As the two women grasped each other for comfort and strength, Dir only stared at the corpse. Clearly, it was evident that his uncle had been beaten – a man who had never harmed anyone and had always sought to live his life in peace. Continuing to stare, Dir experienced mixed emotions of grief, anger, frustration and hurt.

But in those nightmarish days, the young man would only witness more harshness. He tried to remain strong for his mother, aunt, and the little girl. Yet, the insanity only continued and sometimes, it seemed to worsen. Dir noticed how at first the original German occupiers appeared to be a decent lot of men who seemed sympathetic to Lviv's citizenry, assisted its populace, handed out candy to little children and viewed the Brigidky massacre with horror and contempt. But the original occupiers did not stay long and as they left to push further eastward, another group of occupiers arrived. Wearing a different type of uniform, the new occupiers came only to rule and if anyone failed to comply with their demands, swift arrest ensued.

For nearly two years following the murder of his uncle, Dir continued to live with his mother, aunt and cousin. He tried to be a father to the little girl, but as much as he tried, he could never bring back those carefree days of family life. For Dir, himself, life was also uncertain and he secretly feared that one day he might be hauled off to one of Germany's dreaded "volunteer" labor programs. He considered running away, but where could he possibly go? As for linking up with the UPA, the idea of being a guerrilla fighter, although romantic in theory, in the harsh light of reality offered only an ugly way of fighting and surviving. He sometimes wished that he could obtain a weapon. But what good was a weapon without proper training? And besides, in the last year or so, while life under the German occupation was far from secure, the harshness of its earlier days had somewhat abated. Perhaps, hoped Dir, Hitler would some day come to his senses, and after destroying the imperialistic communist state, would pull out of Galicia and allow its people to live in peace.

Yet there was no way Dir could have known that Hitler's eastern campaign was progressively turning for the worse. True, Dir had heard about Germany's defeat at Stalingrad, but that was so far away and besides, Germany's propagandists continued to boast of victory. So for the moment, Dir reasoned he would stay out of trouble, take care of his family, take life one day at a time and hopefully, the situation would eventually improve.

But one day in late April 1943, as he was returning home from work, Dir spotted a proclamation. Addressed to Galicia's youth, the poster proclaimed "that the time has come for us to bar the road to the Ukrainian land from our eternal eastern enemies with a steel wall" and to "volunteer into the ranks of the SS Rifle Division Galicia." Since the poster also proclaimed that "only arms will decide the fates of nations," Dir realized that at last, he had a golden opportunity to strike out against those who would attempt to harm him or his loved ones. Noting when and where the physicals would be given, Dir promptly decided to be there.

Six feet tall, blond-haired and blue-eyed Oleh Dir had no trouble enlisting. Upon receiving his call-up card, he told his weeping mother and aunt that he would enlist. Shortly afterward, Dir reported to the reception center from which a train took him to Heidelager.

At Heidelager, as later at Neuhammer, Dir excelled. His physical strength, above normal to begin with, only increased. He also shot well, so well that he astonished his instructors. No matter how far out the targets were, Dir hit them all. His vision, co-ordination and reflex's were superior and, under "Feldwebel" Walder's guidance, were sharpened in skill and precision.

Walder was the epitome of a true professional. An ex-sniper himself, the German NCO strongly recommended to Dir's company commander that Dir be utilized in a sniper/anti-sniper role. What Dir especially admired in his feldwebel was the man's honesty. The night before Dir left to return to Galicia, Walder confided to him that Hitler was nothing but an idiot, and his policies were morally wrong. The next day, as both men exchanged their goodbyes, Dir knew that he would never forget his instructor.

Continuing to scan the battlefield, Dir firmly grasped his Gewehr KAR 98 rifle. Manufactured in 1938, when weapons craftsmanship was at its peak, the rifle was 43.6 inches in length, and was well-balanced with a weight of 8.6 pounds. Its 7.92mm heavy ball round packed quite a punch. With a velocity of 2,476 feet per second, the round was accurate up to 800 meters. Whether Dir utilized its 4 power "bmj" Hensoldt scope, or shot through the rifle's front barley and rear tangent V sights, the weapon was equally precise. The turned-down bolt handle could be worked both easily and swiftly, and its chances of jamming were virtually non-existent. "If there was anything good about Hitler's Germany," thought Dir, "it was the fact that it produced some excellent arms."

Dir's ash-covered splinter camouflage suit merged perfectly with the ruins. In addition to his rifle, he carried two handguns: a Walther P38 9mm and a 7.62mm Tula Tokarev he obtained from the corpse of an NKVD police officer whom he had eliminated from an incredible range of 600 meters. Inside his right pants pocket, Dir carried a low-gravity paratrooper's knife and a few boxes of 7.92mm ammunition, while his hand-sewn left cargo pocket held a canteen of water, one folded handkerchief, and several iron rations. Extra 7.92mm rounds were carried in a pocket sewn inside his jacket and a camouflaged 1944 forage cap covered his head. Since nothing should hinder his movements because the slightest delay could kill him, Dir discarded his rucksack, blanket, poncho, mess kit and webbing. He took his mission seriously, so seriously that for extra camouflage he even covered his scope and parts of his rifle and cap with pieces of material torn from a burlap bag.

Dir knew that his task was not easy. And a successful sniper has to possess special skills – namely, the ability to be a loner. While, of course, a sniper does belong to a company or battalion, and therefore works with a team, ultimately, the sniper is a loner. On a modern-day battlefield, he often operates alone.

To be alone with one's own thoughts, fears and doubts, in heat and cold, in hunger and thirst, in pain and comfort, to be alone while stalking and fighting, and to possibly die a solitary death requires a special kind of physical and psychological courage. Alone, the sniper "hunts" his prey. And because he is alone, all his senses – his vision, hearing and smell; his intellect and co-ordination, combined with a strong determination to succeed, must be stronger, sharper and more finely tuned than those of the average soldier. A sniper cannot hate his enemy, for hate will inspire him to eliminate as many of his opponents as quickly as possible and only cause him to err. And in combat, the slightest mistake can easily take a man's life – especially if he is alone.

Some have condemned sniper warfare as morally and ethically wrong. But warfare itself is morally and ethically unjust. And during those hot July days at Brody, Dir's extraordinary sniper skills proved to be of tremendous value, saving many a fellow soldier. Continuing to lie in the smoldering ruins, Dir remained invisible, yet, he maintained a commanding view of the whole area.

Searching first to his front and left, Dir spotted a group coming in from the northeast. Identifying it as a "Galicia" group heading southwest, Dir also noted that they were carrying a couple of wounded men on stretchers.

But as he scanned to his right, he spotted a much larger Soviet group heading straight toward the Ukrainian force. Realizing that in a matter of minutes the superior Red Army force would intercept and probably overwhelm the smaller group, Dir readied for action. Dir knew that in some ways he was in an advantageous position. He was on higher terrain, the smoking rubble offered protection, and the setting sun, behind him, completely prevented the blinded Soviets from accurately firing back. Noting their organization and type of weaponry, Dir was especially struck by the fact that the group was headed by just one officer. Dir calculated that once the officer was dropped, the rest would scatter, thus making it easier for him to hold them off and simultaneously, provide extra time for the friendly group to escape.

Dir estimated the Red Army force to be about 500 meters away. He observed the distant tree tops and noted no natural movement. "Good!" thought Dir, "very little to no wind." He intended to allow the Soviets to advance another 200 meters before opening up. Slowly zeroing in on the officer, Dir set his sights on the commander's chest. Simultaneously, his mind automatically raced through the rules for an effective shot: "good, firm grip, place the sights, watch them, breathe deeply, exhale half of it, hold the rest but not for long, maintain the Hensoldt's post sight on him, watch him, and very, very softly squeeeeze" – the crack of the rifle shattered the silence, and as the red-hot 7.92mm round ripped through the Soviet officer's heart and lungs, Dir instantly ejected the spent cartridge, rammed in a fresh round, sighted, and slammed a round squarely into the face of a Soviet soldier who had sought shelter in a slight depression behind a tree and was searching for Dir through a telescopic Mosin-Nagant. So automatic were Dir's actions and so finely honed were his skills, that he moved without pausing to think as he performed his solo ballet of war.

And so it went. Day and night. From point-blank range to distances beyond 500 meters, Dir dropped Soviet officers, snipers, tank commanders, machine gunners, communist guerrillas and NKVD personnel. Virtually every round fired struck home. Entire enemy platoons, companies, and on several occasions entire battalions were held up by his skills. With repeated success, Dir covered withdrawals, breakouts, and retreats. Because of him, many a soldier escaped from the bloody Brody encirclement.

"HURRAH!" "HURRAH!" From all sides, Soviet troops descended upon Liubomyr Zach and his squad. A 30th regimental NCO, known to Liubomyr under the nickname of "Siy," whipped out a P-38 pistol and immediately shot and killed six incoming troopers. After emptying his handgun, Siy reached for his remaining egg-type handgrenade, pulled its pin, pressed it against his body and charged into a communist officer. The ensuing explosion ripped them both apart. Suddenly struck, Liubomyr lost consciousness.

Awakening hours later, Liubomyr found himself lying in a wooded knoll north of Bilyi Kamin with other wounded soldiers, mostly from the Division. As he lay, he heard Russian voices. Surrounded by Soviet soldiers, Liubomyr had no means of escape and within moments, he was approached by several of them.

Fear gripped Liubomyr. He wondered if his captors would release him, as earlier he had released several of his prisoners. But that would not be the case. After stripping him of his possessions, the Soviets lifted him up to his feet, and along with the others who could still walk, Liubomyr was marched off. He wondered what would become of those who could not stand up; the long burst of Soviet submachine gun fire provided the answer. Along with the others, Liubomyr was marched eastward. After a while, they reached an army headquarters. Following a brief wait, Liubomyr and another prisoner were taken inside, where they came face-to-face with Konev and Sokolovskiy. Liubomyr would never forget how everyone just eyed them. Finally, Sokolovskiy broke the silence.

"These are all young boys, and on top of everything, all are volunteers!" Apparently, the 1st Ukrainian Front's headquarters had already received news of the "Galicia" Division, and had ordered a few of its prisoners to be brought to the rear. When their Divisional emblem, the lion patch, was noticed, an order was given to have it cut off. Then Liubomyr chanced to see that his own wallet was lying on a field table where its contents were being carefully examined. Following a brief detention, Liubomyr was pushed back outside to the remaining prisoners.

Marched further to the east, Liubomyr reached a number of railway cars standing on a single track and was ordered into one of them. The moment he entered its sweltering heat, the heavy doors clanged shut. Finding a spot in the semi-darkness, Liubomyr lay down and attempted to sleep. His trip from one hell into another was about to begin.[9]

Shouting "GENTLEMEN, THIS WAY! QUICKLY! THIS WAY!" Freitag caught the attention of Sylenko. Standing beside Lange and an automobile in the village of Kniazhe, Freitag urged Sylenko's group to move rapidly southward.

Kniazhe was devastated. Its streets and yards were filled with dead soldiers, civilians and horses. Virtually every building was burning or smoldering. Wagons, vehicles, and destroyed T-34's and KV's lay scattered around. From the positions of the corpses, it was apparent the fighting had been close with much hand-to-hand combat. Desperate for a drink of water, Sylenko thought about the stream which flowed through Kniaszhe. Approaching it, he changed his mind when he saw it was full of enemy bodies. "They attempted to fall back, but seeing that they could not escape through the open ground, sought cover in it. Doesn't matter, we got them all!" With these words, a German non-Divisional NCO informed Sylenko about what had happened.

South of Kniazhe, the terrain sloped slightly downward and then upward toward a small forest. To stay in Kniazhe was impossible. Just moments before, a Soviet plane had come streaking in, dropping its payload of 80-pound bombs, and killing just about everything in sight. Never would Sylenko forget the sound of single pistol shots by wounded soldiers finishing themselves off. Directing his battlegroup southward, Sylenko pushed on.[10]

Until now, the Division's fusiliers had been fighting the Division's battle. They had been constantly rushed from one critical sector to another and repeatedly, their actions had altered the course of events.

But that was in the past. Now, south of Kniazhe, the fusiliers were fighting their own breakout battle. Led by leaders such as Waffen-Obersturmführer Danylko, the fusiliers once again demonstrated skill in adapting to a difficult situation. Danylko was the epitome of a true combat leader. Adorned in a camouflaged outfit, with belts of machinegun ammunition draped around his body, his hands firmly grasping an MG42 machinegun, a pistol tucked into his waistband, the fusilier officer actually looked like the God of War. Quickly organizing a breakout force of 200 soldiers, Danylko assured the group that success was in sight with such words: "WE'RE GOING FORWARD! WE'RE GOING TO WHERE THERE IS LIFE, FREEDOM AND LOVE!"

And fight they did. Ripping into a Soviet mechanized and NKVD police battalion with a savagery, power, and determination that one can only possess at such a time, the fusiliers totally devastated the threatening force. They shot, bayoneted, clubbed, stabbed and killed with their bare hands. Well-placed anti-armor rounds tore enemy tanks and vehicles into pieces. Since earlier the fusiliers had not been granted any quarter, they now responded in kind. Charging into an NKVD police

Chapter 16: Brody!

trooper who towered well over six feet, Chester Tush would never forget the steel teeth and the smell of sweat and cheap liquor as he plunged a close-combat knife deep into the massive hulk. As the trooper fell forward, Chester actually came face-to-face with him. Propping him up with his left arm, Chester attempted to remove the knife. But the knife had penetrated so deep into the NKVD trooper's upper abdomen that Chester was unable to pull it out.

Dropping the trooper to the ground, Chester noted blood on his hands. Momentarily, he considered removing the corpse's NKVD lapel pin. But after wiping his blood-covered hands on his camouflaged fatigue pants, Chester reached only for the deceased man's Ppsh 41 and its spare drum of ammunition. After all, reasoned Chester, hell could hold many more NKVD men.

Along with the other survivors of the 29th Regiment's Headquarters Company, Vasil Sirs'kyi probed cautiously toward Pochapy from Bilyi Kamin. At approximately 5:30 a.m., Sirs'kyi's group was totally encompassed by a morning fog so thick that one could barely see beyond several meters; yet, from Yaseniw's direction, the men noted that a heavy battle had erupted.

After reaching Pochapy, Sirs'kyi and the others readied for action. By now, the fog had lifted, and from Pochapy's higher elevation, Kniazhe could be seen. Sirs'kyi could not fail to notice the terrain between Kniazhe and Pochapy – it was pockmarked with holes from thousands of shell bursts and bombs.

At Pochapy, Sirs'kyi saw the Division's remaining anti-aircraft personnel. Until now, they had done the best they could. But with their remaining guns totally out of ammunition, the anti-aircraft personnel blew their guns; now, they would fight as infantry. Obtaining a heavy machine gun from a German soldier, Sirs'kyi passed it on to Kul'chytskyi, an anti-aircraft standard bearer, who prepared the weapon for combat. Someone's command of "MACHINEGUNNERS! ANTI-TANK GUNNERS! TO THE FRONT!" was heralded.

Sirs'kyi knew the big moment was approaching. As well, everyone knew that in and around Kniazhe were dug-in Soviet troops. But as Sirs'kyi readied his weapon, he noticed the Soviet prisoners, now unguarded, just milling around. It was obvious that amongst them, there were those who feared to return to their own side.

"O.K. LET'S DO IT!" With these words, the battlegroup moved forward. Enroute to Kniazhe, Sirs'kyi's battlegroup encountered a German battlegroup accompanied by one tank. Its commander, a high ranking Wehrmacht officer, addressed Sirs'kyi's group: "Gentlemen, our situation is tough, but not impossible. Together, let's storm Kniazhe!"

Storming into Kniazhe, the battlegroup encountered success. Clambering aboard an overturned railway car, Sirs'kyi proceeded to fire upon a group of Soviet soldiers who, shortly before, had dug themselves in at the edge of Kniazhe. Others, under various shouts such as "SLAVA!" charged forward. A Soviet sniper killed the Wehrmacht officer with one well-placed shot; within moments, the same sniper who had just killed was himself killed as various members of the battlegroup returned his fire. Noting the deceased officer's cap lying alongside him, Sirs'kyi covered the German soldier's face.

After proceeding through the outskirts of Kniazhe, the combined German-Ukrainian battlegroup halted to rest. Among them were six wounded soldiers – four Ukrainians and two Germans. Since no one wanted to leave them behind, it was decided to bring them along. But suddenly an automobile, its top open, appeared. Driven by a chauffeur, its sole occupant was a German army captain. Seeing the wounded, the captain hopped out of the vehicle and helped to place the wounded into the auto. As rapidly as it had arrived, the vehicle continued southwest to Lakye, with Sirs'kyi and the others following quickly on foot. Enroute to Zhukiv, Sirs'kyi's group encountered another group. Among them was Dern, the 29th Regiment's commander.

The end, however, was not yet over. In the following days, Sirs'kyi would only know the screams of "HURRAH! SLAVA!," the sounds of incoming rounds, explosions, whining bullets, and the screams of the dying. At point-blank range, Sirs'kyi shot and killed Soviet regulars. In hand-to-hand combat, he slashed and fought his way through. Sirs'kyi was determined to survive, and if he had to kill the devil in hell to do so, then he would. Finally, after nearly two weeks of intense combat, Sirs'kyi reached safety.[11]

Through the remaining day and night hours of 23 and 24 July, the remnants of the 13th Corps broke out.[12] Excluding those who perished, and the bulk of the wounded, as well as those who lost the will to participate in a breakout and were left behind, 13th Corps' battle was ended.[13] For those who remained, escape was now virtually impossible. But before moving in for the final kill, Konev's forces unleashed a massive fusillade of firepower into a highly contained area.

The ground trembled, rolled and tore into shreds from the numerous blasts. Buildings, vehicles, trees, horses, wagons – and humans – disappeared in huge blasts of fiery red and orange blasts. So many shells rained in that virtually every foot of ground was struck. As Soviet gunners slammed in shell after shell into red-hot breach blocks, their senses totally numbed by the awesome noises, its gunners were determined to pulverize everything within their designated target areas. In-

deed, so heavy and frantic was their fire that some Soviet gunners actually collapsed from heart failure beside their guns.

It was bad enough for the Red gunners. But for those who were on the receiving end, it was far worse. Theodore Rukh*, for example, never could have imagined that such a hell could exist.

Lying in a roadside ditch obscured by huge trees, Theodore was relieved that
he had found some shelter. He did not want to abandon his wagon, but when he
saw two supply wagons with drivers and horses directly in front of him disappear
in huge blasts, Theodore knew that he had to leap off his wagon and seek shelter.
As he lay in the ditch, massive explosions rocked everything. Looking up, he saw
a smoking crater where just seconds before his wagon and two horses had stood. It
was clearly apparent that some enemy spotter or aerial observer was doing an
excellent job of calling in ground fires.

More screams of incoming shells warned Theodore to remain in the ditch as
massive explosions ripped everything into pieces. "GOD!" shouted Theodore
"PLEASE HELP ME!"

But there was no help, or reprieve, as raining shells continued to explode all
around. With cordite and smoke filling his nose and lungs, Theodore became nau-
seous and craved to get up and escape. Realizing, however, that death was virtually guaranteed if he stood up, Theodore remained in the ditch.

Shells continued to rain in. Earth, stones, gravel, wood, and other debris rained
down upon the grenadier. Without respite, the thunderous barrage showered death
and destruction. Theodore lost consciousness.

Awakening hours later, he was surprised to find himself alive. Lifting his head,
he saw that his helmet was gone. Apparently, as he had lay unconscious, an explosive wind force had blown it away. Rising slowly to his feet, Theodore observed
his tattered clothes. Along with his helmet, his weapon had been blown away.

Theodore detected an eerie silence. Numerous craters pockmarked the terrain, causing the earth's ash-covered surface to resemble a lunar landscape. Not
one tree, or even tree trunk, remained standing. The road had been completely
obliterated. As for the small settlement which Theodore had passed by before driving into hell, it no longer existed. Nothing existed. Nothing at all. Armageddon
had come and gone.

Dejected, exhausted, and unsure of what to do, Theodore crawled into a crater
and fell into a deep sleep. He remained there until a roving UPA patrol came upon
him, awakened him, and took him into their ranks.

When the sun finally set on 23 July 1943, the "Battle of Brody" was over. In
the following day or two, Soviet mop-up forces battled with individuals and small

groups but for the greater part, the battle was over. In honor of the Soviet victory, it is reported that Stalin personally ordered a twenty-four artillery gun salute in Moscow.[14]

At the end of July 1944, the Division had completely withdrawn from Galicia. Until the conclusion of the war almost a year later, the Division would never again operate in Galicia, Ukraine, or any part of the Soviet Union. Consequently, in its second year of existence, the Division could not have been "shooting, raping and robbing civilians, most of them Jews, in the neighborhood of Lvov," and nor could it have been conducting "mass shootings, hangings, beatings, tortures, and medical experiments on live victims" as falsely written by Kurt Fleischmann.[15]

17

An Evaluation of the Division's Casualties at Brody

Arriving in Lviv several days before the Galician capital fell on 27 July 1944 to the troops of the 1st Ukrainian front, Yuriy Krokhmaliuk was shocked to learn from the Military Board that he, as well as the other 10,000 soldiers of the Division, had been "killed-in action."[1]

As Krokhmaliuk examined the lengthy lists of those reported killed, he not only found the names of many soldiers that had successfully broken out, or had not even been surrounded (such as those in the Division's Field Replacement Battalion), but found his own name as well. Stepping back outside, Krokhmaliuk saw crowds of people surrounding those who had accompanied Krokhamliuk; all were inquiring about loved ones within the Division. Indeed, the crowd was so large that Krokhmaliuk had a difficult time in re-entering the military automobile.

Slowly driving westward through city streets filled with civilians fleeing in the same direction, Krohmaliuk was not only distressed and angry about the fact that many of those listed killed were actually alive but, worse, that many families were already informed of their "losses."

So how many were actually killed at Brody? What are the true figures?

"Biy Pid Brodamy" cites that of 11,000 soldiers in the encirclement, 7,000 soldiers and officers were lost. From these, the greater portion were killed, wounded, or fell into communist hands (prisoners-of-war);[2] Savaryn cites "7,000 lost at Brody;[3] "from 11,000 Divisional soldiers and officers, only approximately 3,000 returned from encirclement;"[4] "of 18,000 men roll call revealed 7,000 as missing;"[5] "14,000 went into combat, and 3,000 returned;"[6] "approximately 2,000 returned,;"[7] and "for the ideological armed struggle against the Bolshevik occupation of Ukraine, duty called upon the flower of the youth –7,000 at Brody."[8] Svoboda, a Ukrainian newspaper dated from 2 August, 1952 cited "7,000 fell for an ideology," [9] while the Encyclopedia of Ukraine cites "7,000 killed or captured."[10] An article appearing in an emigre journal regarding the Brody Battle cited "that within the encirclement, over 7,000 of our soldiers were killed;"[11] and an article appearing on 29 May 1991 in the city of Lviv cited "that from 11,000 Divisional soldiers, at Brody 5,000 perished, and approximately 3,000 remained alive."[12] And various former Divisional soldiers have also cited various figures. Reverend (former Chaplain) Nahayewsky cites "approximately 8,000 young Ukrainians perished!"[13] while Volodymyr Molodets'kyi cited "that of 11,000, 5,000 perished at Brody;"[14] Divisional officer Liubomyr Ortyns'kyi cited "around 4,000 perished in the encirclement;"[15] and Yaroslav Tir* stated "almost 10,000 fell!"[16] Numerous other Ukrainian sources cited figures of no less than 7,000 killed-in-action and some, even more. What is the truth?

According to Yuriy Krohkmaliuk, approximately 10,400 troops (including those of the Field Replacement Battalion), deployed to the eastern front from Neuhammer. Of this strength, 3,000 resurfaced after Brody. Krokhmaliuk stated "it is not known how many entered UPA's ranks, " but added "a sizable number did end up in the insurgency." [17] But until the conclusion of the war, Krokhmaliuk carefully recorded the number of soldiers who, in the weeks and months following Brody, reentered the Division either in Neuhammer, Slovakia, Yugoslavia, or Austria. Some of them arrived from the UPA; others, incorporated into various German units as they fought out of the pocket, returned once the front was reestablished; and some returned via the Soviet Army. This occurred when after the breakout some returned home, discarded their uniforms, and attempted to hide out. But they were soon drafted into the Soviet Army. After a period of training, they entered Soviet front-line units as replacements. Defecting to the German side at a moment of opportunity, in due time they returned to the Division. On more than one occasion, shouts of laughter, cheers and various embracing exclamations were heard in Neuhammer and elsewhere as men returned to their former units. "Stefan, you bastard! Welcome back! We thought your were killed!" " I was, but hell was too hot for me. So I decided to come back." "Myhailo's back! Great to see you!" and so forth. However, moments of happiness were frequently shattered when a returnee inquired about a brother, cousin, or close friend. After a period of silence, someone's reply of "Stefan, we buried him at Koltiw;" ... " he never returned. No one ever saw him again;" ... "unless he ended up in the UPA, he's probably dead" erased all moments of jubilation.

Chapter 17: An Evaluation of the Division's Casualties at Brody

As attested by Krokhmaliuk, in the ensuing months after Brody, slightly more than 2,300 returned; altogether, with the 3,000 who returned initially, slightly over 5,300 returned to the Division.[18] However, this figure does not include those who remained in the UPA until the end of the war, and continued to fight within the insurgency until well into the 1950s;[19] nor does it include those who returned home and succeeded in hiding out; or those who remained in a German unit until the war's end.[20]

Yuriy Krokhmaliuk emphasized that the division committed slightly over 10,000 soldiers to Brody, where it encountered massive Soviet ground and aerial forces and, yet, in excess of 5,000 succeeded in breaking out, with many others ending up in the UPA. If one takes these figures into consideration, then it becomes clear that under extraordinarily tough conditions the Division executed a successful breakout, rather than being destroyed at Brody, as is the popular belief. As for the number of those killed-in-action at Brody, the former Divisional staff officer cites a figure of no less than 1,600 but not over 2,000.[21] But as Krokhmaliuk himself stated, this figure does not include the number of those captured who later perished deep in the interior of Russia's slave labor camp system.

Krokhmaliuk's observations and figures are closely substantiated by his brother Roman, according to whom 10,050 soldiers were deployed to Brody.[22] Deducting the 3,000 returnees, the wounded who were evacuated prior to encirclement, the estimated number of those who ended up in the insurgency or returned home, in the end a figure of 2,690 were either killed-in-action or severely wounded.[23] While, of course, this was a huge and tragic loss, it is far lower than the losses assumed by many.

In regards to the Battle of Brody, the Soviets have also provided various figures. But, as usually was the case, their figures were very inflated, and were submitted solely for purposes of propaganda. According to one post World War II count, at Brody eight German divisions were destroyed and 38,000 officers and soldiers were killed and 17,175 were captured.[24] But this figure is obviously tremendously exaggerated because prior to Konev's offensive, the entire 13th Corps, to include the "Galicia" Division, totalled no more than 32,000-35,000 men.

For many years following World War II, no proper figures were available. But with the emergence of "glasnost" and a desire by many Soviet historians to at long last share historical information in an objective manner (not permissible previously by Soviet authorities), at long last accurate and objective accounts, as well as new information, began to surface.[25] One such account, originating covertly in 1989, reveals that UPA Colonel "Kalyna" cited a strength of "almost 3,000 Divisional members reinforced UPA's ranks following the encirclement."[26] It is now known that others also attempted to enter UPA's ranks, but failed to do so. In one instance in August 1944, a strength of at least 300 Divisional soldiers attempted to enter the UPA in the Carpathian Mountains. After establishing contact with a commander names "Hutsul," the soldiers moved to their rendezvous point. Falling into an ambush, no more than 50 escaped.[27] According to Vashchenko, no less than 3,000 Divisional soldiers entered the insurgency.[28] Although in the following weeks and months some left to return to the Division, a high percentage stayed on. In the post-war period, some perished.[29] But some returned to western Europe and later emigrated while others returned home and, in due time, blended into the populace.[30]

According to Yuriy Krokhmaliuk, the "Galicia" Division's soldiers could fill UPA's ranks in such ways: deserting from the ranks during travels to the homeland; by escaping under certain circumstances (i.e. Kampfgruppe "Beyersdorff"); or during the Brody battle and afterwards.[31] In his 1975 study, Krokhmaliuk cited "it may be ascertained, that many of the Ukrainian (Galicia) Divisional soldiers took full advantage of the chaos within the encirclement and entered the ranks of the UPA under the condition to avoid capture."[32] Krokhmaliuk is correct in his ascertain that "many" divisional soldiers ended up in the UPA; however, Krohkaliuk is unable to provide a figure.

Divisional soldiers usually entered the UPA in platoon or group strengths; fewer entered as individuals. But the Divisional soldiers did tremendously bolster the insurgency. According to Krokhmaliuk and UPA documents, following the Brody battle, such newly composed UPA companies were formed: Lisoyna; Burlak; Rydachiv; Druzhynnyky; Halaida I; Halaida II, and others.[33] Within such companies, up to 50 ex-Divisional soldiers frequently provided the nucleus while new volunteers rounded out the strengths.[34] This figure, however, did not include the numerous individuals who served on various battalion, divisional, regional, and even, in Shukhevych's command structure. Such was the case with Volodymyr Yurkevych and Bohdan Hvozdets'kyi, a.k.a. Emir Kor. In the case of Yurkevych, who enlisted in the Division in 1943, in July he left on the fist transport to Heidelager. After completing his recruit training, in October 1943 Yurkeyych left for the Lauenburg (Pommern) NCO Academy. In March, he returned to the Division (now at Neuhammer), as an NCO, where he immediately assumed a Platoon Sergeant's position; within weeks, Yurkevych was sent to an officer's school at Kienschlag. (Bohmen-Mahren). In July 1944, he returned to the Division at Neuhammer as a senior NCO, with orders to be promoted to the officer rank of Waffen-Untersturmführer. Taking the last transport bound for Galicia, that same month at Brody he entered the UPA. Because of his military training, Yurkevych was posted to a regional UPA command headquarter's; there, he remained until the postwar period.[35]

According to former Divisional officer Major Ren, following the breakout battles, "many soldiers of the 1st Ukrainian ["Galicia"] Division entered the UPA and new Druzhny companies were formed."[36] And a former Divisional staff officer, Bohdan Pidhainyi, cites that Divisional staff personnel also entered UPA's main command headquarters.[37]

Ultimately, it appears that no less than 3,000 to as many as 4,000 entered the UPA.[38] Some stayed briefly, but others remained in the insurgency until the war's end. Realistically speaking, German fears of widespread desertion to the Ukrainian insurgency proved correct.

As for Ukrainian sources which cite high fatalities of "4,000, 5,000, 7,000, 8,000," and up, and allege that the "Galicia" Division "was destroyed at Brody," "annihilated," "obliterated," these sources are grossly exaggerated and are solely based on false assumptions, rumors and propaganda. Compounding the matter is the fact that these Ukrainian sources have erroneously been accepted as valid by a number of contemporary western writers who, in turn, have exaggerated the inaccuracy.[39]

18

An Evaluation of the Division's Combat Performance at Brody

At Brody, the "Galicia" Division encountered a Soviet front that was not only superior in numerical strength, but also massively reinforced with armor, artillery, aircraft, and a massive supply system. Ultimately, this superiority played a major role in achieving a breakout, encircling the 13th Corps, and repulsing Germany's AGNU front westward.

In an attempt to defend its homeland, the Division expended a maximum effort. Repeatedly – against an enemy air threat that pulverized the front, against massive armored and mechanized concentrations, whether on the offense or defense, in Koltiw's vicinity or in the attack during the breakout, the Divisions personnel were determined to succeed. During its combat operations, the Division's troops did not panic, drop their arms and cease to resist, or defect to the Soviet side. As Heike himself recorded: "no other unit had even approximately as much responsibility in such unfavorable conditions as had the Ukrainian ["Galicia"] Division... in difficult battles the Division had acquitted itself as well as could have been reasonably expected..." and "during the fighting in the Brody pocket and during the breakout many Ukrainians proved to be extraordinarily brave."[1]

Initially, the Division was ordered to proceed southeastward from a secondary position within the Prinz Eugen defensive system in order to assist German forces in sealing a Soviet rupture in Koltiw's vicinity (known as the "Koltiw corridor") before a major breakout would occur. The moment the Division moved, Soviet aircraft swept in with a fury seldom seen and previously witnessed only at Kursk, and later in the Prussian and Berlin battles. So massive were the aerial

Chapter 18: An Evaluation of the Division's Combat Performance

strikes that many a German veteran later recalled with shock and dismay the severity and effectiveness of the Soviet air force. True, enemy air had been previously encountered, but never in such massive scope as at Brody. Just alone in a five hour period on 15 July, the Soviet 2nd Air Army flew no less than 3,288 aircraft sorties and dropped 102 tons of bombs against the counter-attacking forces.[2] The intensity of the enemy's air and ground firepower was attested to by a former panzer NCO, who fought at the gates of Stalingrad. As recalled years later by Veryha, the panzer warrior stated: "Brody was worse than Stalingrad!"[3] From 13 to 22 July, but especially during the breakout phase, the battle was very closed in and intense; yet, Galicia's volunteers put forth a maximum effort, persisting in their efforts even though a number of the German personnel within the pocket had ceased to resist.

Some have classified the Division as "an inexperienced combat formation," or "a formation lacking combat experience." While it is true that the Division, as a formation, never fought prior to Brody, a number of its soldiers did have varying degrees of combat experience. Some of its personnel had fought the Germans in Poland in 1939; others saw combat within the Soviet Army or had fought in World War I and in its post-war era with either the Galician or UNR's Army. And all of the Division's UPA-infiltrated personnel had previously fought the Nazi occupiers, Soviet guerrillas or both.[4]

Contrary to popular belief, a combat formation, if exceptionally well-trained, does not require prior combat experience to succeed.[5] Once its soldiers are organized around a solid inner core, and its officer and NCO leadership core holds, so, too, will its troops. Prior to Brody, some of the Ukrainian officers and NCOs did have combat experience; additionally, all of the Ukrainian leaders – including even those who previously held leadership positions in other armies – were provided solid training. In a number of cases, even former NCOs and officers were first put through a solid recruit training within the Replacement Army before being dispatched to officer and NCO schools. Virtually unknown is the fact that prior to Brody, a small number of Ukrainian officers, who somehow had completed their training but once within the Division failed to meet unit standards, were dropped out of leadership positions. Whenever this occurred, strong efforts were undertaken to find replacements as soon as possible. In this area, credit must be given to Paliiv, Krokhmaliuk and, even, Freitag who insisted on a solid leadership core. Nevertheless, in regard to the Ukrainian officer's and NCOs' performance at Brody, it not only matched the German leadership but, in some cases, even surpassed it.

As the Division's soldiers advanced to repulse the Soviet front, they encountered demoralized German troops retreating westward. Such an encounter can be very demoralizing for the most experienced troops; yet, it appears the "Galicia" Division was not unnerved by this sight as its soldiers pressed forward. Perhaps the fact that it was fighting in its homeland, coupled with the fear of Soviet capture, compelled the 14th "Galicia" Division to maintain a strong mission awareness.

At Brody, certain units demonstrated exceptional performance. A case in point involves the fusiliers.

In combat, the Division's fusiliers displayed an aggressiveness and tenacity found only within the most elite Wehrmacht, paratroop, and Waffen-SS fusilier units. Repeatedly rushed from one sector to another, whether on the defense or offense, and always against superior odds, the fusiliers not only halted enemy penetrations, but on occasion succeeded in repulsing the enemy and retaking critical terrain, towns and villages. During the Division's breakout and withdrawal, fusiliers frequently spearheaded assaults, and often were reinforcing both those Divisional soldiers holding escape routes, and the rear guard. As Heike attested: "the fusiliers were continuously in the fighting, and acquitted themselves well."

To understand why the Division's fusiliers demonstrated such toughness and tenacity, one must remember that the battalion was itself a unique outfit. Composed exclusively of "double volunteers" (first for the Division and then for the battalion), its soldiers (following recruit training), were afforded a very lengthy, grueling, and practical, period of specialized combat training. Fully aware of his critical mission, each volunteer took his training seriously and by mid-June 1944, had mastered a host of German and Soviet weapons, anti-tank weaponry, mines and grenades. More so than the other Divisional units, fusilier troops underwent a considerable amount of hand-to-hand and close combat training. Commanded by SS-Sturmbannführer Karl Bristot, a highly respected Austrian officer who, in turn, was supported with a staff of German officers very receptive to the battalion's needs, the fusilier battalion developed an exceptionally high esprit-de-corps.

Although successful in its breakout, the battalion did take casualties. Because few, if any, fusiliers were taken prisoner, and because it has never been established how many ended up in the UPA, or were killed, or returned home and somehow managed to hide out, the battalion's exact casualties have never been fully established; the battalion did, however, succeed in breaking out.

Artillery:
At Brody, the Division's four artillery battalions put forth a maximum effort. To move an artillery piece, along with its ammunition over a battlefield under constant aerial and ground dangers, is in itself a major undertaking. The Division's

Chapter 18: An Evaluation of the Division's Combat Performance

artillery frequently suppressed enemy ground targets with deadly precision, thus slowing the enemy thrust within the Koltiw corridor.

Once surrounded, and with its ammunition running out, the Division's artillery could no longer support its own and 13th Corps' efforts. During the breakout, what remained of the artillery was utilized in the breakout. Some notable individuals involved were Sturmbannführer (Major) Palienko and Obersturmführer (Lt) Dlaboha.

Anti-tank:

Whether within the infantry regiments or within the independent anti-tank company, the Division's anti-tank personnel engaged the 1st Ukrainian Front's armor and, as again attested by Heike, "scored repeated hits at close range."

In combat, most men fear the clanking sound of iron; after all, tanks and armored vehicles do possess the capability to exert a tremendous amount of physical – and psychological – damage. To effectively counter such iron threats, especially at point blank, requires nerves of steel coupled with sufficient training.

At Brody, Ukrainian 'panzerjäger's' frequently "crawled up to fight metallic monstrosities at close quarters." Heike's observation is certainly credible since the former major himself witnessed Galicia's volunteers ripping enemy armor into pieces.

At Brody, the Division's anti-tank company was destroyed, and its seal was captured by Soviet forces. But before the company was totally destroyed, its panzerjägers inflicted some serious damage to Rybalko's, Sokolov's, and the 1st Ukrainian Front's armored reserve. Certain individuals displayed exceptional bravery. On one day alone, Volodymyr Chuchkevych, who hailed from Galicia, and SS-Unterscharführer Karl Nielsen, a German-Russian born in Leningrad on 23 November 1920, destroyed no less than six tanks apiece.

Infantry:

Although constantly battered from the air, pulverized on the ground, and always against superior odds, infantry regiments 29, 30, and 31 fought day and night to stem the Soviet offensive. Whether attacking the Soviet breakthrough forces at Koltiw, or fighting fiercely for a number of villages and towns; whether defending Oles'ko, the heights of Pidhirtsi or Opaky, or breaking out of encirclement, the Division's grenadiers never lost hope. Continuously, the three battered regiments were quickly reformed and pressed into combat. By 20 July, the regiments only existed within the various battlegroups; yet, the surviving grenadiers demonstrated true elan in breaking out.

265

Galicia Division

Anti-aircraft:

Well before the Division was ever committed into combat, the Division's anti-aircraft battalion was already engaging Soviet aircraft. From the Division's disembarkation point at Ozhydiv to Bilyi Kamin, anti-aircraft gunners were constantly in action; officially, they were the first to engage the enemy and many of its members, such as Myhailo Lobach, were one of the last ones to break out.

Precisely how many enemy aircraft were shot down remains undocumented; however, it is known that a number of Soviet aircraft were shot down and undoubtedly, others were damaged. In combat, the battalion's 88 guns not only shot down a number of aircraft, but when employed in a ground role against Soviet armor, decimated many a T-34 or KV-I. By 20 July, however, the battalion was destroyed. It is known that its remaining guns fought as late as 21 July to cover the bridges at Bilyi Kamin and Pochapy. But once out of ammunition, its survivors merged into the various battlegroups and participated in the breakout as infantry. According to Roman Hayetskyj: a former anti-aircraft soldier, a number of the Division's anti-aircraft personnel ended up in the UPA.[6]

Support:

Initially, the Division's supply, engineer, communications, support and maintenance units, whether operating themselves, or alongside other units, functioned fairly smoothly in the beginning. But as they were forced into transferring personnel to hastily formed "emergency battle units," or into regular units, and as its casualties mounted, the overworked and battle fatigued engineers, communication and other life-support troops began to reel under the constant enemy pressure. Collapsing at about the time the breakout occurred, its surviving personnel fought, in the end, as regular frontline troops.

Medical:

At Brody, one of the most tragic fates of the Division was experienced by its medical corps.

Until it was surrounded, the Division's medical staff had successfully evacuated 360 wounded and injured personnel.[7] But once surrounded, as always is the case, incapacitated personnel become problematic – especially if the surrounded unit is on the move.

By the rules of warfare, military hospitals – whether in the field or in an established permanent location – are not to be fired upon. But on the eastern front, more than one military hospital was destroyed with no regard for its wounded and medical personnel. Prior to encirclement, the Division's medical personnel were fired upon, the Division's hospital[8] came under repeated aerial and ground attack, and its ambulances were struck. Hence, it became apparent that any captured wounded personnel would suffer a cruel fate.

According to Krokhmaliuk, aerial evacuation, partially successful at Stalingrad and other sites, was impossible because of a lack of German "Auntie Ju" transport aircraft, and because the pocket was not staying in place.[9] Thus, the only remaining choice was to bring the wounded along.

But in battle circumstances, carrying out the wounded is virtually impossible. While there were isolated instances where wounded/injured personnel were carried or driven out, for the greater part those wounded and unable to walk out were left behind. These incapacitated personnel, along with a number of surviving doctors and medical personnel, were taken prisoner.

Doctors Myhailo Hryhorchuk and Zenon Lokach, the artillery regiment's two doctors, were killed at Brody. The regiments third doctor, Osyp Syvenkyi, escaped from the encirclement. Refusing to leave the wounded behind in the wake of a Soviet advance, Dr. Yaroslav Karpevych, Chief Doctor of the 29th Regiment, stayed behind. Shortly afterward, survivors who came upon the destroyed forward-aid station reported that Dr. Karpevych, along with his medical orderlies and male nurses, as well as the wounded, had been killed.[10]

Throughout the battle, the Division's hospital moved from one location to another. Its final location was west of Pochapy;[11] there, with limited medical supplies and under very adverse conditions, aid was administered as best as possible to those breaking out, or those who had to be left behind. Overrun on 21-22 July, its remaining medical personnel and wounded were captured.[12]

Among those captured were surgeon Volodymyr Prokopovych and Divisional surgeon Myhailo Tymchyshyn. Following years of imprisonment, Doctor Prokopovych was released to West Germany as a "German" prisoner. Doctor Osyp Zalyshniy, who hailed from Zolochiv, was presumed killed. After brief service with the UPA, he reentered the Division in November 1944. Dr. Stepan Iaromyr Olesnyts'kyi also ended up in the UPA. But he never returned to the Division. Born 27 December 1914 in Czechoslovakia, he returned with his family to Lviv in 1932. Shortly before the eruption of World War II and the Soviet takeover, Olesnyts'kyi graduated from Lviv's medical school. Because the communist occupants classified many professional people – to include doctors – as "exploiters" and targeted them for arrest, deportation or murder, Dr. Olesnyts'kyi fled to Cracow, Poland; there, he practiced medicine. In early 1944, he entered the Division. Upon the completion of a medical course in Vienna, Austria, he returned to the Division and soon, deployed with the Division to the eastern front. Wounded in the knee, he ended up in the UPA. Within the UPA, he served as a doctor and supervised the training of medics and nurses. Approximately 3 March 1945, Dr. Olesnyts'kyi's medical facility was attacked by NKVD combat police troops and the brave doctor was killed.

But in the case of Doctor Petro Skobelsky, to this day his whereabouts remain unknown. Refusing to leave his wounded patients behind, the brave 30-year-old doctor declined all offers of attaching himself to any of the breakout groups. He was last seen alive with his patients approximately 21 July. In the aftermath of Brody, Doctor Skobelsky never resurfaced into the Division and it is known that he never entered the UPA. It was rumored, however, that the doctor was transported to central Siberia, where he served as a medical doctor. Yuriy Keidovsky, Bohdan Panasiuk, Alexander Farion and Bohdan Pytliuk were among the doctors who avoided death or capture. It is believed that Dr. Farion, who served with the fusiliers, was the last Divisional doctor to break out. With a wounded fusilier slumped over his right shoulder, Dr. Farion reached safety.

At Brody, the Division lost all of its heavy equipment, artillery and anti-aircraft weapons. But, comparatively speaking, under such adverse conditions, it is not uncommon for even the most elite troops to suffer a high, or even total, materiel loss. And once it became apparent that the Division could not be evacuated by AGNU, and as ammunition supplies began to run out, the exhausted troops were unable to haul out their equipment and weapons system. For this, the Division's soldiers could not be held responsible.

At no time did the Division, nor any of its sub-elements, ever panic. While certain individuals and companies did report that continuing enemy pressure could possibly unnerve the already exhausted companies, at no time at Brody did any of the troops drop their weapons, discard personal items, throw off their helmets, and flee screaming. During the breakout, Divisional troops exerted much pressure upon the enemy and by their actions, thwarted Soviet efforts to seal the breakout. On more than one occasion Divisional breakout groups even bypassed mobs of German soldiers who simply lost their will to fight and breakout.

So the question remains – did the Division fail? It appears not. As verified by Lischyns'kyi, at Brody the Division's mission was to engage the enemy and draw Konev's forces into heavy combat; as also acknowledged by Lischyns'kyi, the Division, by itself, could not destroy the entire Soviet force. But the Division did exert much pressure upon Konev's front and for a while, Konev himself feared that perhaps his fronts attempts to break through and achieve operational depth would fail. And once the 1st Ukrainian Front began to penetrate AGNU's defense, Konev was forced to divert a number of Soviet units into the area of Brody to deal with the Division, as well as the 13th Corps, when the encircled units began to strike southwestward into the Soviet rear. In the very end, 13th Corps and the Division did slow Konev's frontal advance.[13]

Committed to one of the two major Soviet breakout points, from the outset the "Galicia" Division was forced to undertake an extremely difficult and unfavorable mission under very adverse conditions. But at Brody, the Division put out a maximum effort. As attested by Heike "no other unit had even approximately as much responsibility in such unfavorable conditions as had the Ukrainian "Galicia" Division, nor could they approach it" and "during the fighting in the Brody pocket and during the breakout, many Ukrainians proved to be extraordinarily brave."

Allegations that "Brody is comparable to Kruty," ... "Brody was another Kruty," and so forth, are totally false.[14] Furthermore, such allegations are always made by those who have no understanding of what occurred at Kruty and Brody.

Under no circumstances can the events of Kruty and Brody be coupled together. To begin with, when the Division deployed to the eastern front in late June and early July 1944 its volunteers, unlike those who marched to Kruty, were professional soldiers exceptionally well-trained, armed and equipped with the most modern arms, equipment, and materiel of that era. The Ukrainians who marched to Kruty and attempted to make a stand were not even soldiers. The vast majority were untrained teenage cadets hastily organized with a weak and, it appears, incompetent core of leaders. Poorly armed and equipped, from the beginning the cadet force stood no chance of achieving any type of success. Indeed, it was such a miserable show of force that when Red Russia's advancing troops encountered the cadet force, they urged the Ukrainian youths to drop their arms and go home. But determined to uphold a rapidly crumbling government, the Ukrainians decided to fight it out. In the ensuing struggle, a senseless massacre occurred.

Unlike those at Kruty, at Brody the Ukrainian military offered stiff resistance and it succeeded in inflicting battle damage to communist forces. On more than one occasion, superior Soviet ground forces were also held up by Divisional elements. And in recent years, this fact has been acknowledged by a number of Soviet military men and military analysts in a number of Soviet military journals and writings.

At Kruty, the inexperienced youths performed poorly; few, if any, emerged as survivors. At Brody, whether on the defense or offense, the Division's soldiers repeatedly lashed out. And although surrounded, unlike those at Kruty, the warrior's who fought at Brody succeeded, against a vastly superior enemy, in achieving a breakout. In the very end the greater percentage of the Ukrainians who fought at Brody survived. As always is the case, survival is attributable strictly to tough, solid training, competent and aggressive leadership (especially at squad, platoon, company and battalion levels), and a strong mission awareness. Clearly, these factors were non-existent at Kruty.

Most of the men who volunteered for the Division knew about the tragedy of Kruty. In an attempt to avert such military unpreparedness and its tragic consequences, the Division's volunteers sometimes cited Kruty as an example.

In combat, a soldier fights to win. In the event it becomes apparent that at the moment a victory cannot be achieved, that same soldier executes some type of action to survive for the future. At Kruty, this never occurred. At Brody, the thousands of soldiers who broke out, or who entered the ranks of the UPA, returned with vital skills and experiences which then strengthened the soon-to-be reformed Division as well as the Ukrainian underground. At Brody, actions were also undertaken, and lessons learned, which can – and actually are – utilized internationally for military studies. In regards to Kruty, Kruty has nothing to offer.

To be sure, those who marched to Kruty did have a positive spirit. But spirit alone does not achieve results. Undoubtedly, had Kruty's defenders been afforded what the Division had, the situation would have been different. But under no circumstances can the events and results of Brody be compared with Kruty.

At Brody, approximately 900 Divisional soldiers were captured. This figure was compiled by Doctor Volodymyr Prokopovych who, as a prisoner-of-war, encountered other Divisional soldiers in person or learned of others through Divisional and non-Divisional members.[15]

Lying inside a darkened railway car, Liubomyr Zach wondered where his ordeal would end as the train began to pull its human cargo eastward. After a week's travel, a starving Liubomyr found himself disembarking outside of Kiev; for the moment, Liubomyr was glad that he had not wound up further east in Kazakhstan or Siberia.

Marched to a large field surrounded by wire and filled with German, Hungarian, Rumanian, and other prisoners, Liubmyr entered the area and found a place where he could lie on the ground. Here and there stood a small solitary tent or half-tent; some men stood, but most sat or lay on the ground. There were no food, water, or medical facilities. Many of the men were in tatters, and some appeared to be crazed. "If there is a hell," thought Liubomyr, "then I have just entered it!"

On the following day, he ran into Osyp, a fellow soldier from the Division. Noting Liubomyr's Divisional collar patch, Osyp immediately informed Liubomyr to remove the emblem, forget that he ever belonged to the Division and "if you know German, speak only German!" From Osyp, Liubomyr learned that NKVD personnel had already removed a few of the Divisional prisoners. Heeding Osyp's advice, Liubomyr portrayed himself as a German national.

Days, and weeks, passed. To commemorate the "heroic October 1917 Revolution," the prisoners were marched out, placed in rows of 12, shoulder to shoulder, and marched through Kiev's streets. Never would Liubomyr forget the eerie silence as hungry, ragged and sick prisoners moved listlessly through the streets of the Ukrainian capital.

On the following day, the prisoners were placed into box cars and deported to various places throughout Ukraine, Russia, and Siberia. Fortune, however, once again befell Liubomyr as he and approximately 2,500 others were sent into Southern Ukraine to rebuild destroyed facilities. In due time, Liubomyr, as a member of a "construction brigade," was dispatched to the Baltic Sea area; there, the harshness of the previous camps were somewhat abated.

Informed by a local woman that across the Polish border was a Polish Repatriation Commission, Liubomyr decided to seek its help. One night in the summer of 1946, Liubomyr fled from the camp and crossed into Poland. Although not specific on what occurred inside the committee, the Repatriation Committee did assist him. Provided papers and a certain amount of Polish currency, Liubomyr headed west. Eventually, he was successful in evading life in the post-war Soviet Union.

Although Liubomyr Zach managed to avoid years of imprisonment, many others were not so fortunate. Well into the 1950s and 1960s, former Divisional soldiers such as Myhailo Bendyna, Bohdan Seniv, Myhailo Pidkivka, Vasyl Kurash, Ostap Chorniy, Ivan Burlakiv, Roman Serkez, Victor Javorskyi, Josef "Ivan" Nakonechny, Dr. Volodymyr Prokopovych and Reverend Chaplain Josef Kladochnyi languished in Siberia's coal mines and in the sub-zero forests and tundras of Russia's interior. How many perished under such horrible conditions has never been established, and probably will never be known. It is known, however, that a number did return to Western Ukraine in the Khrushchev era. But those who returned frequently found no family left, were denied adequate jobs, and were not permitted to emigrate to the west; frequently, in poor health, they languished in poverty until death. But it is known that a number of former prisoners-of-war did survive and currently, are residing in Western Ukraine, Siberia, Poland and other areas.[16]

19

The "Galicia" Division's Withdrawal and Reformation

Crossing the Dnister River northeast of Zhydachiv, the Division's survivors headed southwest into the Carpathians through Stryi, Drohobych, Sambir, Stariy Sambir, Turka, Uzhok, and Uzhhorod to Seredne located in the Transcarpathian region of Carpatho-Ukraine. At Seredne, the Division began to rest and reform itself.

Enroute to the Carpathian Mountains, the Division's survivors moved at a fast pace in order to avoid the advancing Soviet front. On occasion, the Division's column came under aerial attack; in the vicinity of the Dnister River, several skirmishes were fought with Soviet spearheads.[1]

. At Drohobych, the head of the Military Board, Colonel Bisanz, appeared. A former soldier who was always deeply devoted and concerned about the Division's soldiers, Bisanz inquired about the Division's fate in hopes of presenting some favorable news to the Military Board. But after meeting with Freitag,[2] Bisanz left with a heavy heart and tears in his eyes.

In the late hours of 24 July, the Division reached the Uzhotsky Pass. By now, thousands of civilians had joined the column. If not controlled, civilians could pose a threat to the withdrawing force. But once through Uzhotsky, for the first time the soldiers had finally passed into safe territory. Continuing onward, the force of approximately 500 reached the village of Spas overlooking the Dnister River in the Carpathian's northern (or eastern) slopes where a temporary assembly area was established around the Divisional command post located in a foresters cabin. Enroute southwest, the Division marched through UPA territory. Instances arose where Divisional troops found themselves surrounded by UPA guerrillas who urged the Division's soldiers to defect. But few did. And unlike the Wehrmacht's units, which were disarmed, UPA's troops let the Division's personnel pass without further obstruction.[3]

Wachter, the former governor of Galicia, joined the Division at Spas. Terribly upset about the loss of Galicia and reports of "all 10,000 killed," Wachter undoubtedly wanted to personally see for himself what remained of the Division as well as raise morale.

But when Wachter spoke to Freitag, the general immediately denounced the Division in a very coarse and brutal manner. So unprofessional was Freitag's behavior that Major Heike walked away. Heike was especially disgusted by Freitag's epithet of "cowards!" – as he denounced his troops.[4]

Responding to Freitag's cruel allegations, Wachter informed him that both Berlin and the High Command had already concluded that the Division was not a poor formation, and that under the exceptionally harsh circumstances, had performed well. Upon hearing this, Freitag's attitude changed. Softening his merciless attacks, Freitag reversed his position and spoke a little more positively about the Ukrainians.

Once again, as previously at Brody, Freitag demonstrated a low level of professionalism. Beside the fact that Freitag's allegations were incorrect, he also demonstrated poor evaluation skills. The general, who never actually fought alongside his troops at Brody, was mistaken in accusing his troops of cowardice. As previously at Brody, Freitag failed to properly assess the situation. Had he looked around, Freitag would have noted that his troops were all armed. A number of the soldiers even carried out weapons which had run out of ammunition; here and there, anti-armor panzerschreks and even a few pak light guns were found along with various pieces of light equipment. These arms were carried out by soldiers who realized that the weapons had to be preserved for future needs. Soldiers who panic do not carry out weapons and light equipment. Even the automobile Freitag was using had been repaired within the Brody pocket and driven out by Waffen-Haupsturmführer Martyniuk's repair company. Disgusted with Freitag's behavior, Wachter parted with the general on poor terms.

After a short stay at Spas, the Division crossed over the Carpathians and proceeded over to Seredne, approximately 12 miles southeast of Uzhhorod. Since crossing the Dnister River north of Zhydachiv, the Division's survivors had marched no less than 150 miles. A town located on the southern (or western) slopes of the Carpathians, Seredne lay within a region that had declared its independence in 1939 with the proclamation of the Carpatho-Ukrainian statehood. But with Nazi Germany's support and Poland's approval, Hungary's troops, with German military advisors, shattered the republic. Within this region, the Division found sympathy from the inhabitants, who welcomed the soldiers with open arms. In the vicinity of the village of Lynchi, Ostap Veryn even met a girl who, months later, would marry him.

Throughout the entire month of August, the Division rested and reformed itself. Its field replacement battalion linked up, survivors drifted in, and groups of Ukrainian soldiers who had linked up with the 8th Panzer, the 18th Waffen-SS "Horst Wessel" Division and other units appeared. Martyniuk reestablished his repair company, and damaged weapons and equipment were repaired. By the end of August, roll-call revealed a strength of approximately 3,000.[5]

On 1 August 1944, at 5 p.m., as Soviet Russia's armies approached Poland's capital city of Warsaw, Poland's anti-Nazi underground arose in revolt. But because the Poles were also anti-communist, Stalin halted his forces to allow the Germans to suppress the revolt. At this time, the Division's Brody combatants were many miles to the south of Warsaw, totally outside of Poland. The Division's 8,000 man Training and Replacement Regiment was at Neuhammer, while others remained in officer, NCO, and specialist schools in Germany. Therefore, at no time was the "Galicia" Division, or any of its elements or personnel, ever utilized in the Warsaw August insurrection, as falsely implied in the post-war period by such sensationalist and irresponsible authors as V. Beliaiev, M. Rudnyts'kyi, Alexander Rydzinski, Wladyslaw Sdydunski, Valery Styrkul, and Josef Wroniszewski.[6]

At Seredne, both General Freitag and Heike wrote detailed reports and drew diagrams of the Brody battle; in turn, these reports were submitted to the German high command in Berlin. In the concluding days of August, both Freitag and Heike flew to Berlin to submit additional reports. In Freitag's absence, Beyersdorff assumed command.

Meeting personally with Himmler, Freitag noted that the Reichsführer was very interested in the Division's status. Himmler informed Freitag that it had been brought to his attention that at Brody the Division had performed reasonably well. Even Lange, the 13th Corps commander, in submitting his report, underlined certain positive comments and praises regarding the Division at Brody and during its breakout.[7] Himmler took into consideration the heavy odds and firepower directed against the Division, and stressed that under such conditions, more could not have been expected. The Reichsführer emphasized to Freitag that other German divisions were unable to hold the Soviet advance, and praised the formation for its valiant effort. Because the Reichsführer felt the Division could be utilized in future events, Himmler informed Freitag that earlier, on 7 August, he had ordered

Hans Juttner, who headed the SS-FHA, to reform the Division.[8] Himmler also ordered Freitag to rebuild the Division around those assembled at Seredne.

The Reformation of the Division:
Following the Berlin meetings, Freitag and Heike set out for Neuhammer. Because the U.S. Army's 8th Air Corps was once again blasting Berlin's railway and airport, the two men were delayed in their return trip. Once at Neuhammer, final details were worked out with the training camp's commandant for the placement and training of the Division. Afterwards, Freitag and Heike flew in the Divisional Fiesler Storch aircraft to Transcarpathia, where they found the Division in high-spirits, well-rested, and organized into a brigade-sized element. Under Beyersdorff's guidance, the Division was well-taken care of. Permission had been granted for local visits, and among the Ukrainian and Hungarian populace, a very friendly relationship prevailed. Because the railway system was unable to transport the brigade sized unit, trucks transported the soldiers and their equipment, horses and wagons to Neuhammer. By 12 September, the Division was in Neuhammer and once again was within the Replacement system.[1]

On 15 September 1944, the Division began its reformation which was to last until 31 December.[2] By 1 January 1945, the Division was to be combat-ready.

With its withdrawal from Galicia in July 1944, the Division entered a new period of existence which may accurately be referred to as its second phase. During this phase, which lasted until the end of the war, the Division experienced a number of changes in its political, training and organizational structure, as well as its military activities.

In combat, the Division would no longer see action in its native Galician soil; until the end of hostilities, the Division would continue to battle communist forces. But these combat activities would occur in various sites in Europe. In its composition, the Division began to undergo a significant change. Whereas previously its members hailed overwhelmingly from Galicia, beginning in the late summer of 1944 until the end of the war, a number of men entered the formation as refugees from scattered areas of Ukraine, from bombed-out factories, and from various German military, ad-hoc, paramilitary, youth, anti-aircraft, and self-defense groups. In some cases, a number of Galician male refugees, who had earlier enlisted in Galicia but failed to appear when called up, at last found themselves in the Division; however, it is important to note that in many of these cases such "volunteers" only entered the Division to escape from the Wehrmacht, flak units, and from factories, mines, and agricultural sites; to avoid Soviet service; or in fears of being drafted into some German service. In other cases, men only joined because they sought a meal to eat, and out of a desire to be among their own kind during a chaotic time.

For the greater part, these men were untrained and many were poorly educated. Among those who entered the formation through the efforts of the Ukrainian Central Committee, or who drifted into the Division from a bombed-out factory or similar site, a number harbored nothing but a low contempt and even outright hatred for being in military service; simultaneously, there were those who cared very little about the Ukrainian cause, and some even loathed those Galician volunteers who exhibited strong patriotic tendencies. Instances occurred of pro-Russian and, even, pro-Communist sentiments. While of course such "volunteers" did bolster the Division in numerical strength, their level of professionalism would never reach the value of those who had earlier entered the Division and had returned from Brody with combat experience.[3]

On Himmler's orders to rebuild the Division, plans were made to train the new recruits. But with the intensification of the Allied air-war, the constantly approaching western Allied and Soviet land fronts which at first threatened but then began to overrun the Wehrkreiss training areas; with arms, ammunition, and equipment shortages setting in, and with a decline in good instructors – training – both quantitatively and qualitively – began to diminish. While of course Divisional soldiers continued to train as best as possible under the German system, incoming recruits were no longer afforded the same level of training previously afforded to those from July 1943 to the spring of 1944. To improve and raise training standards, Ukrainian commanders enacted their own training. But with an insufficient amount of training time available, and certain equipment shortages, it was difficult for the Division to provide incoming personnel with proper training.

Materiel shortages also arose. Following Brody, the Division was unable to replace certain equipment and heavy weapon systems. One such system was the 88mm artillery, lost at Brody. Never again would the Division be able to replace its coveted 88's.

Arriving at Neuhammer, the Division linked up with its three infantry battalions, the 300 skeleton personnel left behind, and the 8,000 strong Training and Replacement Regiment. When the Division was deployed eastward, the Training and Replacement Regiment was transferred from Wandern to Neuhammer.[4] Along with the Division's remnants, Neuhammer's manpower strength was to play a critical role in reestablishing the battered "Galicia" Division into full Divisional strength.[5]

Chapter 19: The "Galicia" Division's Withdrawal and Reformation

This was especially so in the case of the Division's infantry. According to Veryha, all three Infantry Regiments needed Immediate Replacements. The 30th Infantry Regiment's roll call on 22 September, for example, revealed a strength of 432 returnees[6] from a total strength of 1903 deployed. At Brody, three Ukrainian officers, two NCO's, 24 grenadiers (including one German) for a total of 29 were officially verified as killed. Simultaneously, 17 officers (4 German), 56 NCO's (14 German) and 1,369 grenadiers (3 German) for a total of 1,442, were listed as missing-in-action.[7] In order to rebuild the regiment (as well as the 29th and 31st Infantry Regiments), the communications, fusilier, engineer, artillery, anti-tank, supply and other units, Neuhammer's non-Brody personnel were quickly dispersed throughout the formation.

When it came to leadership, fortune, however, befell the Division. As the Division fought on the eastern front, a number of its personnel were still attending officer and NCO schools. When the Division returned to Neuhammer, no less than 200 graduating officer candidates and 150 NCOs and soldiers dispatched for specialized training returned to the Division.[8] These leaders, along with the leadership which returned from Brody, enabled the Division to maintain a sufficient leadership strength. Additionally, some of the Brody veterans were dispatched to officer, NCO, and specialist schools for leadership and specialist training.[9]

Some have alleged that after Brody, Freitag attempted to develop a leadership corps composed primarily of Germans.[10] To accomplish this, the general requested approximately 1,000 officers and NCOs to fulfill leadership positions.[11]

But luck was with the Division. Because during the month of September it was difficult for the German high command to dispatch a sizable number of its leaders to any formation, of those who arrived, the majority were Volksdeutsche personnel from Slovakia and Hungary. A number had served in the Czechoslovakian Army before being incorporated into the German service, had lived among Slavs, and were sympathetic to their needs. One such individual was SS-Obersturmbannführer Karl Wildner.[12] Transferred to the Division from the Slovak Army in September 1944, "Papa" Wildner would soon become one of the most beloved and respected officers to serve in the Division.[13] Such combat-experienced leaders, reinforced with over 200 (mostly Ukrainian) officer-qualified personnel, along with a number of NCOs and specialists who also arrived just in time, enabled the "new," or "second" Division to avoid the serious hardship of obtaining its leadership as had been experienced in the early phases. To be sure, problems would still be encountered. Certain units, such as the rebuilt communications battalion, would now be composed solely of German leadership[14] and Freitag undoubtedly would have preferred to have more Germans in command throughout the Division. But by late September 1944, Ukrainian leadership was firmly established.[15]

That September, two German rifle battalions were incorporated into the Division.[16] On 20 September 1944, the Division's strength was placed at 261 officers, 673 NCO's, 11,967 enlisted personnel for a total of 12,901.[17] Until the end of the war, the Division basically remained a "Type 44" (1944) infantry division.[18] The only reason why the Division never converted into a "Type 45" is attributable strictly to the Division's command. Insisting that enough manpower existed to maintain a "Type 44" formation (and undoubtedly arguing that any changes would disrupt the Division's training mission), on such grounds the Division won its request to retain its "Type 44" status.

Some changes, however, did occur. Whereas before the Division maintained one full anti-aircraft battalion, in the aftermath of Brody the Division's AA would consist of only one 37mm anti-aircraft battery. While of course a full AA battalion would have benefitted the Division, it was impossible to obtain the required AA weaponry. Brody also proved that the Division would require a strong field security force. As a result, the Divisions military police force was upgraded to company strength. Approximately 50 specially trained Doberman Pincher guard dogs were included. From specially selected riflemen, a sniper/counter-sniper platoon was organized. As for the 8,000 found within the Training and Replacement Regiment, by now most were included into the Division; however, the Training and Replacement Regiment was not disbanded because incoming personnel continued to rapidly fill the Training and Replacement Regiments ranks. Such was the case with the 1,000 personnel rapidly mobilized in mid-July 1944.[19] As previously the others before them, they, and the other newcomers, would complete some type of training prior to placement into a Divisional unit.

During this time, the Division's field hospital was rebuilt. 25 Ukrainian assistant nurses from various parts of Ukraine reinforced the German female nurses who arrived shortly before. Prior to Brody, no female medical personnel were posted to the Division. In the following weeks, additional Ukrainian, as well as some Baltic and Russian female nurses and medical orderlies, would arrive. And until the end of the war, they would undergo all of the Division's ordeals.[20]

In personnel and unit structure, a number of changes occurred in the Division. Freitag remained in command, and Major Heike remained as 1st General Staff Officer. It appears that SS-Sturmbannführer Johann Burkhart, a Divisional staff officer who was reported as missing-in-action at Brody, was never replaced. The

29th Regiment remained under the command of Freidrich Dern as did the 30th under Hans Forstreuter;[21] the 31st, however, was now commanded by SS-Standartenführer Rudolf Pannier (born 10 July 1897; SS-Nr. 465,891/non-party member).[22] All three infantry regiments were rebuilt in August/September 1944; however, no 3rd Battalions are officially recorded in Regiments 30 and 31. And as late as March 1945, when sufficient manpower was available and the regiment's 3rd battalions were actually formed and included into the regiments, neither the 30th or 31st Infantry Regiments officially carried their respective third battalions on any battle rosters;[23] the reasons for this remain unclear.

Beyersdorff remained as the artillery commander; Remberger remained as the engineer commander;[24] Bristot remained with the fusiliers; Martyniuk continued to command the Division's Maintenance and Repair Company; and sometime in September or October 1944, the signal battalion received a new commander, SS-Obersturmführer Heinz. The Division's anti-aircraft battalion,[25] as well as the independent Divisional anti-tank company, were not rebuilt. Anti-aircraft and anti-armor training did, however, continue and each infantry battalion's "heavy" company had its specially formed anti-armor platoons; the Division's Field Replacement Battalion remained and all maintenance, bakery, and field post companies, were reestablished.

The Division chaplain's staff also underwent some changes but still remained under the overall supervision of Chaplain Dr. Vasyl Laba.[26] Chaplain Levenets' was transferred from the 29th Regiment to Divisional staff where he served with Liubomyr Syven'kyi; Sydir Nahayewsky served as the 29th Regiments chaplain; Chaplain Myhailo Ratushyns'kyi served the 30th; Chaplain Bohdan Levyts'kyi, the 31st. Chaplain Emanuel Korduba served the artillery regiment; Chaplain Ivan Tomashivs'kyi served in the medical unit; Chaplain Julian Gabrusevych[27] served the Field Replacement Battalion; and Chaplain's Oleksander Babij, Danylo Kovaliuk, and Oleksander Markevych served the Division's independent Training and Replacement Regiment.[28]

Because Waffen-Haupsturmführer Dmytro Paliiv never re-turned from Brody,[29] a replacement had to be found. In due time, the choice came down to either Yuriy Krokhmaliuk or Liubomyr Makarushka; and the latter was selected.[30]

Always quick to defend the Ukrainian cause and its interests, Makarushka accepted his new assignment with much devotion, enthusiasm, and concern. Very persistent in obtaining what was required, Makarushka, who eventually won Freitag's trust, always strove to elevate the Division to high standards. According to Heike, in some respects Makarushka was more persistent than Paliiv, and frequently was difficult to satisfy.

Galicia Division

As already mentioned, during this period, the Division also obtained its replacements from the 8,000-strong Training and Replacement Regiment. Beginning in July (and prior to the return of the Division's remnants in September 1944 to Neuhammer), the Training and Replacement Regiment began to assign its personnel into the Division's various regiments and units. And once the Division's battered elements returned to Neuhammer, its various elements were immediately reinforced with personnel previously assigned to the respective units. In the long run, such a move proved beneficial because much time was later saved in reorganizing the Division's various regiments and units.

But by no means was the Training and Replacement Regiment disbanded. Incoming personnel continued to appear. In one case alone, approximately 1,000 came in. These youths were obtained in Galicia proper in July 1944 when Divisional officer, Waffen-Hauptsturmführer Boychuk, appeared in the region of Oshydiv and warned the region's youth that if they failed to enter the Division, they would be conscripted into the Soviet army. Transported immediately to Neuhammer, that same July as the 8,000 were placed into the Division, the 1,000 were placed into the Training and Replacement Regiment.

In mid and late September 1944, the Division received a number of awards and decorations to be awarded to its soldiers. Already on 1 August, Anton Stek was awarded the Iron Cross Ist Class and a number of Divisional soldiers, such as Chaplain Myhailo Levenets'; Yaroslav Kinasch; Ostap Chuchkevych; Josef Demkovytsch; Vasyl Janko; Myhailo Dlaboha; Pavlo Zaborowski; Volodymyr Martschuk; and Stefan Batko were among the 23 Ukrainians (7 of whom were officers), designated for the Iron Cross 2nd Class with Ribbon.

Dmytro Ferkuniak; Myhailo Vankevych; Eugen von Nikitin; Myron Lozynskyj; Nicholas Powch; Alexander Maslak; Porfiriy Sylenko; Yaroslav Gaba; Roman Rak; Doctors Fahrian, Panasiuk, Koldowsky and veterinarian Doctor Volodymyr Kischko were among the 34 (10 officer), Ukrainians also nominated on 1 August for the Iron Cross 2nd Class.[31]

On 17 September 1944,[32] Hryhoriy Bobel; Vasyl Biletzkyi; Vasyl Vykluk; Josef Junyk; and Bohdan Hluschko were nominated for outstanding service.

On 26 September, Dmytro Ferkuniak; Myhailo Vankevych; Eugene von Nikitin; Alexander Maslak; Myron Lozynskyj; Mykola Schkira; Ivan Chybuch; Yaroslav Iwaneckyj; Myhailo Mamalyga; Roman Dmytruk; Nicholas Powch; Julian Temnyk; Bohdan Tesluk; Vladimir Kulchytskyj; Eugene Kopijchuk; Dmytro Sadovych; Bohdan Swarych; Volodymyr Andrushchak; Yaroslav Gaba; Volodymyr Slipak; Theofil Mazur; Porfiri Sylenko; Roman Rak, Stanislav Senedeckyi; Leonid Martyniak; Theodore Vynnyk; Pavlo Bakalatsch; Andrij Ivaniv; Stanislav

Chapter 19: The "Galicia" Division's Withdrawal and Reformation

Rusyk and medical doctor's Yuriy Koldewsky, Bohdan Panasiuk, Alexander Farion, along with veterinarian doctor Volodymyr Kischko, were 33 Ukrainians out of a total of 123 nominated and approved by Freitag for the Distinguished War Service Cross, 2nd Class. For the greater part, many of the awards were presented in unit ceremonies. These awards were not final. In following weeks and months, additional awards were issued. And in some cases, such as with Myhailo Lobach, awards were issued to Divisional soldiers for valor as they served in other formations prior to returning to their parent Division.

A number of individuals were also awarded the "tank destruction badge;" in some cases, if five or more verified kills were noted, the tank destroyer badge was awarded in gold crest. Ostap Chuchkevych and Karl Neilson were two of the recipients of this award.

During this time, an effort was also made to notify family members of those killed or missing-in-action. According to Veryha, a German officer, SS-Obersturmführer Hohage, appeared carrying a bag. Emptying the bag's contents on the table, Veryha noted a number of stamped seals. These seals contained various inscriptions which Veryha was to stamp upon letters and envelopes addressed to families notifying them of what had happened to their kin. Picking up one seal, Hohage pressed it against a piece of paper "Gefallen fur Führer und Grossdeutschland!" ("Died for the Führer and Greater Germany!"). Seeing the inscription, the German officer stated "you won't be needing this one because you fought for your homeland, and not for a greater Germany!" Looking over several other seals, Hohage at last found an appropriate seal – "Gefallen fur die Heimat!" ("Died for the Homeland!"). Veryha was instructed to use only that seal.[33]

Together with the Division, the Military Board made strong efforts to obtain as much information as possible about the fate of the Division's personnel; likewise, the Military Board tried to inform the Division's soldiers about the whereabouts of their families in hopes of relieving fears and anxieties as best as possible.

In January 1944, the Military Board and the Ukrainian Central Committee, in anticipation of a possible Soviet occupation of Galicia, moved a part of its bureau and staff to the town of Krynytsi, in the Lemko region of northern Carpathia; in March 1944, with the approach of the 1st Ukrainian Front into the outer edges of Eastern Galicia, the bulk of the Military Board and Ukrainian Central Committee moved to Krynytsi; prior to Lviv's fall in July 1944, the remainder of the Military Board moved to Krynytsi. But in September 1944, both the Military Board and the Ukrainian Central Committee moved to Luben in Silesia. However, the Military Board opened additional branches in Berlin and Vienna. Toward the end of the war, the Ukrainian Central Committee was evacuated to Kufstein, Bavaria, and the Military Board operated from Vienna, Austria.

In mid-September 1944, the Division commenced its training. But unlike in the past where a strong emphasis was placed on offensive tactics, the emphasis now changed to the defensive.

At Brody, the Division's offensive performance exceeded its defensive performance. Psychologically, from squad to regimental level, the Division's soldiers, although massively pounded from the air and constantly pressed by superior ground forces, as in the attempt to seal the Koltiw corridor and during the breakout, responded more effectively to an attack rather than a defensive mission. This was attributable to the fact that at both Heidelager and Neuhammer the Division's soldiers were drilled more extensively in the attack than defense.

According to former Divisional officer Evhen Ren, Germany's reversals would not have been so sudden and its losses so great had it acknowledged the fact that it was no longer on the offensive but rather, on the defensive and, therefore, adapted to the situation by changing its training methods.[34] Ren's observation's are largely correct; however, it must be remembered that although the Ukrainians always viewed the Division as a regular type of division (or even as the "Ukrainian Army"), German planners viewed it as simply another Waffen-SS formation. At the time of its formation, Waffen-SS units were primarily utilized as elite shock troops, and were frequently rushed from one critical sector to another (and even sometimes from one front to another), to reinforce a front or stem a breakout.[35] Although Germany was on the defensive, well-trained offensive units were still in demand. This explains why (prior to July 1944), the "Galicia" Division was trained largely for offensive actions.

But in late 1944, with Germany pressed solely on the defensive, its Waffen-SS (as were the other services), was forced to adjust some of its training. Thus, the Division also revamped its training around the combat lessons learned at Brody. Hand-to-hand; positional warfare; and night marches combined with night maneuvers with live ammunition especially highlighted the training.

At Brody, the Division's supply and service repeatedly found themselves in the thick of battle. Therefore, in addition to receiving their usual mechanical, communication, cooking, baking, supply and technical training, the units personnel were required to undergo no less than two hours of weekly rifle, submachinegun, machinegun, and anti-tank training; as well, they participated in the general maneuvers. All of the training was carried out in the field.[36]

Chapter 19: The "Galicia" Division's Withdrawal and Reformation

The fact that the Division was no longer operating within the territorial borders of its homeland could potentially reduce morale. Thus, to support morale, members of the Military Board and Ukrainian Central Committee, as well as various theater and choir ensembles, and the Lviv opera and ensemble, were brought in. In a similar vein, extended periods of rest and relaxation were afforded, but especially for those previously wounded. The Division also established a health resort at Zakopane. Located in the northern foothills of the Tatry Mountains, this spa, or rest center, was funded by Wachter's exiled General Government and Military Board. Many soldiers (joined by their families in some cases), spent a memorable time at Zakopane.[37]

20

Modlin-Legionowo: Fall 1944

After an advance of nearly 250 miles, the Soviet 1st Belorussian and the southern wing of the 2nd Belorussian Front concluded their summer campaign on the Warsaw front.[1] But after a brief respite, from the end of September to November 1944, Soviet Army Marshal Konstantin Rokossovsky launched a series of offensive actions north of Poland's capital city. These offensives, although limited in scope, were conducted to maintain constant pressure on Germany's eastern front, inflict additional battle destruction, secure bridgeheads for future operations and prevent the Germans from launching any counterattacks into the Soviet rear. In an attempt to outflank Warsaw from the north, from the vicinity of Roznan to Pultusk, Serock, Modlin, and Legionowo, on a front of approximately 55 miles, Rokossovsky's front battled to improve its position.[2]

In the vicinity of the Vistula and Wkra Rivers, approximately twenty miles to the northwest of Warsaw, stood the fortress town of Modlin.[3] Adjacent to Nowy Dwor Maz and a series of critical road, railway, and river canal systems, Modlin would write a chapter in the Division's history.

Modlin was located within the front which ran from Serock to Warsaw's northern suburban town of Praga; in turn, this front was held by the 9th German Army's 4th SS Panzer Corps.[4] Consisting of the battered 5th SS "Wiking" and 3rd SS "Totenkopf" Panzer Divisions, the weak corps was assigned a difficult mission. Since the corps was below strength, the Wehrmacht's 3rd Panzer and elements of the 19th Panzer Division's were shifted to reinforce the 4th SS Panzer Corps' sector. But because neither the 3rd and 19th Panzers were in full strength either, additional manpower was still required. This was especially true in the case of the "Wiking" Division.[5]

To obtain the necessary manpower for this mixed German/western/northern European division, a strength of approximately 1,000[6] soldiers were tapped from the "Galicia" Divisions Gross Kirshbaum (adjacent Wandern) Training and Replacement Regiment to reinforce the "Wiking" Division.[7] Organized into two battalions (each with a strength of approximately 500), in the first week of July 1944 these soldiers were dispatched to the Heidelager training camp where previously, the Division had trained prior to its relocation to Neuhammer in March 1944. Had the Military Board been aware of this, undoubtedly they would have protested the action. But because the move had happened suddenly, it could not be averted. On 8 July, the 1,000 arrived to Heidelager.[8]

Although classified as "soldier's," in actuality the vast majority were nothing but raw recruits. Prior to their arrival to Gross Kirshbaum, they were civilians. Few, if any, had ever served in any military prior to their entry to Gross Kirshbaum and none had served in the "Galicia" Division.[9]

To this day, it has never been explained how these 1,000 were selected.[10] Regardless, upon their arrival to Heidelager, the recruits were immediately issued arms and equipment to commence their training. For the next several weeks, the recruits underwent infantry training.[11]

Suddenly, in the early hours of 26 July, to the accompaniment of whistling alarms and military shouts of urgency, the 1,000 were quickly ordered – with weapons and full battle gear – into formation. In company formation, the soldiers were marched to Debica's railway station. Loaded into railway cars, the soldier's proceeded to Frankfurt-on-the-Oder, a city overlooking the Oder River approximately 95 miles east of Berlin.

Arriving to Frankfurt-on-the-Oder by rail, the soldiers noted one train after another coming and going. Clearly, the town was a major staging point. Departing that location on 28 July,[12] after a six hour train journey they arrived to Kohlow, a training area located southeast of Frankfurt-on-the-Oder.[13] At Kohlow, Galicia's soldiers were subjected to additional training.[14]

According to Yasho Dach,* periods of monotony, coupled with food shortages, disrupted training and lowered morale.[15] These conditions, however, did not last long and on approximately 10 August, the two Galician battalions were railroaded to Straseci,[16] a town west of the city of Kladno, almost adjacent to the city of Prague, capital of the current Czech Republic. At Straseci, under much better training and living conditions, the soldiers trained from approximately 13 August to 10 September in ideal weather and concluded their training in high spirits. Unlike the training previously at Kohlow, the training the Division's personnel received at Straseci was first rate. At Straseci, the recruits mastered various types of weapons such as machine guns, anti-armor weaponry and mortars. A strong emphasis was placed on rifle marksmanship.[17]

In September, they departed.[18] The fact that they were bound for eastern-front combat did not dissuade Galicia's troops. Morale was astonishingly high. Various songs filled the railway cars and numerous drawn symbols and quotations, such as "Slava Ukrainin!" "Death to Stalin!" "Death to the Muscovites!" expressed the soldier's desires to at long last, engage their eastern tyrants in combat.

After a three-day journey through Prussia and Poland, the troops arrived at the fortress town of Modlin via Plock, a town located on the north bank of the Vistula River approximately 40 miles northwest of Modlin.[19] Disembarking one crisp morning not far from Modlin, the men were immediately transported via truck directly to Modlin. Placed into formation, the troops stood and watched as various commanders from the Wiking Division's "Germania," "Westland," and "Totenkopf"[20] regiments selected the number of personnel they needed. Because Yasho Dach fell into the "Germania" regiment, he and the remainder of the Ukrainians were transported to Legionowo, a town approximately 13 miles east of Modlin and also located within the Modlin defense system.[21]

At Legionowo, the Ukrainians were further broken down. In the end, no group contained more than five Ukrainians. After obtaining extra weaponry and filling their rucksacks with extra ammunition, the Ukrainians were moved closer to the front.

The moment the men arrived to their respective platoons and companies, they immediately dug in. As Dach dug a fighting position approximately one-and-a-half miles from the front, artillery shells and rockets constantly screamed over his head. On the following day, a hot meal was brought to him. But as he ate, Dach noted the walking wounded trickling back. "So this is war," he thought.

On the following night, all hell broke loose. With full rucksacks, combat gear, and four extra-issued stick "potato masher" hand grenades, Dach ran with a group of soldiers northeastward to the Narew River in the vicinity of Lake Zegrzynskie. Dach ran so hard that he felt his lungs would explode. For him, the Narew River was significant because it formed the Buh River's tributary: a river which flowed into Dach's lost homeland.

Within moments of spotting the Narew, Dach heard shots and saw a group of soldiers fall. Rushing into a bunker riddled with bullet holes, Dach was initiated into the life of a frontline soldier.

Chapter 20: Modlin-Legionowo: Fall 1944

At Modlin, the Division's soldiers stood side-by-side with Wiking's German, Belgian, Wallonian, Dutch, French, Swiss, Austrian, Swedish, Norwegian, Finnish, Danish, Baltic and other volunteers. Day and night, as they battled the 1st Belorussian Front's 47th Army[22] and the 2nd Belorussian Front's 70th (NKVD) Army,[23] they endured massive artillery and rocket barrages, tank attacks, ground attacks, the screams of men "HURRAH!!!" "POBEDA!!!" and hand-to-hand combat. So close in was the combat one cold late night that Zakhary Blushko*, after emptying his Kar 98 rifle, swung it over the head of an incoming Siberian regular who had attempted to spray him with a Ppsh 41. Removing an MP 38/40 from the hands of a dead 19-year-old Belgian ideologist and Waffen-SS volunteer who seconds before had been killed by the same Siberian eliminated moments later by Zakhary, Zakhary shot and killed four more charging Asians. Emptying the MP's magazine, Zakhary swung the submachine gun to thwart the thrust of a bloodied 18-inch bayonet. Continuing to swing the weapon, Zakhary struck the cursing Russian hulk several times more before dropping him. But before Zakhary could smash the MP down upon the hulk's head, he was struck from behind. Falling down upon the Russian, Zakhary quickly rolled upon his back. As he rolled, Zakhary simultaneously reached for the 9mm Walther pistol tucked into his waistband. Looking up, he glimpsed the eerie background of a night sky lit up by a descending parachute flare, and he momentarily spotted the dark-skinned and wrinkled face of an Asian warrior. Firing the 9mm, Zakhary heard the Asian's screams of pain as the pistol's red-hot bullets tore the life out of a warrior who, just seconds before, had raised upwards a bayonet-tipped rifle in a fruitless attempt to plunge into Zakhary's body. Transported thousands of miles westward to kill and pillage, the oriental would find nothing but a lonely grave upon a distant Polish hill.

Since the night Zakhary broke down the door of a Polish cottage and shot three Mongolians accompanied by an NKVD officer who were in the process of raping a young Polish woman, Zakhary found no objections about killing anyone with slanted eyes, or associated with the NKVD. Never would Zakhary forget the screams of the woman, the insane criminal laughter, and the cries of her pleas as he, a fellow Wallonian, and a German went out late one night to probe for Soviet positions and instead, came upon the cottage...never would Zakhary forget the cigarette burns on her breasts, and the tears in her eyes...never would Zakhary forget the girl's curses as she reached for the dead NKVD officer's revolver...never would he forget how she placed the revolver's barrel tip against the officer's head, and emptied its cylinder...never would Zakhary forget the girl's trembling body covered by blotches of blood as she stood up and cried out for her mother, a murdered woman who lay dead in an adjacent room...never would Zakhary forget how the Wallonian slapped her to quiet her, and how they wrapped her in a blanket and

took her to their lines...never would Zakhary forget the sadness he felt on the following day when a medical doctor informed him that the girl had died from shock...never would Zahkary forget the cold pitch-black nights shattered by gunfire, incoming rounds, explosions, screams, and death... never would he forget the faces and screams of the dark-skinned Siberians, Mongolians, Azerbaijans, Tadzhik's, Tartars and the lighter skinned Soviets as he fought and killed them in hand-to-hand combat...never would Zakhary forget his dead friends...and never would he ever pray or believe in a Supreme Being, for Modlin proved to Zakhary that there is no God.[24]

In the final week of October, the Division's soldiers were withdrawn from the front. Whether this resulted from a stabilized front, or because of the Military Board's diligent efforts to have the troops returned, or a combination of both, is not known. Regardless, on 3 November 1944, they departed to Slovakia to return to the Division.[25] On 4 November, Wiking's Divisional Commander, SS-Standartenführer Ulrich, issued a special divisional order thanking Galicia's volunteers. The order read:[26]

> Volunteer Fighters Against the Bolsheviks!
> Three weeks of difficult, heavy combat lay behind us. You have, in your own capacity, carried out your duty so that the Front has been able to hold against a manifold enemy superiority.
> The Reichsführer-SS has at this time ordered your detachment from the [Wiking] division and your transfer to the Galician SS Volunteer Division. I thank you for your demonstration of resolve in the struggle against the Bolshevik's and wish you "soldier's luck" in the Galician Division until the final victory over our hereditary enemy "Bolshevism."
>
> Signed: Ulrich
> SS-Standartenführer and
> Divisional Commander.

Of the 1,000 volunteers who entered combat three weeks earlier, no more than 700 returned.[27] While a small number would eventually return from hospitals, in the very end, no more than 750 returned.[28] As verified by Krokhmaliuk, these were heavy casualties and: "Ilko" Boyko; Vasyl Borts'; Petro Bobak; Osyp Bordaiku; Volodymyr Babiy; Stefan Bendyna; Vasil Bei and his brother Pavlo; Petro Baran; Myhailo Vosikhovski; Andrei Patrygura; Dmytro Vasyluk; Myhailo Buk; Eugene Bunchash-Grechen; Ivan Fliut; Omelian Salaniak; Stefan Mushka; Albin Zozula;

Chapter 20: Modlin-Legionowo: Fall 1944

Myhailo Kit; 24-year-old Pavlo Mahdan and his 17-year-old brother Volodymyr; Hryhory Danybiuk, whose older brother Mykola was killed at Brody while serving in the 29th Regiment; twin brothers Petro and Oleksa Kruslakhyi, born in 1921, died side-by-side as they attempted to stem a mighty enemy thrust one night in late October; 20-year-old twin brothers Dmytro and Vasyl Kordiak also perished side-by-side; and 34-year-old Stefan Chervak, along with his two younger brothers, 29-year-old Sviatoslav and 17-year-old Hilarko, were amongst the many buried in the frozen plain of central Poland.[29]

21

Slovakia

With the fall of Mussolini and Germany's failure to stem the Soviet advance into Rumania, the Baltic States and Poland proper, the unstable governments of Rumania, Hungary, Croatia and Slovakia either began to seek ways to extricate themselves out of the war or, if their leaders remained loyal to Germany, experienced internal revolts by anti-fascists who sought to end any alliances with Hitler's Germany. Such was the case with Slovakia.

Dissatisfied with President Josef Tiso, General Ferdinand Catlos, head of Slovakia's Defense Ministry, decided to act against him. Whether Catlos' motives stemmed from a pro-Soviet stance, or a hunger for power or a combination of both is irrelevant, for on 23 August 1944, from his headquarters in Byaska Bystrica in central Slovakia, he called for a rebellion. Supported by Slovakian General Golian and approximately 20,000 Slovakian regulars reinforced with Soviet agents and airborne troops, the revolt gained momentum.[1]

For the Germans, the revolt posed a number of serious political and psychological dangers. And from the military standpoint, the revolt would also weaken the eastern front and endanger vital rear-area road, rail, and communication lines. Aware of this potential threat, the Germans immediately reacted.

After disarming the 24,000 strong 1st Slovak Infantry Corps, the Germans proceeded to disarm the other Slovakian units, and quell the revolt. But because the ad hoc "Tatra" Panzer Division, the 178th Panzer Divisional Staff Replacement, SS-Kampfgruppe "Schaefer" from the 18th SS Panzergrenadier Division and a handful of Wehrmacht units were all understrength, supplemental forces were requested. To ensure that Slovakia's newly appointed SS-Chief Gottlob Berger succeeded in restoring order, additional troops from various Wehrmacht and Waffen-SS schools, as well as the "Galicia" Division, were requested.

On 20 September 1944, the Division's strength (minus the strength of its Training and Replacement Regiment), stood at 261 officers, 673 NCO's, and 11,967 enlisted for a total of 12,901.[2]

On 22 September 1944, a Berlin directive ordered the Division to dispatch a battlegroup to Slovakia.[3] Six days later, on 28 September, another Berlin directive ordered the entire Division into Slovakia.[4] But two days before, on 26 September, a battlegroup was enroute.[5] Because the order of 22 September specified that the battlegroup was to be composed of a reinforced battalion, the 29th Regiment's 3rd Infantry Battalion was utilized.[6] In turn, this battalion was augmented with a battery of light artillery, two anti-tank platoons, two platoons of sappers, a signal/communications platoon and a supply section.[7] With a combined strength of 900 soldiers under the command of 47-year-old SS-Obersturmbannführer Karl "Papa" Wildner,[8] Kampfgruppe "Wildner's" mission was to advance into Slovakia, and in the vicinity of the cities of Banska Bystrica and Zvolen, clear its region of any communist insurgency. Because Wildner was a beloved leader and a commander whose men "would follow him to hell," no objections were ever voiced against "Papa" Wildner.

Prior to the battlegroup's departure on 26 September, the 29th's Regimental commander, SS-Standartenführer Dern, assembled the group in a massed formation and spoke to them.

In his speech, Dern stated: "In Slovakia, a communist uprising has occurred. Your families, evacuated during the Bolshevik occupation of Galicia, are being slaughtered by Slovakian and Muscovite communists. They must be destroyed. Already, elements of the German forces are fighting. Our Division must assist by dispatching one reinforced battalion."[9]

Departing from Debica's railway station, the battlegroup passed through Slovakia's capital city of Bratislava in the night hours of 28 September. By the afternoon of 29 September, Kampfgruppe Wildner had successfully disembarked in Slovakia's Zemianske-Kostolany's railway station and, with the order of "Gentlemen, we will now proceed to the village of Pizla!" Wildner's battlegroup immediately commenced its operations. As previously in the Northwestern Ukraine in February/March 1944, the Kampfgruppe moved together as one unit. At no time did it occupy a permanent location or establish a base camp. Because the lessons learned in the Northwestern Ukraine were still fresh, the posted guards and battlegroup scouts maintained a strong vigilance.

Galicia Division

At Pizla, as in other places, Wildner's troops found a population initially somewhat confused by the sight of fellow Slavs in a Waffen-SS formation. Some were at first terrified; most, however, were sympathetic or, simply, remained neutral. But already at Pizla, the battlegroup encountered Slovakian citizens of Ukrainian decent, as well as a number of Slovaks who were in a position similar to that of the Galician Ukrainians within Wildner's group – they wanted to remain free of both Nazi and Soviet rule.

Moving through hills, mountains, plateaus and populated centers such as Nova Banca, Hlinik, Banska Stiavnica, Sasa, Dobra Niva, Zvolen, Banska Bystrica, Brusno, Podbrezova, Hronec, and Brezno, the Kampfgruppe cleared the region of any insurgents, insuring that Slovakia's critical road and railway system was not disrupted. For the greater part, as attested by Heike, the Slovak insurrectionists did not demonstrate a strong willingness to battle any German or foreign force approaching them.[10] Undoubtedly, the fact that Catlos' insurgency was quickly subordinated to Moscow under the control of inserted Soviet officers, specialized personnel and commissars forced the Slovak insurgents into the realization that Catlos had been transformed into nothing but a puppet type of leader. Consequently, the communist resistance became very scattered and uncoordinated.

At the same time Kampfgruppe "Wildner" was preparing for its deployment and commencing its operations, the Division was also preparing to depart for Slovakia. Prior to its departure on 15 October, General Freitag, Heike, and other staff personnel reported to General Hermann Hoffle, who headed the German command in Slovakia.

Hoffle stated that he had submitted warnings of a possible revolt,[11] but they were ignored. Hoffle did, however, strongly condemn Hans Ludin, the head of the German consul in Bratislava, for allowing conditions to deteriorate to the point where a revolt could occur. Hoffle also informed the two men that the revolt was apparently Moscow inspired, but that it was partially supported by nationally-conscious anti-German Slovaks. Because the revolt was being suppressed, its organizers and supporters entrenched themselves in the districts of Banska Bystrica and Zvolen. General Hoffle also correctly reasoned that once these areas were cleared, the revolt, excluding for some mopping-up activities, would basically be quelled.

Seeking a way to prevent the Division or any of its elements from entering the conflict, Freitag immediately emphasized that his Division was still in the process of reforming itself after Brody, that certain amounts of arms, ammunition and supplies were still needed, and the general emphasized the Division's priority was its training.

Although mindful of General Freitag's remarks, Hoffle insisted that simply the mere presence of an additional military formation, even in a weakened condition, would help restore the situation. Hoffle promised Freitag additional supplies and material, and informed him that the "Galicia" Division would be posted into Zilina's district. There, the Division would replace the "Tatra" Panzer Division which had already cleared Zilina's area and than would be moved southeastward for deployment against the insurgent's main base at Banska Bystrica. Hoffle informed Freitag and Heike that once the Division was posted to Zilina, it would defend the town and its area. But because the area's insurgents had been largely destroyed and scattered, the Division would not be massively burdened and could undertake its primary mission of training.

In the end, Hoffle also assured Freitag that excluding Kampfgruppe "Wildner," neither the Division, nor any more of its elements, would be utilized outside of Zilina's area.

On 5 October 1944,[12] Freitag and Heike drove to Zilina. Meeting with the aristocratic General Friedrich-Wilhelm von Loepper, both parties discussed the situation and the necessary measures to ensure a proper, and easy, changeover. But while the men conferred, it became clear that sufficient guerrilla strongholds were still in the areas of Cadca, Ruzomberok, St. Martin, Povazska Bystrica, Zilina, Turzovka; additionally, the Division would have to ensure that the critical road and railway lines running from Upper Silesia to Bratislava to Zilina-Turzovka and Ruzomberok was not disrupted. As for the arms and ammunition requests, the Division was told "we have none. Get them from the partisans!"[13]

On 12 October 1944, the Division's various regiments and units dispatched their quartermaster units to Zilina's vicinity. To ensure a safe and successful operation, quartermaster units' personnel were to secure an area, ensure no dangers (i.e. minefields, explosive sites, poisoned wells, snipers, unsafe terrain, etc.), existed; arrange for the provision of supplies; draw preliminary defense sketches; locate, establish, and recommend suitable headquarters and living sites and, with the arrival of the Division, assist its incoming units.

On 15 October, the Division's first echelons left Neuhammer. Transport of the entire Division, along with its Training and Replacement Regiment, with a combined strength close to 22,000 troops,[14] could have ostensibly been a problem. But proper movement orders and efficient quartering parties ensured a smooth transfer. Upon departure from Neuhammer, many believed that they would soon return to their "home;" sensing otherwise, the moment Ostap Veryn exited the camp's main gate, he immediately turned and looked back. And so it was – never again would the Division return to Neuhammer.

Upon arrival to Slovakia, the Division established its units as follows:

- 14th Divisional Staff – Zilina (Sillein in German);
- 29th Regiment – area to the north of Zilina, with its command post (HQ's) at St. Kysucke Nove Mesto;
- 30th Regiment – area to the west of Zilina, with its command post at St. Velka Bytca;
- 31st Regiment – area to the southeast of Zilina, with its command post at St. Martin;
- Fusilier Battalion – area to the southwest of Zilina, with its command post at Rajec;
- Artillery Regiment – deployed around Zilina, its command post was at Bytrica, approximately 2 miles directly south of Zilina;
- Anti-tank unit – area to the southeast of Zilina, its command post was also in St. Martin;
- Engineer Battalion – north of St. Martin at Vrutky;
- Divisional Supply – along with the mess, baking, veterinary, field hospital and medical companies, were located south of Zilina;
- Field Replacement Battalion – east of Zilina with its command post at Bela;
- Training and Replacement Regiment – located north/ northeast of Zilina with its command post at Cadca, its three battalions were established in such locations: 1st Bn: at Cierna; 2nd Bn: Tuzovka; 3rd Bn: Oscadnica. The Training and Replacement Regiments Replacement Battalion (sometimes unofficially referred to as the "4th" Bn.), was located at Ordca.[15]

By 25 October the Division, minus Kampfgruppe "Wildner," was in place. From north to south, the Division occupied and controlled an area of almost 47 miles, and from east to west almost 65 miles. Within this area, the Division's primary mission was to protect the region's agricultural and factory sites; ensure that sabotage did not disrupt Slovakian civilian life nor destroy the region's road, rail, and communications network, and continue its training. To maintain order, the Division established checkpoints, manned observation posts, and conducted patrol activities around the clock.

Because the insurgents continued to maintain a strong grip north of Banska Bystrica in the vicinity of Ruzomberok (and virtually adjacent to the Division's eastern perimeter), and thus effectively barred the main road and rail system, the Division was forced to conduct a clearing operation.

For this purpose, a strong battlegroup, centered around the 30th Regiments 3rd Infantry Battalion and under the command of SS-Hauptsturmführer Friedrich Wittenmeyer, was organized in the closing days of October 1944.[16] Reinforced with an artillery section, sappers, panzerjägers, communications and supply personnel,[17] Kampfgruppe "Wittenmeyer" rapidly opened the main artery to Ruzomberok. Afterwards, the kampfgruppe began to press the insurgents further into the hills and mountains of High and Low Tatry to the north and northeast of Ruzomberok.

Immediately after Wittenmayer's men cleared Ruzomberok and began to pursue the insurgents, a third battlegroup, Kampfgruppe "Dern," was also dispatched. Organized from elements of the 29th Regiment and commanded by the regimental commander, Dern's men, in the strength of one reinforced company, moved eastward south of Ruzomberok.

Heike does not specify what Dern's mission was. It appears the battlegroup was to possibly reinforce "Wittenmeyer" in the event Wittenmeyer's group encountered stiff resistance in Ruzomberok, or to mop up any insurgents left behind. Keeping in mind that SS-Standartenführer's Dern's group was only in the approximate strength of a company,[18] it undoubtedly had orders to stay within a safe distance of the Division. Encountering no resistance, and unable to establish contact with Wittenmeyer, Kampfgruppe "Dern" withdrew to the Division's perimeter. It was never again used.[19]

Of interest to note is that during these operations, for the first time the Division had aerial support. But this support was not provided by the Luftwaffe; rather, it came from the Division's Fiesler Storch aerial reconnaissance plane. Diving out from clouds or around the sides of mountains, aerial observers spotted and accurately reported guerrilla strengths, activities, locations, directional movements, types of weapons, etc. Sitting beside the pilot was an observer. Through radio messages, dropped messages, or by landing on plateaus, Fiesler Storch aircraft crews constantly relayed much accurate information.

On 27 October, Banska Bystrica, the administrative hub and capital of the leftist insurgency,[20] fell. Although the pressing Germans struck the rebels with light forces in minimal strength, the well-entrenched, well-armed, artillery-supported insurgents, along with their many Soviet advisors[21] and paratroopers, offered little resistance.[22] Pursued rapidly, the insurgents were unable to reestablish an effective resistance; those who were not killed or captured fled into higher terrain.

In this final assault, Kampfgruppe "Wildner" was the only Divisional unit committed into combat by the Germans at Banska Bystrica. Approaching the insurgent stronghold from the south and southwest, Wildner's troops distinguished themselves in the attack. Striking an insurgent force superior in strength,[23] they quickly overran the insurgents; with Banska Bystrica's fall, the battlegroup did not cease its operation. Pursuing the insurgents above the Hron River, Kampfgruppe "Wildner" played an instrumental role in further scattering the guerrillas. Wildner's men finally ceased their operation in the vicinity of Brezno and on the peaks of Chopok, approximately 8 miles north of Brezno.[24] Throughout the whole ordeal, Wildner's soldiers moved on foot. With a rucksack on his back and a mountaineer's walking stick, "Papa" Wildner frequently led the way. Never did his troops complain; after all, they would follow their "Papa" to hell.

At approximately the same time that Wildner's battlegroup had reached its objectives, Kampfgruppe "Wittenmeyer" was continuing its relentless pressure against the insurgents. In desperation, various scattered insurgent groups attempted to flee into higher terrain to reorganize themselves; their efforts, however, proved unsuccessful as Kampfgruppe "Wittenmeyer" continued to pursue them into the snow covered plateaus and mountains of Higher and Lower Tatry. Because Wittenmeyer proved to be a responsible commander who displayed sympathy and concern for the Ukrainians and their cause, Wittenmeyer also won the respect of his soldiers.

Although approximately 200 encircled insurgents succeeded in slipping away in the Waag Valley (east of Zilina and north of the Vah River), Kampfgruppe "Wittenmeyer's" men continued to inflict damage.[25] With the fall of Banska Bystrica and the continuing pressure, the Moscow-supported insurgency began to crumble; injured both physically and psychologically, Catlos' troops began to call it quits. Entire formations began to surrender while others, frequently unsuccessfully, attempted to reach higher terrain. Wittenmeyer's group was especially adamant in totally driving Moscow's artificially inserted forces out of Slovakia. In well-conducted searches through mountainous caves and crevices, Wittenmeyer's soldiers unearthed many hidden caches of arms and equipment. A number of horses, critically needed by the Division, were captured from shattered insurgent units as well as some light artillery pieces and even, several German and Slovakian trucks. At long last, the Division began to replenish itself.

Chapter 21: Slovakia

In the closing days of November 1944, Kampfgruppe "Wittenmeyer" returned to the Division; on 2 January 1945, Kampfgruppe "Wildner" returned. After a brief two-day rest in Zilina, many of Wildner's men remained there as a defense force.

As regards to their campaign, out of a total of 145 days, Kampfgruppe "Wildner" spent 45 days in garrison in Zilina; 46 days marching; 48 days in battle activities; and 6 in rest and relaxation. Altogether, it covered a distance of approximately 991 miles; of this, the battlegroup was transported approximately 333 miles by rail and truck while approximately 658 miles were covered in marching. Of the marching distance, 60 percent was conducted under a forced combat march. A daily march usually covered a distance of no less than 10 miles, but distances of up to 30 miles were not uncommon. An average march totalled nearly 22 miles.[26] But most importantly, good reconnaissance, coupled with good leadership and a strong mission awareness, ensured that Kampfgruppe's Wildner, Wittenmeyer and Dern suffered few casualties.

Once the Division withdrew in entirety into its perimeter, it continued its security mission and training mission. Prior to the Divisions occupation of the Zilina area, insurgents were known to destroy or damage railways, tunnels, bridges; attack members of the Slovak population (especially those who remained neutral or harbored anti-communist sentiments), and strike various facilities. Whereas before it was dangerous to travel even in broad daylight, within days of the Division's arrival it was possible to travel at night.

In Slovakia, the Division's soldiers maintained a harmonious relationship with the Slovak population. Undoubtedly, the fact that these were fellow Slavs with a similar language who harbored little empathy for Nazism contributed to their acceptance by the Slovak populace. In the Division's territory, overwhelmingly the population was exceptionally friendly. On weekends and during periods of rest and relaxation, many a Divisional soldier spent a pleasant day or evening in the home of a Slovak family. Because the area remained calm, and no serious food and liquor shortages had set in, the Division's soldiers enjoyed the local cuisine and variety of beers and wine found in the various restaurants and cafes. The soldiers always paid for the meals and drinks or, if money was unavailable at the moment, some item of exchange was provided. The fact that Slovak guides, usually armed, assisted the Division's battlegroups in repulsing the Soviet-led insurgents proved to the Division's soldiers that many Slovaks hated and feared Stalin's Soviet regime. It is important to note that in addition to having successfully rescued thousands of Ukrainians (who, in due time were also evacuated to the west) caught up in the revolt, the Division also rescued a number of Slovak citizens. This explains why in the concluding weeks of the war and in its aftermath, Ukrainians who were serving in various Czechoslovakian Army units, upon arriving to areas previously occupied by the Division, were informed by the populace that its members behaved cordially and with respect.[27] To be sure, while some minor incidents arose (and if that was the case its perpetrators were punished),[28] no serious or large-scale offenses were committed. This also explains why, to this day, neither the Czechoslovak government, nor the current Slovakian Government, has ever pressed for the extradition of the Division, or any of the "Galicia" Division's members, for war crimes.[29]

On 30 September 1944, General Fritz Freitag received Germany's prestigious Knight's Cross. This award was issued to soldiers for exemplary service only under combat conditions, and its final approval was granted by no less than Adolf Hitler.[30]

On 19 October, General Freitag personally issued a special Divisional Order-of-the-Day. Addressing the "Men of My Division!", Freitag praised the Division's soldiers. After announcing that the Führer himself had issued the award, Freitag also stated:

> The Führer has decorated me with the Knight's Cross of the Iron Cross. I bear this high distinction for all of the brave and model German and Ukrainian officers, NCO's and men of my Division, who in the difficult days at Brody demonstrated their soldierly qualities to the highest value through their actions, tenacity and character, and by so doing, constructed a tradition for the 1st Ukrainian Division to follow.
>
> For the Germans in the Division, my decoration is the receipt of the highest praise and recognition for their constructive performance and courage in the struggle for the eternal future of our people.
>
> An acknowledgement of similar proportions is due to Ukrainians in that the Führer has fully honored their brave deeds, and the fullest recognition has been accorded for the battle actions of the Ukrainians on behalf of their people and homeland, and the continuing efforts to make them free. We will vow to the Führer that in our new undertakings it is our intention to fight through together until victorious over the Bolshevik hordes and their Jewish-plutocrat helpers.

(Signed) Freitag
SS-Brigadeführer and
Generalmajor of the Waffen-SS
and Divisional Commander

Chapter 21: Slovakia

Although Freitag was correct in sharing the credit, whether he was truly sincere will never be known. Possibly, he was motivated to share the credit simply in order to restore some prestige because he was fully aware of the fact that his personal performance at Brody was poor; besides, it was common knowledge that Freitag had unjustly downgraded the Division. But what is especially interesting is the fact that Freitag referred to the formation as the "1st Ukrainian Division," possibly he did this to appease the Ukrainians. Because Freitag also knew that most of the Division's Ukrainians were impartial to the "SS" and its symbol, references to the "SS" were not included. Significantly, neither Wachter, Bisanz, the Military Board nor any important Ukrainian official, congratulated Freitag upon receiving the award.

Desertion, always a problem for any military force, reached its peak in Slovakia. In the brief period that the "Galicia" Division served in Slovakia, 220 of its members deserted.[31]

The largest desertion involved 20 soldiers, all from the Division's medical/field hospital battalion.[32] Although the troops were serving under a German commander who was very cordial to the Ukrainians, a successful desertion nevertheless took place.[33]

Whenever a sizable group of soldiers desert, it is an indication that the desertion was organized. In this case, it was undoubtedly coordinated with an outside force – the UPA. Because the UPA underground was constantly striving to improve its medical services, a number of the UPA's personnel were also serving within the Division's medical services, as was commonly known. Once inside, UPA infiltrators exerted their influence upon others and in the end, 20 medical personnel, loaded down with as much medicine and medical equipment as possible, left the Division.

Heike attributes these individual desertions to the UPA.[34] While undoubtedly some defections did occur to the Ukrainian underground, Yuriy Krokhmaliuk attributed a number of the individual desertions to a very powerful and influential force – love.

Some of Europe's most beautiful women may be found within the Slovak region. And some of the Division's personnel succumbed to them. Krokhmaliuk cited that when he personally investigated the desertions, in several cases he was informed that the deserter is "in the hands of a beauty!" But as Krokhmaliuk also stated, deserters usually took all of their arms and equipment with them. In one case alone, a soldier who "went over the hill" from a patrol, took his MP 38/40, eight to ten magazines, a Walther P38 pistol, and a couple of panzerfaust anti-armor rounds. Such arms, confirmed Krokhmaliuk, were difficult to replace and, of course, were needed for the future. But as also acknowledged by Krokhmaliuk "men do many things for the love of a woman!"[35]

But it was also in Slovakia that some of the Division's first Brody veteran's began to reappear. And one such soldier was grenadier Oleh Dir, who reappeared in the beginning of November 1944.

Late one night in July 1944, from a partially gutted and destroyed German-made mobile Leichte Flakpanzer 38 (t) anti-aircraft gun, Dir scavenged some canned food, a large box of crackers, some chocolate, a blanket, and a full bandoleer of 7.92mm ammunition. Dir was tempted to take the bottle of vodka and cigarettes lying inside. But knowing that alcohol deadens the senses and smoke can be spotted, Dir left those items for the Russians; withdrawing into a wooded area, he found some heavy brush which afforded excellent cover and concealment, 360 degrees of visibility, and good avenues of escape. Knowing he had to rest, Dir decided that unless forced otherwise, he would remain in his location for the next two days.

He ate sparingly and slowly, filling his stomach. The canned fruit and "ersatz" chocolate tasted especially good. He slept soundly, and although it rained one afternoon, Dir did not move an inch. At night, he could hear the distant rumble of artillery; three times he spotted enemy patrols and once, an exceptionally well-armed UPA patrol.

On the morning of the third day, Dir decided to move. He placed his trash into the blanket, rolled it up tightly, and shoved the blanket into a brushy depression, thus totally concealing the items. To return to this location would be suicidal, so from now on he would have to find new places of concealment.

By the end of the day, Dir had linked up with the UPA. His original intent was not to join the Ukrainian underground, but after spying an NKVD patrol setting up an ambush, Dir decided to intervene.

Patiently, slowly, he crawled toward their ambush site, and established himself no further than 100 meters from the patrol's 12.7mm Degtyarev Shk heavy machine gun. Knowing that a sniper was undoubtedly posted amongst their midst, Dir carefully searched the brush. Unable to first locate him, Dir finally spotted a puff of smoke emanating from the brushy depression. Except for the upper part of his camouflaged hood, the sniper lay totally concealed.

From then on, Dir just waited. But he did not have to wait long. Shortly before 7 p.m., he spotted the sniper raise his head, peer through the rifle's scope, place his weapon down, and with his left hand signal the police troops to his left. Continuing to lie as low as he could, Dir searched ahead and through the brush he spotted a UPA officer. Barely visible in the brush, the UPA officer was leading a patrol straight into an ambush.

Slowly shifting the rifle to his right, Dir resighted on the Red sniper; he noted that the sniper was already peering through a PU-4 scope. But the moment the sniper began to squeeze the M1891 Mosin-Nagants trigger in the full belief that he would drop the UPA leader, Dir shattered the sniper's head with a well-placed 7.92mm round.

Automatically, Dir turned to aim toward the machine gun crew to his left and front. After quickly eliminating the weapon's gunner with a head shot, Dir also dropped his assistant; by now, the shouts of "SLAVA!" filled the air as the UPA rushed forward, their weapons blazing death. Continuing to fire, Dir killed several more.

Dir's actions saved the UPA patrol. By eliminating the machine gun, he destroyed no less than 70 percent of the NKVD's firepower. His first shot also warned the UPA, and created havoc among the NKVD. By operating from behind and on the enemy flank, Dir effectively supported the UPA thrust.

"Thanks!" After shaking hands with "Vovk," the UPA leader, Dir accepted his invitation to join their ranks. For the moment, linking up with the UPA was not a bad idea; from them, he could obtain food, extra clothing and 7.92mm ammo.

Many hours later, in a UPA camp deep in the Carpathian Mountains, as Dir cleaned his Kar 98 and listened attentively to what "Vovk" and his commander had to say, Dir was also realizing that the UPA was a much larger and sophisticated underground than he had ever imagined. Accepting Dir into their ranks, the UPA also promised him that he could leave upon request.

On his first long-range patrol, Dir helped to deliver medical supplies to nom-de-guerre Doctor Abraham Kum. Jewish by birth and a recipient of the highest UPA medal for valor, Dr. Kum commanded an underground hospital in Trukhaniv's province. Dir would never forget the doctor's kindness as he treated his patients with tender and loving care.

Around the towns and cities of Bibirka, Drohobych, Halych, Stanyslaviv, Chernivitsi, Lutsk, Rivne and many other smaller towns and villages, Dir fought the NKVD. Side by side with the UPA, he participated in raids and ambushes. As at Brody, he covered attacks, withdrawals and retreats. By his actions, Dir saved many a man and amongst both friends and foes, his reputation spread.

In early October, Dir accepted a highly dangerous one-man mission – to eliminate a ruthless NKVD colonel operating from a village converted into an NKVD base camp near the town of Khust, on the Slovak-Ukrainian border. Because there was danger in approaching the area, Dir's two-man escort was under strict orders to return immediately once they came within several miles of the village. From that point, Dir would be on his own, and would also have to return alone.

In order to kill this ruthless leader, who had been terrorizing people since 1918 in Russia, Ukraine, Poland, Spain, Rumania, Slovakia and countless other places, Dir reasoned that for the first couple of miles he would approach carefully. But for the remaining distance, he would have to virtually crawl, and be constantly on guard for patrols, mines, and lookouts. Of course there would be peril in the entire mission and it would take time, but Dir estimated that on the following day sometime by late afternoon he would be in position. After eliminating the colonel, Dir would utilize the early darkness for escape.

Through a cold, dark and rainy night, Dir crawled toward his aim. By late morning, he had centered himself at the edge of a treeline bordering a small forest 500 meters from where the NKVD colonel was supposedly encamped. As the rain stopped, the sun rose and the foggy mist cleared, Dir spotted a high ranking NKVD officers' automobile parked alongside a house. Patiently, Dir waited for his target to step out.

He waited and waited. NKVD men came, entered, and left the house but their leader never appeared. And as the ground dried and hardened, the sun beat down on Dir, hunger gripped his sides, and his throat felt parched. Relieved that he had drunk a full canteen of water seconds after positioning himself and therefore he had some liquid in his system, Dir only continued his patient vigil. But as the sun began to set, Dir began to fear that perhaps the UPA's intelligence had made a mistake, and that an NKVD patrol would discover him. Deciding to take advantage of the darkness encircling him, Dir inched his way backwards.

The moment he moved, he thought he heard the sound of engines in the distance. Wondering if he had actually heard something, Dir halted. Within moments, in the quickly diminishing light, he spotted a Soviet staff car with a strong-armed escort rounding a bend. But Dir's luck did not hold, and by the time the jeep had pulled up in front of the house, darkness had totally engulfed the area. To make matters worse, the crack of a lightning bolt, followed by an immediate downpour, hurried the NKVD colonel into the house. Desperately wanting to accomplish his mission, Dir decided to hold out one more night. So through another cold, rainy and misty night, Dir continued his lonely vigil.

At the crack of dawn the rain ceased. Thoroughly soaked and shivering, Dir was grateful to see the sun break out. Yet, he also knew that a clear day could bring new dangers, especially since at night he had crawled another 50 meters forward to shorten the distance between himself and the house. True, Dir's camouflage blended thoroughly into the grassy knoll. But the forest's edge was now at least 150 feet to his rear.

Chapter 21: Slovakia

From where he lay, Dir had a perfect view. He estimated the distance to the colonel's dwelling to be no more than 350 meters. But Dir also knew that his first shot would be critical; therefore, from the first crack of light, Dir carefully studied the distant tree tops and prayed for no enemy patrol to appear when the time came to fire.

At approximately 9 a.m., Dir spotted an NKVD private exit the house. "Good!" thought Dir, "the vulture's coming out." He noted that the private had a problem in starting up the staff car, but Dir also realized that this would prove to be advantageous because once the colonel stepped outside, he would not be partially blocked by the vehicle.

At last, Dir's target emerged. Dir immediately recognized him by the peaked red and blue NKVD cap with its hammer and sickle badge. As the NKVD leader stood fully erect, facing the sniper's direction, Dir's mind raced the rules for an effective shot. Continuing to stand, the NKVD man first looked to his left, said something to the driver, placed his right hand into his black leather jacket, and produced a pack of cigarettes. By now, Dir had the scope's post sight planted squarely on the upper part of the short, Asiatic-looking leader's upper chest. To allow for bullet drop, Dir deliberately kept the sight slightly higher. "That's right" thought Dir, "you take your last cigarette break!"

As he lit a match, Dir held his breath; as he raised it to his lips, Dir slowly squeezed. The second the match fused with the cigarette, Dir's rifle cracked. With tremendous force and speed, the 7.92mm round shoved the NKVD man backwards against the house. Clutching his chest and bending over, the colonel attempted to straighten up. But as he did, Dir slammed another round squarely into his stomach. Collapsing to the ground beside his still burning cigarette, the NKVD man never stood up again.

Congratulating Dir on a well-accomplished mission, "Vovk" also presented the sniper with some grim news. As Dir listened, staring into the face of the handsome UPA officer, he noted much sadness in the man's eyes. Between the Reds and Nazis, the man lost his parents, his wife, child, and many of his relatives. "If anybody has really seen much tragedy," thought Dir, "this man surely has."

Vovk, along with a UPA west intelligence officer, debriefed Dir. But at the conclusion of the briefing, Vovk's intelligence officer warned Dir of his precarious situation. "It has been brought to our attention that the Reds have brought a selected team of snipers to eliminate you. They are highly trained, some personally by Zaitsev, yes, the famous Stalingrad sniper, and all have tremendous experience. They're attached to the NKVD, and will be searching for you. Dir, you're either going to have to go into another region, many miles away, or return to your division. You're good, but let's face it, they're good also!" And before Dir could even respond, Vovk immediately added that he would forbid Dir from engaging the Red snipers in any kind of private war. Faced with these options, Dir chose to return to the Division. After resting for several days, he bid his farewells and with a heavy heart and a two-man UPA escort, Dir began his westward journey. Parting with the UPA men, of whom a good number were former Galician troops, was not easy and deep down, Dir knew that he would never see any of them again.

A week later, Dir and his escort neared the German lines. From this point on, Dir would be on his own. "After all, the Germans probably still hold a grudge against us!" laughed one of Dir's escorts as the men exchanged their goodbye's.

That night, the sniper passed through the German lines. Shortly thereafter, he was reunited with his fellow troops, all of whom had believed that he had been killed at Brody. Give or take a handful of NKVD and Red Army personnel, from the period of mid- July 1944 until his departure from the UPA, Dir had eliminated approximately 120 enemy personnel.

Through the discovery of insurgent caches, and the capture of insurgent arms and materiel, the Division succeeded in replacing much of its Brody arms, equipment, and materiel losses. But in November 1944, some arms and weapons did arrive to the Division from German factories.[36]

One such weapon, produced in the latter stages of the 3rd Reich, was the Stg Sturmgewehr MP44 Assault Rifle. As a result of Hitler's personal insistence and combat demands, an "assault rifle" was developed. This selective fire (automatic and semiautomatic) rifle, with a weight of 11.5 pounds, fired a light, but very effective and deadly, 7.92mm "Kurz" round. Officially, this was the first true "assault" rifle. And in the post-war era, the MP 44 altered the course of combat arms development.

Because production on the MP44 did not begin until August 1944, and even then only limited numbers were produced, the weapon was primarily issued to select Waffen-SS and paratrooper units. How many MP44's were issued to the Division is not known. But once issued, the weapon was distributed among selected fusilier and infantrymen.[37] After test firing the weapon, Dir immediately fell in love with its action, and knew that the exotic-looking assault rifle would make an impact on future weapons developments. Of course, Dir kept his telescopic Kar 98 Mauser rifle and his two handguns. Along with four "potato masher" stick grenades, Dir reasoned that in his hands he possessed more firepower than a platoon of 30-40 soldiers in the old Galician Army.

Chapter 21: Slovakia

In mid-November 1944, General Reinhard Gehlen, the eastern front's Chief-of-Intelligence, issued a report on the Ukrainian UPA insurgency.[38]

Titled "The Ukrainian National Resistance Movement – the UPA," the report (with a number of attached enclosures), was lengthy and was subdivided into various sections. Although the report acknowledged that certain information is still lacking pertaining to the UPA, it does provide detailed sections on the historical background and origins of the OUN, various personalities, insurgent concentrations, and UPA's battles with Soviet NKVD and regular army units. Of interest to note is that although the report was written in late 1944, it specifically covered UPA's anti-Nazi activities in the concluding weeks of the Nazi occupation.

In regard to the "Galicia" Division, the report specifically emphasized that contact is continuously maintained between the Division and the UPA. An emphasis is also made on the fact that Divisional soldiers try to do their best to train and equip the UPA.

It is interesting to note that within the period of October to December 1944, the Division, although retaining its "Type 44" organization, was organized into three main battlegroups. In turn, each battlegroup's nucleus was one of the Division's infantry regiments.[39]

This was done to ensure a quick reaction. Therefore, each regiment had an artillery battalion, signal company, engineer company, panzerjäger (anti-tank) platoon, medical company, veterinarian platoon, supply company and other assets specifically assigned to it. For example, if a battlegroup in regimental strength was requested, and if the 29th was dispatched, the following would be deployed as well: the artillery regiment's 1st Battalion; the signal battalion's 1st company; the engineer battalion's 1st company; the veterinarian company's 1st platoon, and so forth. But if a battlegroup in battalion strength was requested, and the 29th Regiment's 3rd Battalion was dispatched, the 1st artillery battalions 3rd battery; the 1st signal company's 3rd platoon; the 1st engineer company's 3rd platoon; the veterinarian company's 3rd platoons 3rd squad with one veterinary doctor, and so forth, would be deployed. As for determining who would deploy first, monthly standby periods were specifically designated for each regiment, along with its sub-units, for instant deployment. For example: December 1944 was covered by the 29th Regiment; January 1945 by the 30th; and February by the 31st. In March, the 29th would resume its assignment. During its month of standby, a regiment and its sub-units would continue to train and perform their required assignments. The only difference was that the standby regiment would be prepared for immediate deployment. And to ensure a speedy and successful deployment, regional German rail and transportation battalions were provided directives on how many railway cars and trucks were needed to transport a certain type of battlegroup and its materiel.

Such organization not only ensured a quick response for the need of a battlegroup from company to regimental strength, but eliminated any unnecessary confusion and waste of time in dispatching a battlegroup. It is noteworthy that this type of organization arose from the Division's own initiative; none of this was proposed by higher command. And by organizing itself in such a manner, the Division became one of the first military organizations in the world to develop itself into a "rapid-deployment" force.

In a continuing effort to break into the critical road and rail network of the Austrian city of Vienna, the Soviets continued to press forward. Determined to succeed, throughout November and December 1944, the Soviets repeatedly struck the Budapest front.

The Budapest front comprised an area to the south/southwest of Budapest, the city itself, and an area to the north/northeast of the Hungarian capital. This front was held by two army groups – Army Group Fretter Pico[40] which consisted of the 6th German and 3rd Hungarian Army, and Army Group Woehler[41] which was composed of the 8th German and 1st Hungarian Armies. But although impressive in name, both Army groups were far from their authorized strengths. As for the Hungarian armies, a combination of manpower weaknesses and a desire to withdraw from the war forced the Germans to conduct the brunt of the fighting. But what also hurt the Budapest front is that on 16 December 1944, against the advice of his generals, Hitler launched a major offensive in the Belgian Ardennes Forest. Besides the fact that the eastern front was stripped of its manpower and armored forces for this totally senseless western offensive, until dictated otherwise by Hitler, the eastern front would receive virtually no reinforcement. As a result, the eastern front could only rely on what it had.[42]

With the fall of Vac, a city directly 14 miles north of Budapest, and Sahy, a town approximately 23 miles northwest of Vac, the 2nd Ukrainian Front, in the period of 5-19 December 1944, drove northwest to the Hron River and created a corridor in the German defense. Soviet spearheads began to approach Revice, a town on the Hron River, and if not contained, would cross over.

From 20-31 December, the Soviets repeatedly attacked to expand the corridor into various directions. 4th Panzer Corps (a part of the 6th Army), and General Friedrich Kirchner's 57th Panzer Corps (this corps, however, was found within the Hungarian 3rd Army), as well as the 8th Army's right (southern) flank, came under exceptional pressure.

To stem this mighty Soviet thrust and halt the attack of the 6th Guards Tank Army (which was battling to secure a bridgehead across the Hron), as well as the 7th Guards and 53rd Armies fighting to expand the corridors, additional forces were called upon. But because these forces, such as the crack – but weak – 96th Infantry Division and the 211th Volksgrenadier consisted of minimal strengths, the 14. Waffen-Grenadier Division der SS (ukrainische Nr. 1), was called upon to immediately dispatch a kampfgruppe.[43]

Organized around Dern's 29th Regiment, within 12 hours Kampfgruppe "Dern's" first elements were rolling southward into the town of Banska Stiavnica (located 22 miles directly south of Banska Bystrica where Kampfgruppe "Wildner" fought its famous battle), and its area; within 24 hours, the whole kampfgruppe was deployed.[44] Proceeding to a point approximately 45 miles directly to the south of St. Martin, Kampfgruppe "Dern" fought in the vicinity of the Hron River in Banska Stiavnica's district where it engaged the forces of the 6th Guards Tank Army's[45] 5th Guards Tank, 5th Guards Mechanized and the 23rd Independent Rifle Corps' as well as elements of the 53rd Army.[46] As for the 23rd Rifle Corps, the Division had previously encountered this independent rifle corps at Brody when the 23rd Independent was attached to the 60th Army.

The moment Kampfgruppe "Dern" entered the area, it immediately entered combat. It appears that Dern's battlegroup was committed to the sector held by the 4th Panzer Corps. Fully realizing that a major Soviet breakout could engulf or overrun the remainder of the Division located to the north, whether on the offense or defense, Kampfgruppe "Dern" served with distinction and soon, the foreign troops earned a tough reputation. Kampfgruppe "Dern's" artillery especially distinguished itself. Although always engaging superior odds, Kampfgruppe "Dern" played an instrumental role in halting, and then repulsing, Soviet attempts to cross the Hron River and advance further westward. In January 1945, Kampfgruppe "Dern" was withdrawn from the front. Returning victoriously to the Division, Dern's men were highly praised for their valor,[47] and a number of the battlegroup's soldiers were decorated with individual awards.

On 12 January 1945, the Soviets launched a major winter offensive. Army Group "A," with its front running from Serok (north of Warsaw) to Rimavska Sabata (east of Zvolen), was especially struck. Breaking through, Soviet strategists planned to conclude the war by capturing Berlin within 45 days.

Prior to this offensive, Colonel-General Heinz Guderian, who commanded the entire eastern front, repeatedly appealed to Hitler to release the eastern front forces designated for the Ardennes back to the eastern front. But because Hitler refused to do so, and persisted in fighting it out in the Ardennes, when the Soviets struck on 12 January, they hit a paper-thin front.

With the front falling westward, the Division was increasingly placed into a perilous position. On 17 January 1945, the Division's main headquarters at Zilina stood no more than 62 miles from the main front line; Divisional units east of Zilina stood much closer. Although the distance might have seemed to be a safe one, if one takes into consideration that an advancing enemy force could reach the Division's perimeter in two or three days, then the Division was indeed in an unsafe position. By now, Soviet air attacks were intensifying, and one day, as General Freitag and Yuriy Krokhmaliuk walked down Zilina's main street, air raid sirens suddenly screamed their warning.

As soldiers and civilians dashed for safety, Freitag continued to walk as if nothing was happening; clearly, he was going to demonstrate that a Prussian had no fears. But Krokhmaliuk, totally unmoved by the bombing, likewise was going to demonstrate that a "Galician" has no fears. So as bombs rained down and explosions levelled buildings and shattered store front windows, both men continued to walk and converse as if no danger existed.[48]

Slowly, but steadily, Army Group "A's" 1st Panzer and 8th Armies continued to be repulsed westward. Since it had become obvious that sooner or later the advancing Soviets would reach the Division's area, the Division intensified its previous efforts to construct fighting positions, fortifications, blocking positions, and engagement areas.

But as the Division was digging in, the higher command was deciding the Division's next course of action. At first it was not known if the Division would remain and defend its area, or be transferred to another frontline area, or further to the west. But on 21 January 1945, the Division received such an order:[49]

"The Ukrainian Division is to transfer immediately to Styria, on foot, where it is to complete its reformation and training and reach complete battle-readiness. The exact district where the Division is to be stationed will be indicated by the Higher SS and Police Leader in Ljubljana. During its training the Division is to continue fighting the many partisan units in its assigned district. The reserve [Training and Replacement] regiment will continue to be attached to the Division and will also transfer to the new district on foot. There is no rail transport available for transfer of the Division at this time. The Division will be subordinated to the local command until such time as it is brought into action."

Chapter 21: Slovakia

The "Galicia" Division would now be posted to the border region of Slovenia, an area in Northwestern Yugoslavia adjacent to the south/southeastern border of Austria, and to Austria's southeastern Steiermark region.

To move into this region, the Division was provided only a limited amount of time to prepare; realistically speaking, the rapidly encroaching eastern front did not provide the Division much time. But because the Division was organized into rapidly-deployable groups, no serious difficulties were encountered in actually moving the formation. Also, because Divisional movement plans were prepared well in advance for a westward march, the plans were simply transferred to the route used by the Division.

To move into its new area-of-operations, the Division would use three March Groups: March Groups A, B, and C. Of these, two would be conducted by foot and one, by rail. The March Groups composition was as follows:

March Group A: Commander: General Freitag.

Units: 29th, 30th Infantry Regiments; most of the communications battalion, elements of the anti-tank unit; the artillery regiment; one engineer company; and most of the supply services.[50]

March Group B: Commander: SS-Standartenführer Rudolf Pannier.

Units: 31st Infantry Regiment; fusiliers; engineer battalion (minus one company),[51] and the Division's field reserve battalion.

March Group C: Commanded by the Division's anti-tank commander, SS-Sturmbannführer Hermann Kascher, the march group supervised the loading of the Division's heavy artillery equipment, and the greater number of the Division's trucks upon railway cars for rail transport to Maribor, Yugoslavia. To ensure that enroute to Maribor the Division's heavy arms and motor transport was not confiscated and would arrive safely, March Group C's railroading personnel, along with most of the Division's Military Police company, travelled by train.

However, one major problem did arise. And that was what to do with the Training and Replacement Regiment which, by mid-January 1945, had again risen to a strength of approximately 7,000-8,000.[52] But it could not be left behind, and a lack of proper training, sufficient leadership, as well as a shortage of arms and equipment did not enable it to be committed to the front. As a result, the Training and Replacement Regiment had to be taken along. It was attached to March Group A.

As attested by Krokhmaliuk, had a way been found somehow to run these men through the German Army's Replacement system within a training Wehrkreis, and if a solid officer and NCO leadership core could somehow have been established by either bringing in additional officer's and NCOs from the outside, or by establishing a leadership core from those inside, or both, a second Ukrainian Division could have been raised. But (as also verified by Krokhmaliuk), although in the beginning of 1945 many German divisions had a personnel strength of at best 8,000 (and in many cases even fewer), it was still impossible to convert the 8,000 strong Training and Replacement Regiment into a division. This was attributable to the fact that in the beginning of January 1945, the Wehrkreis military systems began to be overrun. This prevented the 8,000 from undergoing a 14-16 week period of solid training. Although the men were attired in military clothing, were issued helmets and were armed with rifles and some machineguns, the Training and Replacement Regiment lacked heavier weapons and much requisite equipment. Such disadvantages thus prevented the regiment from being properly organized further into respective units (i.e., a fusilier battalion, anti-tank battalion, communications battalion, etc.). As a result, the Training and Replacement Regiment – in near divisional strength – never evolved into a division.[53]

For any type of military force to be mobile, even a foot marching infantry force, some kind of transport is required. Since it was not possible to move the brunt of the Division's 22,000 men by rail,[54] the Division would have to execute its move on foot. But even if on foot, much of the Division's materiel would need to be transported; additionally, if casualties were incurred, any wounded, injured, or ill personnel would need transport. And because the Division's march was in itself a military operation, proper transport was required.

To conduct a safe and expeditious move, Divisional staff and movement's personnel estimated that approximately 100 extra horse drawn wagons and an additional 800-900 horses would be required.[55] Although the Division had some trucks (primarily light trucks), the bulk of its heavy weaponry and equipment, along with the Division's extra arms, ammunition, food supplies, etc., would have to be pulled by animal power. True, the Division's soldiers would carry some of the materiel. But horses would be needed to carry most of the materiel and haul wagons. Unfortunately for the Division, at Brody the Division had lost most of its horses, wagons and trucks. And it was difficult to replace the needed animals and transport.[56] While it is true that in the anti-guerrilla operations a number of horses were secured from the insurgents, in the end more animals, as well as wagons and motorized transport, was required.

According to Heike "in all, about 1600 horses and more than 300 hundred wagons [in addition to those already within the Division] had been willfully requisitioned, or nearly 800 horses and 150 wagons more than had been deemed necessary by the norms set by staff." In the end, "the Division returned more than 200 horses and 100 wagons."[57]

In his memoirs, Heike claims that despite the "norms set by [Divisional] staff, nearly 800 additional horses" were secured.[58] But, unfortunately, Heike failed to provide a figure for the number of horses the Division had prior to searching for and requisitioning additional horses. Keeping in mind that in mid-January 1945 the Division had approximately 14,000 soldiers and a further 8,000 in its Training and Replacement Regiment,[59] and that this strength was virtually all centered around foot marching formations, with the bulk of its wagons, artillery, and heavy equipment pulled by horses, than no less than 3,000 horses and/or mules were required. It is interesting – and important – to note that although Heike faults requisitioners for obtaining nearly 800 extra horses and 150 wagons, Heike also states "the Division returned more than 200 horses and 100 wagons."[60]

So the question is such: if certain individuals did requisition so many "more" and "additional" horses and wagons, why were not all of the 800 horses, and 150 wagons, returned? Does the possibility exist that Divisional staff itself originally miscalculated the number of horses and wagons required? Were they aware of how many animals altogether were in the Division? The fact that nearly 600 horses and 50 wagons were retained clearly demonstrated that extra transport was required; after all, 600 additional horses and 50 additional wagons can move much. Again, it must be remembered that at Brody, the Division lost virtually all of its horses, wagons and its limited number of trucks that were committed. As the Division's survivors returned to their Neuhammer home base, they discovered there only a limited number of horses, wagons, and trucks. During the anti-guerrilla operations a sizable number of "Red" horses were seized, but many of these animals were in pitiful condition. While of course Dr. Kishko and his veterinarian company succeeded in nursing some of the animals back into proper condition, the remaining horses which could not be restored to army standards were simply provided for the local populace's civilian use. Were Heike, Freitag and the other Divisional staff personnel aware of this? And if so, were they notifying higher command of the urgency of transport needs? Or aggressively seeking animal and wheeled transport? As acknowledged years later by Yuriy Krokhmaliuk "horses, as well as all other forms of transport, was needed and sought."[61] And the fact that nearly 600 horses and additional wagons were retained clearly indicates that something was inconsistent with the Divisional staff's original estimates and that perhaps, the Division's veterinarian 4C section and its veterinarian company were aware of the true picture, whereas Divisional command was not. Undoubtedly, the Division's practical necessities and not (as expressed by Heike), greed, were the factors motivating the requisitioners.

Heike also blamed both German and Ukrainian requisitioners for failing to properly fill out, maintain and provide receipts which caused "the commander of-section 4C [the Divisions veterinary section] and the Division's veterinary officer to waste a considerable amount of time compiling these lists, because in many instances neither the German nor the Ukrainian requisitioners had given out receipts."[62] But again, this allegation must be examined.

By late 1944 or early 1945, it was very difficult, and in many cases impossible, for units to obtain all of their required needs via official routes. Fully aware that horses, wagons, and truck (vehicle) transport were required, that time was running out, and that the Division was in the midst of a life-and-death situation, the Division's supply and requisitioning personnel, whether German or Ukrainian, began to make all kinds of deals; and of course (as in any military force), such deals are often made without anyone's knowledge or consent. Needless to say, the Division was not an exception. Whether Heike or the Divisional staff approved it or not, it must be remembered that such deals were strictly made to better the Division's transport needs.

Worldwide, in any type of army, from battalion to army level, supply orders, distributions, and requisitions are handled by senior ranking non-commissioned officers. While of course unit supply officers are also found, they are fewer in number and when it comes down to it, supply systems are primarily directed by NCOs. And such was the case in the "Galicia" Division.

To ensure that units are provided their necessary goods, supply personnel fill out the necessary paperwork and receipts. Afterwards, they wait and hope that the requested items arrive in time. But as any supply NCO knows, such a method frequently is tedious, involves long periods of wait, paperwork re-submissions, and in the end, an NCO might be simply informed that "no such item(s) are presently available;" therefore, good supply NCOs (especially at a critical time), become experts in "back door," "under the table," and "handshake deals," and if necessary, will resort to the "beg, borrow, steal, or let's make a deal!" method. Good supply NCOs personally know other brigade, divisional, corps and army supply NCOs, and will not hesitate to contact them in time of need. And if a local black market exists, and if it thrives in military goods, a supply NCO will know how to tap into it. Historically speaking (especially during periods of shortages), many a unit maintained its combat effectiveness and readiness on account of such deals. Simply stated, if a supply NCO is unknowledgeable, unable, or unwilling to work in such ways, then he is not a good and competent supply person. So if German units used unorthodox means to secure their supply and transport needs, by no means could supply personnel within the Ukrainian Division be exclusively faulted for adopting such practices.

Chapter 21: Slovakia

Although Heike does not use the words "thievery" and "stealing" directly, he does accuse theft by implication when he asserted "that the Division's staff was flooded with complaints from other divisions that almost all of their horses and wagons had been seized."[63]

Regarding these remarks, it must be noted that some thievery undoubtedly did occur. But that was nothing new. Thievery began since the "Galicia" Division's beginning. The largest factor behind the theft was the Ukrainian underground.[64] But in regard to allegations of theft in Slovakia in obtaining transport, the possibility does exist that some of the reported "seizures" were attributable to various "under the table" deals unknown to Heike. And if some theft in obtaining transport did occur, again, it was due to the urgency of obtaining transport for upcoming events.

22

The Division's March and Its Experiences on the Austro-Yugoslavian Front

To arrive into its new area, the Division would utilize two route marches – March Group A and March Group B.

March Group A: With its starting point (SP) at Cadca, its main check points (CP's) were at Zilina; Povazska Bystryca; Trencin, Piest'any; Malacky; Klosterneuburg; bypass Vienna at Wiener Wald; Wiener Neustadt; Semmering; Bruck; Graz; Leibnitz; to Maribor. Once at Maribor, March Group A's release point (RP) would be found. Altogether, March Group A would cover a marching distance of no less than 316 miles.[1]

March Group B: Starting Point Vrutky; check points St. Martin; Piest'any; Mali Karpaty; Bratislava; Wiener Neustadt; Hartberg; Gleisdorf; and Graz. Its release point was also Maribor. Although March Group B's marching distance was slightly shorter with a distance of approximately 295 miles, its terrain was slightly more difficult. As for March Group C, it would entrain in Zilina and disembark in Maribor.[2]

The above routes were selected because there was a lack of sufficient railway transport and because the main Zilina-Bratislava-Vienna railway line was used extensively for German military movement; thus, the main route was prohibited for Divisional use. But from a military point of view, this was for the better because the main road was coming under increasingly heavy allied air attacks. By utilizing the secondary high-hill mountain routes, the Division, until its arrival to its new area-of-operations, would be utilizing a route far less blasted by allied aircraft.

314

Chapter 22: The Division's March/Austro-Yugoslavian Front

There were, however, many dangers imposed by nature as well as military conditions. To march a distance of approximately 300 miles over high terrain in the coldest time of the year, in heavy snowfalls, combined with poor road conditions; in fog; through periods of low visibility (especially in the higher elevations), with the constant threat of avalanches which took the lives of over 40,000 Austrian, Yugoslavian and Italian soldiers in World War I – all of this could seriously hamper the Division's movements. Additionally, the moment the Division would cross into Austria, the threat of Allied air activity was imminent; as well, those elements crossing into Yugoslavia could be threatened by Marshall Tito's guerrillas.

To enact the transfer as expeditiously and as safely as possible, the Division planned to march no less than 20 to 25 miles per day. Conducted over snowy, cold terrain with steep grades, with the average soldier carrying a load of no less than 40 pounds, excluding the weight of his personal weapons, such a march would require tremendous physical stamina, willpower, and endurance. The fact that troop morale was quite high and no complaints were recorded attests once again to a high mission awareness, unit pride and cohesiveness.

The Division's posting to Slovakia proved invaluable when the time came to march. In Slovakia, the Division rebuilt itself; secured additional arms and equipment (especially from the partisans); gained valuable knowledge and expertise in anti-guerrilla/security operations, and some additional front-line experience against Soviet regulars. And by its exposure to high altitude terrain, the Division's troops reached a high-level of physical standards and endurance, which ultimately benefitted the Division in its westward march. By the time the Division withdrew from Slovakia, as verified by Krokhmaliuk, Veryn, and Heike, it "left as an operational, military unit ready for battle."[3]

After conducting its tactical march, the Division would be dispersed on the border region of Southeastern Austria's Steiermark region and Yugoslavia's Northwestern Slovenia region of Styria.[4] Within Austria, approximately 71 percent of its terrain is mountainous, and this mountainous terrain is divided into the Eastern, Central, and Southern Alps. Elements of the Division would be located in Austria's Southern Alps comprising the Carnic and Karawanken Ranges which border on Italy and Yugoslavia. The average elevation of these ranges exceeds heights of 4,000 feet. As for Yugoslavia, 60 percent of its total land mass consists of hills and ridges up to 3,000 feet, while 20 percent consists of mountains and plateaus over 3,000 feet. Yugoslavia's mountains are primarily located in the southern, southwestern, and northwestern region adjacent to Austria's border. The Julian Alps are among the most rugged mountain ranges in Europe, with peaks averaging from

6,000 to over 9,000 feet. Not far from this rugged northwestern region, the remainder of the Division would be situated.[5]

On 31 January 1945, the Division began its movement. Shouldering his twenty-five-and-a-half pound MG 42 machine-gun, Stefan Medynskyi looked at his watch; he wondered how long it would take. Medynskyi was proud of his watch. The best machine-gunner and the most liked soldier in the 29th Regiment's 6th Company, Medynskyi was presented the watch by the company's beloved commander, SS-Hauptsturmführer Royker, who had himself purchased the watch while on leave in Germany. Medynskyi also noted the location of the battalion's "goulash wagon," and was pleased to see that it was immediately to the rear of his company. While, of course, every soldier was issued a handful of "iron rations," there was no way that an "iron ration" could take the place of a hot meal; after all, Medynskyi knew what every soldier in any army knows – "that a good kitchen is a unit's mother."

The plan was as follows: after a march of several days, each unit would be provided one day for rest. To ensure that the troops were housed in proper quarters with sufficient protection against inclement weather, each battalion, accompanied with a handful of designated personnel from each company, formed a quartermaster unit. Marching well ahead of a battalion, the quartermasters found ample and suitable locations (usually schoolhouses, sizable public buildings, hotels, etc.), for overnight stays and days of rest; additionally, each company had its medics, and engineer and communications personnel were dispersed with each quartermaster and battalion-sized unit to canvas the roads, banks, bridges, crevices, hillsides, for any dangers; to reinforce roads and bridges; and inform regimental and Divisional headquarters on a unit's progress.

As the Division marched in Slovakia, and entered Austria, it encountered no severe problems or even, hardships. But whenever a sizable force marches, especially through rough terrain and in inclement weather, unfortunately, accidents, do occur. In one case, 35-year-old Osyp Kadlubach, a combat engineer NCO who survived Brody, was killed in the vicinity of Neustadt, Austria, when a light truck slid uncontrollably down an icy incline and crushed the engineer. And in another case, a combination of hunger and the misfortune of being caught ransacking for some food cost a young volunteer his life.

An all-encompassing hunger engulfed 17-year-old grenadier Evhen Kulbaby. To avert it, the young grenadier ate his remaining "iron" rations. But as he continued to march through the mountainous terrain, the meager "iron" rations offered no respite against the gnawing hunger.

Chapter 22: The Division's March/Austro-Yugoslavian Front

Hours later, when Kulbaby's battalion halted for the night, and as the men settled down to sleep, Kulbaby, still unable to sleep on account of his gnawing hunger, decided to do something about it.

Knowing that within one of the battalion's supply wagons certain food items were stored, Kulbaby decided to conduct a midnight raid upon it. Of course, the young grenadier knew that his actions were wrong. But it was not his intent to steal all of the food; rather, he would just cut a small chunk of meat and a piece of bread to just hold him over until the next meal.

Sneaking up to the wagon, Kulbaby untied its canvas ropes. Draping the canvas top over, he searched the wagon's contents until he found what he sought. Removing his knife, Kulbaby quickly cut into a chunk of meat and sliced a piece of bread. But the moment he raised the sandwich to his mouth, he felt a strong hand on his shoulder.

Prior to the battalion's departure on the following day, Kulbaby was administered a court martial, found guilty, and was sentenced to death. Asked if he had any final requests, Kulbaby replied "I refuse to die in hunger!" and he requested some meat and bread. Provided the foodstuffs, Kulbaby enjoyed his last meal as several soldiers dug his grave.

Marched to the edge of the grave, the young grenadier refused to have his hands tied; as well, he refused a blindfold. Praising the Lord and his unit, he faced the firing squad with true bravery. At least he didn't die on a totally empty stomach.

From Graz to Bruck, to Maribor Celje, and Laibach, the road came under increasingly heavy allied air attack. The British Royal Air Force was especially determined to disrupt all road and rail movement. As a result, this forced the Division to march southward from Graz only at night even if heavy fogs and snows shrouded the area. But despite the precautions, a small number of soldiers, as well as horses and materiel, were lost as a result of allied air activity.

To further familiarize himself with the region, as well as to see what supplies could be obtained for the Division's future needs, Major Heike drove to see the region's Gauleiter, Dr. Siegfried Uiberreither, in Graz, Austria. Because Heike arrived in the midst of another air raid, he met the gauleiter in a bunker.

As most gauleiters, Uiberreither held an officer's rank. Already angry about the fact that air raids were making life miserable for everyone, Gauleiter Uiberreither's anger rose when Heike informed him that the Division was moving through his region. Uiberreither was especially angered by the fact that no one had previously informed him that a military force was entering his province. Immediately, the gauleiter began to complain that he had no foodstuffs for the Division, and that the force was not required because only "peace and order" reigned in his province.

To counter these remarks, Heike immediately replied that the Division was only following the orders of higher military authorities. Heike assured the gauleiter that the Division would make do with what it had, thus not burdening the region. Determined to get in the last word, Heike also informed Uiberreither that there was no peace, and order, and as proof, Heike cited how it was virtually impossible to travel safely by day on the road from Maribor to Celje.

Exploding in anger, Gauleiter Uiberreither reminded Heike that he was a personal friend of Adolf Hitler, and that he could have Heike shot. Of course, Heike did not take these remarks seriously because to threaten someone is one matter, while carrying out a threat is another matter. And by reasoning with the gauleiter, Heike was able to calm him down.[6] After carefully listening to Heike, Gauleiter Uiberreither accepted Heike's proposal. In due time, Gauleiter Uiberreither developed a more positive attitude toward the Division, and even became pleased that a well-disciplined force was within his province.

As the Division's first elements approached Yugoslavia, they encountered a whole new threat – the Titoists.

Unlike the partisans in Slovakia, Tito's guerrillas were far larger, stronger, and better organized; additionally, much of Tito's leadership was comprised of former Austro-Hungarian and Yugoslavian regulars. These former regulars also understood conventional warfare, and during their attacks, frequently fought conventionally. The fact that the allies dropped much arms, materiel, and on occasion even military specialists and advisors also bolstered Tito's insurgency. Tito's guerrillas knew their terrain, were confident of victory, and exhibited much aggressiveness.

Simultaneously, the Division's command had to keep in mind the allied air campaign, and the eastern front's ever-approaching front. To effectively counter air threats, the Division's elements would be deployed within adjacent smaller towns and villages. A strong infantry regiment, the fusiliers, anti-tank, engineers, and two artillery battalions (including the heavy 4th battalion), were posted south of Maribor to protect the Division's eastern flank.

By 28 February 1945, the Division had arrived. Occupying an area straddling the Austrian/Yugoslavian border region, the following Divisional units were posted into these areas:[7]

Divisional Staff: Selnica (approximately 7 miles west of Maribor);

29th Regiment: the area north and south of Maribor with its headquarters at Slovenske Konje;

30th Regiment: the area southeast of Slovenjgradec with its headquarters at Velenje;

31st Regiment: on Austria's and Yugoslavia's border region north of the Drava River in the vicinity of Radje, Muta, Eibiswald with regimental headquarters established in Saint Lorenzen;

Fusilier Battalion: region of Sloven Bistrica with its headquarters at Zg. Polskava;

Artillery Regiment: Headquarters – co-located with Divisional Staff. 1st Battalion – at Sloven Bistrica; 2nd Battalion – with the 30th Regiment; 3rd Battalion – with the 31st Regiment; 4th Battalion – slightly west of Sloven Bistrica;

Anti-tank: at Sloven Bistrica;

Communications Battalion: located directly south of Selina at Ruse;

Supply: Posted in Austria at Leibnitz;

Engineers: at Muda and Radje along the northern bank of the Drava River;

Field Supply: Posted south of Maribor with its headquarters at Slivnica;

Field Replacement Battalion: Posted in Austria's towns of Eibiswald, Armfels, and Leutschach;

Training and Replacement Regiment: Posted in the area of Deutschlandsberg, Austria, its headquarters was at Deutschlandsberg.

Altogether, the Division occupied an area that from north to south covered approximately 43 miles and from east to west 31 miles. This area, however, was also located within the communist established Fourth Partisan Operational Zone.[8] And within this Fourth Partisan Operational Zone, a total of five communist brigades, three from the 14th Partisan Division,[9] and two independent brigades, the 6th "Slander" and 11th "Zidansek" Brigades, waged their war.[10]

Within this area, the Division's mission was similar to that undertaken in Slovakia: training and the security of a region. But due to the fact that the Division was now operating in mountainous terrain, its soldiers would encounter certain circumstances which are characteristic of mountain operations.

Environmental factors (such as altitude, terrain, wind, snow, and ice); cover and concealment; scouting; dispositions and tactics; and troop movement (in the Division's case primarily on foot), needed to be addressed. As well, the terrain benefitted guerilla and sniper warfare; and a new form of warfare began to be experienced by Divisional soldiers which had seldom been experienced before, and would only make its mark in the postwar period – terrorism.

Galicia Division

According to Yuriy Krokhmaliuk, in the concluding months of the war, and especially in Yugoslavia, the Division began to encounter more and more incidents of activities virtually unknown in the Western, North African and Italian theaters of war. In due time, such warfare would be experienced by French, American, Israeli, Portuguese, and other allied soldiers in Korea, Southeast Asia, the Saharan Region, the Middle East, and Africa.

Such incidents included: the deliberate maiming of soldiers with snipers, homemade bombs and various devices; the placement of explosive devices into automobiles, trucks, or animal-drawn carts; using women and children to lure soldiers or medical personnel into a house, apartment, or alley with urgent cries of help. Once inside, an ambush or assassination team awaited to kill the unwary; poisoning wells, aqueducts and food supplies; kidnapping; and the dissemination of propaganda/defeatism among troops. And these activities did not cease until the Division totally withdrew into Austria. As verified by Krokhmaliuk, modern terrorism, in its current usage, actually originated before World War II but was specifically practiced and improved upon by Soviet Russia which, already in the war years, encouraged and exported terrorism.[11]

The Division's units which were posted to Northwestern Yugoslavia served very briefly in that region. Within their area-of-operations, the units conducted security operations, and guarded roads, bridges, passes, and the regions railway system. Excluding a couple of forays against Tito's guerrillas adjacent to its perimeter, the Division operated primarily within its area. As before in Slovakia, within its limited area-of-operations, the Division's soldiers encountered a Yugoslav population which, once aware that a Nazi hating non-German military force was within their premises, either displayed a friendly attitude or remained neutral; the Austrians found on both sides of the border were mostly receptive to the Division.

Limited combat actions, however, did occur. Prior to the Division's arrival into Gauleiter Uiberreither's region of "peace and order," it was not only unsafe to travel by night, but even by day. The main highway between Maribor and Celje was especially threatened. But with the insertion of approximately 22,000 soldiers into the border region, Tito's partisans faced a strong element; by employing the lessons learned in Slovakia, within days of the Division's arrival, the main highway, as well as all mines and bobby-traps, were cleared.[12] Inside a school-house, Bohdan Tyr identified and cleared a booby-trapped device inside a piano. By establishing outposts, observation posts, and constantly maintaining patrol activities, such round the-clock vigilance kept Tito's warriors at bay.

Soon, Ljubljana's (Yugoslavia) SS-Chief of Police, Obergruppenführer Rosner, although well-disposed toward the Division, began to make certain demands of it. Seeing that the Division had effectively curbed the activities of the "Bachern" guerrilla brigade,[13] and dissatisfied with the way the German police battalions were conducting their anti-guerrilla/terrorist operations, Rosner decided to use the Division for further operations.

As a result of Rosner's persistence, the Division was involved in a couple of short – but sizable – guerrilla operations which involved various elements of the Division. The first one, coordinated with a couple of Wehrmacht regiments, was launched to the south of Ljublanja, in the Menina Planina Mountains. A strong concentration of guerrillas had assembled in that area to pick up a sizable allied aerial arms and food supply delivery. In order to succeed, the Division would have to conduct a forced southwesterly infantry march of approximately 60 miles with full gear. Afterwards, with no more than a few hours of rest, the Division's troops, in an attempt to encircle the insurgents, would advance through mountains exceeding altitudes of 6,000 feet and covered with deep snow. This accomplished, the goal was to press the guerrillas into a confined area where they would either be destroyed or captured.

Leaving behind their horses and a few light supply trucks at the base of the mountains, the Division's soldiers marched strictly on foot through mountainous terrain with no cabins, homes, few trails and no roads and received neither hot meals nor sleep. After several days of continuous operations, no major successes were reported. Excluding a handful of brief skirmishes, the capture of some munitions, and the destruction or capture of some guerrillas, the operation was a failure.[14] For its efforts, the Division suffered one soldier killed and several wounded.[15]

Ten days later, the Division undertook a larger operation – "to secure and clear the districts of Mozirje, Ljubno, Solcava and the area of Boskovec."[16] Within these districts, adjacent to the Division's western and southwestern perimeter, it was reported that a number of Tito's guerrillas were assembling for another aerial resupply.

To arrive into these districts, some of the Division's elements conducted forced infantry marches while others (from the distant northern, central, and eastern areas) boarded trains. Militarily, the operation was similar in scope to the previous Menina Planina operation, but well before its commencement, several problems arose.

To begin with, south of Maribor, the train came under the attack of the RAF. Flying in at low-level, RAF Spitfires, rocketfiring Typhoons and light two-engine Mosquito fighter-bombers strafed and rocketed the column. Jumping out of their railway cars, in some cases while the train was still moving, the Division's soldiers sought cover. Leaping from the train, Stefan Medynskyi looked up and saw an incoming Spitfire, its wings spraying the angel of death. Loudly pleading to God for help, Medynskyi hit the ground and hoped for the best. Within a split second, aircraft rounds splattered all around. Picking himself up, he ran for cover. As he ran, the herculean sound of a massive explosion thundered as a Typhoon virtually jumped up from above tree-top level, sighted in on the train's locomotive, and unleashed a barrage of rockets. Ripping the locomotive into smithereens, the Typhoon's pilot quickly banked to his right, flew below tree level, and exited out from under the cover of trees. "EXCELLENT MOVE, EXCELLENT!" shouted a Divisional NCO. "But too bad he's hitting the wrong people!"

As in the previous operation, it was impossible to conduct a large-scale encircling operation. Apart from the fact that the guerrillas always had knowledge of any large scale movements,[17] the exceptionally harsh terrain made it virtually impossible to effectively coordinate any sizable ground movements. Guerrilla strengths hinged on a thorough knowledge of the terrain, and they could execute, especially in small groups, rapid marches of up to 45 miles daily. What also compounded the problem was that when the Division moved in full force, for the several days that it was outside of its perimeter, guerrilla bands took advantage of the situation, moved in, and struck targets.

From a military point of view, the Division's two large scale operations failed totally. But neither the Division's staff or any of its soldiers could be faulted for this. In their pursuit of the insurgents, the Division's soldiers scaled peaks thousands of feet in height, and ventured into terrain that previously posed serious challenges to the Wehrmacht and police units. During both operations, for several days soldiers operated in tough and climatically adverse conditions, enduring forced marches and combat with no hot meals or rest. In the end, however, it was again proven that in order to effectively counter the guerrillas, the only effective ways of maintaining order within a guerrilla region was through a strong security within a specified area, coupled with strong patrols and occasional assaults by small detachments to ambush and keep guerrillas at bay.

As frequently is the case in any war zone, examples of humanity and needless cruelty may be found. And by no means was Yugoslavia an exception.

From a concealed observation point in the vicinity of the Muta River virtually adjacent to the Austrian border, a team of observers spotted one of Marshall Tito's bands heading for the Drava River. From the looks of the raiding party, it appeared that the Titoists were planning to blow up a bridge or possibly, a pass. Realizing that a destroyed bridge or pass adjacent to the Division's area could cause much hardship, at the crack of dawn on approximately 25 March 1945, a reinforced engineer company picked up the raider's trail. Sensing danger, the Titoists turned to the southwest in an attempt to flee.

Chapter 22: The Division's March/Austro-Yugoslavian Front

For the duration of the day, the battlegroup pursued the raider's. Notifying Divisional command of the guerrilla's movements, from the vicinity of Velenje the 30th Regiment quickly dispersed a small battlegroup westward to assist the engineers in intercepting the raiders. Maneuvering around, ahead, and on the sides of the guerrillas, the Ukrainian pursuers barred their escape. To avoid encirclement and capture, the Titoists fled toward the eastern perimeter of the Kaminske Alps.

For the raiders, the only way out now was by going up. In desperation, they fled higher into the mountains of Bokovec, with heights nearing 5,000 feet and covered with deep snow.

But it was to no avail. The Ukrainian force could not be dislodged. Seeing that escape was impossible, the Titoists readied for action.

But nothing happened. As the two combined Ukrainian battlegroups edged closer to the mountain top, they established their light mortars and prepared to assault its top. But as they readied, the cries of men were suddenly heard as both sides yelled out to one another.

"COMRADES!" "LISTEN UP!" "ENOUGH IS ENOUGH!" "LISTEN, YOU TITOISTS! WHAT HAVE YOU GOT AGAINST US!" "NOTHING!" "UKRAI- NIAN! THIS IS NOT YOUR BATTLE! GO BACK!" Similar shouts filled the air. But when from atop a loud voice heralded "TO HELL WITH THIS WAR! LET'S MAKE PEACE!" both sides immediately lowered their weapons.From among the boulders, tired, hungry, and thirsty men stood up. At first, they moved slowly, cautiously. But as they neared each other, arms were extended for handshakes. The loud voice again proclaimed "TONIGHT, LET THERE BE PEACE!"

In a small cabin located on the top of a mountain, a fire was lit and under a clear night sky blanketed by millions of stars, the men shared their food and water, opened bottles of wine and other spirits, and feasted all night long. Even the German personnel joined in. Throughout the night, the sounds of laughter were heard as men humorously recounted their experiences, drank and told jokes.

At the crack of dawn, the party ceased. Wishing each other health and happiness, the Ukrainians headed back to their assembly areas, and the Titoists returned to their guerrilla base.[18]

But then, there was the tragic case of Dr. Anatoli Puposhynskiy, Chief Doctor of the Division's 30th Regiment. Throughout the regiment and the entire Division, Dr. Puposhynskiy was respected not only for his skills as a physician and surgeon, but for on his insistence on immediate medical care. On more than one occasion, the brave doctor disregarded specific orders to stay back and, instead, ventured forward into dangerous areas to administer medical care. His valiant efforts in fact saved many lives. A true humanitarian, Dr. Puposhynskiy always administered aid not only to civilians but also to any captured enemy personnel in need of medical care.

Appearing once at the scene of a shooting incident, Dr. Puposhynskiy spotted a wounded soldier lying downhill in the middle of the road. Moments before, a communist sniper from one of Tito's bands had shot the young grenadier. To unnerve the troops, the sniper deliberately wounded the soldier; efforts to retreive him had failed.

Hearing the grenadier's screams, Dr. Puposhynskiy declared the young man needed immediate assistance, and that he would go to him. Against the advice of both officers and enlisted personnel, the doctor chose to go. Again, he was urged not to, but to those standing around him, the doctor firmly replied "I am going!"

Alone and unarmed, with a clearly visible Red Cross symbol on his left arm, his left hand clutching a medical bag, his right arm holding upwards a stick to which was attached a white cloth, Dr. Puposhynskiy proceeded down the road. But as he neared the wounded soldier, the crack of a rifle shattered the doctor's life.

The sniper who pulled the trigger clearly saw the doctor and knew that he was firing upon an unarmed medical man. By his actions, the communist sniper had not only violated the most basic rights of human decency, but as well the universal laws of war such as those found in the Geneva Accords in regards to medical personnel.[19]

On 1 March 1945, the Division's strength was set at 14,000.[20] This strength included those on leave, in hospitals, in school or undergoing specialized training. This figure, however, did not include the approximately 8,000 serving in the Training and Replacement Regiment located in Deutschlandsberg, Austria. But the Division's strength would increase several days later when in the vicinity of Graz, Austria, a so-called "Ukrainian Self-Defense" unit joined the Division.[21]

Formed in 1943, this battalion's origins lay with those Ukrainian refugees who had fled into Volyn's wooded Kremianets area in late 1941 and through 1942 to escape Nazi rule. The sympathies of this unit laid primarily with the Melnyk faction of the Organization of Ukrainian Nationalists. Until June 1943, the unit fought the Germans as well as the Soviet and Polish guerrillas. But in June 1943, Volyn's guerrilla harassed German administration concluded an unofficial agreement with the unit – for the cessation of hostilities the Germans would not disarm the guerrilla band, would not imprison any of its members, would release some of its previously captured personnel, and would utilize it for the security of Volyn.[22] In 1943, the Volyn Battalion was commanded by Mykola Medvets'kyi, whose alias was "Khrim."[23] In early 1944, the Volyn battalion was commanded by a former 1917-21 Ukrainian colonel, Evhen Kvitka;[24] however, in June 1944, he was succeeded by Colonel Petro Diachenko.[25] According to Roman Krokhmaliuk, Colonel Volodymyr Herasymenko last commanded the battalion;[26] yet in his memoirs, Heike states that the unit was last commanded by a German Waffen-SS-Sturmbannführer who "appeared to be a dreamer and seemed to be an intellectual rather than a leader of a military formation."[27] Regardless, at the time of its incorporation, the Legion contained a strength of 20 Ukrainian officers, 5 German officers (undoubtedly serving as advisors), and slightly over 600 NCO's and enlisted personnel.[28] Chaplain Job Skakal's'kyi served as the unit's chaplain.[29]

Arriving to the battalion's location with a senior Divisional staff officer and the Divisional band to officially incorporate the unit into the Division, Heike and the others found that the brunt of the battalion had deserted. Taking their arms and equipment, their horses and wagons, the battalion headed toward the forested region of Lenart east of Maribor; there, they planned to link up with the Chetniks and hopefully, with their help, return to Ukraine.[30]

So what was the problem behind this military defection?

To begin with, it appears that the Battalion was unaware of the Division's nature, its mission, and its political-military goals. Keeping in mind that at one time a number of its personnel had openly battled with the Germans, possibly a strong anti-German sentiment continued to exist. Some of the battalion's personnel also aspired to serve with the UPA while others just longed to return home. And prior to the incorporation of the battalion into the Division, it was planned for Makarushka to brief the unit about the Division and the Volyn unit's responsibility within the Division. However, this never transpired because at the last moment the Divisional staff gave in to the SS-Sturmbannführer's request that he himself be allowed to conduct the briefing and orientation. With the German commander's failure to provide a proper briefing, both uncertainty – and fear – prevailed.[31]

Another problem also stemmed from the fact that a number of Volyn's Ukrainian officers were totally incompetent. Among them were those who previously were denied leadership positions upon entry into the Division or once within, were dismissed as a result of incompetence or failure to meet standards. Returning to Volyn, these men then entered the battalion. Now realizing that upon re-entry into the Division they would either be dismissed or reduced to a much lower rank, these leaders agitated against the Division, and sought to retain their titles within some other force – in this case the Chetniks.[32]

On the following day the Division dispatched a company, under Heike's command, to apprehend the Volynians. After the company successfully intercepted the defectors, the men were ordered to fall in, with their arms, for briefing.

With Makarushka translating, Heike personally informed the men that they would not be considered as deserters, and would not be punished for what had occurred because the German commander was mostly responsible for what had transpired. Heike then thoroughly briefed the soldiers on what they failed to know: the Division's mission, its aspirations, that Germany's High Command had officially recognized the formation and any other units (such as the Volyn battalion) that were to be attached to it, and that the Division was now permitted to wear its national insignia. Satisfied that they would not be harmed, and at last fully understanding what was occurring as well as their role within the Division, the soldiers fell in and marched back to the Division. Once within the formation, the Volyn Battalion was dissolved and its members, incorporated into the Division, proved to be capable soldiers.[33]

In addition to the so-called Volyn Battalion, an increasing number of Ukrainian troops found throughout the various districts and armies of the rapidly-collapsing Third Reich, began to look upon the Division as a haven. For the most part, these men only sought to enter the Division for reasons of safety and refuge.[34]

Unfortunately for the Division, much of the incoming personnel would create problems. In addition to the fact that many of the men were untrained, and their sympathies and loyalties were of questionable nature, the backgrounds of a number of these men was also of a dubious nature.

Every repressive system has its repressive institutions. And by no means was Nazi Germany an exception. Well before 1945, it was known within the Division that concentration camps existed because some members of the Division had previously been incarcerated within the camps, while others learned of the camps from German and non-German personnel. Since knowledge of the daily routines of these camps was kept secret from the general military and civilian population, the Division's personnel, as most Wehrmacht and Waffen-SS soldiers, had no detailed knowledge of the camp's location, where the extermination centers existed; the routines of these camps, and so forth. Regardless, within each facility German and foreign personnel were found. And as the Allied armies pressed toward Germany and began to approach the camps, its personnel began to flee.

At this time, the Ukrainian units (such as the Division), "no doubt tended to act as magnets to lost and stray Hiwis, Schutsmannschaft personnel, Ostarbeiter, Oastsoldaten, POW's, refugees, emigres, and others."[35] As well, the possibility now arose that any Ukrainian (or for that matter any Eastern European) concentration camp personnel found within the camps would also attempt to use the Division as an escape valve.

According to Yuriy Krokhmaliuk, Ukrainian officers were fully aware of this. To counter the dangerous possibility that ex-concentration personnel would seek to enter the Division or its Training and Replacement Regiment, on more than one occasion Ukrainian staff officers expressed their concerns to keep any former concentration camp personnel out of the Division, or any of its sub-elements. Regarding this matter, Divisional staff relented to this request.

Although various factors could be cited for excluding former ex-concentration camp personnel, the most important reasons were based on military, political, and morale factors.

From a military viewpoint, most concentration camp personnel were militarily untrained. Because at this time military Wehrkreis' were being overrun, the Division was on the move, and war time shortages were setting in, it would be difficult – if not impossible – to properly train, arm, and equip such personnel.

As for training such personnel, Krokhmaliuk himself stated that in many cases it would have been very difficult, and sometimes even impossible, to effectively train such men because a number of them were physically and/or mentally unfit for military service; hence, their incorporation into the slave system. Among them were the very young, the overaged, and the physically and mentally unfit. There were also those who ended up in the concentration camp system because they were cowards who feared front-line service; some were sadists and some were failures in life who now had a valve through which to vent their personal anger, jealousy, and frustration on innocent beings. Needless to say, such depraved individuals would not be able to undergo the rigors of proper military training, and realistically speaking, would have been totally useless for any kind of professional military force.

Politically, the Ukrainians always dreamed for the day when the Division would break away from its sponsors. Since, ideologically, the Division was fighting solely to improve the conditions of Ukrainians both in and beyond Galicia, any association with Nazi concentration camp personnel could reflect close ties with the sinister deeds of the Third Reich. By now, it was obvious that Nazi Germany would lose the war. And in the ensuing discussions with allied military and political leaders, it would be difficult for the Division to adequately explain its true intent, its exact role, and the nature of its "collaboration" if concentration camp personnel were found within the Division's ranks.

Morally, a number of the Division's personnel had not only experienced German incarceration, but they still had immediate or distant family members or close friends in various Nazi prisons and the remaining concentration camps. By placing ex-concentration camp personnel among the Division's soldiers (especially among those sympathetic to Bandera), ill feelings, possibly resulting in conflicts, would have arisen. And with the incorporation of a criminal element, soldierly trust, always critical for a unit, would diminish while crime, previously unproblematic, would increase. And whenever crime and conflicts arise in a unit, consequently morale, pride, and cohesiveness collapse.

Galicia Division

To counter such problems, the Division began to screen all incoming personnel. Men were thoroughly questioned; in some cases the Division's intelligence personnel were brought in. And cases actually arose were individuals were not accepted. As for the non-Ukrainians: Russians, Byelorussians and other foreign personnel which approached the Division to gain entry, they were immediately denied access. But in addition to the foreigners, a number of Ukrainian's were also denied entry because they possessed backgrounds of questionable nature. As for the Ukrainian's and non-Ukrainian's denied entrance, they either wound up in Vlasov's Russian Liberation Army or, they were inserted into some Wehrmacht or work (construction) battalion.[36]

23

The Division's Days of Uncertainty

On 3 January 1945, the Ukrainian graduates who previously had entered in July 1944 the Posen-Treskau officers school in the vicinity of Poznan, reported to the Advanced Arms Training Center located in Leshany, Czechoslovakia.

Prior to their arrival to the advanced arms center, on 1 December 1944, the candidates took their final examinations and in mid-December, a graduation ceremony was held. By a Berlin decree signed by Dorlfer, the Ukrainian officer school graduates were promoted to the rank of "Standartenoberjunker der Reserve der Waffen-SS."[1] There was, however, one exception. Honor graduate Yuriy Skarupa, who graduated at the top of the entire class from among both the Germans and Ukrainians, was immediately promoted (as was the tradition) to an officers rank – in this case "Waffen-Untersturmführer." (2nd Lieutenant).

To complete an officers school is a very high achievement. A graduate, regardless of class standing, has much to be proud of. For the Ukrainians who graduated from the training, this was especially so if one takes into consideration that some of the candidates had to master the German language while, simultaneously, they were training and undertaking various class courses; there were periods of uncertainty about family and loved ones (especially from the end of July to September 1944 and, as every candidate and instructor knows, bad news from home can devastate a candidate or trainee to the point of failure); and, of course, on top of all of this, there was a sufficient amount of discouraging news about the Division in the aftermath of Brody.

Yet despite these difficulties, strong loyalties and devotion to the homeland, the Division, and one another enabled many a candidate to overcome the burden. Upon the completion of the officers school, the graduates were provided 18 days of leave. On 3 January 1945, the graduates reported to the advanced arms school located in Leshany, Czech region, to study the application of various new and heavy weapons to offensive and defensive operations.

On 12 January 1945, the Soviets commenced a major offensive. With Berlin as their final objective, Stalin's forces struck a front severely weakened by Hitler's Ardennes offensive. Within days, Germany's entire Eastern front was shattered and by mid-March, the various Soviet fronts had recaptured most of Poland, secured much of Prussia, penetrated deep into Hungary and Czechoslovakia, and began to approach Austria.

As all of this was occurring, the Ukrainian Division was still within its occupational area. Subordinated to the Replacement Army, the Division continued to train and maintain its security mission.

In response to intelligence reports that Tito's "Bachern" (affectionately known to the Division as "our friendly friends") partisans had reappeared in the Pohorje region, the Division's command dispatched the bulk of its artillery and the entire fusilier battalion to conduct a four-day, anti-guerrilla operation south of the Sava River 25 miles to the west and southwest of Ljubljana.[2]

In addition to responding to the guerrilla presence, at the very same time various Divisional elements, reinforced with the brunt of the Training and Replacement Regiment, solidly secured the "Kozja" Region's bridges and road network west of Maribor between the Drava River and the area north of Selnica, adjacent to the Austrian border.[3] Although this region was within the Division's perimeter, the extra security precautions were undertaken to ensure that no inserted guerrilla or airborne saboteur forces would threaten the bridges, the narrow mountain passes, the Division's command post, or the vital road and rail links leading to Maribor. Since it was also common knowledge that in the event of any further withdrawals elements of the Division would have to cross into Austria proper, this undoubtedly was the chief factor behind the extra precaution undertaken on the Austro-Yugoslavian border region.[4] Once this was accomplished, elements of the Training and Replacement Regiment were also dispatched southwestward to reinforce the artillery and fusilier units pursuing the "Bachern" Brigade. Such an action would also further intensify the Division's security and assist in curbing the "Bachern" Brigade's activities.

Chapter 23: The Division's Days of Uncertainty

Yet, as these events were unfolding, – in distant Berlin – a new development was unfolding which posed more of a threat to the Division than all of the bombs, bullets and shells expended against it.

Deep in an underground bunker beneath the ruins of the once flourishing capital city of Berlin, Nazi Germany's insane leader was conducting another Führer conference. Surrounded by an entourage of generals and advisors, Hitler sat in a chair in front of a table covered with maps. Totally exhausted by the unceasing strains of the war, Dr. Morell's injections, and the bomb blast of 20 July 1944, Hitler sat stonefaced as another wave of allied bombers unleashed their bomb loads. Amidst moments of silence, the dull thuds of exploding bombs could be heard. But after the bombers flew on, the talks resumed and Germany's critical war needs resurfaced.

In the early morning hours of 24 March 1945, the Eastern front's requirements were discussed in depth. During the ensuing discussion, the names and numbers of various divisions and units affiliated with the Eastern front were cited and at this time Hitler learned of the Ukrainian Division.

Initially to be held in the late evening hours of 23 March, the conference was finally held on 24 March between the hours of 2:26 a.m. and 3:43 a.m. Participants included Generals Below, Bormann, Bruder-Mueller, Burgdorf, Goehler, Guensche, Hewel, Johannmeier, DeMaiziere, Suendermann and Zander.

By now, the war situation was as such: in the East, the front ran from Stettin to Frankfurt-on-the-Oder. Koenigsberg, Danzig and Breslau were cut off and under siege. In the Southeast, Soviet forces were beginning to approach a city very close to Hitler's heart, Vienna, and in the West, an American reconnaissance/scout group grabbed the remains of a blown – but not totally destroyed bridge – at Remagen. Patton began to forge the Rhine in the vicinity of Oppenheim, and Montgomery was attacking at Wesel.

During the ensuing discussion, the names and numbers of various divisions, especially those on the Eastern front, were cited. It was then that Hitler expressed that to his amazement a "Ukrainian SS-Division had suddenly appeared." Continuing on, Hitler stated, "I don't know a thing about this Ukrainian SS-Division" and he inquired about the formation.[5]

Responding to Hitler's inquiry, General Goehler replied "It existed for a long time." Hitler then stated that "no reference was ever made to it in our discussions." But interested in the formation, he asked Goehler "do you remember one?" Goehler responded "No, I don't remember one."

Upon hearing Goehler's response, Hitler slightly changed his previous viewpoint and stated, "I don't know. It may have been reported to me a long, long time ago." Continuing on, the Führer asked "how strong is the Ukrainian Division?" Informed by Goehler that "I'll find out again," as Hitler waited for an answer he stated "either the outfit is trustworthy or its not trustworthy. I can't organize units in Germany because I don't have any weapons. It's just insanity for me to give weapons to a Ukrainian Division which isn't quite trustworthy. I'd rather take their weapons away and raise a new German division. Because I suppose they are splendidly armed, better armed than most of the German divisions we are raising today."

Upon returning to the conference, Goehler was asked by Hitler "so what is this Galician Division anyway? Is that the same thing as the Ukrainian Division?" But before Goehler could respond, General Borgmann replied "I can't say." In response, Hitler immediately replied "there's always a Galician Division floating around. Is that the same as the Ukrainian Division? Because if that [division] is made up of Austrian Ruthenians, the only thing to do is to take their weapons away immediately. The Austrian Ruthenians were pacifists. They were lambs, not wolves. They were miserable, even in the Austrian Army. This is just self-delusion. Now, is this Ukrainian Division the same thing as the so-called Galician Division?"

In response to Hitler's inquiry, Goehler provided an answer. However, his answer was not correct when he stated "No, the Galician is the 30th, the Ukrainian is the 14th. The 30th is being rested, I believe in Slovakia."

"Where did it fight?" asked Hitler. "The 30th, the Galician," replied Goehler, "was originally committed in the Tarnow sector, and hasn't been committed since." And DeMaiziere added "the division was committed in the area of the 1st Panzer Army during the battles around Lvov. At that time, it was attached to, I believe, the 13th Corps and suffered the encirclement, and only some parts of the division came back. As far as I know, it hasn't been used since."

In a questioning but actually more of an implicit manner, Hitler remarked "and they've been resting ever since? Do they have weapons?"

Once again, Goehler stated "I'll have to check on that." Continuing on, Hitler said "we can't afford a joke like this while I don't have enough weapons to equip other divisions. That's ridiculous."

In response to Hitler's question, Goehler replied "the Ukrainian Division has a table-of-organization strength of 11,000, but an actual strength of 14,000."[6] And when Hitler asked "why more actual strength than the T/O strength?" Goehler answered "probably they got more volunteers than the T/O allowed them."

But then Hitler's concern turned to the division's arms and equipment when he asked "and the equipment?" But as previously before, Goehler gave an improper response when he informed Hitler "they gave a large part of their equipment to the 18th SS [Horst Wessel] Division."

Chapter 23: The Division's Days of Uncertainty

Unsatisfied with Goehler's reply, Hitler stated "but if they are ready for combat now, they must have weapons again. I don't want to insist that you can't do anything with these foreigners. Something could be done with them, but it takes time. If you have them for six or ten years, and if you govern their home territories, as the old Habsburg monarchy did, then they will become good soldiers, of course. But if you get the men, and their homelands on the side – why should they fight at all? They are susceptible to every piece of propaganda. I assume that there are still very strong German elements among them."

At this time, Goehler submitted such a report – "they have the following weapons: 2,100 pistols, 610 submachine guns, 9,000 rifles, 70 rifles with telescopic sights, 65 automatic rifles MP-43, 434 light machine guns, 96 heavy machine guns, 58 light mortars, 4 heavy mortars – " interrupting Goehler, Hitler stated "you could equip two divisions with that." Continuing on, Goehler added "22 flamethrowers, 1 medium AT gun, 11 75mm AT guns, 17 light infantry howitzers, 3 heavy infantry howitzers M-33, 9 37mm AA guns, 37 light field howitzers, 6 heavy field howitzers."

Unable to say anymore, and unsure of what the Ukrainian Division was, Hitler stated "I must know what this division is worth. I want to speak to the Reichsführer right away tomorrow. He's in Berlin anyway. We have to investigate exactly what we can expect of a unit like that. If one can't expect anything, there is no sense to it. We can't afford the luxury of keeping units like that."[7]

Whether Hitler ever did speak to Himmler about this matter is not known, but it appears that no further discussions ever arose.

Of course, the information provided to Hitler was not entirely accurate. And had Hitler known the true facts, perhaps his anger and consequently his non-sensical illogical order to disarm the Division, would have never arisen.

While it is true that in the aftermath of Brody the Division was primarily involved in reforming and training, by no means was the entire Division kept totally out of action. Aside from establishing several battlegroups which played major roles in suppressing the Moscow-inspired communist revolt in Czechoslovakia, other battlegroups were utilized as "fire" units during periods of emergencies to reinforce some critical sector of the Eastern front to contain a Soviet attack and breakout. And during such operations, the Division's troops never swayed from a difficult mission or assignment. To the utmost, they performed their front-line duties and responsibilities. And on more than one occasion, their deeds were acknowledged and their valor was honored. Of course, this was not only noted by a number of senior military men but also by Heinrich Himmler, as evidenced in a personal discussion in March 1945 with his private physician, Dr. Felix Kersten.

A Finnish citizen of Estonian origin, Kersten was a cosmopolitan masseur who, prior to the war, had resided in various European nations and had developed a reputation for alleviating nervous pains. His reputation was so highly regarded that Prince Henry of the Netherlands invited Kersten to establish a practice in the Netherlands. Introduced to Himmler in early 1939, on 15 May 1940, the physician was ordered by Himmler to serve as his personal physician. Although an anti-Nazi, Kersten accepted. But perhaps this was for the better. During his personal sessions with Himmler, Kersten frequently appealed to Himmler on behalf of certain individuals and as a result, on more than one occasion, many of Kersten's Dutch, German and Jewish friends were released.

On 19 March, Himmler succumbed to another fit of depression and called for Kersten. As the masseur treated the Reichsführer, Himmler spoke about his Waffen-SS and its losses.

Kersten inquired if this included Europe's foreign volunteers. In a gloomy mood, Himmler informed his physician that "their sacrifices were equally great." Continuing on, the Reichsführer added that "of the 6,000 Danes, 10,000 Norwegians, 75,000 Dutch, 25,000 Flemings, 15,000 Wallonians, 22,000 French and an unspecified number of Mohemmedans found in the Waffen-SS, every third was killed in action." Himmler also spoke of those who hailed from the Baltics and eastern regions; he acknowledged that "wherever the fighting rages their blood has not been spared" and added the "figure is relatively high for the men of the Baltic provinces, the Ukrainians and Galicians."[8]

Of course, Himmler was more than correct in his observations about the Galician Ukrainians. Along with the Wehrmacht, Waffen-SS, and other military forces, the Division's Ukrainians had also experienced high casualty losses. By March 1945, it may be correctly stated that since its inception, the Division's attrition rate – through combat, missing-in-action, desertion, accidents, execution by Nazi personnel, and those who were medically discharged as a result of accidents, injuries, or combat wounds – experienced an overall loss of no less than 30-35 percent. Needless to say, such figures not only represent a high casualty loss but are comparable to the losses suffered by many German divisions. In certain cases, the Divisions casualties even exceeded those of other German and foreign divisions. And in the ensuing days, with further combat, additional casualties would be sustained by the Division.

Approximately two days after the 23 March conference, the Division received an order to disarm and surrender its weapons to newly created German divisions.[9] If enacted, the Division would be placed into a critical situation. But though it is easy to issue an order, carrying it out is another matter. And if one takes into consideration the situation the Division was encountering in the spring of 1945, as well as the general events surrounding it, it soon became apparent that this order could not be carried out.

To begin with, the order specified certain directives. Among them, the Division was to take its arms to a local railway depot, load them upon freight trains, and ship the arms to Nuremberg, where supply and weapon redistributors would redistribute the arms and supplies.

But realistically speaking, the order could not be carried out. As of mid-March, excluding pockets and strongholds of resistance, in all military sense Germany's resistance had ceased to exist on the Western front. General Patch's 7th U.S. Army was also rapidly advancing toward Nuremberg, allied planes were flying at will, and freight trains were one of their priority targets.

And, of course, there was another problem. The old German fears of an armed and trained foreign element becoming virtually impossible to disarm proved correct. So who would actually conduct the disarmament? What SS officials would supervise such a disarmament? And who would believe that this disarmament was "just a temporary disarmament pending the arrival of newer arms" when, in fact, the Division was already armed with some of the newest and most sophisticated arms? Knowing from first-hand experience the tragic consequences of being unarmed, Oleh Dir swore to himself that he would kill the first Nazi who would attempt to take away his prized MP-44, the Kar 98 telescopic rifle he so effectively utilized at Brody and within the UPA, his 9mm Walther pistol, and the Tokarev that he obtained from an NKVD officer.

In addition to the supply and psychological problems, there were also some serious tactical military matters to consider. To disarm a military force in peacetime is one matter. But to disarm it within a region infested with communist guerrillas and within range of the advancing Soviet front is another. Undoubtedly, such matters were identified, and in an attempt to rescind the order, the Division requested confirmation of the order. In the meantime, Freitag himself journeyed to one of Himmler's command posts located in Salzburg to confirm the order and to demand that Salzburg's chief-of-staff raise the issue with Himmler.

In the very end, however, no further disarmament orders were issued. And on 28 March 1945, Salzburg issued an order that the Division was not to be disarmed.[10] Salzburg's order also averted a near tragedy.

Another very confusing matter which arose in the spring of 1945 was whether to convert the Division into a paratroop division, or incorporate the elements of a proposed paratroop division into the Division itself.

Galicia Division

In September 1944, the 10th German Fallschirmjäger (paratroop) Division was ordered to be raised. This order, however, was soon withdrawn but in February 1945, it was reinstated.

Commanded by Colonel (soon General) von Hoffman, the 10th Paratroop was initially to concentrate on the Dutch/German frontier. But in February 1945 its cadre, along with some Luftwaffe personnel, were assembled just north of Maribor in the Feldbach area of Eastern Austria; possibly, the 10th Paratroop was dispatched to that area because west of Budapest, not far from the Austrian border in a town named Papa, the Germans had a jump school. But because at that time Papa was in the process of being overrun, for the moment jump (airborne) training was suspended.

As usually was the case, the 10th Paratroop Division was to be centered around three airborne regiments – in this case the 28th, 29th, and 30th Fallschirmjäger Regiments (each with three battalions). A Fallshirmjäger artillery regiment, and one fallschirmjäger anti-tank and engineer battalion were to round out the Division. Its regimental and battalion commanders were identified, and some of its cadre were jump-qualified. But beside the standard arms and equipment shortages, the biggest problem the 10th paratroop encountered was in obtaining well trained and experienced infantry, artillery, anti-tank, engineer, as well as staff personnel.

In early April, a Luftwaffe general, while enroute to the Division in a Fiesler Storch aircraft, was shot down by allied aircraft.[11] By chance, he was shot down by the Division's supply depot, but he survived the crash. Upon arrival to the Division's headquarters, the Luftwaffe general claimed he had authorization to secure the Division's weapons, and because he only had approximately 1,000 men with no infantry training, he also claimed he had authorization to secure what personnel was required for his 10th Paratroop from the Ukrainian Division.[12]

Heike, Freitag, and the others stared in disbelief. But on the following day, 5 April, Divisional staff received a telegram from the 18th Military District's Headquarters based in Salzburg.[13] Although the Division was not under the 18th's command, 18th Headquarter's ordered the Division to immediately reform itself into the 10th Paratroop Division.[14]

Once again, confusion was created with the appearance of the Luftwaffe general and the ensuing order. But what especially caused the confusion were the following contradictions: the general stated he had "authorization" to "secure weapons and appropriate personnel" while 18th Headquarters issued an order for the Division to convert itself into a paratroop formation. According to Heike, "it was difficult to believe that higher authorities would issue such an absurd directive."[15] But was this really the case?

Chapter 23: The Division's Days of Uncertainty

Had the Division provided some of its weapons and personnel to the 10th Paratroop, the action undoubtedly would have lowered morale. But in regards to converting itself into a paratroop formation – realistically speaking, had time been available and a jump-training site provided, along with the necessary "Auntie Ju" transport aircraft, either the Division or its exceptionally strong Training and Replacement Regiment, could actually have been converted into a paratroop formation.

The backbone of any paratroop division is its infantry. Aside from the fact that the Division's three infantry regiments were all well-trained and sufficiently combat experienced, the Division's fusilier unit was an exceptionally elite combat battalion, and even many of those who were found within the Training and Replacement Regiment had by now been sufficiently trained and had acquired enough combat experience while conducting security and anti-guerrilla activities. But virtually unknown is the fact that some of the Division's members were jump qualified. Prior to World War II, Czechoslovakia had developed an airborne brigade, and some of the Division's troops had served in it. As well, there were those who, after Brody, had volunteered for the "Special Forces Group 'Brandenburg.'"[16] Because this was a commando unit (and one of the requirements of a German commando was to be jump-qualified), those Divisional soldiers selected for commando training underwent jump-training at the Papa jump school. In order to qualify, each candidate had to undertake six jumps from an aircraft in flight. Following the completion of training, additional jumping experience was acquired through further training or during missions. Because in the spring of 1945 those Ukrainians who had served within Brandenburger's units were released, upon their re-entry into the Division they brought back vital airborne experience and knowledge. When the Soviets had occupied Galicia, they exposed a number of Galicia's youth to tower training – a major step toward jumping out of an aircraft in flight. Prior to Poland's fall in 1939, that nation was the first in Europe to undertake anti-paratroop training. Along with the Poles, some of the Ukrainians now serving in the Division had also received that training. Realistically speaking, among Divisional soldiers, varying degrees of airborne knowledge did exist.

The possibility also existed that Germany's high command, or someone within the Luftwaffe, wanted to create either a foreign or a mixed German/European paratroop division. And in the concluding weeks of the war, as a search was launched to determine which sizable unit could be utilized, the Ukrainian Division was eyed.

Regardless of the confusing circumstances, in the very end neither the Ukrainian Division, nor any of its elements or personnel, including the Division's Training and Replacement Regiment, were ever incorporated into the 10th Fallschirmjäger Division.[17] However, in mid-April, the Ukrainian Division did absorb the

10th Paratroop's 2,500 Luftwaffe personnel.[18] For the greater part, these men were untrained and unarmed aircraft technicians and ground personnel but some pilots were found amongst them. Various commanders viewed these new arrivals in different ways, and various proposals on how to best incorporate the new personnel were raised. Freitag, for example, proposed to form three "4th Battalions." Once organized, each infantry regiment would receive an additional battalion.[19] This plan was never realized. However, according to Heike and Krokhmaliuk, a large contingent of these men were placed into one quickly organized battalion and incorporated into the 30th Regiment. In the end, the majority were posted into the Division's reserve Training and Replacement Regiment but a number of the Luftwaffe communication and technical personnel were absorbed into the various communication, repair, and staff sections where their expertise was effectively utilized.[20]

24

Austria and the Final Battles

At about the same time the 18th Military District's Headquarter's was issuing an order that the Division was to be absorbed into the 10th Paratroop Division, Army Group 'South'[1] placed the Division into the 2nd Panzer Army's[2] 1st Cavalry Corps.[3] Unit charts reveal the Division was within the 1st Cavalry Corps on 24 March 1945, but Heike cites 31 March 1945[4] as the date the Division was included into the 2nd Panzer Army. In regards to Heike's observation, the Division was undoubtedly posted by Army Group 'South' into the 2nd Panzer Army just before an official order was issued on 31 March; therefore, Heike is not incorrect in his observation. As for two different headquarters issuing separate orders at approximately the same time, it must be remembered that in the concluding weeks of the war there was a considerable amount of confusion, and it was not uncommon for any military unit to receive various orders and amendments to orders. Because the Division was not an exception, it received various orders from such diverse command posts:[5] Himmler's Headquarter's; the SS-FHA; OKW's operations section along with its quartermaster chief; Army Group's 'South' and 'Southeast;' 18th Military District Headquarter's; 2nd Panzer Army; 6th Army; 1st Cavalry Corps; 4th SS Panzer Corps; and even the newly forming Ukrainian National Army.

On 30 March 1945, Heike travelled to the 2nd Panzer Army's Headquarters where he reported the Division's situation, and battle-readiness, to the Panzer Army's Chief-of-Staff, Major General Ulrich Burker. During the meeting, Heike requested that the Division be deployed with the 2nd Panzer, and this request was granted.[6] Because none of the 2nd Panzer Army divisions were in full divisional strength, and as of 24 March were all classified as either "forming" or in a number "3" or "4" (and most were in the "4" rating), the 2nd Panzer Army's Chief-of-Staff was very pleased that the 2nd Panzer would be possessing a well armed and manned division.

Undoubtedly, Heike's personal visit proved productive because although the Division was a well-armed, relatively well equipped, and strongly manned formation, the German chart of 24 March 1945 classified the Division as "unreliable."[7] To this day, it has never been explained why such a classification was provided. But the possibility exists that in the higher echelons of the 3rd Reich, some erroneously believed that the Division was in the process of being incorporated into the 10th Paratroop (or even some other formation) or, as a result of the Führer Conference's of 23-24 March, believed it would be disarmed. It must also be kept in mind that in the later stages of the war, a number of Germany's undisciplined foreign formations began to disintegrate within themselves. For such reasons the Divisions's status in late March 1945 was not certain and possibly, this explains its classification as "unreliable."

But in reality the Division was far from "unreliable." This was already evidenced by the fact that during this period of uncertainty, the Division did not just idly stand by. East of Maribor, communist reconnaissance patrols from the 3rd Ukrainian Front's[8] 57th Army[9] and the newly created 1st Bulgarian Front were spotted. Likewise, Tito's guerrillas were now rapidly reorganizing themselves into conventional (regular) military forces and fighting as conventional troops. These combined forces began to advance to the west and northwest. Sensing upcoming dangers, the Division began preparations to counter these threats.

Defensive positions around Maribor, but especially to the east of that city were continued. Besides drawing the 29th and 30th Infantry Regiments closer to Maribor's vicinity, the Division's artillery, anti-tank, and sapper units established themselves in and around that city. The fact that the Division undertook such measures on its own initiative without any guidance from higher headquarter's indicates that within the Division, there were experienced analysts carefully viewing and analyzing near-future upcoming situations and that the Division was a well-disciplined force.

With the collapse of the remaining Hungarian forces, Marshal I. I. Tolbukhin's 3rd Ukrainian Front attacked on 31 March 1945 the German front in the vicinity of Feldbach. Within hours, the 3rd Ukrainian Front's 57th Army and elements of the 27th Army[10] had succeeded in rupturing the 2nd Panzer Army's front. Desperate to halt the Soviet advance, late that same day the Division was ordered to advance northward to the vicinity of Gleichenberg and Feldbach[11] approximately 100 miles to the south of Vienna. On April 1, at 6:30 a.m., the Division began its northward advance.[12] Its mission: establish contact with the advancing enemy, halt their advance, and restore the front. Spearheading the assault would be the Division's 29th and 30th Infantry Regiments.

To conduct a forced tactical march over mountainous terrain, to march without respite distances of no less than 40 to 60 miles into immediate combat with no air and armor support and with only minimal intelligence knowledge about enemy strengths and intents, is not only difficult but indeed, a very dangerous task.[13] And in order to accomplish such a maneuver, a unit must be well-conditioned, armed, equipped, possess a high esprit-de-corps and a flexible operations staff ready to make critical split-second decisions and contingency plans. Clearly, the Division possessed such virtues.

By nightfall of 1 April, those Divisional elements which had been posted across the Austrian border in Yugoslavia had crossed into Austria proper to follow those units spearheading the assault. Upon retirement from either Southeastern Austria or Yugoslavia, all civilian centers were left unharmed, no private homes were destroyed, and in lieu of the fact that in the forthcoming days and weeks other retreating units would be utilizing the same roads, railways, passes and bridges, these features were all left behind intact. Of course, the possibility exists that certain targets (such as the bridges protected by Divisional security spanning the Drava and Mur Rivers), were later destroyed by Tito's guerrillas to either hamper the withdrawal of other Axis units from the Balkans, or to secure a specific region. Regardless, upon displacement, no destruction was carried out by the Division which explains why to this day many of the sights may still be observed as they stood in the war years. Perhaps this also explains why in the post-war period neither Yugoslavia, or Austria, ever requested the Division, or any of its elements, or personnel, to be extradited to face any charges of war crimes.[14]

During the Division's brief stay in the Austro-Yugoslavian Styrian Region, 150 soldiers deserted or were captured by the guerrillas.[15] As in previous instances, such factors were attributable to desertion: guerrilla propaganda, a feeling that nothing positive would be gained from further service, a desire to return to loved ones, fear of severe punishment or execution for an infraction, orders to return to the UPA, or falling under the influences of a local girl.

Although on the Austrian-Yugoslavian frontier casualties were very minimal, some losses were experienced and Stefan Wosniak, (6th Co., 30th Regiment and a survivor of the Brody battle); Pavlo Dudka (13th Co., 30th Rgt.); Yuriy Dubijchuk (whose brother Vasyl was KIA at Brody while serving with the artillery); Ivan Viter (7th Co., 29th Rgt); Pavlo Vitek (5th Co., 29th Rgt); artilleryman Stefan Volan; Hryhory Kalytun (13th Co., 29th Rgt); Dmytro Bazylo and Alexander Melnyk (both from 31st Regimental staff); and the well known and respected 30th Regimental doctor and surgeon, Anatoli Puposhynskiy – were some of those who made the supreme sacrifice.

At the start of its offensive, the Division registered such a strength: 14,000 troops[16] and approximately 8,000 in its Training and Replacement Regiment for a total of 22,000.[17] Of this combined strength, 14,000 marched northeast towards Feldbach, Austria.[18] At Straden (approximately 22 miles northeast of Maribor), Forstreuter's 30th Regiment veered to the northeast to contain the Soviet thrust between the towns of Merkendorf and Wilhelmsdorf. Simultaneously, Dern's 29th (on the 30th's left flank), advanced northward on a front between Straden and Rohr but at Krusdorf (approximately 2.5 miles north of Straden), the 29th's 1st and 3rd Infantry Battalions veered to the right of Krusdorf to advance northeast adjacent to Merkendorf and to the right of Waldsberg, a town located approximately 1 mile to the southwest of Merkendorf. Commanding the 29th Regiment's 1st Battalion was the Division's famed "Papa" Wildner, a highly admired and very ambitious soldier; the 3rd Battalion was commanded by SS-Hauptsturmführer Dietz, who also demonstrated sound competence. Fully aware of the dangers of advancing into unknown enemy territory, Wildner dispatched Waffen-Obersturmführer Omelian Kul'chyts'kiy's scout-reconnaissance platoon to probe ahead. Kul'chyts'kiy's scouts probed ahead aggressively, revealed timely information, and succeeded in capturing and delivering a Soviet NCO. As a result, Kul'chyts'kiy's actions revealed that for the moment, the 29th Regiment was advancing against a weak foe in the vicinity of Feldbach, Bad Gleichenberg (also identified as Hill 372), Traummansdorf and an elevated position known as Hill Sultz. Realizing the important significance of Mt. Sultz, Waffen-SS Obersturmführer Volodymyr Kozak, who commanded the 1st Battalion's 3rd Company and whose company had just hours before repulsed the Soviets from Traummansdorf while securing its railway station, decided to take advantage of the situation and continuing to advance forward, secured the critical terrain feature.[19]

Because this was a concentrated effort, the 2nd Panzer Army's entire 1st Cavalry Corps was utilized. On the Ukrainian right (southern) flank operated the 1st Cavalry Corps' 3rd Cavalry Division. But once the Division veered to the northeast, the 5th SS "Wiking" Tank Division, a division within the 4th SS Panzer Corps, 6th Army (and an army which operated to the north and adjacent of the 2nd Panzer Army), appeared. Advancing from the northwest into a southeasterly direction directly to Feldbach and its southern region, "Wiking" fell adjacent to the Division's left (northern flank). To maintain solid tactical control, Divisional headquarters positioned itself closely in the center behind the three regiments and operated strictly on the move. Following its dispersement from Selnica on 1 April, it relocated itself to St. Peter, then to Gnas (approximately 1 mile southwest of Katzendorf), and then into the town of Straden from where a commanding view of the area was found.

In order to prevent the Soviets from developing their initial penetrations into major ruptures, they had to be immediately halted and repulsed. North of Straden in the vicinity of Wilhelmsdorf the 30th encountered Soviet elements, and in the vicinity of Krusdorf and Ebersdorf, the 29th's 1st and 3rd Battalions encountered Soviet spearheads; simultaneously, the 29th's 2nd Battalion, commanded by SS-Sturmbannführer Blakenhorn,[20] in its advance northward and northeastward, encountered Soviet elements south of Katzendorf and in the vicinity of Hofstatten and Gleichenberg. As for the 31st,[21] it encountered Soviet spearheads in the vicinity of Wilhelmsdorf and Hochstraden (approximately two miles directly east of Wilhelmsdorf).

In their sectors, the Ukrainian Infantry Regiments demonstrated true proficiency in successfully repulsing the Soviet spearheads. While it is true that in neither sector was the enemy very strong, if one takes into consideration that the leading regimental spearheads marched straight into battle with minimal strengths, and the various regimental battalions had different objectives to secure and therefore, could not rely on other battalions for immediate reinforcement, then indeed the Divisions regiments demonstrated true bravery and elan.

Although the enemy resistance at first was negligible, it soon stiffened. At the village of Gleichenberg, the 29th Regiment's 2nd Battalion, after repulsing Soviet elements to the west and southwest of Gleichenberg, encountered exceptional resistance. Quickly calling in for heavy and light artillery support, Ukrainian artillerymen responded with accurate fire. After suppressing the enemy positions, the gunners lobbed in smoke rounds, and under the cries of "Slava!" the 29th's 2nd Battalion, reinforced with Kozak's 3rd Company from the 29th's 1st Battalion, seized and secured Gleichenberg.

During this same time, tough Soviet resistance was also encountered north of Gleichenberg where the ancient castle of Gleichenberg overlooked the village and at the look-out points of Stradner-Kogel (vicinity of Hochstraden) and Gleichenberg-Kogel (northeast of Gleichenberg Dorf). Because Kozak had previously dispatched a patrol from his company toward the castle to obtain first-hand information on the Soviet strength, and the patrol returned with information that the castle was occupied by a sizable force with one tank, the advancing Ukrainians knew that they would have to contest the communists for the castle. But the Ukrainian momentum could not be halted and Gleichenberg castle, along with the lookout positions, were secured. By 4 April, south of Graz, the front was stabilized.[22]

By its actions, the Division not only halted the 3rd Ukrainian Front's spearheads but independently, succeeded in repulsing Soviet advances.[23] An aggressive leadership was especially exhibited by those who from July to December 1944 had attended the Posen-Treskau officer's school and in January/early February 1945 had mastered heavy weapons training in the Advanced Arms Training Center. Although the majority of the officer graduates had not yet been promoted to an officers rank, upon arrival to the Division they immediately assumed leadership positions on platoon and even, company levels. And certain soldiers, such as grenadier Evhen Biluk, demonstrated exceptional bravery. Taking charge of Kozak's 2nd Platoon at a critical moment when the platoon's leadership was wiped out as a result of a combat activity, Biluk ensured that the platoon continued its critical mission of supporting the thrust of Kozak's 1st and 3rd Platoons against the Gleichenberg castle. Against stiff communist resistance, critical terrain and lookout points were secured, and Soviet prisoners, arms, and equipment were seized. But most importantly, the Division restored the front and demonstrated that in the offense, it was a formidable force. Consequently, morale rose significantly.

For three days and four nights, the Division moved and fought without respite. During this time no one slept, and those meals consumed were absorbed on the march. Needless to say, such conditions would inevitably exhaust even the most physically conditioned soldier. When a respite in the fighting finally occurred, wherever they happened to be, soldiers plopped down to sleep.

But security still had to be maintained. And those who were immediately posted found themselves in an uneasy dilemma; after all, to stand utterly exhausted with a weapon in hand among a crowd of sleeping soldiers is very difficult and challenging.

To this day, it has never been determined – nor will it ever be – whether the two posted sentries who were found asleep by a roving night patrol succumbed to exhaustion, or intentionally decided to take a chance and fall asleep. But it does not matter because the fact remains that by their actions, numerous lives were placed in danger. Angered by the fact that two of his sentries were awakened by a patrol, SS-Untersturmführer Diemke ordered the maximum punishment – execution by firing squad.[24]

That morning, at 10 o'clock, Yaroslav Liulky and Ivan Liudkevych, two soldiers from the town of Rohatyn, Galicia, were shot on an Austrian plateau. With tremendous sorrow and tears in his eyes, Veryn supervised their burial and wondered how many more would be buried in distant places far from their homeland.

To be sure, the two executed sentries were derelict in their duties, however, death by execution was not called for. If punishment was to be handed out, some other form could have been administered. By executing the two, Diemke exhibited a cold brutality and no concern for the morale of the others.

Following this execution, no other executions took place. Regardless, in the short period of the Division's existence, approximately 200 Divisional soldiers were executed.[25] This figure is not only exceptionally high but indeed, a shocking one. Executions were conducted for numerous reasons ranging from minor infractions such as appearing late from leave or pass or playing a joke, and to the more serious infractions of disobedience of an order, theft, or expressing a defeatist attitude (or what was perceived as such). Cases also occurred where soldiers were ordered to report to a headquarters and after their arrival, were never seen or heard from again. Throughout the Division, it was also common knowledge that if one came across any OUN or UPA literature, it would have to remain well-concealed, otherwise, execution by firing squad would ensue. Perhaps this explains why frequently after a quick glance, such material was destroyed. This also explains why the UPA's inserted personnel were constantly on guard, and were always briefed on where to find immediate shelter in the event that an immediate exit out of the Division was necessary.[26]

The fact that approximately 200 men were executed is not only an astonishing figure but when one takes into consideration that in western armies, composed of millions of soldiers, no army executed so many soldiers, than indeed this is a shocking figure. Yet, this figure would have been higher had it not been for the efforts of Krokhmaliuk, the Ukrainian chaplains, and on occasion, certain German commanders and NCOs. The fact that 200 soldiers were executed is proof that the Division's troops were exposed to severe and ruthless discipline.[27]

Immediately following its successful counteroffensive and the re-establishment of the front, from Hofstatten to Wilhelmsdorf, the Ukrainian Division was holding a frontline distance of 7 miles. But immediate changes to that would be made with the shifting around of certain formations. On its right, the 1st Cavalry Corps moved its 3rd Cavalry Division from the frontline into a reserve position. In turn, the 4th Cavalry Division briefly covered its sector but within days, the 4th Cavalry was replaced by the 16th SS "Reichsführer" Panzergrenadier Division. As for the Ukrainian Division, it basically remained in place but its left wing was slightly extended to the north. Now, the Division held a frontline distance of 8 miles and its front encompassed most of the town of Feldbach southward to a line adjacent to Muhldorf, Untergiem, Obergiem, Hofstatten, Gleichenberger Castle,

Galicia Division

Gleichenberg Dorf, Kirchenberg and Bad Gleichenberg. Divisional headquarters was established approximately half a mile to the northwest of Obergnas. Regimental headquarters were established in such locations: 29th – east of Gnaz in the vicinity of Katzendorf; 30th – west of Feldbach in the vicinity of Oberweisenbach; and the 31st was located west of Kinsdorf. The Division's artillery headquarters was established adjacent to Divisional headquarters. From north to south (Feldbach to Bad Gleichenberg), the front was held by all three infantry regiments in line with the 30th in the north, the 31st in the center, and the 29th in the south. On the Division's right stood the "Reichsführer" Division, while "Wiking" occupied the left.

During the entire time the Division was on the front line, it was constantly bombarded with enemy propaganda. Tolbukhin's front contained a sizable number of Ukrainians; therefore, its propaganda and intelligence sections began to exploit this in a strong effort to induce the Divisions soldiers to surrender.[28] These messages were especially broadcasted at night when homesickness, and a desire to be with loved ones, was at its peak. On occasion, specifically designated messages were also broadcast.

To an extent, the messages were successful. Individuals did cross over, but the possibility also exists that some of the "deserters" were individuals with predisposed communist sympathies, or Soviet-inserted agents who decided to return with information.[29] But the worst case of mutiny occurred one mid-day within the 31st Regiment's 1st Battalion's 1st Company. Under the influence of two Ukrainian NCOs, Pachovskiy and Pankov, more than 30 soldiers bolted to the Soviet side. Later that night, Pankov's voice was broadcasting "today, I am glad I became a Red-army soldier," and he urged others to desert.[30]

Needless to say, this was a very serious matter. Aside from the fact that such desertions could anger the Germans to the point that they might ostensibly dissolve the Division (or if so unable would cease to furnish the Division with further supplies which, at this point, were becoming increasingly difficult to obtain), deserters provide an opponent critical knowledge of defense position locations, unit strengths, and so forth. But in the case of the Ukrainian soldier, it was especially demoralizing because a number of the Division's soldiers still had relatives and close friends in Galicia and other areas now under Communist occupation. In addition to revealing military information, deserters would also reveal the identities of other Divisional soldiers as well as information about their families. In turn, this information would also be utilized by the NKVD to conduct repressive measures against specific family members. And such fears where not groundless. It is known that in the concluding days of the war and in the post-war period, a number of arrests and executions undertaken by the NKVD arose as a result of someone's involvement with the Division.[31]

To counter this threat, the Ukrainian Division reinforced its counter-intelligence efforts, and began to direct propaganda against the enemy.[32] It appears, however, that the Division's efforts were not very successful. According to former Divisional officer Major Ren, the Division's efforts on the Austrian front were weak and ineffective.[33] Although some Soviet soldiers did desert to the Ukrainian side (such was the case when four Soviet soldiers deserted to Orest Yarymovych),[34] in the very end, no more than 98 desertions were recorded.[35] In all, by the conclusion of the war, approximately 600 soldiers, from the period of 1943-1945, deserted.[36]

From the moment the Ukrainian Division re-established the front in its sector, it was clear the Soviets would return. In an effort to break through and overrun Austria, STAVKA ordered its fronts to resume the offensive. It should be noted that these attacks were not just launched against the Ukrainian sector; in April 1945, the entire Eastern front was hampered by a series of massive Soviet attacks. And in their effort to secure Vienna (as further north in Germany Berlin), the Soviets resumed their military operations.

But whereas before, minimal enemy armor and aircraft were encountered, this would no longer be the case. Enemy tanks, to include the new 45-ton Joseph Stalin tank and JSU-122 tank destroyer,[37] along with various aircraft and artillery, reinforced the Soviet 57th and 27th Armies. Elite Soviet airborne troops from the independent 3rd Guards Airborne Division[38] were also rushed in. The lookout points at Stradner-Kogel, Gleichenberg-Kogel, and the Gleichenberg castle itself were especially contested. To secure these critical elevations, the Soviets launched full-scale assaults with strong artillery and rocket firing Katyusha support. In the ensuing struggles, the fighting was always close-in and as on previous occasions at Brody and Modlin, knives, daggers, and handguns were used abundantly. Among the screams of the dying, the sickening oozing sounds of flamethrowers emitting a fiery death were heard day and night. To hold these positions as well as the front-line, the Division utilized the following tactic: minimal numbers of soldiers were positioned at the front. But behind the front line positions, each regiment maintained strong reserves. So the moment the Soviets began to breach the front, the reserves would rush in to contain any Soviet penetrations.

With such a defense, the Division successfully repulsed Tolbukhin's attacks and held their sector of the front. Critical situations, however, did arise. On one occasion, the 3rd Cavalry Division, a division utilized by the 1st Cavalry Corps as its main reserve, galloped in to help the Ukrainians. To supervise the battle from a more advantageous position, General Harteneck, who commanded the 1st Cavalry Corps, re-established himself in the Ukrainian Division's headquarters. But as the battle was waging, General Freitag became unnerved, lost his personal control and, as previously at Brody during a critical moment, announced to the corps general his resignation.

Angered by Freitag's inefficiency and irresponsible behavior, the Corps general not only refused his resignation, but after reprimanding Freitag, ordered Freitag to remain at his post. Side-by-side with the cavalry troops, the Ukrainian soldiers continued the battle. For several hours the battle swayed back and forth, but in the end the Soviet advance was halted and the front held.

It is important to note that throughout much of April, the Ukrainian Division's elite fusilier battalion was not with the Division. Because the 1st Cavalry Corps' 23rd Panzer Division was not in full strength and urgently needed reinforcement, the Ukrainian fusiliers were dispatched to the 23rd Panzer.[39] Had the 900-plus fusiliers been with the Division, the possibility exists that the 3rd Cavalry's reinforcements would not have been required;[40] regardless, the fusiliers were posted to Major General Josef von Radowitz's 23rd Panzer. And during the time the fusiliers served with von Radowitz in the vicinity of Radkersburg,[41] the fusiliers served with distinction. As previously at Brody and in other places, the fusiliers displayed tremendous aggressiveness and tenacity. Wherever committed, the Ukrainian fusiliers accomplished their mission and developed a tough reputation not only within the 23rd Panzer Division, but as well within the entire 1st Cavalry Corps. After a period of service, the fusiliers were recalled to their parent Division. Upon departure, the 23rd Panzer expressed its tremendous gratitude, and von Radowitz not only expressed his positive comments verbally but likewise, a letter of appreciation was forwarded to the Division and the headquarters of the 1st Cavalry Corps.[42]

In mid-April, the Ukrainian Division was transferred from the 2nd Panzer Army's 1st Cavalry Corps to General Hermann Balck's 6th Army;[43] in turn, the 6th Army assigned the Division to its 4th SS Panzer Corps, commanded by SS-Obergruppenführer Herbert Gille. Although officially this was the first time the Division was placed into the 4th SS Panzer Corps, the Division was well known to the corps because previously, in the fall of 1944, approximately 1,000 Divisional soldiers had served with valor within the 4th SS Panzer Corps' "Wiking" Division at Modlin.[44]

On 15 April, at approximately 9 p.m., as Freitag and Heike were resting and eating dinner, a regimental commander notified Divisional headquarters by telephone to report enemy activity along his line; within minutes, the 16th SS Panzergrenadier Division's headquarters also called up. Adjacent to the Ukrainian Division's right sector, the 16th SS reported that everything was quiet in its entire sector but it noticed enemy flares and activity to the front of the Ukrainians. Concerned about any dangers, 16th SS inquired as to what was occurring. They were told to wait.

Suddenly, another call came in, reporting that a strong enemy force was advancing on the positions covering Gleichenberg castle; simultaneously, numerous flares, night signals, tracer rounds, small arms fire as well as near and distant explosions shattered the night's stillness. Though the situation was not yet totally clear, Freitag alerted the reserves.

Still another call came in. The 31st Regiment's commander reported that an assault group had been repelled in his sector, but the commander of the 29th reported that a Soviet force had penetrated his positions near Gleichenberg's castle; however, the castle was still held by the regiment's Ukrainians.

More shells screamed in; simultaneously, various Divisional sectors reported enemy activity. Reports poured in that an enemy force in the strength of a reinforced company with massive artillery and mortar support had succeeded to rupture through the front and was assaulting the castle from both sides. But although the enemy force had broken through and had surrounded the castle, the Ukrainian defense positions centered around the castle were still holding; artillery observers and grenadiers occupying the castle were also resisting.

Clearly, it was apparent that the various small-scale attacks were diversions for the main assault force besieging the castle. But when Divisional headquarters was informed by a regimental commander that a counterattack had failed to breakthrough and relieve the defenders, Divisional headquarters knew it had to act immediately.

It was of essence that the Division retain the castle and the village of Gleichenberg. From the plateau and castle, a defender had a commanding view for many miles and could observe not only the lower elevations of Gleichenberg-Kogel and Stradner-Kogel, but as well the entire Divisional front line and its rear, and the defense areas held adjacent to the north and south of the Division by the other divisions. But most importantly, the entire Soviet front was observed; simply put, the castle was the main lynch-pin in the Division's defense.

But as well, there were other critical reasons for maintaining the castle. Beside the military factor, there were serious psychological and morale factors. Within and around the castle, a number of Ukrainian defenders were continuing to resist. Although for the moment communication was lost with the encircled defenders, the constant heavy staccato of gunfire, explosions, and exploding flares revealed that the defenders, although outnumbered, were still resisting. And because everyone knew that if the castle fell any captured defenders would experience only torture and death, for this reason alone it was just as critical to secure the plateau and relieve its defenders.

An assault force was formed quickly. Composed of two reserve companies, a squad of engineers with flamethrowers and anti-tank personnel, the assault force was accompanied by two artillery spotters. This force was led by the commander of the Division's reserve (Field Replacement) battalion.[45] But as the assault force moved forward, it encountered those troops who earlier had retired from their positions; insisting to rejoin the battle, these soldiers fell in and reinforced the assault group.

On 16 April, at 1:28 a.m., the artillery lay down a two minute artillery and smoke preparation. Careful not to strike the castle, the artillerymen saturated the overrun positions as well as the approaches to the town of Gleichenberg and the castle. At exactly 1:30 a.m., the Ukrainian assault troops attacked. Following a brief but vicious hand-to-hand battle, the Ukrainians repulsed the Soviets. At 2:00 a.m., the commander of the assault force radioed that his objective was secured and the castle's defenders had been relieved.

After mid-April, the front was stabilized. Soviet attacks began to diminish, and those which were launched were considerably weaker. Although a temporary lull ensued, daily mortar and artillery rounds were still directed against the Division, and Soviet snipers posed continuous dangers. Never would Omelian Kulchyts'kyi forget the whistling sounds of a sniper's bullet flying by his head as he ducked and leaped into a ditch for cover, nor would Volodymyr Kozak ever forget how an enemy grenade landed right in front of his feet and without even thinking, Kozak picked it up and threw it away as he dove for cover. To maintain a clear picture of enemy activities, each night Divisional scouts probed for enemy positions or to secure prisoners while long-range reconnaissance teams operated deep behind enemy lines. In a number of cases, such teams stayed for extensive periods of time behind Soviet lines.

During its time in Austria, the Division was also visited by various dignitaries. But these visits were not always pleasant. When Wachter visited, Freitag refused to accommodate the former Galician Governor. Possibly the fact that Wachter and the Ukrainian Military Board had never congratulated Freitag for "achieving" the coveted Knight's Cross had something to do with this. But with Heike's intervention, Wachter was accommodated.

On 19 April, Wachter, Colonel Bisanz and Dr. Arlt appeared. But this time, they were accompanied by a Ukrainian commander, General Pavlo Shandruk.[46]

Chapter 24: Austria and the Final Battles

Shandruk not only headed the Ukrainian National Committee but by a recent order of President Livyts'kyi,[47] was appointed as Commander-in-Chief of the Ukrainian Army.

Tremendously interested in the Division, Shandruk visited all of its units, including even those on the frontline. Outfitted in a Ukrainian Army uniform, the Ukrainian general made a strong and favorable appearance. Although morale was quite high, Shandruk's visit raised it higher. To maintain contact with the Division, Shandruk established his quarters within the reserve Training and Replacement Regiment.

Prior to his visit, Shandruk had planned to rename the Division into the "1st Ukrainian Division." As well, he planned to utilize this force as a base for the formation of the "Ukrainian National Army – U.N.A." Although previously on 12 November 1944 the Division was officially re-designated from "Galicia" to "Ukrainian," many Ukrainians were still unaware of this change and the "Galicia" title was still used. To rectify this matter once and for all, on 27 April, Shandruk issued Divisional Order 71 to officially change the Divisions title to "1st Ukrainian."[48] At this time, the Ukrainians swore a new oath of loyalty to their Ukrainian nation,[49] and that same day, General Freitag officially rectified the Division's name change, transferring the Division to Shandruk's Ukrainian National Army. Amongst the Ukrainian personnel, the German Waffen-SS ranks ceased to exist and Ukrainian ranks, similar to those utilized by western nations, entered. General Myhailo Krat was appointed as Divisional commander.[50]

Because Himmler had previously agreed to transfer the Division to the Ukrainian National Army, no German opposition was experienced and as of 25 April 1945, the Ukrainian Division finally ceased to be a Waffen-SS formation. Until the conclusion of the war, it belonged to the Ukrainian National Army.

25

The Ukrainian National Army[1]

Formed on 15 March 1945 by Order No. 8, the Ukrainian Army was organized around two formations – the 1st Ukrainian (formerly "Galicia") Division with its Training and Replacement Regiment, and the 2nd Ukrainian.[2] According to Shandruk, the UNA reached a strength of 35,000-38,000,[3] but this figure is difficult to verify. Yet in a letter submitted in the immediate aftermath of World War II to British authorities, the Ukrainian prisoners of war cited such corroborating information to their captors in regards to the Ukrainian Army:[4]

"On 17th of March 1945, a solemn declaration was issued by the Committee which called Ukrainians to fight against the Soviets (only against Soviets). On the same day the Commander-in-Chief of the Ukrainian Army, appointed by the Committee, gave detailed instructions about the formation of the Army."

At the beginning the Army would have to comprise four divisions:

1) The first one already existing from 1943;
2) the second from reserved groups;
3) the third from armed brigades which were at the front at Gerlitz; and
4) the fourth one from various small ukrainian units which had refused to fight against Western Powers and therefore, disarmed, were stationed at

Ukrainian NCO's departing a Sunday church service in Slovakia in the vicinity of Cadze. Photo taken in 1944.

Divisional soldiers in training. Three of the soldiers are wearing the 1944 camouflage 'brick' pattern. Initially designed for combat in built-up areas, the tunic soon proved to be effective both in forests and fields. Of interest to note is that the second soldier from the right who appears to be giving instructions and is emphasizing a point with his right hand to the soldier to his right while those to his left are setting up a spotting and aiming periscope, is wearing an Italian camouflage battle smock. This smock was also worn by many Luftwaffe paratroopers and Waffen-SS commandos. Therefore, he is either an instructor tasked to assist in the training of the "Galicia" Division or possibly, is a Ukrainian who had previously been serving in the multi-national "Brandenburg" commando unit but with the rise of the "Galicia" Division, requested reassignment into the Division. This photo was taken in Neuhammer on 3 June 1944.

TWO OPPOSITE: Chaplain Vasyl Laba preparing services for Divisional training recruits. Heidelager, fall 1944. The soldiers in the background are beginning to congregate for the religious service.

Colonel Alfred Bisanz, who headed the Military Board.

Chaplain Doctor Vasyl Laba, Chief Divisional Chaplain.

A recruiting poster. The poster states: "Join the Battle Against Bolshevism in the ranks of the "Galicia" Division!"

Otto Wachter, Governor of Galicia.

Governor Otto Wachter (left), accompanied with Vice-Governor Otto Bayer (adjacent to Wachter with glasses) and other dignitaries leaving St. George's Cathedral in Lviv. 17 July 1943. In February 1944, Bayer was assassinated.

Departing volunteers. 18 July 1943.

Some more departing volunteers. At the extreme left is Vasyl Veryha.

Departing volunteers in the city of Chortkiv, 18-20 July 1943. Upon their departure, the volunteers were dispatched to Lviv from where they departed for the Heidelager training camp.

Some of the symbols drawn on the railway cars. Of interest is the "Buvaite Zdorov Rekliamatsiyni!" (Simple translation: "Stay Healthy, Reclaimed Heroes!") Rekliamatsiyni was a slang term utilized by the Divisions volunteers for the many thousands who earlier pretended to volunteer but when the time came to leave, found various excuses to avoid service. Needless to say, the Divisions personnel looked upon them with distaste, disgust and viewed them as cowards and men with low esteem.

These soldiers appear to be from the communication signal battalion – note the signal wire inside the wagon. They are wearing the 1944 issue pebble/brick style camouflage.

OPPOSITE TOP: Waffen-Obersturmführer Liubomyr Makarushka with members of his 8th Heavy Company, 2nd Battalion, 30th Infantry Regiment. For some unexplainable reason, Makarushka is not wearing the Galician lion emblem on his right collar; however, he appears to be wearing it on his left sleeve. The pictured weapon is an MG42 Heavy Machine Gun. The camouflaged vehicle is the Amphibious Schwimmwagen or le.P.Kw.K.2s (light Panzer Kampfwagen 2nd Model). Each Heavy Company was outfitted with two or three of these light vehicles which had the capability to cross light and medium rivers with a specially designed propeller-shaft. Of interest to note is the M1935 Steel Helmet (Stahlhelm 35) worn by the second NCO to Makarushkas right. Although the older M16 and M18 helmets were effective in World War I, by the early 1930s these helmets were no longer effective and popular. Therefore, a new helmet, the M1935, was developed. Tested in mid-1935, its inside contained an M31 leather head protector made from either sheep or goat leather. This helmet contained no ear cutouts or ventilation lugs but had a higher visor and the rear neck apron and visor sides were shortened. Excluding some very limited attempts to alter this helmet during World War II, the M35 remained in the German inventory. Approximately 25 million of these helmets were produced from 1935 to 1945, with the brunt produced between 1939-1943. Approximately 30,000-32,000 M35 helmets were issued to the "Galicia" Division, its Training and Replacement Regiment, and its four Independent Rifle Regiments. However, in addition to the M35 helmet, some M42 helmets (a version of the M35), as well as some French and Italian helmets, were found in the Division.

OPPOSITE BOTTOM: Makarushka pictured with several of his officers and NCOs. Behind the vehicle are a number of enlisted personnel. Of interest to note are the boots. The leather boot worn by Makarushka, as well as by the officer to his immediate left (with the Galician Lion patch on his left sleeve) and the NCO with glasses standing second on the right from Makarushka), are wearing the so-called "jack boot." Prior to and at the beginning of the war, this boot was the standard boot of the German Army. However, as demonstrated in this and many other photographs, an ankle type of boot was also worn. This boot was actually a British Army boot widely utilized in North Africa and the Mediterranean region. With the German capture of Tobruk in June 1942, a tremendous number of these boots were located in warehouses and tens of thousands of pairs were shipped back to Germany. Because the boot was very comfortable, caused far fewer foot injuries, and with one or two pairs of woolen socks was an ideal late spring, summer and fall boot, it was issued in place of the jack boot. Every officer, NCO, and soldier in the "Galicia" Division was issued this boot. As for the highly polished jack boots worn by some of the Divisions officers and NCOs, it was primarily worn at functions such as graduations and special affairs. If worn in combat, it was solely by an officers or NCOs discretion. Most of the Divisions soldiers which deployed to Brody actually wore the British army boot.

Wachter in discussion with some of the Divisions volunteers. Lviv. May, 1944. It appears that Colonel Bisanz is on the left side of Wachter.

Five members of the "Galicia" Division in Heidelager. Winter, 1943-1944. Four of the pictured soldiers are wearing the M35 steel helmet. A close examination of the helmet worn by the second soldier from the left reveals the slanted "SS" black runes on a white patch. On 12 August 1935, Order I A/O I No. 013570, was issued by the Chief of the SS-Headquarters Berlin. This order designated that a shield with the SS runes in a lightning pattern was to be placed on the right side of the helmet and a swastika on a shield was to be placed on the left side of the helmet. (Silver SS runes on black shields were initially introduced for wear on 23 February 1934). However, the 1935 order was countermanded by the Order of 1 November 1943 Verordnungsblatt der Waffen-SS, 4. Jahrgang, Berlin, 1.11.1943, Nr. 21, Z. 402, which forbade any further wear of the SS runes. Yet numerous photographs reveal that until the conclusion of the war, many Waffen-SS soldiers from various formations continued to wear helmets with the slanted SS runes on the right side. And certain photographs also reveal that on occasion, Divisional soldiers painted the Ukrainian Trident national symbol on the right side of their helmets. This was, of course, done without authorization because as of date, no orders or documents exist to verify that the Trident symbol was to be utilized. But the most interesting find as of date occurred in the early 1980s near the town of Myslenice, in the vicinity of Cracow, Poland. While cleaning out a barn, a woman discovered a World War II German helmet. On its right side are the SS runes. But on the left side a well made metallic dark blue shield decal with a gold rampant lion and three ducal crowns are pictured. Of course, the helmet posed no interest to her. But some family member became very interested in it and took it to a local Polish Army Reserve unit. In due time, the helmet was brought to the military museum in London, England, where curators and military experts verified that the helmet is an authentic M42 (slight variation of the M35) helmet. British experts also confirmed that the metallic shield was an unofficial shield since no order was ever issued for the creation of such a shield. As for who designed the lion shield, it is believed that either a private jeweler or an artist with an ability to work with metal designed the shield for a relative or friend serving in the "Galicia" Division. Of course, such a find is rare and the value of this helmet is in the thousands of dollars.

Chaplin Myhailo Levenets. Pictured here
as a Waffen-SS Untersturmführer.

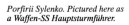
Porfirii Sylenko. Pictured here as
a Waffen-SS Hauptsturmführer.

Yuriy Krokhmaliuk. Pictured here as a
Waffen-SS Untersturmführer.

Liubomyr Makarushka. Pictured here as
a Waffen-SS Obersturmführer.

The Tryzub badge. This badge was to be worn on caps by the Ukrainian Division soldiers. It was introduced by General Pavlo Shandruk in April, 1945.

Divisional sleeve shield patch – a yellow lion on a blue background.

Divisional collar tab – silver lion on a black background.

Metzingen. Beside that were planned the aviation units and some other special services. But military and political events did not permit the realization of all of these designs."

From the above-mentioned information one can see that the Ukrainian National Army was never hostile to Western Powers.

From: Ukrainian Comm. of the Camp 5c.

At the time Shandruk was organizing his Ukrainian Army, approximately 900,000-1,000,000 million Eastern Europeans were within the various German services.[5] Of these, approximately 220,000 were Ukrainians.[6] While of course a high percentage of the Ukrainians were simple labor troops who volunteered only to avoid further starvation in German prisoner-of-war camps, others served individually within various Wehrmacht units or within various Schuma battalions. In such cases, many of these individuals had undertaken German training, and had various degrees of combat experience. In order to built an army, Shandruk sought to somehow gather up and coordinate all of the Ukrainian personnel found within the various German armies, support units, Schuma battalions, and construction units. Once assembled, an army (or at least enough for a nucleus), could be developed.[7]

But General Shandruk's desires were never fulfilled. World events, coupled with various secret agreements conducted between the Western Powers and the U.S.S.R., would ultimately prevent the establishment of any such liberation armies. As well, in the aftermath of World War II, it would have been impossible for Shandruk to raise an army without massive western military assistance and political recognition. Because the Ukrainian units which survived the war were never permitted by the western allies to wage war upon the Soviet Union, they ceased to exist shortly after the conclusion of the war.

As for the Ukrainian personnel who served in the various German armies and services, the fortunate ones merged into the civilian population in the aftermath of the war or, if captured by the western allies, were released with the other prisoners. Often times, Ukrainians accomplished this by impersonating as German, or Western European, soldiers. But in many other tragic instances, they were forcibly handed over to the Soviets in the infamous and disgraceful repatriation campaign known as "Operation Keelhaul."[8]

Beyond the planning stages, nothing ever became of the proposed Ukrainian National Army. Although the 1st Ukrainian Division was officially de-

Galicia Division

tached from German service to be utilized as a nucleus for the proposed army, front-line events never permitted the Division to be withdrawn from the front. In reality, until the very end, the 1st Ukrainian Division remained within the German army.

26

The Final Days of the 1st Ukrainian Division

On 2 or 3 May, General Balck called for a conference. All senior ranking commanders, higher adjutants, and chiefs-of-staff were ordered to attend. Assembling his commanders, Balck informed them that it was his belief that positive results would yet ensue. He also gave instructions to various commanders, ordered an intensification of long-range reconnaissance activities, and stated that for the moment enough fuel and ammunition, as well as supplies, were assured. In regards to the Ukrainian Division, Balck praised it, and urged it to continue its mission. But those who attended the meeting remained skeptical, and were not satisfied with Balck's military assessment – some even totally disbelieved him.[1]

By now, the western allies were advancing in Western Austria.[2] Fueled by false rumors that an exceptionally strong Nazi redoubt hideout was located somewhere in Austria, the Allies were determined to rapidly overrun Austria to prevent any Nazi fanatics from maintaining a hold anywhere on the European continent.[3]

On 6 May, another conference was held at the 4th SS Panzer Corps Headquarters.[4] To his assembled commanders, Gille proclaimed that Germany's fate was sealed, and that it appeared a surrender was imminent. That same day, General Balck again summoned his commanding personnel. He informed them that Germany would surrender, and that in an effort to avoid the capture of both the German and foreign units, commencing on 7 May, the 6th Army's front would disengage from the Soviets and retire as quickly as possible to the west and into the hands of the Americans and British.[5]

Galicia Division

That same day General Shandruk, Wachter, Arlt, and Colonel Bisanz appeared to the Divisions headquarters. Wachter proclaimed that Germany had lost the war, and he wanted the Ukrainians to surrender to the western allies. In an attempt to assist the Division, Wachter immediately travelled to Balck's Army Headquarters in hopes of securing an early withdrawal.

A military withdrawal, especially in the face of enemy pressure, is one of the most difficult – and dreaded – operations to undertake. In order to succeed, a unit must leave the false impression that it is remaining in place, establish a route or a number of routes to be utilized, and ensure that no natural terrain or enemy-inserted personnel will intercept, delay or halt a withdrawal. Likewise, engineers must ensure that roads, passes, and bridges are sufficiently reinforced and, once the withdrawing units pass, must frequently destroy certain sites while emplacing mines and obstacles to delay or halt any pursuing forces. Anti-aircraft units must protect critical crossing sites and scouts – along with flank and rear guard parties – must protect a withdrawal.

Anticipating that the day would soon arrive when the Division would have to conduct a withdrawal, the Division prepared – detailed withdrawal plans – well in advance. And to ensure that contact was made with the western allies, Captain Makarushka and an English-speaking German officer were dispatched to the west to negotiate the transfer of the Division to the allies.

Once the withdrawal would be ordered, it would be conducted in the following manner – the 2nd Regiment (previously the 30th), and elements of the 3rd Regiment (previously the 31st), would withdraw by a northerly route in the vicinity of Feldbach to Gleisdorf to a point south of Graz. The remainder of the 3rd and 1st Regiments (previously the 29th) would withdraw by a southerly route from the vicinity of Gleichenberg and Gnas to St. Stefan towards Graz. At a pre-established point south of Graz, the Division's regiments would cross the Mur River and march to Lieboch, Voitsberg, Pack, and Twimberg. To ensure a speedy withdrawal, at Twimberg some of the Division's units would head southwestward toward Volkermarkt (an area adjacent to Yugoslavia) and Klagenfurt while other Divisional units would move northwestward from Twimberg toward Judenburg and from there, directly to the west.

To ensure a timely and successful withdrawal, speed was of essence. But in order to conduct a speedy withdrawal, it was imperative that Austria's mountainous terrain be overcome in advance so that no problems would be encountered at critical moments. Realizing this, Divisional headquarters and the Division's engineers conducted detailed terrain analyses. In the waning hours of the Division's history, one of its most successful feats was accomplished by the engineers. Sensing that adequate bridges were not available for the entire 1st Cavalry Corps and the 4th SS Panzer Corps (plus any other elements which might suddenly appear), to cross the Mur River rapidly, the Division's engineers requested authorization, and received permission, to construct a bridge for the Division approximately 6 miles south of Graz on the Mur River.[6] Fully aware that Soviet or other allied aircraft could possibly bomb the bridge, the engineers deliberately constructed their bridge in a shaded area between two deep ravines where it would be difficult for allied planes to spot a bridge and fly in to bomb it. To ensure that work was not interrupted, the bridge was largely constructed during the night hours and even painted black. By morning, a light – but sufficiently sturdy 12-ton bridge – was spanning the Mur. In the following days, this bridge would provide the Division a major lifeline when the other bridges became clogged. Combat engineer Lieutenant Bohdan Spivak, who had a reputation throughout the entire engineer battalion for accomplishing any type of critical assignment, played a major role in the construction of this bridge.[7]

On 7 May, at approximately 11 a.m., German units to the Division's left began to withdraw. Concerned about the dangers of an exposed left flank around Feldbach, both Freitag and Heike raised their concerns. In the end, the Division had to acknowledge that nothing could be done. But neither Freitag nor Heike would cease their efforts; continuously, all day long, both soldiers pressed the 4th SS Panzer Corps for a withdrawal time. But always the same reply came back: "Wait. Orders will be issued!"[8]

The Withdrawal!
On 8 May, at approximately 2 a.m., Wachter called. He informed Divisional command that to the best of his knowledge, 6th Army had already been issued orders to withdraw. In turn, Heike immediately called the 4th SS Panzer Corps, but received no orders. Shortly afterwards, at 6 a.m., the Panzer Corps Chief-of-Staff telephoned and ordered the Division to withdraw immediately to the vicinity of Volkermarkt. Of historical significance, this was the last order the Division ever received.[1]

In anticipation of such an order, as early as 6 May the Division had already relocated its supply and logistics far to the west. But as expected, the Soviets soon noted the Division's withdrawal, and began to intensify their activities. Near Feldbach, the 2nd Regiment encountered some difficulties and took some casualties, however, it did succeed in withdrawing. To ensure a speedy withdrawal, the artillery regiment fired their remaining rounds at the approaching enemy, in some cases within 400 meters of the withdrawing Ukrainians, and then rendered their guns useless; all heavy equipment not previously withdrawn, along with tents and other materiel left standing to create a deception, were left behind. Excluding the essential food and medical supplies and personal weapons, the Division's soldiers carried nothing else. Passing several bunkers enroute to the west, Vasyl Motuk noted the "Death to Stalin!" "Slava Ukraini!" "We'll Be Back!" and "You'll Hear From Us Soon!" inscriptions crayoned upon the bunker walls.

Until 10 p.m., the Division's headquarters remained at its location. Afterwards, in the night hours, it quickly reestablished itself on the western edge of the Mur River in a secluded spot selected in advance by the engineers and within the vicinity of the bridge. By the time headquarters moved, most of the Division had withdrawn. Enroute to its new location, the headquarters passed some of the Division's columns. But once within its new location, Divisional headquarters was able to properly direct the withdrawal.

That same day on 8 May, in Berlin, Nazi Germany officially surrendered. After 12 years and 5 months, Hitler's 1,000 year Third Reich had ceased to exist.

The end, however, was far from over for those withdrawing westward. Through the entire day of 9 May 1944, Soviet planes continuously appeared to bomb and strafe the columns. As Lieutenant Volodymyr Tyvoniuk's artillery crew sought cover Tyvoniuk, no novice to aerial attacks, calmly waited out the enemy's aerial attack. A former artillery NCO in the Polish Army, in September 1939 Tyvoniuk's battery frequently fell under Nazi Stuka and bomber attacks; yet, it was one of the last batteries to surrender in Warsaw. To gain freedom and to avoid forced repatriation to the Soviet Union, Tyvoniuk enlisted in the German Army. Serving with Rommel's vaunted Afrika Korps in North Africa, Tyvoniuk repeatedly came under devastating allied air attacks. With the surrender of the Afrika Korps in May 1943, Tyvoniuk was evacuated to Europe; there, he learned about the newly created "Galicia" Division and immediately, Tyvoniuk requested reassignment to it. After completing an artillery officers school, Tyvoniuk was commissioned an officer upon arrival to the Division. As bombs exploded all around, Tyvoniuk patiently waited out the attack. "That's all right," thought Tyvoniuk, "we'll get our chance yet!"[2]

Communist ground forces, reinforced with armor, pursued the Division in an attempt to destroy or surround it. In the vicinity of Volkermarkt, Marks' Training and Replacement Regiment encountered Tito's guerrillas now operating within Austria proper.[3] After a brief struggle, the guerrillas were repulsed. Some casualties, however, were suffered.[4] In addition to Tito's guerrillas, some Austrian civilians were also observed wearing the red colored communist hammer and sickle arm band and shouldering rifles. But unlike the Titoists, they offered no resistance. As he marched past one such group, Motuk thought to himself "that's all right.

Chapter 26: The Final Days of the 1st Ukranian Division

You'll get a dose of communism yet!" But to avoid further contacts and delays, Divisional headquarters ordered all of its units to head northwest upon reaching Twimberg and guides were posted at critical points to ensure that no one ventured into enemy territory. Needless to say, casualties were suffered and in addition to those who perished through combat on 9 May, Lt. Fedir Karasevych (who enlisted under the alias Fedir Koval and fought at Brody), died tragically when he was crushed to death between two withdrawing vehicles.

On 10 May, Wachter suddenly appeared in the Division's headquarters on Mur's left bank. The former Galician governor wanted to see if there was anything else that he could do. Wachter was very pleased to see that the brunt of the Division had succeeded in passing the Mur and that in such a chaotic time, the Division was still holding its own. Prior to leaving, Wachter bid everyone farewell; few would ever see him again.[5]

That afternoon, the Division's headquarters moved again. But whereas before it had stayed primarily in the rear or center to control the withdrawal as well as the Division's rear guard, now it rushed to the front of the columns to Tamsweg, a town in Western Austria. This move was solely undertaken to establish contact with the western allies as soon as possible. That same day, the engineers kept the bridge open as long as possible. By late afternoon, the last of the Division's rear guard had crossed over. To ensure that no stragglers were left behind, the engineers kept the bridge open.

One of the last to cross over was Sergeant Oleh Dir. With a telescopic rifle swung over his back and an MP 44 in his hands, Dir quickly ran over to the engineers. As previously at Brody and with the UPA, now in Austria's mountains Dir was keeping Soviet pursuers at bay with deadly long-range shots. After reporting to the engineers that to the best of his knowledge he was the last one to cross, Dir positioned himself in a location from which he could cover the engineers. Within minutes of Dir's arrival Soviet patrols were spotted and the bridge was blown.[6]

That evening, Divisional headquarters relocated to St. Andrae, approximately 2 miles north of Tamsweg. This would be its last tactical displacement.

Until now, the Division had withdrawn in order. Command and control had been maintained, and those units forced into combat succeeded in repulsing the enemy. However, as frequently is the case in any type of military withdrawal, problems will arise and the Ukrainian Division began to experience its share.

To begin with, it was becoming increasingly difficult to control the long Divisional columns which by now, were interspersed with the numerous withdrawing German forces. And to ensure a swifter withdrawal, many of the Division's soldiers began to hitch rides upon motorized vehicles. In turn, as the vehicles drove off into various directions, commanders began to lose control over their personnel. Clearly, the end was now in sight.

In an effort to establish contact with western forces, Heike personally drove forward. That evening, Divisional headquarters also received news that the Allies were interning the various foreign and Waffen-SS units in the vicinity of Tamsweg. Upon hearing this news (confirmed by one of Wachter's assistants), Heike stated that he would venture forward to the Allied checkpoint located at Tamsweg, but would return. But just as he was about to depart, Wachter suddenly reappeared. Heike quickly informed him, General Freitag and the Division's headquarters staff to await until he returned with further information and instructions. Upon his departure, Heike would never again see either Freitag or Wachter.

Stalled columns, crowded narrow roads, and a crowded pass at Radstadter Tavern hampered Heike. In desperation, Heike ordered his assistant, corporal Nodinger, to return to Divisional headquarters with the request to wait a little longer because Heike needed additional time to scout another withdrawal route. Establishing contact with the engineer battalion commander, Heike was informed by him that General Freitag had committed suicide. In the meantime, Wachter and his assistants had disappeared into the mountains. Establishing contact with an English brigade, Heike was assigned by the British a large field near Tamsweg for the Division's assembly.[7] At this time, Heike was assured that the Ukrainians would not be repatriated to the Soviets, and that those who had already surrendered in the vicinity of Radstadt had nothing to fear.[8]

Amid the confusion and withdrawal on 10 May, the Division's headquarters, as well as the Division itself, had officially ceased to exist. Simultaneously, as the Ukrainian Division marched into internment, it marched into history.

In the following days, many more Divisional soldiers would surrender to the British 5th Corps.[9] That month, approximately 10,000 Divisional personnel entered captivity.[10] But this figure also included the Division's German personnel. Once removed, approximately 9,000 Ukrainian soldiers were counted.[11] In an effort to assist the Division, Major Heike continued to visit the interned Division; he continued his efforts until the Division's transfer to Spittal (approximately 27 miles directly to the southwest of Tamsweg), in Southwestern Austria. At that time, Heike himself was officially interned and placed into a prisoner-of-war facility outside of the Division.[12]

But not everyone surrendered to the British. Proceeding northward, approximately 700 Divisional soldiers crossed the Austrian border into Southwestern Germany. There, in the vicinity of Radstadt, they surrendered to the Americans.[13] In the following days, these soldiers were interned in a camp overlooking a lake in the vicinity of Murnau (approximately 30 miles southwest from Munich at Bad Augling), and finally at Auerbach. (East of Nurnberg).[14] At Auerbach, on 21 September, a letter was submitted to the American authorities.[15] In this short but detailed seven-page letter, the Ukrainians explained their position, and the atrocities and brutalities they had experienced both under Soviet and Nazi rule. The Ukrainians also cited their reasons for enlistment into the 14. Waffen-Grenadier Division der SS (Ukr. No. 1): as they claimed, under the circumstances, it was their only recourse at the time to improve their position. In this letter, the Ukrainians cited a figure of approximately 500 prisoners,[16] and requested the latter be transferred to the location of the other prisoners. The letter was signed by Liubomyr Ortyns'kyi (who, it appears, was the senior Ukrainian leader), Myroslav Maleckiy, and Dr. Radyvil', a medical officer.[17]

In addition to these 500, it is also known that a number of Divisional soldiers were captured individually, or in small groups, by the Americans.[18] Blending in with the other prisoners, it appears that the greater number survived; however, it is known that in the ensuing Operation "Keelhaul," a secret repatriation conducted by the Soviets in concert with the western allies to forcefully extradite both civilians and surviving Soviet prisoners-of-war released from German captivity back to the Soviet empire, some Divisional soldiers were also handed over. In such cases these individuals, if not executed outright within the Soviet zone, were deported to Siberian slave-labor camps to begin an ordeal of agony known only to those sentenced to such a cruel fate.[19]

Yet, as in any army, there are always those who will refuse to surrender. It is virtually unknown that beginning on 8 May, a sizable number of Divisional soldiers – individually, in pairs, or in small groups, drifted into the mountains in an attempt to avoid capture. Amongst them was a disproportionate number of Brody combat veterans.

In the ensuing days, weeks, and months, these individuals would cross into Germany, Switzerland, and France; some would hide out within Austria proper. For the greater part, these ex-soldiers would hide in very rural areas, and would not resurface until months or years later.

In his personal attempt to avoid capture and possible extradition to the Soviet Union, Myhailo Lobach went so high up into the mountains that he actually encountered a long-bearded mountain man who shocked him with the words "I didn't even know a war broke out!" Likewise, Lobach would never forget the kindness of the senior ranking U.S. Army NCO of Ukrainian decent who assisted him and others in their journey through Southern Germany toward Munich.[20] And Oleh Dir would never forget the sadness he experienced when he took his prized weapons to the edge of a mountain crevice and, after slowly feeling each weapon for one last time, dropped them into a deep, and fast-flowing stream hundreds of feet below. But he would feel more sadness on the following night. Changing into civilian attire provided to him by a kindly Austrian woman whose two sons disappeared at Stalingrad, the woman suddenly broke out in tears and stated "You remind me of my oldest son. God! How nice he looked in that suit!" Unable to control his own emotions, Dir stepped outside. But as he stared at the night sky cross-riddled with a million stars, he thought of his home to which he would never return, his mother, his family, and of his murdered uncle; he thought of Heidelager and Neuhammer, Brody, the UPA, the enemy personnel he had eliminated, and the misery that he had witnessed throughout Europe. He tried to remain detached, but every man has a breaking point and Dir, too, broke down and cried.[21]

In the very end, those who ran the gauntlet would always remain deeply indebted to the many kind-hearted Austrian, German, and other civilian men and women who provided shelter, even for just a night; a hot meal, extra food for an upcoming journey, medical care, clothing, or just a sympathetic ear and simple "Good luck, and God bless!" Physically, morally, and psychologically, such assistance raised more than one ex-soldiers spirits and enabled him to overcome the difficult ordeals of the post-war chaos.

27

An Assessment of the Division in Austria

In Austria, the Ukrainian Division proved to be a formidable force. In the end, it was not defeated, but only succumbed to world events totally out of its hands.

Committed to the Austrian front on a minute's notice against an advancing enemy, the Division immediately marched north/northeast with little to no knowledge about enemy strengths, dispositions and intents. Yet, with no armor and air support, the Division's soldiers engaged, halted and repulsed Tolbukhin's spearheads. The fact that this was immediately done following a forced infantry march attests to a true "winning-spirit," elan and high morale.

Once the front was stabilized, the Division remained on the front. Whether on the defense or offense, it performed all of its missions. Against heavy enemy ground pressure, and always against superior odds, as well as against superior enemy firepower, the Division held its front; aggressively, it launched raids far behind Soviet lines, and repulsed all counterattacks. As was usually the case, the Division received no armor and air support. Although at first Soviet armor and air attacks were limited, as the battle for Austria intensified, Soviet armor and air units made a much stronger appearance. Yet the Division continued to hold.[1]

During the time the Ukrainian Division was on the front, various elements were also dispatched to assist other front line divisions. Such was the case with the fusiliers. Attached to Major General Josef von Radowitz's 23rd Panzer Division, through much of the month of April the Ukrainian fusiliers, filling in as infantry, fought with distinction; their feats were noted not only to the Ukrainian Division's Headquarter's, but also to the 4th SS Panzer Corps' Headquarters and the headquarters of the 6th Army. In addition to the fusiliers, the Division's engineers played an important role in helping Marburg's defenders fortify their positions.

But continuous enemy pressure, along with the collapse of Nazi Germany and intensifying supply shortages, finally forced the entire Austrian front to withdraw. At the time of its withdrawal, the Division's artillery regiment had no more than 10-15 rounds per gun. This fact alone attests to the critical shortages – and urgency – for a withdrawal.

Anticipating a withdrawal, the Division began its preparations well in advance. In addition to preparing detailed plans, the Division also began to move its heavy baggage and equipment, along with much of its supply and support, westward. Accomplished mostly at night to prevent the enemy from noting any withdrawal, such a move would ensure an easier withdrawal once the Division was ordered to withdraw.

Once ordered, the Division withdrew from the front line in an orderly manner. As already attested, to withdraw under any circumstances is difficult. But to retire when on the front line is far more difficult. Yet, under adverse combat conditions, the Division performed superbly. Certain units especially stood out: the engineers, artillery and rear guard. And certain individuals, among them Major Heike, demonstrated exceptional loyalty, tenacity, and willingness not only to the very end but actually, beyond the call of duty.

While it is true that in the very end some collapse began to develop, this is attributable to difficult terrain, the fact that various units became intermingled, and some confusion arose when contact was established with the western allies who then began to issue their own orders. Under such conditions, chaos is something which cannot be avoided and, as a matter of fact, must be expected. But the fact that the Division's soldiers were disarmed by the western allied troops prior to entering the prisoner-of-war compounds illustrates that amongst the confusion panic did not occur, and the Division maintained its high level of professionalism.

But as always is the case, in combat there is a price to pay. And Austria was no exception. During the time the Division was in Austria, no less than 1,500 men were killed-in-action.[2] Among the fallen were such: Ukrainian battalion commanders Lt. Colonel's Kuchta and Podlesch,[3] and Lt. Mykola Nedzveds'kyi, a OUN activist and UPA soldier who enlisted under the alias of "Mykola Hrin" and who, prior to his entry into the Division, fought both Nazi Germany and Communist Russia. A number of soldiers were also wounded, amongst them regimental commanders Dern and Pannier. In turn, their commands were assumed by two well-liked and respected battalion commanders: Wildner (who assumed command of the 1st Regiment), and Wittenmeyer (who assumed command of the 3rd Regiment).

Chapter 27: An Assessment of the Division in Austria

Despite its losses, the Division held. And although it was forced to surrender and lay down its colors, it did so honorably. In the brief period of its existence (1943-1945), the Division's soldiers served faithfully. Despite severe hardships, few succumbed to defeat, and the Division's soldiers never faltered. But most importantly, through military service and self-sacrifice, they demonstrated – as previously did the members of the old Galician "Halyts'ka Armiia" of the early 1900s – military pride, devotion to duty, and immense respect for one another as well as to their homeland.

28

Die Ordnungspolizei
(The Order Police)

Prior to the commencement of World War II, some elements of the German police were organized along the lines of the Regular (Wehrmacht) Army.[1] Usually in company strength and motorized, this police formation was known as the Ordnungspolizei – Order Police.

The mission of the Ordnungspolizei was to serve as a mobile reserve for the local and regional police and constables found within Germany's cities and outlying areas. As was the case of the other police forces, the order police was also subordinated to the SS.

In general, the men who entered and served in such companies were often older than those found in the army. However, high physical and mental standards were still required for entry, and were maintained during service. This was deemed necessary because of the anticipation that in the event of hostilities, personnel might be committed into areas of combat.

The first time the order police units were utilized was in the fall of 1939. Although they did not serve in Poland proper in the blitzkrieg of 1939, the order police were posted into Western Germany (in anticipation of a possible British-French attack), for defensive purposes and to evacuate civilians and refugees adjacent to France and Belgium if the need arose. But in the following year during Operation "Yellow" (the German code-name for the offensive against the west), Ordnungspolizei companies ensured that civilians did not obstruct roads required for vehicular traffic, conducted civilian and prisoner-of-war (P.O.W.) evacuation operations, and guarded key intersections, bridges and communications. Because the 1940 blitzkrieg was rapid and the campaign short-lived, the order police saw minimal combat.

A typical battalion was organized into a headquarters unit and four-line companies. Armed with the standard handguns, rifles, machine-guns, and PAK anti-tank guns found in any regular army battalion, such units averaged a strength at approximately 550-600 men. As well, all of these battalions were fully motorized.

But in September-October 1939, the first of a number of major reorganizations took place within the Ordnungspolizei. A number of the independent companies were merged into battalions while the fully mechanized battalions were organized numerically and the first nine battalions were merged into three regiments. Each regiment contained three battalions. Because these regiments were fully motorized, they were soon thereafter incorporated into the newly-created 4th Waffen-SS "Police" Division. With the incorporation of these three regiments into a regular division, the rest of the ordnungs-polizei units remained either in company or battalion strength.

Shortly after the commencement of Operation "Barbarossa," an urgent need arose for additional manpower. By the end of December 1941, most of the independent Ordnungspolizei battalions were rushed to the eastern front. Committed primarily to the front west and southwest of Moscow, the independent battalions (well clothed and equipped for winter warfare), played a major role in containing and halting Zhukov's counter offensive. With the re-establization of the eastern front, the battalions were utilized for security, convoy, and anti-guerrilla operations. Of importance to note is that during this time, none of the ordnungspolizei units were ever employed for either concentration camp or extermination duties.[2]

Although the first three previously established regiments were disbanded, combat demands forced the ordnungspolizei to expand itself. In July 1942, a total of 25 ordnungspolizei regiments were ordered to be raised.[3] Numbered 1, 4 through 27, these regiments were formed in Berlin, Southern and Central Russia, France, Serbia, Croatia, Czechoslovakia, Norway, Bavaria, and in Hamburg, Germany. No reason is officially cited as to why the 2nd and 3rd regiments were not raised in July 1942, but regardless, on October 1942, the 2nd and 3rd were also reconstituted in Wandern, Germany.

By the time the "Galicia" Division was raised, in mid-1943, a number of the police order regiments were disbanded as its personnel were incorporated into various Waffen-SS divisions or training areas. Because the personnel strengths of the original 4th and 5th regiments (previously raised in France and Serbia), and the 6th (raised in Southern Russia in a combat zone), and the 7th (raised in Norway) were all disbanded, the regiments now existed only on paper. Seeking a way to reconstitute manpower into the non-existent regiments, the Germans temporarily placed a number of the Galician volunteers, who had volunteered exclusively for the Division, into the 4th, 5th, 6th and 7th regiments.

In July 1943, the 4th and 5th Regiments were re-activated in Poland; the following month the 6th was re-activated in Southern France; and the 7th was re-activated in Paris, France.

By the time Galicia's volunteers entered them, the majority of the regiments lacked transport and therefore, were not fully motorized. Although the regiments were officially under police control, for the greater part the regimental leaders and cadre personnel did not regard themselves as "policemen" but rather, as soldiers. In lieu of the fact that many of the cadre personnel had experienced front-line action as well as combat against insurgents, while some had actually served in either the regular army or Waffen-SS prior to reassignment to an ordnungspolizei regiment, they were more than correct in their assertion that they were soldiers and not policemen. In the pure military sense, the ordnungspolizei was simply an extension of the regular army – whether Wehrmacht or Waffen-SS.

By January 1944, the 6th and 7th Galician Regiments were disbanded. During this same period, the 4th and 5th Galician Regiments were in the process of disbandment; by June 1944, they ceased to exist. Following this, the regiments were never again re-activated, and no other additional Ukrainian personnel, either meant for the Division or any other formation, ever again entered the Ordnungspolizei.

In the following pages, the short-lived experiences of Galicia's volunteers, as well as the role of the Galician Military Board in relation to the Ordnungspolizei, is revealed.

The Division's Volunteer Regiments:[1]
Despite the fact that the initial volunteer figure of approximately 80,000 fell tremendously, in the initial period of recruitment, it became impossible to take all who did want to enter the Division to Heidelager for recruit training. Therefore, in order to prevent a possible manpower loss, and to save training time, a way had to be found to organize and commence training (even if just on a rudimentary level), prior to placement into the Replacement Army's recruit training center.

Although Himmler himself opposed the placement of Galician volunteers into a police unit by stipulating that the Division was to be "a front-line [combat] infantry division,"[2] by the end of June 1943, it became evident that Himmler's directives could not be fully carried out. In response to the situation, on 24 June 1943, a "Schnellbrief" (Urgent or Quick brief) directive from the Field-Command Post ordered the creation of five independent police regiments.[3] Although from the outset Himmler planned to incorporate the regiments' personnel into the Division, for the moment, the ordnungspolizei regiments did play a historical role within the Division. Himmler's order specified:

> 1) I order that 12,000 Galician volunteers be transferred to form five Police-Rifle Regiments;[4]
>
> 2) The commander of the "Ordnungspolizei" will disband one SS Police Regiment. Its personnel shall be distributed amongst the other Police Regiments and will be utilized as staff (cadre).[5] 500 German officers and NCO's will be posted within each of the police rifle regiments;[6]
>
> 3) The Higher SS and police Führer of the Ukraine will provide arms for the first five regiments;[7]
>
> 4) The commanding officer of the Ordnungspolizei will supply arms for one of the regiments;[8]
>
> 5) The commander of the SS-Fuhrungshauptamtes (SS-Headquarters) will also supply such arms – rifles and machine guns for three of the regiments;
>
> 6) For psychological and political reasons, the regiments numbered 4-8[9] will be titled "Galician SS Volunteer Regiment;"[10]
>
> 7) A formation order for the 5 regiments is also enclosed.

Signed: Himmler

Although the order of 24 June 1943 laid the foundation for the establishment of five independent regiments, it was not explicit in its guidance. To avoid confusion, and to establish a more precise plan of action with regard to the regiments, a series of additional orders followed and actually continued until the regiments were totally disbanded.

Of importance to note is how under directive number 6, Himmler explicitly ordered that for "psychological and political reasons" regiments 4-8 would be titled as "Galizische SS-Freiwillegen Regiments" rather than "SS-Polizei (Schuetzen) Regiments."

Himmler's decision was based on such factors: he was fully aware that among the Ukrainians, there was much open resentment and, on occasion, open hostility was directed against the Nazi police; Himmler feared that any "police" titles would further fuel the arguments presented by those Ukrainians, who opposed the creation of the "Galicia" Division by citing the authorities are claiming they are recruiting manpower for a conventional army force but, in actuality, once recruited, the recruited males are entering not an army unit but rather, a police unit; it could drive more Ukrainians into the UPA; and Galicia's leaders who were supportive of raising the Division would not only oppose the placement of its youth into the police but in the end, could possibly change their minds and side with those who opposed the Division.

Therefore, despite the fact that for the moment some of Galicia's volunteers recruited for the Division would be temporarily placed into the Ordnungspolizei, from the outset Himmler demanded that the Ordnungspolizei conform its training as close as possible to the training provided by, and for, a regular army unit.[11] As for allegations that the "Galician" Police Regiments were formed into a Waffen-SS Division,[12] this is incorrect. At no time were the four independent Galician ordnungspolizei regiments ever utilized as a base, or inner core, for the formation of the Division. Months before its personnel were even disbanded and incorporated into the Division, the Division was already organized and was developing a solid Galician-Ukrainian leadership core. Excluding the Ukrainian chaplains (most of whom held the rank of captain); a very limited number of Ukrainians appointed in due time to low-ranking leadership positions; and the one or two German-speaking Ukrainian liaison officers who were posted from the Division itself into a regiment prior to its disbandment in order to assist its Ukrainian personnel in their transfer to either Heidelager or Neuhammer, within Ordnungspolizei regiments 4-7, the overwhelming majority of the German officers, NCOs, and support cadre personnel were German.[13]

4th Volunteer Regiment:
On 5 July 1943, an order was issued from Berlin's Ordnungspolizei.[1] Clearer in its guidance than most of the previous orders, it specified that the 4th Regiment[2] was to be based in France, in the Alsace region, and the regiments' units were to be posted to the following:[3]

> Regimental staff: Saaralben;
> 1st Battalion: Saaralben;
> 2nd Battalion: Bergzabern;
> 3rd Battalion: to be posted in the Luftwaffe barracks in Ferschweiler adjacent to the city of Trier.

SS-Sturmbannführer Binz was designated as Regimental commander. According to an unpublished account written by Yuriy Krokhmaliuk, the 4th Regiment's strength stood at approximately 2,000.[4] This figure is also substantiated by Liubomyr Makarushka, following a personal visit to the regiment in late November and early December 1943.[5] But there are strength discrepancies – according to Roman

Krokhmaliuk, the 4th Regiments strength stood at 1,264 soldiers,[6] a figure substantiated by others.

Regardless of the discrepancies or changes, on 20 July 1943, a 12 page Berlin "quickbrief" was issued to many Higher SS and Police leaders throughout Europe.[7] Although this directive covered many units and areas, regarding the newly forming 4th Galician regiment, the 20 July directive provided some specific guidance.

In regard to the 4th Regiment, the directive stated that the regiment would be organized in such a fashion with such post numbers:

Regimental Staff: Nr. 51;
Communications Company: Nr. 14b;
Engineer Platoon: Nr. 32;
1st Battalion (1st-4th Co's) Nr. 38;
2nd Battalion (5th-7th Co's) Nr. 38;
3rd Battalion (9th-11th Co's) Nr. 38.

As for the battalion staffs, each staff was under Nr. 37 and the 1st Battalion's Heavy 4th Company was under Nr. 36a.

In regard to the regiment's placement, the quickbrief specified more specific locations for the regiment. These were:

Regimental Staff: Nickolauskaserne in Zabern;
1st Battalion: Schlobkaserne in Zabern;
2nd Battalion: Marokkanerkaserne in Saaralben;
3rd Battalion: Luftwaffenbarackenlager Ferschweiler b. Trier.[8]

The 20 July directive also specified that SS-Sturmbannführer Binz, who commanded the 24th Ordnungspolizei's Regiments 3rd Battalion, would command the 4th Regiment. As for the regiment's cadre, the officers were to be secured from Oranienburg's Police Training Battalion, while the NCOs and soldiers were provided by the 8th Ordnungspolizei's 3rd Battalion. Undoubtedly, both the 24th and 8th regiments were selected because Berlin reasoned that the 24th, raised initially in Lviv in July 1942, and the 8th, formed that same month in Russia proper, were composed of personnel who were more aware of and sympathetic to the needs of an eastern European element.

On 29 September 1943, a Berlin directive was addressed to all of the regiments.[9] It specified that when a regiment is to be trained, the assigned German training personnel will be utilized in full strength. The directive also stipulated that an entire regiment's staff and communications company personnel would not only remain in place but as well, would soon be reinforced.[10]

Clearly, this directive revealed that although the recruits were dispatched two months earlier to be trained, training and other problems still existed not only within the 4th but likewise, within regiments 5 through 7.

In regard to the quality of training the 4th Regiment conducted, there are indications that it did not meet the standards set by the 6th Regiment, nor did it equal that received by Galicia's volunteers in Heidelager or especially at Neuhammer. In a personal discussion with former Divisional officer Yuriy Krokhmaliuk, the latter acknowledged that a couple of the regiments in France did not conduct training satisfactory to the needs of a front-line unit.

Ultimately, the standards an Ordnungspolizei regiment established were determined by its commander. If a regiment was located in a relatively safe and quiet European environment (such as Southern France), versus a unit (such as the 6th) which was much closer to the eastern front with largely an eastern front cadre, then it appears that Krokhmaliuk's observations are more than correct that training in safer areas was not always up to par and during periods of time "the men did absolutely nothing!"[11]

In an effort to access, and to see what could be done if necessary to rectify a situation, Galicia's Military Board decided to conduct personal visits to the regiments.

Prior to the departure of any of its members to France, Galicia's Military Board, along with Wachter, strongly opposed the incorporation of any Ukrainian personnel into the Ordnungspolizei. This protest actually started the moment letters written by volunteers revealed that they were not dispatched to military bases but rather, were dispatched to police training sites. In some cases, letters from France revealed unsatisfactory training, as well as the volunteers' exposure to inefficient and unsympathetic cadre personnel who disillusioned the recruits.[12]

In response to Wachter's and Bisanz's demands for better training and for the personnel dispatched to the Ordnungspolizei to be immediately transferred to Heidelager, Berlin replied that for the moment, it could not enact any transfers. Although the Nazi command acknowledged that Himmler himself had decreed earlier that the volunteers were to be placed strictly into a division designated for front-line combat, Berlin cited recent heavy winter and spring front-line losses, and the critical need to replenish the losses. As a result, by the time Galicia's volunteers stepped in, the army training areas were filled up. Though Heidelager was able to accommodate many of Galicia's recruits, it was immediately clear that others could not be accepted. In an effort not to lose training time and manpower,

Chapter 28: Die Ordnungspolizei (The Order Police)

on 24 June 1944, Himmler ordered the Ordnungspolizei to accept some of Galicia's volunteers. Once within a regiment, basic or rudimentary training would be provided until room was made to move the recruits from an Ordnungspolizei regiment into a regular army training site.

Officially, the Galician Military Boards visits were undertaken for morale purposes, and to reassure the volunteers that they were regarded as equal peers with those dispatched to Heidelager. Unofficially, however, the visits were undertaken to view the living conditions and to obtain first-hand information about the training.

According to a former regimental chaplain, Chaplain Danylo Kovaliuk, the regiment's personnel were visited by Yuriy and Roman Krokhmaliuk, Makarushka, and Galicia's Governor, Dr. Otto Wachter.[13] Kovaliuk does not cite an exact date as to when this occurred, but according to Roman Krokhmaliuk, the 4th Regiment was visited on approximately 28 November 1943 by Myhailo Khronoviat, a former Galician military officer and now, a civilian official within Galicia's Military Board.[14] And Yuriy Krokhmaliuk, along with Vasyl Laba, the Division's Chief Chaplain visited all of the regiments in both the fall and spring of 1943-44. Along with some entertainment and musical groups also brought in from Galicia – these visits did improve morale.

On 23 December 1943, Berlin ordered the Ordnungspolizei to deliver 2,000 Galicians from the various regiments to Heidelager's troop training site.[15] Although there was no specific guidance to the 4th Regiment, the order stated that the 6th and 7th, along with a reserve battalion, were to give up a specified number of personnel, and the 5th was to dispatch its chaplain to Heidelager. But the order of 23 December made it clear that finally, the very unfortunate Ukrainian role with the Ordnungspolizei regiments was at last beginning to end.

How much of an influence Wachter, Bisanz, and the Galician Military Board, as well as the Ukrainian Central Committee – exerted through their constant protest is not – and never will – be known. But because by late October, November and early December 1943 Heidelager's recruits were concluding their training and entering other stages of advanced specialist, NCO, or officer training, it was now possible to move more personnel into Heidelager.

Unfortunately for the 4th Regiments personnel, on 25 January 1944, Berlin directed Stuttgart's and Nimwegen's ordnungspolizei that they were to immediately prepare the transfer of the 4th Regiments 3rd Battalion.[16] Because the order also informed Stuttgart's Ordnungspolizei that it was to inform Berlin on how this would transpire, it appears Stuttgart's Ordnungspolizei was placed in charge with this responsibility.

Sensing that the regiment might possibly be deployed for eastern front combat, on 3 February 1944, Stuttgart's Ordnungspolizei's main headquarters informed Berlin's Ordnungspolizei that the 4th was not, at the immediate moment, prepared to be inserted and employed for combat.[17] This telegraphic message was dispatched in response to Berlin's previous directives regarding the 4th Regiment's march and tactical employment.

Titled "Secret/Confidential," the telegram cited a considerable amount of materiel shortages. Such shortages were especially cited: communications equipment, clothing, uniform patches, medical supplies along with medical field packs, rucksacks, vehicles (such as trucks) and trained drivers, fuel canisters; horses were identified as being in poor condition; saddle and animal covers were also identified as lacking and it was projected the regiment would not receive these items for at least another two-three weeks, and so forth.

But in addition to materiel shortages, Stuttgart's telegram revealed the shocking news that many of the men were still untrained. To stress the seriousness of the matter, the message disclosed that 120 "new [frequently acquired] recruits still need to undergo training."[18]

On 9 February 1944, another urgent Berlin directive was addressed to the Ordnungspolizei in Stuttgart, Danzig, Nimwegen, and Cracow.[19] Signed by an official named Becker, this directive stated that Himmler had ordered the entire transfers of both the 4th and 5th Regiments. Although five directives were included in this order, it is of historical significance that the directive removed the regiments from Stuttgart's, Danzig's, and Nimwegen's Ordnungspolizei control and placed them under Cracow's control. Regarding the regiments' transfer, Cracow would control the time and places of movement. Berlin's directive also informed Cracow to keep Berlin posted on all immediate movements. In regard to the regiment's transfer movements, as usually was the case, Berlin provided no specifics and left this matter to the regional Ordnungspolizei headquarters.

But three days later, on 12 February, Berlin's Ordnungspolizei issued another "quickbrief" directive to various Ordnungspolizei centers.[20] Though titled "Reference: the Disbandment of the Galician SS Free Volunteer Battalion in Heidenheim," (Silesia), the same directive covered other (non-Galician) units; however, in regards to the Ordnungspolizei's Galician units, the directive also ordered the disbandment of the entire 4th and 5th Regiments in France and Poland, including the Reserve Battalion in Tarbes, France. While the order of 12 February 1944 did not dissolve the 4th or 5th Regiment, it did specify that the regiment's days were numbered in France and Poland.

Chapter 28: Die Ordnungspolizei (The Order Police)

What is interesting about the 25 January; 9 and 12 February 1944 directives is that there is no mention of any transfer to Heidelager. But two days later, on 14 February 1944, another secret directive was dispatched from Himmler's field command post to Wachter.[21] The directive informed Galicia's governor that two of the 4th Regiment's battalions were to be directed to Lemberg (Lviv), and that Lemberg's SS would determine exactly where the battalions where to be posted.

In the concluding days of February, the entire 4th Regiment (and not just two battalions), was transferred eastward. Whether this was done on the initiative of the Military Board which previously had been requesting a regimental-sized unit to be utilized for security purposes against the ever-increasing communist-inserted (primarily Soviet) guerrillas and specialized saboteurs, or because of front-line needs will never be known, but by the end of February 1944, the 4th Regiment was in position in Galicia.[22]

Prior to the regiment's transfer, there were German fears that the regiment's personnel would flee into the ranks of the UPA; these fears, however, soon proved groundless as the regiment re-entered Galicia. While some contact was made with the UPA, no serious defections were noted.[23]

At the outset of March 1944, the 4th Regiment, still commanded by Binz, was displaced by battalion-sized units into such areas:

Regimental Headquarters – Zolochiv (approximately 40 miles east of Lviv and 23 miles Southwest of Brody);

1st Battalion – with its headquarters at Radekhiv, the battalion was located in the Radechiv-Lopatyn area (approximately 40 miles northeast of Lviv and 25 miles northwest of Brody;

2nd Battalion – with its headquarters at Koniushkiv, about 3 miles north of Brody), the battalion was displaced in the Koniushkiv-Berlin area;

3rd Battalion – with its headquarters at Zbarazh southeast of Brody, the battalion was displaced in the area of Zbarazh.[24]

Near-by Zolochiv was the town of Strutyn which held the regiment's anti-tank company.

All three battalions were located close to the front. As to why this occurred, no official reason is cited; however, this was undoubtedly undertaken to reinforce the front in anticipation of an upcoming Soviet offensive.

On 2 March 1944, Field-Marshal Manstein accurately predicted that the Soviets would launch an offensive to cut the Lviv-Odessa railway line east of Ternopil.

This offensive would also be undertaken to place the Soviets closer to the Galician capital city of Lviv prior to the spring thaw.

On 5 March, Soviet guerrillas struck the town of Zbarazh, located approximately 12 miles northeast of Ternopil. Undoubtedly, this guerrilla attack was coordinated by the Soviet 1st Ukrainian Front to support an offensive in Ternopil's vicinity, which had begun on the previous day of 4 March.

Although Zbarazh was defended by the 4th Regiment's 3rd Battalion, the battalion offered a very weak resistance.[25] Rushing into the town, the Soviet guerrillas quickly secured it. Prior to this attack, Divisional staff officer Yuriy Krokhmaliuk (who at this time was also a member of the Military Board), arrived to meet with the battalion's personnel. But Krokhmaliuk's stay was very short. Under grave danger from incoming guerrilla fire, Krokhmaliuk, along with a number of other 3rd Battalion staff and line personnel, quickly boarded a moving train in Zbarazh's railway and succeeded in escaping to Ternopil.

Although Yuriy's brother Roman cites in his book "that Zbarazh fell after a short battle to communist guerrillas,"[26] realistically speaking, there was no "short battle." The truth of the matter is that the Ukrainian defense collapsed rapidly. And unlike further to the northwest where an element from Kampfgruppe "Beyersdorff" had been ambushed but then reacted swiftly and effectively to counter a sizable Soviet guerrilla force and, in the process, succeeded in repulsing and inflicting a heavy loss upon the guerrillas, none of this happened at Zbarazh. At Zbarazh, the battalion was quickly routed. Those who were not immediately killed or captured scattered in various directions. In the following days, straggler control picked up a number of its personnel, however, some of the men who hailed from the region, returned to their homes.[27] Undoubtedly, they were overcome with shame and disgust by their poor performance.

Some have alleged that when the Soviet guerrillas struck, they struck in superior strength. Undoubtedly, this is true. And the Soviets surely had a thorough knowledge of the lay of the town. But it must be taken into consideration that the battalion, which had arrived at least four or five days earlier, could have – and actually should have – within just one or two days, organized a sufficient defense to not only repulse an insurgent force but indeed, a conventional attack. And if one also takes into consideration that following the guerrilla attack no immediate and concentrated counterattack was undertaken by either the 3rd Battalion's or 4th Regiment's headquarters to retake the town, and that on the eastern front numerous instances occurred were superior sized Soviet guerrilla units were repulsed by smaller – but ably lead – forces, and instances also arose were first-rate units (such as demonstrated in Slovakia by Kampfgruppe "Wildner" which never fought defensively but always offensively) succeeded in repulsing numerically superior forces in well-fortified positions, than obviously, it is clear that serious problems continued to exist within the 4th Regiment. So the question remains: what went wrong?

As is always the case when such a military disaster occurs, a number of factors may be identified. To begin with, communication equipment shortages, such as cited in the 3 February 1944 dispatch to Berlin's main Ordnungspolizei headquarters, played a role in establishing poor communications. Inadequate intelligence, coupled with weak and ineffective outlying observation and warning posts, as well as equipment shortages, also played a factor. But most importantly, the lack of solid training (in some cases no training whatsoever), in addition to a weak and ineffective German officer and NCO corps, were the primary contributing factors in the swift and sudden disaster. Months later, this was evidenced by an account written by one of the 4th Regiments survivors – grenadier Vasil Petrovskyi.[28]

From the manner in which Petrovskyi's account was written, it appears that a report was requested by higher command. In turn, this report was probably submitted to either the Division's intelligence or some investigative personnel (or possibly both), who wanted to determine as best as possible what had occurred within the 4th Regiment during the days of February-March 1944. In submitting his report, Petrovskyi gave a somewhat detailed view of his background and of the events leading to his service in the Ternopil vicinity.

Born on 28 September 1920 in Yamnitz, Stanislav district, Petrovskyi was a law student in his fourth year in Lviv when, on 29 July 1943, he enlisted into the SS Division "Galicia." Shortly afterward, he was dispatched to the Ferschweiler Barracks in Trier's vicinity for recruit and NCO training, where he remained until 15 January 1944. Afterwards, he was dispatched to Mastricht, Holland, for further training. But because his regiment was ordered eastward, Petrovskyi was not there very long. Sometime in the first half of February 1944, Petrovskyi was transferred to Zbarazh, Galicia. Posted to the 10th Company he served within the 3rd Battalion, 4th Volunteer Regiment.

After a stay of approximately three or four days in Zbarazh, Petrovskyi's company entered what he termed as a "resistance point" at Dobrovogi, located in the vicinity of Zbarazh, where frequent encounters with guerrillas occurred.

On 28-29 February, two platoons from the 10th Company, and one platoon from the 9th, along with a "panzer one" (undoubtedly either a German tank or a command vehicle of some type), traveled to Lopushna, a village located within Volyn and described by Petrovskyi as "Hell!" Soviet armor was encountered and casualties were heavy; one squad alone (from an unidentified platoon and company), lost 6 soldiers. Petrovskyi claimed the men had no anti-armor weaponry with which to engage the advancing enemy armor. A retreat ensued to Zbarazh. Arriving to Zbarazh on 1 March 1944 at approximately 10 o'clock (Petrovskyi does not cite whether a.m. or p.m. but undoubtedly, he utilized military time and because it is known the guerrillas struck in the late morning it appears 10 a.m. is the correct time), within minutes of his arrival, Zbarazh conducted a military evacuation.[29]

According to Petrovskyi, this occurred "when the German officers [leaders] deserted us and departed for Ternopil."[30] It appears that Petrovskyi's German company commander also fled because, Petrovskyi states "company command was taken over by a German. However, he was not interested [in his newly appointed command]." Petrovskyi described the men (undoubtedly those within his company) as "exhausted" but most importantly that "there was no organized defense."[31] Continuing on, Petrovskyi wrote:

"On the morning of 2 March [1944], communist tanks resumed their advance. Everything scattered. I travelled on a horse to Ternopil. After about two days, the boys from the [various] companies gathered in Ternopil. We were designated to defend the northeastern edge of the town facing Brody. On 16-17 March, we were surrounded within a pocket with approximately 4,500 others. But prior to complete encirclement, Ternopil's staff left for Zolochiv. Although I was now a part of that staff, I, along with the others, remained in Ternopil. In Ternopil, I was slightly wounded. Seeking a way to avoid capture, I sought the help of a woman who provided me some civilian clothing. This saved me from captivity [when Ternopil fell to the Soviets].

At first, I decided to lay low and remain in Ternopil prior to attempting to cross the front. But my efforts proved unproductive when, on 21 April, I was ordered to appear for induction into the Soviet Army. That same day I and the other inductees were taken to the village of Bila Tserkva. [White Church].

Upon arrival to Bila Tserkva, I was immediately handed over to the NKVD police. I managed to avoid an arrest by 'lying my way out.' But prior to totally releasing me, the NKVD major proposed that I serve as a [informer] agent within the Soviet army. In an attempt to save myself, I accepted.

But once within the army, I was approached by UPA agents who were operating within the Soviet army.[32] A plan was established to enable me and some of the others to escape on 15 July. But because suddenly on 9 July we were dispatched towards Latvia, the escape plan was foiled.

Following a lengthy trip, I found myself on the Latvian front in the vicinity of Bauska, not far from Riga where I was posted to the 7th "Heroic" Platoon. This platoon was within a penal battalion found within the 43rd Rifle Division, 1st Baltic Front.[33] But during an advance, I and approximately 50 others surrendered to some Latvian troops fighting on the German side. While in captivity, I revealed my true identity to a Latvian intelligence officer. Shortly afterwards, I left Latvia's capital city of Riga aboard a vessel bound for Danzig. [Gdansk]. From Danzig, I travelled through these German cities: Westfalia, Munster, and Unna in the vicinity of Dortmund to an SS Replacement Battalion where I stayed for two months. But a transport bound [for Slovakia dropped me off at the Divisions Divisional headquarters' in Zilina. Along with me these men served in the Soviet Army on the front: Myron Lyshko, who hailed from Truskavtsia and who was wounded; a "Posharniuk;" Dovhan from Stanislaviv; and "Soia" who hailed from Krekhivetz' in the vicinity of Stanislaviv."

A simple review of Petrovskyi's report, which was submitted on 9 January 1945 in Zilina, reveals training of questionable quality, inept leadership, a lack of critical weapons, frequent confusion (undoubtedly attributable to a lack of proper communication equipment and inept personnel), and military shortages. The fact that a number of the 4th Regiment's personnel were fed piecemeal into combat also reveals the regiment lacked the military expertise to engage Soviet forces in entirety.

It was also during this period that a very ugly matter arose which ultimately, also lowered morale and helped to create a further rift between the Ukrainians and their leadership, which was primarily German.

Instead of rationally analyzing why the 4th's performance was so poor, the Germans began to seek scapegoats. In an effort to place the blame on someone, Ukrainian "cowardice" was cited. And to set an example of what would happen to a "coward" and through fear possibly instill a "fighting spirit," an execution was ordered. This execution, which was to take place in the town of Kamianets-Buzhs'kiy in the beginning of March 1944, is mentioned in the memoirs of Chaplain Kovaliuk as he described some of the ordeals of the 4th Regiment's chaplain, Reverend Osyp Karpins'kyi.[34]

Realistically speaking, on a modern-day battlefield, there is no such thing as "cowardice." To begin with, had the individual been a "coward," he would have never volunteered for the Division in the first place, or, if he had, he would have found some way to avoid service as did thousands of others when the time came to depart. But now, on the eastern front, this individual, inadequately trained, armed and equipped, with inadequate German leadership which, furthermore, had fled at the first opportune moment, could not under no circumstances be faulted for "cowardice."

The night before the soldier was to be executed, Chaplain Karpins'kyi offered him the last rites. But on the following morning, when the Nazi execution detail opened the door of the doomed soldier's cell, they only saw that it was empty. Because now again a scapegoat was needed to be held responsible, the 4th Regiment's Chaplain, Chaplain Karpins'kyi, was fingered as the individual who had engineered the escape.

Despite the pressures imposed by the newly appointed regimental commander, SS-Sturmbannführer Klein, and a host of other German commanders to court-martial and punish Chaplain Karpins'kyi, they failed to do so. Through the intervention of Wachter, Colonel Bisanz, and the Galician Military Board, the punishment, and what even appeared to be an attempt to execute Chaplain Karpins'kyi, failed. The fact that the regiment was also in the process of being disbanded undoubtedly also assisted the chaplain. But not to be outdone, and to have the final say, in the end the Germans – although failing in their effort to have the Chaplain court-martialed and possibly executed – released Chaplain Karpins'kyi from service.

Chaplain Karpins'kyi, who from the outset served as the 4th's Regimental chaplain, endured much hardship throughout his entire service within the 4th Regiment. Unlike some of the other chaplains who were posted to regiments commanded by sympathetic and cooperative German commanders, Chaplain Karpins'kyi had the misfortune to serve under commanders who were totally unresponsive and unsympathetic to his, and the other Ukrainian volunteer's, needs. As always is the case in any army unit when its personnel are exposed to consistently brutal treatment, it ultimately takes its toll – both physically and emotionally. Shortly after returning to Vienna, Reverend Karpins'kyi succumbed to a nervous breakdown and passed away.

Initially buried in Vienna, Chaplain Karpins'kyi's remains were transferred and interned in the 1950s in the Divisional cemetery located in Feldbach, Austria. Despite a somewhat uneventful demise, Chaplain Karpins'kyi has justifiably gone down as a true soldier who, in the face of numerous hardships, bravely endured many of the Division's ordeals.

On 22 April 1944, a classified order was issued by Berlin's Ordnungspolizei to Cracow's Ordnungspolizei which ordered the transfer of the entire 4th Regiment to the Neuhammer training site.[35] This order was issued personally by Himmler who wanted the regiment's survivors to undergo a period of solid training. And five days later, on 27 April, a Berlin telegraphic directive ordered that this be done immediately.[36]

Chapter 28: Die Ordnungspolizei (The Order Police)

Despite these two directives, for some unknown reasons an immediate transfer did not take place. By now, the regiment had somewhat recuperated, but it was never again committed to any combat activities. Most of April and May was spent in rest and reformation. But on 9 June 1944, a more detailed "quickbrief" was issued which provided more specifics.[37] The 9 June directive ordered the 4th and 5th Regiments to be disbanded in entirety; its personnel were to be delivered to the Division. Of special interest to note is that both regiments were no longer to be within the Ordnungspolizei.

The 9 June directive may be cited as the date when the 4th Regiment ceased to be a part of the Ordnungspolizei. Who, if anyone, had administrative control of the regiment past 9 June is not known. Regardless, as the men prepared to disembark to Neuhammer, on 17 June, another directive arrived from Berlin.[38] Titled "Transfer of the Galician SS Free Volunteer Regiments 4 and 5 to the Waffen-SS," the Berlin directive informed Cracow's Ordnungspolizei that the transfer of the 4th and 5th Regiments would be conducted SS-Obersturmbannführer Lechthaler. The order also specified that the regiment's foreign (Ukrainian) personnel were to be transferred to Neuhammer while the regiment's German leadership and staff personnel were to be disbanded and were to await further instructions. Upon arrival at Neuhammer, many of the 4th Regiment's Ukrainian soldiers were immediately placed into Neuhammer's recruit training prior to their entry into the Division; few, if any, saw combat at Brody.

Although the 4th Regiment's history was never an exemplary one, its personnel – upon the completion of solid training and placement amongst capable leadership – soon proved to be some of the Division's finest soldiers. In due time, a number even attained officer and NCO positions.[39]

5th Volunteer Regiment:
In an undated but very short Berlin directive of June 1943 titled "Organization of the 5th Galician SS Free Volunteer Regiment," various members of the Ordnungspolizei were informed that on Monday, 28 June 1943, at 9 a.m., a meeting would be held to determine how the regiment was to be organized.[1] Other than also revealing the meeting's location, no other information was provided.

But shortly afterwards, Berlin's directive of 5 July 1943 constituted the raising of regiments 4-8.[2] Although the directive was not totally specific in how this would occur, it was a little more detailed in regard to the 5th Regiment.

Regarding the 5th Regiment,[3] Berlin's order specified that it was to be formed in Poland, and its elements were to be based in these areas:

Regimental Staff – Lager der Ordn. Pol. in Aldershorst b/Gotenhafen;
1st Battalion – Gotenhafen;
2nd Battalion – Lager der Ordn. Pol. in Thorn;
3d Battalion – Umsiedlungslager Kaslin.

The order designated SS-Obersturmbannführer Lechtaler, a police commander, as regimental commander. As with the 4th Regiment, the 5th Regiment's[4] training and administrative cadre was to be provided by the disbanded 32nd German police Rifle Regiment's 1st Battalion.

On 20 July 1943, a Berlin directive addressed to several commanders, including Danzig's Ordnungspolizei's Headquarters, ordered the 5th Regiment to be dispatched to Gdansk (Danzig). The order's date stated 16 July 1943; however, it was not specific as to the locations.[5]

But that same day (20 July), a somewhat lengthy 12-page "quickbrief" was addressed to numerous Higher SS and Police leaders throughout Europe.[6] Signed by Winkelmann, the order covered many areas, and was addressed to various units – both Galician and non-Galician.[7]

In regard to the 5th Regiment, the 20 July directive revealed more details. To begin with, the directive specified that the 5th Regiment would be organized in the same manner as the 4th, and as with the latter, cadre personnel from the 32nd Police Rifle Regiment would be utilized. As previously with the 5 July directive, SS-Obersturmbannführer Lechtaler was identified as the regiment's commander.[8] Reverend Ivan Durbak was the regimental chaplain.[9]

Although the 5 July directive revealed where the regiment was to be posted, the 20 July directive also cited a location. But unlike the 5 July directive, the 20 July directive cited a slightly different location. According to the update "the regiment was to be posted within Prussia, Germany, in the Danzig vicinity, under Danzig's high command, in the following locations:

Regimental Staff – Lager der OP. in Adlershorst by Gotenhafen;
1st Battalion – Lager der OP. in Adlershorst by Gotenhafen;
2nd Battalion – Lager der OP. in Thorn;
3rd Battalion – Lager der OP. in Aldershorst b. Gotenhafen.

The directive also specified that a number of the 32nd Regiment's weapon specialists would be utilized. The 32nd's disbanded medical (sanitation) personnel, along with their medical supplies, would also be attached to the 5th Regiment.

Although the 32nd's staff would conduct the transport of the recruits, Lublin's 17th SS Police Regiment's 3rd Battalion would assist with the transport.

Because by this time the Ordnungspolizei had entirely ceased to be a fully mechanized force, horse transport would be utilized.[10] Thus, the directive also stated that a veterinary specialist (undisclosed) would be sent to Lemberg (Lviv) to see Dr. Magerl, a veterinarian located on 9 Balonova St. The two men would determine the needs of the veterinary unit. In regard to this, Winkelmann requested that he be informed as to what would be arranged.

Regarding pay, the 20 July directive stated that the regiment's recruits would receive the same amount of money which would be paid out to the German families. However, the money would be granted through specially designated bank accounts. The directive also addressed the unit's numerous needs, and listed the numbers of various different pieces of equipment (such as field kitchens, communication equipment, flare pistols, compasses, gas masks, shovels, wire cutters, axes, etc.), to be provided to the regimental staff and various battalions. In a number of cases, such as with the field kitchens, it appears that eight field kitchens would suffice. But in other areas, an examination of the lists reveals shortages did prevail.

In regard to small-arms weapons, the directive specified the 5th's 1st Battalion would receive the arms and equipment of the 32nd Police Rifle Regiments 1st Battalion. But for the regiment's 2nd and 3rd Battalions, as well as its engineer platoon, the 20 July directive specified the following:

	Engineer Platoon	2nd Bn		3rd Bn	
		Staff	5-7 Co's	Staff	9-11 Co's
Light MG 08/15[11]	3	–	36	–	36
Carbine (Karabiner a,k,p,t,y)[12]	30	71	396	71	396
P08 Pistols (Luger)	3	6	39	6	39
7.65mm pistols[13]	6	12	78	12	78
Submachine gun	4	2	48	2	48
Flare pistol[14]	2	2	18	2	18
Rifles 84/98	41	83	537	83	537

From the ammunition roster, one finds this issue:[15]

	Standard Issue Ammunition	Practice Ammunition
Machine Gun	2,000	1,000
Carbine	120	30
Machine Pistol	500	150
P08 Pistol	64	16
7.65mm Pistol	35	15
Flare Pistol	10	5
Hand grenades	1	1
Machine Gun	–	1,500
Carbine	–	20

While undoubtedly in due time more ammunition would be issued, a simple examination of pages 9 and 10 of the 20 July directive reveals serious materiel, arms, ammunition and support service shortages. Although efforts were undertaken to reduce shortages, and in some cases outdated (but effective) arms along with fake ammunition training rounds were issued to cover shortages, the fact remains that (unlike in Heidelager and especially at Neuhammer), shortages did occur. In the very end, these shortages played a major factor in hindering the regiment's training.

According to an unpublished account regarding the 5th Regiment, the regiment's 1st Battalion was formed from volunteers who received their call-up cards to report for the Division "Galicia" on 24 July 1943.[16] From various parts of Galicia, trains took the volunteers to Lviv; there, the recruits disembarked from their various trains and changed to one train.

The recruit's inquiries concerning "what is our destination?" were greeted with the reply: "Gottenhafen!" For many of them, "Gottenhafen" was an unknown place; a look at the maps brought along by several of the men revealed no such location. Since no further answers or details were provided, it was assumed that the men were bound for Germany proper. As it turned out, Gottenhafen was in Prussia.[17]

One thing in particular, however, somewhat unnerved the recruits – the fact that the German personnel wore the uniform of the Ordnungspolizei. Although of course at the time nothing could be done about it, apparently there was some dissatisfaction upon seeing these personnel. For reasons of efficiency, German-speaking recruits were singled out; then, the men were organized into groups of 40 and a German-speaking recruit was placed into each group.

Because Lviv's and Galicia's inhabitants supplied the recruits with sufficient foodstuffs, the train which carried them was amply supplied for a three-day journey. The train departed in the late evening hours of 24 July. Following a brief journey, the recruits arrived late one night at Gottenhafen, located on the Baltic Sea. Exiting the train, the men walked for about one-and-a-half miles to their training center. For the rest of the night and the entire following day, the recruits rested. But on the second day they were organized into squads, platoons, and companies. Uniforms were issued, and the men began to drill.

After two weeks of military drill, the 1st Battalion's 4th Company was dispatched to Danzig for further training.[18] There, for the next several weeks, continued military drills, along with the handling and firing of rifles, submachine guns, light arms, along with a considerable amount of night training and company sized maneuvers, were conducted. Throughout this entire time, Chaplain Durbak accompanied the recruits.

It is difficult to ascertain how thoroughly Berlin's main Ordnungspolizei viewed the training. But on 29 September 1943, a Berlin directive stipulated that all training undertaken by the-4th-6th Regiments would be conducted strictly by the assigned German training personnel. Possibly, this directive was issued in response to reports and complaints of inferior training. At approximately the same time the 4th Regiment was visited by Galician officials and members of the Military Board, the 5th, still in Gottenhafen, was visited by Colonel Bisanz and Governor Wachter. As in the case of the other regiments, this visit was undertaken to view first-hand the training, to raise morale, and to make contact with certain German officials to extract the 5th Regiment out of Gotenhafen to the Division proper. At this time, the 5th Regiment's strength stood at 1,372 personnel.[19] But this figure also encompassed the regiments' cadre personnel, which was strictly German.

On 23 December 1943, a Berlin directive ordered the various Ordnungspolizei regiments to give up 2,000 of the men to Heidelager's troop training center. Although this directive was addressed primarily to the 6th and 7th Regiments, the order provided explicit guidance that the 5th Regiment's chaplain, Ivan Durbak, was to be transferred to Heidelager.[20]

Shortly afterward, on 9 February 1944, another Berlin directive was issued.[21] Addressed to the Ordnungspolizei's Headquarters in Stuttgart, Danzig, Nimwegen and Cracow the directive, titled "Transfer of the Galician SS-Free Volunteer Regiments 4 and 5," stated that the 5th Regiment will no longer be under Danzig's command. As for the 4th, the directive stated that on Himmler's order, the 4th Regiment would be moved in entirety, its soldiers are to be notified of monetary changes, food supplies are to be provided to Cracow for feeding purposes, and that Cracow was to control the regiment's place of transfer and times of movement. Of essence is to note that the 9 February order was not specific, and Berlin requested to be kept posted as to the movement.

Three days later, on 12 February 1944, another Berlin directive, in "quickbrief" format, was issued in regard to a number of the Ordnungspolizei units.[22] In regard to the 5th, the Regiment was to be disbanded. But that same day, a telegram was dispatched from Danzig's Main Ordnungspolizei Headquarters to Berlin.[23] Titled "One's Readiness for Action of the Galician Free Volunteer Regiment 5," Danzig's high command identified critical shortages, and stated in short "the front-line effectiveness of the 5th Regiment cannot be expected any sooner than 15 March 1944." Among the problems identified were such: 90 unsuitable horses; veterinarians stated that the horses would not be expected to recuperate until the end of March; two more veterinarians, along with an additional dentist and one foreign doctor were needed; 20 soldiers to fill various critical specialty positions were also needed, as well as three additional German staff personnel and one communications officer. In addition to identifying the personnel shortages, equipment shortages were also cited such as communications gear, cooking utensils, wagons, and other related items.

To this day, it has never been properly explained why Danzig responded in the manner it did. Perhaps, Danzig's command obtained information from some unofficial source, or it feared that once control of the regiment was passed to Cracow's Ordnungspolizei, Cracow's command would dispatch it to the front line in Eastern Galicia as it was dispatching the 4th. In an attempt to possibly avert a disaster, Danzig notified Berlin.

Clearly, Danzig's urgent response revealed that (as with the 4th) the 5th Regiment was not combat ready. Danzig was honest in its admission: a lack of proper instructors, along with modern arms, ammunition, communication equipment and support service shortages had prevented Danzig from creating an elite force – even though it had control of the regiment for approximately eight months. Needless to say this did not go unnoticed by the Galician Military Board. Aside from the fact that no one in Galicia wanted the volunteers to be placed into the Ordnungspolizei in the first place, Galicia's Military Board was also not pleased with the Ordnungspolizei's training. Consequently, the Military Board constantly agitated Wachter and various other officials to have the regiment disbanded and its personnel transferred to an established military base.

As a result of Danzig's directive, the 5th Regiment remained in place. But on 23 April 1944, Berlin dispatched another directive.[24] Unlike the previous ones, which made no specific reference as to where the 5th Regiment was to be posted, the 23 April directive made it clear that the regiment was to be dispatched to the Neuhammer training site.

Chapter 28: Die Ordnungspolizei (The Order Police)

On 9 June 1944, Berlin issued another "quickbrief." Titled "Transfer of the Galician SS-Free Volunteer Regiments 4 and 5 in the Waffen-SS," Berlin's directive specified that the 5th Regiment is no longer within the Order Police. The directive, however, was not totally specific and itself stated that "further guidance will be provided."[25] Officially, 9 June 1944 is cited as the date the regiment was officially disbanded.[26]

But on 17 June 1944, another Berlin directive was issued.[27] Addressed to Cracow's command, the directive specified that the 5th Regiment was to be immediately transferred to Neuhammer.

With this directive, the regiment's personnel were transferred to Neuhammer. As for the regiment's non-Ukrainian cadre and administrative personnel, they were informed by the 17 June directive to await further orders.

In the latter part of June 1944, the disbanded 5th's personnel arrived at Neuhammer. At this time, the Division's Neuhammer personnel were departing for the eastern front. Because the regiment's personnel were not on par with those trained at Heidelager and Neuhammer, and a lack of time prevented the regiment to be incorporated into the Divisional units bound for the front, the former regiment's personnel were not deployed; instead, most were placed into recruit training, although some were dispatched to various NCO schools.

While in Prussia proper, the regiment's personnel only trained. When deployed for a very brief period to Kholm, the regiment only conducted security operations to protect itself and Kholm's Ukrainian citizens from intensified guerrilla activities. At no time did the regiment even conduct any sizable anti-guerrilla operations. Likewise, the regiment was never deployed further west to Poland's interior, nor was its personnel ever utilized as guards in any concentration or prisoner-of-war camps.[28]

6th Volunteer Regiment:

Prior to his entry into the Division, former Divisional soldier Myhailo Protsakevych served in the 6th Regiment. Because Protsakevych served with the 6th from its inception to its disbandment, his experiences are reminiscent of all those who served in the 6th.

On 23 July 1943, in a Peremysl railway station, many Galician Ukrainians bid their volunteers a joyous farewell. According to Protsakevych, the average volunteer was 21-years-old, he had no previous military or police service, and over half were high school graduates. Overwhelmingly, the men hailed from the region of Peremysl, Yaroslavshchyna, and the area northwest of Lviv. But of these, approximately 80 percent hailed from Yaroslavshchyna.

Following a one night stopover in Lviv, Protsakevych and approximately 500 others boarded a transport bound for a destination north of Lublin. After a three-day journey, the recruits arrived to a railway depot outside of Graewo without any difficulties. Upon disembarking from the train and stepping on the ground, each volunteer immediately entered a new world.

Berlin's directives of 24 June and 5 July 1943 officially constituted the re-establishment of the 6th Regiment.[1] But on 6 August 1943, an order was specifically issued in regards to the 6th.[2] It should be noted that at the time the 6 August order was issued, the 6th Regiment was already in the process of being formed. Regardless, the order officially specified a number of directives of which the most important were as such – the regiment was to be commanded by SS-Obersturmbannführer Kuhn, and was to be displaced into these areas in Northern Poland:

Regimental Headquarters and Staff – Nordkaserne;
1st Battalion – Sudaven (Barackenlager);
2nd Battalion – Wehrmacht Barackenlager Fichtenwalde b. Gumbinnen;
3rd Battalion – Wehrmacht Barackenlager Grajewo.[3]

The order also specified the following strengths would be maintained in these areas:

Sudauen:	700;
Fichtenwalde:	550;[4]
Grajewo:	550;
Total:	1,800[5]

Finally, Reverend Ivan Holoida, who hailed from the Carpathian Lemko region, was appointed as the regimental-chaplain.

Disembarking from the train, the volunteers were met by officers and non-commissioned officers in police uniforms. Immediately, Protsakevych, as well as the others, experienced a feeling of dissatisfaction, hopelessness and even outright anger for being dispatched to a police training center rather than an army base. After all, Protsakevych and the others had enlisted to serve in the army, and not in a police capacity.

As previously in Lviv, those who were proficient in German were asked to step forward. Afterward, the police company commanders began to form their own companies. In all, 10 companies, each with approximately 160 recruits, were formed. Protsekevych went into the 9th Company. Looking around, he noted most of the youths hailed from Peremysl. Marched to what prior to the war was a Polish cavalry post, the recruits were then assigned to their various barracks, which were spacious and comfortable with bunk beds. In the center of the barracks stood one building which served as a mess and lecture hall. Following a quick meal, military clothing was issued, the recruits were showered, disinfected for lice, and put to bed.

The next morning, the companies were re-organized into four platoons – 3 platoons of infantry with 1 support platoon. Once accomplished, SS-Hauptsturmführer Fischer introduced himself. Through a translator, Fischer also introduced his trainers, his assistant, SS-Untersturmführer Koch, and the company's 1st Sergeant. Fischer also informed the recruits that their 9th Company was a part of the 6th Regiment, and that their police uniforms would be immediately turned in for the field uniforms worn by the Waffen-SS. After all, as Fischer himself stated, "you are not policemen – but soldiers!" But when the recruits were issued Soviet arms, tremendous dissatisfaction was once again aroused.

Fischer was the epitome of a true professional. Along with his staff, he displayed a proper attitude toward the Ukrainian volunteers. He created an atmosphere of mutual respect. Although the recruits of the 9th Company trained hard, at no time were they ever abused, and the instructor's attitude was termed "fatherly." In order to establish mutual trust and form a bond, Fischer and his training cadre ate their meals in the mess hall together with the recruits. And at no time were any of the recruits ever designated for mess hall duties. Local civilians were utilized for cooking and cleaning, and they produced adequate meals.

According to Protsakevych, physical activities were emphasized, with a special emphasis being placed on running and jumping. As they developed strength and endurance, the recruits began to run with arms and equipment, and the running distances were increased. Along with the physical training, modern hand-to-hand and close-in combat techniques, referred to as "judo," as well as knife fighting, were extensively emphasized.

Following one month of such training, the recruits went to the rifle range. In due time, each soldier became proficient with a German rifle, the Russian Mosin-Nagant rifle, a Soviet Ppsh submachine gun, and a heavier Soviet machine-gun. Some of the recruits especially excelled. Praised upon the successful completion of the first part of their training, the recruits toasted each other with a choice of either beer or alcohol.

Galicia Division

On 29 September 1943, a Berlin directive specified that during training, German personnel would be utilized.[6] This directive was issued not only to the 6th Regiment, but as well as to the 4th and 5th Regiments. But as previously mentioned, to this day it has never been properly explained why this order was issued. Perhaps the exceptionally low training standards found within the 4th and 5th Regiments is what compelled Berlin to issue the directive. Undoubtedly, Berlin's directive was extended to the 6th Regiment to ensure that if the 6th was not conducting proper training, its cadre would reverse their position and proceed with proper training. Clearly, Berlin was making a stronger effort to ensure that training was being conducted in accordance to military standards.

At the end of October 1943, a soccer match between the Wehrmacht and Waffen-SS was staged at Byelostok. Selected to participate, Protsakevych encountered at that location a number of Galician volunteers from the other companies and even, regiments.

To maintain morale, Fischer encouraged the recruits to write and receive mail. But not all of the mail was optimistic. Soldiers received letters which revealed family members arrested by the Gestapo, of family members forcefully coerced for "volunteer" work programs in Germany and, on occasion, tragic notices of relatives and close friends shot for various infractions. Needless to say, such news was not merely demoralizing, but could, in some cases, disrupt training; emotionally shattered recruits could not train effectively. Desperately seeking a way to voice their frustrations, in due time the recruits began to approach their instructors with their qualms.

But when the volunteers were forbidden to sing certain patriotic songs, and they encountered a period of inadequate meals, they decided to express their dissatisfaction in unison. One evening, following a day of training, the recruits sat down to dinner. But because they were conducting a "hunger strike," following Fischer's rallying cry of "Smachnoho!" ("Enjoy!"), no one ate. Needless to say, Fischer and his staff noticed the air of dissatisfaction, but they continued with their meals.

Following the meal, the recruits where assembled for a formation. A good commander will always immediately confront a problem or disruptive situation. Now, Fischer wanted to know what factor or factors were behind the hunger strike.

Openly, and straight to the point, the recruits complained about the recent meals, and expressed their desires to be transferred to the Division, and their need to have contact with a representative from the Galician Military Board. After hearing the recruits out, Fischer provided the following response: although both he and his staff were posted to a police regiment, in actuality, he and his personnel were soldiers whose mission it was to train the volunteers; the Ukrainians must realize that their posting into the Ordnungspolizei was only a temporary posting prior to transferring into the Division; for the moment better meals could not be provided; and as for their desires to establish contact with the Military Board, this request would be immediately passed on to higher command.

But, as with any commander confronted with such a situation, Fischer was also forced to address the strike. In a professional manner, he informed the recruits that this matter would be forgotten, and that no punishment would be meted out. However, he did warn the recruits that within the Waffen-SS, disobedience of orders was punishable by death. To what extend, if any, the recruits grievances were addressed is not known. But in due time, 9th Company's personnel noted an improvement in the quality of the meals, contact was established with the Military board, and training resumed with no further incidents.

Despite the fact that the 6 August 1943 order specified that the 6th Regiment was to be formed and trained in Poland, it was not to remain very long in that country. In November 1944, rumors began to surface that the regiment was soon to be displaced. Within days, the regiment began its preparations to relocate to its new training location – the Pao and Tarbes region in Southern France, adjacent to the Pyrenees Mountains.

In the period of late November and early December 1943, the regiment – in its entirety – arrived in Southern France. The regiment's personnel were housed in the so-called "Marshall Foch" barracks where, prior to the German occupation, Morocco's legionnaires were quartered.

According to Protsakevych, the Marshall Foch barracks was one huge building with large windows. But the moment the soldiers arrived, the training resumed. This time, however, it acquired a new character.

Unlike previously in Poland, there were far fewer drills. Field training, in unit strength, was emphasized, along with urban warfare training. Map and compass reading, terrain orientation, learning to approximate the time of day by observing the sun, battle formations along with the different movements utilized in forested and open terrain, camouflage, and anti-sniper warfare were all part of the training. Unlike previously, when Soviet weapons were utilized, German weapons were issued and marksmanship training was emphasized. The soldiers found the training interesting; the temperate climate also favored the training, although pure white snow covered the distant mountain tops.

Although a relatively high percentage of the soldiers were in varying degrees proficient in German, translators were still utilized. But now in France some Ukrainians, who had either resided in France prior to the war or had learned French at the translators' school, were posted to the 6th Regiment. Protsakevych's company received two such French-speaking Ukrainians.

From 26-30 November, the 6th Regiment was visited by various members of the Military Board. On 28 November, Governor Wachter, Colonel Bisanz, Chief Divisional Chaplain Reverend Laba and Yuriy Krokhmaliuk, who was now serving as an officer on the Divisional staff, visited the 6th Regiment. As always was the case with any visiting dignitaries, morale increased and all of the dignitaries were tremendously welcomed.

On 23 December 1943,[7] the Ordnungspolizei received such an order from Reichsführer Heinrich Himmler – that 2,000 men be immediately dispatched to Heidelager for training. Signed by Flake, one of Himmler's adjutants, the order was issued because Himmler, who personally objected to having the Galician volunteers placed into any type of police units in the first place, was now rapidly moving to place the volunteers into their respective combat division. Himmler's order of 23 December was concurrently addressed to the various regiments, and it provided directives to several of the regiments and a replacement battalion. 6th Regiment was ordered to dispatch 1,200 of its personnel to Heidelager. To ensure an expedient transition, the order specified the volunteers were to travel in uniform, but minus their arms. For traveling purposes, each man was to bring the following items:

> 1 coat or jacket;
> 1 hat ;
> 1 pair of pants;
> 1 belt;
> 1 pair of shoes;
> 1 pair of socks;
> 1 pair of extra underwear; and
> 1 blanket.

As for the remaining personnel of the 6th Regiment which would not immediately be traveling to Heidelager, the order specified that they (along with those remaining from the 7th Regiment), would be organized into a replacement battalion within France. In conclusion, the order also specified that further directives were forthcoming.

On 31 January 1944, the 6th Regiment was disbanded.[8] With the transfer of its 1,200 personnel to Heidelager, the regiment ceased to exist.[9] Because at the last

Chapter 28: Die Ordnungspolizei (The Order Police)

moment it was decided to leave behind a small group in Pao, France, to serve as a security force for Pao's administration and command, a small number of the 6th's personnel were dispatched to the city of Tarbes. Upon arrival to Tarbes, the group augmented the remainder of the 7th Regiments personnel who remained behind in Tarbes when the 7th was also officially disbanded in January 1944 and the majority of its personnel departed to Heidelager.[10]

Upon receiving the news that the 6th would be disbanded and its personnel would at last be incorporated into the Division proper at Heidelager, there was much jubilation. But as the 9th Companies soldiers prepared to depart, and bade their farewells to Fischer and the instructors who had accompanied them from Poland to France where they, along with the French based-instructors, continued to work and train together, jubilation suddenly turned into sorrow. The soldiers were proud to hear as Fischer, shaking each man's hand and personally wishing him continuing success, recalled that in his twenty years of service, he had never served with finer soldiers. Following Fischer's remarks, other cadre members spoke and, at this time, the departing soldiers listened in awe as Fischer's assistant, Koch, spoke fluently in Polish!

Accompanying his departing soldiers to the train station, Fischer watched his soldiers board the train. But as it began to pull away, those who had served in the 9th Company scrambled to the windows to view, for one last time, their beloved commander. Never, would they forget the final sight of the tall, elegant Fischer as he stood alone on the platform in his highly polished black knee-high boots staring at the departing soldiers.

Though Fischer was never seen again, and his whereabouts in the aftermath of World War II remain unknown, the former company commander would never be forgotten. Later, in such places as Brody, Slovakia, the Hron River in Banska Stiavnica, Yugoslavia, and Austria; or within the UPA, or in the frozen, snow-covered mountains of North Korea in the winter of 1951, or in the steamy plateau of Dien Bien Phu in the late spring and summer of 1954, many a former soldier from the 9th Company would experience feelings of shame and gratitude – shame that he had ever resisted mastering communist weaponry; and gratitude that Fischer had forced him to master both Soviet and German arms and equipment.

Upon re-entry into the Division, many of the highly trained soldiers of the 6th Regiment were immediately dispatched to various NCO schools. Some of the former 9th Company's personnel soon entered the officer school at Poznan-Treskau, while a number volunteered for the Division's fussilier battalion which began forming in January 1944 and was seeking well-trained soldiers with a thorough knowledge of both German and foreign weaponry.

Galicia Division

On 25 January 1944, the 6th Regiment's former Chaplain, Ivan Holoida, wrote a letter to further inform Galicia's Military Board about what had transpired in the final days of the 6th Regiment.[11]

Titled "Report," the letter stated:

With this, I report that the 6th and 7th Regiments are disbanded. From the remainder of the grenadiers, a reserve battalion was formed, which is lodged in Tarbes. The battalion's strength is set at approximately 900 personnel.[12] A smaller portion was redirected into the 4th Regiment, but the remainder entered the Division at Heidelager.

For the moment, the regimental staffs are intact and are continuing their mission, awaiting further directives.[13] Some instructors and non-commissioned officers were dispatched to Italy to train Italian elements. But the reserve battalion is currently in the organizational stage; its future status is uncertain.

Currently, two chaplains [Kovaliuk and Holoida], are still in place. For the moment, which one will remain behind is not known. But in all probablility, it will be Chaplain Kovaliuk. As well, all of our doctors are still here in place. Any periodicals/letters for the battalion may be forwarded care/of the following address:

Feldpost No. 05477A.

The [regimental] records have been gathered together and placed at the battalions disposal. But currently, we are also awaiting for approximately 200 pieces of various records.

The boys are feeling somewhat depressed because they were disbanded, and as of yet have not reestablished a united camaraderie.

The Christmas packages finally arrived on 16 January. Because not that many remained behind [in Tarbes], each grenadier received two packages. We immediately presented these gifts. Our boys were delighted tremendously.

Mail, however, continues to arrive late. And the news from Galicia is not always good. As for further information [regarding those still in France], Reverend Dr. Laba and engineer Yuriy Krokhmaliuk have probably already revealed more.

Chapter 28: Die Ordnungspolizei (The Order Police)

A final observation: The style and orthography [of the regimental records], are left in their original. From these texts we note the difficulties that were experienced on numerous occasions as recollected by the two regiments stationed in France.

Glory to Ukraine!

Chaplain Holoida's letter of 25 January 1944 stands as one of the last documents available on the remnants of the former 6th and 7th Regiments now based in Tarbes. And excluding a Berlin directive of 25 February 1944, which only makes a brief reference to the former 6th Regiment's veterinary personnel,[14] no further orders or letters regarding the 6th Regiment were issued after early January 1944.[15]

7th Volunteer Regiment:
Initially organized in Norway in July 1942, the 7th Ordnungspolizei was soon disbanded. But in October 1943, it was reconstituted in Paris, France.

Yet despite its reconstitution in the latter half of 1943, in actuality the 7th Regiment was not reformed. It only existed in the planning stages. Although references to the 7th may also be found in the Berlin decrees of 24 June and 5 July 1943, and on 12 August 1943 it was somewhat organized in an unofficial manner, it was not until 29 September 1943 that a Berlin directive set the wheels in motion for the re-establishment of the 7th Regiment. This directive revealed that forthcoming information will yet be dispatched regarding the respective fates of both the 7th and 8th Regiments, and where both regiments are to be posted.[1] Generally speaking, 29 September 1943 is the date usually accepted as the date of the regiment's official re-establishment since its disbandment in 1942.[2]

According to a report published in the aftermath of a meeting held by Galicia's Military Board in the capital city of Lviv on 14 January 1944,[3] the 7th was identified with a personnel strength of 1,671.[4] Along with this data, Ukrainian and other sources identify Reverend Danylo Kovaliuk as the 7th's Chaplain.[5]
However, the 7th Regiment was still late in forming. Exactly when it was finally formed is not known. But according to Myhailo Protsakevych, a former 6th Regimental soldier, the 7th was finally formed in the latter part of 1943.[6] And if one takes into consideration that as late as 29 September 1943 Berlin's directive stated that information regarding the 7th Regiment would still be forthcoming, Protsakevych is correct in his observation that the 7th Regiment was finally formed in the concluding months of 1943.

During the time that Chaplain Kovaliuk served in the Division, he served primarily in its Training and Replacement Regiment. Nevertheless, Kovaliuk did maintain close contacts with the other Divisional units. And in addition to serving within the Training and Replacement Regiment, Chaplain Kovaliuk was also posted for awhile within the short-lived 7th Regiment. This occurred when a chaplain was needed, and the Training and Replacement Regiment was tapped to provide one.

In the aftermath of World War II, Kovaliuk wrote an account about the Division, which was primarily based on a diary which the chaplain maintained during his period of service.

According to the former chaplain, the 7th Regiment (as well as the other regiments), was a separate regiment independent of the Division.[7] Posted to the Southwestern French region of Salier de Bearn[8] (vicinity Bayonne) the regiment's staff, along with its entire 1st Battalion, was quartered there while the 2nd and 3rd Battalions were posted in the vicinity of Orthez.[9] In his memoirs, Chaplain Kovaliuk described Salier de Bearne as a Basque region. Because Chaplain Kovaliuk became closely acquainted with the Basques, he affectionately described them as a people who, in addition to living on both sides of the Pyrennes Mountains in the border region of Northern Spain and Southern France, possessed a distinct language and culture.

7th Regiments entire headquarters staff was composed of German personnel. Commanded by SS-Obersturmbannführer Huber Gubert,[10] a former front-line officer who fought in World War I, the Colonel hailed from Baden-Baden, Germany. Kovaliuk described Colonel Gubert as a cultured man who despite the fact that he never attended Mass, was a deep believer. Kovaliuk also cited that the Colonel was correct towards him as well as toward the regiments Galician soldiers. This could not, however, apply to all of Gubert's officers.

The regimental staff's headquarters was located in an old, but beautiful European castle where, at one time, Imperial Russia's tsars were quartered during their travels to France.

When the recruits first arrived, the local populace, in the mistaken belief that the regiment's personnel were German, viewed the men with suspicion and hostility. But this attitude immediately changed when the region's inhabitants learned that the recruits were Ukrainian, and noted their religious Sunday services. And soon, Chaplain Kovaliuk was warmly welcomed by the local French and Basque padres. Although some of the regiment's cadre repeatedly proposed that the religious services be conducted strictly outdoors and within the regiment's premises, Chaplain Kovaliuk remained adamant that the services be held in a local church and Gubert acquiesced to Kovaliuk's request. Up until the regiment departed, every Sunday morning a number of the regiment's personnel could be seen and heard in the countryside as they marched to a local church.

Aside from the fact that Reverend Kovaliuk quickly established warm relationships with the local French citizens for personal, collective, and humanitarian reasons, his actions were also undoubtedly based on reasons of security. Fully realizing that the local French and Basque inhabitants were not truly under a "French Vichy" government but rather, were within the Third Reich's zone of occupation, Chaplain Kovaliuk, in an effort to ensure that no local partisan/guerrilla or allied-inserted sabotage team would pose as a threat, constantly emphasized to the local inhabitants that the regiment's soldiers were friendly, posed no threat to the region's civilian inhabitants, were anti-Nazi, and served within a German-sponsored formation only because for the moment, that was their only way to improve their position which was ultimately, in defense of their Galician homeland.

In his observations, Kovaliuk did not specify what type of training the recruits received. But there are indications that it did not meet the standards as those of, for example, the 6th Regiment. Keeping in mind that the 7th was formed at a time when the Ordnungspolizei itself was experiencing shortages, and that the intention was always for the 7th's (as well as for the other regiments) Ukrainian personnel to be incorporated into the Division as soon as possible, then from these two factors alone it is apparent that the 7th Regiment was not trained on the high level of standard found first at Heidelager, but especially later at Neuhammer.

In late November 1943, the 7th was visited by Governor Wachter, Yuriy Krokhmaliuk, Makarushka and Bisanz. Following a Mass conducted by Chaplain Kovaliuk, several of the visiting dignitaries spoke and the day was marked by much festivity. Governor Wachter was especially pleased that the soldiers were exposed to proper health and welfare conditions.

On 23 December 1943, a Berlin directive was issued in regards to several of the regiments:[11] the 7th was ordered to immediately dispatch 745 of its personnel to the Heidelager troop training center. The soldiers were to travel light, bringing no more than the same items as did the 6th. As for the 7th's remaining personnel, they were to be merged with the remnants of the 6th and together, both were to be utilized for the establishment of a reserve battalion in France.

On 31 January 1944, the 7th was officially disbanded; however, it is known that well before 31 January, the brunt of the 7th was dispatched to Heidelager because in a report submitted shortly after the 14 January 1944 meeting held in Lviv by the Military Board, it was recorded that 2,000 grenadiers, from both the 6th and 7th transported earlier from France, had already arrived at Heidelager.[12]

Upon arrival at Heidelager, the disbanded 7th's personnel were soon diverted into the Division's Training and Replacement Regiment located in Wandern. As for the 7th Ordnungspolizei Regiment, it was never reconstituted.

8th Volunteer Regiment:
Although the 8th Regiment is positively identified in various Berlin directives, such as on 24 June and 5 July 1944, none of them provide any specific guidance and, as a matter of fact, even state that additional information in regard to the 8th will yet be forthcoming.

Initially raised by the Ordnungspolizei in July 1942 in Russia on the eastern front, the 8th was soon disbanded but reconstituted in mid-1943. Proposals were offered to fill the ranks of the 8th with some of the Galicians who had volunteered for the Division but at the moment, could not be dispatched to Heidelager.

Despite such proposals, a combination of upcoming recruitment difficulties, along with other war-time exigencies, prevented the 8th from ever being formed. Ultimately, never created, at no time did the 8th ever contain Ukrainian volunteers from either Galicia or any other Ukrainian regions.[1]

Polizei-Regiment "Galizien":
This unofficial unit, proposed by Colonel Alfred Bisanz to test the receptiveness of Galicia's youth towards the creation of a military unit, registered on 20 March 1943 a strength of 3,500.[1] It must be remembered, however, that this figure was only a pre-indictment figure, and as far as the "3,500 volunteers" were concerned, they were not yet even medically examined for a military call-up. Excluding its brief existence strictly for test and possible propaganda purposes, in actuality, Polizei Regiment "Galizien" never existed.

Tarbes (France's) "Galicia" Division's Reserve Battalion:
On 31 January 1944, a Berlin directive ordered the establishment of a Divisional Reserve Battalion to be formed in Tarbes, France.[1]

Although the directive did not specify what the battalion's troop strength was to be, it did specify that the battalion was to be under the control of Paris' Ordnungspolizei, and that its personnel were to be armed with an unspecified number of Karabiner carbines. The directive also requested veterinarians from both the 6th and 7th Regiments.

The battalion's strength stood at approximately 740. This figure was derived from the minutes of the 14 January 1944 Lviv meeting which revealed a strength of 600 remained within a reserve battalion which was soon to be moved to Tarbes to link-up with the approximately 140 already dispatched to Tarbes.[2] According to Ordnungspolizei records, the Tarbes reserve battalion was formed from the remnants of the 6th Regiment;[3] however, it is known that some members of the 7th (such as Chaplain Kovaliuk), did, for a brief time, augment the reserve battalion. (When the bulk of the 7th was dispatched to Heidelager, a chaplain was still needed to maintain troop welfare for those remaining behind in Tarbes. Chaplain Kovaliuk was ordered to assume responsibilities of the battalion's spiritual matters).[4]

According to Kovaliuk's memoirs, Tarbes was not a large city but it was very beautiful. The birthplace of a number of historical figureheads such as Marshall Foch, Tarbes was also the seat of a French bishop and historically, of French Christiandom.

Unfortunately for Kovaliuk and the remaining Ukrainian personnel from the disbanded regiments, the units commander, SS-Sturmbannführer Fosten[5], a former philosophy professor in civilian life, was not a sympathetic individual; as well, he was an atheist who held a low contempt for the Ukrainian personnel, and was clearly dissatisfied with his assignment.

Clearly, Fosten's negative attitude was displayed during his first meeting with Kovaliuk. Amidst a very uncomfortable atmosphere, Fosten sharply demanded answers to a number of questions, and before Kovaliuk could even reply, Fosten himself provided the answers – albeit incorrect ones.

Needless to say, Fosten's attitude would never change. Nevertheless, in spite of this negative attitude, Kovaliuk quickly established a warm relationship with the Tarbes chief Bishop, who personally knew Galicia's Metropolitan Sheptytskyi. In addition, the chaplain also established friendly relations with two Ukrainian medical officers (previously from the disbanded French-based 6th and 7th Regiments), Doctors Kovalskyi and Havrysevych, who were also posted to the battalion. It was also at Tarbes that Kovaliuk encountered a German NCO, known to everyone as "Sergeant H" because of an exceptionally long last name. And one day, "Sergeant H" confided to Kovaliuk that when he had served on SS-General Dietrich's staff, he actually read a Berlin order which stated that the Ukrainian intelligentsia was to be destroyed.

In addition to Fosten and "Sergeant H," Chaplain Kovaliuk would also have the opportunity to meet and speak with a highly respected soldier on the international arena – Field-Marshal Erwin Rommel.

The first time Kovaliuk ever spoke to Rommel, the famed "Desert Fox" asked, in a jocular manner, "since when do priests defend the SS?" But after carefully listening to Kovaliuk, the marshal finally understood who Kovaliuk was, what he and his fellow soldiers represented, and that their sole reason for enlistment was to defend their native homeland from communist terror. Years later, the former chaplain still felt that he had adequately satisfied Rommel's interest and inquiry.[6]

Shortly after the establishment of the battalion, on 12 February 1944, a Berlin "quickbrief" was issued.[7] Dispatched to various commands, the directive specified that a number of units were to be disbanded. The "quickbrief" provided some guidance regarding the disposal of certain personnel, arms, equipment, communications gear, and so forth. Along with the units identified for disbandment was the Tarbes-based Galician Battalion still under Paris' command. Of interest to note is that in regard to guidance provided for foreign personnel, a Doctor Hryzyschye (undoubtedly this was a typing error; the name may have been spelled "Havrysevych"), was to accompany the battalions personnel during the transfer of the battalion.

On 25 February 1944, another Berlin directive was issued. Like many of the others previously issued, it was not explicit and was composed of only two short paragraphs. Basically, it was an update to the directive of 31 January 1944, which had stated that it would yet be determined in the near future how the battalion's troops would be armed.[8]

At Tarbes and its vicinity, the reserve battalions personnel conducted virtually no training exercises. The battalion's relationship with the local inhabitants was very positive; not once did a problem or conflict ever arise between the Ukrainian soldiers and the civilians. There was, however, a serious threat – the French maquis underground.

Because in Southern France the German occupational forces were at low strength and thinly spread, the underground was able to operate with relative ease, especially during night hours. To counter the maquis threat, whenever the Ukrainians found themselves in any part of occupied France, they immediately announced their identity, and explained their cause. The fact that their position was anti-Nazi was strongly heralded in private discussions with local and regional non-German civilian leaders (with the knowledge that this revelation would in due time be transmitted to any local/regional insurgency), and that they harbored no enmity toward any of the local inhabitants. The Division's chaplains especially played a key role in this area. Wherever they were posted, they found ways to meet with the local and regional church and civilian leaders. As already stated, this was done for security reasons and to inform any existing local and regional insurgencies that the Ukrainians posed no threat to the French.

But in addition to the nationalist maquis, the Spanish communists also operated in the southern region of France. Previously defeated by Franco in the Spanish Civil War, the remnants of this fanatical communist movement had fled to the Pyrenees Mountains of the Spanish-French border region. On occasion, these communists crossed into France proper and by either linking up or coordinating their activities with the French communist guerrilla faction, launched raids and ambushes against both the Germans and the forces of Vichy France.

In the first several years of the German occupation, for the greater part the insurgents assassinated targeted SS and Gestapo leaders, as well as local and regional French collaborators. They planted bombs in police stations, and conducted propaganda and spy activities. But as the insurgents grew in numerical strength and received sizable supplies of allied arms and equipment, their area-of-operations began to spread. Increasingly, the guerrillas began to operate throughout France, planting many more mines and explosive devices, and intensifying their attacks until they actually began to strike regular German army units and facilities. And as an increasing number of the central and southern French-based German units were diverted northwards to the vicinity of Normandy in anticipation of the allied landings, and once when the Battle of Normandy developed in earnest, the insurgents especially intensified their activities. From where the Ukrainians were posted in Tarbes, nightly gun battles could be heard between outlying German Wehrmacht and police units versus the insurgents.

To be sure, this was a dangerous situation. Besides the fact that mines do not discriminate, the communist insurgents held a different outlook from those who were just fighting in the Maquis insurgency for national liberation. In their viewpoint, anyone who was not a Stalinist would be targeted.

Needless to say, this matter was addressed to Wachter, to the Military Board and was even brought before Berlin's Ordnungspolizei. Along with demands that the remainder of the Division's disbanded 6th and 7th Regimental personnel be removed to Heidelager as soon as possible, the insurgent threat was always emphasized.

One day, Tarbes received information that a sizable communist guerrilla force was planning to attack Tarbes itself. Within minutes, the Ukrainians were ready for action; a group was dispatched to secure a wooded area which, it was believed, might possibly be utilized by the insurgents as a final staging area prior to attacking Tarbes. This group, as well as those left behind in Tarbes, was led strictly by German officers and NCOs. Excluding Chaplain Kovaliuk and the two doctors who held officer's rank, and a handful of very low-ranking Ukrainian NCOs, the bulk of the officer and NCO leadership was German.

As the soldiers approached the wooded area, a Ukrainian, sensing danger, stated that the woods might already be infiltrated by partisans awaiting to launch an ambush. "SINNLOSIGKEIT!" replied a German officer. But right at that moment, small arms fire suddenly rocked the wooded area.

Scattering for cover, the Ukrainians awaited further orders. But none came. Seeing a dangerous situation, and knowing that something had to be done, a Ukrainian soldier, spotting the German officer now to the rear, ran through a gauntlet of small-arms fire to reach the officer. Insisting that the officer lead the troops forward like an officer should, both men surged forward together. The others followed.

The guerrillas withdrew. Although no partisans were killed, two were captured. The Ukrainians' losses were light, but still grievous. Kovaliuk only recalled that the soldier who fell was named Hychai, and that at one time he was associated with Lviv's Seminary. The German officer, meanwhile, was relieved from the battalion; his Ukrainian counterpart, however, was granted an award.[9]

In the meantime, Fosten and a number of the battalion's cadre personnel were ordered to Paris. Neither Kovaliuk, nor anyone else, ever saw these men again. In his writings, Kovaliuk (nor anyone else for that matter), ever identified who was now officially in charge; possibly, no one was. But in the following days, as the Ukrainians heard the Germans increasingly talk of the impending Allied invasion, they simultaneously noted that more and more of the battalions cadres were being dispatched to other parts of France. In due time, only about 25 German battalion staff, company and support personnel remained.[10] As for the battalion itself, it was now organized into three companies.[11]

According to Kovaliuk, the Germans who remained behind did only two things – drink and sleep. As for the Ukrainians, they just milled around. Rumors continued to persist that the battalion's Ukrainian Galician personnel would soon be returned to the Division.

During periods of personal travel outside of Tarbes, Chaplain Kovaliuk noted the results of the intensified allied air and guerrilla activity. Shattered railway cars, burned-out trucks, dead horses, overturned wagons, along with an occasional decomposing burned corpse, began to litter the French countryside. Finally, it appeared that there was some truth behind he rumors of an allied invasion. And as the tranquillity of the French countryside began slowly transforming into a world of hell, Kovaliuk began to fear increasingly for his boy's safety. Daily, the chaplain prayed fervently for providence and their safety.

On 8 May 1944, Chaplain Kovaliuk's prayers were answered. In a directive captioned "Urgent!", Berlin ordered Tarbes personnel to be immediately transferred to Neuhammer's troop-training area.[12] Because it was common knowledge that the reserve battalion was to be disbanded any day, Berlin's directive surprised no one. As in the previous directives, guidance was provided on transport and personnel gear but actually, very little was brought along by Galicia's personnel enroute to Neuhammer. Within 72 hours of the 8 May directive, the men moved out. But by no means would it be an easy journey.

By now, France's railway system was being systematically blasted by strong allied air attacks and occasional guerrilla activity; roads and bridges were pulverized, and certain railway centers disappeared totally from the face of the earth. What previously took a day or two to traverse now required a minimum travel time of a week.

For Chaplain Kovaliuk, this final journey proved to be an especially trying ordeal. Aside from the sadness he experienced when saying good-bye to his French clerical and non-clerical friends, Kovaliuk was especially saddened to see the destruction of his men. On more than one occasion following an allied air raid, tears could be seen in his eyes as the brave chaplain hunched over the shattered remains of a 17, 18 or 19-year-old and removed the deceased's identification tags and other personal items. And in the following weeks at Neuhammer, Chaplain Kovaliuk would frequently stay up late into the night writing condolence letters to deceased soldiers' loved ones.

By rail, foot, and vehicle transport, Kovaliuk and the rest reached Neuhammer. Upon arrival, they were soon placed into the Division's Training and Replacement Regiment. On 9 June 1944, another Berlin "quickbrief" was issued. Again addressed to Europe's various Ordnungspolizei commands, the directive informed them that the short-lived Galician Reserve Battalion based in Tarbes had been disbanded.[13] By now, the allies were fighting in Normandy, there were no Ukrainian soldiers in France,[14] and the Galician Ukrainian volunteers were in Neuhammer. Chaplain Kovaliuk, meanwhile, remained with the Division and endured its ordeals until the very end.[15]

The "Galicia" Division's Volunteers Within France's Maquis
The numerous resistance units which comprised France's main underground – the Forces Francaises de Interieur (F.F.I.) or, as it was simply known – the Maquis, was associated with a French acronym for a thorny and tough bush which grows in various parts of France.

By mid-1944, the Maquis had expanded throughout entire France. As usually is the case with any sizable underground, in due time foreign personnel will eventually be included. With the insertion of the Ukrainian Volunteer Regiments into the French interior, it would not be long before a number of Ukrainian personnel, initially meant for the "Galicia" Division, would find themselves serving, fighting, and in some cases dying, within the Maquis for the liberation of France. A point in case is that of Lieutenant Osyp Krukovsky.

Prior to World War II, Krukovsky journeyed to France. In the region of Sans, he was employed as an agricultural worker. Proud of his heritage, Krukovsky established contact with other Ukrainians, joined a Ukrainian organization and eventually, became its head.

With the eruption of World War II, Krukovsky, on 7 September 1939, enlisted into the French Army. Following the completion of his training, Krukovsky, along with some other Ukrainian and foreign personnel, transferred into France's elite French Foreign Legion. In the rank of sergeant, he served in Northern France, and along with the other legionnaires, fought a successful rear-guard action at Dunkirk.

Avoiding capture, he returned to Sans, and soon resumed his work. But within a year after the eruption of the German-Soviet War, Krukovsky decided to return home. Thus, in 1942, he found a homeland devastated by various occupants.

In 1943, Krukovsky enlisted in the "Galicia" Division. Though passionately anti-Nazi, Krukovsky enlisted under the same auspices as did many others: to avoid a "volunteer" work program or a concentration camp; to distance oneself from Gestapo harassment; or to assist a loved one. But most importantly, to obtain arms for self-preservation.[1]

Placed into the 6th Volunteer Regiment, in due time Krukovsky found himself once again in France, in the vicinity of Tarbes and the Pyrenees Mountains. Obviously sympathetic to France as a result of his previous French residency, citizenship, military service and fluency in the language, Krukovsky, as an "older Frenchmen," quickly established contact with a local Maquis unit through a local Maquis agent code-named "Liafaria."

In the ensuing weeks, Krukovsky actually formulated plans for the entire regiment's three battalions to be incorporated into France's anti-Nazi underground rather than remain with the 6th Regiment. But unfortunately for Krukovsky, Tarbes local Gestapo and SS leaders learned of his plan. Arrested along with a number of other Ukrainians, Krukovsky and his fellow POW's were placed into solitary confinement.

In early July 1944, shortly after the last Ukrainians had departed from France, Krukovsky and his followers were packed into a cattle car and deported northward to an unknown destination. But enroute to wherever they were headed, in the vicinity of Tur, the train came under a heavy allied air attack. In the ensuing explosions, derailment, strafing and general confusion, Krukovsky and his followers broke free from the car, secured some weapons, hand grenades, extra ammunition and even, four horses. Fleeing into the hills, the Ukrainians established contact with some local Maquis commanders: Captain "Tuder" and Lieutenant "Massier." With their assistance, Krukovsky and his men were placed into the F.F.I. According to Krukovsky, the F.F.I., which was operating in the Tur region, was headed by

Chapter 28: Die Ordnungspolizei (The Order Police)

a Major "Liegrand," a former regular French Army officer who, in 1940, had escaped to England via the successful Dunkirk evacuation but in due time, had been reinserted into the Tur region by parachute to help organize and command the area's underground.

From 4 August until 30 September 1944, Krukovsky, now in the rank of 1st Lieutenant, and his fellow Ukrainians, fought side-by-side with the Maquis. Until the allied liberation, Krukovsky and his men participated in every French insurgent operation. The Nazi transport system was especially targeted. During such raids, Krukovsky, as an officer within the Maquis, always ensured that any Ukrainian, French, or Eastern European laborers found amidst the derailed transport were not harmed, but provided with proper care. With the conclusion of the German occupation, Krukovsky and his men participated in a ceremony held in L'osh, a town just liberated by a mixed Ukrainian-French Maquis force.

Reentering the regular French Army as a Lieutenant, Krukovsky soon rejoined the French Foreign Legion's Ukrainian Battalion headed by Major Lev Hloba. Posted into General de Lattre's 1st French Army the Ukrainian Battalion fought and pursued Nazi Germany's 19th Army in France's Vosges Mountains and Alsace Region; it also fought in the Black Forest region in Southwestern Germany. As for Krukovsky, a combination of trench foot and a leg wound suffered in the Vosges Mountains in the winter of 1944-45, ended his days as a warrior.[2]

But by no means was Lieutenant Krukovsky an exception. As already presented, within the various French Maquis units, a sizable number of Ukrainians were to be found. Included amongst them were those personnel who had previously enlisted into the "Galicia" Division but while dispatched to France, for whatever reason, deserted from the Ordnungspolizei and ended up within the Maquis.

To adequately cover this topic alone would, indeed, require an entire study of considerable length. But some of this historical material should be included here. In addition to Krukovsky and his followers, there was actually an entire Ukrainian unit which, denied access into the Division, found itself posted to France. Dissatisfied with their posting and the treatment they had undergone, the unit had revolted and defected into the French underground. And their drama must be unfolded.

In the early days of 1944, Nazi Germany faced both a disastrous eastern front and an extensive insurgency in various European nations. In a desperate effort to secure manpower, Germany's military machine redirected many non-German European males, initially conscripted by force for labor purposes, into its military.

Galicia Division

Such was the case in the East Prussian region of Deutsche Elau when a German police major suddenly appeared and informed the assembled Ukrainian men that every healthy male between the ages of 18 to 30 years was "now going to be mobilized into the German army and as soldiers, would be dispatched to France to battle French terrorists!"

Amongst those mobilized, there were mixed feelings. While on one hand there was jubilation because initially, the prospect of military service seemed to offer some haven from forced labor and a condition of limited freedom, on the other hand, the Ukrainians did not savor the idea of being pitted against a nation toward whom they harbored no enmity. But then, as every Ukrainian knew, France was also fighting to liberate itself from Nazi rule. So in the event they were deployed to France, perhaps the Ukrainians could desert to the French underground. But because by now every Ukrainian had heard of the "Galicia" Division, it was hoped (and actually believed) that sooner or later, the drafted soldiers would be channeled into their Division.

Through various channels, the Ukrainian Central Committee, as well as Galicia's Military Board, learned of this forced mobilization. Concerned about the fate of these young men, and strongly opposed to the usage of Ukrainians in any of Nazi Germany's pacification operations (as well as to the use of any Ukrainian personnel within European nations with whom, historically speaking, the Ukrainians had no quarrel), the UCC, as well as representatives of the Military Board, strongly protested this forced mobilization.

With their complaints falling on deaf ears, the UCC, along with the various other committees, appealed directly to the Germans to divert the Ukrainian manpower into the "Galicia" Division itself. The UCC was not only concerned about the danger of Ukrainian males being utilized for an unproductive and unworthy non-Ukrainian cause but, also, that the Ukrainians would be minimally armed, poorly trained, and strictly under unsympathetic – and even brutal – German leadership. Therefore, the UCC strove instead to channel the Ukrainians into the Division, where better arms, equipment, training and leadership were the guaranteed norm.

But ultimately, nothing positive was gained. On 2 February 1944, the Ukrainians commenced some form of training in East Prussia. After a training period of approximately six months,[3] Nebeliuk stated that the Ukrainians were incorporated into the 30th Infantry Division's[4] 1st Regiment's 3rd Battalion.[5] Although at this time the 30th Division contained a number of Balts, Russians and even Cossacks, Nebeliuk writes that Ukrainians comprised the entire 1st Regiment's 3rd Infantry Battalion.[6] But when it came to leadership, the battalion's entire officer and NCO leadership was composed of German personnel, with the exception of one Ukrainian officer, Lev Hlobda (who actually was more of a spokesman rather than as a military leader).

Detached from the 30th Infantry, the Ukrainian battalion was deployed westward. In mid-September 1944, it entered Eastern France in the vicinity of Belfort.[7] But as the battalion neared this eastern French city,[8] the sudden sound of a massive explosion by saboteurs halted for the moment all further railway movement.

In the ensuing delay, as railway personnel repaired the damage, Major Hloba appealed to the battalion's Germans leadership to release the five innocent French civilians who, in the aftermath of the explosion, were swept up to be shot as a reprisal. Hloba successfully convinced the Germans that nothing positive would be gained by execution and the five civilians were released.[9] Following the repair of the railway system, the Ukrainians were moved deeper into France, and posted into the vicinity of the Confrancon Forest.

In this area, the village of Confrancon was located. Although seemingly an unimportant village not far from the Swiss-German borders, a critical road system was found in its area which connected to a series of roads to the main Paris-Basle highway system. In the event of any efforts to dispatch reinforcements to central, southern or northwestern France, or in the event of any withdrawal, Confrancon's road system would play a major role.

But it was also within this forested area that a Maquis unit was operating. Realizing the dangers of any insurgent interdictions, the Germans decided to, once-and-for-all, destroy the Maquis threat. To accomplish this mission, a German Wehrmacht officer, Major Hanenstein, who commanded the Ukrainian battalion, was dispatched to establish order.

Through spies, agents, and Maquis intelligence, allied intelligence learned of these "Russians." But by now, allied intelligence was fully aware of the fact that a number of foreign personnel, including Russian deserters from the German army, were also operating within the Maquis ranks. In an effort to determine the intricacy of the situation, and to further develop an intelligence gathering center in eastern/southeastern France, America's Office of Strategic Services (OSS), decided to insert a five-man team in September 1944 into Southeastern France.[10]

Headed by Lieutenant-Colonel Walter "Wally" Booth, the team consisted of Michael Burke, a well-known University of Pennsylvania football player, two French army officers, and Lieutenant Walter Kuzmyk, an American paratrooper of Ukrainian descent who hailed from Boston, Massachusetts, and who previously had parachuted into Normandy on D-Day, 6 June 1944, with the 101st "Screaming Eagles" Airborne Division. Kuzmyk, who claimed a proficiency in the Russian language but was actually fluent in Ukrainian, was selected on the basis of his language abilities.

In the meantime, as the team was being assembled, and the Germans were planning to eliminate Confrancon's Maquis, Major Hloba was secretly negotiating with the French insurgents.[11] Because previously French-based Ukrainian personnel within the 4th, 6th, and 7th Volunteer Regiments had established contact with the Maquis, while other Ukrainians bound for the "Galicia" Division ended up as anti-Nazi freedom fighters within France's F.F.I., such prior interactions proved to the F.F.I. that French-based Ukrainian personnel were not hostile to France and its people, and that Ukrainians could be trusted.

Between the Ukrainians and the Maquis, such a deal was negotiated: enroute to the Confrancon Forest, the Ukrainians would revolt, overpower the German cadre, and flee into the forest. Major Hloba and Commander "Simon" established that the revolt would occur during the night of 25 and 26 September, and that Hloba would rendezvous at exactly 12 midnight with Simon.[12] At this time, Simon also informed Hloba that F.F.I.'s leadership acknowledged his rank, and would support him.

On the day the revolt was to be staged, the Germans decided to transport the battalion to a new location. For the moment, the pre-arranged revolt was suspended. But again, changes occurred, and in the end, it was decided to utilize the Ukrainian force in an operation against the Confrancon Forest.

Within the Confrancon Forest, a strength of approximately 200 well-armed and equipped Maquis insurgents were found.[13] Against this force, the Germans dispatched Major Hanenstein's battalion. With 30 officers on horseback and 87 German NCOs directing the 700 Ukrainians, the force marched against the insurgents. Despite the abandonment of the previous plan, the Maquis and the Ukrainians quickly formulated a new plan. As the force approached the forest, the Ukrainians rebelled, wiped out the Germans, secured their arms, and fled into the forest.[14]

In the ensuing days, the mixed French-Ukrainian insurgent force continuously struck the road systems around the forest. Day and night, German troops and supply convoys were harassed. In lieu of the fact that the German front in France was shattered and Nazi forces were withdrawing, these disruptions were especially damaging. In an effort to re-establish control and prevent further disruptions, the Germans assembled a sizable force of approximately 4,000 soldiers 100 miles to the northeast of the forest at Luxeil-les-Bains. Reinforcing them with armor and artillery, they proceeded southwestward with the aim of ultimately destroying the insurgents.

Chapter 28: Die Ordnungspolizei (The Order Police)

In the meantime, as this was occurring, the five-man OSS team had established contact with the French-Ukrainians. Amongst the insurgents, the OSS team found out that the "Russians" were not Russians but actually, Ukrainians.[15] As for Kuzmyk, although former OSS officer William Casey does not cite his nationality but mentions he spoke Polish, Kusmyk was described by the Ukrainians as being "American in uniform, but in his heart and spirit, a true Ukrainian."[16] As it turned out, Kuzmyk's parents hailed from Kremianen, a town from which a number of the Ukrainian soldiers also hailed from.

For the next several days, the combined American, French and Ukrainian force fought a desperate and difficult battle against a superior Nazi force. According to OSS reports, it was indeed a difficult battle, as the allied force was out-numbered no less than four to one, with one Nazi attack continuously following another.[17] Although the allied force successfully repulsed the ground attacks, the situation did become critical for the defenders; indeed, so desperate that the defenders began to contemplate a surrender.

Good fortune, however, befell the insurgents. Just as their ammunition was about to run out, the exhausted defenders noted a German withdrawal.

While the Franco-Ukrainians were fighting the Nazis, General Alexander Patch's 7th U.S. Army was advancing north/northeastward toward the German border. Spearheading one such thrust was the 117th Cavalry Reconnaissance Troop. This unit was commanded by Colonel Charles Hodge, a former Wall-street lawyer who, prior to the war, had enlisted into the U.S. Army's Reserve to ride horses and play polo. Hodge was the epitome of a true cavalry-reconnaissance commander. Although by 1944 tanks, mechanized half-tracks and scout cars had replaced horses, the old cavalry-horse spirit still prevailed. And Hodge's lived and fought as his cavalry predecessors did decades before in the American Civil War and in the west. Smoking a cigar and adorned in a cavalry trooper's hat, Colonel Hodge's was pushing deep and far ahead of Patch's army into "Injun' Country."

Following the German withdrawal, the American, French, and Ukrainian combatants emerged from the forest and entered the nearby town of Haute-Savoie. Its civilians, jubilant about the German withdrawal and that the insurgents had survived, poured out into the streets. Wine bottles were opened, the Ukrainians prepared borscht (one of Kuzmyk's favorite dishes), French, American, and Ukrainian songs filled the air, and Burke produced a football and organized a game. Simply put, an international party with thousands of participants was underway.

Driving into the midst of this scene, Colonel Hodge could not understand what zone he had just entered. As he stood in his jeep amongst cheering civilians, Maquis fighters, Ukrainian insurgents dressed in bits and pieces of German uniforms, two regular French army officers, a famous football player and a Ukrainian-American airborne officer, Hodge was undoubtedly contemplating whether this was reality or a dream. But since at least no one was shooting at him and his men, Hodge's radioed his observation to 7th Army Headquarters, hoped that no one at headquarters would think that he had turned into a lunatic, and then joined the party.

Of course, General Patch's headquarters could not make out what this was all about. Appearing in person, Colonel Booth explained the situation and the OSS acknowledged the Ukrainian bravery. Needless to say, this moment would not be soon forgotten and in the upcoming decades, on occasion French civilians and military dignitaries would commemorate the event. Such was the case on 12 May 1985, when at Versailles, various French and Ukrainian political and military representatives honored the 1944-45 Franco-Ukrainian alliance. Notables included Mayor Georges Gruio who, along with Danylo Klym, Ivan Slozhuk, Volodymyr Avram, Andrei Marchenko and former French resistance officer Colonel Victor Peshi, laid a wreath at the base of a monument commemorating those Ukrainians who perished in France while serving with the Maquis. Such names are found on the monument: Semon Matsenko, Myhailo Pavlyk, Ivan Bodnar, Mykola Sydorenko, Petro Goshniak, Bronislav Lozynskyi and Petro Prytula. These names represent just some of those Ukrainians who made the supreme sacrifice within the ranks of the French resistance.[18]

Following the liberation of Paris, a number of foreign embassies re-established themselves in the French capital. Amongst them was the Soviet embassy. Noting that a number of Ukrainians were serving within the Maquis as well as in the regular French Army, the Soviets immediately began to agitate against them, seeking a way to repatriate them.[19]

Realistically speaking, this anti-Ukrainian agitation actually began even before France was totally liberated and it continued right at the moment Ukrainian personnel were fighting and, in a number of cases dying, to liberate France from Nazi rule.

In an effort to seize these Ukrainians, the Soviets portrayed them as "deserters!", "traitors!", "Nazi henchmen!", "renegades!", and "collaborationists!" In addition to these high-sounding distortions, Moscow's French-based personnel began to submit "evidence," "documents," and "eye-witnesses" which began to portray the Ukrainians in a negative and even, slanderous manner. Stories began to surface that Ukrainians had "terrorized" French civilians, that Ukrainian personnel were brought to France to "guard concentration camps," and Ukrainian soldiers fought the western allies in Normandy and France.[20] The "Galicia" Division was especially targeted.

Of course, Moscow's allegations were not only totally false and totally groundless but indeed, totally idiotic. And whenever any French, western allied military, or civilian agency inquired into any "Ukrainian massacres" and "crimes," or allegations that the "Galicia" Division fought the western allies, they found none.

In the immediate aftermath of World War II, numerous investigations were undertaken by both allied and French authorities to determine what crimes were perpetrated in France. In a number of cases, certain individuals and units were identified and brought to trial. If found guilty, punishment was meted out. In some cases, this even included native Frenchmen. But in the case of the Ukrainians, not one soldier (such as those who served in the 4th, 6th and 7th Volunteer Regiments), or any Ukrainian unit, or the "Galicia" Division itself, were ever implicated by the French.

Yet, despite the fact that up to the present no French administration has ever implicated the Division, or any of its Ukrainian personnel, and despite the fact that no American or other western allied military or civilian agency has ever implicated the Ukrainians, until the collapse of the Soviet Union in 1991, Soviet propagandists would repeatedly allege that Ukrainian personnel had committed "war crimes" when stationed in France.[21]

Notes

Notes Introduction

1. It is not always necessary to use the various titles of the Division. For purposes of clarity, whenever references are made to the Division, the word will be capitalized.

2. UPA - Ukrainian Povstans'ka (Insurgent) Army. During World War II, this guerrilla army fought both Nazi Germany and Soviet Russia.

3. Some individuals requested to remain anonymous. Therefore, when a reader notes an asterisk above a particular name, it indicates a factual individual, but an unfactual name.

Notes Chapter 1

1. Christopher Chant, *Hitler's Generals and Their Battles* (London: Salamander Books, Ltd, 1976), p. 78. This number only included the immediate attack and reserve divisions used in the opening phases of Barbarossa. In the following weeks and months more German, Hungarian, Rumanian, Finnish and other European units would be incorporated into the struggle. As a result, by the conclusion of 1941, approximately 207 German and satellite divisions and brigades had invaded Soviet Russia.

2. John Keegan, *The Waffen-SS* (NY.: Ballantine Books, Inc., 1970), p. 76. At the outset of Operation Barbarossa the twelve mechanized divisions were immediately reinforced with two additional Wehrmacht mechanized divisions, thus bringing the total number of mechanized divisions to enter Russia in 1941 to fourteen. See also *Illustrated World War II Encyclopedia* (H.S. Stuttman, Inc., 1990), Vol. 4, pp, 436-438. Hereafter referred to as *World War II Encyclopedia* with appropriate volume and page. According to the encyclopedia, 17 panzer and 12 panzergrenadier divisions comprised the front line strength, and two panzer and panzergrenadier divisions were in the rear. (Page 438).

3. John Keegan, *The Waffen-SS*, p 76.

4. John Erickson, *The Road to Stalingrad* (NY.: Harper and Row, 1975), Vol. 7, p. 98.

5. George H Stein, *The Waffen-SS, Hitler's Elite Guard at War, 1939-45* (N.Y.: Cornell University Press, 1966), p. 120. Although by the conclusion of 1941 the five Waffen-SS divisions were reinforced with the 6th SS "Nord" Mountain Division and a handful of independent Waffen-SS regiments, the overall strength of the fighting SS was still very small when compared to that of the Wehrmacht.

6. Erickson, *The Road to Stalingrad*, p 98; Matthew Cooper, *The German Army, 1939-45: Its Political and Military Failure* (N.Y.: Bonanza Books, 1984) cites the strength of the Wehrmacht in June, 1941, at 3,800,000.

Notes

(P.275). Of this strength 165,000, or approximately three percent of the whole army, consisted of the Waffen-SS. (P. 449).

7. *The International Military Tribunal, Trial of the Major War Criminals* (Germany, 1948), Vol 22, p. 512. Hereafter referred to as *IMT* with appropriate volume and page.

8. Heinz Hohne, *The Order of the Death's Head* (NY.: Ballantine Books, 1971), p. 65; IMT, Vol 22, p. 512; Keegan, *The Waffen-SS*, cites its strength in April 1929 as 280. (P. 31).

9. The son of a Roman Catholic teacher, Heinrich Himmler was born on 7 October 1900. In the closing months of World War I, he served as a cadet in the 11th Bavarian Regiment. Years later the neurotic, bespectacled man who suffered from emotional and physical problems, would claim front-line combat duty on the western front. (To this day, however, no records or accounts can substantiate his claim).
Initially, Himmler's relationship with Nazism was sporadic at best. In 1922, after obtaining a diploma from Munich's Technical Gymnasium, he worked as a salesman. The following year, he participated in the November Putsch but with its failure (and the collapse of Hitler's group), Himmler left the party. Returning in 1925, he joined the SS under number 168. But in 1927, Himmler married and went into the chicken business. With the collapse in early 1929 of both his business and marriage, he again returned to the party. Displaying abilities as a cold but capable and efficient organizer, Himmler took charge of the SS in April 1929. In addition to the SS, he headed virtually everything to include the Police, Gestapo, the concentration camp system, the Political Intelligence Department, the Waffen-SS, from 1944 the Wehrmacht's Reserve Army (against the Wehrmacht's protest), and in the concluding months of the war served briefly as a front commander in Northwestern Europe and in February, 1945, he commanded the Eastern Front's 'Army Group Vistula.' As a military commander, Himmler was totally inept.
Captured by British troops, he was imprisoned to stand trial for war crimes. But on 23 May 1945, the "expert on racial theory" committed suicide by swallowing cyanide poisoning.

10. Keegan, p. 34; Jeremy Noakes and Geoffrey Pridham, ed.'s, "The SS-Police System. The SS Take-over of the Police 1933-36" in Naz*ism: A History In Documents and Eyewitness Accounts," 1919-1945* (N.Y.: Schocken Books, 1984), Vol. 1, p. 499.

11. James Lucas and Matthew Cooper; *Hitler's Elite: Leibstandarte SS* (London: MacDonald and Jane's Co, Ltd., 1975), p. 12; Bruce Quarrie, *Hitler's Samurai: The Waffen-SS in Action* (England: Patrick Stevens Ltd., 1986), p. 23, *World War II Encyclopedia*, Vol. 20, p. 2763.

12. This unit would become the first Waffen-SS division.

13. Until 1942, Hitler himself opposed any major expansion of the Waffen-SS. There was to be no SS army corps, and Hitler insisted that the strength of the Waffen-SS was never to exceed 5 to 10 percent of the Wehrmacht's peacetime strength. Hohne, *The Order of the Death's Head*, p. 516; Cooper, *The German Army*, p. 450.

14. One may cite many reasons for the German failure: the fact that Operation Barbarossa was delayed from its original date of 15 May 1941 to 22 June; Germany's tremendous underestimation of Soviet Russia's strength; poor tactical planning; tough, unexpected Soviet resistance at critical points; German military weaknesses; and ruthless Nazi crimes against Soviet Russia's populace are just some of the factors contributing to the German failure For excellent accounts of combat on the eastern front from June to December 1941 see Hans von Luck's *Panzer Commander: The Memoirs of Hans von Luck* (N.Y.: Praeger, 1989); Heinz Guderian's, "The Campaign In Russia, 1941" in *Panzer Leader* (N.Y.: Ballantine Books, 1980), 7th ed., pp. 115-210; Colonel Albert Seaton, *The Battle for Moscow* (N.Y.: Playboy Press, 1980); and Janusz Piekalkiewicz, *Moscow: 1941. The Frozen Offensive* (London, England: Arms and Armour Press, 1985).

15. According to post-war allied investigations, by the conclusion of the war the Waffen-SS was estimated to have developed into a strength of some 580,000 men organized in 40 divisions *IMT*, Vol. 22, p. 513; Quarrie, *Hitler's Samurai*, pp. 30-34; Charles Sydnor, Jr., *Soldiers of Destruction: The SS Death's Head Division. 1933-1945* (N.J.: Princeton University Press, 1990), p. xviii. See also Colonel Albert Seaton's, *The Fall of Fortress Europe*, 1943-1945 (N.Y.: Holmes and Meier Publishers, Inc., 1981), pp. 18-19.

16. Quarrie, *Hitler's Samurai*, pp. 30-34; M.R.D. Foot, *Resistance: European Resistance to Nazism*, 1940-1945 (N.Y.: McGraw-Hill, 1977), p. 237; *World War II Encyclopedia*, Vol. 20, p. 2788.

17. Son of an Estonian mother and Lithuanian father, both of German extraction, Alfred Rosenberg was born in Reval (now Tallinn) in Estonia on 12 January 1893. Rosenberg studied engineering in Riga and in 1917, obtained an architecture degree from Moscow's State University. With the collapse of Imperial Russia, Rosenberg fled to Paris but shortly afterwards, he moved to Munich. In Munich, Rosenberg involved himself with the anti-Bolshevik emigre movement but in 1919, he joined the Nazi party. Rosenberg participated in Hitler's Munich "Beer Hall" Putsch. With Hitler's rise to power in January 1933, Rosenberg was appointed to head the Foreign Affairs Department. Rosenberg, who always envisioned a "great Nordic empire" under German leadership, was in reality nothing but a weak, blundering and incompetent administrator. Although he espoused some degree of separatism and autonomy for certain East-

ern European states, and on occasion did protest the brutal treatment of Eastern Europeans (such as his letter to Field-Marshal Keitel, OKW Chief, on 28 February 1942 regarding the brutal treatment of Soviet prisoners of war), by no means was Rosenberg a humane Nazi. During the Nuremberg Trials, Rosenberg's Chief Counsel, Alfred Thoma, argued that it was Bormann, Himmler, and Erich Koch who frustrated Rosenberg's "good and fair intentions." (For much of what Thoma said see *IMT*, Vol. 18, pp. 73-80). Regardless, Rosenberg was found guilty of war crimes and on 16 October 1946, was hanged at Nuremberg.

18. Gerald Reitlinger, *The House Built on Sand: The Conflicts of German Policy in Russia*, 1939-45 (NY.: Viking Press, 1960), p. 169; and *The SS: Alibi Of a Nation*, 1922-1945 (N.Y.: DaCapo Press, Inc., 1989), p. 205. See also Anthony Read and David Fischer, T*he Deadly Embrace: Hitler, Stalin, and the Nazi-Soviet Pact, 1939-1941* (N.Y.: Norton and Company, 1988), pp. 590-591.

19. On 31 March 1941, Hitler appointed Rosenberg to head the "Political Office For the East" On 20 April, it was redesignated "Central Department For the Treatment of Eastern Questions" and on 17 July 1941, it became a ministry headed by Rosenberg. *IMT*, Vol. 18, p. 75; *Read and Fischer*, p. 590.

20. Reitlinger, *The House Built on Sand*, p 169; *Read and Fischer* pp. 590-591.

21. William Shirer, *The Rise and Fall of the Third Reich* (NY.: Simon and Schuster, 1960), p. 798; Read and Fischer, p. 590.

22. Reitlinger, *The House*, p 169; *IMT*, Vol 4, pp. 10-11.

23. Reitlinger, *The SS*, p 205; and *The House*, pp. 134 and 169.

24. *IMT*, Vol. 18, p. 75; Alan Clark, *Barbarossa: The Russian-German Conflict*, 1941-1945 (N.Y.: Quill Publishers, 1985), pp. 64-65; Raphael Lemkin, *Axis Rule In Occupied Europe. Laws of Occupation/Analysis of Government/Proposals For Redress* (Washington: D.C., 1944), p. 7; Foot, p. 286; Wolodymyr Kosyk, *The Third Reich and the Ukrainian Question. Documents: 1934-1944* (London: 1991), p. 15.
Who was Erich Koch? Was he a Nazi fanatic, or a Soviet agent operating within the higher circles of the Third Reich? An honorary SS Lieutenant General, Gauleither of East Prussia and Reich Commissar of Ukraine from 1941 to 1944, Koch was born in Ebberfeld, Prussia, on 19 June 1896. Koch, a poorly disciplined soldier who adopted "revolutionary socialism" in the trenches of the Russian front (Reitlinger, *The House Built on Sand*, p. 78), left the army at the conclusion of the war after undistinguished military service. Supposedly, Koch's pro-left sympathies were short-lived because in 1921, he joined "Freikorps Rossbach," a violently pro-nationalist and anti-communist paramilitary group. Whether Koch joined the Freikorps to obtain easier entry into the Nazi party and to eliminate any doubt about his leftist sympathies may only be speculated. From 1921 to 1933, Koch held various party leadership positions in the Ruhr and East Prussia. In September 1933, he was promoted "Oberprasident" of East Prussia. Ruthless with his critics, Koch was also unpopular with East Prussia's peasants because he advocated agricultural collectivism. As Reich Commissioner of Ukraine, Koch ruled with particular brutality and thus, alienated Ukraine's populace against Nazi Germany.
In 1944, he fled from the advancing Soviets to Prussia. Shortly afterwards, Koch disappeared. Arrested in May 1949 by British authorities, Koch was extradited to Warsaw, Poland, for war crimes on 14 January 1950. Yet his "trial" did not begin until 19 October 1958. At that time, Koch was only charged with crimes against Poland. At no time was he ever tried for crimes against the Ukrainian, Jewish, and other inhabitants of Ukraine. On 9 March 1959, a Polish court sentenced him to death; his sentence, however, was soon commuted to life imprisonment on the grounds of "poor health." Until his death, Soviet authorities never requested his extradition, nor did they ever pressure Poland's authorities to carry out the original death sentence. Although in "poor health," Koch lived a long and comfortable life in Barczewo, Poland. He died 12 November 1986.

25. *IMT*, Vol 18, p. 75; Lemkin, *Axis Rule*, p. 7. The Reich Commissariat for Ukraine was headquartered in Rowne and was divided into six commissariats: Zhitomir, Kiev, Nikolaiv, Chernihiv, Dniepropetrovsk, and the Crimea.

26. *IMT*, Vol 18, p. 75.

27. Reitlinger, *The House*, p 169.

28. *Ibid*; *Kosyk*, p. 15. For Hitler's views on colonizing and exploiting Ukraine, as well as his opposition for Ukrainian independence and Ukrainian education, see H.R. Trevor-Roper. *Hitler's Social Conversations, 1941-1944* (N.Y.: Farrar, Straus and Young, 1953). See especially pp. 13,24,26,28-29,39,45,76,465,501-502,506,557.

29. On 1 September 1939, Germany invaded Poland. Shortly afterwards on 17 September, Germany's short-lived ally, Soviet Russia, struck Poland from the east. Outnumbered and poorly equipped, the Polish Army was soon defeated. On 12 October 1939, Hitler ordered Poland to be organized as a "General Government" and he divided that country into four districts: Cracow, Lublin, Radom, and Warsaw. (Lemkin, *Axis Rule*, pp. 225-226). But in 1941, with the forceful incorporation of Galicia into the General Government, five provinces were now established. Alexander Dallin, *German Rule in Russia* (London: MacMillan and Co., Ltd., 1957), pp. 71 and 90, and Lemkin, *Axis Rule*, p.226.

Notes

30. In a conference attended by Hitler, Lammers, Goering, Keitel, Rosenberg and Borman on 16 July 1941, Hitler announced "that the former Austrian part of Galicia will become Reich territory" (On 17 December 1945, Captain Samuel Harris, Assistant Trial Counsel, presented to the Nuremberg Court Document No. L-221, Exhibit No. USA-317, dated 16 July 1941. Initialed by Borman, this document revealed Nazi plans for Galicia. *IMT*, Vol. 4, pp. 4, 10-11). See also *Lemkin*, p. 226; Reitlinger, *The SS*, p. 204.

31. Commander of Army Group "South's" Rear Administration.

32. "If I put up a poster for every seven Poles shot, the forests of Poland would not be sufficient to manufacture the paper for such posters!" So boasted Hitler's former lawyer, Hans Frank. With such a mentality, Frank ruled Poland. In personal discussions with Hitler, such as on 2 October 1940 (*IMT*, Vol. 7, pp. 223-227), Poland's place in Europe's "New Order" was established. During this discussion, Frank also informed the Führer that Nazi activities against the Poles and Jews in the General Government could be termed as "successful." Viciously, Frank ensured Hitler's decree that "Poland's gentry and intelligentsia be eliminated and that Poland be nothing but a labor camp for Germany." (Ibid. See also *IMT*, Vol. 39, Document No. 172, pp. 425-429). But Frank's disillusionment with Hitler's Third Reich began in late 1942 when Nazi authorities arrested and shot Dr. Karl Lasch, a former president of Germany's Law Academy. Angered by the loss of a close friend, Frank condemned Nazism and publicly demanded a return to constitutional law. As a result, he was stripped of all Nazi Party honors and positions, and was only permitted to serve as Poland's Governor General, a position which Hitler regarded as the lowest. With the collapse of the Third Reich, Frank was tried as a war criminal. At Nuremberg, he condemned Hitler, confessed his guilt, and pleaded for mercy. Regardless, Frank was found guilty. Born on 23 May 1900, he was executed on 16 October 1946.

33. In actuality, Galicia's first governor was Dr. Karl Lasch (who was also the former president of Germany's Law Academy). But following his dismissal as a result of a scandal, Wachter (an Austrian by birth on 8 July 1900 and the son of an Austrian army general) assumed the position.

34. For a detailed study of the German-Austrian influence in Galicia and Ukraine see Enc*yclopedia of Ukraine* (Toronto University Press, 1988), Vol II, pp. 42-56.

35. *Ibid.*

36. "Nimts'i Pro Halychynu" [German's About Galicia], *Svoboda* Ukrainian Daily, 14 November 1979, p 2. But under the Soviet occupation, many German Galicians were repatriated to Germany between December 1939 and February 1940.

Notes Chapter 2

1. Piotr S Wandycz, *The Lands of Partitioned Poland, 1795-1918* (Seattle and London: University of Washington Press, 1974), p. 249.

2. Dmytro Doroshenko, *A Survey of Ukrainian History* (Winnipeg, Canada: Trident Press, Ltd., 1975), p. 567; Roland Gaucher, *Opposition In the USSR, 1917-1967* (N.Y.: Funk and Wagnalls, 1969), p. 159; Petro Grigorenko, *Grigorenko Memoirs* (N.Y.: W.W. Norton and Company, 1982), pp. 344-345.

3. This 'ukaz' even prohibited the importation of Ukrainian works published abroad John S. Reshetar, *The Ukrainian Revolution, 1917-1920* (N.Y.: Arno Press, 1972, p. 7). See also *Wandycz*, p. 249.

4 A prime example is that of Professor Myhailo Drahomaniv Deprived of his position at Kiev University, Drahomaniv and a number of other Ukrainian political exiles sought refuge in Geneva, Switzerland. After establishing a publishing house in Geneva, they made contact with Galicia's Ukrainian movement. In due time, they transferred their publishing activities to Eastern Galicia.

5. Soviet Russia's invasion of Ukraine was based on practical and ideological reasons. Although initially Lenin and the Bolsheviks recognized the Ukrainian Republic, they soon realized they needed Ukraine for its economic and strategic position. As Europe's "breadbasket," and rich in natural wealth, Ukraine was deemed essential for the economy of the newly established Bolshevik state. Ideologically, there were two reasons: preaching "world revolution," the Bolsheviks would need Ukraine as a springboard for exporting revolution into Europe, the Middle East, and Africa; additionally, Ukraine's democratic socialism, as practiced by the Ukrainian government, offered an ideological threat to Marxism-Leninism. In the event that communism would fail in Red Russia, many Russians would look upon Ukrainian socialism as an alternative. For these reasons, Russia's Bolsheviks had to suppress the Ukrainian state.

6. Also known as the National Democratic Party. Founded in 1897, the party stressed grass roots work in every field of activity in preparation for independence. Strongly anti-German, it also took an uncompromising attitude in regards to Jews and Ukrainians. M.K. Dziewanowski, *Poland In the 20th Century* (N.Y.: Columbia University Press, 1977), p. 57. Josef Buszko, *Historia Polski, 1864-1948* (Warszawa: Panstwowe Wydawnictwo Naukowe, 1984), p. 202, cites the organization was very anti-German. The nationalist organization 'Zwiazek Ludowo-Narodowy' (ZLN),

Galicia Division

also took a strong anti-German, Ukrainian, and Semitic stand. (*Ibid.*, pp. 220-221). See also Stewart Steven, *The Poles* (N.Y.: MacMillan Publishing Co., Inc., 1982), pp. 312-313.

7. Richard M. Watt, *Bitter Glory: Poland and Its Fate, 1918-1939* (N.Y.: Simon and Schuster, 1982), p. 55. See also Ferdinand Czerin, *Versailles 1919* (N.Y.: 1964), p. 218; H.W.V. Temperley, ed., *A History of the Peace Conference of Paris* (London: 1920), Vol. 1, p. 335. Hereafter referred to as *History of Paris Peace Conference*, with appropriate volume and page.

8. With the collapse of Imperial Russia on 7 November 1917, on 22 January 1918, the Ukrainian National Republic (UNR) proclaimed its independence With Austria's demise in late 1918, on 1 November 1918, the East Galician Ukrainians proclaimed an independent Western Ukrainian Republic. But two months later, on 22 January 1919, on the first anniversary of UNR's independence, the UNR and the newly created Western Ukrainian Republic's merged into one nation.

9. As early as 1848, when the Slavic Congress was held in Prague, the East Galician Ukrainians sought the division of Galicia into two separate parts: Western Galicia to be Polish and Eastern Galicia to be Ukrainian (*Wandycz*, pp. 144-145). The following year, Galicia's population (both western and eastern but excluding Bukovyna), was officially set at 4,920,000. Of this figure, 2,258,000 were Poles; 2,303,000 were Ukrainian; 323,000 were Jews; 27,000 were Germans; and 9,000 were of other nationalities. But in Eastern Galicia's twelve districts the Ukrainians (known at that time as Ruthenians - or Rusyny), were the largest national group. Here, out of a total of 3,313,000, 71 percent were Ukrainian; 20.4 percent Poles; 7.9 were Jews; 0.6. were Germans; and 0.1 were undetermined. Jan Kozik, *The Ukrainian National Movement In Galicia: 1815-1849* (Canada: University of Alberta, 1986), p. 17. See also Orest Subtelny, *Ukraine: A History* (Toronto: University of Toronto Press, 1988), p. 248; and Josef A. Gierowski, *Historia Polski, 1764-1864* (Warszawa: Panstwowe Wydawnictwo Naukowe, 1984), pp. 253-254.

10. The Peace Conference proceeded from the principle that in Europe the frontiers most likely to prove just, satisfactory, and durable were those that conformed to ethno-graphic divisions. Edward House and Charles Seymour, *What Really Happened at Paris: The Story of the Peace Conference* (N.Y.: Charles Scribner Sons, 1921), p. 68.

11. This was the Kingdom of Poland formed by Tsar Alexander I of Russia.

12. Kay Lundgreen-Nielsen, T*he Polish Problem At the Paris Peace Conference; A Study of the Policies of the Great Powers and the Poles, 1918-1919* (Odense University Press, 1979), Vol. 59, p. 34; Stephan Horak, *Poland And Her National Minorities, 1919-1939* (N.Y.: Vantage Press, 1961), p. 31.

13. *Lundgren-Nielsen*, pp. 35-36. See also *Horak*, pp. 32-33.

14. *Lundgren-Nielsen*, pp. 35-36; *Horak,* pp. 32-33; Laurence J. Orzell, "A Hotly Disputed Issue: Eastern Galicia at the Paris Peace Conference, 1919" in *The Polish Review,* Vol.XXV. No.1, 1980), p. 51. See also Subtelny, p. 371.

15. *Lundgreen-Nielsen*, pp. 35 & 45; *Horak*, pp. 34-35.

16. *Dziewanowski*, p. 58; *Horak*, pp. 32-33.

17. *Lundgreen*, p. 36; M.K. Dziewanowski, *Joseph Pilsudski: A European Federalist, 1918-1922* (Ca.: Hoover Institution Press, 1969), p. 248. Regarding Byelorussia, Dmowski theorized that if Poland took the whole of Byelorussia, it would not only be difficult to assimilate and control but worse, would lead to Russian hostility. But if Poland surrendered the whole region to Russia, this would create future problems for Poland. And if Byelorussia became independent, Dmowski feared it would come under foreign influence. Therefore, to best resolve the matter, Poland would divide Byelorussia between itself and Russia. (*Lundgreen*, p. 36). See also *Horak*, pp. 34-35.

18. Stephen Bonsal, *Suitors and Supplicants: The Little Nations at Versailles* (N.Y.: Prentice-Hall, Inc., 1946), p. 135. An American Army translator fluent in a number of European languages, Lieutenant Bonsal was America's official translator and recorder of the daily discussions for President Wilson and Colonel House during the Paris Peace talks. In due time, Lt. Bonsal became very sympathetic to the Ukrainian cause.

19. Galicia's first inhabitants came from the south-central Ukraine during the Middle Paleolithic period. In the era of European tribal migrations (A.D. 300-800), Galicia's history is not well known. The Primary Chronicle, written in Kiev Rus' from the early 12th through 13th century (based on princely, monastic, and foreign accounts collected throughout Kiev and its principalities such as Galicia), speaks of several Slavic tribes inhabiting Eastern Galicia: White Croatians (who later migrated southwestward into the Balkans), Lutychi, and Tivertsi. Ethnically, culturally, and linguistically, Galicia's Slavs were related more closely to Kiev's Slavs than to the Slavs living further in the west, such as the various Polish tribes inhabiting regions northwestward of them. It is also known that these three tribes were a part of the Kievan Rus' state and that in 907, all three participated in Kievan Prince Oleh's campaign against Byzantium.

Notes

In 981, Kievan Prince Volodymyr the Great (who in 988 accepted Christianity), fought with the Poles. In 1054, Grand Prince Yaroslav the Wise died and the Kievan State began to disintegrate into separate principalities, such as Galicia. By the time the Mongols struck in 1240, the Kievan State was so weak that it was shattered.

Eastern Galicia's city of Lviv was founded in approximately 1250 by the Galician Ukrainian ruler King Danylo. In 1272, Lviv became the capital of Galicia. Ukrainians, to this day, refer to Galicia as "Halychyna," the name deriving from the Eastern Galician city of Halych founded in the mid-12th century by Volodymyrko, a direct descendant of Yaroslav the Wise. Throughout the 13th and early 14th centuries, Galicia's rulers faced internal rivalries and external pressures from Polish, Hungarian, and Mongolian rulers as they vied for Galicia. In 1340, when Poland's King Casimir III attacked Lviv, Poland's position became increasingly dominant until 1772 when Austria, Prussia, and Russia partitioned Poland. That same year, Austria claimed Galicia on the grounds that its Empress, Maria Theresa, had at one time ruled Hungary and, in turn, the Hungarian State had briefly occupied the Galician principality in the early 13th and late 14th centuries. Austria's new province, referred to as the 'Kingdom of Galicia' and 'Lodomeria' (called "Galicia" by the Austrians in memory of the ancient Ruthenian Dukedom of Halych, see Roman Dyboski, Poland *In World Civilization*, N.Y.: Barrett Corp., 1950, p. 138), comprised an area of 83,000 square kilometers and 2,800,000 inhabitants. See also *Encyclopedia of Ukraine*, 1988, Vol. II, p. 6.

20. *Laurence J. Orzell*, p. 50. Cited also from E.L. Woodward and Rohan Butler, *Documents on British Foreign Policy, 1919-1939, First Series* (London: H.M. Stationary Office, 1949), Vol. 3, pp. 842-843. Whereas in West Galicia, out of 2,693,000 people, 2,384,000 (88%) were Roman Catholic; 87,000 (3%) Greek Catholic; 213,000 (8%) were Jewish. The majority of Galicia's Ukrainians were Greek-Catholic.

21. H.J. Patton, "Poland At the Peace Conference," in Temperly's *History of Paris Peace Conference*, op. cit., Vol. 6, pp. 267-268. The term "Ruthenian" was also used to describe Ukrainians who previously had inhabited Austria's Empire.

22. *Ibid.*

23. *Ibid.*

24. *Papers Relating to the Foreign Relations of the United States: 1918, Supplement I, The World War* Vol. I (Washington, D.C.: Government Printing Office, 1933), Vol. I, pp. 405-413. Hereafter referred to as *Foreign Relations*, with appropriate volume and page. In turn, Colonel House submitted this report to President Wilson. See also *Lundgreen*, p. 86.

25. Watt, B*itter Glory*, p 69; *Lundgreen*, pp. 35 & 39; Foreign *Relations*, Vol. III, pp. 78; 781-782.

26. *Foreign Relations*, Vol III, pp. 781-782.

27. *Lundgreen*, p. 54; Dziewanowski, *Joseph Pilsudski*, pp. 245-246; O. Dotsenko, *Litopys Ukrains'koi Revoliutsii [Chronicle of the Ukrainian Revolution]*, (Lviv, 1924), Vol. II, op. cit., n. 13, p. 253; M.K. Dziewanowski, "Joseph Pilsudski, the Bolshevik Revolution and Eastern Europe," in *Essays on Poland's Foreign Policy, 1918-1939*, ed. Thaddeus V. Gromada (N.Y.: Pilsudski Institute of America, 1970), pp. 17; 23-24.

28. Lundgreen, pp. 54-55.

29. Dziewanowski, *Joseph Pilsudski*, p. 246; and *Joseph Pilsudski, the Bolshevik Revolution and Eastern Europe*, p. 24. Pilsudski was not an exception. Poland's federalists also favored the establishment of an independent Ukraine. See Roman Debicki, *Foreign Policy of Poland, 1919-1939. From the Rebirth of the Polish Republic to World War II* (N.Y.: Frederick Praeger, 1962), pp. 25; 27-28. Of interest to note is that on 28 October 1918, a conference of Austrian-Polish representatives met at Cracow. Although no Ukrainian representatives appeared (possibly none were invited), nor were any Jewish representatives present, the conferees stressed for the incorporation of Western Galicia in accordance with President Wilson's "territories inhabited by indisputably Polish populations" into Poland proper. But in regards to Eastern Galicia, this was not the case. *History of Paris Peace Conference*, Vol. 4, p. 104.

30. Dziewanowski, *Joseph Pilsudski*, p 246; *Foreign Relations*, Vol. 12, p. 368.

31. Jiri Louda, *European Civic Coats of Arms* (London: Paul Hamlyn, Ltd, 1966), p. 174. In 1789, Emperor Joseph II added a star and mount (Mount - 'Berg') on the 14th century Galician Lion's (Lem's) crest, thus giving the second half of the town's German name of Lemberg. (*Ibid*). See also Olena Stepaniv, *Suchasnyi Lviv v 700 littia zasnovannia Mista L'vova* [Current Lviv in 700 years of the Founding of the City of Lviv], (Howerla Publishers, 1953), pp. 3, 5, and 8.

32. Steven L. Guthier, "The Popular Base of Ukrainian Nationalism In 1917," in *Slavic Review*, Vol. 38, No. 1, March, 1979, p. 31. See also *Horak*, p. 87.

33. *Guthier*, p. 31.

Galicia Division

34. During the Paris Peace talks, the Allied group consisted of five Principle Allied and Associated Powers simply known as PAAP: the United States, Great Britain, France, Italy, and Japan

35. *Lundgreen*, pp. 65; 68-69;. *Subtelny*, p. 371; *Horak*, p. 48; *Foreign Relations*, Vol. III, pp. 642; 672.

36. Orzell, p. 54; *Foreign Relations*, Vol. IV, p. 410. In regard to Eastern Galicia, Balfour even suggested that Poland's representatives be gathered and told "they must limit their actions to the protection of indisputable Polish territory against invasion from without, "and that" the ultimate frontiers of Poland should be left to the Peace Congress." *Foreign Relations*, Vol. III, p. 672.

37. *Lundgreen*, pp. 65-69; 186. Of Jewish parentage, Louis Bernstein-Niemirowski (Namier) was born in Russian Poland on 27 June 1888. As a child, he moved with his family to East Galicia in 1890. Educated at Lemberg, Lausanne, and Oxford Universities, Namier became a naturalized British subject in 1913.

38. *Ibid*, pp. 187; 414. However, some Frenchmen did support the Galician Ukrainians. (See p. 187).

39. *Ibid*, pp. 69-71.

40. Although on 22 January 1919 the Ukrainian National Republic formally united with the West Ukrainian (Galician) Republic, many Galician Ukrainians firmly believed that their chance for some kind of international recognition (and possibly the establishment of an independent state), was better than that of Ukraine proper; therefore, they continued to maintain their own autonomy and army.

41. Clarence Manning, *Twentieth Century Ukraine* (N.Y.: Bookman Associates, 1951), p. 68; William Chamberlain, *The Ukraine: A Submerged Nation* (N.Y.: MacMillan Co., 1944), p. 50. See also Dziewanowski, *Poland In the 20th Century*, p. 81.

42. Ernest Dupuy and Colonel Trevor Dupuy, *The Encyclopedia of Military History* (NY.: Harper and Row, 1970), p. 991. See also *Manning*, pp. 67-70.

43. *Dupuy and Dupuy*, p. 991; *Manning*, p. 68; *Chamberlain*, pp. 50-51.

44. Michael Yaremko, *Galicia-Halychyna, A Part of Ukraine From Separation to Unity*. Published by the Shevchenko Scientific Society (Toronto-New York-Paris, 1967), p. 223; William Chamberlain, *The Ukraine: A Submerged Nation*, pp. 65-66. This included the whole of Eastern Galicia. At this time, Poland also abandoned Petliura. As for Ukraine, it was divided between Poland and Russia. (Dziewanowski, *Poland In the 20th Century*, p. 83).

45. For the allied viewpoints, see *Lundgreen*, p 86; *Foreign Relations*, Vol. 1, pp. 411-412; and "Treaty Between the Principle Allied and Associated Powers and Poland," in *Foreign Relations*, Vol. XIII, pp. 793-795. See also Chamberlain's, *The Ukraine: A Submerged Nation*, p. 65; and Raymond J. Sontag, *A Broken World, 1919-1939* (N.Y.: Harper and Row, 1971), p. 64. Since a solution could not be achieved, a mandate (against Poland's demands) was proposed by those such as Sir Eyre Crowe, Britain's Under-Secretary of State, and a staunch advocate of uniting Eastern Galicia with Ukraine or even, Russia. In order for the Galician issue to be resolved in the near future, a mandate was set for a period of 25 years after which the League of Nations would determine the final status of Eastern Galicia. (*Reshetar*, pp. 296-298; *Orzell*, pp. 64-68).

46. "The Question of the Bukovina: First Phase" and "The Question of the Bukovina: Second Phase," pp. 102-107 and pp. 126-127, in Sherman D. Spector's, *Rumania At the Paris Peace Conference: A Study of the Diplomacy of Ioan I.C. Bratianu* (N.Y.: Bookman Associates, 1962). With regard to Eastern Galicia, Spector cites that it would be supervised by the League of Nations and its final destiny would be determined after a period of twenty-five years. (*Ibid.*, footnote no. 79, p. 316).

47. The UNR's delegation was headed by Gregory Sidorenko and included Alexander Shulgin, Serhi Shelukhin, and the eminent and respected Ukrainian-Jewish scholar, Dr. Arnold D. Margolin. The Galicians had their own delegation headed by Dr. Vasyl Paneyko, Dr. Myhailo Lozynsky, and Colonel Dmytro Vitovsky. *Reshetar*, p. 271. See also Arnold D. Margolin, *From A Political Diary: Russia, Ukraine, and America, 1905-1945* (N.Y.: Columbia University Press, 1946).

48. Anthony Polansky, *Politics In Independent Poland, 1921-1939* (Oxford: Clarendon Press, 1972), p 33; *Dyboski*, p. 234, cites over 4 million Ukrainians in Southeastern Galicia. According to Polish statistician A. Krysinski, more Ukrainians existed than acknowledged by official Polish statistics. As of January 1928, 4,865,000 Ukrainians were found in Poland. See *Horak*, p. 84.

49. For a chart of the structure of the national groups in Poland, see *Horak*, p 100. See also Stewart Steven, *The Poles*, p. 277; and *Watt*, p. 173.

50. Herbert A. Gibbons, *Europe Since 1918* (London: Jonathan Cape, 1923), p. 235.

Notes

51. Arnold Toynbee, *The Eve of War, 1939, Part I*, Introduction (London: Oxford University Press, 1958), p 9. For an interesting account condemning Poland's actions in partitioning its neighbors see Peter Brock's "Boleslaw Wyslouch, Founder of the Polish Peasant Party," in *The Slavonic and East European Review* (December, 1951), pp. 143-144; Wladyslaw Studnicki, *Das Oestliche Polen* (Gottingen, 1953), pp. 76-77. Translated by Dr. Wilhelm von Harpe.

Although the Treaty of Riga was welcomed by the war weary Poles, a number of serious (and very negative) consequences, lay behind it. Aside from the fact that the treaty was achieved at the expense of the Ukrainians and Byelorussians, it could not solve Poland's eastern security question. This was already evidenced in early 1924 when a number of German military and political envoys (based in the Soviet Union) were informed by Soviet officials that Moscow was speaking of pushing Poland's border back to its "ethno-graphic frontiers." See Piotr S. Wandycz, "The Treaty of Riga: Its Significance for Interwar Polish Foreign Policy," in E*ssays On Poland's Foreign Policy, 1918-1939*, ed. Thaddeus Gromada, pp. 31-36. See also *Lundgreen*, p. 414; *Manning*, p. 72; *Horak*, pp. 142-143; and Len Deighton, *Blitzkreig: From the Rise of Hitler to the Fall of Dunkirk* (N.Y.: Ballantine Books, 1980), pp. 63-65.

52. Polish (and even Rumanian) promises of "autonomous" status for its minorities were never fulfilled. Eastern Galicia was referred to as "Little Poland" and Ukrainian schools, cultural centers, political organizations and in general, the Ukrainian way of life was subjected to "Polonization." Yet, even succumbed to it. Poland itself never evolved into a full democracy and, factually speaking, in the early 1930's moved increasingly toward totalitarianism and neo-fascism. By 1935, Poland's military clique, headed by Pilsudski, reduced the Sejm's power by half. The League of Nations accords regarding the protection of minorities was revoked, and a concentration camp was established at Bereza Kartuzka. (*Doroshenko*, p. 724; *Buszko*, pp. 286, 312, 325, 340; "Poland: Current Situation in Poland" in U.S. Army Intelligence (G-2) Summary for 28 May 1937. (Unclassified). (Washington, D.C.), p. 16198. For a factual political, economic, and social study of Poland in 1937 see pp. 16197-16204. See also Chamberlain, pp. 66-68).

Needless to say, such measures only worsened the Ukrainian position and created further hardships for those involved in such organizations as the Ukrainian National Democratic Union (UNDO), which lobbied Poland's parliament in behalf of its minorities. See also Robert Kee, *1939: In the Shadow of War* (Boston: Little, Brown and Co., 1984), pp. 62 and 315; and Philip Friedman, "Ukrainian- Jewish Relations During the Nazi Occupation" in *YIVO: Annual of Jewish Social Science* (N.Y.: 1958-59), No. 12, p. 261.

53. See also Articles 7-11 in *Foreign Relations*, Vol. XIII, pp. 799-801; *Watts*, pp. 172-174. Officially, however, on an international level, only Western Galicia was recognized as an integral part of Poland. As for Eastern Galicia, it was decreed that it would remain under Poland's control until a future plebiscite (in which only Eastern Galicia's populace would participate), would determine the outcome. But this never occurred because of World War II. See *Margolin*, p. 140; and Reverend I. Hazapko, "Rishennia Rady Ambasaderiv 1923" [The Decision of the Ambassadors in 1923], in *The Light Almanac* (Toronto: Basilian Press, 1973), p. 92; and *Chamberlain*, pp. 65-66. A last minute personal appeal by the former president of the Ukrainian Republic, Evhen Petryshevych, along with Premier I. Levytsky, failed to produce any successful results in Paris.

Notes Chapter 3

1. Most Latynnycky's were Ukrainians who had converted themselves from Greek Catholic to the Polish Roman Catholic.

2. *Ethnic Groups of the South-Western Ukraine (Galicia) on the 1st of January, 1939* (Memoirs of the Scientific Shevchenko Society, Published in London-Munich-Paris-New York, 1953), p. 11. At that time, Poland's administration referred to Eastern Galicia as "Little Poland." (Malopolska Wschodnia). As for the Ukrainians, they were the majority in Stanislaviv, Ternopil, and the Lviv districts which constituted Eastern Galicia. Jan T. Gross, *Revolution From Abroad: the Soviet Conquest of Poland's Western Ukraine and Western Byelorussia* (N.J.: Princeton University.Press, 1988), p. 4. And if the territory of Volyn, which was 70 percent Ukrainian were also included, the Ukrainian majority was overwhelming. (*Ibid*). According to a post World War II U.S. Army study "as of the beginning of 1939, the Polish state had a total population of 34.75 million, of whom 22 million were ethnic Poles. The large minorities were the Ukrainians (3.25 million), Jews (2.75 million), Ruthenians (2.25 million), and Germans (.75 million). Smaller numbers of Russians, Lithuanians, Slovaks, and other Slavic groups comprised the remainder of the minorities resident within Poland's borders." Major Robert M. Kennedy's,"Population and Economy, Poland's Position and Germany's Preparation For the Attack" in *The German Campaign In Poland, 1939*, DA Pamphlet No. 20-255 (Washington, D.C.: April, 1956), p. 48. See also *Deighton*, p. 64.

3. Besides targeting the Ukrainian leadership, the Kremlin also planned to exterminate the patriotic Polish, Byelorussian and Jewish element. See Dziewanowski, *Poland In the 20th Century*, p. 115.

4. Ronald Hingley, *The Russian Secret Police* (NY.: Simon and Schuster, 1970), p. 185; Boris Levytsky, *The Uses of Terror: the Soviet Secret Police, 1917-1970* (N.Y.: Coward, McCann and Geoghegan, Inc., 1972), p. 149. In a number of cases, the NKVD police (as did later Hitler's gestapo), obtained the names of many individuals by simply going through the Polish police files. See Myhailo Il'kiv, *Nimets'ki Kontsentratsiini Lagery (Spohad)* [German Concentration Camps (Memoirs)] (Canada: Harmony Printing Ltd., 1983), p. 14.

Galicia Division

5. Irena and Jan Gross, *War Through Children's Eyes, The Soviet Occupation of Poland and the Deportations, 1939-1941* (Hoover Institution Press, 1981), preface xxii; Dziewanowski, *Poland In the 20th Century*, pp 115-116. Of the 1.2 million, 880,000 were forcibly deported during such four major waves of deportations: February, April, and June of 1940 and in June, 1941. *Gross*, preface xxii. Boris Shub and Bernard Quint, *Since Stalin: A Photo History of Our Time* (N.Y.: Swen Publications, Inc., 1951), p. 84, cites some 1,500,000 were deported to Northern Russia, Central Asia, and Siberia. According to J. Lee Ready, *The Forgotten Axis: Germany's Partners and Foreign Volunteers in World War II* (N.C.: McFarland and Co., Inc., 1987), p. 121, the NKVD arrested 1.5 million. Ready's figure is substantiated by Oleg Gordievsky, a former NKVD officer who cited that by June 1941, approximately 1.5 million were deported to Siberia and Kazakhstan. Of these, nearly half perished. See Christopher Andrew and Oleg Gordievsky, *KGB: The Inside Story* (N.Y.: Harper Collins, 1990), pp. 248-249 and 252-253.

6. Gross, *War Through Children's Eyes*, preface xxiii. The above figures did not just include Poles, but also included Ukrainians and Jews. Almost one-third were workers and peasants. *(Ibid)*. See also *Levytsky*, pp. 152-153.

7. For harrowing accounts regarding the widespread arrests and deportations, see Alexander Solzhenitsyn's, *The Gulag Archipelago, 1918-1956* (N.Y.: Harper and Row, Publishers, 1973); and Karlo Stajner, *Seven Thousand Days in Siberia* (N.Y.: Farrar, Strauss and Giroux, Inc., 1988). See also Amy Knight, *Beria, Stalin's First Lieutenant* (N.J.: Princeton University Press, 1993).

8. Initially, this even included many Jews. John Toland, *Adolf Hitler* (N.Y.: Doubleday and Co., Inc., 1976), Vol. II, p. 775. It should be noted that at that time anyone (and not necessarily the Germans), that would have entered the communist-occupied areas would have been hailed as liberators.

9. In June 1941, Eastern Galicians were again subjected to mass arrests. So many were arrested, and the jails were so crowded, that it was virtually impossible for the prisoners to lay or sit down. Initially, the NKVD planned to deport the prisoners deeper into Russia and Siberia, but the Nazi invasion interrupted this plan. Lacking time to deport the prisoners and unwilling to release them, Soviet NKVD police personnel went from one prison cell to another machine-gunning their prisoners. Afterwards, the prison buildings were set on fire. In such a manner, an estimated 10,000 Ukrainian political prisoners were murdered in the so-called "Lviv Massacre." Doroshenko, *A Survey of Ukrainian History*, p. 746; Hingley, *The Russian Secret Police*, p. 191; *Ready*, p. 144, cites that just alone in Lviv's main prison 3,500 corpses were found. And according to Jack Fleisher, a New York Times reporter who personally viewed the cells following the Soviet withdrawal, Fleisher reported that he had witnessed as many as 20-30 corpses contained within each cell ("Soviet Lays Waste Abandoned Cities" in the *New York Times*, 7 July 1941, p. 2). In addition to slaughtering those in Lviv, the NKVD also attempted to herd a number of its prisoners eastward in prisoner columns. But as they lagged or faltered behind, they were shot down. See John Erickson, *The Road to Stalingrad*, p. 166. For additional information on prisoner columns see Gross, *Revolution From Abroad*, pp. 183-186; n. 117, pp. 297-298. According to Gross, of approximately 13,000 arrested in June 1941, only about 600-700 survived the ordeal in Lviv. (P. 181).

10. Lemkin, *Axis Rule*, p. 9; Colonel Albert Seaton, *The Fall of Fortress Europe, 1943-1945* , p. 41.

11. The origins of the Organization of Ukrainian Nationalists (OUN) date back to the early 1920s when Colonel Evhen Konovaletz, an exceptional organizer trained in the military, organized the Ukrainian Military Organization ('Ukrains'ka Viis'kova Organizatsiia'- UVO). Politically, the UVO championed the Ukrainian cause and on occasion, carried out acts of sabotage in Eastern Galicia and throughout Ukraine. In 1929, under Konovaletz' leadership, the UVO was reorganized into the OUN. (*Gaucher*, p. 277). But on 23 May 1938, after meeting with and receiving a "gift" from an individual who posed as a friend and sympathizer named "Wallych" in the Cafe Atlanta in Rotterdam, the Netherlands, Konovaletz was torn apart by an explosive device. Undoubtedly, Wallych was a Soviet agent; yet, OUN activities did not cease.
Internal differences caused the OUN to split into two factions in 1940: Melnyk's faction (OUN-M), composed primarily of older members and nicknamed the "Old Guard," and Bandera's "Young Turks," the OUN-B. From 1941-1944, the OUN fought a constant battle with Nazi Germany, its SS and Gestapo, various fascist powers and the Soviet state; from 1945 until the collapse of communism in 1991, resistance was offered to Soviet rule.
During and after World War II, Soviet propagandists have viciously attacked the OUN as being a "pro-fascist" organization which collaborated with the Nazis. Its leadership, they claimed, consisted of "class enemies of the workers and peasants, individuals under the pay of foreign agents, sadists, and torturers." *Ukrains'ka RSR u Velykii Vitchyznianii Viini Radians'koho Soiuzu, 1941-1945* [The Ukrainian Soviet Republic In the Great Patriotic War of the Soviet Union, 1941-1945] (Kiev: Vydavnytstvo Politychnoi Literatury Ukrainy, 1968), Vol. II, p. 163; V. Styrkul, *The SS Werewolves* (Lviv: Kamenyar Publishers, 1982); *Nazi Crimes In Ukraine, 1941-1945: Documents and Materials* (Kiev: Naukova Dumka Publishers, 1987), are just a few of the many accounts attacking the OUN. Unfortunately, many western historians and writers, relying on the abundance of Soviet propaganda, half-truths and lies, have erroneously fallen prey to such communist distortions. (See Christopher Simpson, *Blowback: America's Recruitment of Nazis and Its Effects On the Cold War* (Weidenfeld and Nicholson, 1988), p, 163; Mark Arons and John Loftus, *Unholy Trinity: the Vatican, the Nazis, and Soviet Intelligence* (N.Y.: St. Martins Press, 1991), p. 139; and Peter Hamill, "Its Links Include Nazi Faithful," in *N.Y. Post*, 3 October 1988, p. 4. To make matters worse, they have continued to write and spread the deliberate Soviet inaccuracies. While it is true that in the late 1930s some collaboration did arise between certain Eastern Europeans and some German officials, this relationship arose out of a need by

Notes

Germany's Abwehr intelligence to utilize ethnic Germans and various Eastern Europeans as translators, propagandists, and saboteurs in so-called "fifth column" units. (*IMT*, Vol. 7, pp. 272-273); simultaneously, because the OUN was desperately searching for assistance, certain members (including Bandera), did cultivate those Germans receptive (or pretending to be receptive) to the Ukrainian cause. But it is important to note that the OUN never adopted - nor ever espoused - Nazism and, as a matter of fact, as early as 1934 certain OUN leaders, such as Evhen Onatsky, openly condemned Hitler and Nazism as "imperialistic, racist, and anti-Christian." Bohdan Krawchenko, "Soviet Ukraine under Nazi Occupation, 1941-44," in *Ukraine During World War II, History and Its Aftermath*, ed. Yuriy Boshyk (Edmonton: University of Alberta, 1968), p. 18. And once Nazi Germany invaded the USSR and exposed its true intentions, a break immediately developed between the OUN and the Third Reich. For a condemnation of the "Soviet Disinformation Campaign Against Ukrainian Nationalists," see Herbert Romerstein, "A Time For Re-examination: the Soviet Role In the Demjanjuk Case," in *Human Events*, 4 April 1992, pp. 12-18.

12. Gaucher, *Opposition In the USSR*, p 356; Reitlinger, *The SS*, p. 204; Yaroslav Stetsko, *30 Chervnia 1941* [30 June 1941] (London: 1967), p. 19; Orest Subtelny, Ukraine, A History, pp. 465-468; Friedman, *Ukrainian-Jewish Relations*, p. 266; and Myhailo Il'kiv, *German Concentration Camps*, p. 5.

13. In late 1939 Germany's Abwehr, in an agreement with Bandera's OUN-B faction, established two Ukrainian anti-communist volunteer battalions: "Nachtigall" (Nightingale, its name deriving from a choir within the unit), and "Roland" Recruited from Ukrainians who in 1939-41 had fled westward from Soviet terror, and from Ukrainian prisoners-of-war who had previously been serving in the Polish Army, each battalion consisted of four companies with a strength of 120-160 per company. Among the Ukrainians, these units were known as the "Druzhyny Ukrains'kykh Natsionalistiv" (DUN - Units of Ukrainian Nationalists). Volodymyr Kubiyovych, U*kraine: A Concise Encyclopedia* (Toronto: University of Toronto Press, 1963), Vol. II, p. 1087. See also Colonel Evhen Pobihushchyj-Ren, *Mozaika Moikh Spomyniv (My Life's Mosaic)* (London: Association of Former Ukrainian Combatants in Great Britain, 1982), pp. 66-76; John Armstrong, *Ukrainian Nationalism* (N.Y.: Columbia University Press, 1963), 2nd ed., p. 74; Myroslav Yurkevich, "Galician Ukrainians in German Military Formations and in the German Administration," in *Boshyk*, ed., p. 71. In the opening phases of "Barbarossa," both groups succeeded in creating a considerable amount of havoc in the Soviet rear. Erickson, *The Road to Stalingrad*, p. 166; Paul Leverkuehn, *German Intelligence* (N.Y.: Weidenfeld and Nicholson, 1954), pp. 164-165.

14. The proclamation of independence was issued on 30 June 1941. Undoubtedly, that same day some kind of radio announcement regarding the proclamation must have been made. But on the morning of 1 July, at 11 A.M., the proclamation was officially announced over Lviv's Konovaletz Radio Station. See *The Trident*, July-August, 1941, Vol. V, No. 6, p. 1. (In 1941, "The Trident" was a Ukrainian-American journal published in New York City, N.Y.).

15. Stetsko, *30 Chervnia 1941*, pp. 319-320; English synopsis, p. 462. Shortly after his arrest, Stetsko was deported to the Sachsenhausen Concentration Camp. (*Ibid*). Friedman, p. 266, cites 12 July 1941 as the day that Stetsko and his minister, Roman Ilnytzky, were arrested and deported to Germany. According to Stetsko in "Colonial Policies in Ukraine Result in Germany's Collapse," *Ukrainian Echo*, 24 April 1985, p. 6; and *30 Chervnia 1941*, p. 320, he and a number of his colleagues were deported to Sachsenhausen at 3 A.M. on 24 January 1942. (See also p. 462). For additional details of the arrest see O. Koval's, "Ukraina v Borot'bi za Svoiu Derzhavnu Nezalezhnist" [Ukraine in Battle for Its National Independence], *Liberation Path* (Great Britain: January 1991), p. 7; Wolodymyr Kozyk, *The Third Reich and the Ukrainian Question. Documents: 1934-44* , pp. 14, 53; and "What Were the Real Facts of the Situation?" and "The Democratic Basis of the Ukrainian Government of 1941" in Yaroslav Stetsko's, *Ukraine and the Subjugated Nations: Their Struggle for National Liberation (Selected Writings and Speeches by Former Prime Minister of Ukraine)* (N.Y.: Philosophical Library, Inc., 1989), ed. John Kolasky, pp. 543-546. See also p. 7.

16. Revolutionary, politician, and a fiery patriot, Stepan Bandera was born on 1 January 1909 in Uhryniv Staryi, Galicia. The son of a priest, from his early youth Bandera took an active role in community and Ukrainian affairs. Although a non-military man, he joined the Ukrainian Military Organization (UVO) and later, the OUN. A strong orator with a fluency in a number of languages, Bandera headed the OUN's propaganda section.

In June 1934, Bandera was tried by Polish authorities for allegedly participating in the assassination of Poland's Minister of Internal Affairs, Bronislav Pieracki, and for the murder of a fellow OUN executive. Sentenced to death, Bandera was transported to Warsaw to await his sentence. But there, his sentence was commuted to life. With Poland's collapse in 1939, Bandera escaped. At no time was Bandera released by Soviet authorities as incorrectly stated by Khruschev in his memoirs, *Khruschev Remembers* (Boston: Little, Brown and Co., 1970), p. 140.

Because Bandera was anti-communist, he was not able to return to Soviet-occupied Galicia. Remaining behind in German occupied Poland, Bandera soon began to associate himself with certain German officials who had expressed an interest in the Ukrainian cause. But little did Bandera realize that these Germans not only had no say in the politics of the Third Reich but, as Bandera was negotiating with them, in the higher circles of Nazi Germany Adolf Hitler himself was making plans for Ukraine's future. And Hitler's plans were completely different from what Bandera, the OUN, or anyone else had in mind.

For his refusal to rescind the 30 June 1941 proclamation of a Ukrainian state, and for his condemnation of Nazi excesses, Bandera was arrested on 15 September 1941. (*Ukrainian Echo*, 24 April 1985, p. 6; *Friedman*, p. 266). For the next three years, until his release in late 1944, Bandera's "home" consisted of imprisonment in Cracow, strict one man confinement in cell 29 in the gestapo's centralized prison at 8 Prince-Albert Place in Berlin, and from 28 March

1943, various concentration camps such as Sachsenhausen. Danylo Tshaikovsky, "Liudyna, Borets', Providnyk" [Human, Fighter, Leader] (N.Y.: 1970), p. 36. See also Il'kiv, *German Concentration Camps*, pp. 75-76.

Tragically, Bandera (as well as many of his followers), have been falsely accused of taking a pro-Nazi stand. (See Hamill's, "Its Links Include Nazi Faithful," *N.Y. Post*, 3 October 1988, p. 4). But little do such writers know that Bandera (who had a reputation for speaking his mind freely), had not only concluded by early 1943 that Nazi Germany was going to lose the war but that Bandera had actually expressed this viewpoint to his captors; furthermore, the Ukrainian leader had also witnessed the destruction of much of his family by German rule. And this included Bandera's two brothers: Vasyl, arrested 14 September 1941 in Stanyslaviv and murdered in Auschwitz in July 1942; and Dr. Alexander Oleksa Bandera, who also perished in Auschwitz. (Roman Malanchuk, "The First German Strike, 14 September 1941," *Ukrainian Echo*, pp. 3-4). Malanchuk, Vasyl Bandera and two others were arrested on Bilinsky Street in Stanyslaviv on Sunday, 14 September 1941. After lengthy interrogations in that city by SS-Hauptsturmfuhrer Krueger regarding "war crimes" committed by the OUN against the Fuhrer, the men were transferred, on 18 September, to a prison in Cracow and shortly after, were moved to Auschwitz. Malanchuk was the only one who survived. For a photo of Vasyl Bandera, tatooed with No. 49721 in a concentration camp suit, see Petro Mirchuk's *Revoliutsiinyi Zmah Za USSD* [Revolutionary Struggle for Ukrainian Self-Determination and Statehood] (New York-Toronto-London, 1987), Vol. II, p. 209. With the conclusion of the war, Bandera remained in the OUN. Elected to its head in 1947, Bandera held that position until his murder on 15 October 1959 by a fellow Galician and Soviet agent, Bohdan Stashinsky. See also Ladislav Bittman's. *The KGB and Soviet Disinformation: An Insider's View* (International Defense Publishers, 1985), p. 67.

17. Roger J. Bender and Hugh Page Taylor, *Uniforms, Organization and History of the Waffen-SS* (Ca.: Bender Publishing Co., 1975), Vol. 4, p. 14. According to *Friedman*, (p. 267), some of Melnyk's followers were arrested at the end of November, 1941, when they organized a large conference to commemorate the anti-Soviet Ukrainian fighters killed by the bolsheviks in the concluding months of the 1918-1921 Civil War. Utilizing the occasion to their advantage, the Germans arrested over twenty organizers of that conference. Shortly afterwards, they were executed. Simultaneously, the Nazis shattered Melnyk's groups throughout the region while Melnyk himself was arrested and dispatched to Sachsenhausen. *(Ibid)*.

By the thousands, OUN members and their supporters were arrested, deported to various concentration camps (notably Auschwitz or Sachsenhausen), or shot. See Steven Hendrickson's "Survivor Recalls Nightmare..." *Los Angeles Times*, 30 October 1983. Hendrickson's short but powerful article recounts the ordeals of a Ukrainian patriot, Petro Boyan, at Auschwitz; Petro Kovalskyj's (Auschwitz tatoo no. 154791), "In Memory of My Friend Vlodko," *The Ukrainian Echo*, pp. 5-6; Yaroslav Stetsko's "Colonial Policies In Ukraine Result in Germany's Collapse," *Ukrainian Echo*, pp. 3-6; and Mirchuk's "Auschwitz: In the German Mill of Death," *Ukrainian Echo*, p. 4. See also O. Dans'kyi, *Khochu Zhyty! Obrasky z Nimets'kykh Kontsentratsiynykh Taboriv* [I Want to Live! Images from Nazi Concentration Camps] (Munich: Ukrainian Publishers, 1946). Vividly, these accounts describe the hardships and ordeals of Ukrainian patriots under Nazi rule and incarceration.

18. *IMT*, Vol. 39. pp, 269-270; Koval', p. 7; *Ukrainian Echo*, p. 4; Armstrong, *Ukrainian Nationalism*, pp. 69-70. For detailed accounts of the OUN-Nazi struggle see Kost Pankiwsky, *Roky Nimets'koi Okupatsii 1941-44* [Years of the German Occupation, 1941-44](East Side Press, 1965). See also *Levytsky*, p. 152; *Romerstein*, p. 16; and Colonel Trevor Dupuy's, "The Ukraine," in *European Resistance Movements* (N.Y.: Franklin Watts, Inc., 1965), p. 72. At no time did the OUN make a "significant contribution" to Germany's war effort as erroneously implied by Scott Anderson and Jon Lee Anderson in *"Inside the League: The Shocking Expose of How Terrorists, Nazis, and Latin American Death Squads Have Infiltrated the World Anti-Communist League"* (N.Y.: Dodd, Mead and Co., 1986), p, 35.

19. Reitlinger, *The House Built on Sand*, p 169; Leverkuen, *German Intelligence*, pp. 165-166; Colonel Evhen Pobihushchyj-Ren, *My Life's Mosaic*, pp. 71-76. Hereafter Ren will only be used. On pages 72-73, Ren's ten memorandum's issued to German authorities in regards to Ukraine are presented. As for "Roland," it never entered combat. Posted to Rumania for deployment, the unit remained there until it was disarmed. See Roman Kolisnyk's, "Organizatsiia Viis'kovoi Upravy" [The Organization of the Military Board] in *Ukrains'ka Dyviziia i Viis'kova Uprava "Halychyna." Nimets'ka polityka vidnosno ukrains'koho natsional'noho viis'ka 1943-1945 (Prodovzhennia)* [The Ukrainian Division and the "Galicia" Military Board. German Politics Corresponding to the Ukrainian National Army 1943-1945 (Continuation)], *Visti Kombatanta*, (Veterans' News). (N.J.: Jersey City. Published jointly by United Ukrainian War Veterans in America, Brotherhood of Former Soldiers of the 1st Ukrainian Division Ukrainian National Army (UNA) in association with: Brotherhood of Ukrainian Sichovi Stril'tsi, Former Members of the Ukrainian Insurgent Army, Inc., and the Ukrainian War Veterans' Association in Canada), 1987, No. 2, p. 56. Hereafter referred to as *Visti* with appropriate year, issue, title of work and pages.

20. *Bender and Taylor*, Vol. 4, p. 14; *Ren*, p. 72; Kolisnyk, *Visti*, 1987, No. 2, p. 56, cites this incorporation took place in October, 1941. At this time Ren, in the rank of major, was designated as the units commander.

21. *Bender and Taylor*, Vol. 4, p. 14.

22. Because the unit also refused to involve itself in any police actions against civilians, this further complicated the units relationship with German authority Petro Mirchuk, *Roman Shukhevych (General Taras Chuprynka)*

Notes

Komandyr Armii Bezsmertnykh [Roman Shukhevych: Commander of the Army of Immortals] (London: Ukrainian Publishers, Ltd., 1970), pp. 100-101; *Ren*, pp. 100-103.

23, *Ren*, pp 100-107; Kolisnyk, *Visti*, No. 2, p. 56. See also *Bender and Taylor*, Vol. 4, pp. 13-14.

24, Mirchuk, *Roman Shukhevych*, p. 101; Reitlinger, *The House*, pp. 169-170; *Ren*, p. 102; *Visti*, 1987, No. 2, p. 56.

25, *Ren*, p. 102; *Visti*, 1987, No. 2, p. 56; Mirchuk, *Roman Shukhevych*, p. 101, cites 1 December 1942 as the date the legion was formally disbanded.

Notes Chapter 4

1, *Gaucher*, p. 354; Major (Retired) Petro R. Sodol, *UPA: They Fought Hitler and Stalin* (N.Y.: 1987), p. 19; Dupuy, *European Resistance*, pp. 73-74; Mirchuk, Revoliutsiinyi Zmah, p. 114; Marta Dmytrenko; *Mykhailyk* (Canada: Harmony Printing Ltd., 1981), p. 7; Stepaniv, *Suchasnyi Lviv*, p. 134; *Koval'*, pp. 7 and 119; Vasyl Veryha, *Along the Roads of World War II, Legends of Ukrainian Participation In the Warsaw Uprising of 1944 and the Ukrainian Division "Galicia."* (Toronto: New Pathway Publishers, 1980), p. 182; Kost' Bondarenko and Yuriy Kyrychuk, "Do 50-richchia UPA" [To 50 Years of the UPA], in *Viis'ko Ukrainy* [Ukraine's Military] (Kiev: 1992), pp. 54-55. See also p. 53; and Reitlinger, *The SS*, p. 204. See also John Kolasky, *The Shattered Illusion: The History of Ukrainian Pro-Communist Organizations in Canada* (Canada: Peter Martin, Ltd., 1979), p. 89; and Foot, *Resistance*, p. 12. At no time did Nazi Germany organize the UPA in a desperate effort to harass the Soviet advance as erroneously stated by the Anderson authors in *Inside the League*, p. 25.

2. By the spring of 1942, Germany's military and police authorities were fully aware of the Ukrainian patriotic resistance and began to compile a series of reports on it. *Widerstandsbewegung In Der Ukraine*, Der Chef der Sicherheitspolizei und des DD, Kommandostab, Berlin, den 22 Mai 1942, R58/687, was one of the first reports compiled in Berlin from the eastern front region. This report, divided into three sections, identifies Bandera and Melnyk as resistance leaders, and identifies the Polissia Sich as a "Ukrainian Freikorps" established in November 1941. See also Reitlinger, *The SS*, p. 204; and Peter Kleist, *Zwischen Hitler und Stalin* (Bonn: 1950), pp. 186-190.

3, Mirchuk, *Roman Shukhevych*, pp. 109, 190-191; Enrique M. Codo, "Guerrilla Warfare In the Ukraine," in *Modern Guerrilla Warfare*, ed. Franklin Mark Osanka (N.Y.: Glencoe Free Press, 1967), p. 114; James K. Anderson, "Unknown Soldiers of an Unknown Army," in *Army* (Magazine), May, 1968, p. 63; Mirchuk, *Revoliutsiinyi Zmah*, p. 57; M. Sulyma, "Ukrains'ka Povstans'ka Armiia" [The Ukrainian Insurgent Army] in "Partyzanshchyna!" [Partisan Warfare!] in *Visti*, 1979, No. 5-6, p. 67; and *Gaucher*, p. 356. That same year, the UPA issued a proclamation titled "What does the UPA Fight For?" For an understanding of the UPA's viewpoints in regards to liberation, foreign domination, human, minority, cultural and educational rights see "Prohrama Ukrains'koi Povstans'koi Armii (UPA) [Program of the Ukrainian Povstans'ka Army, UPA], *Visti*, 1982, No. 4, pp. 54-56. For its English translation see *Boshyk*, pp. 192-195. The UPA republished this proclamation in 1949.

4. Shukhevych was born on 17 July 1907. In his youth, he became an active member of the OUN. In the mid-1930s, he served briefly in the Polish Army and in 1936, he served as a military advisor to the independently established - but short-lived - Subcarpathian Ukrainian People's Republic. With Carpatho-Ukraine's demise, Shukhevych returned to Galicia. But with the Red occupation of Galicia in 1939, Shukhevych fled west. Recruited by Germany's Abwehr, Shukhevych returned to Galicia and Ukraine as an officer within Nachtigall. For the "crime" of protesting the arrest of Bandera, Stetsko, Melnyk and Nazi Germany's policies toward Ukraine, Shukhevych was relieved of duty and placed under military arrest. (Yaroslav Bilinsky, *The Second Soviet Republic: The Ukraine After World War II* (N.J.: Rutger's University Press, 1964), p. 122; Mirchuk, *Roman Shukhevych*, pp. 107, 115, 117; *Gaucher*, p. 356). Escaping, he fled into the ranks of the UPA and shortly afterwards, assumed command. See also Mirchuk's *Revoliutsiinyi Zmah*, p. 57.

5. In addition to the four regions, independent urban operational groups conducted propaganda, sabotage, intelligence gathering, and assassinations throughout the Donets Basin, Kharkiv, Lviv, Odessa, the Crimea and many other cities and towns According to Anderson in "Unknown Soldiers,"*Army*, p. 67, the strength of an independent operational group was composed of approximately 2,000 fighters.

6. On 25 June 1943, Koch wrote a personal letter to Alfred Rosenberg to inform him that certain Ukrainian regions were retaken by Ukrainian insurgents or communist guerrillas (Der Reichskommissar Fur Die Ukraine V-I-7422, Tgb. Nr. 378/43 geh. *Betr.: Derzeitiger Stand der Bandenlage*, Rowno, den 25 Juni 1943). According to Colonel Dupuy..."under the skillful leadership of [General] Taras Chuprynka, the UPA gradually gained control of much of the rural Ukraine. The Germans concentrated their forces on the main routes and at the communication centers." See *European Resistance*, pp. 73-74. According to a report submitted by Zhitomir regions district leader, Commissioner General (General-Kommissar) Leyser to Rosenberg 30 June 1943, approximately 1,400,000 hectares (or 80%) of the forests and 60% of the arable land found in District Zhitomir was controlled by Ukrainian guerrillas. Leyser also reported that the guerrillas disrupted the region's road and rail system and assisted the peasants with their food

Galicia Division

production. *Mundlicher Lagebericht des Generalkommissars Leyser uber den Generalbezirk Shitomir, gehalten in einer Dienstbesprechung vor dem Herrn Reichsminister Rosenberg in Winniza am 17. Juni 1943.* Der Generalkommissar, Geheim! Shitomir, den 30. Juni 1943 in *IMT*, Vol. 25, Document No. 265-PS, pp. 319-323. The report is signed by Leyser. For an English study of this report see Clifton J. Child's, "Occupied Eastern Europe: The Ukraine Under German Occupation, 1941-44" in T.R.V. Toynbee's, ed., *Survey of International Affairs: Hitler's Europe 1939-45* (Oxford University Press, 1954), pp. 632-633.

7. Ready, *The Forgotten Axis*, p 274. See also p. 275; Yuriy Tys-Krokhmaliuk, *UPA Warfare In Ukraine: Strategical, Tactical and Organizational Problems Of Ukrainian Resistance in World War II* (Vantage Press, 1972), pp. 227-228.

8. *Codo*, p. 115; *Gaucher*, p. 357; *Ready*, p. 275; Krokhmaliuk, *UPA Warfare In Ukraine*, pp. xii-xiii; 142, 175-176, 227 and 297; *Sodol*, p. 20. In his 1944 New Year's message, Koch not only admitted that Ukrainian patriots had been fighting the Germans, but also acknowledged the fact that he (Koch) had lost many of his "Verwaltungsfuhrer's" to Ukrainian "bandits." See "British Foreign Office Research Department Memorandum on 'Liberated Ukraine,' 29 March 1944, Discussing Ukrainian-Russian Relations and Ukrainian Nationalist Resistance Movement" in Lubomyr Y. Luciuk and Bohdan S. Kordan, *Anglo-American Perspectives On the Ukrainian Question, 1938-1951 (A Documentary Collection)* (N.Y.: Limestone Press, 1987), p. 150.

9. Krokhmaliuk, *UPA Warfare*, pp. 228-229; 233; 239-243. See also p. 286. In German "BB" stood for Bandenbekampfung or "Battle Against Bands." According to Anderson "Heinrich Himmler himself appointed Bach-Zalewski, the famous SS anti-partisan chief, the mission of destroying the UPA." See *Unknown Soldiers*, p. 63.

10. *General Roman Shukhevych* (N.Y.: Published by the OUN, 1966), p. 63.

11. In mid-July 1943, an extensive report, *National-Ukrainische Bandenbewegung*, Bfh H. Geb. Sud., Abt. Ic Nr. 168/43, Rh 22/22, was published by "South Russia's" Police and SS command. This detailed report covered the Ukrainian underground's origins, expansion, growth; its destruction of Nazi administrative and police centers; raids and battles with Germans; and raids on Polish settlements and Ukrainian propaganda methods against the established Nazi civilian administration. Of interest is also the fact that the report emphasizes that the Ukrainian's main struggle is against the Nazi civilian administration and Police. In regard to the common German soldier serving in the Wehrmacht, the report states that "captured German soldiers are disarmed, wounded are provided first aid, and prisoners released." And former eastern front General Ernst Kostring, in a postwar debriefing report to Allied authorities, stated that UPA guerrillas "fought almost exclusively against German administrative agencies, the German police and the SS in their quest to establish an independent Ukraine controlled neither by Moscow or Germany." "*Debriefing of General Koestring,*"Department of the Army (Washington, D.C.), 3 November 1948, MSC - 035. Cited from *Sodol*, p. 58. Also of interest to note is that in 1947-48, a committee of former German eastern front commanders revealed at the allied established European Historical Division Interrogation Enclosure located in Neustadt, Germany, that "the Ukrainian Nationalist Movement (UPA) formed the strongest partisan group in the east except for the Russian Communist bands, which fought bitterly." See "Non-Russian Partisans," in *Russian Combat Methods In World War II* (Washington, D.C.: U.S. Army Center of Military History, 1950. Republished 1988), chap. 18, p. 111. See also *Ready*, pp. 274-275.

12. Krokhmaliuk, *UPA Warfare*, p. 227; 242. Personal discussion with Vashchenko and other former UPA guerrilla soldiers.

13. "Karpats'kyi Reid," [The Carpathian Raid], in *Radians'ka Entsyklopediia Istorii Ukrainy* (Holovna Redaktsiia Ukrains'koi Radians'koi Entsyklopedii, 1970), Vol. II, pp. 314-315; *Codo*, p. 115; John Armstrong, *Soviet Partisans in World War II* (Wisconsin: University of Wisconsin Press, 1964), p. 745.

14. Armstrong, *Soviet Partisans*, pp. 116, 749; *Codo*, p. 115; *Gaucher*, p. 357; Anderson, "Unknown Soldiers," p. 63. Recent accounts regarding Kovpak's raid will be found in contemporary Soviet writings, along with an admission of intense combat with Ukrainian patriots. (See *Ukrains'ka RSR u Velykii Vitchyznianii Viini Radians'koho Soiuzu, 1941-1945*, pp. 169-171; 270-271). Kovpak's forces also battled German security and Wehrmacht forces.

15. Der Chef der Sicherheitspolizei und des SD-Kommandostab, Meldungen aus den besetzten Ostgebieten, Nr 46. Berlin, den 19 Marz 1943. Geheim! *Ukrainische Widerstandsbewegung.* This report revealed that Ukrainian security personnel have deserted to the UPA underground with an estimated 15,000 rifles, 1,550 pistols, and 45,000 hand grenades.

16. Krokhmaliuk, *UPA Warfare*, p. 229. According to *Sodol*, p. 59, a UPA battalion commander and a company commander were courtmartialed and executed in early 1944 for negotiating and dealing with enemy forces.

17. Shankowsky's figure of 60,000 is substantiated by various former UPA soldiers. However, this figure includes only UPA's combat personnel and not UPA's support, it's agents, spies, and the so- called "eyes and ears" found throughout much of Ukraine.

Notes

18. *Bilinsky*, pp. 117-118.

19. Mirchuk, *Revoliutsiinyi Zmah*, p 66.

20. *Codo*, p. 116.

21. T Brimelow and B. Miller, "War Office Report on Ukrainian Nationalist Movement and Resistance in Ukraine, 13 December 1945," in *Luciuk and Kordan*, pp. 167-177. This report, however, was not able to confirm whether the UPA continued to be centered around divisions of 10,000, but did specify that reports indicated organized strengths of 2,000-5,000. (See p. 173).

22. *Ibid*, p. 173.

23. "UPA Ochyma Nimtsiv" [The UPA Through German Eyes], *Visti*, 1982, No. 4, pp. 49-50; *Kolasky*, p. 89.

24. *Gaucher*, p. 361. According to *Vii'sko Ukrainy*, in 1946-47, UPA's strength reached 300,000 personnel. Of this strength, 50,000 made it to the west. (P. 57). In all, throughout its existence, upward to 700,000 men and women passed through UPA's ranks. *(Ibid)*.

25. Personal discussion with Vashchenko, a former UPA intelligence officer.

26. *Gaucher*, p. 361. While serving in the UPA, revolutionary writer Marta Dmytrenko wrote a fictional story titled "Mykhailyk."
Mykhailyk portrays the ordeals of a young boy who reconnoitered for the UPA. Although the account is fictional, it does actually portray the life of many a child or young teen involved with the UPA. On 29 December 1948, Dmytrenko was killed-in-action in the village of Lubohir, in the Carpathian Mountains after she personally shot and killed several NKVD officers. Her body was recovered by the UPA, and the bloodied text of "Mykhailyk" found on her possession, was later smuggled to the west. It was first published in 1960 in book format.

27. UPA's leadership constantly strove to avoid combat with Germany's foreign personnel. An example which may be cited is how the UPA established in the summer of 1942 a relationship with Hungary's security troops in UPA's Northern (Belorussian) region. By releasing its captured Hungarian personnel, the UPA was able to quickly establish a secret agreement with the Hungarians. And for better understanding and mutual cooperation, the Hungarians even dispatched Lieutenant-Colonel Jeno Padanyi to serve as a liaison officer to UPA-North. *(Sodol*, p. 21. For a photo of the Hungarian officer with a number of UPA and OUN leaders see p. 23). At first, the Germans had no knowledge of such agreements, but by the winter of 1944 their intelligence was aware of the UPA-Hungarian truce and issued a report titled *"The Attitude of the Hungarians Towards the UPA."* Issued on 16 February 1944, this report not only confirms a truce has been concluded, but that the UPA was also using Hungarian weaponry. Abt. Fremde Heere Ost (I/Bd) Vortragsnotiz, H 3/478. *Veraltnis der Ungarn zur National-Ukrainischen Aufstandsbewegung.*

28. Friedman, p. 285, ibid. no. 59; personal discussion with Vashchenko. Of special interest to note is that in 1983, a book was published in the Soviet Union which acknowledged that Jewish personnel served in UPA's ranks. Titled "Anatomy of Treason," the books pages are filled with the standard anti-Ukrainian, anti-OUN/UPA rhetoric; however, the book reveals that "during the Great Patriotic War of 1941-1945, many Zionists were members of the Ukrainian Insurgent Army (UPA)" who fought both the Nazis and even, communists. Among those identified were UPA fighters Haim Sigal (alias Sigalenko), Margosh, Maximovich and Kun (undoubtedly Doctor Kum). See *Human Events*, 4 April 1992, pp. 14-15.

29. Shankowsky's 7 March 1958 letter to Friedman (*Friedman*, p. 285, ibid. no. 60). Freidman himself cited how after the war he met a Jewish physician who, along with his wife, served within a "Bandera (UPA) group and thus, were saved." *(Ibid.)* See also the testimony of Dr. Shmuel Specktor (also spelled Spector) on 22 June 1987 in *"State of Israel vs Ivan (John) Demjanjuk,"* Criminal Case No.373/86, p. 6187. (Specktor refers to the UPA as the "Ukrainian National Partisan Movement").

30. *Friedman* pp. 283-285; Krokhmaliuk, *UPA Warfare*, p. 95. See also Leo Heiman's, "We Fought for Ukraine - The Story of Jews Within the UPA," in *Ukrainian Quarterly* (Spring, 1964), pp. 33-44.
Yet, various erroneous accounts have surfaced accusing the UPA of crimes against Jewish personnel. One, written by Betty Eisenstein-Keshev and published in 1957, suggests that when the Soviet Army approached two UPA camps in Porycj and Kudrynki in the Northwestern Ukrainian region of Volyn in June 1943 the UPA, just prior to abandoning their camps, slaughtered their Jewish personnel. "Di Yidn in Volin, 1939-1944," in *Fun Noentn Ovar (From the Recent Past)*, (New York, 1957), No. 3, pp. 62-64. But Eisenstein's account may be faulted in a number of ways. To begin with, in June 1943, Volyn was under Nazi occupation and the German-Soviet front line was hundreds of miles to the east of Volyn on the Russian-Ukrainian frontier. Regular Soviet Army units did not even begin to approach Volyn until 1944. While, of course, the UPA did engage Soviet guerrillas in 1943, the UPA seldom, if ever, abandoned a camp upon the approach of Red guerrillas. To be sure, UPA guerrillas did, on occasion, disband camps. But only when confronted by the arrival of superior Soviet NKVD police and regular army units or, as in the June 1943 incident, with the approach of superior German forces. As Friedman himself noted, the UPA was forced to

425

abandon the two Volyn camps under Nazi pressure and not, as Eisenstein incorrectly claims, with the arrival of the Soviets. (*Friedman*, p. 286). And, of course, any captured personnel, whether Ukrainian or Jewish, were undoubtedly shot.

32. John Erickson, *The Road to Berlin* (Colorado: Westview Press, Inc, 1983), pp. 181-182; Krokhmaliuk, *UPA Warfare*, pp. 296-297. Krokhmaliuk cites 19 March 1944 as the day of the attack. Sodol, pp. 60-62; and *Velikaia Otechestvennaia Voina* [The Great Patriotic War] (Moscow: 1970), p. 273, cites 29 February 1944 as the date UPA struck Vatutin.
In the beginning of April 1944, the German 4th Panzer Army's command reported that UPA's forces had decreased their anti-German activity but had increased their activities in the Soviet rear. *UPA Hinter Der Front Der Roten Armee*. Ober Kommando der 4. Panzerarmee, Abt. Ic Nr. 765/44 geh. A.H. Qu., den 1.4. 1944, T313/406.

33. The UPA, however, occasionally conducted joint operations with Poland's anti-communist undergrounds such as the WIN (Wolnosc i Niepodleglosc - Freedom and Independence), and the NSZ (Narodowe Sily Zbrojne - the National Armed Force). Both of these Polish undergrounds remained active for some time after World War II.

34. Realistically speaking, Czechoslovakia's and Hungary's forces, composed primarily of paramilitary and frontier guards, never demonstrated a strong desire to battle the UPA. As a matter of fact, sizable numbers of its soldiers and populace demonstrated a friendly attitude towards the UPA. Thus, the battle against the UPA was primarily conducted by Russia's and Poland's communist forces.

35. Anderson, *"Unknown Soldiers,"* p. 64; personal discussion with Vashchenko.

36. *Gaucher*, pp. 369-370; *Zmah*, pp. 2; 183-184; Mirchuk, *Roman Shukhevych*, pp. 7;184; *Levytsky*, p. 238; Anderson, *Unknown Soldiers*, p. 66. However, in recent years, information has been resurfacing that Shukhevych was killed not in a hospital but in the streets of Lviv by Vasil Kuk (alias Vasil Koval), a UPA Colonel and one of Shukhevych's operational officers who (it is believed), turned into an NKVD operative. In the aftermath of Shukhevych's death, Kuk himself revealed to western OUN operatives that Shukhevych was killed-in-action in an underground bunker in the vicinity of the village of Bilohorska, Lviv region. See Vasyl Veryha's, *Losses of the Organization of Ukrainian Nationalists During the Second World War* (Canada: New Pathway Publishers, 1991), p. 159.

37. Although 1956 is generally cited as the year armed resistance ceased, sporadic reports of "industrial/railway accidents," "hooliganism," and "burglaries," along with confirmed reports of assassinations, bombings, and revolts in Siberian slave labor camps continued well into the 1980s. (*The Ukrainian Review*, Vol. xviii, No. 3, 1962; *Gaucher*, pp. 449-550). According to "Great Escapes From the Gulag," *Time Magazine*, June 5, 1978, pp. 91-92, "leadership [for such escapes and revolts], was provided by prisoners from the Western Ukraine, former guerrillas who had alternately fought the Nazis and Soviets in a desperate effort to gain their independence." See also Colonel Dupuy's, *European Resistance*, p. 74; Nicholas Riasanovsky's, *A History of Russia* , 2nd ed. (N.Y.: Oxford University Press, Inc., 1973), p. 582; and "Soviet Divisions Said to Fight Ukraine and Caucasus," *The New York Times*, 29 January 1948. For a Polish viewpoint see Brigadier Ignacy Blum's, "Udzial Wojska Polskiego w Walce o Utrwalenie Wladzy Ludowej: Walki z Bandami UPA" [The Share of the Polish Army In the Struggle for the Stabilization of People's Government: Actions Against the UPA Bands]. (Wojskowy Przeglad Historyczny - Review of Military History), Vol. 4, No. 1, (January-March 1959). For a Soviet viewpoint and acknowledgment of the fierce clashes between Soviet government forces versus Ukrainian (and Baltic) opposition groups see Colonel General Dmitri Volkogonov, *Stalin: Triumph and Tragedy (The First Glasnost Biography)*, Trans. Harold Shukman (N.Y.: Grove Weidenfeld, 1991), pp. 504, 508, 531.

Notes Chapter 5

1. *IMT*, Vol. 38, p. 87, Document no. 221-L; David Littlejohn, *The Patriotic Traitors: The History of Collaboration In German-Occupied Europe, 1940-45* (Garden City, N.Y.: Doubleday and Co., Inc. 1972), p. 293; James Lucas, *The Last Year of the German Army. May 1944-May 1945* (London: Arms and Armour Press, 1994), p. 128; *Ready*, pp. 164 & 194; Kolasky, *The Shattered Illusion*, pp. 89-90; Sviatomyr M. Fostun, *"U 50-Richchia 1-oi UD UNA"* [50 Years In the Rise of the 1st Ukrainian Division, Ukrainian National Army], *Visti*, 1993, No. 4, p. 23.

2. According to General staff estimates, by the spring of 1942, approximately 2.5 million men were required. Walter Gerlitz, *History of the German General Staff, 1657-1945* (N.Y.: Praeger, 1961), p. 411; *Ready*, pp. 164; 193-194, 272; Reitlinger, *The House Built on Sand*, p. 249; Lucas, *The Last Year of the German Army*, pp. 128-129. (See also pp. 112-113).

3. Alexander Solzhenitsyn, *The Gulag Archipelago*, 1918-1956, p. 254. See also Earl F. Ziemke and Magna E. Baur, "Accomplices Against the Bolshevik System?" in *Moscow to Stalingrad: Decision In the East* (Washington, D.C.: 1987), pp. 217-219; Ready, pp. 164-165, 193; and F. H. Hinsley, *British Intelligence In the Second World War: Its Influence on Strategy and Operations* (Cambridge Univ. Press, 1988), Vol. 3, p. 30.

Notes

4. Such fear were not just groundless. As late as April 1944, Germany's Abwehr prepared a report stating that some of the Galician Ukrainian intelligentsia, although willing to support the establishment of Ukrainian army units within the German army, were still very critical of Germany's policies toward the Ukraine; furthermore, the report also warned that the majority of Galicia's population, and as much as 90% of its Ukrainian youth, were sympathetic towards the UPA. *Zur Frage Der Nationale Bewegungen In Galizien.* [AMT] Abwehr, Abwehr-abteilung III/Walli III [B. Ia?] 2847/44 geh, (C/Ausw. 25)), O.U., an 22.4.44 H3/474, T78/565.

5. Ready, p. 272. According to various Ukrainian sources, the idea of forming an armed force in February 1943 originated strictly with Wachter. See Pankiwsky, The Years of the German Occupation, p. 221; Myroslav Malets'kyi, "Z Nahody 50-Littia" [In Occasion of 50 Years], p. 8; and Volodymyr Mykula, "Dyviziia "Halychyna" – 1-sha Dyviziia Ukrains'koi Natsional'noi Armii" [The Division "Galicia" – the 1st Ukrainian Division In the Ukrainian National Army], p. 10, in *1943-1993. 1-sha UD UNA, 50 Littia* [1943-1993. The 1st Ukrainian Division In the Ukrainian National Army] in Roman Hayetskyi, Yaroslav Zakaliak, Antin Tymkevych, Evhen Shypailo, *1943-1993. 1-sha UD UNA, 50 Littia* [1943-1993. The 1st Ukrainian Division, 50 Years] (N. J.: Computorprint, 1993). (Published by the Brotherhood of Former Soldiers of the 1st Ukrainian Division of the Ukrainian National Army), pp. 11-12. According to Mykula, Wachter raised the Division to steer Ukrainian potential for Germany in a more positive manner and to halt the Ukrainian underground's influence in Galicia. According to Ready, pp. 273-274, the German Army and not the Waffen-SS, was set to initially raise the "Galicia" Division. But because Himmler was both frustrated and jealous by his previous inability to grasp complete control of the so-called "Russian Liberation Army" (ROA) from the Wehrmacht (along with a personal desire to expand the Waffen-SS), Himmler moved quickly to place the proposed new division under his control.

At no time did the organization of the "Galicia" Division begin after a speech by the Luftwaffe Marshall Hermann Göring, in the Berlin Sports Palace on 14 October 1942, as alleged by Hromads'kyi Holoc in "Desiat' Povishenykh"[The Executed Ten], No. 23, 1 December 1946, p. 4; nor was the Division raised by a Ukrainian General named Pavlo Shandruk who then handed the formation to the "Hitlerites" as claimed by the Soviet propagandist writer Marko Terlytsia in *Pravnyky Pohani. Ukrains'ki Natsionalisty v Kanadi* [Ugly Jurists. Ukrainian Nationalists in Canada], (Kiev: Radians'kyi Pys'mennuk, 1960), p. 181.

6. *Bender and Taylor,* Vol. 4, p. 15; Basil Dmytryshyn, "The Nazis and the SS Volunteer Division "Galicia," in *The American Slavic and East European Review,* Vol. XV, No. 1, February, 1956), p. 4. A letter from Wachter to Himmler on 30 July 1943 contains the only record of the 1 March conversation; Yuriy Krokhmaliuk, "Zminy Nazv Ukrains'koi Dyvizii "Halychyna," [The "Galicia" Division's Title Changes]*Visti,* No. 5-6, 1977, pp. 47-48; Kubiyovych, "Dyviziia "Halychyna" (Do Istorii ii Povstannia),"[The "Galicia" Division. (The History of Its Origins)], *Visti,* No. 3, 1963, pp. 10-11.

7. In March 1943, Germany's armies were in need of no less than 700,000 troops. Cooper, *The German Army,* p. 452. Fully realizing that it would be difficult to obtain manpower in Germany proper, the organization of various indigenous units began in earnest. This improvisation was undertaken to strengthen Nazi Germany's fighting power. Units began to be organized in the occupied and friendly countries, especially by the Waffen-SS. "The Manpower Problem: Maintenance of Combat Efficiency" in *Military Improvisations During the Russian Campaign,* CMH Pub 104-1 (Washington, D.C. 1983 and 1986), p. 79.

8. Roger Manvell and Heinrich Frankel, *Himmler* (N.Y.: G.P. Putnam's Sons, 1965), pp. 164-165. SS-Obergruppenführer Gottlob Berger, the "Duke of Swabia," who headed the main SS recruiting office, strongly pushed (and probably originated), the concept of creating the Waffen-SS into an international army. (Reitlinger, The SS, pp. 153-154). As early as April 1941, Berger proposed the establishment of a Ukrainian Waffen-SS unit from Ukrainian prisoners-of-war captured from the Polish Army. (*Bender and Taylor,* Vol. 4, p. 14). But Himmler forbade the plan on "racial grounds." (Ibid). It is interesting to note that besides Berger, many front-line SS commanders strongly protested the racist doctrine that Slavs were "sub-human." Heinz Höhne, *The Order of the Death's Head,* p. 569. And General Felix Steiner, while commanding the 5th SS "Wiking" Division in Russia, personally told Himmler that such "a war could only be won if people such as the Ukrainians were granted autonomy and allowed to fight at the side of the German army against the Soviet enemy." But Himmler totally rejected the idea and told Steiner "Do not forget that in 1918 these splendid Ukrainians murdered Field Marshal von Eichhorn." (*Ibid*). See also Felix Steiner's, *Die Armee der Geachteten* (Plesse Verlag, Gottingen, 1963), p. 179.

9. *Wachter to Himmler,* Lemberg, 4 March 1943. Cited from *Bender and Taylor,* Vol. 4, p. 16; and *Visti,* No. 5-6, 1977, p. 48.

10. *Bender and Taylor,* Vol. 4, p.16; *Visti, No. 5-6, 1977 p. 48,* Reitlinger, The SS, p. 202; Roman Kolisnyk, *The Ukrainian Division 'Galicia' and Its Military Board: Work and Responsibilities of the Military Board 'Galicia' and the German Political Attitudes Regarding the Ukrainian Armed Forces In 1943-1945* (Canada: Shevchenko Scientific Society, 1990), p. 12: Kolisnyk, "Tvorennia Dyvizii Halychyna" [Creating the Galicia Division], *Visti,* 1986, No. 4, p. 90; Roman Fedoriv, "Khlopchi z-Pid Znaku Leva" [The Boy's Under the Lion Patch], *Visti,* 1993, No. 2, p. 57. According to Fedoriv, in the summer of 1943, Hitler authorized the establishment of the "Galicia" Division.

11. *RFSS to Wachter, Field Command Post,* 28 March 1943, Tgb. Nr. 35/37/43; Visti, 1986, No. 4, p. 90; *Bender and Taylor,* Vol. 4, p. 16; Kolisnyk, *The Ukrainian Division "Galicia, "* p. 12. See also Cooper, *The German Army,* p. 450.

Galicia Division

According to Reitlinger, a German radio broadcast on 24 March 1943 announced the forming of a Ukrainian Military Committee in Kharkiv to form a Ukrainian Army. (The SS, pp. 200-203). But because Kharkiv is in the Eastern Ukraine, undoubtedly this broadcast had nothing to do with the proposed "Galicia" Division. In conclusion, it must also be emphasized that no "Ukrainian Army" was ever organized in Kharkiv, the Eastern Ukraine or, for that matter, in Galicia or itself in Germany in 1943-44. If a Ukrainian Military Committee did arise in Kharkiv, its existence was very brief and it had no connection whatsoever to the "Galicia" Division and its Military Board. As well, at no time did Hitler agree to raise the "Galicia" Division on proposals submitted by nationalists as alleged by Soviet propagandists V. Belipiev and M. Rydnyts'kyi in *Pid Chuzhymy Praporamy*, [Under Foreign Flags] (Kiev: Padians'klyi Pys'mennyk, 1956), p. 94.

12. In the early stages of the discussions, certain Galician leaders sought to establish a panzergrenadier (Mechanized Infantry) division. (*Pankiwsky*, p. 226). But the strength of such a division centered on the Schutzenpanzerkampfwagen Sdkfz 251. (Armored personnel carrier – or wagon – 251). Because there was an insufficient number of such vehicles, and because the average Ukrainian in Galicia did not know how to drive, the idea was quickly discarded. Therefore, the 14th Waffen-SS Division became the first Waffen-SS division to be strictly a marching and horse powered infantry division.

13. Contrary to popular belief, Nazi Germany's armies were never fully mechanized. Throughout the war Germany's armies (as well as Russia's), resorted extensively on animal power. During World War II, approximately 2,700,000 horses were utilized by Germany's forces compared to 1,400,000 in World War I. (*Cooper*, p. 163). Worldwide, horses and mules were widely used by all belligerent powers to include even that of the United States.

14. Dmytryshyn, *"The Nazis and the SS Volunteer Division "Galicia"*, p.4.

15. *Bender and Taylor*, Vol. 4, p. 16.

16. "We'll see about that!" With these words, Colonel Alfred Bisanz would storm out of a Ukrainian meeting to confront German officials about German-Ukrainian grievances. A Galician Ukrainian of German ancestry, Bisanz was born in 1890 in Liubin Velyki, Eastern Galicia. With the proclamation of Eastern Galicia's independence, Bisanz, a former officer in the Austro-Hungarian Army, immediately joined the Galician Army and rose to the rank of Lieutenant-Colonel. During the Civil War, he first commanded the Galician Army's crack 7th "Lemberg" Brigade and in June 1919, a combat group which fought at Berezhany and Korosten in Ukraine. At the conclusion of hostilities, Bisanz remained in Galicia. In 1943, with the forming of the "Galicia" Division, Bisanz became the head of the Galician Military Board. With Galicia's fall to the Soviets in July 1944, Bisanz fled west. Arrested in April 1945 in Vienna, Austria, he was deported to Siberia and disappeared. It is alleged that he died in 1950, but other accounts cite 1953 as his date of death. Some have also alleged that Bisanz was secretly returned to communist Poland from Siberia and executed in that nation.

17. A number of former Galician military men did, however, oppose proposals for raising the "Galicia" Division. Amongst them was Colonel Dashkevych.

18. *Fernschreiben, An SS-Brigadeführer Dr. Wachter, Lemberg, 16.4.1943.*

19. *Brandt to SS-Brigadeführer Wachter*. Field Command Post, 10 April 1943. See also *Bender and Taylor*, Vol. 4, pp. 16-17 and *Dmytryshyn*, p. 5.

20. *Bender and Taylor*, Vol. 4, p. 17; *Visti*, No. 3, 1989, p. 43. A personal letter signed by Wachter cites 12 April 1943 as the date of the conference. Yet in a letter from Kruger to Himmler on 16 April 1943 regarding the "Galicia" Division, 14 April is the cited date of this conference. Since Kruger's name is not cited on Wachter's roster of the individuals attending the 12 April meeting, there is a possibility that Kruger mistook 12 April for 14 April or that another meeting was also held on 14 April in Lviv and was attended by Kruger or someone representing Kruger. Regardless of the exact date, it is known that a conference (and actually a series of meetings) did take place through this period of time. According to Vashchenko, the UPA was informed of these conferences by an agent operation within Wachter's staff.

21 The attendees of the 12 April conference consisted of : Galicia's Governor Otto Wachter; Generalleutnant Der Polizei Pheffer-Wildenbruch; Chef des Amtes Bauer; SS=Brigadeführer und Generalmajor der Polizei Joseph Stroop; Chief of Administration Oberstleutnant Wenerer; Major Degener; SS-Sturmbannführer Sielaft (who directed the reinforcement section); Colonel Bisanz; Abteilung Propaganda Leader Toscher; and Leiter des Prasidialamtes (Director of Presidium Administration) Dr. Neumann. These names are cited from Page I of Wachter's 12 April report. See also *Visti*, No. 4, 1986, p. 91. It should be noted that not one Ukrainian attended this meeting.

22. Roman Kolisnyk, "Ukrains'ka Dyviziia i Viis'kova Uprava "Halychyna." Nimets'ka Polityka Vidnosno Ukrains'koho Natsional'koho Viis'ka 1943-1945." (Z Dokumentiv Pro Tvorennia Ukrains'koi Dyvizii). [The Ukrainian Division and the Military Board "Galicia." German Politics Corresponding to the Ukrainian National Army 1943-1945." (From Documents Concerning the Ukrainian Division)], *Visti*, 1989, No. 3, pp. 43-47, contains the Ukrainian translation of the original German text.

Notes

23. The German Nazi Party acknowledged five racial groups: 1) pure Nordic; 2) dominant Nordic; 3) harmonious mixed breeds from the first two groups with small admixtures from the Alpine, Dinarian or Mediterranean groups; 4) mixed breeds predominately of the Eastern or Alpine type; 5) mixed breeds of non-European origin.

24. This so-called "Polizei-Schutzen-Regiment "Galizien" never existed. While four independent regiments were trained from an excess number of volunteers (and eventually incorporated into the Division itself), these units should not be confused with Berger's experimental "Polizei-Schutzen-Regiment "Galizien." Exhaustive studies of both German Military and Police Order of Battle's (such as George Tessin's "Die Stabe und Truppeneinheiten Der Ordnungspolizei," Tiel II of "Zur *Geschichte der Ordnungspolizei 1936-1945*" (Bundesarchiv, Koblenz, 1957), along with primary English, German, and Ukrainian sources, show that no such unit every officially existed.

25. *Bender and Taylor*, Vol. 4, p. 18.

26. *Himmler to Wachter*, Field Command Post, 16 April 1943. The directive was signed by Brandt. Additionally, the directive informed Galicia's governor that he would be receiving further instructions from either Brandt or Berger regarding this matter. Undoubtedly, Wachter feared that perhaps Himmler was changing his mind and would either postpone or even completely cancel the idea of establishing the "Galician" Division.

27. *Wachter to Grothmann, Lemberg*, 19 April 1943. (Cited from *Bender and Taylor*, Vol. 4 p. 18). On 16 April 1943, a telegram was sent from Berger to Himmler informing the Reichsführer that 20 April would be the date of the proclamation. (*Visti*, No. 4, 1986, pp. 90-91). But shortly afterwards, the proclamation date was brought up to 28 April.

28. *Bender and Taylor*, Vol. 4, p. 19; Henri Landemer, *La Waffen-SS* (Balland Press, 1972), p. 200; Roman Kroklmaliuk, *Zahrava Na Skhodi* [The Glow In Eastern Europe] (Toronto: Kiev Printer's Ltd., 1978), p. 25; Yurkevich in *Boshyk*, p. 76; Wolf-Dietrich Heike, *Ukrains'ka Dyviziia "Halychyna." Istoriia Formuvannia; Boiovykh Dii, 1943-1945* [The Ukrainian Division "Galicia" : The History of Its Formation and Combat Operations, 1943-1945] (Toronto: Kiev Printers, Ltd., 1970), Ukrainian ed., p. 17. For the English translation see Heike's, *The Ukrainian Division 'Galicia," 1943-45, A Memoir* (Toronto-Paris-Munich: The Shevchenko Scientific Society, 1988), p. 4; "Nainovisha Istoriia Ukrainy, 1943-1963, 28 Kvitnia 1943" [the Newest Ukrainian History, 1943-1963, 28 April 1943], *Visti*, 1963, No. 3, pp. 6-7; and Osyp Holynskyj, "40-Richchia Postannia Dyvizii "Halychyna" [40th Anniversary of the Rise of the Division "Galicia"], *Visti*, 1983, No. 4, p. 20.

29. An internationally renowned geographer and demographer, Volodymyr Kubiyovych was born 23 September 1900 in Novy Sancz, Poland. After completing his secondary studies in 1918, Kubiyovych enrolled in the Jagiellonian University in Cracow in 1919, majoring in geography and history. In 1923, he concluded his studies with a doctoral degree. Until 1928, he taught in a gymnasium (high school) in Cracow, and from 1928 until 1939, he lectured on Eastern European geography in the Jagiellonian University. During the time, Kubiyovych was active in such educational societies as the "Shevchenko Scientific Society" (named after Taras Shevchenko, 1814-1864, a Ukrainian poet), and was on the Ethnographic and Geographic Commission of the Polish Academy in Cracow.

As an educator, he produced around 90 scholarly works pertaining to geography, anthro-geography and demography. Kubiyovych's works were published in English, French, German, Czech, Polish, Rumanian, Ukrainian and other languages. With the Eruption of World War II, Kubiyovych was residing in Cracow. He relocated in 1940 to Prague, Czechoslovakia, where he briefly lectured at the Ukrainian Free University establised in that city. But shortly afterwards. he returned to Cracow to head the Ukrainian Central Committee, a post he held until the termination of World War II.

After World War II, Kubiyovych resided briefly in Germany. Moving to Sarcelles near Paris, France, Kubiyovych headed the European Shevchenko Society. He was editor-in-chief of the 13 volumes of the Encyclopedia of Ukraine (published in Ukrainian) and the driving force behind the 5 volume Ukrainian Encyclopedia currently being published in English. Until his death on 2 November 1985, Kubiyovych remained active in Ukrainian affairs. His "Ukrainian's In the General Government, 1939-44" remains a classic study of Ukrainian life in the General Government.

Notes Chapter 6

1. Kubiyovych, Ukraintsi *v Heneral'nii Hubernii, 1939-1944. Istoriia Ukrains'koi Tsentral'noi Komitii.* [Ukrainians In the General Government 1939-1944: History of the Ukrainian Central Committee] (Chicago: 1975), p. 47; Myroslav Yurkevich "*Galician Ukrainians in German Military Formations,*" in *Boshyk*, ed., p. 73; Gross, *War Through Children's Eyes*, pp. 15, 16, 19 and *Revolution From Abroad*, p. 31; Milena Rudnytski, ed. *Western Ukraine Under the Bolshevik's 1939-41* (Shevchenko Scientific Society, 1958),p. 193.

2. Kubiyovych, "Dyviziia Halychyna, (Do Istorii ii Postannia)" [Division Galicia (To the History of Its Rise)],*Visti*, 1963, No. 3, p. 10.

3. At first (April 1940), it was known as the Ukrainian National Union. But in June 1940, it was renamed as the Ukrainian Central Committee (UCC). Similar organizations existed for the Poles and Jews.

429

4. Kubiyovych, *Visti*, No. 3, 1963, p. 10.

5. One such letter was presented to the Nuremberg Court on Wednesday, 12 December 1945, by Mr. Thomas J. Dodd, Executive Trial Counsel for the United States, during the continuing trial of Poland's ex-Governor General, Hans Frank. This lengthy letter, classified as Document Number 1526-PS, USA-178 was, according to Prosecutor Dodd, written by the Chairman of the Ukrainian Main (Central) Committee at Cracow on 25 February 1943. (See *IMT*, Vol. 3, p. 416). Reading the document's English translation and beginning with the second paragraph on the third page of the English text (the same passage may be found in Kubiyovych's original text on page 2, paragraph 5), Mr. Dodd quoted: "The general nervousness is still further increased by the wrong methods of labor mobilization which have been used more and more frequently, in recent months. The wild and ruthless manhunt is practiced everywhere in towns and country, in streets, squares, stations, even in churches, as well as at night in homes, has shaken the feeling of security of the inhabitants. Every man is exposed to the danger of being seized suddenly and unexpectedly, anywhere and at any time, by the police, and brought into an assembly camp. None of his relatives knows what has happened to him, and only weeks or months later one or another gives news of his fate by a postcard." (*IMT*, Vol. 3, pp. 416-417). Continuing to read, Mr. Dodd quoted: "In November of last year an inspection of all males of the age – classes born in 1910-1920 was ordered in the area of Zaleeszczut (District of Czortkow). After the men had appeared for inspection, all of those who were selected were arrested at once, loaded into trains, and sent to the Reich. Similar recruitment of laborers for the Reich also took place in other areas of the district. Following some interventions, the action was stopped." (*Ibid*). Kubiyovych's letter, in its full German text, is found in *IMT*, Vol. 27, pp. 298-306. From pp. 307-324, various other protests provided by Kubiyovych to German authorities are also cited. See also *IMT*, Vol. 12, p. 119; and Kubiyovych's book, *Meni 70*.

6. Kubiyoych's remarks regarding this matter are also cited from a statement that he wrote to American Allied authorities in Germany after World War II. (See Krokhmaliuk's, *The Glow In Eastern Europe*, p. 265).

7. Krokhmaliuk, *The Glow*, pp. 265-266. Kubiyovych's entire statement is found between pp. 264-274.

8. From 9-12 August 1941, America's President Franklin Roosevelt and Britain's Prime Minister Winston Churchill, in the first wartime conference off Newfoundland's coast, drew up the "Atlantic Conference." Issued jointly, it somewhat resembled Woodrow Wilson's Fourteen Points. Among a number of pledges, the Charter pledged that "sovereign rights and self-determining governments would be restored to those who had been forcibly deprived of them" and it promised that in the postwar period it would "afford that all men in all the lands may live out their lives in freedom from fear and want." The Charter also shunned any ideas of territorial expansion by any nation in the postwar period, and stressed "all people's rights to self-determination within a wider and permanent system of general security." John A. Garraty, *The American Nation: A History of the United States Since 1865* (N.Y.: Harper and Row, Inc., 1971) 2nd Ed., p. 393; Joseph L. Morse, ed., *Funk and Wagnall's Standard Reference Encyclopedia* (N.Y.: Standard Publishing Co., Inc., 1959), Vol.3, pp. 765-766; Document No. 70, "The Atlantic Conference, August 1941," in *Roosevelt and Churchill, Their Secret Wartime Correspondence*, ed. Francis L. Lowennheim (N.Y.: E.P. Dutton and Co., Inc., 1975), pp. 153-155. See also Joel Colton, *A History of the Modern World* (N.Y.: Alfred A. Knopf, Inc. 1978), 5th ed., p. 820: and Adam B. Ulam, *Expansion and Coexistence: The History of Soviet Foreign Policy, 1917-67* (N.Y.: Friedrich A. Praeger, 1968), p. 331. Of course, Soviet leaders viewed the Atlantic Charter with suspicion. (*Ibid*).

9. *Funk and Wagnalls*, Vol. 10, p. 3667.

10. Throughout Europe, but especially in Germany, Eastern Europe, and Russia, there was a widespread belief that once Nazi Germany was defeated, a military conflict would immediately develop between the Western Allies and Russia. And Stalin himself held that belief. (Colonel V. Sekistov, "Why the Second Front Was Not Opened in 1942" (*Soviet Military Review*, Moscow: Krasnaya Zvesda, No. 8, August, 1972), pp. 50-52. Hereafter referred to as *SMR*, with appropriate year and volume.
Moscow's leaders never forgot how after 22 June 1941, certain American officials, including Missouri's Senator Harry Truman, had expressed delight toward the conflict between the two totalitarian powers. (*Ulam*, p. 331; Graham Lyons, ed., *The Russian Version of the Second World War* (N.Y.: Facts on File, Inc., 1976), p. 29. And throughout the War, the Soviets constantly maintained (and continued to do so till their collapse), that the sole reason the Western Powers postponed the second front until 1944 was to allow both Nazi Germany and Soviet Russia to exhaust and weaker each other to the point where "the imperialists of the USA and England," after Germany's defeat, could better consolidate "their domination of the world." (*Lyons* pp. 43-44. For Soviet suspicions and allegations of Allied betrayals see *Lyons*, pp. 7-13; 29-30; 43-47; 66-69; 95-99; 100-103; 108; 100-114; Anthony C. Brown, *Bodyguards of Lies* (N.Y.: Harper and Row, 1975), pp. 99-100; 384; 801-802; Ladislas Farago, *Burn After Reading* (CA.: Pinnacle Books, 1978), pp. 173-174; and *Kolasky*, p. 90.

11. Kubiyovych, *Visti*, No. 3, 1963, p. 13; Veryha, *Along The Roads*, pp. 182-183; Hryts' Lurakovs' kyi, "Tak Tse Ne Bulo Naspravdi" [It Truly Was Not That Way], *Visti Kombatant*, July, 1951, No. 7 (9), p. 13; *1943-1993. The 1st Ukrainian Division*, pp. 8-9; Myroslav Malets'kyi, "Rokovyny Odnoi Viis'kovoi Odynytsi" [Anniversary of One Military Formation], *Visti*, 1993, No. 2, pp. 3-4. For other reasons cited in support of the establishment of the Division, see *Visti*, 1993, No. 4, pp. 24-25; 28.

Notes

12. Armstrong, *Ukrainian Nationalism*, pp. 170-175; see also *Ukrainian Nationalism*, 3rd ed., pp. 127-131; Doroshenko, *A Survey of Ukrainian Nationalism*, pp. 754-758. See also Veryha, *Along The Roads*, pp. 182-183; Hryts' Lurakovs'kyi, "It Truly Was Not That Way," *Visti Kombatant*, July, 1951, No. 7 (9), p. 13; *1943-1993. The 1st Ukrainian Division*, pp. 10-11; *Visti*, 1993, No. 2, p.4.

13. "The "Galicia" Division," *Visti*, No. 3, 1963, p. 12.

14. Kubiyovych, *Meni 70* (Paris-Munich: Shevchenko Scientific Society, 1970), p. 59. See also *Visti*, No. 3, 1963, pp. 12-13. According to *Ready*, p. 273, the Divisions personnel enlisted out of a desire to at least obtain autonomy, if not full independence, within Germany's sphere and to control their own national, cultural, and religious freedoms. Although at that time such desires could have only been achieved by serving in a German force, at no time did the Divisions soldiers view themselves as SS soldiers; rather, they only viewed themselves as soldiers of a free Ukraine. (*Ibid*).

15. Years later, on 18 April 1968, in Toronto, Canada, during a commemoration ceremony honoring the 25th anniversary of the founding of the 1st Ukrainian Division (originally known as the "Galicia" Division) Dr. Kuybiyovych, as a guest speaker, spoke about the Division's turbulent days.
In his speech, Kubiyovych emphasized the point that a Ukrainian formation would have eventually had an influence on Germany's policies against those who opposed any co-operation with the Ukrainians such as Erich Koch in the Reichskommissariat's Ukraine. Kubiyovych stated that Galicia's Governor, Otto Wachter, encountered difficulties when he proposed to establish the Division, and that Wachter had to proceed cautiously because the Division was organized without Hans Frank's (Poland's General Governor and Wachter's superior), approval, support and cooperation. Additionally, the organizing of the Division worried the Soviets because they feared that this was the beginning of a German political change in the east. As a result, claimed Kubiyovych, they dispatched one of their most able guerrilla commanders, Sidor Kovpak, on a raid into Galicia to demonstrate German weakness. Yet, the communists were unable to demoralize the Division's volunteer. In conclusion, Kubiyovych accurately stated the "Galicia" Division might have arisen without Ukrainian leadership but simultaneously, without some kind of Ukrainian involvement, it would not have benefitted the Ukrainian cause. Kubiyovych emphasized the fact that the Division did strengthen the Ukrainian position in Galicia and eventually, it would have strengthened the Ukrainian position beyond Galicia. The former UCC leader also stressed that at that time, a well-trained and armed Ukrainian force could only have been organized within Germany's armed forces. And once organized, it could have been utilized as a nucleus for a future Ukrainian army.
In summation, Kubiyovych added that for the sake of historical truth, Governor Wachter did carry out most of the proposals presented to him. Asking his audience if the Division fulfilled its mission, Kubiyovych himself replied "yes and no. No. because we are not celebrating its 25 anniversary on our dear land but yes, because it went down in Ukrainian history with all other armed formations: the Ukrainian Rifle Shooters, the Ukrainian Galician Army, the UNRA, and the UPA which after Brody secured hundreds if not thousands of Divisional soldiers. The actions of the Division stand as a true statement that under all circumstances we want to live for Ukraine, and when necessary, to die for her." (For Kubiyovch's speech in its entirely see the Ukrainian quarterly *Surmach* (London: 1968), No. 1-4, pp. 31-34).

16. *IMT*, Vol. 29, p. 605; *IMT*, Vol. 12, p. 148; Noakes and Pridham, *Nazism*, Vol. 2, pp. 980-981. See also Helmut Kraus-Nick, Hans Buchheim, Martin Broszat, Hans-Adolf Jacobsen, *Anatomy of the SS State* (N.Y.: Walker and Co., 1965), p. 510.

17. Personal discussion with Yuriy Krokhmaliuk and Ostap Veryn.

18. *Visti*, 1963, No. 3, pp. 13-14; Veryha, *Along the Roads*, pp. 54-55 and English synopsis, pp. 184 and 205; Yurkevych, "Galician Ukrainians in German Military Formations," in *Boshyk*, ed. p. 77; Krokhmaliuk, *The Glow*, p. 24; Armstrong, *Ukrainian Nationalism*, pp. 169-170; Liubomyr Ortyns'kyi, "I-sha Ukrains'ka Dyviziia na tli Politychnykh Podii Druhdi Svitovoi Viiny" [The 1st Ukrainian Division on the Political Background Events of the Second World War] in Oleh Lysiak, ed., *Brody: Zbirnyk Stattei i Narysiv* [Brody: A Collection of Articles and Narratives] (Published by the Brotherhood of Veteran's of the 1st Ukrainian Division). (N.J.: Computorprint Corp., 1974), p. 43: Myroslav Prokop,"U Sorokrichchia 3-oho Nadzvychainoho Velykoho Zboru OUN" (The 40th Anniversary of the 3rd Great General OUN Conference) in *Suchasnist*, 1987, No. 3 p. 394; and *Naperedodni Nezalezhnoi Ukrainy. Sposterezhnnia; Vysnorky* [On the Eve of Ukraine's Independence. Observations and Conclusions] (Kiev: Shevchenko Scientific Society, 1993). "The UPA's Group "Hoverlia" in *Litopys UPA*, ed. Sodol, Vol. 18, p. 19; General Pavlo Shandruk, *"Geneza i Militarno-Politychne Znachinnia 1-oi Ukrains'koi Dyvizii UNA v Zmahanniakh za Ukrains'ky Dershavnist"* [The Origins and the Military-Political Meaning of the 1st Ukrainian Division UNA in the struggle for Ukrainian Statehood], p. 7 (Unpublished work).
At no time did Bandera or the OUN raise "several SS divisions" as erroneously stated by authors Scott Anderson and Jon Anderson in *Inside the League*, p. 35.

19. "Dovkruhy CC Strilets'koi' Dyvizii "Halychyna" "Biuleten Kraevoho Provodu Organizatsii Ukrains'kiv Nationalistiv -S.D." [Bulletin From the State Leadership of the Organization of Ukrainian Nationalists – S.D.], No. 11, 1943, p. 3. (This bulletin was an underground publication). For the full text of the denunciation see *Suchasnist'* (Munich: Buchdruckerei und Verlag, 1963), No. 10, (34), pp. 106-110). See also Veryha, *Along the Roads*, pp. 54-55. The initials "CD" stood for "Samostiinykiv Dershavnykiv" (Independent Statehood), which was also the name of Bandera's OUN-B faction of Ukrainian Nationalists. (*Ibid*, p. 54). Initially published in 1943, "Dovkruhy CC Strilets'koi

431

Galicia Division

Dyvizii 'Halychyna' was reprinted in its original 1943 format exactly twenty years later in 1963 by the Ukrainian journal "Suchasnist.'"

20. *Suchasnist'*, (1963), p. 110. See also *Subtelny*, p. 472.

21. *Ibid*. Factually speaking, from the outset the Germans provided no political guarantees. Certain promises – such as the Division would be exclusively utilized for eastern front combat; religious observances; and an independent Galician identity with a mixed Ukrainian-German officer cadre, were kept. Volodymyr Kubiyovych and Zenon Kuzeli, *Entsyklopediia Ukrainoznavstva v Dvokh Tomakh* [Encyclopedia of Ukrainian Studies In Two Volumes] (Munich-New York, 1949), Vol. 1, p. 589.

22. Bohdan Pidhainyi, "UPA–Dyviziia "Halychyna," Nimchi, i Stanovyshche OUN i UPA do Dyvizii" [UPA-Division "Galicia," the Germans, and the Position of the OUN and UPA towards the Division], *Visti*, 1990, No. 3, p. 63.

23. Petro Mirchuk, *Revoliutsiinyi Zmah*, p. 126. Mirchuk's book largely deals with the Ukrainian struggle against Nazi Germany, but between pages 125-130, *"Proty Vsiiakoi Spivprachi z Hitlerivs'koiu Nimechchunoiu" [Against All Cooperation With Hilter's Germany]*, specifically covers the various viewpoints regarding the Ukrainian opposition to the "Galicia" Division.

24. *Ibid*, Veryha, "Mashcruiut' Dobrovol'tsi ... Ity Chy Ne Ity" [Volunteers Are Marching ... To Go or Not To Go], *Visti*, 1977, No. 4, pp. 57-58. According to Veryha, OUN agitation was especially strong against the Division. See the English synopsis in Veryha's, *Along the Roads*, p. 184. Lev Shankowsky, "UPA i Dyviziia" [UPA and the Division], *America*, July 1954, pp. 70-71. According to "Nabir do Dyvizii i Vyshkil" [Recruitment to the Division and Training] in *1943-1993. The 1st Ukrainian Division*, "following a short period of indecisiveness, the OUN, under Stepan Bandera, issued a call not to volunteer for the Division." (P. 14). See also Bohdan Pidhainyi's "Dva Shliakhy. Odna Meta" [Two Paths. One Goal.], in *Brody: Zbirnyk Stattei i Narysiv*, ed. Oleh Lysiak, pp. 113-114; and Mirchuk's *Revoliutsiinyi Zmah*, p. 126.

25. Mirchuk, *Revoliutsiinyi Zmah*, p. 126-127. I

26. General M. Kapustians'kyi,"Persha Ukrains'ka Dyviziia i OUN" [The 1st Ukrainian Division and the OUN], *Visti*, 1967, No. 1, p. 6.

27. Volodymyr Kubiyovych, "Dyviziia Hayychyna" [Division "Galicia"], *Visti*, 1963, No. 3, pp. 13-14.

28. Armstrong, *Ukrainian Nationalism*, 3rd ed., p. 127; personal discussion with Yuriy Krokhmaliuk.

29. Personal discussion with Krokhmaliuk.

30. Armstrong, *Ukrainian Nationalism*, 3rd ed., p. 169; Krokhmaliuk, *The Glow*, p. 24; Yurkevich in *Boshyk*, ed. p. 77; Mirchuk, *Revoliutsiinyi Zmah*, p. 126.

31. Mirchuk, *Revoliutsiinyi*, p. 126, Yurkevich in *Boshyk*, ed. p. 77; Krokhmaliuk, *The Glow*, p. 27; Kubiyovych, *Meni 70*, p. 65, Armstrong, *Ukrainian Nationalism*, 3rd ed., p. 127.

32. According to Veryha, *Along the Roads*, p. 56, the OUN-M faction did not take a clear viewpoint and, as a matter of fact, its members were divided on this issue. But according to Pankiwsky, *The Years of the German Occupation*, "leaders of both OUN groups viewed the matter (in regards to the Division) negatively." P. 224.
Although there were those within Melnyk's faction who opposed the Division, overall, Melnyk's faction, unlike the OUN-B, was much more receptive to this venture. See also "Ukrains'ka Dyviziia i Viis'kova Uprava "Halychyna" [The Ukrainian Division and the Military Board "Galicia"], 1987, No. 2, p. 57. According to *1943-1993. The 1st Ukrainian Division*, "Melnyk's OUN neither supported – or opposed – the Division." (Pp. 12 and 14).

33. Veryha, *Along the Roads*, p. 56; *Visti*, 1990, No. 3, p. 63.

34. Armstrong, *Ukrainian Nationalist*, 3rd ed., p. 127.

35. Yurkevich in *Boshyk*, p. 77; Krokhmaliuk, *The Glow*, pp. 40- 41; Mirchuk, *Revoliutsiinyi Zmah*, pp. 1125-130; and *Roman Shukhevych*, p. 121; Veryha, *Along the Roads*, p. 55; Heike, *Ukrainian ed.*, pp. 38, 48-49 and *English ed.*, p. 4. See also introduction section, p. xx; Sodol, *They Fought Hitler and Stalin*, p. 22; *Armstrong*, 3rd ed. p. 127; Liubomyr Ortyns'kyi, "I-sha Ukrains'ka Dyviziia Na Tli Politychnykh Podii Druhoi Svitovoi Viiny" [The 1st Ukrainian Division on the Political Background Events of the Second World War], in *Brody: Zbirnyk Stattei i Narysiv*, Oleh Lysiak, ed., pp. 45-46; and Shankowsky's, "UPA and the Division," in *America*, July 1954, p. 70. According to Shankowsky, the UPA never agitated the Division. Rather, the UPA initially opposed the concept for the creation of the Division. (*Ibid*). According to Pidhainyi, UPA's leadership (as OUNs) took a negative position against the division. See *Visti*, 1990, No.3, p. 63.

Notes

36. Angered by UPA's strong agitation, Wachter personally addressed the matter to the Military board. In an angry fit, Wachter denounced the UPA and stated that the Ukrainian insurgency is a force composed of "Bandit's!" In response to the Governor's remark, Roman Krokhmaliuk stated: "They are Ukrainian sons which possibly took the wrong position." Unsatisfied with Krokhmaliuk's reply, and knowing that the Military Board's sympathies also lay with the UPA, Wachter replied: "Look! You can't play two instruments at the same time!" See Krokhmaliuk's, *The Glow*, p. 296.

37. According to Vashchenko, the UPA first learned of the proposals for the creation of the "Galicia" Division in early 1943 from one of Governor Wachter's most trusted secretaries and from a corrupt Nazi propagandist who, for a bottle of good vodka or a sum of wartime marks (money), passed along any kind of information.

38. Organized 15 April 1943 even before the Division itself was created (Kolisnyk, "Ukrains'ka Dyviziia i Viis'kova Uprava "Halychyna") [The Ukrainian Division and the Military Board "Galicia"], *Visti*, 1987, No. 2, p. 60), Galicia's Military Board was established to deal with matters pertaining to the interests and needs of the Division's soldiers and their families. (See also Yurkevich in *Boshyk*, ed., p. 77; Heike, *English ed.*, pp. 4-5; Krokhmaliuk, *The Glow*, pp. 22-23; 183-185). At first, the Military Board was headed by Volodymyr Kubiyovych. But shortly afterwards, he was replaced by Colonel Alfred Bisanz, an individual better qualified for truly understanding the needs of soldiers. In turn, the board was subdivided into various specific departments such as the Department of Health, Legal Affairs, Culture, Refugee Control, etc. Its main headquarters was located on 10 Parkova St., Lviv, but regional, city, and town offices were also established throughout Galicia. (For a list of its members and the various sections within the organization see Krokhmaliuk's, *The Glow*, pp. 22, 183-185; *Visti*, 1987, No. 2, pp. 63-64).

39. Krokhmaliuk, *The Glow*, p. 40; and personal discussion.

40. *Ibid*, pp. 40-41. Much of the "unqualified personnel" who fled into the ranks of the UPA did so on account of UPA's efforts to dissuade Galicia's manpower from the "Galicia" Division.

41. Reverend Ivan Hryn'okh, "Dyviziia "Halychyna" i Ukrains'ke Pidpillia" [The Division "Galicia" and the Ukrainian Underground], in *Brody: Zbirnyk Stattei i Narysiv*, ed. Lysiak, pp. 78-81; and personal discussions with Yuriy and Roman Krokhmaliuk. For an interesting account of the Division's relationship with the UPA, see pp. 69-71. See also Yurkevich in *Boshyk*, ed., p. 77.

42. Yurkevich in *Boshyk*, ed., p. 77. See also *Armstong*, 3rd ed., p. 128.

43. Mirchuk, *Shukhevych*, p. 122.

44. The two men would never again see each other. Shukhevych was killed in action in March, 1950, and Krokhmaliuk emigrated to the west. (Personal discussion with Roman Krokhmaliuk).

45. One such lengthy meeting was held on 3 April 1943. Volodymyr Kubiyovych, "Pochatok Ukrains'koi Dyvizii "Halychyna" [The Origins of the Ukrainian Division "Galicia"], *Visti Kombatant*, 1954, No. 3-4 (41-42), pp. 2-5. At no time did Kubiyovych travel to Berlin in February 1943 to meet with high-ranking Nazi officials to discuss any kind of military cooperation as alleged by Polish communist propagandists such as Antoni B. Szczesniak, *Droga Do Nikad: Dzialalnosc Organizacji Ukrainskich Nacjonalistow; Jej Likwidacja w Polsce* (Warszawa: Wydawnistwo Ministerstwa Obrony Narodowej, 1973), p. 122.

46. Kubiyovych, *Visti Kombatant*, 1954, No. 3-4, pp. 4-5; Krokhmaliuk, *The Glow*, pp. 21-22; Kolisnyk, "Ukrains'ka Dyviziia i Viskova Uprava "Halychyna," *Visti*, 1987, No. 1, p. 79; *Pankiwsky*, pp. 225-228; Reverend Dr. Sydir Nahayewsky, *A Soldier Priest Remembers* (Toronto: Ukrainian Book Co., 1985), p. 33. For a highly objective Polish account as to why the Division arose, as well as the problems its organizers encountered, see "Historyczna Prawda o Ukrainskiej Armii Narodowej" [Historical Truth of the Ukrainian National Army], in *Stosunki Polsko-Ukrainskie 1917-1947, od Tragedii do Wspolpracy* [The Polish-Ukrainian Relationship, 1917-1947; From Tragedy to Cooperation]. (Wydawnictwo "Perturbancii," 1990), pp. 773.

47. Armstrong, *Ukrainian Nationalism*, p. 172; Yurkevich in *Boshyk*, ed., p. 77; Krokhmaliuk, *The Glow*, p. 21; *Ready*, p. 273; Pankiwsky, p. 226. At no time was the "Galicia" (Ukrainian) Division, or any of its elements or personnel, ever employed in France against French "Maquis" Resistance fighters, in Norway, in the 1941-42 Babi Yar massacres, in the April/May 1943 Warsaw Ghetto, against the western allies in Normandy in 1944, in the 1944 Polish Warsaw Uprising, or in any concentration/ extermination camps as alleged by some.

48. *Ready*, pp. 272-273. This would eventually occur but not immediately as will be seen.

49. *Ibid*.

50. At that time, some of Nachtigall's imprisoned officers were held in Lviv's jails. *Pankiwsky*, p. 227; Bohdan Stasiv, "Tragediya Pid Brodamy" [Tragedy at Brody], *Visti*, 1992, No. 3, p. 52, cites Kybiyovych strove to obtain a general amnesty for all Ukrainian political prisoners, to include Bandera and Melnyk.

Galicia Division

51. *Ready*, p. 272. Although Kubiyovych requested that the Division be a part of the Wehrmacht, it was Himmler who finally determined that the Division would be incorporated into the ranks of the Waffen-SS. (Kolisnyk, *Visti*, 1986, No. 4, p. 91). See also *Pankiwsky*, p. 226. At no time was the Division "Galicia" ever a "police" division; nor was it ever referred to, or titled, as the "Galician Police Division" as falsely stated by author's Aaron and Loftus in *Unholy Trinity*, p. 180; and nor was the Division ever an "anti-partisan police unit" as alleged by the sensationalist Nazi-hunter Sol Littman in "These Aging Men Were Monsters Once" in *The Windsor Star*, Tuesday, 16 July 1985.

52. Initially, the Military Board was headed by Kubiyovych. But he was soon replaced by Colonel Bisanz.

53. *Bender and Taylor*, Vol. 4, p. 19; Heike, *English ed.*, p. 4; Veryha, *Along the Roads*, p. 54; English synopsis, p. 183; Samuel Mitcham, Jr., *Hitler's Legions: The German Army Order of Battle, World War II* (N.Y.: Dorset Press, 1987), p. 456; *Pankiwsky*, p. 228; *1943-1993. The 1st Ukrainian Division*, p. 12; Holyn skyj, *Visti*, 1983, No.4 p. 20.

54. In a 438 page restricted book published by the U.S. Military Intelligence Service in April 1943 and titled *"Order of Battle of the German Army,"* the 14th Waffen-SS "Galicia" Division was not yet identified; however, the Division's first commanding officer, Walter Schimana, is identified as holding rank in the General SS and Police but not in the Waffen-SS. By this time, America's Intelligence Service had positively identified the first 10 Waffen-SS divisions and a number of its independent brigades. But no reference is yet made to the 14th Waffen-SS Division.

55. Kolisnyk, "Verbuval'na Aktsiia" [The Recruitment Action] in "Ukrains'ka Dyviziia i Viis'kova Uprava "Halychyna." Nimets'ka Polityka Vidnosno Ukrains'koho Natsional'noho Viis'ka 1943-1945 (Prodovzhennia).' [The Ukrainian Military Board "Galicia." German Politics in Relation to the Ukrainian National Army, 1943-1945 (Continuation)] in *Visti*, 1987, No. 5-6, pp. 48-49.

56. General-Gouvernment, Der Governeur des Distrikts Galizien, Tgb. Nr. 104/43 g. Gehaim, Lemberg, den 28 April 1943; An die Krieshauptleute o.V.i.A., An der Stadthauptmann in Lemberg o. V.i.A., An die Stadt-und Landkommissare-direkt (NA).

57. Wachter's words signified the changing policies of the Third Reich in 1943 versus its policy in 1942 when just one year earlier, on 23 March 1942, a Berlin propaganda directive titled "Basic Principles for Propaganda Directed Toward Armed Forces and Peoples of the Soviet Union" and was published by the Armed Forces High Command (OKW) and signed by Jodl. This directive was issued to eliminate confusion pertaining to the many suggestions, requests and critiques offered by various agencies regarding German propaganda towards the Soviet Union's populace. A number of points were established, and all propaganda was to be centered around these points. What is especially interesting is that the 1942 directive unequivocally declared "that Ukrainian manpower could not be utilized for the front line." And point No. 3 specified: "Plans provide for considerable postwar independence only for the Turkic nations and the peoples of the Caucasus. For that reason, volunteer legions and active participation in the war of liberation against Bolshevism may be considered for members of those ethnic groups while the Baltic peoples, Ukrainians, etc., remain eligible only for police duties but not for commitment at the front." Source: *Heersgrupe Nord Propaganda befehle (75131/104)*, p. A-61. For the full text of this propaganda directive see Captain John H. Buchsbaum, General Staff, U.S. Army, *German Psychological Warfare On the Russian Front, 1941-1945* (Washington, D.C., 1953), pp. A60-A63.

58. Kubiyovych's appeal was published in various newspapers throughout Galicia. It must be noted, however, that in a few of them, Kubiyovych's words were slightly reworded. In Lviv's (Lemberg's) newspaper "Lvivski Visti," where Kubiyovych's appeal was also published, the words "Muscovite-Jewish Bolshevism" were inserted whereas in Kubiyovych's original appeal, no such words were stated by him. Kubiyovych's exact words may be found in the newspaper "Krakivski Visti," published 16 May 1944. The reason why certain words were inserted into Kubiovych's appeal in Lviv's newspaper is because the Ukrainian press in Lviv was officially under the auspices of the General Government's Press and Journal Publications branch and as such, was directed by George Lehmann, a Nazi official who also headed all of Eastern Galicia's broadcasts and press publications; whereas in Cracow, Poland, the press "Krakivski Visti" was under the management of the "Ukrains'ke Vydavnytstvo" (The Ukrainian Publishing House), which had close ties to Kubiyovych's Ukrainian Central Committee, (*Boshyk*, p. 185) and therefore, was subject to limited press censorship. For a similar but shorter appeal, see *Pankiwsky*, p. 229, or *Krakowski Visti*, 1 May 1943, No. 89.

59. On 29 January 1918, a small contingent of approximately 500 Ukrainian cadets was hastily organized and set to Kruty, a town east of Kiev located on the Moscow-Kiev railway line. At Kruty, the Ukrainian cadets attempted to stop a numerically superior Red Army force commanded by General Mikhail Muraviov and Rudolf Eidemann (a former general in the Imperial German Army who adopted the Red cause), as they advanced westward toward Kiev. Although classified as a "battle" by many Ukrainians, what really happened at Kruty was in reality no battle but a tragic and senseless massacre which only disclosed military incompetency, faulty leadership, and a weak military organization within the Ukrainian National Republic.

60. *Visti*, 1987, No. 2, p. 58. Personal discussion with Yuriy Krokhmaliuk.

61. *Visti*, 1987, No. 2, p. 58.

62. *Ibid.*

63. Although German propagandists claimed the Waffen-SS was a volunteer "freiwillegen" service and certain formations carried before their divisional names the title of "freiwillegen" ('Free Volunteer') in reality, this was just a propaganda lie. In both German and Foreign Waffen-SS divisions, much of the manpower was secured through conscription. (Höhne, *The Order of The Death's Head*, p. 518). Certain German Waffen-SS units were primarily raised by conscription, such as the 9th SS "Hohenstauffen" and 10th SS "Frundsberg" tank divisions. (*Bender and Taylor*, Vol. 3, p. 46, cites that "70 percent of "Hohenstauffen" was conscripted while Keegan, T*he Waffen-SS*, p. 91, cites between 70-80 percent for both divisions). By no means did the draft system apply only to German units. In Travik, Croatia, additional "volunteers" for the 13th SS "Handschar" Division were even secured by such methods as dragging unwilling Moslem men out of their Mosques in the midst of worship services. (*Bender and Taylor*, Vol 3, p. 140). And much of the manpower for the German sponsored 15th SS "Freiwilligen" Latvian (1st Latvian) and 19th SS Latvian (2nd Latvian) Divisions was secured by conscription. (*Bender and Taylor*, Vol. 4, pp. 71, 75, 82; and Vol. 5, pp. 14-17). See also *Höhne*, pp. 534-537; *IMT*, Vol. 22, pp. 513-514; *IMT*, Vol. 42, pp. 83-85; and *Himmler*, p. 165.

In 1943, America's war-time intelligence correctly concluded that the Waffen-SS was no longer a volunteer force. "Since the beginning of 1943, strenuous efforts have been made to induce boys of 16 and 17 to join the Waffen-SS" ... " There is reason to believe that in many cases the pressure on the youths to "volunteer" is tantamount to compulsory enlistment." In a sub-paragraph titled *"Outside Germany,"* the report also correctly identified that in Croatia, Estonia, and from Russian Volksdeutsche, men were conscripted for Waffen-SS service. See "Recruitment of the Waffen-SS," in *Tactical and Technical Trends, Military Intelligence Division* (Washington D.C.), Number 35, 7 October 1943, pp. 49-55.

64. During an advance, the Soviets always scoured the countryside for manpower and materiel. To cite an example, in the fall of 1943, the German 6th Army (rebuilt after Stalingrad), estimated that the Soviets had conscripted approximately 80,000 men from towns and cities previously occupied by German rule. (Earl F. Ziemke, *Stalingrad to Berlin: The German Defeat in the East* (U.S. Army Historical Series, Washington, D.C.: Government Printing Office, 1971, pp. 172-173). These draftees were usually outfitted with just an army jacket or a pair of military pants and, if lucky, they might have received a rifle and bayonet. Organized into assault waves with very little or no training, the green conscripts were often used for "cannon-fodder" to spare the better armed, equipped and trained Soviet troops. (*Ibid*, p. 206). In another period between July and mid-October 1943 the Soviets, after reoccupying German held areas, secured some 500,000 to 600,000 men. (*Ibid*, pp. 214-215).

According to a British War Office report of 13 December 1945, the Soviets undertook massive conscriptions. "The reoccupation of every village was followed within a few days by a call-up of all men between 18-50, usually conducted by an officer of the NKVD. They [the draftees] were given 5-10 days of training and were sent ill-armed and ill-clothed in the most dangerous part of the front; casualties and desertions seen to have been heavy." See "War Office Report on the Ukrainian Nationalist Movement and Resistance in Ukraine, 13 December 1945" in *Luciuk and Kordan*, pp. 173-174. Ziemke's and the British War Office observations are substantiated by many former German eastern front veterans. "Russian Battle Techniques" in *Russian Combat Methods in World War II*, chap. 5, pp. 24-26; and "Partisan Warfare," chap. 16, p. 105, vividly describes how women and children were also utilized by Soviet authorities in violation of international law.

65. Realistically speaking, the so-called "anti-Bolshevist crusade" was not, as the Waffen-SS liked to envision it, a popular political/military European movement. Most who volunteered cared nothing about Hitler's "Great" or "New Europe;" rather, they enlisted to better their own personal and national character.

66. *Hohne*, p. 539; *Ready*, p. 273. Ready's remark is substantiated by Ihor Fedyk who wrote: "We did not have a nation, but we wanted it. That is why our youth perished for their ideal in a foreign army – in hopes that through the formation of their own Ukrainian Army, they will form a Ukrainian nation." Ihor Fedyk "Chy Buly Dyviziinyky Koliaboratoramy?" [Were Divisional soldiers Collaborators?], *Visti*, 1993, No. 1, p. 58. See also Sviatomyr M. Fostun, "U 50-Richchia Postannia 1-oi UD UNA" [On the 50 Anniversary of the Rise of the 21st Ukrainian Division, Ukrainian National Army], *Visti*, 1993, No. 4, pp. 23-24. According to Osyp Holynskyj, "Galicia's Ukrainians had no desire to rescue Hitler's Germany. Rather, the Ukrainians had their own plans (for self-liberation)." Holynskyj, "40th Anniversary of the Rise of the Division 'Galicia,'" *Visti*, 1983, No.4, p. 20.

67. Little did they realize that in future months, America and Great Britain would renege on their promise of national freedoms (as proclaimed in the Atlantic Charter) and instead, at Yalta in February 1945, would officially permit the Soviets to control the region. See also Veryha, *Along The Roads*, pp. 57-58.

68. *Bender and Taylor*, Vol. 4, pp. 19-21. Although in mid-1943 German authorities had no intention of organizing a "Ukrainian Army," many Ukrainians erroneously believed that in addition to the "Galicia" Division, the Germans were actually organizing a "Ukrainian Army."

69. *Hohne*, p. 539; *Ready*, p. 273.

70. *Bender and Taylor*, Vol. 4, pp. 19-21; personal discussion with Yuriy Krokhmaliuk; Reitlinger, *The SS*, p. 204. However, as verified by Reitlinger, a number of the released Ukrainians were soon rearrested by Nazi authorities because they boycotted the Division. (*Ibid*).

Galicia Division

71. Such was the case of Colonel Evhen Pobihushchyj-Ren. On Saturday, Easter weekend, Colonel Bisanz appeared in Ren's cell. Bisanz informed the imprisoned ex-Roland warrior that a Ukrainian "Galicia" Division was in the process of being raised and that officers were needed for the Division. Faced with the option of either volunteering or rotting inside a German prison, and realizing that the Ukrainian cause could only improve its position with an army of its own, Ren volunteered.

However, many Ukrainian political prisoners were still not released. Certain leaders, but especially those such as Bandera, were still considered too dangerous to be released.

72. *Armstrong*, 3rd ed. pp. 127-128; Oleh Lysiak, "Fragmenty Spohadiv z Dyvizii" [Fragmentary Remembrances From the Division] in *1943-1993. The 1st Ukrainian Division*. p. 34; and *Visti*, 1993, No. 2, p.57. According to Vashchenko, Shukhevych at first was not receptive towards the Division. But from the outset, Vashchenko concluded that the Division could not only be utilized for intelligence gathering, but to secure arms, ammunition, equipment as well as tactical, mechanical and communications training. Therefore, Vashchenko urged Shukhevych not to interfere with its formation.

73. *Bender and Taylor*, Vol. 4, p. 21. According to Veryha, Kubiyovych managed to extract a promise that the Ukrainian Division would only be utilized against Soviet armies on the eastern front. Veryha, *Along The Roads*, English synopsis, p. 183.

74. As already presented, much of the manpower secured for German and foreign Waffen-SS units was through conscription. See also *Hohne*, pp. 535-540; and *Ready*, pp. 304-305 and footnote no. 92.

75. Usually after a dose of eastern front combat, many such men sought various ways to evade further service, or simply left when their service time expired.

76. Yurkevich in *Boshyk*, p. 77; Heike, *Ukrainian ed.*, p. 25; *Ready*, pp. 272-273; Veryha, *Along the Roads*, pp. 57-58; English synopsis, p. 184; Evhen Shypailo, "Brody i My" [Brody and Us], *Visti*, 1965, No. 3, pp. 3-4.

On 21 February 1947, nineteen months after World War II, a report regarding the Division was submitted by L.D. Wilgrest, a High Commissioner within Canada's Refugee Screening Commission. Titled "Refugee Screening Commission Report on Ukrainians in Surrendered Enemy Personnel," the report also covered reasons for enlistment into German service. Wilgreat's report cited four main reasons: 1) The hope of securing a genuinely independent Ukraine; 2) Without knowing exactly what they were doing because other Ukrainians whom they knew had already volunteered; 3) As a preferable alternative to forced labor, etc., or to living in Soviet controlled territory, and 4) to have a smack at the Russians, whom they [the Ukrainians] always refer to as "Bolsheviks." See "Refugee Screening Commission Report On Ukrainians In Surrendered Enemy Personnel," (SEP) Camp No. 374, Italy, LACAB/18RSC/RIC, 21 February 1947. For a copy of the entire report see *Boshyk*, pp. 233-240.

77. *Ready*, p. 272; Veryha, *Along the Roads*, pp. 57-58 and English synopsis, p. 184, cites "many nationally conscious young men and women."

78. While it was forbidden to accept a recruit under 17 years of age, it is known that a small number of 16-year-old's did succeed in entering the Division.

79. Yurkevich in *Boshyk*, p. 77; Heike, *Ukrainian ed.*, p. 25. The Division was not recruited from "many Ukrainian collaborationist police and militia units that had enthusiastically participated in anti-Semitic and anti-Communist pogroms" as erroneously claimed by *Simpson*, p. 180; nor was the Division "an amalgam of auxiliary police battalions before it was absorbed into the SS" as erroneously stated by Aarons and Loftus in *Unholy Trinity*, p. 189; and at no time did "many policemen volunteer" into its ranks. (*Ibid*, p. 180).

80. Veryha, *Along the Roads*, p. 57 and English synopsis, p. 184; Heike, *Ukrainian ed.*, p. 25.

81. According to Myroslav Prokop, "U Sorokovi Rokovyny Proty Nimets'koi Borot'by" [On the 40th Anniversary of the Anti-German Struggle], "the volunteers enlisted out of a desire to serve the Ukrainian fatherland, and not the Third Reich." See *Suchasnist'*, October, 1981, No. 10, p. 55.

82. *Bender and Taylor*, Vol. 4, p. 22.

83. *Ibid*.

84. Telegram sent by Berger to Himmler, 11 May 1943. Cited also from *Bender and Taylor*, Vol. 4, p. 22.

85. Kruger to Berger, 11 May 1943. *See Bender and Taylor*, Vol 4, p. 22.

86. *Ibid*, Vol. 4, p. 22.

87. Heike, *Ukrainian ed.* p. 247. For a synopsis of the "Galicia" Division in the English language, see pp. 245-253.

Notes

88. *Bender and Taylor*, Vol. 4, p. 22.

89. Berger to Himmler, Betr.: SS-Schutzen Division Galizien, Zwischenneldung 21 Juni 1943; *Bender and Taylor*, Vol. 4, p. 22. Several days later, on 24 June, Hitler forbade the recruitment of Poles; therefore, at no time were Poles recruited for the Division. See also *Bender and Taylor*, Vol. 4, p. 22.

90. Berger to Himmler, Betr.: Freiwilligen-Legion Galizien, 29 Juni 1943. In this letter, Berger also emphasized the importance of posting a strength of approximately 4,000 in Galicia for maintaining order. Once formed, these men would not be sent into the Division. Although Berger suggested such an idea, this never happened. In regards to the term "Legion," this was the first and only known instance of the "Galicia" Division ever being referred to as a "Legion." Because this term was never officially used, Berger must have simply erred.

91. Berger to Himmler, Berlin, 2 July 1943. See *Bender and Taylor*, Vol. 4, p. 22.

92. Kubiyovych, *Meni 70*, p. 62.

93. *Doroshenko*, p. 756; Nahyewsky, *A Soldier Priest Remembers*, cites over 80,000 as volunteering. (P. 34).

94. Krokhmaliuk, *The Glow*, p. 34; and *Veryha*, p. 57, cite the same figure. Of these, 52,875 were accepted by the commission, but a total of 29,124 were rejected. *Ibid*.

95. George Stein, *The Waffen-SS: Hitler's Elite Guard at War, 1939-1945* (N.Y.: Cornell University Press, 1966), p. 185; *Dmytryshyn*, p. 6; *Hohne*, p. 570; K.G. Klietmann, *Die Waffen-SS: Eine Dokumentation* (Osnabruck, 1965), p. 194; Martin Windrow, *The Waffen-SS* (Revised Edition), (England: Osprey Publishing Ltd., 1985), p. 14, cites 30,000 were accepted.

96. *Luciuk and Kordan*, p. 148. This report provided no numerical figure, but its report that "four were said to have been formed and to have left for the front by November, 1943" was inaccurate. At the same time, this report extensively covered the Ukrainian struggle against the Nazi occupation, and cited Reichskommissar Koch's New Year's message as an example of the German-Ukrainian struggle. (For a full text of the report, see pp. 146-150).

97. "Commission of Inquiry On War Criminal," *Alliancer*, 30 May 1985, p. 9.

98. Krokhmaliuk, *The Glow*, p. 34.

99. *Ibid.*

100. *Ibid.* Yurkevich in *Boshyk*, p. 77.

101. Krokhmaliuk, *The Glow*, p. 34; Yurkevich in *Boshyk*, p. 77; Heike, *Ukrainian ed.*, p. 25; English synopsis, p. 247. But in the ensuing months, until approximately June 1944, more men would be called up for training. Such arrivals would bolster the Division's strength to a figure o 15,299 by 30 June 1944. *Bender and Taylor*, Vol. 4, p. 48.

102. *Bender and Taylor*, Vol. 4, p. 22; Heike, *Ukrainian Ed.*, English synopsis, p. 247.

103. Although by 1943 the Waffen-SS had lowered its height restriction, its standards were still higher than those of the Wehrmacht's. The minimum height for enlisting into the "Galicia" Division was 160-164 cm. (About 5 ft. 5 in.). One can see that height restrictions eliminated many from a letter written by Berger to Himmler on 21 June 1943. The recruiting chief reported that out of a total of 26,436 men so far examined, 12,874 were found unfit. Of these, exactly 7,139 failed to meet the minimum height restrictions. Berger to Himmler, Betr.: SS-Schutzen Division "Galizien," Zwischenneldung, 21 Juni 1943. See also Kolisnyk, "Verbuval'na Aktsiia" [The Recruitment Action], *Visti*, 1987, No. 5-6, p. 53. Needless to say, the reaction to being disqualified as a result of height restrictions varied. Some were pleased, but others felt shamed. One man, when told he was to short, broke down and cried. Of interest to note is that America's intelligence correctly identified a minimum height of 5 feet, 5 inches for the Waffen-SS foreign personnel. See *Tactical and Technical Trends*, 7 October 1943, p. 54. America's intelligence also correctly summed this observation: "Recruiting notices ask for men between 17 and 45 years of age, Aryan, with no criminal records, and mentally and physically fit. This is now the general standard for the foreign SS recruits." (*Ibid*).

104. In reality, although Ukrainian patriots were theoretically barred from the formation, unless a man's past was fully known or he possessed an arrest record for "nationalist" activities, there was no reliable way of separating the "nationalists" from the "non-nationalists."
In Martin Windrow's *Waffen-SS*, pp. 18-19, author Windrow incorrectly presents how SS authorities began to use "Ukrainian nationalists in areas now behind the German lines in Russia." Factually speaking, the recruitment of so-called "Ukrainian nationalists" for the "Galicia" Division was never encouraged by Nazi authorities. Daluege's letter of 14 April 1943 is just one of a number of letters which opposed the recruitment of those perceived to be "nationalist."

Galicia Division

105. As late as 30 June 1944, in a letter addressed and signed by Myhailo Khronoviat (who was also a member of the Military Board), it was written that many men (including ex-officers and non-commissioned officers), when called for service to the Division were using various excuses to dodge service. Aktenvermerk Fur Herrn, Oberst A. Bisanz. Leiter des Wehrausschusses Galizien. Lemberg, den 30. Juni 1944.

106. Stein, *The Waffen-SS*, p. 186.

107. A ruthless figure but an excellent police organizer, Daluege was the second most powerful policeman in the SS, surpassed in rank only by Reichsführer Himmler. Born on 15 September 1897 in Upper Silesia, Daluege served as Commander-in-Chief of the German Reich's Police. Following Heydrich's assassination in Czechoslovakia in 1942, Daluege became Deputy Protector of Bohemia and Moravia. Held responsible for the destruction of Lidice, Daluege was executed by the Czechs on 24 October 1946.

108. Undoubtedly, when Daluege mentioned to Himmler the matter of a "Police Rifle Division," Himmler at first did not know what Daluege was referring to because Himmler never instructed, nor authorized, the establishment of a "Police Rifle Division" from Galicia.

109. Der Chef der Ordnungspolizei SS-Obergruppenführer Kurt Daluege: An General-Leutnant Winkelmann, Berlin, z.Z. Feld-Kommandostelle, den 14.4.43.

110. But this never happened. Unless a volunteer had a record, there was no way of distinguishing a Ukrainian patriot from one who was not. Because skilled military personnel who possessed a fluency in both the German and Ukrainian languages were desperately needed for a cadre, German officials in Poland and Galicia overlooked the so-called "patriots." In the end, a high number of Ukrainian patriots did in fact enlist into the "Galicia" Division.

111. Ren, *My Life's Mosaic*, pp. 114-115; Liubomyr Otyns'kyi, "Persha Ukrains'ka Dyviziia na tli Politychnykh Podiy Druhoii Svitovoii Viiny" [The 1st Ukrainian Division on the Political Decay of the Second World War] in *Brody, Zbirnyk Stattei i Narysiv* [Brody: A Collection of Stories and Essays], ed. Oleh Lysiak. (Munich: 1951), pp. 26-27; 145; and *Brody: Zbirnyk Stattei i Narysiv*, 1974, ed., p. 44; Sviatomyr Fostun, "50 Years In the Rise of the 1st Ukrainian Division, Ukrainian National Army." *Visti*, 1993, No. 4, p. 25. According to Veryha, Along the Roads, English synopsis, p. 184, "the Germans were not in a hurry to for the [Galicia] Division because there were voices questioning Ukrainian loyalty, saying that arms given to the Ukrainians, sooner or later, would be turned against the Germans themselves."

112. Der Gebietskommissar, VI 91/43 geheim; Gorochow, den 19. Juni 43; An den Herrn Generalkommissar fur Wolhynien und Podolien in Luzk; gez. Harter (Abschrift); Der Generalkommissar fur Wolhynien und Podolien, VI 29/43 g. Luzk, den 29 Juni 1943; An den Herrn SS-und Polizeiführer in Luzk. (Cited also from *Visti*, 1987, No. 1, p. 86). See also Kolisnyk's "Ukraintsi" chy "Halychany?" ["Ukrainians" or "Galicians?"], *Visti*, 1987, No. 1, p. 81.

113. Der SS-und Polizeiführer fur Wolhynien und Podolien, Luzk, den 30.6.43; An den Hoheren SS und Polizeiführer BB in Kiew. I.A. Oberlt. d. Sch. (Cited also from *Visti*, 1987, No. 1, p. 86. See also *Visti*, 1987, No. 1, p. 81).

In 1941, Himmler appointed two HSSPF (Senior SS and Police Commanders) to serve as his principle representatives in Russia. Gruppenführer Hans Prutzmann of HSSPF 'North' was in Riga, and HSSPF Gruppenführer Erich was in Kiev. In mid-1942, SS Brigadeführer Gerret Korsemann served briefly as HSSPF for the Caucasian region. After the German withdrawal from Caucasia, Korsemann was reposted to Central Russia. (*Höhne*, pp. 410, 469).

114. Der Hohere SS-und Polizeiführer Russland Sud. Wolfsheide, den 8.7.1943; An den Reichsführer SS. (Signature illegible). SS-Obergruppenführer und General der Polizei). (Cited also from *Visti*, 1987, No. 1, p. 86). See also *Visti*, 1987, No. 1, p. 81).

115. Jurgen Thorwald, *The Illusion: Soviet Soldier's In Hitler's Armies* (N.Y.: Harcourt, Brace, and Jovanovich, 1975), pp. 135-136. Hitler also cited Ludendorff's World War I failure with the so-called "Polish" Legion. Because none of those attending the evening's conference dared to challenge Hitler's fallacious comparisons of the World War I period to the events of 1943, the matter was once again dropped.

116. Koch not only opposed the Division throughout its entire existence but he was one of the first high ranking Nazi officials to oppose the proposals for the establishment of the "Galicia" Division.

117. COSS HA/Be/We. Adjtr-Tgb. Nr. 685/43. Kds. Betrift: Galizische Division. Bezug: Schreiben des Reichskommissars Ukraine, den 10.12.1943. (Simple translation: "Reference: Galicia Division. Letter of the Reichskommissar Ukraine.").

118. *Bender and Taylor*, Vol. 4, p. 26; *Visti*, 1987, No. 1, p. 80; *Visti*, 1977, No. 5-6, p. 49; *Pankiwsky*, p. 226; Heike, *English ed.*, p. 4. According to Heike, Himmler also explicitly ordered that there was to be no mention of Ukrainian independence.

Notes

119. Landemer, *La Waffen-SS*,p. 199; *Visti*, 1987, No. 1, p. 80; *Pankiwsky*, p. 226. Himmler's decree ran contrary to what Wachter had stated earlier on 28 April: "That the name [of the Division] will be Ukrainian." (*Visti*, 1977 No. 5-6, pp. 49-50). The deception, however, fooled no one – Himmler included – and in the end the Division was composed mostly of patriotic Ukrainians. See also Stein, *The Waffen-SS*, p. 186; and Heike, *English ed.*, p. 4.

120. Der Reichsführer SS, Tgb. Nr. 48/10/43 g.; Geheim. Feld- Kommandostelle, den 14.7.43; An alle Hauptamtchefs; "Bei der Erwahnung der galizischen Division verbiete ich, jemals von einer ukrainischen Division oder vom ukrainischen Volktum zu sprechen." (Cited also from *Visti*, 1987, No. 1, p. 86). See also Heike, *English ed.*, p. 4.

121. Generalgouvernment Der Gouverneur des Distrikts Galizien; Lemberg, den 30. Juli 1943; Geheim. Dr. Wa/Ra,Z1. 19/43 g. Personlich; An den Reichsführer-SS und Chef der Deutschen Polizei Heinrich Himmler, Berlin Sw11, Prinz Albrech-Strasse Nr. 8. (Here, the nine points have been condensed into seven. For the full nine points see *Visti*, 1987, No. 1, pp. 82-83 and p. 86.

122. Der Reichsführer SS, Tgb. Nr. 48/10/43 g. Geheim. 11 August 1943. Feld-Kommandostelle; An den Gouvernor des Distrikte Galizien SS-Brigadeführer Dr. Wachter, Lemberg. (Cited also from *Visti*, 1987, No. 1, p. 86).

123. *Ibid.* See also *Visti*, 1987, No. 1, p. 83-85; and *Dmytryshyn*, pp. 7-8.

124. Generalgouvernment Der Gouverneur des Distrikts Galizien; Lemberg, den 4. September 1943. Dr Wa/Ra; Zl. 19/43; Geheim; An den Reichsführer-SS. (Cited also from *Visti*, 1987, No. 1, p. 86).

125. Wachter, persistent in his convictions, continued to address the matter to Himmler as late as October, 1943. Wachter to Brandt, Lemberg, 13 October 1943; Wachter to Himmler, Lemberg, 30 October 1943. As earlier, Wachter's requests fell on deaf ears.

126. A.D. Skada, *Radians'ka Entsyklopediia Istorii Ukrainy* [Soviet Encyclopedia of Ukrainian History], (Kyiv: Akademia Nayk URSR, 1972, Vol. 1, p. 1656.) See also Veryha, *Along the Roads*, p. 63.

127. Among Ukrainians, Bohdan Khmelnytsky is regarded as a liberator of Ukrainians from foreign rule and tyranny.

128. Such was the case with Kovpak's guerrilla force. In December 1943, this unit was redesignated as the "1st Ukrainian Partisan Division." (*Radians'ka Entsyklopediia*, Vol. 1, p. 2706; Veryha, *Along the Roads*, pp. 63-64). In reality, the bulk of this "Ukrainian" Division was composed of non-Ukrainians under Russian command. (*Veryha*, pp. 64-65).

129. The allegation that the "Galicia" Division was dispatched to Norway to conduct a "new order" (See Yaroslav Gallan, *Tvory u tr'okh tomakh* [Stories In Three Volumes], Kiev: Derzhavne Vydavnytstvo Ukrainy, 1960, Vol. 2, pp. 336-337; cited also from Veryha's *Along the Roads*, pp. 66-67), is totally false. At no time did the "Galicia" Division, or any of its elements or personnel, ever serve in Norway or in any Scandinavian nation.

130. For Gallan's remarks see Veryha, *Along the Roads*, pp. 65-66. Parts of Gallan's speech were later published in the leftist Ukrainian newspaper *Holos*. See "Ukrains'ka Halychyna v Boiakh z Nimtsiamy" [Ukrainian Galicia In Battle With the Germans], 15 August 1944, No. 16, p. 8. Of interest to note is that at approximately the same time that Gallan was denouncing the Division, a Moscow supported organization titled "Obshasne Komanduvannia Narodnoi Gvardi" [The Regional Command of the People's Guards], began to circulate in mid-1943 various leaflets specifically addressed to Galicia's Ukrainian populace regarding the Division. One such leaflet, titled "Ukrainian" proclaimed that "not one Ukrainian patriot will enter Hilter's dog Division. But those that will go – they are traitors to their homeland." Continuing on, the leaflet urged "every [Galician Ukrainian] to enter the ranks of the People's Guard!" Urging "Death to the German occupant!" the leaflet also denounced the Hitlerites for advocating a military force to be utilized against "our brothers." But along with a denouncement of the Division, the leaflet also issued such a warning: "Those who go, they will not be granted mercy when the time comes for a payback!" (A copy of this leaflet was provided to the author by Roman Kolisnyk. Originals may be found in the Divisional archives located in Toronto, Canada.).

131. Veryha, *Along the Roads*, p. 67; M. Kyrah, "Ukrains'ka Dyviziia "Halychyna" v Nasvitleni Bol'shevyts'koi Propangandi" [The Ukrainian Division "Galicia" as illustrated in Bolshevik Propaganda], Visti, 1959, No. 1, p. 71.

132. Alexander Werth, *Russia at War, 1941-1945* (N.Y.: E.P. Dutton, Inc., 1964), pp. 185-186; 639-642; 652. See also Jan M. Ciechanowski, *The Warsaw Rising of 1944* (Cambridge University Press, 1974), pp. 3-5.

133. Richard Collier, *The War That Stalin Won* (Great Britain: Hamish Hamilton, Inc., 1983), pp. 40-41. See also pp. 192-194.

134. In the end, this actually happened.

Galicia Division

135. This treaty was, in fact, violated by Stalin on 23 August 1939 when Molotov signed the Hitler-Stalin Pact with Nazi Germany.

136. Dziewanowski, *Poland In the 20th Century*, p. 122. For a map of Poland's planned postwar borders see p. 146.

137. Stewart Richardson, *The Secret History of World War II: The Ultra-Secret Wartime Letters and Cables of Roosevelt, Stalin, and Churchill.* (N.Y.: Richardson and Steirman, 1986). See especially: Message from Churchill to Stalin (Most Secret and Personal), 1 February 1944, pp. 156-159; Stalin to Churchill, pp. 160-162; Churchill to Stalin, pp. 163-167; Stalin to Churchill, p. 168; Churchill to Stalin, pp. 169-170; and Stalin to Roosevelt, pp. 187-188. See also *Chamberlain*, p. 78.

138. As evidenced by certain allied reports. See *Luciuk and Kordan*, "Note Prepared for the Yalta Conference by B.E. Pares, Northern Department, British Foreign Office, 23 February 1945, Dealing with Ukrainian Minority in Poland. Included Minutes," pp. 156-158.
Point 1 of this 6 point report presents how "Poland's eastern frontiers presents not simply a Russo-Polish issue, but a triangular situation in which Poland's national minorities constitute the third party; and the record of Poland's relations with the Ukrainians has been anything but a happy one."

139. The Division was usually addressed by the Poles and Ukrainians as "Ukrainian" rather than "Galicia." But there were exceptions. One leaflet, issued by the Polish underground, was titled "Instruktsiia v. Spravakh Tvorennia Dyvizii Ukrains'koi. Del', Analiza, Plian, Vykonane, Kontrolia." [Instructions In Matters Pertaining to the Creation of the Ukrainian Division. Viewpoint, Analysis, Plan, Action, Control]. Under "Viewpoint," it acknowledged that the Ukrainian Division would be titled as "Galitsia" (Galicia), with a military personnel strength of 15-20,000. Especially of interest to note is that the writer's of this leaflet correctly identified that "the 'Galicia' Division's personnel are to be used on the front." Under "Action," the underground charged (as did Roman Dmowski over two decades earlier during the Paris Peace Talks) that the "Ukrainian element is primitive and politically undeveloped." Continuing on, the insurgents claimed "the Division is in the interest of the clergy. They have paid 3 million zlotys to urge men to enlist." Under "Control," the underground urged its followers to carefully monitor the Division's recruitment, propaganda, the reaction of the populace towards the creation of a military force, etc. Of interest to note, however, is that under "Analysis," the writers of the leaflet acknowledged that "a strong Ukraine is in the interests of Poland" and that "the OUN attempted to negotiate with the Poles the settlement of the border region and to work together against communism." (Published underground, the leaflet contained a Polish text with the Ukrainian alphabet. It appears a Ukrainian typewriter was utilized).

140. For the original Polish and Ukrainian texts see Veryha, *Along the Roads*, pp. 216-220. To counter any anti-Polish activities amongst its "minorities," Colonel Stefan Grot-Rowecki proposed to Sikorski new military, political, and social changes for Poland. Conceding the fact that in the pre-war era Ukrainians and Byelorussians constituted the majority in Poland's eastern provinces, Grot-Rowecki urged the exiled government to re-examine its minority policy and issue a declaration guaranteeing Poland's "minorities" cultural autonomy, social/economic changes and full citizenship. Grot-Rowecki also warned that if such measures were not implemented, the Soviets would use these eastern "minorities" to further their own cause and political plans. See *Ciechanowski, The Warsaw Rising of 1944*, p. 140.

141. Curiously enough, Poland's strongest condemnation of the "Galicia" Division occurred in the aftermath of World War II. Communist Poland disseminated a number of vicious articles which accused the Division of various "war crimes." But in recent years, a number of highly objective and historically accurate accounts regarding World War II have appeared in Poland. In truth, these works have exonerated the Division from the previously published false accusations.

142. Personal discussion with Yuriy Krokhmaliuk.

143. Scholar, intellectual, humanitarian and an internationally respected Church leader of Galician aristocracy, Count Roman Alexander Sheptytskyi was born 29 July 1865 in Pryblulach, Galicia. His father, Ivan, was a Galician Count of Polish-Ukrainian extraction and his mother Sophia was a countess of French nobility.
After graduating from a secondary school in 1883, Count Sheptytskyi immediately joined the Austrian Army and served in its cavalry corps. Following army service, Sheptytskyi studied law in the University of Cracow as well as in Breslau, Germany.
In the spring of 1886, the young count travelled to Rome. There, he experienced a religious revival; he requested – and was granted – permission to meet with Pope Leo XIII. Returning to Cracow, he graduated in 1888 with a Degree in Law but immediately returned to Rome in June 1888 to begin his theological studies. Ordained as a priest four years later, he chose the spiritual name of Andrei.
On 24 March 1899, Pope Leo XIII appointed Sheptytkyi Bishop of Galicia's Stanislyviv Region and on 17 January 1901, he was appointed Archbishop and spiritual leader of Lviv's Archdiocese. As head of the Archdiocese Sheptytskyi was not only known for expanding theological studies throughout the whole of Galicia, but also for his humanitarian work. The Archbishop expanded and built hospitals, closely monitored the activities of Ukrainians in America and Canada and assisted them with their needs. Because the Archbishop had a soft heart for children, inva-

lids, and those who suffered from incurable illnesses, he often contributed his own money for such projects. Most importantly, Sheptytskyi constantly promoted goodwill among Galicia's various nationalities, and strongly opposed any acts of hatred and violence.

When Imperial Russian troops occupied Lemberg in early September 1914, Sheptytskyi protested the occupation. For this he was arrested and deported east to Kursk and later to Suzdal, Russia. Strong Papal and world condemnation forced the Tsarist Government to release Sheptytskyi; yet, he was not permitted to return to Galicia until 1917. Up to the time of his return to Galicia, Sheptytskyi served in a monastery in Suzdal.

From 1917 until his death on 1 November 1944, Archbishop Andrei Sheptytskyi directed Galicia's Archdiocese. For an account of the Metropolitan's life see Lonchyn Tsehel'skyi's "Metropolyt Andrei Sheptytskyi (Korotkyi Shyttepys i Ohliad Ioho Tserkovno-Narodnoi Diialnosti – Metropolitan Andrew Sheptytskyi: A Short Biography and Review of His Church and National Activities) (Published by America, 1937); and Paul Robert Magocsi, ed. *Morality and Reality: The Life and Times of Andrei Sheptytskyi* (Canadian Institute of Ukrainian Studies, 1989).

144. This 'Open Letter' was titled as "Pastyrs'kyi Lyst." *Ekran*, (Ukrainian Magazine for Youth and Adults), January-April, 1978, No. 67-68, p. 3.

145. *Armstrong*, p. 173; *Friedman*, p. 291. Members of the Galician clergy were also subject to arrest. Such was the case of Reverend Johann Peters, a Galician Ukrainian priest of German extraction and a close friend of Shepytskyi. Arrested in 1942, he was dispatched to the Dachau concentration camp. See "Slovo o. Johanna Petersona, Prysviachenyi Sluzh Boshomy Andrievi, Vyholoshenniau Minheni,"*The Patriarchate* (N.Y.: Meta Publishing Co., January, 1989), p. 30.

146. *Friedman*, p. 291; *The Patriarchate*, pp. 28-29.

147. *Armstrong*, p. 173; *Friedman*, p. 291. See also "Metropolitan Sheptytskyi was Church's Spiritual Leader," *America*, (Ukrainian Catholic Newspaper), 12 November 1987, p. 2; and *The Patriarchate*, p. 29; "Andreya Sheptytskoho, Arkhiepiskopa L'vivs'koho Ukrains'koho Mutropolyta Halyts'koho Episkopa Kammianchia-Podil's'koho," *Artkyly*, Rym, 1958), pp. 27-28. Shortly after writing to Himmler, in early 1943, Sheptytskyi wrote directly to Hitler. In his letter, the Metropolitan protested the Gestapo's attacks against the Ukrainian populace and the destruction of Soviet prisoners. (*Ibid*, p. 28). Whether Hitler every received the letter remains unknown.

148. *Friedman*, p. 291.

149. *Ibid*.

150. According to *Friedman*, p. 292, Sheptytskyi (who was fluent in Hebrew and always sympathetic to the Jews), boldly reproached "Dr Frederic." for the way the German administration inhumanely treated the Jews. The Metropolitan also told his visitor that he knew of such brutalities not only from Jewish leaders but also from those who had personally witnessed such crimes and cited as an example, one Ukrainian participant who, sickened by what he had assisted in, confessed his guilt to Sheptytskyi. (*Ibid*, pp. 292-293).

151. "Dr. Frederic's" report accurately reflects the Metropolitan's attitudes and largely substantiates other accounts, such as those by Stepan Baran, "Metropolitan Andrei Sheptytyskyi" (Munich: Vernyhora Ukrains'ke Vydavnyche Tovarystvo, 1947), pp. 114-115; and Reverend Mykhailo Sopuliak's, "Pamiati Velykoho Metropolyta" [Recollections of the Great Metropolitan], in *Chas*, 14 December 1947, p. 3. See also *Armstrong*, p. 173; *Friedman*, p. 292; and *America*, 12 November 1987, pp. 1-2.

In addition to the report submitted by "Dr. Frederic's" verifying Sheptytskyi's criticism of Nazism, Sheptytskyi also wrote directly to Pope Pius XII. In a lengthy letter submitted to the Vatican in the summer of 1942, Sheptytskyi strongly denounced Nazism, its occupational policies, and its brutal mistreatment of Ukraine's populace. "Today, our entire nation agrees that German rule is just as harsh, if not harsher, than that [previously experienced] under the Bolsheviks. Throughout the year, there has not been a day without crimes, executions, theft, plunder, confiscations and coercion ... Within just our land 200,000 Jewish inhabitants have been murdered. Jews have even been slaughtered on the streets in full view of its inhabitants. In Kiev, up to 130,000 men, women and children were slaughtered ... Our youth is arrested and subjected to deportation to Germany where they are forced into factory or agricultural labor ... Christians have perished by the hundreds of thousands and are continuing to perish. Daily, they die from hunger or die in concentration camps ... Daily, entire company's of prisoners-of-war perish as a result of deliberate negligence – within the next several months, the greater portion of the prisoners will perish." (Sheptytskyi's letter was titled "Andrej Sheptytskyi. Lyst Do Papy Piia XII. 1942, 29-31 VIII L'viv." [Andrei Sheptytskyi's Letter to Pope Pius XII, 29-31 August 1942, Lviv]. Sheptytskyi's entire letter was published in the Jewish newspaper *Shofar*, a Jewish daily which appeared in Lviv in the aftermath of the collapse of the Soviet Union. Under the title of " ... I Muzhnii Holos Prolunav" [And the Courageous Voice Heralded], a brief synopsis of Sheptytskyi's valor is also noted. The Metropolitan is praised for rescuing Lviv's (and Galicia's) most eminent rabbi, Dr. Kahane, and it mentioned how in Israel a monument was enacted in honor of the late Metropolitan. "... And the Courageous Voice Heralded" may be found on pages 10 and 13). (Unfortunately, the person who produced a copy of this letter from the original newspaper failed to cite the exact date of publication. He believes, however, that it was sometime in 1992).

152. *Friedman*, p. 292; *The Patriarchate*, pp. 29-30.

Galicia Division

153. *Friedman*, p. 293.

154. *Ibid*, p. 291; *Baran*, pp. 114-115; *Human Events*, 4 April 1992, p. 15.

155. *Friedman*, ibid. #79, p. 293; *America*, 12 November 1987, p. 2.

156. *Friedman*, p. 293. According to Rabbi Kahane, approximately 300-400 Jews, mostly children, were rescued. See also Kolisnyk's "Ukrains'ka Dyviziia i Dukhovna Opika" [The Ukrainian Division and Its Spiritual Guardianship], *Visti*, 1988, No. 4, p. 32.

157. *Friedman*, p. 293.

158. *Ibid*.

159. *Armstrong*, p. 173. Former Divisional chaplain Reverend Doctor Ivan Nahayewsky cited such two main reasons for the establishment of the Division: (1) in the event both Nazi Germany and Soviet Russia collapsed, there would be a critical need for an effective military force for establishing an independent Ukrainian republic; and (2) a force was needed to protect and preserve Ukraine's populace and its church. The former chaplain also cited that the NKVD terror of 1939-1941 was still vivid in the minds of Galicia's inhabitants. See Nahayewsky, *A Soldier Priest Remembers*, pp. 16-17. See also p. 30.

160. Soldier, priest, academic, humanitarian, and a linguist proficient in ten languages, Dr. Vasyl Laba was born in Bibilka, Galicia, in 1887. Graduating from Lemberg's gymnasium, he studied theology in Innsbruck, Switzerland, in Vienna, Austria, and Lemberg University. In 1914, he completed his studies with a doctoral degree.
During World War I, he served as a field chaplain in the Austrian Army. Insisting that a chaplain's place "is with the troops," Laba disregarded orders to remain behind in safety. He frequently served under enemy fire, survived poison gas attacks and administered spiritual and medical aid to both Entente and Allied captured personnel. For his valor, he was awarded the Iron Cross, 2nd Class, being one of the few chaplains to win this award. At the conclusion of the war, he was confined to an Italian prisoner-of-war camp. Fluent in Italian and Latin, he served as a spokesman for the prisoners and frequently negotiated with higher authorities in defense of the prisoners.
In 1919, he joined the Galician Army. With the death of Chief Chaplain Father Mykola Lucak in 1919, Laba assumed his post. Until 1922, through "hell and high water," Laba endured all of the army's ordeals.
Between the war years he taught in various seminars, schools, and orphanages. From 1943 until 1945, he served as the Galicia/Ukrainian Division's Chief Chaplain. He constantly took care of soldiers' needs, their families' needs and, after the July 1944 Brody Battle, he worked endlessly on behalf of the wounded, the missing-in-action, their families and refugees.
From 1946-1950, he was a rector at a Ukrainian Seminary in Germany. In 1950, he emigrated to Canada. Shortly afterwards, he was appointed by Bishop Cur Neil as Edmonton's Vicar. Until his peaceful death in the early morning hours on 10 November 1976, Laba remained active in theology and the academics. Never forgetting a soldier's needs, he continuously participated in the Division's affairs and held positions in various Canadian War Veteran's groups. Until the very end, Father Laba remained "with the troops." See also *Armstrong*, p. 174; *Bender and Taylor*, Vol. 4, p. 29; Kolisnyk, *Visti*, 1988, No. 4, pp. 31-37; *Nahaywesky*, p. 33.

161. *Bender and Taylor*, Vol. 4, pp. 29-30. To secure Himmler's approval, Berger personally approached Himmler with this matter. Whether Himmler ever regretted having granted permission for the Chaplain's corps has never been established; however, it is known that Himmler wrote to Kaltenbrunner that he was entrusting Berger to clarify to Sheptytskyi the role of the Ukrainian priests with this warning: "As long as the priests maintain a good influence on the troops, they will remain. But if they incite the troops [against Germany] we will dismiss them, and place the whole blame on the Metropolitan." Der Reichsführer-SS, Personlicher Stab, Tgb. Nr. 42/78/43, Bra/Bn; Feld-Kommandostelle, den 16 Juli 1943; An den Chef der Sicherheitspolizei und des SD SS-Obergruppenfuher Dr. Kaltenbrunner, Berlin. (Cited also from *Visti*, 1988, No. 4, p. 37. See also Visti, 1988, No. 4, pp. 31-32). Himmler was also responding to Kaltenbrunner's previous charges that Metropolitan Sheptytskyi would be continuing anti-Nazi "politics" within the Division. Der Chef der Sicherheitspolizei und des SD; IV B 3-416/43 Berlin SW 11, den 28 Juni 1943; An den Reichsführer-SS. Betr.: Eintritt griechisch-katolischer Geistlichen in die SS-Schutzen-Division-Galizien. (Signed: Kaltenbrunner). Cited also from *Visti*, 1988, No. 4, p.37.

162. Der Reichsführer-SS, Chef des SS-Hauptamtes, Cd SS/Be/Ra. Vs- Tgb. Nr. 4659/43 g. Adjtr. Tgb. Nr. 8372/43g. Berlin-Wilmersdorf 1, den 26.7.1943; Geheim; An den Reichsführer-SS. Personlicher Stab SS-Oberstumbannführer Dr. Brandt. (Signed by Berger). (Cited also from *Visti*, 1988, No. 4, p. 37). Berger also wrote that he had discussed the matter personally with Laba. (See also *Visti*, No. 4, 1988, pp. 33-34). In a personal discussion on 10 December 1987 with Yuriy Krokhmaliuk, Krokhmaliuk stated that although initially 12 (including Laba) chaplains were accepted, the actual number of chaplains tended to fluctuate as a result of battle casualties, requests for dismissal, etc. Krohkmaliuk also confirmed that Zennheim, in France's Alsace region (then under German occupation), was the priests training site. Of interest to note is that a publication from the Soviet Ukraine, Ukrains'ka RSR u Velykii Vitchyznianii Viini Radians'koho Soiuzu, 1941-1945 rr.,Vol. 2, pp. 171-172, cites a total of 19 chaplains and three priests. In this account, Laba is identified as a spiritual leader but his rank is incorrectly cited as that of a "nationalist general." (P. 172).

442

Notes

163. Ren, *My Life's Mosaic*, pp. 159-160.

164. Vasyl Laba, "Dukhovna Opika Nad Stril'tsiamy 1-oi U.D." [Spiritual Guardianship Over the Riflemen of the 1st Ukrainian Division], *Visti Kombatant*, 1952, No. 10-11 (24-25), October-November, p. 8.

Notes Chapter 7

1. FM 22-100, *Military Leadership* (Department of the Army, Washington, D.C., October, 1983), p. 44; and FM 17-95, *Calvary* (Department of the Army, Washington, D.C., 1981), p. L-1.

2. Excluding the premier Waffen-SS Division "Leibstandarte SS-Adolf Hitler" which in the beginning of 1943 had an officer strength of 678 (Lucas, *Hitler's Elite*, p. 40), the average number of officers within a Waffen-SS and Wehrmacht Division was from approximately 342 to about 387 officers and officials. For a breakdown of what was found in a 1944 German infantry division, to include its personnel strength, see *Handbook On German Military Forces*, TM-E30-451. (Published by the War Department, Washington, D.C.: 15 March 1945), pp. 11-16 and 11-19).

3. Heike, *English ed.*, pp. 8-9.

4. *Ibid.* Galicia's volunteers were not the only ones subjected to harsh German cadre personnel. Various other European and non-European volunteers and draftees also experienced hardships when they found themselves in the midst of German personnel who had no proper understanding of their national aspirations. Indeed, so many hardships were experienced that in due time, numerous complaints of mistreatment reached Himmler. See *Höhne*, p. 538.

5. Roman Kolisnyk, "Ukrains'ka Dyviziia i Viis'kova Uprava "Halychyna" [The Ukrainian Division and the Military Board "Galicia"], *Visti*, No. 3, 1988, p. 35.

6. Heike, *English ed.*, p. 9. And by seeking to enlist, these men also inflated the recruitment figures. See also *1943-1993. The 1st Ukrainian Division*, p. 14.

7. Cooper, *The German Army*, pp. 451-452; *Höhne*, p. 534; personal discussion with Yuriy Krokhmaliuk.

8. Between the period of 1 July 1942 and 1 July 1943, a total of 55 Wehrmacht, Luftwaffe and Waffen-SS divisions were established. Hence, the need for more leaders.

9. Heike, *English ed.*, p. 10; personal discussion with Yuriy Krokhmaliuk.

10. Yurkevych in *Boshyk*, p. 77. Yurkevych, however, does not provide any figures about the number of ex-Nachtigall/Roland officers entering the Division.

11. Paul Lungen, "War Crimes Link Possible? Rodal Traces Ukrainian Units Role," *The Canadian Jewish News*, 8 October 1987. In this extracted report, Lungen presented a number of Alti Rodal's viewpoints. While neither Rodal nor Lungen officially state that "Nachtigall or Roland" committed atrocities and note "that Soviet allegations against the two [units] have been particularly severe," they also fail to clear the units of any alleged criminal accusations.

12. *Ibid.*

13. Roman Bojcun, "Legion DUN (Drushyn Ukrains'kukh Natsionalistiv)" [Legion DUN (Troops of Ukrainian Nationalists)], *Visti*, 1982, No. 5-6, p. 47; Kolisnyk, "Ukrains'ka Dyviziia i Viis'kova Uprava "Halychyna." Nimets'ka Polityka Vidnosno Ukrains'koho Natsional'noho Viis'ka 1943-1945" [The Ukrainian Division and the Military Board "Galicia." German Politics Regarding the Ukrainian National Army 1943-1945], *Visti*, 1987, No. 2, p. 56, cites Bojcun's figure. According to Kolisnyk, of the 22 officers, 9 entered the "Galicia" Division. (*Ibid*).

14. Bojcun, *Visti*, 1982, No. 5-6, p. 47.

15. *Ibid.*

16. Colonel Evhen Pobihushchyj-Ren, *My Life's Mosaic*, pp. 73-75. (Hereafter Ren will be used). Ren refers to this unit as the "Legion." Of these 18, 17 were staff and combat officers and one was a medical officer. (Ren's rank of Colonel was achieved in the aftermath of World War II. The highest rank he held in the Division was that of Waffen-Sturmbannführer – Major).

17. *Ren*, pp. 102 and 109. Ren's, as well as Bojcun's officer strength figures are correct if one takes into consideration the fact that both Nachitgall and Roland were organized on the lines of a German infantry type battalion with a headquarters staff and four line companies. Such a number of officers was approximate to what was found in a World War II German infantry battalion.

443

Galicia Division

18. *Visti*, 1982, No. 5-6, p. 51; Kolisnyk, *Visti*, 1987, No. 2, p. 56, substantiates that number.

19. Of these nine, one was relieved of duty shortly afterwards because of age and of the remaining eight, one included the field chaplain. Excluding these two, seven combat officers were found in the Division. According to Bojcun, five were posted to the infantry, one to a light infantry gun platoon and one went into the heavy artillery battalion. But of these seven, one defected to the UPA. (Bojcun, *Visti*, 1982, No. 5-6, p. 51.) Excluding these three out of the nine, one can see how Ren arrived at a figure of six in his memoirs. Of the six officers, three were later killed at Brody. For a list of the six officers, see *My Life's Mosaic,* p. 108.

20. In a personal discussion with the Krokhmaliuk brothers, neither Yuriy nor Roman could recall an exact figure. Because the author did not have access to neither Bojcun's nor Ren's works until months following the interviews, the above figures were not discussed. But the question of the number of ex-Nachtigall and Roland officers found within the Division was raised; Yuriy (who served as a staff officer within the Division's personnel section), stated that "excluding the chaplain and the one who defected to the UPA, and the one or two who were relieved of duty for health, age, or political reasons, no more than five or six ex-Nachtigall/Roland officers were found in the Division up to the time of Brody. After Brody, no more ever showed up." Yuriy repeatedly emphasized that the Division's officer corps was raised from scratch, that at first it had a greater percentage of German personnel but as time went by, more and more Ukrainian soldiers were trained (or gained experience through combat), to fulfill the Division's leadership needs. In due time, many of the German officers were replaced by Ukrainian leadership. Yuriy's brother, Roman, corroborated Yuriy's Statements.

In addition to the allegation that "war criminals" from the Roland Nachtigall entered the Division, there is also the false allegation that the "Galicia" Division, or members of it, participated in suppressing the heroic Jewish Warsaw Ghetto Uprising of April-May 1943. (Charles Ashman and Robert J. Wagman, *The Nazi Hunters: The Shocking True Story of the Continuing Search for Nazi Criminals* (N.Y.: Pharos Books, 1988), p. 249; Sol Littman, "Agent of the Holocaust: The Secret Life of Helmut Rauca," in *Saturday Night,* July 1983, p. 23).

Officially, this revolt commenced in the evening hours of 18 April 1943 when German forces, along with Polish police personnel, commenced to surround the Warsaw Ghetto. By the morning of 19 April, additional reinforcements, composed of Lithuanian, Latvian, Volksdeutsche, Jewish, Ukrainian, and other gendarmes and police personnel, were sent in. (Reuben Ainsztein, *The Warsaw Ghetto Revolt* (N.Y.: Holocaust Library, 1979), pp. 102-102. Ainsztein's study, massively researched with years of intense study, is also noted for its objectivity and historical accuracy).

As already presented, some Ukrainians were found among the foreign personnel. But a review of the exact units involved in the suppression of the revolt reveals no "Galicia" Division (or any of its elements/sub-elements or personnel), as ever being used in the suppression; indeed, no Ukrainian military or police unit is identified at all. (See *Ainsztein*, pp. 105-106). As for the reported "Ukrainians" (excluding those few positively identified by name), how many actually were Ukrainian is also questionable. It is now a commonly known postwar fact that many non-German (foreign) personnel in uniform were erroneously identified as "Ukrainian." (See Wilfred Strik-Strikfeldt, *Against Stalin and Hitler, 1941-1945* N.Y.: John Day Co., 1973, p. 67); and noted European scholar, Hans von Krannhals, has also indicated in his studies how Ukrainians were frequently accused of perpetuating crimes even though they were not involved. As an example, von Krannhals cited the Warsaw Uprising of August 1944. For whatever reasons, Warsaw's general population was convinced the atrocities were committed by Ukrainian personnel. This explains why in numerous testimonies provided in the immediate aftermath of such uprisings, the "Ukrainians" were cited as being the perpetuators and criminals when in reality, the greater percentage of the crimes were inflicted by the numerous non-Ukrainians found in German service. (See Hans von Krannhals, *Der Warschauer Aufstand 1944*, Frankfurt am Main, 1962, pp. 317-318).

In actuality, some of the "Ukrainians" utilized in the ghetto in 1943 were not exclusively Ukrainians but rather, men from various other nationalities among whom some may have been Ukrainian. How many Ukrainians were actually utilized in the Warsaw Ghetto is not known, but certainly Ukrainians as a group cannot be held accountable.

In regard to the ghetto revolt of 1943, one of the best sources of information which may be cited (and one widely utilized in the Nuremberg War Crimes trials), is the original submitted by Warsaw's Chief Police Leader, SS-Brigadeführer and Police Generalmajor Joseph Stroop. Written to his superior, SS-Obergrupenführer and General of the Police Walther Kruger, Stroop's report was titled "The Jewish Quarter of Warsaw Is No More!" This extensively detailed and comprehensive report covers the day-to-day events regarding the suppression of the valiant Jewish uprising, and Stroop's personal involvement in quelling the rebellion. Basically, the report is divided into three parts: Part I cites the various units utilized, their casualties, and information pertaining to the revolt; Part II provides a daily assessment of events from the period of 20 April to 16 May 1943; and Part III is a conclusion. Along with this report, Stroop submitted 18 photographs.

Stroop's full report may be found in the Nuremberg War Crimes volumes. And this report was not only utilized against Stroop at the Nuremberg trials by allied prosecutors but likewise, the source is used to study life in Warsaw under Nazi occupation. (For the full context of Stroop's report, see *IMT*, Vol. 26, pp. 628-694. Stroop's photographs follow p. 694. For the entire English translation see Sybil Milton's *The Stroop Report: The Jewish Quarter of Warsaw Is No More!* (N.Y.: Pantheon Books, 1979).

On pages 628-632, Stroop provides a casualty list of those killed and wounded in suppressing the revolt. A close examination reveals that among the primarily German personnel, some foreign personnel are included. Of these, approximately seven names appear to be Ukrainian. But most importantly, Stroop identified the units which were utilized.

In suppressing the uprising, Stroop used these units:

Notes

Einsatzkrafte

Durchschnitts-Tageseinsatz

Waffen-SS:	
SS-Pz. Gren.Ausb.u.Ers.Btl. 3 Warschau	4/440
SS-Kav.-Ausb.-u.Ers.-Abt. Warschau	5/381
Ordnungspolizei:	
SS-Pol.-Rgt. 22 I. Btl.	3/94
III. Btl.	3/134
Technische Nothilfe	1/6
poln. Polizei	4/363
poln. Feuerloschpolizei	166
Sicherheitspolizei:	3/32
Wehrmacht:	
Leichte Flakalarmbatterie III/8 Warschau	2/22
Pionierkommando d. Eisenb. Panzerzug-	
Ers.-Abt. Rembertow	2/42
Res.-Pionier-Btl. 14 Gora-Kalwaria	I/34
Fremdvolkische Wachmannshaften:	
1. Batl. Trawnikimanner	2/335

An examination of Stroop's handwritten account reveals that not only were no Ukrainian units utilized, but as well, from the casualty lists, few individual Ukrainians were indeed utilized. Furthermore, in the other Nuremberg volumes, no reference is made to any Ukrainian units, or Ukrainian personnel, as ever being utilized in the Warsaw ghetto.

But what is especially important to note is that in Stroop's entire report, not once is the word "Ukrainische" (or any other German variation of "Ukrainian"), utilized. Clearly, Stroop's personal, on-the-scene report, proves the fact that if Ukrainians were indeed utilized, they were not in unit strength but were very minimum in number.

In addition to the German reports, various Jewish sources may also be cited. One of the best eyewitness accounts produced is by the eminent social historian, Emmanuel Ringelbaum, who was born in 1900.

Residing in Warsaw during the Nazi occupation, Ringelbaum was personally intimate with the events of that era. But most importantly, he kept a journal of life – both individual and collective – of the events, people, ideals, experiences, heroism, and suffering. (See Emmanuel Ringelbaum, Notes *From the Warsaw Ghetto: The Journal of Emmanuel Ringelbaum*, N.Y.: McGraw-Hill, 1958).

Ringelbaum survived the Ghetto Uprising. But on 7 March 1944, he was executed on the ruins of what had once been the Ghetto. Although in his memoirs Ringelbaum identifies the various German and non-German military and police forces found within Warsaw, and cites some Ukrainians were found among the occupants, no mention is made of the "Galicia" Division or, for that matter, of any Ukrainian unit as being posted to assist in quelling the ghetto rebellion.

As for the Ukrainians who helped to quell the uprising, it is known that none of them every entered the "Galicia" Division in the aftermath of the revolt. This is substantiated by World War II German records and former Divisional staff officer Yuriy Krokhmaliuk.

According to Krokhmaliuk, no Ukrainian personnel were every recruited for the Division from among those who had served in any German police, SS, gendarme, or Wehrmacht unit stationed in an around Warsaw. In addition, Krokhmaliuk emphasized that German World War II records reveal that the "Galicia" Division could never have been utilized in the April-May 1943 uprising because at that time, the "Galicia" Division only existed on paper and as a plan in the minds of those such as Wachter.

Krokhmaliuk also stated that most of the Division's personnel first heard about the 1943 Warsaw uprising (as they did about many other world war-related or otherwise events), only until after the war's conclusion. (Personal discussion with Yuriy Krokhmaliuk).

21. Der Reichsführer SS, Tgb. Nr. 35/88/43g. RF/Bn., 5. Juli 1943. This order also specified the number of officer candidates, NCO's, and volunteers to depart and cited the call up to be effective no later than 15 July 1943.

22. Krokhmaliuk, *The Glow*, p. 37; Roman Cholkan, "Vyshkoly Ukrains'kykh Starshun i Pidstarshyn Intendatury i Ikhnia Sluzhba v Dyvizii" [The Training of the Ukrainian Officers and Non-Commissioned Officers and Their Service In The Division], *Visti*, 1992, No. 4, p. 84; Kubiovych, *Meni* 70, p. 62, Veryha, "V Oboroni Dobroho Imeni Dyvizii "Halychyna" [In Defense of the Good Name of the Division "Galicia"] *Visti*, 1981, No. 4, p. 21; Nahayewski, *A Soldier Priest Remembers*, p. 34; "Nainovisha Istoriia Ukrainy, 1943- 1963 – 18 Lypnia 1943" [The Newest Ukrainian History, 1943-1963 – 18 July 1943], *Visti*, 1963, No. 3, pp. 7-8; *1943-1993. The 1st Ukrainian Division*, p. 14. According to Lucas in *The Last Year of the German Army*, p. 100, the "Galicia" Division was raised in July 1943.

23. Krokhmaliuk, *The Glow*, p. 37; Nahayewsky, *A Soldier Priest Remembers*, p. 34; *Visti*, 1963, No. 3, p. 8. In Volume 2 of *Ukrains'ka RSR u Velykii Vitchyznianii Viini Radians'koho Soiuzu 1941-1945*, a photograph between pp. 160-161 shows the "vicar of the Division SS "Galicia" Vasyl Laba delivering a sermon before the departure of [Divisional] elements to the front, July 1943." Regarding this, the photograph's caption is incorrect because at no time did any Divisional elements depart for the front in July 1943.

24. "The Newest Ukrainian Ukrainian History, 1943-1963–18 July 1943." *Visti*, 1963, No. 3, p. 8; *Pankiwsky*, p. 241; personal discussion with Yuriy Ferencevych.

At no time were "the ranks of the Division filled with conscripted police officers who, accustomed to an easy life of robbery and murder, wholly tried to avoid the front,"...nor was "The Division's personnel recruited from unemployed, unskilled people lacking an interest in Ukrainian statehood,"...nor were "The Division's ranks filled with Lithuanian, Latvian, and Estonian Nationalists and criminals" as alleged by Beliaiev and Rudnyts'kyi in *Pid Chuzhymy Praporamy* [Under Foreign Flags], pp. 96-97.

25. Yurkevych in *Boshyk*, pp. 77-78; Veryha, *Along the Roads*, p. 121. See also English synopsis p. 184; *Bender and Taylor*, Vol. 4, p. 24; Evhen Shypailo, "Starshyns'ki Vyshkoly: Kurcy v Beneschau-Hradischko-Kienschlag traven' veresen' 1944" [Officer Training in Beneshau Hradischko-Kienschlag May-September 1944], *Visti*, 1992, No. 3, pp. 89-90. According to Vashchenko, UPA's first infiltrators also departed on 18 July. Fully aware that Gestapo and intelligence agents would be undoubtedly monitoring the Division from the outset to counter any anti-German activity, the UPA briefed its departing personnel on what to expect and where to seek safety in the event a rapid exit was needed.

26. Although 20 August 1943 was initially cited as the day the Division's chaplains were to depart for training, some chaplains actually left on 18 July 1943. (Nahayewsky, *A Soldier Priest Remembers*, p. 36). Undoubtedly, this was done for psychological reasons and to develop a closer unity with the first departing recruits.

27. Established late 1942 in the "Prorektorat Bohmen and Mohren" (Bohemia and Moravia), this Wehrkreis comprised the whole of Bohemia and Moravia. Within this mostly hilly and mountainous area of 48,902 square kilometers, an estimated population of 7,500,000 (mostly Czech) were found. The capital city of Prague served as its main headquarters.

28. Wladyslaw Razmowski, "Akcja Treblinka," in *"Dzieje najnowsze Kwarttalnik poswiecony historii XX wieku"* (Warszawa: Instytyt Historii Pan, 1969), rocz. 1, Nr. 1, pp. 169-170. See also Veryha, *Along the Roads*, p. 118-120. While undoubtedly some Ukrainian collaborationist personnel did serve within Treblinka, at no time did troops from the 14th Waffen-SS ever serve there. The "Galicia" Division's manpower, at this time, was comprised of nothing but unarmed personnel who, in the closing days of July 1943, were just beginning to depart to Heidelager and Europe's various schools. And once inside their training areas, at no time were the recruits ever dispatched to Treblinka or, for that matter, to any other concentration camp. Razmowski's account may also be faulted because he identified the guards' language as "Russian." (Surely Razmowski was correct in his language identification because Slavs from Poland, Ukraine and Russia, especially of that era, could distinguish between languages). If Russian was used, the men could not have been "Galician" troops because although "Galicia's" men could identify the Russian language, most were not fluent in it. As well, Russian was never spoken in the "Galicia" Division; therefore, if the guards had been "Galician" they would have spoken either Ukrainian or possibly, even German, but never Russian.

Along with Razmowski, an article titled "U Vrat Bab'ego Iara," *Novoye Russkoye Slovo* (Russian Daily News), Friday, 11 October 1991, p. 14, by Irina Babich alleges that in September 1941, soldiers of the "Galicia" Division played a major role in exterminating innocent lives in the ravines of Babyn Yar outside the Ukrainian capital city of Kiev. Babich's allegations are totally false because it is a historical fact that the "Galicia" Division never existed in 1941. In addition to the numerous German and allied World War II records which reveal that the "Galicia" Division was raised in 1943-44, numerous Soviet works – both military and propaganda – also substantiate the fact that the "Galicia" Division was created in 1943-44. And highly detailed works pertaining to Babi Yar (such as the work by Anatoly Kuznetzov, *Babi Yar: A Documentary Novel* (N.Y.: Dell Press, 1967)), make no reference to the "Galicia" Division.

29. Dr. K.G. Klietmann, *Die Waffen-SS, Eine Dokumentation*, (Osnabruck, 1965), p. 194. According to Veryha, the initial 2,000 recruits were soon augmented by additional recruits. As a result, approximately 2,500 began training in Heidelager. "Vyshkil'nyi Tabir 'Heidelager' ["Heidelager" Training Base], *Visti*, 1977, No. 4, pp. 61-62; Roman Cholkan, "The Training of the Ukrainian Officers and Non-Commissioned Officer Candidates and Their Service In the Division", *Visti*, 1992, No. 4, p. 84, cites 2,500 recruits entered Heiderager in the period of July 1943; Littlejohn, *The Patriotic Traitors*, p. 315, cites that approximately 300 candidates were dispatched to the Bad Tolz officer training school and 2,000 NCO candidates went to various NCO schools. (In some of his writings, Kleitmann has also cited that the 300 Ukrainian Galician officer candidates were dispatched to Bad Tolz). Regarding the 300, at this time, none of the 300 were dispatched to Bad Tolz. In actuality, very few Ukrainian officer candidates attended Bad Tolz; those who did entered the school in the latter part of 1944 and early 1945.

As for the 300 officer candidates, they were dispatched to the "Truppenuebungsplatz Beneschau," south of Prague. Within this training area, three officer schools were located: the artillery school at Beneschau, where 50 Ukrainians arrived; the engineer (pioneer) school at Hradischko, adjacent to the villages of Hradischko, Pikwitz, Brunscchau and Zavist in the vicinity of the Moldau and Sassau Rivers and to where approximately 25 candidates arrived; and the infantry and heavy arms school at Kienschlag, in the vicinity of Teinitz adjacent to the river Sassau,

Notes

where over 200 Ukrainian candidates arrived. Evhen Shypailo, "Officer Training. Courses In Beneschau-Hradischko-Kienschlag May-September 1944," *Visti*, 1992, No. 3, pp. 89-91. Shypailo was one of the 300 officer candidates dispatched in July 1943 for officer training. According to Kolisnyk, at this same time some Ukrainian officer candidates were also dispatched to the officer school at Pozen Treskau.

Notes Chapter 8

1. Mitcham's Hitler's Legion's, p. 32. See also Victor Madej's, *The German Army Order of Battle: The Replacement Army, 1939-1945* (Penn.: Game Publishing Co., 1984), pp. 7-62. However, in 1939, Wehrkreis areas XIV, XV, and XVI ceased to exist. Basically, 18 Wehrkreis' existed until late 1944.

2. From 1938 until 20 July 1944, Colonel General Frederick Fromm commanded the system. From 21 July 1944 until the conclusion of the war, Reichsführer Heinrich Himmler took charge.

3. To cite an example, in September 1939, 90 percent of Nazi Germany's approximately 3,000 tanks were obsolete and in general, the German Army's equipment was not the best.

4. Cooper, *The German Army*, pp. 152; 155-156; 163-164; 180; 210- 213. See also Albert Speer, *Inside the Third Reich* (New York: Macmillan Publishing Co., 1971).

5. Victor Madej, *Hitler's Elite Guards*: Waffen-SS, Parachutist, U-Boats (Penn.: Game Publishing Co., 1985), p. 74.

6. *1943-1993. The 1st Ukrainian Division*, p. 14; personal discussion with Yurily Krokhmaliuk.

7. Parts of Poland were also incorporated into Wehrkreis I, VIII, XX and XXI.

8. U.S. Military Intelligence Division, *The German Replacement Army (Ersatzheer)*(Washington, D.C.), February, 1945, pp. 268-270.

9. *Verordnungsblatt der Waffen-SS*, 4. Jahrgang, Berlin, 15.3. 1943, Nr. 6, Z. 107). See also *Bender and Taylor*, Vol. 4, p. 24.

10. *Order of Battle of the German Army, April 1943* (Washington, D.C.: 1943), p. 41.

11. *Order of Battle of the German Army, 1944* (Washington, D.C.: 1944). (Republished in New York in 1975 by Hippocrene Books, Inc.). Page B29 identifies General Haenicke.

12. Heike, *English ed.*, pp. 8-9; *Bender and Taylor*, Vol. 4, pp. 25- 26.

13. According to Veryha, the approximately 2,500 volunteers who first arrived were organized into 12 training companies. All instructors and administrative personnel belonged to the Waffen-SS. Both the cadre and recruits were centered around the 14th SS-Ausbildungs-Batallion "Galizien" z.b.V. (zur besonderer Verfugung), training battalion. See "Vyshkil'nyi Tabir "Heidelager" [Training Camp "Heidelager"], p. 166, *Visti*, 1977, No. 4, pp. 61-63. *Bender and Taylor*, Vol. 4, p. 27, cite the SS-Ausbildungs-Bataillon z.b.v. (SS-Freiw. Div. "Galizien") was an SS Special Purpose Training Battalion which served as the Division's nucleus.

14. According to Evhen Shypailo, the first recruits who arrived to "Heidelager" in July 1943 underwent a solid period of infantry recruit training which concluded at the end of October 1943. Shypailo's observation is substantiated by Roman Cholkan who cited that the first incoming recruits (July 1943) received three months of training which concluded in October 1943. "The Training of the Ukrainian Officers and NCO's...,"*Visti*, 1992, No. 4, p. 84.
    In an unpublished account titled "U Vyshkilnumu Tabori" [In the Training Camp], V.K. (for some reason the author of this account only used his initials) cited that the approximate 1,500 recruits (of whom V.K. claimed the greater number hailed from rural areas), were all quartered in new barracks. "Just by entering them you can smell the aroma of everything being new. New beds, tables, closets, benches. In each barracks was found a large and convenient bath and shower area. Hardly did we arrive when we were told to take off our clothes, fold them, and shower. Immediately after the shower, we were dressed in fresh clothing. Than, each man [recruit] was issued three uniforms – one set for work, one for training and the third for general wear. The sequence of a day was as such: at 4:30 a.m., wake-up. One hour for cleaning ourselves, the barracks and latrine areas; one hour for breakfast, half-hour of calisthenics and running. Afterwards, until 12 o'clock, military training; from 12 to 14 [2 p.m.] lunch; from 14 to 16 [4 p.m.], more training. From 16 until 20 [8 p.m.] dinner, followed by more training. And prior to sleep, some free time.
    Within the camp is a canteen [military store] were essential items may be purchased but most importantly, where a soldier may purchase and drink some beer. The boys praise the camp's commander and as one individual stated – it would be a sin if I complained about the fact that I am here. It is good for me here. True, during training they give us some hardships, but that is how a soldier is made."
    "With these few lines," concluded V.K. "I present my experiences in the training camp of the SS Rifle Division 'Galicia' to my dearest readers."

Galicia Division

15. Heike, *English ed.*, p. 12, cites high morale and a strong spirit of camaraderie amongst the recruits. Within the Waffen-SS, trainees did not possess locks to lock drawers and lockers. This was deliberately done to help create a spirit of total unity and trust. Galicia's volunteers also followed this rule; yet, very few instances of theft arose among the trainees. (Ibid).

16. See also Krokhmaliuk *The Glow*, p. 65. In actuality, most of those who were dispatched to officer and NCO academies, as well as to specialist schools, did so only after completing recruit training.

17. Upon arrival to an officer's school and halfway into the course, a foreign (non-German) officer candidate held the title of Junker, equivalent to the rank of an Unterscharführer, or a Senior Corporal. After the mid-terms, a junker was promoted to Standartenjunker, equivalent to the rank of a Scharführer, or Sergeant. Upon graduation, Standartenjunkers were upgraded to Standartenoberjunkers, a title equivalent to Hauptscharführer, or a Company Sergeant. With this title and rank, candidates returned to their units. After a period of approximately two months, German graduates were appointed to SS Untersturmführer's, or 2nd Lieutenant's. For non-Germanic foreigners, as in the case of the "Galicia" Division, the rank of 2nd Lieutenant was Waffen-Untersturmführer and not SS-Untersturmführer. There was, however, an exception to this. If a candidate was an honor graduate, he returned to a German unit as an SS-Untersturmführer; to a foreign unit as a Waffen-Untersturmführer.

18. Most of the Division's officer candidates underwent training in such places: Beneschau-Hradischko-Kienschlag in Wehrkreis Bohmen-Mahren (Czechoslovakia); Klagenfurt in Wehrkreis XVIII (Austria/Northwestern Yugoslavia); and Posen-Treskau in Wehrkreis XXI (Eastern Germany/Western Poland). In the concluding months of the war, a small number underwent training in Bad Tolz, Wehrkreis VII (Southern Germany). The Division's doctors underwent an eight week introductory course and a three-four week medical course in the Waffen-SS' Medical Academy at Graz, Austria, also located in Wehrkreis XVIII. Personal discussion with Yuriy Krokhmaliuk. See also Shypailo's "Officer Training...," *Visti*, 1992, No. 3, p. 92; and Madej's *Hitler's Elite Guards" Waffen-SS, Parachutists, U-Boats*, pp. 79-82.

19. This order, however, was not issued until 9 September 1943. SS- FHA, Amt II Org.,Abt. Ia/II, Org. Tgb. Nr. 1300/43 g. Kdos., v. 22.9.1943, Neugliederung der SS-Freiw. Div. "Galizien." See also *Bender and Taylor*, Vol. 4, p. 28. Interesting to note is that in December 1944, the "new type" was renamed as the "Infantry Division, 1944 Type" ("Infanterie-Division Kriegestat 44"). See also *Handbook on German Military Forces: War Department Technical Manual TM-E 30-451 (Restricted), (1945)*, pp. 11-12 through 11-16.

20. An "old type" comprised: 3 infantry regiments, each with 3 battalions. Each battalion had 3 infantry companies and 1 "heavy" or machine gun company for a total of four. The "heavy" company consisted of 4 platoons: 3 platoons of MG34/42 machine guns (each with 4 machine guns) and 1 platoon with six 81mm mortars. This heavy company would be dispersed throughout the other 3 line companies. In addition to the three battalions, each infantry regiment had 1 infantry howitzer company with 4 platoons: 3 platoons with two 75mm light guns (for a total of 6), and one platoon with two heavy 150mm howitzers; and each regiment had 1 anti-tank gun company with 4 platoons: 3 platoons (each with four 37mm antitank guns for a total of 12 guns) and 1 signal platoon. These weapons, in turn, were utilized by whatever battalion(s) needed additional artillery and/or anti-tank support. Within a division, each infantry platoon also had one 50mm mortar.
Every division had 1 regiment of artillery. This regiment in turn had 3 battalions of 105mm artillery and 1 "heavy" 150mm artillery battalion; each 105mm battalion had 3 batteries of artillery. (An artillery company is referred to as a battery). Each 105mm battery had 4 guns for a total of 12 guns. With twelve 105mm guns per battalion, and with 3 such battalions, a total of thirty-six 105mm guns were found within the 3 battalions. As for the "heavy" artillery battalion, it usually comprised 3 batteries – each with four 150mm guns for a total of 12. A typical artillery regiment had 48 artillery pieces. (This figure does not include the guns found in an infantry regiments infantry howitzer and anti-tank companies).
In addition to the above, each "old type" division had an engineer battalion of 5 or 6 engineer companies (plus 1 engineer supply "train"); a signal/communications battalion which possessed a headquarters company and two signal companies as well as a small signal "train"; an anti-aircraft battalion with 3 companies, each with twelve 20mm anti-aircraft guns for a total of 36; a medical battalion which consisted of a horse drawn company, a motorized medical company, a field hospital company and two ambulance platoons; a quartermaster (supply) battalion with 4 companies; an independent medical battalion with 4 companies: 3 companies each with twelve 75mm anti-tank (AT) guns for a total of 36 guns and one anti-aircraft (AA) company with twelve 20mm guns. (This AA company was found within the anti-tank battalion). A veterinary company; a military police unit (usually one or two platoons or one large platoon); and a field post (mail) platoon rounded out a division.
The above, of course, tended to fluctuate. While all "old type" divisions were similar, no division was totally the same as another. For a further explanation and breakdown of a 1942 German "old type" division see Colonel Louis N. Phillip, The German Foot Infantry Division," in *Military Review*, July, 1942, pp. 34-37; and "Infantry: Notes on the German Infantry Division" in *Tactical and Technical Trends*, 23 September 1943, No. 34, pp. 24-29. For a further breakdown of what comprised a German infantry regiment, battalion and company, see "The German Infantry Regiment; the German Infantry Battalion; the German Rifle Company" in *Tactical and Technical Trends*, 13 January 1944, No. 42, pp. 38-47.

21. *Handbook On German Military Forces, 15 March 1945*, pp. 11-13/11-14 and 11-16.

Notes

22. Born on 12 March 1898 in Troppau, Austria-Silesia, Walter Schimana was the son of a newspaper publisher who published the "Altdeutscher Korrespondence." In World War I, Schimana entered the Imperial Austro-Hungarian Army. Following recruit training, Schimana saw combat on the eastern and southern (Italian) fronts.

In the closing months of 1918, Schimana was selected for officer training. But with the collapse of the Austro-Hungarian Empire and the deactivation of its army, Schimana left the military. In 1919, he moved to Bavaria, Germany.

In 1926, Schimana joined the Nazi Party; in the 1930s, he served as a police officer in the Ordnungspolizei. Deployed to the eastern fronts central sector in the fall of 1941, Schimana conducted security operations and fought Soviet stragglers, guerrillas and airborne inserted personnel.

On 15 July 1943, Schimana was posted to command the 14th Waffen-SS "Galicia" Division, a unit existing at that time only on paper. More as an administrator rather as a commander, Schimana held command until 19 October 1943. It appears that during this time, Schimana exercised very little control because most of Galicia's volunteers were undergoing recruit, NCO, or officer training.

Following this command, Schimana was posted to the SS District "Donau." (Danube region). In 1944, Schimana held the rank of SS Gruppenführer and General-Lieutenant of the police. Captured by the Americans after the war, Schimana was soon charged with various war crimes; none, however, could be established positively. In the vicinity of Nuremberg where the trials were held, Schimana simply disappeared one day.

Returning to his home Bavaria, for the next several years Schimana lived an uncertain life. But in 1948, a Bavarian police officer (reportedly a former Ordnungspolizei comrade who served with Schimana on the eastern front) informed the former police commander that American authorities were preparing to arrest and try him. Believing this, Schimana produced a handgun and shot himself. He was buried in Bavaria. Of interest to note is that neither the American – or any other allied authorities – were at that time interested in re-arresting Schimana. It can only be speculated as to why such information was presented to Schimana.

23. While it is true that in the concluding years of the war fewer criminal proceedings were undertaken against those who allegedly committed some type of offense, and certain units such as the notorious "Dirlewanger" Brigade seldom, if ever, conducted legal proceedings, the historical fact remains is that Wehrmacht and Waffen-SS soldiers were held accountable for crimes and criminal deeds against soldiers and civilians. At the conclusion of the war, certain ex-German military personnel (including Waffen-SS), were tried by Allied authorities using captured German records, court martial proceedings, and war-time testimonies. Such was the case of Fritz Knochlein, a former company commander in the 3rd Waffen-SS "Totenkopf" Divison. Knochlein, according to a preliminary German investigation report, ordered and supervised the machinegunning of a number of British soldiers near the village of Le Paradis in Normandy in June 1940. This slaughter caused a negative reaction within the "Totenkopf" Division and following the German investigation, Knochlein was brought up on charges. A court martial date was set, but because the "Totenkopf" Division was deployed for "Barbarossa," Knochlein, who was relieved of duty pending the matter, was ordered back to duty pending a future court date.

But the matter was never readdressed because of the prolonged struggle. Knochlein survived the war, being one of the few Waffen-SS officers of the 1940 period to do so. Arrested in 1948 by British authorities who learned of the massacre largely through captured German records, Knochlein's trial finally began in late 1948. Found guilty, he was hung in West Germany on 21 January 1949.

24. Heike, *Ukrainian ed.,* p. 31. See also Mitcham's, *Hitler's Legion's,* pp. 15-16.

25. According to Roman Kolisnyk, throughout September 1943 until the end of October 1943, in Heidelager the Division's recruits were found in their respective 12 training companies. There was no sign of the three regiments. Kolisnyk feels that the regiments only appeared on the organizational charts.

26. SS-FHA, Amt II Org. Abt. Ia/II, Tgb. Nr. 1574/43g. Kdos., v. 22.10.43. Bezeichnung der Feldtruppenteile der Waffen-SS.

27. SS-FHA, Amt II Org. Abt. Ia/II, Tgb. Nr. II/9542/43 geh., v. 12/11/1943. Bezeichnung der Feldtruppenteile der Waffen-SS.

28. Beyersdorff remained in command of the Division's artillery regiment until the end of the war.

29. Palienko was born on 30 August 1896 in Skvyr, vicinity of Kiev. After graduating from a Kievan school in 1914, he entered Kiev University to study physics. But with the entry of Imperial Russia into World War I, the following year on 1 November 1915, Palienko entered an artillery officers school. On 1 April 1916, in the rank of a lieutenant, he deployed to the eastern front.

With the collapse of Imperial Russia in 1917, Palienko returned home. On 10 December 1918, he voluntarily entered the Dniprovs'kyi Brigade, a brigade formed within the Ukrainian National Republic Army (UNRA). For the next several years, Palienko participated in many combat actions. Along with the remnants of the Galician Army, Palienko (now in the rank of major as a result of a promotion on 29 December 1919) surrendered to the Poles.

Following a period of internment, he relocated to Czechoslovakia. In 1927, he completed his education in the Ukrainian Academy (known also as the Ukrainian Free University) and achieved a degree in chemical engineering. Recruited in 1928 by the Polish Army as a contract officer in the rank of captain, Palienko remained in the Polish Army until World War II. From 1932-1934, he attended the Higher Officer's Military School in Warsaw, graduated in

Galicia Division

1934, and was promoted again to major in 1938. In September 1939, Palienko fought the Nazis. With the destruction of Poland and its army, Palienko returned to Czechoslovakia and found employment in a sugar company.

In July 1943, he entered the Division and was one of the first to be dispatched for training. At Beneschau, Palienko first underwent an artillery officers refresher course and then he remained as an instructor at the artillery school. In early 1944, he entered the Division at Heidelager, and soon afterwards he deployed to the Lviv region with Kampfgruppe "Beyersdorff." In June 1944, Palienko deployed to Brody. In the ensuing breakout, as Palienko directed artillery fire to suppress Soviet positions in the village of Knyashe, he collapsed and died. It appears he succumbed to a heart attack. See also Dr. Oleksa Horbach, "Maior Mykola Palienko" [Major Mykola Palienko], *Visti*, July, 1951, No. 7 (9), p. 13.

30. Because the 4th Battalion was armed with 150mm artillery pieces, it was referred to as the "heavy" battalion.

31. Mitcham, *The German Army*, p. 20.

32. Allied Force Headquarters, Office of the Assistant Chief of Staff, G-2. Intelligence Notes, No. 59, 16 May 1944, p. A-6.

33. Roman Bojcun, "Fiuzilers'kyi Kurin'" [The Fusilier Battalion], *Visti*, 1992, No. 2, p. 88.

34. *Bender and Taylor*, Vol. 4, p. 46.

35. Personal interview with Shuhan on 8 October 1988. See also Bojcun, *Visti*, 1992, No. 2, p. 88.

36. Personal discussion with Shuhan on 8 October 1988. See also Bojcun, *Visti*, 1992, No. 2, p. 88.

37. Ren's service with the fusiliers, however, was brief. By mid- 1944, he was again serving with the infantry.

38. Unfortunately, neither Shuhan, nor anyone else, could recall the names of the two German officers.

39. Yuriy Krokhmaliuk, "Spomyny: Dr. Med. Khirurg Volodymyr Prokopovych. Likar 1-oi Ukrains'koi Dyvizii 'Halychyna'" [Remembrances: Medical Surgeon Dr. Volodymyr Prokopovych. A Dr. of the 1st Ukrainian Division "Galicia"], *Visti*, 1981, No. 1, pp. 65-66; Kolisnyk, "The Ukrainian Division and the Military Board "Galicia," *Visti*, 1988, No. 3, p. 39.

40. Such as in the case of Dr. Alexander Bandera, brother of the Ukrainian patriot leader, Stepan Bandera. Dr. Bandera was murdered in Auschwitz in 1943.

41. Kolisnyk, "The Ukrainian Division and the Military Board "Galicia," *Visti*, 1988, No. 3, p. 39.

42. *Ibid.*

43. *Ibid.* See also Krokhmaliuk's "Recollections," *Visti*, 1981, No. 1, p.66. According to the former staff officer, 14 doctors selected for service were under 30 years of age. (*Ibid*).

44. Kolisnyk, *Visti*, 1988, No. 3, p. 39.

45. *Ibid.*

46. *Ibid.*

47. *Ibid.* According to Roman Kolisnyk, Dr. Bilozar also headed the Military Boards medical department.

48. *Ibid.* In the end, however, neither Bilozar's nor Makarushka's proposals were carried out.

49. According to Yuriy Krokhmaliuk, the Infantry Division "Galicia" should have had 50 doctors, excluding those in its Training and Replacement Regiment. See *Visti*, 1981, No. 1, p. 66.

50. *Mitcham*, p. 21.

51. The care of horses was of essence. Of the 1,500,000 horses lost by Germany on the eastern front, most were lost in combat or through overexertion, forage shortages, and inclement weather. See "Transportation and Troop Movements. Draft Horses," chap. 6, Section III, p. 22, in *Effects of Climate On Combat In European Russia*, CMH Publication 104-6, Center of Military History, U.S. Army (Washington, D.C., 1952).

52. Kolisnyk, *Visti*, 1988, No. 3, p.39. In addition to Dr. Kischko, some sources also identify a Dr. Anderson as being the veterinarian company's commander. Although it is known that Dr. Anderson served briefly on the Division's

veterinary staff section, no accounts or records identify him as commanding the Division's veterinary company. It is known that Dr. Kischko did command the Division's veterinary company.

53. "The German Foot Infantry Division" in *Military Review*, July, 1942, No. 85, p. 34. For a pictorial breakdown of the foot (infantry) division to include its supply and support see Chart I, p. 35 and Chart II, p. 36.

54. Personal discussion with Veryha. See also *Bender and Taylor*, Vol. 4, p. 46.

55. It should be noted, however, that after the Training and Replacement Regiment reached a very large strength of 8,000-10,000, training standards depreciated significantly.

56. Heike, *English ed.*, p. 25.

57. *Nahayewski*, pp. 40-41. Chaplain Sapryn's service with the "Galicia" Division, however, was very brief because he was soon posted to a Luftwaffe anti-aircraft unit much to Chief Chaplain Laba's dissatisfaction.

58. *Ibid*, pp. 55-56.

59. At no time did the Division every incorporate, or possess, a "31st Punitive Detachment" in its ranks as erroneously stated by Soviet propagandist V. Styrkul and the sensationalist Nazi hunter Sol Littman. See Sol Littman's, "These aging men were monsters once" in *The Windsor Star*, July 16, 1985.

60. Kolisnyk, "Ukrains'ka Dyviziia i Vii'skova Uprava "Halychyna" [The Ukrainian Division and the Military Board "Galicia"], *Visti*, 1988, No. 2, pp. 47-50.

61. The initial figure of 82,000 was the final figure compiled from all of those who had signed up. This figure, however, was not accurate because some, in an effort to create confusion to avoid military service, had signed up in two or three different places (thus helping to inflate the figure); as well, this figure was established before any volunteers were summoned for any interviews or physical evaluations.

62. Of the original figure of 82,000, at least 10,000 never appeared. Of those who appeared, nearly 20,000 men (over/under aged, physically/mentally handicapped, potential lawbreakers, uneducated men who could not read or write, suspected homosexuals, those deemed of OUN activities, etc.) were disqualified. In the end, 53,000 were permitted to undergo an examination.

63. But of the 53,000 permitted to be examined, another 11,000 failed to show up, hence the 42,000 figure.

64. As before, a number of the 42,000 who appeared were immediately sent home after a cursory glance. A lack of time and facilities did not enable others to be examined, and they were told to await another examination date.

65. This figure included those who were initially examined and not accepted, but eventually reexamined and accepted. A number of doctors, medical personnel, support personnel and translators later included in the Division fell into this category.

66. This included those found suitable (excluding the reclaimed), for the Division and placed into a "call-up" category.

67. Of the suitable and accepted manpower strength of 25,600, a total of 19,047 were notified to appear by 30 October 1943.

68. Of the 19,047 notified, approximately 6,000 failed to appear when summoned for training. According to a number of sources, in spite of the initial figure of approximately 80,000 volunteers, when the time came, one heard many a "volunteer" (in an attempt to now avoid service), exclaim "and what kind of guarantees do the Germans provide?" Among those who did enter the Division, it was believed that those who refused to enter the Division would (as they themselves claimed) enter instead the UPA. But as it turned out, the same "volunteers" who shortly before had flocked to the various rallies to enlist into the Division but then refused to enter the formation for "political" reasons, now found "tactical" faults with the UPA and, in the end, never entered either service. See also Osyp Holynskyj's, "40th Anniversary of the Rise of the Division "Galicia", *Visti*, 1983, No. 4, pp. 20-21.

69. Well before Brody, the Division lost some men through accidents. One such volunteer was 17-year-old Stepan Tkach, who drowned while swimming in the Oder River in Breslau (now Wroslaw) with a group of friends. His body was recovered on the following day, and the young volunteer was buried in a Breslau cemetery.

70. This figure also included those in the remaining independent rifle infantry regiments but excluded those found in the Divisions Training and Replacement Regiment stationed in Wandern.

Galicia Division

71. Although it was planned to bring in another 6,150 men from Galicia for training in the period of 1-13 November 1943, many of the 6,000 did not enter the Division from Galicia until 1 January 1944, and some entered as late as July 1944.

Notes Chapter 9

1. According to former Divisional Chaplain Nahayewsky, it was anticipated that Colonel Pavlo Shandruk would be appointed as the commander of the "Galicia" Division. (*A Soldier Priest Remebers*, p. 33). But Shandruk, a former Ukrainian officer in the Polish Army, was at that time still under Nazi house arrest.

2. Although Yuriy Krokhmaliuk had never met Schimana, Krokhmaliuk was informed by General Freitag that Schimana himself had requested to be terminated from Divisional command. See "Kommandyr Dyvizii" [The Division's Commander], *Visti*, 1983, No. 3, p. 51; personal discussion with Yuriy Krokhmaliuk.

3. Heike was never a Waffen-SS officer. He held rank only in the Wehrmacht and his refusal to change service and even wear a Waffen-SS uniform caused friction between him and Freitag.

4. Heike, *English* ed., pp. 6-7.

5. *Ibid.*

6. Ren, *My Life's Mosaic*, pp. 124-125. See also *Bender and Taylor*, Vol. 4, pp. 24-26. According to *1943-1993. The 1st Ukrainian Division*, "Freitag was a stern, diligent, ambitious but non-trusting person. In the presence of the softer Slavic character of the Ukrainian soldier, he needed [to exhibit] more generosity, and more proper scope and skill. His positive strengths were that he personally cared for the Division's interests, defended them, and from its officers he demanded honesty and worthy conduct. Severe punishment was meted out to those who displayed an otherwise attitude." (P. 15).

7. By July 1944 at Brody, the situation had not changed much. At Brody, most of the companies only had one officer; few had more than two.

8. Kolisnyk, "Ukrains'ka Dyviziia i Vis'kova Uprava "Halychyna" [The Ukrainian Division and the Military Board "Galicia"], *Visti*, 1988, No. 3, p. 36.

9. Yuriy Krokhmaliuk entered the Division in early 1944; Liubomyr Makarushka arrived shortly after In due time, Makarushka accepted Paliiv's position.

10. 22 January 1944 protocol report to the Military Board See also *Visti*, 1988, No. 3, p. 37.

11. "The Ukrainian Division and the Military Board "Galicia," *Visti*, 1988, No. 3, p. 37.

12. *Ibid.*

13. *Ibid.*

14. *Ibid.*

15. Although conscription was ruled out, a few men actually found themselves drafted Such was the case with Oleksa Javorsky, who was drafted in the spring of 1944. Although 48-years-old and under medical care for a heart problem, Javorsky's episode began one day when a messenger from the Security Service arrived at his Cracow apartment. Javorsky, a former lieutenant in the Austrian and Galician Army, had not sought to enlist because he knew he was too old, by profession was a lawyer, and was in questionable health. Javorsky also knew that some of the older men who had previously enlisted were, after a brief training stint, terminated of duty and returned to civilian life.
Immediately informing the messenger that "this is either a mistake or someone's joke, because only volunteers are accepted," Javorsky soon learned that it was no mistake or joke. To avoid any hardship for his family, Javorsky set forth to Neuhammer.
Somehow, he made it through the three week refresher course. Afterwards, Javorsky reported to Paliiv and was informed that a lawyer was urgently needed to be involved with the "Galicia" Division's family members' concerns. Seeing that he did not have much of a choice and help was needed, Javorsky agreed to it. However, Javorsky felt that his former army rank should be restored, and he protested the policy which forbade former officers from having their previous ranks restored.
Regardless, Javorsky was soon promoted to the rank of Waffen-Oberscharführer (1st Sergeant) and until the end of the war, he was posted to the "Bureau of Soldier's Needs." As a liaison NCO between the Division and the Military Board's Soldier's Bureau, he was constantly involved in legal matters, soldiers affairs, civilian assistance programs, and evacuation matters.

Notes

Of course, Javorsky's assignment was a very difficult one. Frequently, the Soldier's Bureau was forced to relocate and operate under very adverse and extraordinarily tough conditions. After the war, the Bureau continued to involve itself in soldier, family and civilian matters until the end of the 1940s. As for Javorsky, he became so dedicated to his responsibility that until the very end of his life, he remained active in various Divisional functions.

16. In Heidelager, Freitag established a two-month officers training course for 26 Ukrainian officer candidates. According to Shuhan (who was one of the attendees), the course was attended solely by former officers and NCOs who had graduated from recruit training and various specialized courses. All 26 completed the course and were commissioned as officers at Heidelager shortly before the Division relocated to Neuhammer. This course was possibly established with Paliiv's encouragement because Paliiv constantly reminded Freitag that the leadership problem stemmed not only from the Ukrainian side but simultaneously, there was a lack of German leadership both numerically and qualitatively. See also Yuriy Krokhmaliuk, "The Division's Commander," *Visti*, 1983, No. 3, p. 53.

17. Heike, *English ed*, pp. 6-7; Yuriy Krokhmaliuk, *Visti*, 1983, No. 3, p. 52. Krokhmaliuk also expressed this viewpoint to the author during a personal interview.

18. *Visti*, 1983, No 3, p. 52; personal discussion with Yuriy Krokhmaliuk.

19. *Ibid.*

20. Personal discussion with Yuriy Krokhmaliuk.

21. *Ibid* See also *Visti*, 1983, No. 3, pp. 53-56.

Notes Chapter 10

1. Yurkevich in *Boshyk*, p. 78. See also Krokhmaliuk, *The Glow*, p. 65. Of the 29 Waffen-Untersturmführers most, if not all, arrived as Waffen-Standartenoberjunkers and were commissioned shortly thereafter in Heidelager. It was also in mid-October 1943 that the Division's first chaplains concluded their training. After a brief period of leave, the Chaplains reported to Heidelager in November 1943. (*Nahayewsky*, p. 40).
Because officers of "non-Germanic" origin could not become full-fledged members of the SS officer corps, they were not permitted to carry the "SS" symbol preceding the word "Waffen." (*Handbook On German Military Forces*, 15 March 1945, pp. 111-112). This explains why the none of the Ukrainian officers carried the "SS" runes on their uniforms, and were not titled as "SS."

2. *Wachter to Himmler*, 30 October 1943. In his invitation, Wachter cited a strength of "13,000 men under arms." Undoubtedly, Wachter's figure also included those in the independent rifle regiments numbered 4-7. Wachter's figure, however, did not encompass those in the independent Training and Replacement Regiment found in Wandern, Germany.

3. Heike, *English* ed, p. 9.

4. According to Heike (*English ed*, pp. 25-26), the Training and Replacement Regiment was organized in April, 1944, in Wandern, Germany. (Heike refers to this unit as a "reserve-training regiment"). The regiment was, however, actually formed much sooner.

5. Heike, *English* ed., p. 26.

6. Personal discussion with Roman Krokhmaliuk. Roman's brother, Yuriy, substantiated the figures.

7. On 21 February 1947, L.D. Wilgress, a High Commissioner within Canada's Refugee Screening Commission, submitted a report titled "Refugee Screening Commission Report on Ukrainians in Surrendered Enemy Personnel." The report's findings were also derived with the assistance of Major Jashkevych, a prisoner-of-war from the 1st Ukrainian Division. (Formerly known as the "Galicia" Division).
In this report, the Division's various units are broken down into their respective strengths. The "Recruiting Regiment's" (previously known as the "Training and Replacement Regiment") strength was cited at 2,230 personnel. Of this strength, Major Jashkevych reported "that a fair proportion of them were really civilians, such as Todt workers, who had attached themselves to the regiment, as a means of escaping from the Germans." From this regiment, 30 individuals were randomly selected to be interviewed. Of these, nearly a third stated that they had been working in various factories in Germany prior to entering the Training and Replacement Regiment.
In conclusion, the commission's report stated that of the four main motives found for enlisting into the Division, one included "as a preferable alternative to forced labour, etc." (For the complete report see *Boshyk*, pp. 233-240).

8. Personal discussion with the Krokhmaliuk brothers.

Galicia Division

9. B. Hnativ, "Spomyny" [Remembrances], *Visti*, 1980, No. 2, p. 74. Deported to Nazi Germany in 1941, Hnativ was taken to Leipzig where, along with 200 Ukrainians and 30 Poles, he worked as a coalminer. In a desperate effort to escape, Hnativ volunteered for the Division.

10. Personal discussion with Yuriy Krokhmaliuk. As attested by many, the intent of the various Ukrainian relief agencies and the Ukrainian Central Committee was based on this factor: to protect its people as best as possible; therefore, as its representatives went around to as many of the German farms, factories, shipyards and mines as permissible, the Ukrainian representatives reasoned that at the moment one of the best ways to save and secure the Ukrainian manpower was through military service. Undoubtedly, the Ukrainian representatives must have created some confusion because as the ex-forced labor showed up at Wandern, the deportees were speaking of a Ukrainian "viys'ko" (army) rather than a "division." Unfortunately, while the Ukrainian intent was a good one, problems were created. Of those released, many were unfit for military service. Had a Ukrainian "viys'ko" instead of just a division been raised, then much of this raw manpower could have been utilized for labor troop purposes which, at that time, was found in any army worldwide. But as it turned out, only a limited number of those released for the "Galicia" Division could be utilized at the moment.

11. "The Development of the Waffen-SS" in *Tactical and Technical Trends* (Washington, D.C.: Military Intelligence Division, 30 December 1943). (Restricted). No. 41, pp. 35-37.

12. Abt. Innere Verwaltung Bevolkerungswesen und Fursorge nn.IV 702-02 Bi/Schu. 11.November 1943. An den Kommandeur der Sicherheitspolizei und des SD. Lemberg. Betr.: Verhafteten Johann Lutschyn z.Zt. in Auschwitz. This letter was in regard to an earlier verbal appeal by Mrs. Lutschyn to Galicia's Bureau of People's Concerns and Welfare.

13. Also known as Auschwitz. Although Mrs. Lutschyn might have been informed that Oswiencim was a camp for internees, undoubtedly at that time she was unaware that Oswiencim (known soon to the world as Auschwitz), was a major concentration camp. Lutschyn Paraskewie in Kamionka Strumilowa. An Hoch Geehrter Herr Regementskomandant Biesans in Lemberg. Kamionka Strumilowa den 2. XII. 1943.

14. On 16 December 1943, her letter was stamped by the seal of the Generalgouvernement Der Governor Distrikt Galizien, Abt. Innere Verwaltung Bevolkerungswesen und Fursorge, 16.12.43, Aktenz 702-02/4253). [General-Governments People's Concern and Welfare Bureau on 16 December 1943 under Document No. 702-02/4253].

15. Abt. Innere Verwaltung Bevolkerungswesen und Fursorge Inn.IV 702-02. 21.Dezember 1943. An den Kommandeur der Sicherheitspolizei und des SD Lemberg Herbststr. Betr.: Verhafteten Johann Lutschyn, z.Zt. in Auschwitz.

16. Kamionka Strum., den 19.1. 1944. An Herrn Obst., Leiter fur Fursorge der Familienangehorigen der SS Gal.Division in Lemberg. (Signed Lutschyn, Paraskewie).

17. Der Kommandeur der Sicherheitspolizei u. des SD fur den Distrikt Galizien. B. Nr. IV C 2a-4043/43/ Schutsh.Nr. 949, 31.1.44. An den Gouverneur des Distrikt Galizien-Abt.Innere Verwaltung-Bevolkerungswesen und Fursorge in Lemberg. Betrifft: Johann Lutschyn, geb. am 12.6.17 Vorgang.: Dort.Schreiben vom 11.11.43 Inn.IV 702-02.

Notes Chapter 11

1. Roman Krokhmaliuk, *The Glow*, p 49; O. Gorbach, "Periodychni Publikatsii Dlia Voiatstva I-oi UD." [Periodicals Published For the Troops of the 1st Ukrainian Division], *Visti*, 1993, No. 1, pp. 89-90.

2. "Periodicals Published For the Troops," *Visti*, 1993, No. 1, p. 89.

Notes Chapter 12

1. *Bender and Taylor*, Vol. 4, p. 48.

2. Heike, *English ed.*, p. 12; Heike, "Persha Ukrain'ska Dyviziia – z Nahody Proholoshennia Dekliaratsii Suverenitetu Ukraini v Lypni 1990" [The 1st Ukrainian Division–On the Occasion of the Proclamation of Ukrainian Sovereignty in July 1990], *Visti*, 1990, No. 5-6, p. 21.

3. Especially at Kutno, along the Bzura River line. (North of Lodz). Here, the 30th helped to encircle Polish Army Group Kutno, but then came under a devastating attack from the Group as it attempted to break out. So hard hit and pressed was the 30th that General Briesen, after gathering up what reserves he could, personally led a counterattack to repulse the Poles.

Notes

4. From August 1945 until May 1947, Heike was kept in British internment under suspicion that he had served at one time as an SS company commander; Heike vehemently denied the suspicions.

Although Heike served as an officer in the "Galicia" (known later as the Ukrainian 1st Division), Heike never held rank in the Waffen-SS. He consistently opposed all attempts to change his Wehrmacht rank of Major to its Waffen-SS equivalent of SS-Sturmbannführer. During captivity, Heike wrote his memoirs from which evolved his book. After his release in May 1946, Heike studied agricultural science and industrial management. From 1950 until his retirement in 1975, he was employed by the Audi automobile firm in Dusseldorf, and later in Ingolstadt, Germany. He was an Assistant Director, chief of Personnel and Administration, and company director. Additionally, he volunteered his time and services for many worthwhile causes such as : Chairman of the Employer's Association; Chairman of the Board of Statutory Health Insurance in Ingolstadt; member of the Bavarian Red Cross; and member of the Supervisory and Community Building Board in Ingolstadt. For postwar service to his country, Heike was conferred the Federal Cross of Merit with Ribbon in 1975.

Heike fully understands the tragedy of war. In addition to his personal experiences and the loss of personal property and death of relatives, Heike also lost his two brothers on the Eastern front. To seek a proper understanding of the causes of war and obtain solutions to avoid conflict, Heike founded the Association for Military Studies in Dusseldorf, Germany.

5. Personal discussion with Veryha. See also Veryha's, *Along the Roads*, p. 103; and English synopsis, p. 185. Vershyhora's group was an element from the 1st Ukrainian Partisan Division commanded by Kovpak.

6. At that time, Poland's border extended further to the east. Thus, the region of conflict occurred within its territories.

7. Since no sympathy existed amongst the various anti-communist and communist factions, the guerrillas not only fought the Germans and other Axis troops, but each other as well.

8. Heike, *English ed.*, p. 20. In the English translation of Heike's book, the term "task force" is used whereas in the German edition "kampfgruppe" (battlegroup) is used. In the World War II German Army, the proper terminology only used was "kampfgruppe" which translates into "battlegroup." For reasons of accuracy, "kampfgruppe" or "battlegroup" should only be used. Undoubtedly, the translator of Heike's account utilized "task force" as this term is used more readily by western military ground and naval forces. For the exact German order, see Heike's *Sie Wolten Die Freiheit. Die Geschichte der Ukrainischen Division 1943-1945* (Podzun-Verlag, 1974), p. 57.

9. Heike, *English ed.*, pp. 20-21. according to *Ready*, p. 342, the order was initiated by Lviv's Higher SS and Police Leader.

10. The Division was informed some days later that Himmler had not only never issued such an order, but that he actually had no knowledge of it. While it is true that during one of Koppe's and Himmler's previous discussions Himmler mentioned to Koppe the possible usage of the Division for extreme emergency situations, in actuality Himmler always planned to use the Division solely as a combat force on the eastern front. Koppe, however, when pressed to the wall – "under whose authorization?" – falsely replied "Himmler's." By then it didn't matter, for the battlegroup was on its way. (See also Heike, *English ed.*, pp. 21-22).

11. *Ready*, p. 342, cites that the order originated from Lviv's Higher SS and Police Leader. Possibly, Lviv's police leader did press Cracow's Higher SS commander to engage the roving communist guerrillas north of Lviv's vicinity. Regardless, the order did, in fact, originate in Cracow.

12. Myhailo Dlaboha, "Boieva Grupa Bayersdorffa" [Battle Group Beyersdorff], *Visti*, January, 1969, No. 131. According to Dlaboha, a former artillery officer within the battlegroup, the first order arrived at the end of January 1944 (no specific date was cited) and the second order arrived on 15 February 1944. (P. 101). Dlaboha is not specific about the contents of the order, but writes that the battlegroup was to be ready within 48 hours. Of interest to note is that Dlaboha states the second order arrived from Berlin (p.101), whereas Heike (*English ed.*, p. 21) maintains that "we received another order from Himmler and the Cracow SS and Police." It appears that Heike is correct.

13. Heike, *English ed.*, p. 20.

14. Krokhmaliuk, *The Glow In the East*, pp. 67-68. Unfortunately, information regarding which regiment provided the two battalions is not given by the Krokhmaliuk brothers, Heike, Veryha, Taylor, or any other sources. It appears, however, that they were pulled from the 29th Infantry Regiment. As for Rembalovych, he was one of the highest ranking Ukrainian officers in the Division.

15. According to Heike, *English ed.*, p. 21, the Kampfgruppe consisted of one infantry battalion, one battery of light artillery, some engineers, one demolition and one anti-armor platoon, and was accompanied with communications and supply personnel. It is known that the engineer section and communications personnel evolved around the infantry. Although Heike cites one infantry battalion as the basis of this kampfgruppe, Roman Krokhmaliuk cites two infantry battalions; undoubtedly, a second infantry battalion (or at least a good part of it), was utilized since it is known that its commander did participate in Kampfgruppe Beyersdorff's deployment. The fact that a strength of

Galicia Division

2,000 is also recorded indicates that two (or nearly two) full infantry battalions must have ben utilized as the battlegroup's nucleus.

16. Heike, *English ed.*, p. 21, maintains that higher authorities were informed that the unit was not ready for action, and was "ill-prepared for winter fighting." Along with Heike *Ready*, p. 342, cites the battlegroup was not supplied with adequate winter clothing. But Heike's and Ready's views may be strongly contested because photographs, as well as personal accounts, reveal that the soldiers were clad in winter clothing (such as heavy wool coats and various winter white camouflaged parkas) and were superbly armed.

17. Krokhmaliuk, *The Glow*, p. 67; Veryha, *Along The Roads*, p. 103. Personal discussion with Yuriy Krokhmaliuk.

18. Simultaneously, such an activity would also enable some of the Division's personnel to attain some combat experience. For an excellent study of the military aspects of Russian and Eastern European forests and swamps, to include tactics, intelligence/reconnaissance, troop movements, combat deployments, offensive/defensive operations, retrograde (withdrawal) operations, combat under special conditions along with a conclusion, see *Combat in Russian Forests and Swamps* (Washington, D.C.: Department of the Army), 31 July 1951, No. 20-231.

19. Over two-thirds of Ukraine lies at a level between 170-180 meters above sea level. See also Professor Myron Dolnyts'kyi, "Geografiia Ukrainy" [Ukraine's Geography], (Detroit: 1953), pp. 9, 16-25. For a German study see "European Russia: A Natural Fortress," Section II, pp. 4-5; and "Operations In Woods and Swamps," Section V, pp. 28-43, in *Terrain Factors In the Russian Campaign*, CMH Publication 104-5, Center of Military History, U.S. Army (Washington, D.C., 1982. Reprinted 1986).

20. Heike, *English ed.*, p. 21 According to Dlaboha, problems were also encountered in securing equipment, horses, and food stuffs for the deployment. And as the soldiers approached the train station outside of Heidelager where the loading was to be conducted, Major Heike, clearly dissatisfied with the way the artillery battery's preparation was being conducted, took Dlaboha aside and scolded him. Unable to explain the situation, and seeing that Heike was impatient with the way the railroading was proceeding, Dlaboha simply replied "Jawohl!"

21. Personal discussion with Yuriy Krokhmaliuk. See also Dlaboha, *Visti*, 1969, No. 131, p. 101. According to both men, Group "A" was commanded by Rembalovych and Group "B" by Bristot.

22. According to Vasyl Yashan, "Strilets'ka Dyviziia 'Halychyna.' Stanyslavivs'ka okruha v rokakh 1943-44" [The Rifle Division 'Galicia.' Stanyslav Region In the Years 1943-1944], *Visti*, No. 5-6, 1968, p. 58, "... parts of the Division travelled through Lviv in their eastward movement to the area (occupied) by Red partisans. One such company, in its visit to the Galician district, was even addressed by the Governor [Wachter]." According to Dlaboha, the battlegroup's infantry moved through Lviv. (*Visti*, 1969, No. 131, p. 102). Dlaboha, however, cites no reason for such a move.

23. On 28 February 1944, a report was submitted to the Military Board by Ivanna Gardetzka, a member of the Women's Auxiliary Board of Galicia's Military Board regarding the distribution of food items and gifts for Beyersdorff's troops during their movement from Lviv to the northern front from the period of 18-26 February 1944.
   A total of 2,000 packages were distributed containing cookies, baked goods, meat, bread and cigarettes; additionally, for those who wanted it (and most did), beer was also provided. The report stated the follow amounts of foodstuffs were utilized for the distribution of the provisions: 375 pounds of flour; 75 pounds of sugar; 50 pounds of butter; and 500 pounds of sausage meat. A total of 25,000 cigarettes and 1,927 bottles of beer were also distributed. Numerous newspapers, and reading material, was also provided. "Bericht des Hauptfrauendienstes beim Wehrausschuss Galizien in Lemberg uber Verteilung der Geschenke fur die Freiwilligen der SS-Division Galizien wahrend ihrer Durchreise durch Lemberg in der Zeit vom 18 bis 26.2.1944."

24. Personal discussion with Yuriy Krokhmaliuk and Veryn.

25. Veryha, *Along the Roads*, p. 104. Although Veryha cites that the anti-guerrilla action commenced on 13 February 1944, he also states the battlegroup did not arrive into its operational area until sometime in late February 1944. Veryha, when using the date of 13 February, refers to the date of the initial order.

26. This is especially true in the case of the Soviet guerrillas. "The Soviets began raiding villages in a forced recruiting campaign. Those who refused to join the guerrillas were shot as German agents." See Colonel William A. Burke's, "Guerrillas Without Morale: The White Russian Partisans," in *Military Review*, September, 1961, pp. 64-71. For additional information on full-fledged guerrilla conscription drives conducted behind the German front as well as partisan cruelty, see "Operations In Woods and Swamps" in *Terrain Factors In the Russian Campaign*, pp. 42-43.

27. This was the Division's first action. At no time did the "Galicia" Division ever battle Soviet guerrillas in the summer of 1943 as erroneously claimed by certain Soviet sources such as *Ukrains'ka RSR u Velykii Vitchynianii Viini Radian'koho Soiuzu, 1941-1945*, Vol. 2, p. 162; and the *Radians'ka Entsyklopedia Istorii Ukrainy* [The Soviet Encyclopedia of the History of Ukraine] (Kiev: 1969), Vol. 2, p. 315. Such sources are obviously incorrect because if one takes into consideration that the first untrained recruits departed for their training and schools in the second half of

Notes

July 1943 (and that at this time the Division still existed mostly on paper), it is obviously cleart that neither the Division, nor any of its elements or personnel, could have been utilized the summer of 1943.

28. Dlaboha, *Visti*, 1969, No. 131, p. 103, cites a number of skirmishes but writes of only one serious engagement.

29. Skirmishes took place with the guerrillas for the remainder of the day and throughout the night.

30. According to Dlaboha, in the successive days, village inhabitants reported that the guerrillas had suffered heavily. In their withdrawal, they removed a number of their dead and wounded. (*Visti*, 1969, No. 131, p. 103). But the fact that the guerrillas did not remove all of their dead and failed to immediately bury those who they did remove, indicated that the guerrillas felt threatened and immediately retreated to preserve their remaining force. As for the sporadic fighting which took place throughout the remainder of the day and into the night, this probably occurred with the Soviet guerrilla band's rear guard.

31. *Ready*, p. 342, cited that one platoon fell into an ambush and incurred heavy losses.

32. According to Yuriy Krokhmaliuk, the two bodies were examined that day by two medical doctors, who submitted independent reports.
Both reports conclusively established that in the initial ambush, the two soldiers had been shot in the legs. No bullet wounds were noted above waist level. As a result, they were unable to retire with the others. Unlike the other dead who remained fully clothed, the two had been stripped to their waist, and repeatedly slashed with vertical bayonet thrusts in the legs, arms, chest, stomach, shoulders, neck and face. One man had both of his eyes gouged out by bayonet thrusts. Since neither suffered any bullet wounds above their legs, deep bayonet wounds were the cause of death; undoubtedly, these were inflicted upon the two when the guerrillas were force to retire. The two medical reports were initially submitted to the Divisional staff, and then forwarded (with some additional copies) to various agencies such as the Red Cross. Krokhmaliuk, unfortunately, was not able to recall where the reports were submitted and no copies exist in the Division's archives; therefore, this atrocity is only recorded in personal written accounts. As for those killed-in-action, the bodies were returned to Galicia for family burial.

33. Dlaboha cited a guerrilla force of up to 1,500. According to Dlaboha "our German commanders, along with Beyersdorff, had no understanding of [communist] guerrilla warfare." Yet, there were those within the battlegroup, such as Rembalovych, who understood communist guerrilla warfare. In addition to battling Red Guerrillas as a soldier, in the early 1920s Rembalovych himself fought as a guerrilla when he participated in two anti-Soviet winter expeditions. Unfortunately for the battlegroup, Beyersdorff failed to heed their advice. Compounding the situation was the trust and eager acceptance of the advice of certain Polish-born German 'Volksdeutschers' found within the battlegroup. But some of the Volksdeutscher's sympathies lay not with the battlegroup but with Poland and even, with the Soviet underground. As a result, sharp quarrels arose between Beyersdorff and his Galician Ukrainian commanders. See *Visti*, 1969, No. 131, p. 103.

34. L.S. "Spomyn: Yak Zvychaino u Kadri" [Memoir: How Usually It Was In the Cadre], *Visti*, 1986, No. 3, p. 69. Yuriy Krokhmaliuk, in a personal discussion, stated that the Kampfgruppe had strict orders to refrain from misconduct, and its men were immediately to report any incidents of misconduct.

35. According to Vashchenko, only a few UPA agents defected. Those who did, only did so with UPA's full knowledge and consent. A handful also deserted because they were dissatisfied with military life and sought to exit out of a very disciplined environment.
The possibility also exists that a few of the deserters could have reentered the communist side. In a personal discussion with Myhailo Lobach*, a former 88 weapons specialist and later reconnaissance/intelligence officer within the Division, cases of individuals disappearing, or being "captured" and reappearing after the war, did occur. Occasionally, information surfaced that the Division, in addition to being infiltrated by OUN and UPA members, was also infiltrated by communist agents.

36. Heike, *English ed.*, p. 22.

37. *Ibid.* Later on, communist Poland would raise allegations of war crimes. And one of the most famous allegations is the one which cited that a Divisional battlegroup massacred an entire village in February 1944. Because this allegation (which, incidentally, was never raised against the Division during the war years but suddenly appeared in the cold war era) must finally be examined in depth.
On 16 February 1944, the Division deployed a battlegroup, Kampfgruppe "Beyersdorff," from Heidelager to the northwestern area of Eastern Galicia and Volyn adjacent to Poland to combat communist partisans. And Antoni Szczesniak, a Polish communist propagandist and Ukrainian hater, alleges that a "battlegroup from the Ukrainian Division SS Galicia, in the vicinity of Brody, conducted a pacification action against the peaceful town of Huta Pieniacka on 27 February 1944. In the ensuing action, Huta Pieniacka was levelled and around 500 innocent Polish inhabitants were slaughtered." (Antoni B. Szesniak, *Droga Do Nikad: Dziatalnosc Organizacji Ukrainskich Nacjonalistow; jej Likwidacja w. Polsce*, [The Road to Nowhere: The Activities of the Organization of Ukrainian Nationalities and Its Liquidation in Poland], p. 127. For the English synopsis, see Veryha, *Along the Roads*, p. 195).

Galicia Division

Along with Szczesniak, propagandist Mieczyslaw Juchniewicz, *Polacy w. radzieckim ruchu podziemnym i partyzanckim 1941-1945* [Poles in the Soviet Underground and Partisan Movement, 1941-1945] (Warszawa: Ministerstwo Obrony Narodowej, 1973, p. 153), has also voiced this allegation.

Since these allegations have been made Szczesniak's, as well as the other allegations, must be examined.

To begin with, Szczesniak does not provide any specifics. An examination of his allegation reveals nothing but an accusation that during a pacification, "Galicia SS-men herded women and children into several buildings which were then set ablaze." (*Szczesniak*, p. 127).

Szczesniak also alleges that "around 500 Polish inhabitants were slaughtered." How does Szczesniak arrive at that figure? And who established this figure? How does Szczesniak conclude that the women and children were herded into several homes and then burned alive? Were there competent witnesses? Did an international commission comprised of coroners, doctors, and others physically view the site of this alleged atrocity? Remembering that the area of Brody was already in Soviet hands in July 1944, there was more than enough time, and relatively fresh evidence, for an international or neutral Red Cross commission to be invited to examine the site; yet, no one did. Does the possibility exist that if Huta Pieniacka was every examined by a neutral commission they would reveal information totally contrary to what Szczesniak and company claim? And by such an independent revelation embarrass Szczesniak?

So the question remains – why does Szczesniak cite a figure of around "500 inhabitants" when, prior to the war, Huta Pieniacka never even had that many inhabitants? And how does Szczesniak obtain the figure of 500 when Mieczyslaw Juchniewicz cites "several hundred women, children, and older [senior] citizens" were either burned alive or shot. (M. Juchniewicz, *Z dzia alnosci organizacyjno-bojowej Gwardii Ludowej w obwodzie lwowskim*, [From the Activities of the Organization and Fighting (Group) of the People's Guard in Lvov's District],Wojskowy przeglad historyczny, ch. 13, Nr. 4 (48), 1968, p. 153). Why 300? And how does Juchniewicz arrive at this figure? There is a significant difference between 300 and 500. And why just "women, children, and older citizens? What every happened to the young men? There is not only a large numerical discrepancy between Szczesniak and Juchniewicz's figures, but whereas Szczesniak implies men of various ages were at Huta Pieniacka, Juchniewicz cites just "older citizens."

But Szczesniak and Juchniewicz are not the only ones who have written on Huta Pieniacka. One of the best accounts is provided by Dmitriy Medvedev, a former Soviet guerrilla leader whose band, code-named "Krutikov," operated in the vicinity of Huta Pieniacka. According to Medvedev, his guerilla group, composed of Ukrainian, Polish and Russian fighters, departed Huta Pieniacka on 29 February 1944. Three days later, the village was levelled by the "Hitlerites." According to the former guerrilla commander, "17 men, who miraculously survived, managed to establish contact with our group Krutikov. 17 reported that Casimir Wojciechowski, the self-defense commander of Huta Pieniacka, was tied up, doused with gasoline, and burned." (D. Medvedev, *Sil'ni Dukhom* [The Strong In Spirit], Kiev: 1963, pp. 458-460. See also Veryha, *Along the Roads*, p. 114).

In his version, the former communist guerrilla leader makes no mention of any "SS Galicians," "Ukrainians," nor does he make any allegations that any members of the "Galicia" Division destroyed Huta Pieniacka. What is also very interesting – and of critical importance to note – is that Medvedev (who was regarded as one of the most effective and bravest communist guerrilla commanders in World War II), implicated the "Hitlerites" as the village's destroyers. In Soviet World War II terminology, "Hitlerites" was a term which strictly designated the Germans. Had it been brought to Medvedev's attention that the Galician SS had levelled Huta Pieniacka, one can be well assured that Medvedev would have stated so.

But Medvedev's account can further be utilized to discredit Szczesniak's and Juchniewicz's versions. Whereas the two men cite the date of Huta Pieniacka's destruction as 27 February, Medvedev indicates that his element was still within the town on 27 February. It was several days after their departure, on 29 February, that Huta Pieniacka was struck in early March. So what is the exact date? Dates are critically important because in the military, especially during operations, units are frequently on the move. Besides the fact that neither Kampfgruppe "Beyersdorff" nor any other Galician battlegroup operated in February or March in the vicinity of Brody and Huta Pieniacka in the period of 27 February to 3 March (and, therefore, never attacked out the place), the Division's battlegroup was much further to the northwest and, as a matter of fact, did not even move out to commence its operations until 28 February. And during its operations, at no time did the battle group remain concentrated for approximately one week in any given area.

Medvedev does not give a casualty figure; however, he cites 17 male survivors. Why 17 male survivors? And how could these 17 have linked up, after a period of several days, with an insurgent group? Realistically speaking, had the 17 men been just ordinary innocent civilians, under no circumstances would they have been able to successfully link-up with an insurgent body that had departed several days earlier. Amongst the 17, some, if not all, were insurgent personnel.

Of importance to note is that Medvedev states that "Commander Wojciechowski was captured and burned alive." But what was a "self-defense commander" doing in a village termed by Szczesniak as "peaceful and innocent."

In order to approximate an answer, it is important to examine the evaluation of the Polish Ministry of Foreign Affairs, Poland's wartime, London-based government-in-exile, about what had occurred at Huta Pieniacka.

According to a memorandum signed by Minister Bronislaw Banaczek in the aftermath of the destruction of Huta Pieniacka, "... on 24 February 1944, the German Military Field Police (Geheime Feld Polizei-GFP), while operating in the vicinity of Huta Pieniacka's inhabitants, who erroneously took the force for a Ukrainian [guerrilla] band. In the ensuing gunfire, 6-8 Germans were killed. On 27 February, the GFP conducted an expedition, totally destroyed the town, and murdered around 500 persons." ("Sprawozdanie sytuacyjne z ziem polskich," Nr. 12/44, p. 45. Cited from Veryha's *Along the Roads*, p. 113). But shortly afterward, in another disclosure by the exiled Ministry of Internal Affairs, one reads about "Ukrainian SS-men." (Sprawozdanie sytuacyjne z ziem wschodnich, Nr. 15/44, p. 24. Cited from Veryha's *Along the Roads*, p. 113). According to the updated version, as the Ukrainians prepared to search the area, the Polish inhabitants resisted and fired. By the time the shooting concluded "over 500 Poles were slaughtered." Of the entire population "only 49 survived." (*Ibid*).

Important in these two accounts is the fact that neither account specifically implicates the "Galicia" Division in the destruction of Huta Pieniacka. Although the second version cites "Ukrainian-SS men," it is not explicit. Does it refer to the non-German personnel found among the German Field Police, or does the terminology encompass the foreign (possibly Ukrainian?) personnel dispatched to reinforce the German force? But most importantly, the London-based accounts verify what Medvedev stated – that within Huta Pieniacka, a sizable guerrilla threat did exist. Soviet and Polish sources are not the only ones to positively identify Huta Pieniacka as a partisan/guerrilla stronghold. According to former UPA intelligence officer Vashchenko, "Huta Pieniacka was not only well-known to UPA-West, but likewise, to the top UPA command as a major communist guerrilla stronghold. Beside being massively fortified with inner and outer mine fields, and defensive positions, the town was also a staging/assembling area for incoming and outgoing guerrilla forces. Our inserted personnel also revealed that much arms, equipment and ammunition was stored within Huta Pieniacka. Its women and children were utilized not only for intelligence-gathering purposes, but in the production of mines and explosive devices. Huta Pieniacka was comparable to many of the "innocent" villages and hamlets found later in the Vietnam conflict – nothing but communist strongholds." (Personal discussion with Vashchenko).

Vashchenko's observations that Huta Pieiacka was a well-fortified communist guerrilla nerve center is substantiated by Juchniewicz. In his writing, Juchniewicz stated that throughout the spring of 1943 and the winter of 1944, Huta Pieniacka " fought off several strong attacks." (*Juchniewicz,* p. 153). Along with Juchniewicz, Polish author A. Korman cited "how in Huta Pieniacka a strong guerrilla element was organized along the 8th Ak Company." According to Korman, "Wojciechowski personally selected each fighter. But in addition to the self-defense unit, the village inhabitants also assisted Soviet guerrillas with shelter, intelligence information, clothing, guides, medical supplies and repair services." (For Korman's observations see V. Gotskyi's, "Pro Dvi Mirky" [About The Double Standards], *Visti*, 1993, No. 2, pp. 23-24). On occasion, Huta Pieniacka was known to shelter entire guerrilla battalions of up to strengths of 600 fighters. (*Ibid*)

As attested by various Polish, Soviet and UPA sources, Huta Pieniacka was far from being a "peaceful" and "innocent" village. It is also now known that the Germans knew of Huta Pieniacka's activities much sooner. But the main reason they failed to move against the stronghold is because the Nazis benefitted from the Polish-Ukrainian struggle; this way, the more the various anti-communist and communist insurgents fought amongst themselves, the less (or so it was believed by the Nazis), would the insurgents battle the German occupant. But as the eastern front approached Galicia proper, and a German force came under fire, the Nazis began to realize that Huta Pieniacka was also coordinating their activities with Moscow. And in order to retain and defend Galicia, the Germans could no longer tolerate any guerrilla threat. For this reason, they struck the guerrilla stronghold. And in the ensuing operation, the Germans employed their field security troops; possibly, some Ukrainian personnel were mixed in with the security force. But if such personnel were utilized, they were either those within the German force, or, from some sort of Ukrainian self-defense unit under German control. According to Veryha, *Along the Roads*, "although a Ukrainian detachment participated in that punitive action, that detachment was not a part of, or subordinated to, the Ukrainian Division "Galicia." (See English synopsis, p. 195). Simply put, under no circumstances was the "Galicia" Division, or any of its elements, or personnel, ever employed in this operation.

As for the casualties at Huta Pieniacka, to this day no proper record exists on how many inhabitants were actually lost. Figures range widely from several hundred to over 500. How many of these were actually guerrilla and guerrilla support personnel, and how many were innocent civilians, will never be established. Tragically, in warfare, but especially in such anti-guerrilla operations, civilians frequently are caught in the midst; under combat conditions, sometimes they become casualties.

Allegations that a number of people were "burned alive" is undoubtedly nothing but a propaganda lie. Frequently, ugly and cruel incidents will be utilized to portray or exaggerate an incident for propaganda or defamatory purposes. In this case, a burning incident would fit in perfectly with the cries of "SS-Henchmen," "Galician-SS men," "SS marauders," "bandits," and so forth.

In conclusion, it must be noted that when OSI director Ryan, utilizing Styrkal's work "We Accuse" as a source, cited Huta Pieniacka as a site of supposed war crimes committed by the "Galicia" Division, Poland's ministry never responded favorably to Ryan's inquires, or to Styrkal's allegation.

38. The night before the battlegroup withdrew, a Ukrainian officer committed suicide. Dlaboha could not recall the officers name, but described the officer as an honest, ambitious, and righteous person. Apparently, the suicide arose out of allegations that someone within his section had plundered a pig from a farm. During the investigation, the officer swore up and down that his section was not responsible. When the pig was later found cooking in the mess section, the young Ukrainian officer was overcome with remorse. Needless to say, self-execution was not warranted, since a simple troop rebuttal, or punishment of the thieves, would have sufficed. After writing a letter to his mother which stated: "death is my only way out of such a dishonorable event," the officer ended the letter with the words "your loving son." Then he shot himself. (Personal discussion with Veryn. See also Dlaboha, *Visti*, 1969, No. 131, p. 103. (Dlaboha, however, did not identify the officer by name).

According to Roman Kolisnyk, the rank and name of the Ukrainian officer who shot himself was Waffen-Obersturmführer Sobolevskyi. It must be remembered that within Germany's officer corps, if an officer gave his word it was accepted as a word of honor. In the event that it was later proven to be not so, the only "honorable" recourse left was suicide.

39. But the soldiers of Beyersdorff's group did not enter Neuhammer immediately. For several days, they stayed at "Tsaizaf" (Kolisnyk spells it as "Zeisau") a former prisoner-of-war camp shut down months earlier. As the troops walked into the dirty, airless, lice and rodent infested barracks surrounded by crumbling wired fences, many felt as if they were actually being incarcerated. Quickly, the soldiers cleaned the barracks, established hygiene, and deloused the premises. Believing that this was to be their permanent home, they even repaired the broken windows, water pipes, fixed the latrines, and restored electrical power. But just as they started to settle down into their nice and comfortable quarters, they were ordered to move into Neuhammer proper. "Oh well," grumbled the troops, "someone will have a nice place to live in!"

Notes Chapter 13

1. *Pankiwsky*, p. 423. According to Roman Krokhmaliuk, the assassin, disguised in the uniform of a senior Gestapo officer, approached Bayer on a street with an urgent message. As Bayer opened the letter, the assassin quickly produced a concealed revolver, shot both men dead, and fled in an automobile. At first, there were some in Lviv (including a number of long-time German residents) who believed that an internal German political or personal strife was the factor behind the assassination. But after the war, Soviet authorities acknowledged that one of their agents, Nikolai Kuznetsov, a specialized assassin operating from Medvedev's guerrilla group, assassinated both men. See also Krokhmaliuk, *The Glow*, pp. 50-52.

Of interest to note is that prior to World War II, Bayer had resided for a number of years in the United States and it was even rumored that he was a naturalized American citizen. Returning to Germany just before the eruption of the war, Bayer was unable to go back to the United States; later, he was known to confide to close associates that he deeply regretted that he had left what he regarded as his true homeland. Although an anti-communist, Bayer, who had relatives serving in the U.S. Army, harbored no love for Nazism. Undoubtedly, such factors played a major role in Bayer being posted into the Polish general-government, an area reserved by key Nazi leaders for those who were perceived to be untrustworthy, incapable, and unreliable. According to a post-war interrogation study, in addition to Bayer, a Lieutenant-Colonel and one sentinel were also killed by the same Russian agent who was disguised as a German officer. See "Deception" in *Russian Combat Methods In W.W. II*, p. 89.

2. Mackyi, unfortunately, did not cite what parent battalion or regiment the company belonged to.

3. Personal discussion with Veryha. See also Veryha's "Spomyny. Masheruiut' Dobrovol'tsi..." [Recollections. The Volunteers Are Marching...], *Visti*, 1977, No. 5-6, p. 75.

4. Years later, Myhailo Lobach would recall such an episode: As the train he was riding in pulled into Peremysl, he witnessed a terrified young boy, perhaps no more than 16 or 17 years of age, being led down the platform by two rifle-toting SS Policemen and one Gestapo or security officer in civilian attire. Stepping off the train, Lobach immediately appeared in front of the group. With an MP38-40 in his hands, he announced to the captors in fluent German "Release the boy!"

The Germans balked, and it looked as if the argument would actually end in gunplay. But suddenly, the shout of "SWINEHUNDS! YOU HEARD THE MAN!" came from behind the group. Turning around, the captors saw another Galician soldier, pistol in hand, facing them. Immediately, they released the boy, who quickly fled down the platform past Lobach. To ensure that he escaped Lobach (as did the other soldier) waited on the platform until the whistle of the train was heard and it began to move.

5. Krokhmaliuk, *The Glow*, p. 77. Younger males were to be conscripted into a paramilitary force prior to entering the Wehrmacht.

6. *Ibid.* p. 77.

7. It is known, however, that in mid-June 1944, a number of men received conscription notifications with a reporting date of 21 June 1944. Amongst them was Volodymyr Gotskyi, a linguist who resided in Peremysl. Addressed directly to Gotskyi, the telegram was from the Districts Police and Security Commander. The notification was short but straight to the point:

"An Herrn Gotskyj Wolodymyr, Premysl, Kusmanek str. 5. Sie werden ersucht am 21.6.1944 um 14.30 Uhr auf der hiesigen Dienststelle der Sicherheitspolizei u. S.D. Macken str. 29 zu erscheinen. Das Erscheinen ist Pflicht." ("You are requested to appear at the office of Security Police and Security Service at 29 Macken St. at 2:30 p.m. on 21 June 1944. Your appearance is mandatory." Signed Hauptsturmführer – name illegible).

Although Gotskyi knew that in its initial stages the Division was composed of volunteers, in mid-1944 he (as well as others) would learn that German authorities, in a desperate effort to secure manpower for certain critical military specialties, began to obtain volunteers under coercion and fear of reprisal against loved ones. Realizing the negative consequences one could suffer if he failed to appear, Gotskyi appeared. Surviving the war, Gotskyi would learn years later that a family member had saved his draft notice. It was republished in its exact form in a Visti issue. See Volodymyr Gotskyi, "Dva Dokumenty" [Two Documents] , *Visti*, 1990, No. 4, p. 23.

Notes

8. *German Army Order of Battle, 1944*. (Washington, D.C., 1944). Pp. F4-F11.

9. Krokhmaliuk, "Tragichnyi vypadok z. St. Hyhortsevym" [The Tragic Incident of Stepan Hryhortsiv], *The Glow*, pp. 52-53.

10. *Ibid*, p. 53.

11. Kolisnyk, "Nabir Dobrovol'tsiv" [The Recruitment of Volunteers], *Visti*, 1988, No. 2, p. 48.

12. *Ibid*.

13. Personal discussion with Yuriy Krokhmaliuk.

Notes Chapter 14

1. *Bender and Taylor*, Vol 4, p. 48. According to Ivan Kedryn, on 1 December 1944. the Division's personnel strength stood at 12,634. By the spring of 1944, it would increase. "Ukrains'ka Dyiziia – Yak Viis'ko i Problema." [The Ukrainian Division. As an Army and a Problem], *Visti*, No. 5-6, 1983, p. 50. This strength figure did not include the Training and Replacement Regiment's strength at Wandern.

2. *The German Replacement Army (Ersatzheer), February, 1945*. (The Military Intelligence Division, War Department, Washington, D.C., [Restricted], February, 1945), pp. 130-133.

3. *Ibid*. A considerable Polish population was found within Upper Silesia. Czech's comprised the Sudeten and Teschen regions.

4. *Ibid*. See also Madej's, *The German Army Order of Battle: The Replacement Army, 1939-1945*, p. 42.
   In an article condemning "Ukrainian Bourgeoisie Nationalists," Volodymyr Hrytstiuk chastised those who had first betrayed, and then fled, from their homeland. (Volodymyr Hrytsiuk, "Osyni Hnizda. Trydiashchi tavruiut' han'boiu Ukrains'kykh burzhuaznykh natsionalistiv." [Autumn Nests. The Visible Brand of Shame of the Ukrainian Bourgeoisie Nationalists]. Hrytsiuk's work, published in the mid-1980s, was both distributed in leaflet form and published in various Soviet news sources).
   Aside from the fact that Hrytsiuk's work is filled with extraordinary sensationalism, regarding the Division, Hrytsiuk cites such "facts": "The Galicia Division murdered thousands in extermination camps" and "in the city of Neuhammer, formerly in the territory of East Prussia, the SS Division also guarded a concentration camp." Along with the other propagandists and sensationalists, Hrytsiuk's "facts" provide no exact dates or specifics; he fails to identify any specific extermination camps and so forth. But in regard to his allegation that the Division guarded a concentration camp in Neuhammer, Hrytsiuk should be informed that within Neuhammer's training area, there was no concentration camp. Likewise, he should be provided a geography lesson because Neuhammer was in Silesia, many miles away from East Prussia.

5. Whether the move was also conducted to further the distance between the Division and the UPA has never been substantiated; undoubtedly, it was done strictly for training purposes.

6. From the publishers. "Fakty Pro Ukrains'ku Dyviziiu" [Facts About the Ukrainian Division], *Visti*, No. 4, 1985, p. 26. At no time was the "SS Galizien Division a special Ukrainian unit commanded by German Gestapo officers;" nor was "the division used to punish the [Ukrainian] population and round up Jews for extermination in the Ukraine, Slovakia, and Yugoslavia" as erroneously stated by former KGB officer Pavel Sudoplatov in *Special Tasks: The Memoirs of an Unwanted Witness–A Soviet Spymaster* (Boston: Little, Brown & Company, 1994), p. 250.

7. At Neuhammer, for example, the Division's anti-aircraft was finally completed. Commanded by SS-Hauptsturmführer Serge Von Kuester (born in Russia 12 December 1896, SS-Nr. 314,013/non-party member), Kuester was proficient in German, Russian, and he had a relatively strong command of the Ukrainian language. Kuester's anti-aircraft battalion was centered around a headquarters battery and three gun batteries. Each battery was organized around a different number and type of weapons system.
   The 1st "light' battery had a personnel strength of 200 soldiers organized around 4 platoons, each with three 20mm four-barrelled light anti-aircraft guns for a total of 12 guns; however, 6 heavy MG-42 machine guns, converted for an anti-aircraft role, supplemented 1st battery. 2nd "medium" battery, also with a strength of 200, had 3 platoons, each with three 37mm one-barrelled guns for a total of 9 guns as well as 6 heavy MG-42 machine guns. The 3rd "heavy" battery, with a strength of 180, was organized around 1 platoon of four 88mm guns and one platoon of two light 20mm anti-aircraft guns for protection against low flying aircraft. Personal discussion with Roman Hayetskyj, a former Divisional anti-aircraft gunner, and Yuriy Krokhmaliuk. Yuriy Krokhmaliuk's "Organizatsiia I-oi UD UNA" [Organization of the 1st Ukrainian Division] (unpublished work), also substantiates the above organization.
   According to Bohdan Nebozhuk, who on 9 September 1943 was transported to Heidelager for recruit training, following a "very solid period of recruit training," in the latter part of December 1943, the majority of Nebozhuk's company was dispatched to Munich's "SS-Flak Kaserne" for anti-aircraft training. Posted as an observer to a heavy

battery, Nebozhuk received extensive training in various observatory equipment. Concluding their training in March 1944, Nebozhuk and the others returned to Neuhammer; there, they received their anti-aircraft weaponry and equipment. Bohdan Nebozhuk, "Brody," *Visti*, 1992, No. 2, p. 72.

In addition to the Division's anti-aircraft battalion, the Division's fusilier battalion was officially organized in early March 1944. Its non-commissioned corps was composed primarily of Ukrainian leaders who, in 1943, had completed recruit training and were dispatched to various NCO schools. A disproportionate number of the NCO's were graduates of the Radolfzell and Lauenburg NCO schools. Roman Bojcun, "Fiuzilers'kyi Kurin'" [The Fusilier Battalion], *Visti*, 1992, No. 2, pp. 88-89.

8. Heike, *English ed.* p. 25; Ren, *My Life's Mosaic*, p. 127.

9. Nahayewsky, *A Soldier Priest Remembers*, pp. 47-48.

10. Decades later, one could still see the emotion Krokhmaliuk exhibited when describing the showdown with General Freitag. Realizing that neither he or Paliiv would succeed in changing Freitag's mind, at approximately 7 a.m., Krokhmaliuk stated such words to Freitag: "General, this murder will never be forgotten. Some day, sir, it will be recorded in Ukrainian history. In the future, unborn Ukrainians will be reading about this tragedy." Krokhmaliuk's prophecy proved to be correct.

11. Realistically speaking, the NCO's death could possibly have been the result of a feud with some fellow German, at the hands of the communists, or even at the hands of local criminals. The fact that the NCO's murder occurred several weeks following Burlak's death fueled rumors that Galicia's troops were the guilty party.

According to Yuriy Krokhmaliuk, Galicia's troops endured more than their share of abusive and uncalled for behavior from certain cadre personnel because they all knew that in the end, such negative behavior would cease with the rise of a strong Ukrainian cadre. Additionally, as verified by Krokhmaliuk, a number of the Germans who entered the Division in 1943 and early 1944 were "from the bottom of the leadership barrel!" Unwanted by other regular army, Waffen-SS and even most police units, they were channeled into foreign formations such as the "Galicia" Division. So until a Ukrainian cadre arose, the Division's Ukrainian's had to do with what they had.

12. *Bender and Taylor*, Vol. 4, p. 31.

13. *Ibid.*

14. Personal discussion with Veryha. See also Veryha's "Dmytro Paliiv – Voin i Patriot" [Dmytro Paliiv – Warrior and Patriot], *Visti Kombatanta*, 1968, No. 5-6, p. 44. According to Dmytro Ferkuniak, a former Divisional officer, "Captain Paliiv was the Ukrainian spirit within Divisional staff. He exerted his influence upon Freitag, whom he always convinced and compelled to succumb to his [Paliiv's] plans. Paliiv is to be praised because [on account of him] approximately 600 of our youth graduated from officer school and became officers, and approximately 2,000 of our youth completed all types of non-commissioned courses." For Ferkuniak's observations see also, "Komandnyi Sklad Shtabu Dyvizii" [The Division's Command Staff], *Visti Kombatanta*, 1965, No. 4, pp. 27- 28.

15. Heike, *English ed.*, p. 23.

16. Personal discussion with Veryha.

17. Veryha, *Visti*, 1968, No. 5-6, p. 42. Veryn stated that the trident flower-bed was not only replaced but that in the following weeks, more appeared through Neuhammer.

18. Heike, *English ed,* p. 23. Personal discussion with Veryha, Krokhmaliuk, Hayetskyj, Veryn, and others.

19. *Ibid.*

20. Years later, Myhailo Lobach, a radio communications specialist with an 88mm gun battery, would recall the superb training. In response to allegations of "insufficient training at Neuhammer," "poor weapons," "poor leadership," etc., Lobach always refuted such remarks. As Lobach himself stated: "the training that I received was first rate. Not only was I proficient with the communications equipment and various small arms, but I knew everything about the 88."

21. Personal interview with Yuriy Krokmaliuk. And Liubomyr Stek*, a former high-ranking NCO within the Division's supply and support, stated that "following Himmler's inspection and review, excellent modern arms were additionally provided."

22. Personal discussion with Yuriy Krokhmaliuk.

23. Keegan, *The Waffen-SS,* p. 143, appears to imply this when he states "most of the east European SS was riff-raff with the exception of the Latvian and Estonian divisions;" *Windrow*, p. 19, refers to the Division as a "hang-dog unit;" and *Littlejohn*, p. 322, cites the Division was "inadequately trained." Along with such critics, there are some

Notes

Ukrainian's who, to this day, maintain the false notion that the Division was nothing but a "cannon-fodder" type of formation.

24. See Ren, *My Life's Mosaic*, pp. 127-130; Osyp Holynskyj, *Visti*, 1983, No. 4, p. 21. Personal interviews with Yuriy Krokhmaliuk, Veryha and other Divisional veterans substantiate the fact that the soldiers who deployed to the eastern front in mid-1944 were all exceptionally well-trained.

25. Ren, *My Life's Mosaic*, pp. 127-130. Ren's observations are substantiated by Ready who verifies the Divisions personnel received extensive training. (P.273). Ready was also more than correct in his observation that "Himmler was determined that the unit would not be committed to battle until it was fully trained." (*Ibid*). According to Evhen Shypailo, a former Divisional soldier, "the first recruits who arrived to Heidelager in July 1943, underwent a solid period of infantry recruit training which concluded at the end of October 1943." Shypailo's observation is substantiated by Roman Cholkan who cited that the first incoming recruits underwent three months of solid training which concluded in October 1943. Although Cholkan does not cite the exact dates of the training period, he does imply that the recruits training commenced shortly after their departure on 18 July 1943. For Cholkan's observation see *Visti*, 1992, No. 4, p. 84.

26. Ren, *My Life's Mosaic*, p. 128. In describing the Division prior to its deployment, Heike used such classifications: "a modern infantry division; "...'complex'... a mighty military unit." See *English ed.*, p. 35.

27. Ren, *My Life's Mosaic*, p. 128.

28. Ivan Kedryn, "Ukrains'ka Dyviziia – Yak Viys'ko i Problema" [The Ukrainian Division – As an Army and Problem], *Visti*, 1983, No. 5-6, p. 50; Yaroslaw Semotiuk, *Ukrainian Military Medals* (Canada: Shevchenko Scientific Society, 1991), p. 1, cites: "This formation [the "Galicia" Division] had modern combat training;" and former Divisional soldier and Brody combat veteran Hryts' Lychakovs'kyi cited how for over one year prior to Brody "Ukrainian soldiers, the officers and grenadiers of the Division, underwent a systematic and very intensive period of training. With the newest arms and equipment, the Division achieved very high standards. And these standards were ensured by tough German [training] inspectors who, right up to the time of the Division's deployment, ensured high quality." According to Lychakov'skyi, "just alone in the months of January and February 1944, 40 officers and 400 soldiers were dismissed from the Division because they failed to meet the required standards, either physically or training wise." *Visti Kombatanta*, July, 1951, No. 7 (9), pp. 12-13. In a personal discussion with Yuriy Krokhmaliuk, the former Divisional staff officer himself emphasized that the Division was not only exceptionally well-trained, armed and equipped, but that throughout its training, officers, NCO's, and soldiers were occasionally dismissed and sent home as a result of poor performance.

29. Personal discussion with various former Divisional soldiers.

30. In Normandy, the Huertgen Forest, the Ardennes and other places, many Allied soldiers committed into combat were just civilians no more than three to six months before. Replacements perished so frequently that "oldtimers" used to gripe and say "Don't send us any replacements. We only bury them!" See Richard Holmes, *Firing Line* (London: Butler and Tanner, Ltd., 1985), pp. 36-37; and *World War II: A 50th Anniversary History* (N.Y.: Holt and Co., 1989), pp. 258-259.
Evhen Krause,* a Brody veteran who in the aftermath of World War II emigrated to the United States and in 1950 entered the United States Army and fought in Korea, acknowledged that in certain aspects, the training he received in the American Army surpassed that received in the German training system, especially with the emphasis on individualism. But overall, the training he received from the period of July 1943 to June 1944 within the German military system was more thorough.

31. On approximately 10 May 1944, the Division's staff was informed that Himmler would be making an appearance.

32. Stein, *The Waffen-SS*, p. 186; *Bender and Taylor*, Vol. 4, p. 31; Veryha, *Along the Roads,* p. 132; *Visti*, 1968, No. 5-6, p. 42; Rede des Reichsführers auf dem Appell des Führerkorps der Galizischen SS-Freiw.-Infanterie-Division in Neuhammer am 16. Mai 1944.

33. Stein, *The Waffen-SS*, p. 186; *Bender and Taylor*, Vol. 4, p. 32. For most of Himmler's speech on 16 May, see Yuriy Krokhmaliuk's "Taini Promovy Himmlera" [Himmler's Secret Speeches], *Visti*, 1982, No. 2, pp. 44-45.

34. Veryha, *Visti*, 1968, No. 5-6, p. 42.
In an article titled "The Brand of Criminals" (*News From the Ukraine*, 1986, May 20, No. 20, pp. 7-8), propagandist Olexander Vasylenko alleges that when Himmler addressed the Division's officer corps at Neuhammer on 14 May 1944, "he [Himmler] congratulated them on that the division's personnel had considerably rid the Ukraine of Jews."
Beside the fact that Vasylenko cited a wrong date, and was incorrect in his observation when he asserted that Himmler addressed the officer corps because the brunt of the Division's officer corps (German and Ukrainian) was not at Himmler's address, it must be brought to Vasylenko's attention that Himmler's words were recorded. An

Galicia Division

examination of his speech reveals that the Reichsführer made no references to any exterminations, nor did Himmler "congratulate" anyone for "ridding" any specific nationality or group of people.

To begin with, Himmler could never have made such a remark because until his arrival to Neuhammer in mid-May 1944, excluding Kampfgruppe "Beyersdorff's" limited deployment to what was then Northeastern Poland, Himmler was fully aware that the Division was strictly training and had never operated in Ukraine. This is evidenced by a series of training organizational orders issued by none other than Himmler himself.

As for Vasylenko's remarks about what Himmler said in Neuhammer, Styrkul (another Soviet propagandist) offers a totally different version. Styrkul writes: "In his [Himmler's] address to the command personnel, Himmler praised the Division's willing participation in slaughtering the Polish population. But the address was not free of reproach: for it was on our own initiative (said Himmler) that the Jews in Galicia had been wiped out. Too bad! The residents of Galicia, now in the SS, should have shown more initiative in these undertakings even before, let alone after, they joined the ranks." (Styrkul, *We Accuse*, Kiev: Dnipro Publishers, 1984), p. 206.

So whereas Vasylenko cites how Himmler congratulated the Division's personnel for "considerably ridding the Ukraine of Jews," Styrkul cites how Himmler "praised" the Division's willing participation in slaughtering the Polish population but then scolded the Division's personnel for lacking "initiative" in slaughtering Jews before and after joining the Division.

Clearly, between Vasylenko and Styrkul, two major contradictions exist. But Styrkul's remark that "Himmler praised the Division's participation in slaughtering the Polish population" is, as Vasylenko's remark, totally false. While Himmler did state that if he ever released the Division, the Galician volunteers would probably slaughter the Poles, his remark was refuted by Paliiv, one of the few Ukrainian officers at the reception and one proficient in German. Reminding Himmler that Galicia's volunteers did not join the Division to slaughter Poles, Paliiv simultaneously chastised the Nazi policy of instigating Poles and Ukrainians against one another.

For historical clarity, at no time during Himmler's address did the Reichsführer ever praise, or chastise, the Division for either "slaughtering" or "lacking an initiative" to slaughter Poles, Jews, or anyone else.

35. *Visti*, 1968, No. 5-6, pp.'s 42-43. See also Veryha's, "Nasha Voenna Memuarystyka" [Our Military Memoirs], *Visti*, 1984, No. 3, p. 81. Personal discussion with Yuriy Krokhmaliuk. Krokhmaliuk, who was not present at the speech, stated that he learned of Paliiv's rebuttal later that same day.

36. *Visti*, 1968, No. 5-6, p. 43. Krokhmaliuk, who did not witness the above incident, could not recall the name of the officer who congratulated Paliiv.

37. On 5 April 1944, strictly for reasons of tactical simplicity, Army Group 'South' was redesignated into two Army Groups: Army Group 'North Ukraine' and Army Group 'South Ukraine.'

38. One such maneuver involved a counterattack against a fictitious Soviet army – the 15th Mechanized Army. With a fictional 57th Infantry Division on its right flank and the 2nd Tank Division on its left flank, the "Galicia" Division was to halt and repulse a communist advance against the city of Strans. In the ensuing counterattack, in which the entire Division participated, the Soviet thrust was repulsed. Liubomyr Ortyns'kyi, "Polkovi Vpravy" [Regimental Maneuvers], *Visti Kombatanta*, 1951, June, No. 6 (8).

39. Do Viis'kovoi Upravy Halychyna. Viddil Naboru i Dopovnennia u L'vovi. Ch: 39/44. L'viv, dnia 17, travnia 1944. Sprava: Dobrovol'tsia Shupianoho Myhaila. [To the Galician Military Board's Recruitment and Replacement Section. Reference: Volunteer Shupian, Myhailo. No. 39/44, Lviv, 17 May 1944]. (Signature illegible).

According to Roman Hayetskyj, prior to the 1941 Nazi-Soviet War, Shupian had become a strong OUN sympathizer. Hayetskyj was unsure to what extent, if any, Shupian was involved with the OUN, but it was rumored that Shupian was a possible OUN informant and/or courier to the UPA.

40. Heike personally learned of this operation from Gunther D'Alquen, the editor of an SS newspaper entitled 'Das Schwarze Korps' (The Black Corps). In 1944, Himmler also appointed D'Alquen to run the Wehrmacht's propaganda campaign. For additional information on D'Alquen and his role in the Nazi hierarchy see Robert Wistrich's, *Who's Who In Nazi Germany* (N.Y.: Bonanza Books, 1982), pp. 42-43.

41. Heike, *English ed.*, p. 28. According to Yuriy Krokhmaliuk, members of the Division, including Krokhmaliuk, were sometimes involved in anti-Soviet broadcasts. In a humorous manner, Krokhmaliuk recalled how once, in Austria in 1945, as he began to broadcast with a bull-horn, he immediately heard from the other side this reply: "Good morning, Mr. Krokhmaliuk. Listen, we've heard it all before. So either you come up with something new, or just forget it!" Krokhmaliuk never did state which course of action he took.

42. Heike, *English ed.*, p. 28.

43. *Ibid.*

44. *Ibid.* Heike, unfortunately, did not elaborate on what areas were discussed but undoubtedly, these topics were covered: the Division's strengths and weaknesses; its combat capability; deployment problems; UPA's effect on the Division; possible desertions; and the positive and negative consequences of the Divisions return to Galicia.

Notes

45. Heike, *English ed.*, p. 36.

46. *Ibid.* Although Heike makes no reference to the 'Prinz Eugen' system, Heike cites the Division would "entrench in the second line in the Brody district." (P. 37). This second line encompassed the 'Prinz Eugen' system.

47. Verordnungsblatt der Waffen-SS, 5. Jahrgang Berlin, 15.8.44, Nr. 16, Z. 476; Yuriy Krokhmaliuk, *Visti*, 1977, No. 5-6, p. 51; *Bender and Taylor*, Vol. 4, pp. 8-9; 32-33.

48. *Visti*, 1977, No. 5-6, p. 51; *Bender and Taylor*, Vol. 4, pp. 8-9.

49. Heike, *English ed.*, p. 36; Oleh Lysiak, ed., *Brody – Zbirnyk Stattei i Narysiv* [Brody: A Collection of Stories and Essays] (Munich: Published by the Brotherhood of Soldiers of the 1st Division of the Ukrainian National Army, 1951), p. 65; Veryha, *Along the Roads*, cites "by the end of June 1944, the Division completed its training and was deployed to the eastern front." (P. 186). In a personal discussion with Krokhmaliuk, the former staff officer recalled "excluding Freitag and a few others who left shortly before, the Division began to move eastward on 28 June, and continued to do so for nearly a week afterwards." According to *Ready*, p. 369, the Division received its combat orders on 28 June 1944. Reports of the Division being on the Pidhirtsi-Zolotschiv road on 13 June 1944 are incorrect.

50. At no time did the "Galicia" Division, or any of its members, ever serve in Normandy, or France, in the summer of 1944 against the western Allies as alleged by Dimitri Simes in "The Destruction of Liberty" in *Christian Science Monitor*, 13 February 1985.

51. Der Hohere SS und Polizeiführer im Generalgouvernment, Befehlahaber der Ordnungspolizei. Akt. Z.: Abt. IIIb (1) 2795 d – Tgb. Nr. 1441/44 (g.). Betr.: Obernahme des Schutzmannschafts-Batl. 204 in die Galizische SS-Freiwilligen-Division. Krakau, den 22 Jan. 1944. (Signed Himmler). A copy of this order was also dispatched to Berlin. According to Roman Kolisnyk, the possibility exists that the actual transfer was delayed by Cracow's Higher Police Leader. According to V. Tatars'kyi, the 204th Schutzmannschaft Battalion was transferred to the Division "Galicia" in mid-1944. See *Pid Chotyrma Praporamy* [Under Four Flags], (Munich: Buchdruckerei u. Verlag, 1983), p. 148. As for the battalion's officers and non-commissioned officers, of whom the majority were German, Tatars'kyi cites that they were transferred to the 205th Schutzmannschaft Battalion. (Ibid). For additional information on the 204th Battalion, as well as the difficulties its Ukrainian personnel experienced with German cadre personnel, see pp. 133-148.

52. According to Tatars'kyi, the 204th was actually formed in Heidelager. (*Pid Chotyrma Praporamy*, p. 133).

53. Reports of men (or members of their families) bribing both German and Ukrainian officials to avoid military service are true. To cite an example: shortly before Easter in 1944, a woman appeared in an examination center. Her intent was to remove her son who, the day before, was examined and found medically fit for military service and was still on the premises awaiting to be shipped out to Neuhammer. Seeing her pleas were falling on deaf ears, the woman returned shortly afterwards with a young and healthy pig. Informing the doctor that "Easter is approaching and a meat shortage is in existence," the doctor got the hint. Picking up the telephone, he called for the volunteer to be sent back for "re-examination." Informing the woman to leave the pig and return home, the doctor "re-examined" the young man, stamped his papers as "unqualified for military service" and sent the crying volunteer back to his mother. Perhaps the matter would have remained hushed-up, but in the ensuing days, the woman went around the county bragging about her success and encouraging others to do likewise. (Personal discussion with Roman Hayetskyj).

54. Unknown to Khronoviat, the 8,000 at Wandern were in the process of being sent to Neuhammer.

55. Needless to say, Khronoviat's job was not an easy one, and under no condition could Khronoviat be faulted for the very large numbers of men who earlier had enlisted in grand ceremonies, inflated the figures to 80,000, but later sought every imaginable excuse to avoid army service.
As late as 29 June 1944, Khronoviat received letters regarding recruitment difficulties. One such letter, addressed to Lviv's Military Board by Artymovych, an engineer by profession who assisted the Military Boards recruitment in Peremysl, warned and urged the Lviv Military Board to immediately take action on a number of individuals (some mentioned by name) who succeeded to avoid military service; otherwise, wrote Artymovych, "a negative influence will be reflected upon the other graduates and doctors who are to appear." Artymovych also wrote "that a number of men, upon failing to obtain deferments within their own districts, travelled to Lviv to obtain deferments." And such activities, warned Artymovych, "strongly demoralizes further recruiting actions." Viskova Uprava Halychyna Okruzhnyi Povnovlasnyk Peremysl, No. 301/1944 r. Peremysl, 29.6.1944 r. Do Viis'kovoi Upravy "Halychyna." [Military Board "Galicia" in Peremysl's Recruitment Region, No. 301/1944. Peremysl 29.6.1944. To: The Military Board "Galicia" in Lviv]. Signed Artymovych.

56. Aktenvermerk fur Herrn. Oberst A. Bisanz. Leiter des Wehrausschusses – Galizien. Lemberg, den 30. Juni 1944 [Document Note from the Military Board Galicia for Colonel Alfred Bisanz. Lemberg. 30 June 1944].

57. Volodymyr Motyka, "Starshyns'kyi Vyshkil v. Posen-Treskau lypen'-hruden' 1944" [Officer Training in Posen-Treskau in July-December 1944], *Visti*, 1992, No. 4, p. 93.

58. *Ibid.*

59. Motyka cites the date of this promotion as 1 August 1944.

60. *Ibid.*, p. 94. Motyka cites 1 October 1944 as the mid-point of the course.

Notes Chapter 15: (The following are separated by sub-chapter sections).

The Eastern Front: January 1943 – July 1944.
1. Ziemke, *From Stalingrad to Berlin*, p. 277; Cooper, *The German Army*, p. 473.

2. *Ibid.*

3. Sergei M. Shtemenko, *The Soviet General Staff At War, 1941-1945* (Moscow: Progress Publishers, 1981), Book II, p. 48.

4. For excellent accounts and maps of 1943-44 combat on the eastern front, see Brigadier General Peter Young, ed., *Atlas Of the Second World War* (London: Widenfeld and Nicolson, 1973); Ziemke's, *From Stalingrad to Berlin*; Chant's, *Hitler's General's and Their Battles; Russian Combat Methods of World War II; Marshall Zhukov: An Outstanding Military Leader* (Moscow: Planeta Publishers, 1987); and Alex Buchner's, *Ostfront: The German Defensive Battles on the Russian Front 1944: Cherkasy, Ternopol, Crimea, Vitebsk, Brody, Bobruisk, Kischinev, Jassy* (Pa.: Schiffer Publishing Co., 1991).

The Soviet Army
1. According to James Lucas, "The Red Army of Workers and Peasants" in *War On the Eastern Front, 1941-1945. The German Soldiers in Russia* (N.Y.: Bonanza Books, 1979), p. 49, the strength of Soviet infantry divisions rose from 175 in June 1941 to 513 in 1943. Unlike the German divisions, these divisions were raised in near or full strength.

2. Ziemke, *From Stalingrad to Berlin*, p. 144. This was actually a gain of about 1.5 million men since September 1942.

3. Ziemke, *From Stalingrad to Berlin*, p. 214. Simultaneously, from the period of July to October 1943, Nazi Germany lost nearly 1,000,000 men. Of this strength, fewer than half were replaced. Seaton, *The Fall of Fortress Europe*, p. 61.

4. Ziemke, *From Stalingrad to Berlin*, p. 214. See also *Istoriia Velikoi Otechestvennoi Voine Sovetskogo Soiuza 1941-1945* (Moscow: 1960-1963), Vol. 4, p. 20.

5. Simultaneously, with the withdrawal of the Italian, Hungarian, Rumanian, Bulgarian, Finnish, Spanish and other nationalities, Germany's manpower strength would plummet further. See also Ziemke, *From Stalingrad to Berlin*, pp. 213-217.

6. Ziemke, *From Stalingrad to Berlin*, p. 146.

7. John Campbell, ed., *The Experience of World War II* (N.Y.: Oxford University Press, 1989), p. 158.

8. *Ibid.*, p. 159. See also pp. 160-162. Certain small arms weapons systems, such as the Ppsh submachine guns, were not only improved upon but no less than 5 million were produced during the war. See also Duncan Crow, ed., *Armored Fighting Vehicles of Germany* (N.Y.: Arco Publishing Co., 1978), p. 2. In addition to quantity, the Soviet's began to produce arms, tanks and equipment which quality wise, surpassed that produced by Nazi Germany. See Ziemke, *From Stalingrad to Berlin*, p. 501; Lucas, *War On the Eastern Front*, p. 47; and B.H. Lidell Hart, *History of the Second World War* (N.Y.: Putnam's Sons, 1970), p. 486.

9. Ziemke, *From Stalingrad to Berlin*, p. 501.

10. *Ibid.*; Hart, p. 486. See also F.W. von Mellenthin's *Panzer Battles* (University of Oklahoma Press, 1955), p. 278. Von Mellenthin was a former eastern front Wehrmacht general.

11. A tank corps comprised a strength of approximately 189 to 200 tanks with a personnel strength of 10,500; a mechanized corps maintained a strength of around 189 tanks but its personnel strength (primarily mechanized infantry), stood at 16,000. See B.H. Lidell Hart's, *The Red Army: 1918-1945; the Soviet Army* (N.Y.: Harcourt, Brace and Co., 1956), pp. 314-315; and Colonel Richard N. Armstrong's "Battlefield Agility: the Soviet Legacy" in *The Journal of Soviet Military Studies*, No. 4, December 1988, p. 506. Hereafter referred to as *SMS* with appropriate year, number, and page.

Notes

12. Major General Ivan Krupchenko, "Tanks In the Offense" in *Soviet Military Review* (Moscow: Krasnaya Zvezda Publishing House). September (No. 9), 1971, pp. 40-43; and Colonel N. Kobrin, "A Tank Army in the Offensive," in *Soviet Military Review*, January (No. 1), 1976, pp. 47-49. Hereafter referred to as *SMR* with appropriate year, number, and page.

13. Although the problem was already identified in 1941, Field-Marshal Guenther von Kluge once again raised the issue in 1943 and 1944 that, in addition to dwindling divisional strengths, troop qualities also depreciated. See also Ziemke, *From Stalingrad to Berlin*, pp. 215-216.

14. Hart, *History of the Second World War*, p. 487.

The First Ukrainian Front
1. Lev Shankowsky, "Biy Pid Brodamy v Nasvitlenni Sovets'kykh Dzerel." [Battle At Brody In Current Soviet Sources], *Visti*, 1963, No. 1, p. 9; Kazimierz Sobczak, Przewodniczacy, *Encyklopedia II wojny swiatowej* (Warszawa: Wydawnictwo Ministerstwa Obrony Narodowej, 1975). p. 234.

2. *Ukrains'ka RSR u Velykii Vitchyznianii Viini Radians'koho Soiuzu, 1941-1945 rr*, Vol. 2, p. 492. See also Map No. 10 between pp. 344-345; General Sergei M. Shtemenko, *The Soviet General Staff At War* (Moscow: Progress Publishers, 1985), Book 1, p. 255; *Marshal Zhukov*, p. 151.

3. Shtemenko, *The Soviet General Staff at War*, Book 1, p. 299; Colonel-General David Dragunsky, *Pages From the Story of My Life: A Soldier's Memoirs* (Moscow: Progress Publishers, 1983), pp. 175-176; Colonel A. Zvenzlovsky, "The Lvov-Sandomir Operation," *SMR*, August, No. 8, 1974, p. 50; Erickson, *The Road to Berlin*, p. 231; Colonel M. Polushkin, "L'vovsko-Sandomirskaia nastupatel'naia operatsiia 1-go Ukrains'kogo fronta v tsifrakh (13. 7-29. 8. 1944 g.)" in *Voenno-Isstoricheskii Zhurnal* [Military Historical Journal] (Moscow: 1969), No. 8, p. 54; Marshal Konstantin Rokossovsky, "Operation Bagration," in *Battle's Hitler Lost and the Soviet Marshalls Who Won Them* (N.Y.: Jove Books, 1988), p. 129. For an entire review of "Operation Bagration" see Chapter 8, pp. 127-140; I.S. Konev, *Zapiski komanduiushchego frontom 1943-1945* [Memoirs of a Front Commander, 1943-1945] (Kiev: Izdatel'stvo politicheskoi literatur'i Ukrain'i, 1987), p. 244. For a fairly detailed analysis and viewpoint of the Lvov-Sandomir Operation by Konev, see "L'vovsko-Sandomirskaia Operatsiia," pp. 236-304, in *Zapiski komanduiushchego frontom 1943-1945*.

Army Group North Ukraine
1. Ziemke, *Stalingrad to Berlin*, p. 286. The conversion, however, began on 30 March 1944. But on 5 April, Hitler officially renamed Army Group's 'South' and 'A' into Army Group's 'North' and 'South' Ukraine. In all, AGNU's front stretched for a distance of 219 miles.

2. Organized during the winter of 1943-44, the Hungarian 1st Army appeared in the spring of 1944 on the Galician front. Despite some very good soldiers and a relatively solid Hungarian cadre with eastern front experience, a lack of arms, equipment and transport, as well as an inability for both Hungary and Nazi Germany to provide that army its essential needs, prevented the Hungarian 1st from developing into a formidable force. Increasing dissatisfaction with Nazi Germany, along with Hungary's uncertain future political situation, also took its toll.
In a desperate effort to prop up the Hungarians, AGNU placed the Hungarian 1st under its own operational and tactical control, and dispatched a number of German liaison officers to influence military operations and ensure tighter supervision and control of the Hungarians. Of course, such a move offended the Hungarians, provoked opposition, and further deteriorated a relationship which, realistically speaking, was never strong from the beginning. (See Burkhart Mueller-Hillebrand, *Germany and Its Allies in World War II: A Record of Axis Collaboration Problems* (MD: University Publications of America, 1980), pp. 214- 219). Destined to reinforce the Galician front, in the very end the Hungarian 1st Army not only failed to bolster AGNU's defense but in actuality, drained some of AGNU's desperately needed manpower and materiel.

3. Ziemke, *From Stalingrad to Berlin*, p. 319. However, on the eve of Konev's offensive, this strength would drop as will be seen.

4. Throughout 1943 and 1944, General Guderian complained that many of the newly created divisions were not only understrength and below par of those raised previously, but the formations consumed excessive amounts of transportation and logistical support. Ashley Brown, *Modern Warfare, From 1939 to the Present Day* (N.Y.: Crescent Books, 1986), p. 91.

5. Alexander McKee, *Last Round Against Rommel: Battle of the Normandy Beachhead* (N.Y.: Signet Books, 1966), pp. 162-163; Gordon A. Harrison, *Cross-Channel Attack, the United States Army In World War II, the European Theater of Operations* (Washington, D.C.: Center of Military History, U.S. Army, 1951), p. 411; Heike, "Biy Pid Brodamy" in *Brody: Zbirnyk Stattei i Nanyciv*, ed. Lyciak, p. 135; *World War II Encyclopedia*, Vol. 12, p. 1554; and "Zone Defense Tactics" in *Military Improvisations During the Russian Campaign*, p. 35.

6. Stalin constantly emphasized the fact that Silesia was "Gold!" Ivan Konev, *Year of Victory* (Moscow: Progress Publishers, 1969), p. 5. See also David Dragunsky's, *A Soldier's Memoirs*, pp. 175-176. According to Lt. General Ivan

Galicia Division

I. Dremov, a former eastern front commander, the Soviets considered it critical to liberate the remainder of Ukraine, enter the Carpathian region, force the Vistula River, and bring the war into Poland proper. (I.F. Dremov, *Nastupala Groznaia Bronia* [The Formidable Strength Advanced] (Kiev: Izdatel'stvo Politicheskoi Literatur'i Ukrain'i, 1981), p. 90.

7. According to Colonel Andrei Sidorenko, Germany's forces, following their defeat at Stalingrad, changed over to a deeper positional defense. The main defense line, established about 5 to 6 miles (8-10 km's) from the forward edge, was about 2.5 to 3.5 miles (4-6 km's) in depth and the second 1.5 to 2 miles (2-3 km's) in depth. These two lines usually made up the so-called tactical defense zone. Up to 80 percent of the defender's strength was concentrated within the lines. See "Development of the Tactics of Offensive Battle From Experiences of the Great Patriotic War," *SMR*, October No. 10, 1979, p. 20. For a German analysis of how Galicia's terrain, especially how the Dniester and Buh Rivers were incorporated into the defense, see "European Russia: A Natural Fortress" in *Terrain Factors In the Russian Campaign*, pp. 4-5.

8. Dupuy, *Encyclopedia Of Military History, p. 1115; Ziemke, From Stalingrad to Berlin*, p. 286; Seaton, *The Fall of Fortress Europe*, p. 99; *World War II Encyclopedia*, Vol. 10, pp. 1344-1345. 2 April 1944 is the date cited that Model assumed command of AGNU. (P. 1345).

9. Von Mellenthin, *Panzer Battles*, p. 281. Mellenthin's observation was substantiated by General Balck, who commanded the 48th Panzer Corps found within AGNU. See *World War II Encyclopedia*, Vol. 10, p. 1345.

10. *Mellenthin*, p. 283.

11. *Ibid.*, pp. 283-285. For an analysis of what type of commander Model was during this period of time, see Seaton's, *The Fall of Fortress Europe*, pp. 137-138.

12. Operation "Bagration" was divided into two phases. The first phase was to be launched in Byelorussia on 22 June 1944, and the second phase was to be launched in the Western Ukraine in mid-July. As for the code-word "Bagration," it was named in honor of Prince Peter Bagration, an Imperial Russian Army officer who fought Napoleon's armies in 1812. Of interest to note is that despite a massive amount of planning, no one came up with a code-name. Even when on 20 May 1944 Lieutenant-General Alexei I. Antonov, Chief of the Operations Department and Deputy Chief of the General Staff, placed his signature indicating approval of the plan submitted to him several days earlier, he some how failed to note that a code-name was missing. Shortly afterward, Stalin was briefed on the Byelorussian aspect of the plan. At the conclusion of the briefing, Stalin stated that a code-name had not been mentioned and he asked the assembled commanders and briefers for its name. At this time, everyone just stared at one another. Sensing that none had been provided, Stalin suggested "Bagration." Embarrassed into silence, Stalin's assembled officers immediately accepted the name.

13. Erickson, *The Road to Berlin*, p. 231; Shankowsky, "Battle At Brody In Current Soviet Sources," *Visti*, 1963, No. 1, pp. 10-11. One of the reasons why the operation was launched in Byelorussia was to divert forces from the Western Ukraine and Galicia northwards. According to Ziemke, *From Stalingrad to Berlin*, p. 330, AGNU immediately lost three panzer and two infantry divisions as a result of the Soviet offensive in Byelorussia. According to *World War II*, AGNU was ordered to deploy to Army Group Center four panzer and three infantry divisions. (Vol. 12, p. 1659). Undoubtedly, such an order was issued but regardless, it is known that in addition to the three panzer divisions immediately dispatched, another panzer division, the 5th SS "Wiking" Division, was also transferred to the Byelorussian front. In the end, AGNU dispatched a total of seven divisions (four panzer/three infantry) to Army Group Center.
Needless to say, the transfer of these divisions (but especially the four panzer divisions) would seriously weaken AGNU in its effort to halt the 1st Ukrainian Fronts upcoming offensive. See also Seaton, *The Fall of Fortress Europe*, p. 135.

14. Marshal Konstantin Rokossovsky, "Operation Bagration," in *Battles Hitler Lost*, p. 137; personal discussion with Yuriy Krokhmaliuk.

15. Colonel B. Panov, "Lvov-Sandomir Operation" in *Selected Readings In Military History: Soviet Military History, Volume I: The Red Army, 1918-1945.* (Fort Leavenworth, Kansas: U.S. Army Command and General Staff College, 1984), p. 374.

16. Erickson, *The Road to Berlin*, p. 231.

17. Ziemke, *From Stalingrad To Berlin*, p. 506.

18. *Cooper*, pp. 485-490. Perhaps this explains why in 1944, Hitler was known to utter: "I need more divisions!" (Ibid., p. 485). See also Liddell Hart's, *History of the Second World War*, pp. 485-486.
A report submitted in January 1944 to various members of the German high command revealed that from the period of June 1941 to December 1943, German casualties totaled 3,513,000 on the Eastern Front. Personelle blutige Verluste vom 22. Juni 1941 bis 31 December 1943, 4 Jan 44 OHH/Generalquartiermeister, der Heeresarzt, OKH/Org.

Notes

Abt., Arzt Meldungen, Monatsmeldungen ab 1.VII.43. Cited from Gordon A. Harrison, *Cross-Channel Attack*, p. 142.

19. Ziemke, *From Stalingrad to Berlin*, p. 506. According to Mitcham, *Hitler's Legions*, by 1943, each panzer division was authorized a strength of approximately 165 tanks. (P. 21). But in actuality, none of the panzer divisions on the eastern front at that time had so many. (*Ibid*). According to Cooper, 1944 was a dismal year for Nazi Germany's panzer force. Despite the increase in tank production, unit strengths continued to decline. An armored division was fortunate if it possessed over sixty tanks. (See *The German Army*, pp. 487-488). According to Walter Kerr, because of severe losses, in the spring of 1942, Nazi Germany was forced to reorganize its panzer force. Now, a typical German panzer division's armored strength was reduced to the point where it was authorized only one regiment of 130-150 tanks. See *The Secret of Stalingrad* (N.Y.: Doubleday & Company, Inc., 1978), p. 53. And Harrison, *Cross-Channel Attack*, cites that an OKH order of Battle in December 1943 identified ten panzer divisions on the Russian front as being of negligible combat value. (See p. 143).

20. W. Victor Madej, *Russo-German War: Summer 1944 (Destruction of the Eastern Front)* (PA: Valor Publishing Co., 1987), p. 62.

21. Ziemke, *From Stalingrad to Berlin*, p. 319, acknowledges that prior to 22 June 1944, AGNU had a total of eight panzer divisions. However, on p. 330, Ziemke concedes that AGNU lost (as a result of the Soviet offensive in Byelorussia) three of its panzer divisions. (Ibid). AGNU's charts of 8-15 July 1944 reveal a total of five panzer divisions. (1st Panzer, 8th Panzer, 16th Panzer, 17th Panzer, and the 5th SS "Wiking" Panzer). However, the charts reveal that the 5th SS "Wiking" Division, posted in the 4th Panzer Army's Rear Reserve, was departing. (See also Madej, *Russo-German War: Summer 1944*, p. 62). At the time the 1st Ukrainian Front Struck on 13 July, the brunt (if not the entire) 5th SS "Wiking" Panzer Division had departed. In actuality, the independent 509th Tiger Tank Battalion, on the eve of Konev's offensive, AGNU's panzer strength had dwindled to four panzer divisions. (1st Panzer, 8th Panzer, 16 Panzer, and 17th Panzer). Various accounts and sources, as well as AGNU's charts for the periods of 8-15 July 1944, substantiate this. (See also Seaton's *The Fall of Fortress Europe, 1943-1945*, p. 138. According to Seaton, AGNU's strength had fallen to a strength of twelve Hungarian brigades and 31 German Divisions of which four were panzer). But in addition to this, as verified by a host of former German commanders and eastern front veterans and postwar historians (see Buchner's "Brody: XIII Army Corps. An End in the Pocket," in *Ostfront: 1944*, p. 223), all of AGNU's four panzer divisions were operating on unauthorized strengths.

22. Madej, *Russo-German War: Summer 1944*, p. 62. The "+" symbol indicated that reinforcements were on the way, or that a full accounting was not yet completed. Regardless of the true number, the 17th Panzer Divisions tank strength was considerably short of its authorization. According to Major Heike, a former Divisional staff operations officer, the 4th Panzer Army possessed no more than 40-50 tanks, and it was a "panzer" army only in name. Wolf-Dietrich Heike, "Biy Pid Brodamy" in *Brody: Zbinyk Stattei i Naryciv*, ed. Oleh Lysiak, p. 135. According to Stasiv, "Tragedy at Brody", *Visti*, 1992, No. 3, p. 53, "... when it came to armor, the Germans altogether had few tanks."

23. Madej, *Russo-German War: Summer 1944*, p. 62.

24. *Ibid.* For a breakdown of the various divisions and units found within AGNU's armies in June-July 1944, see pp. 62-63.
   As for its personnel strength, a German "Kraftegegenuberstellung" and "Front und frontnah" chart of June 1944 reveals that AGNU possessed a troop strength of 437,000, with an additional 196,000 in reserve. The reservists (supposedly) were posted near the front. This figure was also substantiated in a personal letter to the author by Colonel David M. Glantz. (*Letter of 17 March 1992*).
   However, it must be remembered that prior to the 1st Ukrainian fronts offensive in July 1944, no less than seven entire German divisions (as well as various specialists and military personnel from other units and AGNU's depots) were dispatched to Army Group Center to assist that group in reestablishing a front line. Although it appears that no figures are available as to the number of soldiers departing AGNU, if one takes into consideration that the average strength of a German division was between 8,000 to 10,000 soldiers, with the departure of no less than seven divisions, it may be safely assumed that a strength of no less than 60,000 to possibly as many as 70,000 soldiers were dispatched from AGNU. With their departure few, if any, were immediately replaced. Needless to say, in the upcoming battle, many a commander regretted that AGNU had lost such a critically needed combat strength.

25. In order for the German High Command to maintain a better understanding and working knowledge of the strengths and capabilities of its divisions, a numerical system was developed and utilized. Beside each divisions number and/or name, a number was inserted. "1" indicated the best: the division was capable of offensive and defensive missions; "2" indicated a limited attack capability; "3" showed only full defensive capabilities; and "4" indicated a limited defensive ability. A "?" adjacent a division showed that its capabilities were unknown.

Konev's Plan

1. Konev's right hand was the gifted General Sokolovskiy. According to contemporary Soviet writers, it was Sokolovskiy who conceived and developed the July 1944 Lviv-Sandomir Operation. A gifted tactician, Sokolovskiy characterized the operation by high mobility, aviation, and deep penetration. See Colonel A. Orlov's "Marshall Vasily Danilovych Sokolovskiy, 80th Birth Anniversary" in *SMR*, July No. 7, 1977, p. 43.

Galicia Division

2. P. N. Lashchenko, *Iz Boia v Boi* [From Battle to Battle] (Moscow: Voennoe Izdatel'stvo Ministerstva Oboron'i SSSR, 1972), pp. 278-279; Erickson, *The Road to Berlin*, p. 231; Colonel Armstrong, "Battlefield Agility" in *SMS*, December, 1988, p. 508; B. H. Liddell Hart, *History of the Second World War*, p. 581; and Konev, *Zapiski komanduiushchego frontom 1943-1945*, p. 245. For Konev's analysis and viewpoints of the Lviv-Sandomir Operation, along with his role in the operation, see "L'vovsko-Sandomirskaia operatsiia" pp. 236-304.

3. Until the very end, Stalin leaned in favor of Zhukov's original proposal of one massive shattering strike towards Lviv. To resolve the matter once and for all Stalin, on 22 June 1944, ordered Konev to appear personally in Moscow with his operations officer. Although the two-pronged thrust had not yet been finalized, on 8 July, Konev and Sokolovskiy briefed Stalin, Zhukov, and several members of STAVKA and the Politburo. (See Ian Grey, *Stalin: Man of History* (N.Y.: Doubleday and Company, 1979), p. 397). Stalin, who was in a neurotic state when briefed, only paced up and down; continuously, he proposed and defended Zhukov's proposal. Eventually, Stalin relented. But Stalin warned Konev that he (Konev) was personally responsible for it and that the operation would be conducted without any mishaps. (Konev, *Zapiski komanduiushchego frontom 1943-1945*, p. 249); and Erickson, *The Road to Berlin*, p. 231.

4. Indeed, Konev's forces were so massively reinforced that Zhukov actually proposed to Stalin to shift some of the 1st Ukrainian Front's strength northward to the other fronts. But Stalin totally refused. Insisting on the importance of overrunning Galicia and penetrating into Eastern Europe proper, Stalin maintained Konev's strength. (Grey, *Stalin*, p. 397. See also *Marshal of the Soviet Union, Zhukov: Reminiscences and Reflections* (Moscow: Progress Publishers, 1985), Vol. 2, p. 284).

5. Colonel Andrei Zvenzlovsky, "The Lvov-Sandomir Operation," *SMR*, August No. 8, 1974, p. 51. According to Colonel N. Svetlishin, the 1st Ukrainian Front, which Konev commanded from May 1944 until the conclusion of the war, contained 10-12 armies with a troop strength of 1,000,000 to 1,200,000; 15,000-17,000 guns and heavy motors; 2,500-3,300 aircraft and 2,200-3,500 tanks. Colonel Svetlishin, "[Konev] Commander of Unbending Will" in *SMR*, December, No. 12 (36), 1967, p. 49.

6. Portuhal'skii, *Marshal I.S. Konev*, (Moscow: Voennoe Izdatel'stvo, 1985) p. 135. According to V.E. B'istrov, *Velikaia Otechestvennaia Voina 1941-1945* [The Great Patriotic War 1941-1945] (Moscow: Izdatel'stvo Politicheskoi Literatur'i, 1970], p. 304, "1st Ukrainian Front was significantly strengthened. It contained 1,200,000 men, 13,900 artillery and mortars, 2,200 tanks and self-propelled guns, and over 2,800 aircraft.

7. *Portugal'skii*, p. 135; Gregory Zhukov, *Marshal of the Soviet Union*, Vol. 2, p. 284. According to *World War II*, Konev had 16,213 artillery pieces and rocket launchers, 1,573 tanks, 463 assault guns, and 3,240 aircraft. As well, Konev's front possessed some of the most experienced tank commanders. (See Vol. 12, p. 1659).

8. Colonel Albert Seaton, *The Russo-German War Encyclopedia, 1941-1945* (London: Prescott C. Tinling and Co., Ltd., 1971), p. 446; and *The Fall of Fortress Europe 1943-1945*, p. 138. According to Zhukov, the 1st Ukrainian Front's strength comprised 80 rifle (infantry) divisions, 10 armored and mechanized corps. 4 separate armored and self-propelled gun brigades and 3,250 aircraft. Zhukov, *Marshall of the Soviet Union*, Vol. 2, p. 284.

9. Lt. Colonel Myhailo Lishchyns'kyi, "Nastup Sovets'koi Armii i Boi Pid Brodamy" [The Soviet Army Advance and the Battle at Brody], in *Surmach* (England: 1968), No. 1-4 (38- 41), pp. 22-23. (While serving in the Division, Lishchyns'kyi held the rank of Waffen-Obersturmführer. Shortly after World War II, he was promoted to the rank of Pid Polkovnyk (Lt. Colonel) by the Ukrainian Government-in-Exile).

10. Panov, *Lvov-Sandomir Operation*, p. 377. According to "Partisan Combat Methods" in *Russian Combat Methods in World War II*, "prior to large-scale Russian offensives, strong bands would often migrate to areas that the Red Army soon hoped to take. Prior to the beginning of the large-scale Red Army offensive in East Galicia in July 1944, for example, numerous bands worked their way into the Carpathian Mountains southwest of Lwow, which were among the objectives of the Soviet operations." (Chapter 16, p. 103)). "The bands were generally organized into groupments of from 3,000 to 5,000 men each. Smaller groups, varying greatly in strength, comprised at least 100 men. Attached to each groupment was a number of these smaller partisan groups." (*Ibid.*, p. 104). It is important to note that women fighters also served in these bands.

11. *Velikaia Otechestvennaia Voina 1941-1945 v Fotografiiakh i Kinodokumentakh, 1944* [The Great Patriotic War 1944-1945 in Photos and Cinema, 1944] (Moscow: Planeta, 1979), p. 361.

12. Panov, *Lvov-Sandomir Operation*, p. 377.

13. Predecessors of the Soviet Guards was the Red Guard. According to Soviet historians, in the Russian Civil War of 1918-22, the Red Guard displayed constant selfless heroism. During the Battle of Smolensk in August and September 1941, certain Soviet units also exhibited constant selfless heroism. As a result, on 18 September 1941, four Soviet rifle divisions were retitled as "Guard." Others followed. On 21 May 1942, a Guards Badge was instituted and Guards military ranks were introduced. See Lt. Colonel Victor Mikhailov's, "The Soviet Guards" in *SMR*, September, No. 9, 1981, pp. 37-38; *Shtemenko*, Book 1, p. 451.

Notes

14. Only the most gifted, daring, and mission minded generals were chosen to command tank armies. General Pavlo Semenovych Rybalko was one such commander. Following World War II, Rybalko was appointed Chief Commander of the Soviet tank forces. Until his sudden death on 28 August 1948, he played an instrumental role in the development of Soviet armor and armored warfare. For an excellent study of Soviet Russia's top six tank commanders (to include Rybalko), see Colonel Richard N. Armstrong's *Red Army Tank Commanders: The Armored Guards* (Pa.: Schiffer Publishing Co., 1996).

15. On 17 March 1945, the 4th Tank Army was awarded the honorary title of "Guards."

16. "Pror'iv na Rava-Russkom..." in *Velikaia Otechestvennaia Voina 1941-1944 v Fotografiiakh i Kinodokumentakh, 1944* , p. 363.

17. General D. T. Yazov, *Vern'i Otchyzne* [Faithful to the Fatherland] (Moscow: Voenna Isdatel'stvo, 1988), p. 253; Aviation Marshall S. Krasovskiy, "2-ia vozgushnaia armiia v L'vovsko-Sandomirskoi operatsii" [The 2nd Air Service Army in the Lvov-Sandomir Operation] in *Voenno-Istoriches'kyi Zhurnal* (Moscow: Izdatel'stvo "Krasnaia Zvezda"), 1964, July, No. 7, p. 31; Shankowsky, "Biy Pid Brodamy", in *Brody: Zbirnyk Stattei i Naryciv*, ed. Lysiak, p. 58. Shankowsky also cites that prior to the July 1944 offensive, the 8th Air Army, commanded by General Zdanov, was also brought in. In all, no less than 9 aviation corps' were found to include the 9th Guards Air Division where some of Soviet Russia's leading airmen and aces were found. (*Ibid.*); Von Hardesty, *Red Phoenix: The Rise of Soviet Air Power 1941-1945* (Washington, D.C.: Smithsonian Institution, 1982), p. 222, cites that as many as 1,500 to 2,500 combat aircraft were concentrated in the breakthrough zones during the Lvov-Sandomir operation. For a breakdown of what was found within the 2nd Air Army and 8th Air Army, see Appendix 7, pp. 245 and 247.

18. Erickson, *The Road to Berlin,* p. 232; Panov, *Lvov-Sandomir Operation,* p. 376.

19. *Panov,* p. 376.

20. *Ibid.* According to *World War II Encyclopedia,* "One of Marshal Konev's advantages was that his forces were so powerful and so numerous that he could give his offensive two centers of gravity." (Vol. 12, p. 1659). During the summer of 1944, Soviet artillery was also utilized effectively. See "Artillery" in *Russian Combat Methods in World War II,* Chapter 4, pp. 19- 21.

21. Major General V.A. Matsulenko, A.A. Beketov, A.P. Belokon, and S.G. Chermashentsev, "Operational Camouflage In the Offensive Operations of 1944" in *Camouflage, Operational Camouflage of the Troops, Camouflage of Actions by Ground Force Subunits, A Soviet View.* (Translated by the U.S. Air Force, 1976), pp. 87-100. For a detailed example of how the 1st Guards Army conducted its deceptive and camouflage measures, see Appendix 5. "Plan of Operational Camouflage in the Zone of Operations of the 1st Guards Army in the Lvov-Sandomierz Operation (4-20 July 1944)," pp. 162-165. See also Armstrong's *SMS,* p. 506.

22. "Operations In Forests and Swamps. A Historical Perspective," in *The Soviet Motorized Rifle Company* (Washington, D.C.: Defense Intelligence Report, October 1976), p. 91; "Combat Under Unusual Conditions. Forest Fighting" in *Russian Combat Methods in World War II,* p. 78.

23. Colonel Zvenzlovsky, "The Lvov-Sandomir Operation" in *SMR,* August, No. 8, 1974, pp. 51-52. Lt. Colonel Lishchyns'kyi cites that 70% of the Soviet infantry and 90% of its armor went into the two Soviet assembly areas. "Nastup Soviets'koi Armii i Boi Pid Brodamy" in *Surmach,* 1968, pp. 23-24; and "Ot L'vova do Sandomira" [From Lvov to Sandomir] in *Velikaia Otechestvennaia Voina 1941-1945,* p. 304, also cites 70% of the 1st Ukrainian fronts infantry and 90% of its tanks were concentrated at the breakout assembly areas. For an analysis of what Konev inserted into the two breakout groups, see *Zapiski komanduiushchego frontom 1943-1945,* p. 245.

24. Konev, *Zapiski komanduiushchego frontom 1943-1945,* pp. 245-236. According to Konev, the Lutsk group would attack a front of 12 kilometers; the Lviv group would strike a front of 14 kilometers (*Ibid.*) In "Vhliad v problemu Ukrains'koi Dyvizii i ii Velykoi Bytvy Pid Brodamy" [A Viewpoint in the Problem of the Ukrainian Division and its Great Battle at Brody] in *Brody: Zbirnyk Stattei i Naryciv,* ed. Lysiak, p. 105, Lishchyns'kyi substantiates Konev's observation that two massive blows would be conducted at a distance of 12 and 14 kilometers for a total of 26 kilometers. See also Colonel Orlov's, "V.D. Sokolovsky" in *SMR,* July, 1977, No. 7, p. 43.

25. Zhukov, *Marshal of the Soviet Union,* Vol. 2, p. 284. According to Colonel-General G.F. Krivosheev, "L'vovsko-Sandomirskaia Strategicheskaia Nastupatel'naia Operatsiia" [The Lvov-Sandomir Strategical Advance Operation] in *Grif Sekretnosti Sniat. Poteri Vooruzhenn'ikh Sil SSSR v Voinakh, Boev'ikh Deistviiakh i Voenn'ikh Konfliktakh* [Secrets Removed: USSR's Armed Losses and Strength's in Wars, Military Activities and War Conflicts] (Moscow: Voennoe Izdatel'stvo, 1993), p. 204, the Lviv-Sandomir Operation was divided into two phases: the first phase would be characterized by penetration, encirclement, destruction of enemy forces by the Soviet forces advancing on the Rava-Russka and Lviv axis' and the liberation of towns and cities such as Lviv, Rava-Russka, Peremysl, Stanislav and others. This phase would last from 13-27 July 1944; during the second phase, exploitation of the breakout with an emphasis to cross the Vistula River in the vicinity of Sandomir (Sandomierz) located in Poland proper and approximately 110 miles south of Warsaw. This phase as to last from 28 July-29 – August 1944. In all, the

operation was to last 48 days. The 1st Ukrainian front was to advance on a front of up to 440 kilometers, and attain a depth of 350 kilometers. (For additional information on the strengths of the 1st Ukrainian Front see p. 205).

At the conclusion of the war, the Soviets classified their operations into a defensive/offensive category. Of the 55 major operations, the Lviv-Sandomir Offensive fell under such a category:

Fourth Year of the War

No.	Name of Operaton Date Conducted	Fronts, Fleets, Detached Armies	Spatial Range* (in k's)
38	Lvov-Sandomierz 7/13 - 8/29	Ist Ukrainian	48 300 350

* Spatial Range comprised 48 days; a front line range of no less than 300 kilometers, and a depth of 350 kilometers. For the above, see Colonel Vasily P. Morozov and Captain Aleksey V. Basov, "Important Soviet Military Operations of the Great Patriotic War" in *The Soviet Art of War*, ed.'s Harriet Fast Scott and William Fontaine Scott (N.Y.: Praeger Co., 1982), p. 119.

Notes Chapter 16

Wednesday, 28 June – Wednesday, 5 July.
1. Contrary to what some Ukrainians believe, the Soviet build-up did not develop as a result of the Division being posted into Brody's vicinity; rather, it occurred as a result of Konev's and Sokolovskiy's plan for a two-pronged thrust to penetrate the front of AGNU and to achieve operational depth. According to *World War II Encyclopedia*, 13th Corps mission was to cover Lviv from the Brody region. (Vol. 10, p. 1341).

2. Despite the fact that AGNU'S charts for the period of 8-15 July 1944 reveal the Division was posted into the 3rd Panzer Reserve Rear, in actuality, the Division never entered the 3rd Panzer Reserve Rear because with its arrival to the eastern front, the Division was immediately posted to the 13th Army Corps.

3. Heike, *English ed.*, pp. 36-37; *German ed.*, pp. 91-94; *Ukrainian ed.*, p. 65; Klietmannn, p. 194; Yurkevich in *Boshyk*, p. 78; Buchner, *Ostfront 1944*, p. 238; General Pavlo Shandruk, "Brody" in *Brody: Zbirnyk Stattei i Naryciv*, ed. Lysiak, p. 25; Roman Krokhmaliuk, *The Glow*, pp. 97 and 98; From the Editors: "Fakty Pro Ukrains'ku Dyviziiu" [Facts About the Ukrainian Division], *Visti*, 1985, No. 4, p. 25; Ren, *My Life's Mosaic*, p. 168-170, and personal discussion with Yuriy Krokhmaliuk. Incorrectly, *Stein*, p. 186; and Reitlinger, *The SS*, p. 203, cited the Division as being in the 14th Corps; nor was the 13th Corps a "cavalry" corps as stated by former Divisional Chaplain Nahayewsky in *A Soldier Priest Remembers*, p. 80; and neither was the Division ever a part of 8th Corps as stated by Petro Savaryn in "U 70-Richchia Vymarshu UCC-v na Front, U 40-Richchia Boiu l-oi UD UNA Pid Brodamy, U 30-Richchia Stanytsi k. Voiakiv l-oi UD UNA u St. Keteryns" [In the 70th Anniversary of the March of the USS (Ukrainian Sichovi Striltsi) to the Front; In the 40th Anniversary of the Battle of the 1st Ukrainian Division, UNA (Ukrainian National Army) at Brody; In the 30th Anniversary of the former Soldiers of the 1st UD, UNA in the St. Catherines post], *Visti*, 1984, No. 5-6, p. 19.
The 13th Infantry Corps (not to be confused with the 13th SS Corps) was formed during 1936-37 in Wehrkreis XIII. Nuremberg was its home station. In September 1939, the 13th Corps fought in Poland as a part of Blaskowitz' 8th Army serving in von Rundstedt's Army Group 'South.' In central Poland, the corps participated in the encirclement of a sizable Polish force between Osorkov and Lavitch west of the Vistula River. In 1940, it participated in the western campaign. Committed to the eastern front, it fought in Russia and in the defensive battles north and west of Kiev. In early 1944, 13th Corps was on the southern sector. Destroyed at Brody in July 1944, the corps reappeared as a part of "Corps Felber" in the Ardennes in late 1944 or early 1945. Disappearing in the Ardennes in early 1945, it never resurfaced.

4. The 349th Infantry Division was formed in October/November 1943 from Kampfgruppe "Kamalkueste" and elements of the battered 376th and 384th Infantry Divisions. It was first posted in the area of Calais, France, where the division was utilized in the construction of rear and coastal defense positions. In late March 1944, the 349th deployed to Galicia. Surrounded at Brody, it broke out but as a result of heavy losses, was disbanded on 1 August 1944. On 14 September, it was reconstituted but on the following day, 15 September, the 349th absorbed the 567th Infantry Division. Deployed to East Prussia on 19 December, the 349th was incorporated into the 551st Volk's (People's) Grenadier Division. The Division ceased to exist in Prussia.

5. Organized in the fall of 1943 in Denmark, the 361st Infantry Division was dispatched to the Eastern front in March, 1944. Encircled at Brody, elements succeeded in breaking out, but the brunt of the 361st was destroyed. A number of its soldiers were captured. Withdrawn into Poland, the remainder of the 361st was returned to Germany. Shortly afterwards, the 361st was reorganized as a Volksgrenadier Division. It participated in the Arnhem battles against the Allied "Market-Garden" Operation, and fought in Eastern France. Posted to the Vosges Mountains, the 361st Volksgrenadier incorporated the remainder of the 553rd Volksgrenadier Division (minus its headquarters) but in turn, the 361st Volksgrenadier was incorporated into the newly forming 559th Volksgrenadier Division in January, 1945. Although plans were initiated to re-establish the 361st, nothing ever became of it.

Notes

6. Formed in March 1941 in Wehrkreis VIII from the 454th Infantry Division, the 454th Field Security conducted anti-guerrilla and rear area security missions in Northern Ukraine and Byelorussia. Combat included battles with the UPA. Attached to the 13th Corps in early 1944, the 454th Security at first successfully defended Rivno, a critical railway center, but constant enemy pressure forced it to withdraw. Encircled and destroyed at Brody, its survivors were disbanded.

7. Formed 5 November 1943 in Ivankov, Russia, from the battered remains of the 183rd, 217th and 339th Infantry Divisions, Corps Formation C ('Korpsabteilungen') had, at best, the equivalent fighting strength of one infantry division. The retention of the divisional titles was maintained strictly for deceptive purposes to portray a large number of divisions, and, hopefully, deceive the Allies as to their real strength; additionally, the "divisional" titles were maintained because it was planned to rebuilt them once again into divisional strength. (Cooper, *The German Army*, p. 490; and Seaton, *The Fall of Fortress Europe*, p. 55) According to a number of former German generals and staff officers, a Korpsabteilung was defined as such: "A provisional unit of divisional strength formed by three weakened infantry divisions, each organized into one regiment." (Chapter 3, "Spoiling Attack" in *German Defense Tactics Against Russian Breakthroughs*, p. 18). Once established, the new division was designated Korps Abteilung and was distinguished by a letter, such as A,B,C, etc. (Chapter 15, "The Organization of Special Units" in *Military Improvisations During the Russian Campaign*, p. 86.) Yet, despite the fact that the so-called Korps Abteilungen's proved to be an emergency measure that sometimes proved helpful in deceiving the enemy, and the provisional corps had the combat value of an infantry division and, on occasion, fought well, in the long run they actually proved to be more of a handicap than an asset. For a further analysis of the advantages and disadvantages of Korps Abteilungen, see pp. 86-87.

8. Such a distance, of course, was not only too extensive but actually, violated the German Army's defense doctrine regarding a defensive length. Depending upon the terrain and the estimated strength of the defenders versus attackers, a 1944 division with a strength of 10,000 normally held a frontline distance of 6,600 to 11,000 yards or, approximately 3.5 to 6.5 miles. (*Handbook On German Military Forces*, TM-E30-451, p. IV-21). Realistically speaking, what the Division was covering was not an exception. As acknowledged by a number of former eastern front German commanders, "by 1944, a frontage of 30 miles for an infantry division no longer caused even a raised eyebrow." (See Section IV: "Operations At River Lines" in *Terrain Factors In the Russian Campaign*, p. 25.). In addition to overextended divisional front lines, along much of the German 1944 eastern front entire gaps remained open between various divisions and army corps. These gaps arose as a result of overextended frontages and manpower shortages. (For additional information to include information on Retrograde (Withdrawal) Movements, see Chapter 9: "Delaying and Blocking Actions" in *German Defense Tactics Against Russian Breakthroughs*, p. 57).

9. Volodymyr Kubiyovych, *Encyclopedia of Ukraine* (Munich: Shevchenko Scientific Society, Inc., 1955), Vol. 1, p. 177. According to *1943-1993. The 1st Ukrainian Division*, p. 19, 13th Corps strength stood at 32,000-35,000 soldiers. Of this strength, one-third was from the "Galicia" Division.

10. In the summer of 1944, UPA Group "Druzhynnyky"("Brotherhood"), under the command of Commander "Chernyk," operated in Brody's region. (Ren, *My Life's Mosaic*, p. 165).

In *UPA and the Division*, p. 76, UPA historian Lev Shankowsky alleges that initially, Germany's military command planned to commit the Division to the vicinity of Kolomei. (Carpathian Region). "Unfortunately [for the UPA], this plan was never carried out. The Germans understood that to utilize the Division in this area, in which the UPA was quite strong, was a number one risk for them. At this time, in the Carpathians, in addition to the officer's school "Oleni" and the non-commissioned school "Berkuty," there existed no less than 12 organized UPA companies in addition to other UPA elements." Therefore, concludes Shankowsky, "the Division was unexpectedly committed to the Brody area where UPA's strength was minimal." (*Ibid.*). Simply stated, Shankowsky claims the Division was redirected to Brody because of Nazi fears that in the event the "Galicia" Division was posted to a heavy UPA region, it would desert in entirety to the insurgents.

Regarding this observation, Shankowsky is totally incorrect. To this day, no World War II German or Ukrainian documents, along with credible witnesses, can substantiate that the Division was posted solely to Brody because of fears that its soldiers, if posted into a heavy UPA region, would defect in mass to the Ukrainian insurgents. In a personal discussion with Yuriy Krokhmaliuk, the former Divisional staff officer stated that in the aftermath of World War II, he had also heard "how the Division was going to desert to the UPA but just as it was about to cross over, it was surrounded [by Soviet forces]." Krokhmaliuk acknowledged that most of the Division's soldiers were sympathetic to the UPA. But many of the Division's soldiers volunteered to serve in a conventional unit as a result of an unwillingness to serve in the insurgency; therefore, had suddenly an announcement been made to "flee to the UPA!" the possibility exists that many (if not most) of the Division's soldiers would have opposed this move. Militarily, it would have been impossible to conduct a massive desertion without losing the brunt of the Division's artillery, anti-aircraft weaponry, heavy equipment, vehicles, etc. Simultaneously, a massive desertion would have jeopardized those left behind in Neuhammer, those serving in the Training and Replacement Regiment, and those attending Europe's various schools. Politically, it would have placed the Ukrainians in a very awkward situation at a moment when some positive measures were finally being exerted from the Nazi occupant; and at the moment it would have denied the Ukrainian liberation movement its sole access in obtaining conventional military training, arms and equipment.

11. One of the first units to arrive was the Division's anti-aircraft. Immediately, the AA established positions around Ozhydiv. (Bohdan Nebozhuk, *"Brody,"* *Visti*, 1992, No. 2, p. 72). For another interesting account of how the

Galicia Division

Division's anti-aircraft defended Ozhydiv's railway station and the Division's embarkation point, see Markian Fesolovych's, "Na Oboroni Statsii Ozhydiv" [Defending the Ozhydiv Railway Station], *Visti*, 1972, No. 3, pp. 28-30).

12. By the close of the war, Bohdan would dismantle exactly 35 more bombs – 23 Soviet and 12 western Allied; additionally, 95 artillery, rocket and mortar shells, some of which were buried into the ground by guerrillas for mine warfare, were successfully removed or deactivated by him. Bohdan also discovered numerous mine fields and potential mining sites and, together with his team, identified, disassembled, removed, or destroyed with explosives well over 50,000 mines and unexploded devices.

Bohdan's expertise with explosives did not conclude in 1945. In civilian life, he worked as a licensed demolitions explosives construction specialist, and helped to develop and perfect the technique of urban demolition. With the emergence in the late 1960s and early 1970s of various leftist revolutionary movements such as the Weathermen, Bohdan voluntarily taught bomb safety and removal techniques to various U.S. police departments, state agencies, and to Reserve/National Guard forces. Despite his forced retirement as a result of rheumatism in his hands and, as he jokingly says "show me an old man who can see, hear, smell, and touch like he should!" Bohdan's fascination with explosives remains strong.

Thursday, 6 July – Tuesday, 11 July:

1. In *1943-1993, the 1st Ukrainian Division*, p. 19, a front line distance of approximately 30 kilometers (18.6 miles) is cited; Heike, *English ed.*, p. 38; and "Biy Pid Brodamy" in *Brody: Zbirnyk Sattei i Naryciv*, ed. Lysiak, p. 130, cites a distance of 36 kilometers.

In addition to manning a position about 22 miles in length the Division occupied an area where few, if any, defensive positions were found. Knowing that if the Soviets attacked and penetrated the front the Division would have to stop their advance, the Division immediately began to construct primary, secondary, and even, supplementary defense positions. In addition to that, the Division established observation points, target reference points, fields of fire, engagement areas, supply areas and constructed obstacles.

2. Yuriy Krokhmaliuk, *"Polevyi Zapasnyi Kurin' Pid Brodamy"* [The Field Replacement Battalion At Brody], *Visti*, 1952, No. 2-3, p. 12.

3. Bender and Taylor, Vol. 4, p. 48. This figure included those in the Division, and those on military, convalescent, and emergency leave or schooling. It did not include those in the Training and Replacement Regiment based in Wandern, or those undergoing recruit training within the Replacement system.

4. Personal discussion with Yuriy Krokhmaliuk. In Roman Krokhmaliuk's book *The Glow*, p. 99, Roman cited that a strength of over 11,000 soldiers deployed to the eastern front. However, in a personal interview with the author, Roman conceded that previous figure was incorrect and that approximately 10,000 actually deployed.

5. From the publishers: "Fakty Pro Ukrains' ku Dyviziiu" [Facts About the Ukrainian Division], *Visti*, 1985, No. 4, p. 25. Again, this figure is slightly overestimated.

6. Heike, *English ed.*, p. xxiii.

7. "Tym, Shchto Vpalu...," [To Those Who Fell...], *Visti*, 1961, No. 3, p. 43.

8. Personal discussion with Yuriy Krokhmaliuk; Reverend Stepan Kleparchuk, "Druha Bol'shevyts'ka Okupatsiia Brids'koho Povitu 1944 r. Ukrains' ka Dyviziia "Halychyna" Pid Brodamy" [The Second Bolshevik Occupation of the Brody Region in the year 1944 and the Ukrainian Division "Galicia" at Brody] in *Dorohamy i Stezhkamy Bridshchyny. Spomyny*. [Fording Through the Encirclements Roads and Paths. Remembrances]. (Toronto, Canada: Kiev Printers Ltd., 1971), p. 213. A number of Ukrainians also served on Divisional staff, and each regiment and battalion had Ukrainian staff officers. (Personal discussion with Yuriy Krokhmaliuk).

9. *Reverend Kleparchuk*, p. 213. Undoubtedly, Reverend Kleparczuk's figure also includes the Division's chaplains and doctors which held a military rank.

10. Dmytro Ferkuniak, "Komandnyi Sklad Shtabu Dyvizii" [The Division's Command Staff], *Visti*, 1965, No. 4 (20), pp. 25-26. Ferkuniak was a former captain in the 1st Ukrainian (Galicia) Division. For additional information on the Divisions staff, as well as a breakdown of what constituted the Division prior to and in the aftermath of the Brody Battle, see Yuriy Krokhmaliuk's "Organizatsiia 1-oi UD UNA" [The Organization of the 1st Ukrainian Division, Ukrainian National Army], *Visti*, 1963, No. 3 (11), pp. 15-18.

11. Heike, who was posted into the Division from the Wehrmacht, continued to maintain a non-Waffen-SS rank.

12. Also spelled as Shaff. Two unidentified Germans also served alongside Shaaf.

13. Despite his military rank and position in Staff Section 1C, in actuality Wiens was a Russian and Polish speaking Gestapo agent who was posted into the Division to neutralize the Division's "Banderites." (Those who

Notes

allegedly were sympathetic to the OUN or UPA). Unknown to the gestapo, Wiens (a German who had resided in eastern Europe for a number of years prior to the war) had very strong pro-Russian, pro-Polish but especially pro-communist sympathies. A sadist who despised Ukrainians but especially the Galician volunteers, Wiens was a man who could never be trusted and he was also despised by a number of his fellow Germans. UPA's agents operating within the Division identified Wiens as a Soviet agent. He disappeared at Brody. For an interesting analysis of the various personalities of the German staff officers serving within Divisional staff, see Do Ferkuniak's "The Division's Command Staff," *Visti*, 1965, No. 4, pp. 25-29.

14. Lenard's (on occasion the name is spelled as Leonard) position was also described as that of a standard bearer. (In Ukrainian, "Bunchuzhnyi"). In itself, "bunchuzhnyi" is not a rank. However, a person designated as a standard bearer also helps to maintain a unit's personnel records and deals with matters pertaining to the safety, health, and welfare of a unit's soldiers. Lenard was, however, an officer.

15. In *Visti*, 1965, No. 4, p. 26, Ferkuniak cites Chaplain Nahayewsky as being posted on Divisional staff. At the time then the Division deployed to the eastern front, Nahayewsky remained behind in Neuhammer. Chaplain Stetsiuk was posted to Divisional staff.

16. Bohdan Pidhainyi, "UPA – Dyviziia "Halychyna" – Nimtsi" [The UPA – the "Galicia" Division – the Germans] , *Visti*, 1990, No. 3, p. 65; Ren, *My Life's Mosaic*, p. 166; personal discussion With Yuriy Krokhmaliuk.
According to Vashchenko, UPA's intelligence was fully aware of the massive Soviet buildup in the Lutsk-Ternopil areas, and had accurately concluded that the Division was being positioned into an exceptionally dangerous area. Efforts were made to inform certain Ukrainian Divisional officers of the upcoming dangers, but rapidly moving events, and the fact that the UPA could not operate freely within the 13th Army corps and AGNU, thwarted UPA's efforts.

17. According to Mykola Fylynovych, at Brody, the Fusilier Battalion contained such a command: Battalion Commander – SS-Hauptsturmführer Karl Bristot; 1st Co. – Waffen-Obersturmführer Mykola Horodyts'kyi; 2nd Co. – Waffen-Obersturmführer Stepan Huliak; 3rd Co. – Waffen-Obersturmführer Petro Duda; 4th Heavy Co. – Waffen-Obersturmführer Roman Bojcun. "Z Fiuziliramy Pid Brodamy" [With the Fusiliers at Brody]. (Unpublished memoir). In addition to these officer's, one German adjutant and one German supply officer and two Ukrainian assistant company commanders – Waffen-Obersturmführer's Stefan Shuhan and Myhailo Danylko, rounded out the battalion's officer personnel. (*Ibid.*).

Wednesday, 12 July 1944:
1. Madej, *Russo-German War, Summer 1944*, p. 62; personal discussion with Yuriy Krokhmaliuk.

2. Personal discussion with Yuriy Krokhmaliuk.

3. In a personal discussion with Roman Krokhmaliuk, the three non-committed battalions maintained a combined strength of 1,750.

4. Lange, *Korpsabteilung C* (Vowinckel, Neckargemund: 1961), p. 104. In personal discussions with Yuriy Krokhmaliuk, Veryha, and other former members of the Division, all attest that the Division deployed to the Eastern front as a well-armed and equipped formation.

Thursday, 13 July:
1. P.M. Portugal'skii, *Marshal I.S. Konev* , p. 140; Panov, *Lvov-Sandomir Operation*, p. 376; *Shtemenko*, Book II, p. 69; David Irving, *Hitler's War* (N.Y.: Viking Press, 1977), p. 656; Ziemke, *From Stalingrad to Berlin*, p. 332; *Marshal Zhukov: An Outstanding Soviet Military Leader* (Moscow: Planeta Publishers, 1987), p. 164; Buchner, *Ostfront 1944*, p. 223; *World War II Encyclopedia*, Vol. 12, pp.'s 1659-1660, cite 13 July 1944 as the date Konev commenced the Lvov-Sandomir Operation.

2. "Pror'iv Na Rava-Russkom"[Penetration into Rava-Russka] in *Velikaia Otechestvennaia Voina, 1944* [The Great Patriotic War, 1944], p. 364.

3. Lashchenko, *From Battle to Battle*, p. 299; Major-General K.V. Sychev and Colonel M.M. Malakhov, "Nastuplenie 15-vo Strelkovogo Korpusa s Pror'ivom Podgotovlennoi Oboron'i Protyvnika Strelkovogo s Pror'ivom Podgotovlennoi Oboron'i Protyvnika Ivzhnee Brod'i (14-22 iiulia 1944 g.) Obstanovka i Zadacha 15-go Strelkovogo Korpusa [Offensive of the 15th Rifle Corps in the Breakthrough of the Prepared Defenses of the Battle of Brody (14-22 July 1944). Situation and Task of the 15th Rifle Corps]. (Hereafter referred to as *Offensive of the 15th Rifle Corps*) in *Naztuplenie Strelkovogo Korpusa* (*Sbornik Takticheskikh Primerov iz Velikoi Otechestvennoi Voin'i*) [Advance of a Rifle Corps (A Collection of Tactical Examples from the Great Patriotic War]). (Moscow: Voennde Izdatel'stvo Ministerstva Oboron'i Soiuza SSR, 1958), p. 38. For a detailed account of the 322nd, 336th and 148th Rifle Divisions, as well as the 15th Rifle Corps, see pp. 7-59. See also Robert G. Poirier and Albert Z. Conner, *The Red Army Order of Battle in the Great Patriotic War* (Ca.: Presidio Publishing Co., 1985), p. 139.
The immediate mission of the 15th Rifle Corps was to attack the front at a distance of 5-6 k's (3.1-4 miles), penetrate it, seize hills (Heights) 375 and 396, and advance and destroy all enemy forces in the vicinity of the villages

and towns of Tros'tsianets Mal'i, Skvarzava, Kruhiv, Perepel'niki, Koltiw and Sasiv. Once the corps reached the highway which ran from Sasiv southward to Zolochiv, its subsequent mission was to advance westward to a line north and south of Skvariava. If successful, 15th Rifle Corps would create a sufficient penetration to enable the brunt of Rybalko's 3rd Guards Tank Army to achieve operational depth. See *Offensives of the 15th Rifle Corps*, pp. 7-10.

Friday, 14 July:
    1. Various morning times are cited, but all correspond to approximately the 4-5 a.m. period. According to Lashchenko, the 322nd Rifle Division's 1087th Regiment's 1st Battalion, following a 30 minute artillery preparation, attacked at 5 a.m., to secure Hill 396.0. (Lashchenko, *From Battle to Battle*, p. 299).

    2. Divisional historian Veryha cites the Division's 30th Infantry Regiment actually received its marching orders in the late evening hours of 13 July to advance to the area of Sasiv. (Vasil Veryha, "Pershyi Den' Boiv Pid Brodamy" [The First Day of Battle at Brody] (Toronto: Kalendar-Al'manakh, Novoho Shliakhu, 1984), p. 103; but cites 15 July as the date the 13th Corps ordered the remainder of the Division to counterattack the communist breakout developing in the area adjacent to Koltiw. See also Veryha's "Dmytro Paliv – Voin I Patriot" [Dmytro Paliv – Warrior and Patriot], *Visti*, 1968, No. 5-6 (36-37), p. 43.

    3. According to Bohdan Pidhainyi, a former Divisional officer, the 30th Infantry Regiment was notified on 13 July, at approximately 11:30 p.m., that it was to conduct an immediate forced infantry march into the area of Koltiw-Lykavets' to establish a defensive line to counter the Soviet thrust by no later than 4 a.m., 15 July. Pidhainyi, "Dva Shliakhy – Odna Meta" [Two Roads – One Objective], in *Brody: Zbirnyk Stattei i Naryciv*, ed. Lysiak, p. 115.
    According to Pavlo Sumarokiv, Wittenmayer (who commanded the 30th Infantry Regiments 2nd Battalion), held a quick battalion briefing at the command post shortly after 9 p.m. (13 July). During his briefing, Wittenmayer informed his company and staff commanders that the 30th Infantry Regiment was to immediately march to occupy a defensive position in the 'Dark Forest' between Lykavets' and Koltiw to assist the Wehrmacht in halting the Soviet penetration in the vicinity of Koltiw. Immediately following the briefing, Sumarokiv's 6th Company (along with the entire 2nd Battalion), commenced its march at 9:30 p.m. (Pavlo Sumarokiv, "V Otochenni Pid Brodamy. Proryv 2-ho Kurinnia 30-ho Polky U.D. Halychyna." [In the Encirclement at Brody. The Breakout of the 2nd Battalion, 30th Regiment, Ukrainian Division "Galicia."], *Visti*, 1961, No. 103 (Munich). p. 70. See also pp 70-74.

    4. *The Great Patriotic War*, p. 364.

    5. Although on p. 300 in *From Battle to Battle*, Lashchenko mentions that at 1430 hours (2:30 p.m.), 14 July, a heavy pre-attack bombardment took place, on the previous page (299), Lashchenko also mentions how the 322nd Rifle Division's 1087th Regiment's 1st Battalion attacked earlier to secure from the Germans Height (Hill) 396.0. Undoubtedly, Lashchenko is correct in his observations because certain Soviet divisional and corps commanders, realizing that Konev would soon be ordering an attack south of Brody once the fog lifted, began their own preparations to improve their position prior to Konev's main attack.

    6. The brunt of the Soviet attack fell on the 349th's 913th Infantry Regiment.

    7. Veryha, *Pershyi Den'*, p. 103; *Offensives of the 15th Rifle Corps*, p. 11; I. Konev, "Zavershenie Osvobozdennia Sovetskoi Ukrain'i i Vykhod na Vislu" [The Complete Liberation of the Soviet Ukraine and the Appearance on the Vistula] in *Voenno-Istoricheskii Zhurnal [Military History Journal]* (Moscow: Red Star Publishers, 1964), No. 7, p. 10.

    8. The regiment's 3rd Battalion remained behind at Neuhammer.

    9. Personal discussion with Veryha, 3 November 1987. See also Veryha' s, "Spomyny. I Znovu Noyhammer" [Remembrances. And Again Neuhammer], *Visti*, 1978, No. 4, p. 71.

    10. *Ibid.*

    11. *Ibid.*

    12. Incorrectly, some members of the Division maintain the view that the German front fell back as a result of the assassination plot against Adolf Hitler. Remembering that the attempt to kill Hitler occurred in the afternoon of 20 July 1944, and that Konev's attack commenced on 13 July, the retreating troops encountered by the advancing Divisional soldiers stemmed from Konev's blows, and not as a result of any assassination attempt.

    13. World War II German doctrine emphasized that a battalion on the defense (in European type terrain), should occupy a defensive area from approximately 880 to 2,200 yards. In turn, the battalion sector was subdivided into several company defense areas.
    Generally, each company held an area extending over 400 to about 1,100 yards (average was 750 yards) in length and 300-350 yards in depth. As always is the case, terrain and a battalions man-power strength dictated defense distances. Within a defense area, troops organized a defense against an attack from any direction. Main, and alternate, positions were prepared for each weapons system and if time permitted, mines, obstacles, and wire were also placed.

Notes

Because the "Galicia" Division was following German military doctrine, it appears that the 30th Regiments 2nd Battalion (as also the 1st Battalion), occupied a defensive area ranging from about 1,000 to 2,000 yards in length.

Saturday, 15 July:
1. According to Veryha, the Soviets struck the 30th at approximately 8 a.m. (*Pershyi Den'*, p. 106). But according to General Lashchenko, *Iz Boia v Boi*, p. 305, the Soviets attacked at 8:30 a.m., following an intense artillery preparation. Remembering that Veryha uses an approximate time and at that time Lashchenko was a staff officer within the 322nd Rifle Division, regarding the time, Lashchenko is undoubtedly correct.

2. General Petr Kurochkin, "Pror'iv oboron'i protivnika na l'vovskom napravlenii" [Breakthrough of the Enemy Defenses in the L'vov Direction], in *Military History Journal* (Moscow: Red Star Publishing, July No. 7, 1964), p. 28. According to Kurochkin, "element's of the 14th Infantry Division SS "Galicia," accompanied with assault weapons and tanks from the 300th Assault Brigade, concentrated in the area of Koltiw and strove to break the efforts of the 15th and 23rd Rifle Corps at Nushche." See also *Offensive of the 15th Rifle Corps*, p. 40. (See also maps 2,3, and 4). Various other Soviet war-time sources cite they encountered the "Galicia" Division's 30th Regiment on 15 July 1944.

3. *Offensive of the 15th Rifle Corps*, pp. 14, 17, and 19. According to *Offensive of the 15th Rifle Corps*, the 336th Rifle Division's organic artillery regiment was reinforced with 36 152mm heavy artillery pieces from the 33rd Artillery Brigade; 20 57mm and 40 76mm (for a total of 60) guns from the 7th Guards Anti-tank Brigade; 24 76mm guns from the 408th Artillery Regiment; 53 82mm and 15 120mm heavy mortars; 14 76mm, 4 105mm, 12 122mm artillery pieces from the 359th Rifle (Reserve) Division; and 35 120mm heavy mortars from the 9th Mechanized Corps' 616th Mortar Regiment. (See p. 17).

4. Colonel David M. Glantz, *The Soviet Conduct of Tactical Maneuver: Spearhead of the Offensive* (England: Frank Cass and Co., 1991), pp. 170-172. According to "The Defensive. Zone Defense Tactics" in *Military Improvisations During the Russian Campaign*, "The 1944 battle for Lvov was decided by a major Russian breakthrough north of Lvov...to which the enemy shifted his main effort." See Chapter 2, p. 35.

5. Army Group North Ukraine's organizational charts for 8-15 July 1944 reveal both the 1st and 8th Panzer Divisions to be within the 3rd Panzer Reserve Rear, 1st Panzer Army.

6. Zhukov, Vol. 2, p. 284; Ziemke, *From Stalingrad to Berlin*, p. 332.

7. The Germans did anticipate a heavy ground attack, but all were surprised and shocked by the Soviet Air Force's massive, and overwhelming, air superiority. Until now, few of Germany's Eastern Front veterans had ever seen or experienced anything like it. See Seaton's, *The Russo-German War*, p. 446; and *The Fall of Fortress Europe*, p. 138.

8. *Panov*, p. 376. According to I.G. Viktorov et al., *SSSR v Velikoi Otechestvennoi Voine 1941-1945* [SSSR in the Great Patriotic War 1941-1945] (Moscow: 1970), p. 590, "the 2nd Air Army flew 3,288 air sorties against the enemy's two tank and one infantry divisions. The [German] enemy lost up to 75% of its armor." (Hereafter referred to as *SSSR, 1941-1945*). In the aftermath of World War II , General Mellenthin would acknowledge that in addition to the armor loss, "all hope of counterattack disappeared." See *World War II Encyclopedia*, Vol. 12, p. 1659. For a detailed account of the Soviet air war in the Lvov-Sandomir operation, see Marshal of Aviation S. Krasovskiy's "2-ia Vozdushnaia Armiia v L'vovsko-Sandomirskoi Operatsii" [The 2nd Air Army in the Lvov-Sandomir Operation] in *Military History Journal*, 1964, No. 7, pp. 34-41.

9. Zvenzlovsky, *Soviet Military Review*, August, No. 8, 1974, p. 52; Shtemenko, *Book II*, p. 470, cites the corridor as being "nearly 6 km's wide." However, the corridor's length and width would be expanded. Colonel Armstrong cited the corridor attained a width of 6 kilometers and a depth of 20 kilometer's. (*SMS* December, 1986), pp. 506-507. Colonel Seaton cites the Koltiw corridor was 3 miles wide and 10 miles deep. *The Fall of Fortress Europe*, p. 138.

10. Shtemenko, *Book II*, p. 470.

11. According to *Ready*, p. 369, the Ukrainians began to counter-attack. Prior to this, they had successfully repulsed Soviet cavalry charges. Veryha, *Pershyi Den'*, p. 113, states that the 29th and 31st Infantry Regiments received their marching orders in the evening of 15 July. According to "Defensive Pincers" in *German Defense Tactics Against Russian Bread-Throughs*, during the July 1944 battle near Lvov, the Germans were forced to hold two fronts twenty-five miles apart. In order to contain the Soviet penetrations, pincer attacks were launched against the flanks of the attacking Soviet forces. See Chap. 4, p. 24.

12. According to Colonel Zvenzlovsky, Konev's thrust was slowed because "the enemy command committed on the second day his operational reserves – two tank and one infantry divisions, the counterattacks followed one after another. The advance of the Soviet forces was slowed down." Zvenzlovsky does not identify the two tank or infantry divisions, but the infantry division he refers to was the 14th Waffen-SS "Galicia" Division. See Zvenzlovsky, *The Lvov-Sandomir Operation*, p. 52. Years later, Marshal Zhukov would acknowledge that "[the offensive] initially did

Galicia Division

not proceed as well on the Lvov sector as the Front Command and GHQ had expected"; and "on the Lvov sector, our troops advanced slowly." Zhukov, *Marshal of the Soviet Union*, pp. 285 and 290. For another Soviet acknowledgment of the difficult fighting in the Koltiw Corridor, and to include combat against the "14 Infantry Division SS "Galicia," see "Koltovskii Koridor" [Koltiw Corridor] in *Velikaia Otechestvennaia Voina, 1944*, pp. 367-373. See also John Erickson, *The Road to Berlin: Continuing the History of Stalin's War With Germany* (Colorado: Westview Press, 1983), pp. 234-235.

13. *Lashchenko*, p. 306.

14. *Panov*, p. 376; Colonel Armstrong, *SMS*, December, 1986, pp. 507-508. According to Colonel Svetlishin, Konev's decision demonstrated that as a commander, Konev was "resolute, daring and capable of taking a calculated risk." *SMR*, 1967, December, No. 12, p. 50.

15. *Lashchenko*, p. 306.

16. *Ibid.*, p. 307.

Sunday, 16 July:
1. Erickson, *The Road to Berlin*, p. 235. According to *Lashchenko*, p. 306, the decision had been made by Konev himself at the end of 15 July. In "The Complete Liberation of the Soviet Ukraine and the Appearance on the Vistula," Konev provides this information: that although the 60th Army had not yet reached its objectives, Rybalko's 3rd Guards Tank Army began to move on the morning of 16 July, despite the fact that some of Rybalko's armor was already committed on 15 July to support the 60th Army. (Ibid.). Konev also states that Rybalko personally called him at 3 a.m. on 16 July for authorization to commit the remainder (and brunt) of the 3rd Guards Tank Army into combat. See *Military History Journal*, 1964, No. 7, p. 10.

2. In his memoirs, Heike does not specify where the order originated from; undoubtedly, it either came from the 13th Corps, from the 1st Panzer Army Headquarters, or even from AGNU.

3. Heike, *English ed.*, p. 41.

4. On 1 June 1944, the 29th Regiment was organized in the following manner: Regimental Staff; Headquarters Company. 1st Battalion – Battalion Headquarters with four line companies: 1/29; 2/29; 3/29; 4/29; 2nd Battalion – Battalion Headquarters with four line companies: 5/29; 6/29; 7/29; 8/29; one company of field artillery organized around three platoons of 75mm light PAK guns and one platoon containing two heavy 150mm artillery pieces. Because the regiment's 3rd Battalion was not yet formed, the artillery company was unofficially designated as the "13th" Company; additionally, an anti-tank company, organized around two platoons armed with anti-tank teller mines, panzerfausts/panzerschreks and anti-armor hand grenades and two platoons armed with 75mm PAK guns was found. Every platoon had a machine gun section. Within the entire regiment, the "panzerjäger" company was the only fully motorized company. Its troops rode in the 1.5 ton, V-8, air-cooled Styr-Daimler-Benz truck produced under the "Schell-Programm," and the "Protzkraftwagen" (Kfz. 69), a 6-wheeled light truck which towed either the 37mm or 75mm gun and an extra ammunition trailer. Excluding the 4th and 8th "Heavy" Companies (organized with additional mortar and machinegun support), each line company was organized around 4 platoons – 3 rifle platoons, each platoon with 3 rifle squads), and 1 "grenade-throwing" platoon. Two 80mm light mortars (with one horse driven 2-wheeled wagon containing extra mortar ammunition) was found within each 4th platoon. Each line company was commanded by no more than 1 or 2 officers, and averaged – 148 soldiers (officers including).
On 1 June 1944, the 29th Regiment was commanded by SS-Standartenführer Friedrich Dern. The regiments 1st Battalion was commanded by a Galician Ukrainian, Waffen-Hauptsturmführer Myhailo Brygider with one German adjutant; the 2nd Battalion was commanded by SS-Hauptsturmführer Wilhelm Allerkampf. At the time of deployment, the entire regiments line, artillery and anti-tank companies were commanded by Ukrainian officers, who also served in staff positions. Out of 42 officers, 34 were Ukrainian and 8 German. (Yuriy Krokhmaliuk, "Obsada Starshyns'kykh Funktsii v 29. Polky 1-oho Chervnia 1944 r." [Officer Leadership Positions and Functions Within the 1st Ukrainian Division's 29th Regiment on 1 June 1944], *Visti*, December, 1951 – January, 1952, No. 12 (14) – 1 (1 5), p. 13; and Liubomyr Ortyns'kyi, "Pikhotnyi Polk 1-oi U.D. Organizatsiina Skhem I Zavdannia Poodynokykh Funktsyii" [The Infantry Regiment of the 1st U.D. Its Organizational Schism and the Mission of Its Independent Functions], *Visti*, December, 1951 – January, 1952, No. 12 (14) – 1 (15), pp. 12-13). Ortyns'kyi, who served in the 29th Regiment and deployed to Galicia in late June 1944, substantiates Krokhmaliuk's officer roll call of 1 June 1944. And when the 29th Regiment deployed to Galicia in late June 1944, it deployed with its 1 June standing. (Personal discussion with Yuriy Krokhmaliuk).
In a post-war account published by former 29th Regimental Chaplain Myhailo Levenets', Levenets' also substantiates Krokhmaliuk's writings and verifies that Brygider commanded the 29th Regiments 1st Battalion and Allerkampf commanded the regiments 2nd Battalion. For a detailed account of the 29th Regiment in combat, see Levenets' "Z Arkhivy 1-oi U.D." [From the Archives of the 1st Ukrainian Division], *Visti*, July, 1951, No. 7, pp. 5-9.

5. According to Lishchyns'kyi, a former Divisional officer and Brody veteran, the Division incurred heavy casualties from air attacks. "Nastup Sovets'koi Armii i Boi Pid Brodamy" [The Advance of the Soviet Army and the

Notes

Brody Battles], *Surmach* (Great Britain: Association of Ukrainian Former Combatants in Great Britain, 1968), p. 25. For an excellent account of the difficulties experienced by the Division's anti-aircraft personnel at Brody, see Arkadiy Veremenchuk's "Brody-Polon-UPA" [Brody-Captivity-UPA], *Visti*, 1993, No. 2, pp. 70-74.

6. According to Lishchyns'kyi, Rybalko's armored thrust was preceded by intense Soviet artillery and air attacks. *Surmach*, 1968, p. 25.

7. Heike, *Ukrainian ed.*, pp. 76-78; English ed., pp. 44-45; personal discussion with Yuriy Krokhmaliuk and Veryha.

8. Veryha, *Pershyi Den'*, p. 112.

9. Makarevych's fate, however, remains unknown. For decades, it was believed that the 8th Company Commander was killed-in-action. But in the mid-1990s, information began to surface that Makarevych was actually wounded and captured. According to former Divisional soldier and Brody combat veteran Evhen Lopushans'kyi (who served in the 5th Co., 2nd Bn., 29th Rgt. and was captured at Brody), Lopushans'kyi encountered Makarevych in a prisoner-of-war hospital in the Eastern Ukrainian city of Kharkiv. But Lopushans'kyi provides no further information on Makarevych's fate and undoubtedly, has no further knowledge. As for Lopushans'kyi, he was shortly afterwards transported back to the vicinity of Ternopil, Western Ukraine, where, on 14 November 1944, he was placed on "trial" for "voluntary service with the Division Galicia." Sentenced to death by firing squad, Lopushans'kyi's sentence was soon remanded to hard labor. After fifteen years of imprisonment, Lopushans'kyi was released. He currently resides in Ternopil's vicinity. Evhen Lopushans'kyi, "Poruchnyk Petro Makarevych Ne Zhynov Pid Brodamy" [Lieutenant Petro Makarevych Did Not Perish at Brody], Visti, 1996, No. 2, p. 97.

10. Ren, *My Life's Mosaic*, p. 173; Heike, English ed., pp. 44-45.

11. G. Krivokhizhin, "Bugni Razvedchika" [Routine Reconnaissance Scouts], in *Zvezd'i Soldatskoi Slav'i* [Stars to Soldier Glories] (Kiev: Izdatel'stvo Tsk Lksmu "Molog'", 1980), pp. 21-29.

Monday, 17 July:
1. Heike, *English ed.*, p. 44.

2. In a personal discussion with Yuriy Krokhmaliuk, the former staff officer stated that up until his death, Chaplain Stetsiuk revived, assisted and administered the last rites to many a wounded soldier, both Divisional and enemy, until his death at the hands of a German NCO. But *In A Soldier Priest Remembers,* former Divisional Chaplain Nahayewsky, who upon the Division's return to Neuhammer, made a strong effort to pinpoint the exact cause of Stetsiuk's death, provides a slightly different version. According to Nahayewsky, a German NCO informed him that although he was not fully aware of the details, it was brought to his attention that a German officer (and not an NCO) had shot Stetsiuk. This incident had supposedly occurred as a result of Stetsiuk's refusal to leave a transport carrying some of the wounded during a heavy onslaught of communist tanks, Katyusha rockets and aircraft. But the NCO who related the account to Nahayewsky either did not reveal more (or perhaps Nahayewsky did not provide further details), on what exactly happened. If the NCO's version is correct, perhaps the officer who issued the order feared that if Stetsiuk would refuse to retire, others would also stay behind; hence, he was shot. (See *A Soldier Priest Remembers,* pp. 77-78, 84).
Yet, in Roman Krokhmaliuk's book, *The Glow,* a slightly different version is provided. According to Roman, Stetsiuk was executed on 7 July 1944 in the village of Terebezha near Zolochev. This execution was allegedly carried out because the Chaplain failed in his duty to assist the wounded on the front line. (See *The Glow*, p. 250). But in a letter dated to Visti Kombatanta, dated 30 March 1978, Reverend Myron Holovins'kyi, a former neighbor and close friend of Stetsiuk and his family, stated he had been provided three versions: A) After the Division had been surrounded at Brody, a German General (Holovins'kyi could not recall his name), assembled a number of officers amongst whom was Chaplain Stetsiuk. In the ensuing discussion Stetsiuk, who was known to be a very truthful and straightforward person, expressed doubt that a breakout could succeed. Angered by the Chaplain's remark, the general ordered the priest to be shot; B) Ordered on a patrol, Chaplain Stetsiuk refused and some general ordered the chaplain to be executed; C) Stetsiuk feared to assist the wounded. For this, he was executed.
Regarding the third version, Holovins'kyi totally disregards it and believes something close to one of the first two versions occurred. Holovins'kyi also emphasized that it must be remembered that Stetsiuk is not alive to defend himself; therefore, the whole truth will possibly never be known. Holovins'kyi also emphasized that since Chaplain Stetsiuk was a courageous and spiritually conscientious individual, nothing would have stopped him from assisting those in need. (For the full letter, see *The Glow*, p. 251). Dr. Laba also received a copy of Holovins'kyi's letter.

3. Formed initially as the 96th Mountain Rifle Division in Vinnitsia in Kiev's Military District in December 1923, the 96th Mountain Division was reformed as the 14th Guards Rifle Division in January 1942. That same year in July (possibly in Baku), the 96th was raised again but after Stalingrad, in February 1943, was renumbered and retitled as the 68th Guards Rifle Division. From March 1943 until July 1944, it served with the 17th Guards Rifle Corps, 38th Army. The 68th evolved around the 196th, 199th, and 201st Guards Rifle Regiments and 138th Guards Artillery Regiments.

Galicia Division

4. Regarded as a crack division under the command of Vlasov in August 1940, the 99th was formed in Uman, Kiev's Special Military District between 1936-38. Winner of the "Challenge Red Banner," and designated by General Timoshenko in August 1940 as "the best division in the Red Army," under Vlasov, the 99th retook Peremysl in July 1941, thus being the first Soviet division to strike a success against the German invader. Further combat occurred in Ukraine and Russia. Destroyed at Izyum (Kharkiv region), in May 1942, the 99th was raised again at Balachov, in the Volga Military District in August, 1942, from the divisions survivors. After combat in Stalingrad, the division was reformed as the 88th Guards Rifle Division in April 1943. Raised again in May 1943 around the 99th Brigade, the 99th remained an independent division. In January 1944, the 99th was posted into Ukraine and into the 1st Ukrainian Front's Reserve. Because the 99th Division was still regarded as a crack outfit, it was designated by the 1st Ukrainian Front to serve as a spearhead force.

5. Raised in the North Caucasus in October 1943 from elite navy and marine personnel, the 117th Guards Rifle Division was centered around the 333rd, 335th, 338th Guards Rifle Regiments and the 308th Guards Artillery Regiment. The 117th Guards fought primarily in the Azov and Black Sea regions. In November 1943, it participated in the Kerch landing. Noted for its ability to conduct seaborne and major river crossing operations, the 117th Guards was posted into the 1st Ukrainian Front to assist the front in river crossing operations.

6. Formed in Gorkiy, Moscow's Military District in November, 1941, around the 1128th, 1130th, 1132nd Rifle Regiments and the 909th Artillery Regiment, that same month the 336th Rifle Division was posted into the 60th Army. The following month (December, 1941), the 336th participated in the Moscow counteroffensive and with the 5th Army, retook Mozhaisk, a critical road and rail junction approximately 70 miles west of Moscow. Throughout 1942 and 1943, the 336th fought in Russia and Ukraine with the 5th and 61st Armies. In January 1944, the division reentered the 60th Army and was posted to the army's 15th Rifle Corps. Further combat actions included Ternopil where the Division's 1130th Regiment received the honorary title of "Ternopil." Divisional titles included "Zhytomyr" and "Katowice."

7. The 322nd was formed at Gorkiy, Moscow's Military District in July 1941. In December 1941, the 322nd Rifle Division (serving first within the 10th Army and later the 16th Army), participated in the Moscow counteroffensive. Surrounded at Sukelnichi in February 1942, the 322nd successfully held its position until its relief in August, 1942. In January 1943, it was posted into the 60th Army's 15th Rifle Corps. Further combat actions included Kursk, the Pripyat River Front, Kiev, Zhytomyr, and Ternopil.

8. The recipient of several Orders of the Red Banner, the 148th Independent Rifle Division was raised in the Volga Military District in mid-1941. Initially posted to the Soviet reserve, in September 1941, the 148th was deployed to the Central Front. In January 1943, it was committed to the Voronezh Front. That same year in the month of July, the 148th Independent, as a part of the 18th Guards Independent Rifle Corps, 13th Army, fought in the Battle of Kursk. Crossing the Dnieper River in September 1943 with the 18th Guards, in July 1944 the 148th was posted to the 60th Army's 15th Rifle Corps. Prior to the commencement of the 15th Rifle Corps' advance on 14/15 July, the 148th's entire 326th Artillery Regiment was dispatched to the 336th Rifle Division to assist the 336th's attack. As for the division's 496th, 507th and 654th Infantry Regiments, beginning on 16 July, its personnel were committed as reinforcements for both the 322nd and 336th Rifle Divisions as well as Rybalko's armored units. Throughout the German-Soviet War, the 148th remained as an independent division and it served in various armies.

9. Identified first in Finland with the 13th Red Army in December 1939, the 15th Rifle Corps served and fought throughout Russia and Ukraine. Notable battles occurred at Kiev in September 1941 where the corps was encircled but succeeded in breaking out; Pavlograd (February 1943); and Kursk in July 1943. In March 1944, the 15th Corps fought at Ternopil with the 60th Army but it also briefly reinforced the 13th Army. The 15th Rifle Corps' two organic divisions were the 322nd and 336th Rifle Divisions. But in anticipation of the summer offensive of 1944, in July the 15th Rifle Corps was reinforced with the 148th Rifle Division, an independent rifle division.

10. Initially, the 6th Guards Tank Corps was known as the 12th Tank Corps. The 12th was formed in Moscow, Moscow Military District, in May 1942. Combat actions included Kharkiv in February and March, 1943. Badly mauled by Manstein's winter counteroffensive which recaptured Kharkiv in March 1943, the 12th was pulled from the front and reformed. Recommitted into combat at Kursk in July 1943, on 26 July 1943, the 12th Tank was reorganized as the 6th Guards Tank Corps. Posted into the 3rd Guards Tank Army in November 1943, the 6th Guards Tank fought at Kiev, Fastov, Zhytomyr, and Ternopil. The recipient of the Lenin Order, the Red Banner and Bohdan Khmelnytsky awards, the 6th Guards Tank Corps was regarded by Stavka as one of its most elite tank corps.'

11. Along with the 6th Guards Tank Corps, the 7th Guards Tank Corps was also formed on 26 July 1943. The 7th Guards Tank Corps, a highly trained and combat experienced tank corps, was initially organized in Belorussia in 1938 from an experimental mechanized infantry corps. Following a period of combat on the Bryansk Front, in October 1943, the 7th Guards Tank was posted into the 3rd Guards Tank Army. It fought at Kiev, Fastov, Zhytomyr, and Ternopil. The 7th Guards Tank Corps was also regarded as a highly elite tank corps.

12. Identified as a reserve army corps in the Kiev-Zhytomyr area within the Kiev Military District, the 9th Mechanized Corps was mobilized in June, 1941. Throughout 1941-1943, the 9th Mechanized Corps fought in Ukraine and Russia. In September 1943, the corps was incorporated into the 3rd Guards Tank Army and in the following

Notes

months of October and November, fought in Kiev and Zhytomyr. In the spring of 1944, the 9th Mechanized Corps was committed into combat to repulse the efforts of the 2nd Waffen-SS Panzer Corps in its advance toward the encircled 1st Panzer Army. Removed from the front, in June 1944 the 9th was reconstituted and placed into the RVGK reserve. However, it was immediately reposted into Rybalko's 3rd Guards Tank Army and remained in that army until the duration of the war. During the summer offensive of July 1944, it fought side-by-side with the 6th and 7th Guards Tank Corps.'

13. Formed in Byelorussia's Military District in August 1939, Poland. Fought in Finland with the 13th Army; reactivated in Transcaucasia in 1940 as the 23rd Mechanized Corps, in July 1941, the 23rd Mechanized Corps was utilized as a nucleus for the 45th Red Army. With the incorporation of the mechanized corps into an army, a new 23rd Independent (but non-mechanized) Rifle Corps was raised. First appearing on the Voronezh Front in January, 1943, the 23rd Independent fought throughout Russia and Ukraine with various armies. In January 1944 the rifle corps was posted to the 60th Army but in June 1944, was redirected to Belorussia to participate in Operation "Bagration," the Soviet code name for the destruction of Nazi Germany's Army Group 'Center.' Reshifted into the 60th Army in July 1944, it arrived in time to participate in the Lvov-Sandomir Operation.

14. Organized in the Siberian Military District, in June 1941, the 52nd Rifle Corps was incorporated into the 24th Army. Appearing on the Smolensk Front in the summer of 1941, the 52nd repeatedly held its own. In September 1941, a couple of its divisions were the first to receive the honorary title of "guard." Further combat actions included Kursk in July 1943, and the Southwest Ukraine in the winter and spring of 1944. During the Lvov-Sandomir Operation, the 52nd Rifle Corps served in the 38th Army.

15. First identified in the summer of 1944, in July 1944, the 102nd Rifle Corps served in the 13th Army along with the 24th and 27th Rifle Corps.

16. Appearing at the Battle of Kursk in July 1943, the 17th Rifle Corps displayed outstanding gallantry. Decorated as a "guard" corps, further combat actions included Kharkiv (August 1943), Kiev, the Dnieper crossing in September 1943, and the Southwest Ukraine in the spring of 1944. Posted to the 1st Ukrainian Fronts reserve, during the initial breakout, the 17th Guards Rifle Corps was subordinated to the 38th Army. Its most elite division, the 68th Guards Rifle, was one of the first divisions to be committed into combat.

17. "Sokolov's" Mechanized Group was formed in late 1943 by the incorporation of the 31st Independent Tank and 6th Guards Cavalry Corps. During the Lvov-Sandomir Operation, General Sokolov's group reinforced Rybalko's 3rd Guards Tank Army.

18. The 31st Independent Tank Corps was established in July 1943 from elements of the 1st Tank (soon to be redesignated "guards") Army. The 31st first fought at Kursk in July 1943 and in the following month (August, 1943) fought with the 1st Tank Army at Kharkiv. Reappearing in July 1944 in the 1st Ukrainian Front, along with the 6th Guards Cavalry Corps the 31st Independent Tank Corps comprised "Sokolov's" Mechanized-Cavalry Group.

19. Previously known as the 7th Cavalry Corps, the 6th Guards Cavalry Corps first appeared in Northern Donets in February 1943. Throughout the first half of 1943, the 6th Guards Cavalry Corps remained in reserve status in Novy Oskol. Appearing in August 1943 in Stavka's Western Fronts Reserve, the 6th Guards Cavalry Corps participated in the Korsun-Cherkassy Operation of January 1944. Shortly afterwards, it appeared near Rovno and in February 1944, was posted into the 1st Ukrainian Front. Along with the 31st Independent Tank Corps, the 6th Guards Cavalry Corps comprised "Sokolov's" group. A powerful force, in January 1944 it was identified with the following units: 8th Cavalry, 8th Rifle and 13th Guards Divisions; 136th, 154th, and 250th Tank Regiments.

20. The first experimental combined-arms army ever developed in the communist world, the 3rd Guards Tank Army (formerly the 3rd Tank Army), was organized in May 1942 with three tank corps, three rifle divisions, and an independent tank brigade. Commanded by P. Romanenko, it fought at Tula in 1942, bypassed Kharkiv in February 1943, but was almost totally destroyed in the "Krasnograd" Pocket southwest of Kharkiv in March 1943. Withdrawn from the front, it was reformed in Plavsk, Russia. In May 1943, Rybalko assumed command which he held until the end of the war. In July 1943, the 3rd Tank Army participated in the Orel Operation. Along with the 40th Army, it was the first to reach the Dnieper River in Kiev's vicinity. Retitled as "guards" in November 1943, the 3rd Guards Tank Army fought in Kiev's vicinity, and in March 1944, fought the 4th Panzer Army in Shepetovka. In January 1944, the army was composed of the 6th Guards Tank Corps, 7th Guards Tank Corps, and the 9th Mechanized Corps which served as a reserve in Kiev's Special Military District. Each tank corps had three guards tank brigades and one guards motorized rifle brigade while the 9th Mechanized Corps had three mechanized brigades and three tank regiments. In addition to the 6th Guards, 7th Guards, and 9th Corps, the 91st Independent Tank Brigade, commanded by Colonel I.I. Yakubovskyi, as well as engineer, artillery, anti-tank, rocket, communication and support personnel, bolstered the 3rd Guards Tank Army to a strength of approximately 60,000.

21. Activated as the 13th Army by Trotsky in March 1919 from a 'Group of Forces" composed of die-hard Marxist revolutionaries, foreign interventionists, and red-guardists, the 13th was deactivated in November, 1920. Reactivated in June 1941, it went into the RVGK reserve system that same month. The 13th fought at Smolensk, Moscow, Bryansk, Kursk, Dnieper River, Kiev, Zhytomyr, Rivne, Shepetovka and Lutsk. In July 1944, it contained the 24th, 27th, 102nd Rifle Corps and the 1st Guards Breakthrough Artillery Division.

Galicia Division

22. Activated in August 1941 around the 8th Mechanized Corps, that same month the 38th Army took a beating at Lake Ilmen. Annihilated at Kharkov in September 1941, it was rebuilt shortly afterwards. Further combat occurred on the Bryansk and Kursk defensive and offensive sectors. Entering Ukraine in November 1943, the 38th frequently acquired its manpower from "booty" Ukrainians forged around NKVD police battalions. In July 1944, the 38th Army was organized around the 52nd and 107th Rifle Corps; however, for additional support, the 17th Guards Rifle Corps was subordinated to the 38th Army shortly before 13 July 1944.

23. Activated in Moscow's Military District in August 1941, the 60th Army was re-designated as the 3rd Shock Army in December 1941; shortly afterwards, it was again re-designated as the 3rd Reserve Army. Again re-designated as the 60th Army in July 1942, the army was placed in Stavka's Reserve. (RVGK). Committed to the Voronezh Front in January 1943, the 60th fought at Kursk, Kiev, the Yasnogorodka Bridgehead, Korosten, Zhytomyr (where its headquarters was overrun by the 48th Panzer Corps in December 1943), Rivne, and Ternopil. In July 1944, it consisted of the 15th, 23rd, 28th Rifle Corps' and the Independent 148th Rifle Division. But for additional reinforcement, the 106th Rifle Corps was also posted to the 60th Army. In July 1944, the 60th was commanded by Colonel-General Petr A. Kyrochkin.

24. First identified at Kursk in July 1943, the 7th Breakthrough Artillery Corps saw action in Bryansk, Bukrin and Kiev. It was incorporated into the 1st Ukrainian Front in June, 1944, and in the following month was posted to the 38th Army.

25. On 1 March 1943, the 1st Artillery Division was reformed and on that date, was redesignated as the 1st Guards Breakthrough Artillery Division. In July 1943, it fought at Kursk in support of the 13th and 70th Armies. Further combat actions included Glukhov, the Dnieper River crossing, and Kiev with the 60th Army. During the Lvov-Sandomir operation, the 1st Guards Breakthrough Artillery Division was posted to the 13th Army.

26. In July 1944, the 3rd Guards Rocket Barrage Division contained the following units: 4th, 19th, 32nd Rocket Barrage Brigades and the 312th and 313th Guards Rocket Regiments. That same month, the 3rd GRBD served as a reserve within the 1st Ukrainian Front.

27. First appearing in Kiev in November 1943, the 13th Breakthrough Artillery Division remained in Stavka's reserve for the duration of the war. Placed into Konev's front in late spring 1944, in June 1944 the 13th Breakthrough Artillery consisted of such units: 42nd Light Artillery, 47th Howitzer, 88th Heavy Howitzer, 91st Heavy Howitzer, 101st Heavy Howitzer and the 17th Rocket Barrage Brigade.

28. Formed in March 1943 in Moscow's region as the 17th Artillery Division, that same month the 17th Artillery served with the 8th Army. With the inclusion of the 97th Heavy Howitzer and the 108th Super Heavy Howitzer Brigades, the 17th Artillery Division was redesignated as the 17th Breakthrough Artillery Division. From August 1943, it fought in Orel, Kiev, Zhytomyr, and served in the Korsun-Shevchenkivs'kyi Operation. In the spring of 1944, Stavka assigned the 17th Breakthrough Artillery into Konev's 1st Ukrainian Front. Further re-designations took place but in June 1944, it consisted of the 37th Light Artillery, 39th Gun Artillery, 108th Heavy Howitzer Artillery, and the 22nd Rocket Barrage Brigades.

29. To cite as an example, approximately 40 percent of the 38th Army's infantry was composed of "booty Ukrainians."(See Ziemke's *From Stalingrad to Berlin*, p. 279). But according to the *Red Army Order of Battle*, in March 1944, 80 percent of its infantry was composed of "booty Ukrainians." (See page 55). Although of course various sources will cite various figures, it may be correctly stated that no less than 50 percent of the 38th Army's infantry was composed of "booty" Ukrainians prior to the Soviet offensive of 13 July. And during the fighting, it is known that other armies, such as the 60th Army, replenished its ranks with conscripts which received nothing more than a rifle, a pair of army pants and jacket and fifty to one hundred rounds of ammunition. With no training whatsoever, the terrified conscripts were thrown in to reinforce units depleted by combat casualties.

30. Directed by General Abukomov, penal battalions were found in every Soviet rifle division and most armor and mechanized corps also contained one or two penal battalions. Organized from nonpolitical criminal conscripts, the units were led by volunteer NKVD police officers. For those who volunteered to lead such units, the rewards were very high. Its police officer commanders, however, wore the uniform of regular army officers. Possibly this was used as a disguise but regardless, most (if not all), knew it was the NKVD, and not the army, who supervised the units. Penal battalion conscripts received no training, and were only armed prior to an attack. Their sole purpose was to draw enemy fire and expose their positions. Promised vodka, loot, and the enemy's women, penal battalions surged forward under NKVD police coercion. Unless ordered otherwise, penal battalions never took prisoners. Seriously wounded or injured penal personnel were always shot by their officers or NKVD personnel.

31. To cite as an example, at Pidhirtsi and Kniazhe, Soviet troops in camouflaged smocks were encountered. Either these were airborne, specialized troops or both. If so, they possibly were from the 2nd Guards and 6th Guards Airborne Divisions which, in the spring of 1944, were identified in the Dniester River area with the 1st Ukrainian Front.

32. Personal discussion with Yuriy Krokhmaliuk, Ostap Veryn, and various other former Divisional soldiers. According to L.Z., of 12 prisoners captured south of Brody, one older "soldier" reported to his captors that his son was

Notes

serving in the Division. (L.Z., "Remembrances, 38 Years...," *Visti*, 1982, No. 5- 6, pp. 54-55). And according to S.M., "Spomyny, Horiachi Dni Pid Brodamy" [Remembrances: The Hot Days at Brody], *Visti*, 1979, No. 3, pp. 43-44, "from Kamyanets-Podolsk a number of Ukrainians, many well into their 40's, were also captured [by Divisional troops]. In fear, these "booty Ukrainians" pleaded to remain with their Ukrainian captors for they feared death or mistreatment if handed over to the Germans." According to Yuriy Krokhmaliuk, "whenever at Brody our soldiers captured any Ukrainians forcefully pressed into the Soviet army, they released the poor and miserable looking conscripts to return home. In some cases, medical care, food, and other provisions were even provided to the returnees."

33. Myron Baran never fully recovered from his experiences. Months of intense inner reflection and visits to the chaplain did help, but the pain obviously remains to this day. "The day I die, is the day I will forget!"is how Myron explained it.

34. Raised in October 1941 in the North Caucasian Military District, the 359th Rifle Division fought in November 1941 with the 28th Army. In December 1941, it was held in reserve status with the 39th Army. In December 1941, it was committed into Rzhev (northern Russia) and the Kallinin Front and saw action in both places. In January 1944, the 359th was moved into Ukraine and placed into the 47th Independent Rifle Corps; in turn, this corps served in both the 40th and 6th Guards Tank Army's and fought at Korsun-Cherkassy. In July 1944 the 359th, still within the 47th Independent Corps, was placed in the 1st Ukrainian Fronts reserve. At first, the 359th was held in reserve. But with the intensification of the fighting in Koltiw and its area, the 359th was committed to reinforce the breakout forces.

Tuesday, 18 July:
1. Krokhmaliuk, "Polevyi Zapasnyi Kyrin' Pid Brodamy" [The Field Replacement Unit At Brody], *Visti*, 1952, February-March, No. 2-3 (16) (17), p. 12. That morning, Krokhmaliuk was one of those whose breakfast was interrupted by the appearance of enemy armor.

2. According to Panov, operational depth was achieved toward nightfall on 18 July; additionally, "some units of the 3rd Tank Army reached the region of Drevlyany, where they made contact with General Baranov's cavalry-motorized group and completed the encirclement of eight enemy divisions in the region of Brody." Panov, *Lvov-Sandomir Operation*, p. 376; *SSSR, 1941-1945*, p. 592. By this time, Soviet forces had advanced approximately 30-50 miles. See also *Marshal Zhukov*, p. 164; General S.P. Platonov, *Vtoraia Mirovoia Voina, 1939-1945* [The Second World War, 1939-1945] (Moscow: 1958), pp. 598- 600; Ziemke's, *From Stalingrad to Berlin*, p. 322; and *Velikaia Otechestvennaia Voina*, 1944, p. 364.

3. Soviet sources reveal the pocket encompassed such an area: from the west to the east, 15.5 miles; from north to south, an average of 13 miles. The pocket lay north of the Buh River, with the village of Bilyi Kamin (on the Buh River), at the base of the pocket. According to Colonel V. Kravetz', the 13th Corps was surrounded within such an area: Ozhydiv, Oles'ko, Huta, Maidan, Opaky, Ruda, Khylchychi, Kniazhe, and Krasne. However, as a result of intensified enemy pressure, by 19120 July, the corps area would shrink considerably. Now, 13th Corps base would lie adjacent to Bilyi Kamin. Colonel Kravetz', *Surmach*, (1964), No. 1-2 (25-26), p. 7.

4. Panov, p. 332; *Marshal Zhukov*, Vol. 2, p. 285; and *Marshal Zhukov*, p. 164; *SSSR, 1941- 1945*, p. 592.

5. Ziemke,*From Stalingrad to Berlin*, p. 322, cites five German divisions and the Waffen-SS "Galicia" Division. Yuriy Krokhmaliuk "Materiialy Do Istorii I-oi Ukrains'koi Dyvizii" [Sources For the 1st Ukrainian Division] cites seven German divisions. Krokhmaliuk's figure is correct if Lange's and "Korps Abteilung C's" three divisions and the "Galicia" Division is included in the numerical figure. (See *Visti*, 1978, No. 3, p. 35). Veryha, *Along the Roads*, p. 186, cites "after several days of heavy fighting, the Soviet units on 18 July encircled the 13th Army Corps consisting of four German divisions and the fifth, the Ukrainian Division "Galicia." Robert Goralski, *World War II Almanac, 1939-1945* (N.Y.: Putnam's Sons, 1981), pp. 333-334, cites that in Western Ukraine in 1944, five divisions were trapped west of Brody.

6. Seaton, *The Russo-German War*, p. 447; and *The Fall of Fortress Europe* p. 138, cited 13th Corps strength from 35,000 to 40,000. Undoubtedly, the figure Seaton utilizes was that of the 13th Corps prior to the Soviet movement of 13 July. At the time of encirclement, no less than a third of the corps strength was already eliminated. (Personal discussion with Yuriy Krokhmaliuk).

7. Krokhmaliuk, *The Glow*, p. 99. In a personal discussion with Yuriy, the above figure was corroborated.

8. According to Ren, the moment the 29th Regiments two battalions advanced to Pidhirtsi, they came under heavy and constant enemy attacks. Yet, on 17 and 18 July, against heavy Soviet attacks reinforced with artillery and armor, the 29th held its own. But as its casualties mounted, the 29th was forced to withdraw. Between the morning hours of 6 and 8 a.m., 18 July, the 29th began to retire towards Oles'ko. (Ren, *My Life's Mosaic*, pp. 178-179). Ren, however, does not provide an exact time or date of Pidhirtsi's fall. But his account is substantiated by former Divisional Chaplain Levenets'. According to Levenets', "throughout 17 and 18 July the Soviets advanced all day and night." Chaplain Levenets' stated the 29th's 1st Battalion was to commence its withdrawal on 24 hours (midnight) 18 July, and the 2nd Battalion was to withdraw four hours later commencing at 4 a.m. Levenets', "From the Archives of the 1st Ukrainian Division," *Visti*, 1951 , No. 7 (9), p. 5.

483

9. Presently, these elite troops are known as spetsnatz. "Spetsial'ni Naznachenni Voiska" (Specially Designated Troops). Missions include the elimination of high-ranking military and/or civilian personnel.

10. To cite an example of the difficult conditions the doctors labored under: after examining the 29th Regiment's 1st Battalion's 1st Company commander, Waffen-Obersturmführer Lishchyns'kyi, Dr. Volodymyr Prokopovych concluded that in order to save the commander's life, he would have to amputate the shattered right arm to retard further gangrene. With shells exploding nearby, and lacking proper medical supplies, Prokopovych conducted the operation. Following the operation, Lischyns'kyi was placed on an auto transport with several other wounded. He reached safety and survived. Yuriy Krokhmaliuk, "Doktor Volodymyr Prokopovych, Likar 1-oi UD UNA" [Doctor Volodymyr Prokopovych, Surgeon in the 1st Ukrainian Division, Ukrainian National Army], *Visti*, 1981, No. 1, pp. 65-66.

11. Chaplain Leshchyshyn's death was confirmed.

12. Although Chaplain Durbak was classified as "killed-in- action," his "death" was never officially verified. Serving with the Division's medical unit, the chaplain was last seen assisting the wounded at Pochapy, where the battered medical battalion reestablished itself for one last time. Because Chaplain Durbak never reentered the Division (or the UPA) in the aftermath of Brody, it was assumed that he was either killed in the last hours of fighting or, in the event the more seriously wounded were ordered to be slaughtered after the field hospital was overrun, the possibility exists the chaplain, in the process of protecting the wounded, was himself murdered. In the event this occurred, his body would have been thrown along with the others into one large unmarked grave.
But in the 1950s, stories began to surface in the west that the former chaplain not only survived, but was practicing his faith deep in the Carpathian Mountains. Chaplain Durbak was also reported as being seen in Siberia near China's northern border, as well as in various regions of Ukraine. Of course, the possibility exists that Chaplain Durbak might have ended up in the Gulag system; if so, he might have been moved around to various camps and regions which explains the various different sightings. A rumor also emerged in the late 1980's that Chaplain Durbak was living in Ukraine under an alias, but stories also surfaced that in approximately 1991, an aged – and senile – man passed away in the Carpathian Mountains. Prior to his death, this man claimed to have been a priest who witnessed combat on the eastern front. Of interest to note is that Chaplain Durbak's younger brother, 23-year-old Vsevolod Durbak, also disappeared at Brody. Vsevolod served with Vasyl Veryha in the 7th Company, 2nd Battalion, 30th Infantry Regiment. (Personal discussion with Veryha).

13. Struck in the upper left part of his back by a sizable piece of shrapnel during the breakout phase, Chaplain Josef Kladochnyi's initial reaction was that another soldier had collided into his back as the group came under another massive artillery barrage. But after several steps, Chaplain Kladochnyi collapsed. Unable to move, Chaplain Kladochnyi suddenly realized that he had been wounded.
Several soldiers ran up. Calling for a medic, within seconds a "doctor" appeared. (Chaplain Kladochnyi identified the medical soldier as "Doctor Dakur." However, a close examination of the Divisions medical officers reveals that no doctor by the name of "Dakur" ever served in the Division. Remembering that worldwide in virtually every army medics are referred to as either "doc" or "doctor," the possibility exists that "Doctor Dakur" in actuality was a medic). Amidst exploding shells and gunfire, the medic announced to those squatting and standing around the chaplain "there's no need to bandage him! He will die quickly!" Decades later, the former Divisional chaplain would recall those words and feel disappointment that at least a dressing of some type had not been quickly applied.
As more artillery rounds came screaming in, the medic ran off. Realizing that nothing would be done, the chaplain ordered those around him to flee the devastating fire.
With blood flowing from the wound, the chaplain remained in place. More artillery rounds exploded around him. Dirt rained upon him. A group of German soldiers came running by. One stopped to assist the chaplain. Realizing also that nothing could be done, after a brief exchange of words, the soldier proceeded after the others.
After lying on the ground for an unknown period of time, Chaplain Kladochnyi began to crawl into the direction of a road pointed out earlier to him by the German. Despite the loss of a considerable amount of blood and his inability to move his left arm, the semi-conscious chaplain succeeded in reaching the road. Noting a damaged cottage, he crawled inside.
Within minutes, another massive artillery barrage rained in more shells. A shell exploded adjacent to the cottage. Pieces of the cottage fell upon the chaplain. Noting that the cottage was on fire, Chaplain Kladochnyi crawled out. He lost consciousness.
Years later, the chaplain would recall how someone had come upon him. Within hours, a priest by the name of Iliarii Fenchyns'kyi had been informed that a Divisional chaplain had been wounded and needed immediate attention. Although Father Fenchyns'kyi was fleeing ahead of the communist onslaught in a refugee column, upon receiving word of the wounded chaplain, he immediately went to see what could be done. Along with Fenchyns'kyi came a young girl named Maria Lopatyns'ka who, prior to the war, had studied to be a medical technician. Finding the chaplain, they rendered first-aid.
Because Chaplain Kladochnyi could not be moved, he found himself under communist occupation. For several weeks he remained delirious. Various brave individuals rendered him assistance.
In the ensuing months, Chaplain Kladochnyi regained his strength. But he would only experience more agony. Arrested by the NKVD, the chaplain experienced nothing but incarceration, ruthless interrogations, and beatings. Deported in a cattle car to the arctic region of Vorkuta, in the ensuing years, frequently in sub-zero temperatures, he worked as a slave laborer in a coal mine.

Notes

Released in the Khruschev era, Reverend Kladochnyi returned to Lviv. Within several weeks of his return, he wrote an account of his experiences. Unable to have it published under Soviet rule, and fully realizing that if Soviet authorities ever learned of it he would be re-arrested, for decades the former Divisional chaplain concealed his account. Although it still has not been published, "V Obiimakh Smerty Pid Brodamy" [Embracing Death At Brody] has been photocopied and is an excellent true study of the ordeals of a brave infantry chaplain. As for the chunk of shrapnel which tore into Reverend Kladochnyi's body, it remained in him until his peaceful death on 14 September 1994. Excluding only the first-aid treatment he received, nothing else had been done. Post-war surgeons informed the priest that the chances of someone surviving such a serious wound is virtually unheard of. In the Divisions history, Chaplain Kladochnyi will always be honored as a true soldier, patriot, and man-of-God.

14. Vasyl Sirs'kyi, "Molod Druhoi Svitovoi Viiny" [The Youth of the Second World War], *Visti*, 1988, No. 1, p. 82. Although some ended up in the UPA while others successfully evaded capture by hiding out, the majority perished. In a personal discussion with Yuriy Krokhmaliuk, the former Divisional staff officer acknowledged that the 29th Regiment took the heaviest losses of the three regiments.

15. After Dern was wounded, regimental command fell to Dern's adjutant, SS-Hauptsturmführer Weiss. But in the aftermath of World War II, Chaplain Levenets' cited Dern's adjutant was a major named Dietz. Levenets', "From the Archives of the 1st Ukrainian Division," *Visti*, 1951, No. 7.

Wednesday, 19 July:
1. *SSSR, 1941-1945*, p. 592. In a personal discussion with Yuriy Krokhmaliuk, it is generally recognized that after 19 July, AGNU's chances of containing the Soviet offensive had ceased to exist.

2. Heike, English ed., p. 47; cites the 8th Panzer and the 20th Panzergrenadier Divisions were brought up for an attack to assist the 13th Corps. However, Heike indicates that increasing enemy pressure forced the two divisions to withdraw. *(Ibid)*. Hence, their efforts to assist the encircled corps in the long run proved largely ineffective. *Mellenthin*, pp. 286-287, cite's only the 8th Panzer as being used. In addition to the above forces, it was later reported (but never officially confirmed), that a reinforced battlegroup was hastily raised around the 18th SS "Horst Wessel" Panzergrenadier Division's 40th SS
Panzergrenadier Regiment to assist in the defense of Lviv. *(Klietmann,* p. 215). Commanded by SS-Sturmbannführer Ernst Schafer, little is known of its efforts but allegedly, a "Kampfgruppe Schafer" did assist the 8th Panzer in extraditing the 13th Corps. See also *Bender and Taylor*, Vol. 4, pp. 171-172. According to *Ready*, p. 370, several German units, such as the 18th SS Division and an understrength Waffen-SS French assault brigade, were utilized to assist the 13th Corps breakout.

3. In his memoirs, von Mellenthin (p. 286), cites the evening of 17 July as the date when he attempted to reach the encircled corps by radio, 17 July as the date of his briefing, and 18 July as the date of the attack to relieve 13th Corps. Although von Mellenthin is correct in his sequence of events, he erred on his dates, and is off by one day. All sources cite 18 July as the date of the encirclement and 19 July as the date of Mellenthin's attempt to reach the encircled 13th Corps.

4. In addition to using freshly inserted divisions such as the 359th Rifle Division, various other air and ground forces, including NKVD combat police troops, attacked the encircled corps. According to Colonel Anderson, one entire tank corps from Rybalko's 3rd Guards Tank Army was committed to contain the encirclement. *SMS*, December 1986, p. 507,

5. Personal discussion with Yuriy Krokhmaliuk and other members of the Division.

6. At this time, the "Galicia" Division also organized its first breakout groups. These were formed in the event the escape route was sealed, or a flank needed reinforcement, or certain key terrain features needed to be retaken as the Division itself proceeded through the "funnel."

Thursday, 20 July:
1. Realistically speaking, the exact date of Hauffe's death is not known but it appears that 20 July is the date. It is known that on 19/20 July, General Lange assumed command of the 13th Corps because Hauffe was nowhere in sight. But in the 1960s, a German priest, Chaplain Bader, who officiated in the 454th Field Security Division, returned to West Germany from Soviet captivity. According to the former chaplain, he (Bader) saw General Hauffe on the afternoon of 22 July in the northern part of the town of Kniazhe. Bader described the general as being in a state of depression. According to Bader, Hauffe remarked such words: "Their [the Soviet] superiority is too great, there's no sense in going on. We can't continue to allow the men to be slaughtered uselessly. Perhaps we'll wait until night. The situation is hopeless!" For an interesting account of Bader's experience, as well as what occurred within the pocket in the final hours, see Buchner's, *Ostfront 1944*, pp. 234-236. According to Heike, *English ed.*, p. 51; and "Biy Pid Brodamy," in *1943-1993. The 1st Ukrainian Division*, p. 21, it was reported that General Hauffe was killed in an ambush at Holohory, a town south of Kniazhe. But neither Heike's nor the Division's description of Hauffe's death is clear; it appears that the information pertaining to Hauffe's death was presented to either Heike (or the Divisional staff) in the aftermath of the Brody breakout. In a personal discussion with Yuriy Krokhmaliuk, the former Divisional staff officer stated that to the best of his knowledge, General Hauffe was no longer in command when the first

breakout attempt commenced on 20 July. According to Nahayewsky, *A Soldier Priest Remembers,* p, 83, General Lange was already in command of the encircled corps on 20 July because Hauffe was dead. Regardless of the exact date, it is known that from 20 July onward, Hauffe was no longer in command of the 13th Corps. Of interest to note is that in recent years, information has surfaced that General Hauffe was actually captured and transported to Moscow. Interrogated by the Soviets, during his interrogation Hauffe allegedly acknowledged to his interrogators that the Soviet air force played a major role in destroying the 13th Corps. Although Hauffe's fate remains unknown to this day, perhaps the 13th Corps general was captured. *World War II Encyclopedia,* Vol. 12, p. 1660, cites that Hauffe was taken prisoner on 23 July 1944.

2. Sylenko broke out. His 17-year-old son, Mykola, was killed-in-action toward the end of the war.

3. Personal discussion with Yuriy Krokhmaliuk. See also *Lashchenko,* pp. 318-319; and *SSSR, 1941-1945,* p. 593. On that day, the Ist Ukrainian Front occupied various sizable towns and cities such as Vladimyr-Volynski, Rava-Russka, Peremysl, and Zboriv. But as this was happening, "west of Brody, Soviet forces were conducting a battle to eliminate the surrounded forces and prevent elements of the opposing forces from breaking out of encirclement." (*Ibid,*).

4. Indeed, it turned out to be one of the most vicious battles on the eastern front.

5. Neither Shuhan or Yuriy Krokhmaliuk could recall the officer's name. By his actions, the supply officer not only demonstrated true loyalty to the unit, but saved many lives as well.

6. Heike, English ed., pp. 48-49; Ukrainian ed., pp. 88-89; *The Glow,* p. 98; Nahayewsky, *A Soldier Priest Remembers,* pp. 80-81; personal discussion with Yuriy Krokhmaliuk.

7. Ren, *My Life's Mosaic,* p. 177,

8. *Ibid.*

9. Personal discussion with Yuriy Krokhmaliuk, Veryha, and Veryn. Heike, English ed., pp. 45-46, also substantiates this.

10. Heike, *English ed.,* p. 48.

11. Krokhmaliuk, *The Glow,* p. 98.

Friday, 21 July:
1. Krokhmaliuk, who recounted this episode to the author, could not recall the name of the soldier who died attempting to save the child. It is believed, however, that the soldier who rushed forward was a medic from the 29th Regiment who, somehow, became attached to the fusiliers.

Saturday, 22 July – Monday, 24 July:
1. L.Z., "38 Pokiv" [38 Years], *Visti,* 1982, No. 5-6, p. 55.

2. According to Bohdan Levyts'kyi, enroute through Pochapy, he witnessed rows of wounded lying adjacent to Pochapy's cemetery and its church. At the moment, the church was being utilized as a makeshift hospital. Doctors and medical orderlies were seen taking care of the wounded. Until the last moment, strong efforts were made to evacuate the wounded. But after 22 July, when it became virtually impossible to conduct any further evacuations, those not removed were overrun by Soviet ground forces. See Levyts'kyi's, "Pochapy (Prolom z Okruzhennia)" [Pochapy (Breakout from Encirclement)], in *1944 Brody - 1964 New York* (N.Y.: East Side Press, 1964), p. 10.
At approximately the same time the Divisions remnants were breaking out, the UPA dispatched a number of medical nurses and orderlies, some of them girls no older than 15 and 16 years of age, into the battle area to assist the wounded and injured. UPA's personnel were observed at Pochapy. Under very adverse conditions, UPA's personnel also displayed true humanitarianism. UPA's medics rendered medical aid not only to the wounded soldiers of the "Galicia" Division, but as well as to the German and captured Soviets who required medical assistance.

3. It is known that Chaplain Durbak never entered the UPA.

4. Ren, *My Life's Mosaic,* pp. 174-175. The corridor was, however, expanded on several occasions, See also Heike, *English ed.,* p. 51.

5. Some of the missing and those presumed to have been killed reappeared to the Division in the following weeks and months, Many, however, remained unaccounted for.

6. Levyts'kyi, "Pochapy (Prolom z Okruzhennia)" [Pochapy (Breakout From Encirclement)], in *1944 Brody - 1964 New York,* pp. 10-11. According to Reverend Kleparczuk, the main breakout was through Pochapy, Belzets', Skvariava, and Kniazhe. "Dorohamy i Stezhkamy Bridshchyny. Spomony." [Fording through the Encirclements Roads

Notes

and Paths. Remembrances], p. 213. In a personal discussion with Yuriy Krokhmaliuk, the former Divisional staff officer substantiated the breakout largely occurred through these places. See also Heike's, English ed., pp. 47-53; *Ukrainian ed.*, pp. 99-104.

7. *SSSR, 1941-1945*, p. 593. According to this Soviet source, throughout the entire day of Saturday, 22 July, Soviet forces fought to eliminate the encircled forces in the vicinity of Brody. Although the source acknowledges that the encircled force lost most of its personnel and equipment, it is clearly evident that the fighting was also very difficult for the Soviets by the number of air sorties flown that day against those still resisting inside the pocket. (*Ibid.*).

8. Apparently, what remained of the 91st Independent Tank was simply just incorporated into other Soviet tank units. A close examination of Soviet military units in various Red Army Orders of Battle reveal the tank brigade to be non-existent from August, 1944.

9. For a fascinating account of L.Z.'s capture, imprisonment, and escape, see "38 Rokiv" [38 Years], V*isti*, 1982, No. 5-6, pp. 53-55, and *Visti*, 1983, No. 1, pp. 74-76.

10. For a personal account of the difficulties experienced during the entire Battle of Brody to include the breakout phase, see Sylenko's, "Za Proryv z Otochennia" [Breakout From Encirclement], in *Brody: Zbirnyk Stattei i Naryciv*, ed. Lysiak, pp. 255-264.

11. See also M. Vysots'kyi's, "Spomyn: V Richnytsiu Boiu Pid Brodamy" [Remembrance: Hand-to-Hand Combat at Brody], *Visti*, 1978, No. 3, pp. 63-64. For another excellent account of the difficulties experienced by Divisional troops during the breakout phase, as well as the viciousness of the fighting, see Yuriy Kopystians'kyi's, "Proryv z-Pid Brodiv" [Breakout From Brody], *Visti*, 1994, No. 1, pp. 94-103.

12. Contemporary, Soviet sources acknowledge that heavy fighting occurred in Kniazhe. See *Lashchenko*, pp. 318-319. According to Lashchenko, hundreds of German prisoners were recorded just alone in Kniazhe.
Various authors have also acknowledged that in the final stages of the breakout battle, there was a considerable amount of close-in and hand-to-hand combat. This was substantiated not only by Yuriy Krokhmaliuk, Veryha, and a host of Divisional Brody combatants, but as well by contemporary sources such as Madej's, *Russo-German War: Summer 1944*, pp. 53-58; *Ready*, p. 370; and the German Wehrmacht communiques of 18-23 July 1944. See *Ostfront 1944*, pp. 236-238. *World War II Encyclopedia*, Vol. 12, p. 1660, accurately described the Brody pocket as a "moving pocket from which several thousand men managed to escape during a night attack of hand-to-hand combat."

13. One of the last ones to breakout was Liubomyr Ortyns'kyi. After organizing a battlegroup and breaking out, he linked up with a Major Ziegler and a Wehrmacht commander named von Fessel. Both commanders had also organized breakout groups. Combining the three groups into one, the strengthened force succeeded in reaching safety.

14. Veryha, *Along the Roads, English synopsis*, p. 186.

15. Kurt Fleischmann, "Conspiracy to Conceal" in *World War II Investigator* (London: England, 1989), Vol. 1, No. 10, p. 10.
Of interest – and importance – to note is that in 1987, a massive work regarding World War II war crimes appeared in Ukraine. Initially published in Russian, the work was soon translated into English. Titled *Nazi Crimes In Ukraine, 1941-1944* (Kiev: Naukova Dumka Publishers, 1987), this book was sponsored by the Academy of Sciences of the Ukrainian SSR, Institute of State and Law.
Nearly 400 pages long, the book identifies numerous German and foreign individuals, units, and organizations alleged to have been involved in the conduct of "war crimes" in Ukraine. Within its pages, numerous military individuals from privates to generals; policemen of various ranks, and civilian collaborators who allegedly committed various types of crimes are identified. Dr. Wechtel (Wachter) is cited as an "organizer of forced labor camps." Yet, no mention is made of the "Galicia" Division or Wachter's relation to the Division.
Certain Waffen-SS divisions (such as the Leibstandarte SS-Adolf Hitler) are mentioned in entirety. But once again, in the entire book, there is no mention of the "Galicia" (or "Ukrainian") Division.
So why is this? Are Soviet propagandists finally realizing that their attacks against the "Galicia" Division are baseless, unwarranted and, therefore, totally useless? Possibly they themselves have finally realized the many contradictions? Or did the Deschenes Committee, directly or indirectly, exert some type of influence? Or perhaps is Vasylenko, Styrkul and company awakening to the fact that their contradictory accounts are totally groundless, untrue, idiotic, and therefore, ineffectual?

Notes Chapter 17

1. Personal discussion with Yuriy Krokhmaliuk.

2. *Biy Pid Brodamy*, p. 157. This figure encompassed the dead, wounded, and captured.

Galicia Division

3. Petro Savaryn, "... UNA u St. Keteryns...," *Visti*, 1984, No. 5-6, p. 18.

4. "Fakty Pro Ukrains'ky Duviziiu" [Facts About the Ukrainian Division], *Visti*, 1985, No. 4, p. 25.

5. *Ready*, p. 370.

6. "Komisiia Dlia Rozshuku Voennykh Zlochyntsiv (Komisiia Deshena)" [The Commission for the Search of War Criminals (The Deschenes Commission)], *Visti*, 1987, No. 2, p. 47.

7. I.T., "Biy Pid Brodamy" [Battle at Brody], *Visti*, 1984, No. 3, p. 74.

8. Ivan Kedryn, "Problema Dyvizii" [The Divisions Problems], *Visti*, 1958, No. 5-6, p. 15.

9. O. Lysiak, "Biy Pid Brodamy" [Battle of Brody], *Svoboda*, 2 August 1952, pp. 50-51. The figure of approximately 7,000 killed is also substantiated by "Biy Pid Brodamy" in *1943-1993. The 1st Ukrainian Division*, p. 21.

10. Kubiyovych, *Encyclopedia of Ukraine*, Vol. 1, p. 177.

11. Detroit Novynuk, June, 1988, No. 188.

12. Anatoliy Nedils'kyi, "Yak Vy Umyraly, Vam Dzvony Ne Hraly" [When You Were Dying, the Bells Did Not Ring for You], in *Za Vil'nu Ukrainu* (For a Free Ukraine), Wednesday, 29 May 1991.

13. Nahayewsky, *A Soldier Priest Remembers*, p. 84.

14. Molodets'kyi's figure was cited by A. Nedils'kyi in the 29 May 1991 article appearing in *Za Vil'nu Ukrainu*. [For a Free Ukraine].

15. Liubomyr Ortyns'kyi, *Brody, 1944-1964* (N.Y.: East Side Press, 1964), p. 9.

16. Personal discussion with Tir.

17. Personal discussion with Yuriy Krokhmaliuk.

18. Personal discussion with Yuriy Krokhmaliuk. Such is an example of how some Divisional troops returned to their Division: on 21 July 1944, Colonel Neumeister, from the 1st Panzer Division, made one last effort to rescue as many soldiers from the embattled pocket as possible. Striking into the Soviet rear, northeast of Holohory, Kampfgruppe Neumeister succeeded in extraditing about 3,000 soldiers, of whom 400 were from the "Galicia" Division. (*Ostfront 1944*, p. 231). In due time, these 400 returned to their Division.

19. Thus, the ex-troops of the 14th Waffen-SS "Galicia" Division hold the longest record for combat activities. See also *Gaucher*, p. 354.

20. Because a number of the Galician Germans who succeeded in breaking out never returned to the Division, it is assumed they remained within German units.

21. Personal discussion with Yuriy Krokhmaliuk. According to Osyp Holynskyj, over 3,000 Divisional soldiers succeeded in breaking out and this strength was utilized as a nucleus for the reconstruction of the Division. (40th Anniversary of the Rise of the Division "Galicia," *Visti*, 1983, No. 4, p.21). Although Holynskyj acknowledges that casualties (especially during the breadout phase) were heavy, Holynskyj also cites that a number returned to civilian life while others entered the ranks of the Ukrainian UPA insurgency. (*Ibid*).

22. Roman Krokhmaliuk's review of Reverend Nahayewsky's book, "A Soldier Priest Remembers," in *Visti*, 1985, No. 3, p. 69.

23. Personal discussion with Roman Krokhmaliuk. If one takes into consideration that the Division's Field Replacement Battalion was in the rear and was not encircled, than fewer than 10,000 actually ended up on the front line. Roman's figures were derived from various military Divisional documents and reports, information obtained from German archives, and returnees from Soviet captivity and the Ukrainian UPA insurgency.

24. *Istoriia Velikoi Otechestvennoi Voini Sovetskogo Soiuza 1941-1945* [History of the Great Patriotic War of the Soviet Union 1941-1945], (Moscow: 1962), Vol. 4, p. 214; *SSSR, 1941-1945*, p. 593, cites 17,000 soldiers and officers were captured.

25. One such Ukrainian account regarding the Brody encirclement reveals that the surrounded enemy (the Division "Galicia" is also identified), was destroyed and altogether 15,000 were killed and another 2,500 Hitlerite soldiers and officers were captured. *Istoriia Mist i Sil' Ukrains'koi RSR, L'vivs'ka Oblast* [History of the Ukrainian

Notes

SSR's Towns and Villages in Lviv's Region] (Kiev: Holovna Redaktsiia Ukrains'koi Radians'koi Entsyklopedii, 1968), p. 125. While as of date no official figures have been properly determined, the Ukrainian account of 1968 appears to be the closest to accuracy.

26. Vitaly Vunohrads'kyi, "*I Nastav Svitanok*" [And the Dawn Arose] (Lviv: October 1979), pp. 48, 58; Vasyl Sirs'kyi, "Dyviziinyky v UPA – Desiatnyk Evhen Smyk" [Divisional Soldiers In the UPA – Sergeant Evhen Smyk], *Visti*, 1990, No. 1, p. 75. According to Sirs'kyi, Smyk always stated that he only entered the Division to obtain military training, and that once on the front, he would defect.

27. *Visti*, 1990, No. 1, p. 75. Hutsul was either an agent, or someone on his staff was working for the Soviets.

28. Personal discussion with Vashchenko. For another interesting account of the Division's impact on the UPA, see Yuriy Krokhmaliuk, "Voiaky Dyvizii "Halychyna" v. Ukrains'kii Povstans'kii Armii" [The Division's "Gailicia" Soldiers in the UPA], *Visti*, 1975, No. 6, p. 32.

29. One such soldier was Hryts' Goliash (alias "Hryts' Bei," "Hryts' Shalom," and "Bulba Hryts"). Born 19 August 1910 in the village of Vyshky, Galicia, in his youth Goliash became active in various Ukrainian organizations. Drafted into the Polish Army, he graduated from an NCO academy. Surviving the blitzkrieg of 1939, he returned to Eastern Galicia (now under Soviet occupation) and entered the Ukrainian underground. Shortly after the Nazi occupation, he entered the UPA and fought the Nazis.

In 1943, he left the UPA and enlisted into the "Galicia" Division under an alias. Although there were dangers in this, upon the completion of recruit training, he was trained as a weapons specialist. Immediately after the Battle of Brody, he reentered the UPA. In 1946, he assumed command of a company.

Exactly what year, and for what purposes, Goliash returned to Lviv is not known. Regardless, his identity was somehow revealed and in the summer of 1954, the NKVD came to arrest him.

By no means would this be an easy arrest. After entering the apartment building where it was alleged that Goliash was residing at, the four NKVD policemen proceeded with their search.

They never again saw the street. For the remainder of the day, bursts of automatic gunfire were heralded through the streets of Lviv as the former Polish/Divisional/UPA specialist fought it out singly with Lviv's entire NKVD. Exhausted, his ammunition running out, Goliash removed his remaining hand grenade, pulled its pin, pressed it against his body and hurtled himself out of a four story window. The ensuring blast tore him apart.

30. Personal discussion with Yuriy Krokhmaliuk. However, some continued a passive type of resistance. Such was the case of Iakiv Maliaryk. In the aftermath of Brody, he entered the UPA and stayed within the insurgency until well into the 1950s. Returning to civilian life, he concealed his true identity under an alias. And until the collapse of the Soviet Union, Maliaryk continued his resistance through propaganda measures.

31. Personal discussion with Yuriy Krokhmaliuk.

32. Yuriy Krokhmaliuk, "The Division's Soldiers in the UPA," *Visti*, 1975, No. 6, p. 32.

33. Ren, *My Life's Mosaic*, p. 165.

34. *Ibid.*, pp. 165-166.

35. In addition to Yurkevych, there was Bohdan Hvozdets'kyi (alias Emir Kor) who, as a radio communications specialist, was personally posted by Shukhevych to UPA's top command to head UPA's communications. And Bohdan Bilas (born 1916), after breaking out of encirclement, entered the UPA. He served as a medical assistant to a UPA doctor. Captured by the Soviets in the aftermath of World War II, Bilas was sentenced to 18 years of hard labor. He endured most of his ordeal in Vorkuta's harsh slave labor system. Released in the early 1960s, Bilas returned to his home town of Truskavtsi, in Western Ukraine. He remained there until his death on 22 November 1993.

36. Ren, *My Life's Mosaic*, pp. 165-166.

37. In many of his writings and in a persona discussion, Yuriy Krokhmaliuk cited that "many ended up in the UPA, but the figure is unknown." However, in "Materiialy Do Istorii 1-oi UD UNA" [Materials for the History of the 1st Ukrainian Division, Ukrainian National Army], *Visti*, 1978, No. 3, pp. 35-36, Krokhmaliuk cites that "over 2,000 [Divisional soldiers] were found within the UPA's units."

38. To commemorate the 50th Anniversary of the UPA, a conference was held in Kiev, Ukraine, in 1992. During this conference, various individuals spoke about UPA's struggle, and it was revealed that approximately 3,000 Divisional soldiers entered the UPA in July and August 1944.

This figure, however, does not include whose who entered the UPA via the Division prior to the Brody Battle; nor does it include those who entered the UPA after August 1944. According to UPA's former intelligence officer Ostap Vashchenko, approximately 3,000 entered the UPA immediately after Brody. But hundreds more entered the Ukrainian underground via the Division prior to, and after, July-August 1944. Of interest to note is that on 22 August 1947, the Military Board held its last conference in the "Wolfgangseiche" Restaurant in the city of Munich. And one

Galicia Division

of the guest speakers was Stefan Levyts'kyi, a Divisional artillery officer who, during the breakout phase, fled into UPA's ranks. After serving for 16 months as an artillery and mortar advisor to the UPA, Levyts'kyi returned to West Germany. Although he did not cite a figure of the estimated number of Divisional soldiers who served within the ranks of the UPA, Levyts'kyi acknowledged that "during my 16 month stay in the 'forest' ['forest' was the slang term for the UPA] not once did I ever encounter any UPA element which did not have at least several of our boys from the Division." Levyts'kyi even spoke of the critical medical support provided by the Division's doctors to the UPA. For Levyts'ky's experiences, see "Minutes of the Meetings of the Military Board "Galicia," 22 August 1947, pp. 160-161.

39 Certain western writers, however, have acknowledged that the "Galicia" Division did succeed in breaking out, although sustaining a loss. See Keegan's, *The Waffen-SS*, p. 107; D.S.V Fosten and R.J. Marrion, *Waffen-SS. Its Uniforms, Insignia and Equipment, 1938-1945*, (London: Almark Publishing Co., 1972), p. 27; *Bender and Taylor*, Vol. 4, p. 34; and Mitcham, *Hitler's Legions*, p. 456.

Notes Chapter 18

1. Heike,*English* ed., p. 54. In his memoir, Heike wrote how shortly after the Battle of Brody, he, General Freitag, and some of the other commanders of the 13th Corps were invited to dinner by General Raus. During dinner, Raus praised the various units to include the "Galicia" Division.

2. *SSSR, 1941-1945*, p 590. Needless to say, this is an awesome amount of explosive which actually exceeds the bomb tonnage of the two nuclear blasts at Hiroshima and Nagasaki. Although *SSSR, 1941-1945* does not identify exactly the two tank and one infantry divisions conducting the counterattack on 15 July, the "Galicia" Division was the infantry division dispatched for the counterattack.

In the aftermath of World War II, German commanders acknowledged that usually, Soviet air support was weak, negligible, and was even known to "disappear." However, there were exceptions to this. And one such exception was in the summer of 1944, when "mass sorties were repeated in the Battle of Lwow." See "A Ground Force Evaluation. Tactical Employment," in *Russian Combat Methods In World War II*, p. 99. According to Colonel Seaton,in the summer of 1944, the Red Air Force possessed a supremacy seldom experienced by the Germans. See *The Fall of Fortress Europe, 1943-1945*, p. 138.

3. Personal discussion with Vasyl Veryha.

4. Personal discussion with Yuriy Krokhmaliuk. In a personal letter from author H.P. Taylor, the author writes: "The men who fought at Brody were well-trained (or should have been), probably well-armed, with some of them combat-experienced." (Letter dated 15 October 1988). And Dr. Hryts' Luchkovs'kyi, a former Brody veteran, strongly disputes the allegations that "the Division was poorly trained...;" "the Germans used it to cover their withdrawal...;" "the [Divisions] commander and his staff fled and left the Division" by presenting a fairly detailed evaluation of the Divisions training prior to Brody, the combat events, and breakout. See "Yak tse bulo Naspravdi" [How It Really Was], *Visti*, 1951, No. 7 (9), pp. 12-13. But perhaps the harshest opponent of the Divisions critics is Brody veteran Oleh Lysiak. Condemning the so-called "rekliamatsiyni" (those who were going to enlist but than under various excuses avoided service and, in the aftermath of Brody and World War II became one of the Division's - and UPA's - harshest critics) for circulating various untruths and condemnations of the Division to justify their cowardice and low-esteem, Lysiak charged "as our Divisions soldiers were fighting for two weeks in a bloody and vicious struggle, the 'rekliamatsiyni' had time to pack their trophies, family crests and personal belongings, and ship themselves from Lviv to Krynytsi, and from there either to Slovakia or Vienna." "Biy - ne Katastrofa" [Combat - Not a Catastrophe], *Visti*, 1951, No.7 (9), p. 2. Lysiak's observations are supported by a number of former Divisional soldiers and their families.

5. Cases have actually been known to occur were well-trained fresh units have performed better than combat-experienced formations For an interesting study of why this occurs see, Richard Holmes' *Firing Line*, pp. 214-223.

6. Personal discussion with Roman Hayetskyj.

7. Personal discussion with Roman Krokhmaliuk. The figure of 360 was submitted to Roman Krokhmaliuk by a former medical officer who served at Brody.

8. Personal discussion with Yuriy Krokhmaliuk and several former Divisional medics. According to Roman Kolisnyk, the Divisions field hospital was officially formed after Brody. Prior to Brody, it was referred to as a medical clearing station. Although Kolisnyk is correct in his observation, in actuality the Divisions medical clearing station was staffed not only with medics but with doctors, surgeons and skilled orderlies who possessed tents, ambulances, beds, field X-ray equipment, medical equipment and various supplies sufficient to conduct, if necessary, surgical operations. In consideration of this, it is not incorrect to classify the Divisions medical clearing station at Brody as a field hospital. A German World War II Order-of-Battle also identifies a "Feldlazarett" (field military hospital) as being at Brody. See also *Bender and Taylor*, Vol. 4, p. 47.

9. Personal discussion with Yuriy Krokhmaliuk.

Notes

10. Along with Dr. Karpevych, it is believed that Dr. Liubynets'kyi, who also served with the 29th Regiment and to this day is missing-in-action, was killed. According to former 29th Regimental Chaplain Levenets', Levenets' last saw Dr. Liubynets'kyi in the village of Yasenivtsi. "Z Arkhivu 1-oi U.D." [From the Archives of the 1st Ukrainian Division], *Visti*, 1951, No. 7 (9), p. 5.

11. According to Levyts'kyi, as he was breaking out, he witnessed rows of wounded lying adjacent to Pochapy's cemetery which was adjacent to a church This church now served as the Divisions main medical point. It appears that a strong effort was made to evacuate the wounded, but as it became impossible to conduct further evacuations, a number of the casualties were left behind at Pochapy. See Levyts'kyi's "Pochapy" (*Brody*), p. 10. At this time, some of those who were tending to the casualties were UPA's medical personnel who were dispatched to assist the Division's battered medical service. Among them were girls no less than 16 years of age. UPA's medics displayed true bravery and humanitarianism as they treated under very adverse conditions not only the Division's wounded and injured, but as well the German and Soviet casualties found within the makeshift medical center.

12. It is known that if a doctor survived his capture, within a matter of hours he was separated from the wounded. Afterwards, different doctors endured different fates. One may cite the case of Dr. Tymchyshyn.

Deported to a Siberian slave labor camp in a cattle car, shortly after his arrival to the Gulag, he was posted into its medical service. But in the early 1950s, Dr. Tymchyshyn returned to Lviv where he directed Lviv's Medical Institute and taught surgery and X-ray analysis. He maintained his position until his death in late 1969. Buried in Lychakivskyi's Cemetery, his funeral was attended by many. In the ensuing obituary, Dr. Tymchyshyn was highly praised.

Of course, there was no mention of his service in the "Galicia" Division. And the fact that the doctor was able to maintain in that era such a position left many bewildered. So how did he do it?

Prior to his death, rumors first surfaced in the West Ukraine and later abroad that when in Siberia, Dr. Tymchyshyn was approached by a high-ranking NKVD officer who desperately, was seeking medical help for his dying wife or daughter. Previous efforts by a host of Soviet doctors produced only unsuccessful results. A true humanitarian, Dr. Tymchyshyn performed a proper medical evaluation and a very difficult and delicate operation; his surgical skills saved and cured his patient. In turn, the communist officer reimbursed the doctor by promptly returning him and his entire family (who in the aftermath of Dr. Tymchyshyn's capture at Brody were also deported to Siberia) to Lviv. In the ensuing years, the entire family was left alone.

13. For Lischyns'kyi's observations, see *Surmach*, 1968, p. 26.

14. For an example of one such comparison, see Anatoli Nedil's'kyi's, "Yak vy umyraly, vam dzvony ne hraly.." [When You Perished, the Bells Did Not Ring For You], *Visti*, 1991, No. 3, p. 54. According to Nedil's'kyi, some former Divisional soldiers feel that "Brody is the second Kruty."

15. In turn, this figure was provided to the author in a personal discussion with Roman Krokhmaliuk.

16. In the aftermath of the collapse of the Soviet Union, a number of these former prisoners have re-established contact with the ex-Divisional soldiers residing throughout the world Never forgetting their former comrades-in-arms, the Divisions veterans organization has even sought to assist them financially and medically. Various fund raising activities are also conducted.

Notes Chapter 19

1. As attested in the post-war period by a number of former Divisional soldiers, a breakout from the Brody pocket did not necessarily ensure safety because any breakout forces were now operating in Soviet occupied territory. See "From the Archives of the 1st Ukrainian Division," *Visti*, 1951, No. 7 (9), p. 5; Heike, *English ed.*, p. 51; personal discussion with Yuriy Krokhmaliuk, Ostap Veryn, and other ex-Brody fighters.

2. It is not known, nor will it ever be known, on what exact date Freitag resumed command of the Division. Remembering that his resignation on 20 July 1944 was done voluntarily and unofficially, no official orders would be required to reinstate Freitag. Avoiding death or capture during the breakout, in its aftermath Freitag somehow linked up with the Division's main body. Because he held the highest rank, Freitag immediately resumed command.

3. According to Reitlinger, *The SS*, p. 204, when the Division retreated through the Carpathian passes, the Ukrainian UPA (Reitlinger uses the word "Benderovce") collected their arms. This is largely true; however, this was not done under fear or duress. Immediately in the aftermath of Brody, the Division's survivors began to scavenge for arms and equipment. Extra arms, light mortars, hand grenades, anti-armor weaponry were handed over to the Ukrainian guerrillas. Personal arms, however, were retained.

4. Heike, *English ed*, p. 52.

5. Personal discussion with Yuriy Krokhmaliuk and Veryha. See also Veryha's, *Along the Roads*, English synopsis, p. 186. Heike, *English ed.*, p. 53; *Ukrainian ed.*, p. 96. See also Heike's "Biy Pid Brodamy" in *Brody: Zbirnyk Stattei i Naryciv*, ed. Lysiak, p. 157; Ren, *My Life's Mosaic*, p. 184; and *Bender and Taylor*, Vol. 4, p. 37.

Galicia Division

6. The most famous allegation ever made claims the "Galicia" Division was involved in the suppression of the Warsaw Uprising's gallant insurgents in August-September 1944. Although such charges are patently false, they continue to persist. Therefore, it is important to at long last examine this allegation in depth.

In an account published in 1970, Josef Wroniszewski alleges that in the city of Warsaw, prior to the revolt of 1944, "over 300 soldiers from one SS company and one company of fascists from the SS Division Galicia were quartered" within the building of the Academy of Political Studies, located on 56 Wawelski St., in the Slovatski Gymnasium (high school), and several villas on Dantushka St. (J.K. Wroniszewski, *Ochota 1944*, Warszawa, Wydanictwo Ministerstwa Obrony Narodowej, 1970, pp. 36-37). Wroniszewski alleges that the above mentioned forces were utilized in the ensuing revolt and as "proof," cites how amongst the Nazi casualties, "Galician" personnel were identified.

To begin with, it would be helpful if Wroniszewski would someday define what is the difference between an "SS" company versus one composed of "fascists." Aside from the high-sounding sensationalism, a close examination of his accusations reveals a number of faults. According to Polish author Adam Borkiewicz, the author of T*he Warsaw Uprising of 1944* (Warszawa, 1957), p. 41), about 300 soldiers from an SS unit occupied the Higher School of Political Studies; among this strength, one company was composed of Ukrainians. But Borkiewicz does not identify the company as a Divisional element. (A.J. Borkiewicz, *Powstanie Warszawskie 1944*, Warszawa, 1957, p. 41). And throughout his book, of the numerous divisions, regiments, independent battalions and companies cited by numerical designation and titles, neither the "Galicia" Division, nor any of its elements, are identified. As for the allegation that there was a "Ukrainian" company, does the possibility exist that this company is cited as being composed of Ukrainians because many in Warsaw referred to Germany's foreign personnel as "Ukrainian?" Does the possibility exist that these particular troops were in actuality "Hiwis" (men recruited from Soviet prisoners-of-war), as presented by von Krannhals in his intensive and objective study (see *Von Krannhals*, p. 265) rather than Ukrainians?

Wroniszewski's allegation can also be suspect because while he cites the Division was committing war crimes in Warsaw in the period of August-September 1944, others cite that during this same period of time the Division was committing crimes in other places. Kurt Fleishmann alleges that at this time the Division is committing crimes in Lviv (Fleischmann, "Conspiracy to Conceal" in W*orld War II Investigator*, Vol. 1, No. 10, p. 10); Dimitri Simes alleges that the entire Division is fighting in France against the western allies when he charged "the SS division Galitchina [sic]... fought for Hitler in France" ("The Destruction of Liberty," in *Christian Science Monitor*, 13 February 1985); Volodymyr Hrytsiuk cites "how immediately after Brody the Division's remnants were diverted far to the west [Hrytsiuk does not specify an exact location but undoubtedly refers to western Europe] where they found themselves posted to imperialistic reconnaissance [units]," (Volodymyr Hrytsiuk, *"Osyni Hnizda. Trudiashchi mavruiut' Han'boiu Ukrains'kykh burzhuaznykh Natsionalistiv."* Hrytsiuk's one-page propaganda leaflet was circulated among the emigres and various papers published in both Russia and Soviet Ukraine in the mid-1980's); V. Beliaiev and M. Rudnyts'kyi, *Pid Chuzhymy Praporamy* [Under Foreign Flags], p. 98, cite that after Brody the Divisions personnel "could be found in the base of the Alps as guards in the Hitlerite concentration camp of Mathausen;" Yaroslav Gallan charges the Division is in Norway, pacifying the region for the "new order" (cited from Veryha's *Along the Roads*, p. 66); and authors Aarons and Loftus charge that "the survivors [after Brody] were reformed into various military units under KONR and the Committee for the Liberation of the Peoples of Russia, led by General Vlasov," in *Unholy Alliance*, p. 187. So which is it?

Reichsführer Himmler's orders of August and September 1944 specified the Division was to be immediately reformed at Neuhammer. (Der Reichsführer-SS, RF/m. Tgb. Nr. 111/1294/44 g. Kdos., v. 7.8.1944; SS-FHA, Amt II Otg.Abt. Ia/II, Tgb.Nr. 2880/44g. Kdos., v. 5.9.1944, Neuaufstellung der 14. Waffen-Gren. Div. der SS (galizische Nr. 1). At the time Himmler was issuing orders, the Division was in the Carpathian Mountains, outside of Poland, and far away from Warsaw. So as Poland's brave insurgents battled it out from the ruins and sewers of their nation's capital while Stalin gleefully viewed the massacre of the anti-Nazi and anti-communist insurgents, the "Galicia" Division was many miles away.

To fully present the situation in an objective manner, it must be noted that prior to the Division's eastward deployment from Neuhammer, a number of Divisional NCOs were dispatched to an officer's school in Posen-Treskau, in the vicinity of Poznan. In the second half of August, Divisional staff dispatched one officer, Waffen-Obersturmführer Bohdan Pidhainy, to serve as a liaison officer and keep the Division posted on the progress of their training. Upon his arrival to the school, Pidhainy was informed by the Ukrainian officer candidates that the school's command had dispatched 10 individuals to serve as linguists/translators for various German Wehrmacht elements in Warsaw's vicinity.

In response to this, Pidhainy immediately reported to the Divisional command about what had transpired and personally, protested the transfer of the ten candidates to the school's commandant, SS-Brigadeführer Bailoff. Following an official protest from the Divisional command, in the latter part of August 1944, nine of the ten officer candidates returned to their school. These soldiers reported that upon their arrival to Warsaw, they were held up within a German command post because the German command did not know what to do with them. Apparently, someone (probably a front line unit or intelligence section), had previously requested German-Slavic translators. Of the ten soldiers, none ever participated in any combat activity within Warsaw, and none of the nine ever served as translators. Simply put, all they did was hang around a command post on the outskirts of Warsaw.

But one of the NCOs, a native of Warsaw, never returned. He told his nine compatriots that out of concern for his family, he would attempt to reach and remove them as right at that moment, they were in a part of Warsaw under heavy fire. Upon his departure, he was never seen again. Because he never reappeared and nothing was ever heard of him again, it is believed he perished within the war-zone in an attempt to reach his family.

Undoubtedly, this NCO is the same one Wroniszewski mentions whom the insurgents recovered. Following several attacks against their positions, a number of dead personnel lay on the streets. As usually is the case with

Notes

insurgents, they run out to retrieve arms and equipment. In an attempt to possibly identify who they were up against, they dragged one of the corpses back to their position. A check of the documents recovered from the body revealed him to be an NCO from the "Galicia" Division. (Wron*iszewski*, pp. 140-141; Veryha, *Along the Roads*, pp. 126-127; personal discussion with Ostap Veryn.).

Regardless of the above isolated incident, Wroniszewki's account was published in 1970 - twenty-six years after the uprising. By then, a number of accounts by numerous Polish, German and other historians, as well as by a number of former Warsaw combat participants, had appeared. One may cite the following excellent sources: Jerzy Kirchmayer's, *Powstanie Warszawskie*, Ksiazka i Wiedza, 1964 and *Geneza Powstania Warszawskiego*, Spoldzielnia Wydawnicza "Czytelnik" Luty, 1946. (Kirchmayer not only wrote extensively on the Warsaw Uprising of 1944 but even went so far as to present in his massive 531 page *Powstanie Warszawskie* excellent maps and documents such as the surrender agreements between SS-Obergruppenführer Erich von dem Bach-Zalewski and the Polish insurgents); Alexander Dallin's, *The Kaminsky Brigade, 1941-44* (Cambridge, Mass.: Harvard University Russian Research Center, 1956); Stefan Korbonski's, *Fighting Warsaw: The Story of the Polish Underground State, 1939-1945* (Mass.: Harvard Univ. Press, 1956. Korbonski was the last Chief of the Polish wartime underground); George Iranek-Osmecki's, *The Unseen and the Silent: Adventures From the Underground Movement Narrated by Paratroops of the Polish Home Army* (N.Y.: Sheed and Ward, 1954); General T. Bor-Komorowski, *The Secret Army* (N.Y.: Macmillan Co., 1951); Major Alojzy Dziura-Dziurski, *Freedom Fighter: A Saga of Fighting the Nazi and Communist Oppressions* (Australia: J.A. Dewar Publishers, 1983. Major Dziurski was an underground liasion officer to the various underground factions operating within Poland during World War II); social historian Emmanuel Ringelbaum, *Notes From the Warsaw Ghetto*; Wilfred Strik-Strikfeldt's, *Against Stalin and Hitler, 1941-1945* ; the Nuremberg War Crimes volumes known as *The International Military Tribunal Volumes*; and the London based Polish Historical Institute General Sikorski's, *Polskie Sily Zbrojne w Drugiej Wojnie Swiatowej - Tom II, Armia Krajowa* (London: Instytut Historyczny im. Gen. Sikorskiego, 1950). Published by Komisja Historyczna Polskiego Sztabu Glownego w Londynie. [All three volumes graphically cover the history of the Polish Home Army]; J. K. Zawodny's, *Nothing But Honor: Story of the Uprising of Warsaw, 1944* (Ca.: Hoover Institution, 1978; and MacMillan in London, England, 1977); John Prados', "Revolt of the Polish Underground, 1944," pp. 16-24 and 41-42; Luja Swiatowski's "The Political Situation In Poland on the Eve of the Warsaw Uprising," pp. 43-44 in *Strategy and Tactics: Revolt of the Polish Underground* (Wisconsin: Dragon Publishing Co., Nr. 107, May-June 1986); and Field-Marshal Heinz Guderian, a former eastern front commander, himself exonerated the Waffen-SS when he wrote in his memoirs: "Some of the SS units involved - which, incidentally, were not drawn from the Waffen-SS - failed to preserve their discipline. The Kaminsky Brigade was composed of former prisoners of war, mostly Russians who were ill-disposed towards the Poles; the Dirlewanger Brigade was formed from German convicts on probation." Guderian, *Panzer Leader*, p. 282. See also p. 283. While of course other works are also available, these are just a few of the highly informative, thoroughly researched, documented and objective accounts devoted to the 1944 Warsaw insurrection. While in these accounts references are frequently made to the foreign Kaminski and Dirlewanger units, no allegations or references are made that the 14th Waffen-SS "Galicia" Division was ever utilized in the 1944 suppression of the Warsaw rebellion. Indeed, in most of these accounts, the "Galicia" Division is not even mentioned. The few references made only refer as to why the Division was raised, where it fought, and its surrender in 1945.

In a work titled The Poland We Don't Know (*Polska jakiej nie znamy; zbior reportazy o mniejszosciach narodowych*) (Krakow, 1970), p. 70; see also Veryha, *Along the Roads*, pp. 191-192), noted Polish historian Jerzy Lovell has denied any Ukrainian participation in the Warsaw Uprising of August 1944. Lovell states: "Nobody at any time had ever stated that in combating the Warsaw uprising any military units such as the Division SS-Galicia, or even any units of the Ukrainian police, participated. All Polish sources, however, openly implicate the General Vlasov's soldiers and those of the Kaminski RONA brigade, both of which were Russian."

Lovell's account is not the only one which represents an honest Polish viewpoint. In a letter to a UPA veteran's organization located in Canada, Mr. Z. Czahorski, a military historian and community activist, wrote: "Soldiers of the SS Division 'Galicia,' its soldiers believed that the Ukraine would arise, and though he fought on the German side, he fought well and many perished, especially in the Brody battle. Yet the soldier of the "Galicia" Division, in his conduct with civilian populations, acted accordingly." (Mr. Czahorski's letter of 28 November 1971).

According to Soviet propagandist and disinformation specialist V. Styrkul, the Division itself was never utilized in the Warsaw Uprising. However, in a book published by Styrkul in the Soviet Ukraine in 1980, Styrkul stated: "It is recorded in numerous official documents that 'auxiliary units' made up of Ukrainian nationalists and attached to the SS, and units which later were incorporated into the SS Halychyna [Galicia] Division, participated in the suppression of the Warsaw uprising." V. Styrkul, We *Accuse*, p. 275.

Clearly, Styrkul's allegation reveals that by 1980, the element within and outside the Soviet Union which had until now constantly accused the Division of various "crimes" within Warsaw, now began to realize that the Division, as a formation, was never utilized in the Warsaw Uprising. But not to be outdone, and knowing that it would be more difficult to prove that certain individuals and auxiliary units were not in Warsaw, Styrkul began citing the "fact" that Ukrainian "nationalists" (prior to entering the Division), "participated in the suppression of the Warsaw Uprising."

Ultimately, who are these people? If Styrkul knows that they existed, why can't he identify them by name? And once again, besides the "nationalists," "auxiliary units" are also cited. But once again, precisely what "auxiliary units" is Styrkul referring to? Under whose command were these units subordinated to when in Warsaw? Under what name or numerical designation do they fall? Where, among the voluminous German Orders-of-Battle, are these units identified? And why is it that numerous reputable Polish, English sources and the official World War II German Army and Police Battle-of-Orders (also widely utilized by reputable historians, scholars and academics), cite no Ukrainian companies, battalions, and "Auxiliary units" as being utilized in the 1944 Warsaw revolt?

For historical clarity, it should also be finally mentioned that some Ukrainians did serve in the 1944 Warsaw uprising - on the Polish side, as insurgents.

Galicia Division

At the outset of the revolt, Warsaw's insurgents stormed the Pawiak Prison, releasing its captives. The numerous Russian, Jewish, Ukrainian, Georgian, Slovak, French, and other prisoners, as well as a Royal Air Force pilot named John Ward who previously had escaped from a German prisoner-of-war camp but upon recapture was transported to Warsaw and placed into the prison, immediately joined the insurgents. (See *Strategy and Tactics Magazine*, Nr. 107, May-June, 1986, p. 21). Among the Ukrainians were the patriots from Bandera's faction previously arrested in Poland by Nazi authorities. And until the very end, these Ukrainians fought side-by-side and endured all of Warsaw's hardships along with Poland's Armia Krajowa and the other foreign insurgents.

To commemorate the 25th Anniversary of the 1944 Warsaw uprising, the U.S. Government conducted a study of the uprising. Headed by Senator James O. Eastland, Chairman of the Committee, the commission prepared a report to objectively study this historic event.

Titled "The Warsaw Insurrection: The Communist Version Versus the Facts," this document is divided into three parts: Part I was written and presented by Senator Thomas J. Dodd; Part II, titled "A Study of the Warsaw Insurrection" was prepared by Miss Irene Lazutin, a Foreign Affairs Analyst at the Library of Congress; and Part III consisted of a statement put out by the Polish Communist Embassy in Washington, D.C., on the 25th Anniversary of the Warsaw Uprising. (Washington, D.C.: U.S. Government Printing Office, 1969).

Although various commanders and units which suppressed the revolt are mentioned, in this entire three-part study not one word is directed against the "Galicia" Division nor, for that matter, against any Ukrainian unit or personnel. And it is noteworthy that although the "Kaminsky" Brigade is mentioned, it is finally correctly identified as a brigade formed from "Soviet prisoners who had been freed to enlist as units in the German Army." (See p. 11). Despite the fact that Kaminsky (born in Poznan, Germany, in 1896), was an individual who despised his Polish-German Jewish background (see Major Dziurski's *Freedom Fighter*, p. 127; *Ready* p. 219), a number of western writers have - and continue - to erroneously cite Kaminsky's nationality as being "Ukrainian," and that his brigade was a "Ukrainian" outfit.

Because this report was produced by the American Federal Government, Senator Dodd personally insisted on historical accuracy. Thus it can be assumed with absolute certainty that had the "Galicia" Division been utilized at Warsaw, the report would have stated so. On 24 October 1969, the report was approved by the 91st Congress' 1st Session.

In conclusion, the historical record is such: at no time was the "Galicia" Division, or any of its elements or personnel, ever utilized in the suppression of the 1944 Warsaw Revolt.

7. In addition to General Lange, General Raus also offered his praise. Prior to the Divisions relocation from Ushorod to Seredne, Heike accompanied Freitag to General Raus' 1st Panzer Army's Headquarters where Freitag was to submit his report. Invited to dinner by Raus, both Freitag and Heike were pleased to hear Raus speak positively about the entire 13th Corps, to include the Division "Galicia." See Heike, *English ed.*, p. 52.

8. Der Reichsfuhrer-SS, RF/M, Tgb Nr. III/1294/44 g. Kdos., v. 7.8.1944. (Himmler an Juttner). Aus dem Stamm der 14. Division sowie aus dem Ersatz-Rgt. u. den aufgestellten dritten Bataillonen der Inf.Rgter. ist die 14. Division sofort wieder aufzustellen. Aufstellungsort: Neuhammer. This order, however, was not officially issued until early September. SS-FHA, Amt II Org. Abt. Ia/II, Tgb. Nr. 2880/44 g. Kdos., v. 5.9. 1944, Neuaufstellung der 14. Div. ist mit sofortiger Wirkung auf dem Tr.Ub.Pl. Neuhammer neu aufzustellen. The order of 7 August 1944 specified "the 14th Division shall be immediately formed from the cadre of the 14th Division as well as from the Reserve [Training and Replacement] Regiment and the already formed third battalions within the infantry regiments. Formation site: Neuhammer." The 5 September 1944 order specified: "The 14th Division is to be reformed with immediate effect on the Army training grounds (place) of Neuhammer."

At no time were the survivors of the Brody battle ever "reformed into various military units under KONR, a Committee for the Liberation of the Peoples of Russia, led by General Vlasov," or placed into Vlasov's army as erroneously stated by Aaron and Loftus in *Unholy Alliance*, pp. 186-187.

The Reformation of the Division

1. The exact date when the Division ceased to be a part of the 1st Panzer Army and Army Group North Ukraine (AGNU) is not known; however, since the Division was listed on AGNU's charts on 8-15 July 1944, but was no longer classified on AGNU charts on 22 July, the Division must have ceased to be a part of AGNU sometime between 15 and 22 July. Further examination of AGNU's charts of 31 July; 15 August; and 16 September 1944 reveal the Division is no longer a part of AGNU. On 23 September, AGNU was redesignated as Army Group "A." Unofficially, this was an admittance that until otherwise in the future, the German Army would no longer operate in Ukraine. It is interesting to note, however, that in late December 1944, an Axis roster issued by the high command identified every division destroyed in the summer of 1944 and its status (rebuilt, re-organizing, disbanded, etc.), by December 1944. In this listing, the 14th Waffen-SS "Galicia" Division was not classified as being destroyed in the summer of 1944. Perhaps the fact that a reasonable part of the Division broke out and it was known to the German High Command that its Neuhammer-based three infantry battalions, along with the 8,000 strong Training and Replacement Regiment and a number of officer and NCO personnel were immediately available to reinforce the 3,000+, kept the Division from being classified as a "destroyed" division.

2. Heike, *English ed*, pp.'s 62 and 69. According to Veryha, the reformation commenced on 16 September 1944. Veryha, "I Znovu Neuhammer" [And Again Neuhammer], *Visti*, 1978, No. 4, p. 72.

Regarding war crimes, one of the most sensational (and undoubtedly bizarre), accounts presented about the Division was written by V. Beliaiev and M. Rudnyts'kyi. Titled *Pid Chuzhymy Praporamy* [Under Foreign Flags],

Notes

within this book numerous pages are filled with false information, innuendos, derogatory distortions and, even, outright lies about a number of Ukrainian figureheads and leaders (excluding, of course, those of the Ukrainian Communist Party) from the pre-Austro-Hungarian era to World War II. Needless to say, the Division is also targeted.

To evaluate everything on the Division alone would require many pages; therefore, an evaluation will only be made on some of the more serious allegations.

"Ukrainian SS men from this [Galicia] division saw themselves in the ruins of Warsaw during the suppression of the Warsaw uprising. Along with the Hitlerite elements, these traitors went against the uprising Poles. They threw grenades into the destroyed Warsaw buildings, overcrowded with women and children, and on the outskirts of the city, shot thousands of its [Warsaw's] inhabitant's..." (p. 98), and "Ukrainian fascists, those who fled after the destruction of the Division, could be found in the base of the Alps as guards in the Hitlerite concentration camp of Mauthausen. They transported to that area the remaining incarcerators from Majden and Auschwitz; they deported the honest patriots to a quarry in San Georgen and there, slaughtered the unfortunate, weakened people with rocks. They [the Divisions soldiers] were loyal and trustworthy assistants of commandant Bahmayer, and here, dealt brutally with captured prisoners-of-war, who died of hunger and persecution." (Ibid).

Once again, major distortions may be found. To begin with, as already presented, the Division was never involved in the Warsaw Uprising of 1944. And the allegation that in the aftermath of the Warsaw Uprising the Division was dispatched to "Mathausen for concentration camp duties" is also totally false.

So where, specifically, are the original World War II German orders, documents, or directives specifying the transfer of the Division to that camp? Are Beliaiev and Rudnyts'kyi aware of the various orders issued by Germany's high command specifying that the "Galicia" Division is to be rebuilt and reformed for front-line combat in the immediate aftermath of Brody? Are they aware of the various U.S. Army intelligence reports which reveal the "Galicia" Division's various locations during the years of 1943-45, none citing Mathausen? Why is it that no German, Ukrainian, or allied records, memoirs, and reports, as well as Mathausen's concentration camp survivors, ever place the "Galicia" Division as being in Mauthausen? Remembering that the Americans liberated Mathausen, why is it that in the aftermath of its liberation among the numerous documents and records found, none mention the "Galicia" Division?

In conclusion, such a historical fact remains: at no time did the "Galicia" Division, nor any of its elements or personnel, ever serve in the Mathausen concentration camp or, for that matter, in any Nazi concentration or extermination camp.

3. Krokhmaliuk, *The Glow*, p. 129; *Bender and Taylor*, Vol. 4, p. 40; Heike, *English ed.*, pp. 63-64; personal discussion with Yuriy Krokhmaliuk.

4. *Bender and Taylor*, Vol 4, p. 37, cites 8,000 were transferred to the Division. In a personal discussion with Roman Krokhmaliuk, Roman stated that by the time the Division moved eastward (summer 1944), the Training and Replacement Regiment had grown to a strength of approximately 10,000 men. (This figure was also verified by Roman's brother, Yuriy). But from this strength, around 2,000 were dismissed as unfit for military service just prior to the Training and Replacement Regiments transfer into the Division. Roman Krokhmaliuk was not certain what happened to those who were released but undoubtedly, they returned to the German labor system.

5. Krokhmaliuk, *The Glow*, p. 128; Ren, *My Life's Mosaic*, p. 184. At this time, Ren was an assistant to SS-Standartepführer (Colonel) Marks, who was promoted in the late spring of 1944. Ren cites the strength of the Training and Replacement Regiment was approximately 8,000, and its personnel were utilized for the reformation of the Division. As for the Training and Replacement Regiment, it continued to exist.

6. Veryha, "And Again Neuhammer," *Visti*, 1978, No. 4, p. 71.

7. *Ibid.*

8. Ren, *My Life's Mosaic*, p. 184, cites 200 officer and NCO graduates arrived to the Division in time to bolster the leadership lost at Brody. Roman Krokhmaliuk, "Novi Knyzhky" [New Books], *Visti*, 1985, No. 3, p. 69, cites 200 officer graduates; Heike, *English ed.*, p. 63, cites 200 officer candidate graduates. (These 200 returning officer graduates must not be confused with the 200 officer candidates who were dispatched to the Posen-Treskau officer candidate school in late June 1944 as the Division deployed to the eastern front. These candidates would not return to the Division until 1945).

9. Personal discussion with Yuriy Krokhmaliuk and Vasyl Veryha

10. Ren, *My Life's Mosaic*, pp. 184-185.

11. *Bender and Taylor*, Vol. 4, p. 38, cites them all as NCOs. In his memoirs, Heike wrote "another one thousand German officers and NCOs were to be assigned to it [the Division] as well, to constitute the so-called 'skeleton-personnel' corps. Only under these conditions did Freitag agree to remain as commander of the Division." (Heike, *English ed.*, p. 63). Heike does not, however, specify whether all, if any, of the requested 1,000 actually arrived.

12. Affectionately known as "Papa," Wildner was born on 27 August 1897. A non-party member, during World War I Wildner served on the eastern front in the Austrian Army and before World War II, was a career officer in

Galicia Division

Czechoslovakia's Army. Of mixed nationality (his mother was a Slovak), Wildner was very sympathetic to the Ukrainians and their cause. It is even stated that while in the replacement pool, Wildner requested an assignment into a foreign unit based in Slovakia; hence, his assignment into the "Galicia" Division. An officer who believed that a commander always leads from the front, Wildner quickly earned a lovable reputation; indeed, so high that soldiers were known to remark "I'll go to hell for him!" In the aftermath of World War II, Wildner continued to maintain contact with his soldiers until his death on 18 October 1960 in Unterstein, Germany. Surviving ex-Divisional soldiers who ever served with Wildner continue to hold him in high esteem.

13. Personal discussion with Yuriy Krokhmaliuk, Veryha, Veryn, and others.

14. Realistically speaking, perhaps this was for the better. At Brody, from the outset, the communications battalion was unable to assist the Division, or for that matter 13th Corps, effectively. The major reason for this was because many of the battalions personnel were not proficient in the German language. Although in the initial recruitment period a sizable number of proficient or near proficient German speaking Ukrainian personnel had entered the Division, for some unexplainable reason few German speaking Ukrainians were placed into the communications battalion. A high percentage of the Ukrainians found within the communications battalion, including those in lower ranking leadership positions, were not able to converse in German. Although they had successfully mastered their communications equipment, they were hindered by the German language. And because in a combat environment the least kind of communication problems will destroy a unit, this is why from the outset at Brody the communications battalion failed in its mission. Perhaps this also explains why on 5 September 1944, the two-page Berlin directive pertaining to the Division's various units specified that the communication battalion was to consist of no less than 60 percent of German personnel. SS-Fuhrungshauptampt Amt II Org. Abt. Ia/II. Tgb.Nr. 2880/44 g. Kdos. Berlin-Wilmersdorf, 5 Sep. 1944. Betr.: Neuaufstellung der 14. Waffen-Gren.Div. der SS (galizische Nr.I). Roman Kolisnyk verified that the order of 5 September 1944 specified that the reconstituted communications battalion was to comprise a strength of no less than 60 percent German personnel.

15. Personal discussion with Yuriy Krokhmaliuk.

16. Krokmaliuk, *The Glow*, p 129; Heike, *English ed.*, p. 64.

17. *Bender and Taylor*, Vol 4, p. 48.

18. At no time was the Division ever redesignated and reformed into a "Type 45" division, as incorrectly implied by several sources. When ordered to convert to the Type 45, the Division's command requested to retain its "Type 44" status on the grounds that enough manpower existed to maintain a Type 44 formation and because a change would disrupt the formation's stability. See also Heike, *English ed.*, pp. 67-68.

19. No one has ever officially stated where these 1,000 men came from but undoubtedly, most came from the vicinity of Oshydiv, Galicia. Approximately 13 July 1944, Waffen-Hauptsturmführer Boychuk appeared and stated the situation was as such: either enter the Division or fall into Red hands. Faced with such a grim situation, approximately 1,000 volunteered and they were immediately transported to Neuhammer. As the 8,000 were placed into the Division, the 1,000 were moved into the Training and Replacement Regiment. On 19 September, the July recruits were provided uniforms and equipment to commence their training.

20. The Division's two motorized ambulance platoons were never rebuilt; it also appears the Division's chemical/gas warfare decontamination platoon was never re-established either.

The Division's women's medical service may be cited as originating on 1 June 1944 when a group of 40 young women volunteers departed from Lviv to the town of Krynytsi "full of enthusiasm and hopes!"

Tragically, none of these 40 would ever see the Division. Despite the concerns and efforts of the Military Board and the Ukrainian Central Committee, the 40 volunteers were shuffled around to various German hospitals, refugee centers, and cities frequently under Allied bombing. Years later, Mrs. Stefa Matsiv-Balahurtrak would recall how on more than one occasion, she and the other women were treated by certain German administrators as "untermenschen." At the conclusion of the war, the volunteers found themselves in Bavaria. For an interesting but tragic account of the ordeals undertaken by the 40 nurses, see "Spohad Medsestry" [Recollections of a Medical Nurse], *Visti*, 1994, No. 2, p. 91.

21. It is known that for a very short period of time after Brody the 29th Infantry Regiment was commanded by Forstreuter, and the 30th Infantry Regiment was commanded by Dern. What caused this change of command has never been explained. Despite the temporary change of command, it is known that by the end of September 1944 Dern resumed command of the 29th and Forstreuter regained command of the 30th. Various Ukrainian and non-Ukrainian memoirs and soldierly accounts published about the Divisions events from September 1944 onwards again identify Dern as being the 29th's commander and Forstreuter as commanding the 30th Regiment.

22. Pannier was a Wehrmacht officer who had transferred into the Waffen-SS in the early years of the war. From 1942 until virtually the end of the war, he served only on the Russian front. Wounded in Austria in 1945 while serving with the Division, Pannier never returned to the Division. He was the recipient of the Iron Cross 2nd Class, the Iron Cross Ist Class, and the Knight's Cross. (See also Jost W. Schneider, *Their Honor was Loyalty! An Illustrated Docu-*

Notes

mentary History of the Knights's Cross Holders of the Waffen-SS and Police, 1940-1945 (CA.: R. James Bender Publishing, 1977), pp. 264-265).

23. See *Bender and Taylor*, Vol 4, pp. 45-46. Veryha substantiates Taylor's and the German charts by identifying Klokker as the 30th Regiment's 1st Battalion and Freidrich Wittenmayer (born 19 April 1914, SS-Nr. 422,184/ Party No. unknown), as the regiment's 2nd Battalion commander. See "And Again Neuhammer," *Visti*, 1978, Nr. 4, p. 69).

24. At Brody, the engineer battalion's two top commanders, Remberger and Rembalovych, succeeded in breaking out. But their three line company commanders, Murs'kyi, Savdyk, and Dygdalevych (who commanded respectively the 1st, 2nd, and 3rd engineer company's) were killed-in-action. All three company commanders held an officers rank.

25. According to I.T., the Division's anti-aircraft registered a strength of 860 soldiers found within the three line batteries and support assets prior to the Brody battle. Of this strength, only 81 returned. "Biy Pid Brodamy" [Battle of Brody], *Visti*, 1984, No. 3, p. 74. However, I.T. does not cite how many were actually killed-in-action. According to Myhailo Lobach, of the 123 soldiers serving within his 88 battery, only three returned to Neuhammer. Everyone else was killed. But Lobach's figure is disputed by Roman Hayetskyj, a former Divisional anti-aircraft gunner. Although acknowledging that the Division's anti-aircraft battalion did take a pounding at Brody, Hayetskyj also stated that many of the battalion's personnel, to include those within Lobach's 88 battery, ended up in the UPA. (Personal discussion with Hayetskyj).

26. Kolisnyk, *The Ukrainian Division "Galicia" and Its Military Board*, pp. 89-91. In a letter to the author, Mr. Kolisnyk stated that Chaplain Dr. Laba headed the religious department found within the Military Board. As for the title of "Chief Chaplain," this title was reserved for the chaplain which served on Divisional staff. In the aftermath of Brody, it was Chaplain Levenets'. Chaplain Laba, however, maintained close ties to the Division.

27. Chaplain Julian Gabrusevych joined the Division on 17 July 1944. Upon the completion of his training, he deployed to the Modlin front in the fall of 1944.

28. For an interesting account of the Chaplain's ordeals - to include SS-Obergruppenführer Kaltenbrunner's and Heinrich Himmler's denunciations of Metropolitan Sheptytskyi, see Kolisnyk's "Dukhovna Opika" [Spiritual Guardianship], in *The Ukrainian Division "Galicia" and Its Military Board*, pp. 85-91.

29. One of the last ones to see Waffen-Hauptsturmführer Paliiv alive was former grenadier Vasyl Veryha. On 21 July, as Veryha and a small group passed through a massive enemy artillery barrage in the vicinity of Bilyi Kamin seeking a weak point to break out, Veryha encountered Paliiv south of Bilyi Kamin between Pochapy and Khylchychi shortly before sundown. Paliiv had deliberately remained behind in an effort to gather and assist as many of the Division's soldiers as possible in their efforts to break out.
  Ordering the approximately eight soldiers to follow him, Veryha and the rest followed Paliiv quietly in single file to a small orchard; there, amongst a small group, stood General Freitag and one or two other generals. Ordering the men to rest, Paliiv left them and approached the group. It is not known what was said, but when Paliiv returned, he informed Veryha and the others to stay put until further notice. Veryha feels that this was probably the last time that Paliiv spoke to Freitag. That night (Veryha cites a date of 21-22 July), a strong effort was undertaken to break out. Veryha succeeded in breaking out, but neither he, nor anyone else, ever saw Paliiv again. Veryha, however, is convinced that Paliiv was killed-in-action. (See Veryha's "Dmytro Paliiv," *Visti*, 1968, No. 5-6, p. 43).
  According to Oleksa Jaworsky, in the fall of 1944 two Ukrainian officers, who also had been classified as "killed" at Brody, re-surfaced in the Division. They stated that following the encirclement, they encountered Paliiv, sitting on a cottage step in some village. Paliiv, who was drinking milk from a jug, offered it to the men. Because they were within the encirclement, they decided to stay for the night in the cottage. As the three slept in a room, Soviet soldiers appeared; to protect the threesome, the cottage owner stated that the room was occupied by his sons suffering from typhus. Afraid of contamination, the Soviets left. On the following day, the owner led the two officers to the UPA, but for some reason, Paliiv decided to stay behind.
  For the next ten weeks, both officers trained UPA's insurgents. But because their wives and families were in the west, the officers requested to be released. Through an underground route designated as "Cracow," the two returned to the west and re-entered the Division. In submitting their reports, both officers stated unequivocally that Paliiv was killed in the village by Soviet forces. (See Oleksa Javors'kyi, "Ya Dyviziinyk" [I Am a Divisioner], *Visti*, 1983, No. 4, pp. 50-51).
  But than, there is the account submitted by Ivan Nokonechny. A member of the veterinary company, Nakonechny was wounded and taken prisoner. Because his wound was not serious and his captors planned to interrogate him, Nakonechny was taken to a hospital for Red Army personnel; there, he was placed in a wing which held foreign personnel but mostly, Russian's who had joined the German side.
  Nakonechny admits that he did not know Paliiv very well. But a couple of decades later in Canada, when he was shown various photos of Paliiv to include some of the last photos taken of Paliiv in 1944, Nakonechny is convinced that he had conversed with Paliiv while in captivity. According to Nakonechny, Paliiv was wounded in the foot. Although Paliiv did not provide his name to Nakonechny, he informed Nakonechny that he was an officer from the Division. He also told Nakonechny that he would soon be interrogated by the NKVD and he feared for his life. Taken away, Nakonechny never again saw the captive.

Galicia Division

It is known that Paliiv never entered the UPA. According to Veryn, someone once mentioned to him that a UPA patrol came across the body of an older Divisional soldier by a villager's cottage surrounded by a handful of dead Soviets. The possibility exists that Paliiv, after assisting as many as he could during the breakout, decided to make a final one-man stand in his native land. Regardless of his fate, Paliiv, who prior to Brody was in poor health but was highly respected for his courage and warrior's spirit, played a major role in the Division's history.

30. Makarushka remained at this post until the conclusion of the war.

31. The 1 August 1944 awards chart reveals a total of 240 Iron Cross 1st and 2nd Classes were awarded. Of these, a total of 58 (24%) were issued to Ukrainian Divisional soldiers while a total of 182 (76%) were issued to the Divisions German personnel.

32. This date is approximate.

33. Personal discussion with Veryha. See also Veryha's, "And Again Neuhammer," Vis*ti*, 1978, No. 4, pp. 70-71. (Hohage has also been spelled as Gogage).

34. Ren, *My Life's Mosaic*, p. 176. See also *Handbook on German Military Forces*, TM-E30-451 (Restricted), 15 March 1945, pp. IV-1.

35. Factually speaking, despite the fact that from 1943 onwards Nazi Germany was on the defensive, simultaneously, from 1943 Hitler began to rely more and more upon the Waffen-SS' offensive capabilities to reinforce critical front line sectors and stem any major Allied attacks and penetrations, especially on the eastern front. See also Charles Sydnor, *Soldiers of Destruction*, p. 291.

36. Personal discussion with Yuriy Krokhamliuk.

37. Heike, *English ed.*, p. 67; personal discussion with Yuriy Krokhmaliuk.

Notes Chapter 20

Modlin-Legionowo: Fall 1944.
1. Simultaneously, Konev's 1st Ukrainian Front had achieved its Sandomierz objective and the 1st Ukrainian Front was in Poland proper.

2. According to Shtemenko, Stalin was deeply concerned about the stability of the 1st Byelorussian Front, and the Soviet dictator feared that from the area north of Warsaw, German forces would launch a counterattack into the Soviet rear. Therefore, he ordered Stavka to maintain military pressure against the area of Praga and Serok. See Shtemenko, *The Soviet General Staff At War*, Book II, pp. 105-106.

3. Constructed in the years 1655-56 by Swedish warriors as a defense position against the Poles, for centuries fortress Modlin was contested by various armies. Prior to the German blitzkreig of 1 September 1939, Modlin was the staging area for 'Army Group Modlin,' one of Poland's army groups. For an interesting historical study of Modlin, see *Wielka Encyklopedia Powszechna PWN* (Warszawa: Panstwowe Wydawnictwo Naukowe, 1966), No. 7, (Man-Nomi), pp. 399-400.

4. Formed in Poitiers, France, on 1 June 1943, the 4th SS Panzer Corps was rushed to the eastern front's central sector in July 1944 as a "fire" unit to contain the Soviet summer advance of 1944. From than on, the 4th SS Panzer Corps only fought on the critical sectors of the eastern front (such as at Modlin north of Warsaw), and on many occasions halted Soviet attacks and advances. On 24 December 1944, it was recalled by Hitler to the Hungarian front; there, the 4th SS Panzer Corps spearheaded various counterattacks but under constant enemy pressure, was forced to withdraw to Austria. On 8 May 1945, it surrendered to the western allies in the vicinity of Radstadt, Austria. From its inception to the end of the war, the 4th SS Panzer Corps was commanded by SS-General Herbert Gille.

5. According to Yuriy Krokhmaliuk, "Wiking" Division's three panzergrenadier regiments entire infantry strength at this time did not exceed more than 1,500 soldiers. (Personal discussion with Krokhmaliuk). Indeed, the "Wiking" Division's infantry strength was so low that prior to reinforcement, it was not uncommon for one soldier to hold 100-200 meters of the front. See Will Fey, *Armor Battles of the Waffen-SS, 1943-45* (J.J. Fedorowicz Publishing Co., 1990), p. 114. Translated by Harri Henschler. Originally published in German as *Panzerkampf*, by Munin Verlag, Osnabruck.

6. Different authors, however, have cited various figures. In a personal discussion with Yuriy Krokhmaliuk, the former Divisional staff officer cited a strength of 1,000 deployed to the "Wiking" Division. In "Komentari i Zavvahy do Bytvy v Riadakh Dyvizii Zbroi CC Viking" [Commentaries and Observations of Combat In the Ranks of the SS Division Wiking] (Unpublished personal documentary researched and written by Yuriy Krokhmaliuk), the former Divisional staff officer cited that two battalions were formed and deployed to the "Wiking" Division. (P. 2). Krokmaliuk,

however, did not cite a specific figure as to how many soldiers were actually found within the two battalions but on page 3 of his work, Krokhmaliuk implies a strength of 1,000 deployed when he cites "approximately 750 returned to the Division "Galicia" but 250 were lost." According to Y.D., a "Wiking" combat veteran, a strength of 1,000 deployed to the "Wiking" Division. "Viking" [Wiking], (Unpublished text). But Oleksa Javors'kyi, "Ya Dyviziinyk" [I Am a Divisioner], *Visti*, 1983, No. 4, p. 50, cites a strength of 1,300 were deployed from Gross-Kirshbaum to the "Wiking" Division. Yet Chaplain Julian Gabrusevych, who in the fall of 1944 was deployed to officiate over the soldiers deployed to the "Wiking" Division, cites various figures. In "Bachyv Ya Bachyv, Ranenoho Druha" [I Saw, I Saw, a Wounded Comrade] (Unpublished personal account by the former Divisional chaplain), Chaplain Gabrusevych cited a strength of approximately 1,000 deployed. (P. 1). But in a report he submitted to the Military Board (dated 9 January 1945) regarding his brief participation with those who deployed to the "Wiking" Division, Chaplain Gabrusevych cited a strength of 700. (See Document No. 38, p. 256, in Krokhmaliuk's, *The Glow*). O. Gorbach, "Pikhotni Polky chch. 5-8" [Infantry Regiments No. 5-8], *Visti*, 1993, No. 1, p. 89, cites that in the summer of 1944, approximately 700 were mobilized and deployed from training camps from the vicinity of Frankfurt-on-the-Oder and Prague to the "Wiking" Division. In a personal letter to Roman Kolisnyk from Volodymyr Gockyj, a former Divisional soldier who at the time was serving within the Training and Replacement Regiment, Gockyj cited a strength of 800 was dispatched to the "Wiking" Division. (Letter of 24 October 1993). But Mr. Lew Babij, a former participant in the defensive battles at Modlin, cites a strength of 1200 deployed to the "Wiking" Division. (Letter to the author dated 21 February 1994). Babij also uses this figure in an unpublished account titled, "Grupa Chleniv Dyvizii "Halychyna" Na Vyshkoli i Fronti u Dyvizii "Viking" 1944 Roku" [A Group of Participants of the Division "Galicia" on Their Training and Front Experiences in the Division "Wiking" in the Year 1944], pp. 1-3. It appears, however, that Yuriy Krokhmaliuk's figure of 1,000 is the most accurate and because it is substantiated by others, the figure of 1,000 will be used.

7. Gross-Kirshbaum was located approximately 150 miles north/northwest of Neuhammer near Frankfurt-on-the-Oder. As for the soldiers who were dispatched to Heidelager in early July 1944 for training prior to their transfer to the "Wiking" Division, none had ever previously trained in either Heidelager or in Neuhammer. (Babij's letter to author).

8. This date is cited by Mr. Babij.

9. According to Babij, the soldiers left Gross-Kirshbaum on 6 July 1944, and arrived to Heidelager on 8 July. But Yuriy Krokhmaliuk cites 27 June 1944 as the date the two battalions departed. ("Commentaries and Observations...," p. 3).

10. According to Babij, the brunt of the soldiers hailed from the districts of Bereshan, Pidhaets', Rohatyn, and Buchach.

11. Babij's letter of 21 February 1994.

12. *Ibid.*

13. *Ibid.*

14. *Ibid.*

15. Y.D., "Wiking." In "A Group of Participants of the Division "Galicia"..." Babij acknowledged that although the training continued in Kohlow, the meals were very sparse, it frequently rained, and the soldiers tents were drenched.

16. Also known as Nove Straseci and Neustraschitz.

17. Babij's letter of 21 February 1994 verified that at Straseci, "the training was, overall, very good." According to Babij, if one takes into consideration the training time afforded at Heidelager, Kohlow, and Straseci, the departing soldiers received approximately three months of training. Excluding the brief and somewhat ineffectual training at Kohlow, the Ukrainian recruits did receive (prior to the interruption of their training at Heidelager), a solid three weeks of training at Heidelager with first rate instructors and no less than four weeks of solid training from 13 August to 10 September 1944 at Straseci. Factually speaking, if one takes into consideration that the Ukrainian's received no less than seven to eight weeks of very solid training, than Babij's observation that the training was "very good" is correct. In a personal discussion with Yuriy Krokhmaliuk, Krokhmaliuk stated that in addition to the training provided at Heidelager, Kohlow, and Straseci, a number of the soldiers who had ended up in the "Wiking" Division had also received some training while serving with the Training and Replacement Regiment at Gross-Kirshbaum. Krokhmaliuk was confident that the "Wiking" bound soldiers did receive sufficient training. According to Chaplain Gabrusevych, while in Czechoslovakia, the Ukrainians were housed in military barracks utilized by the former prewar Czech Army. Unfortunately, Chaplain Gabrusevych did not identify the German commander by name and rank. However, the former chaplain described the German commander as a professional leader who behaved very correctly toward the Ukrainians and especially, toward the Chaplain. On Sundays, Chaplain Gabrusevych even conducted religious services. Of importance to note is that at first, the local Czech population could not understand why the Ukrainians were at Straseci, and what they wanted to accomplish. To ensure that there would be no misunderstanding and possible

conflicts between the Ukrainians and the local Czech's, Chaplain Gabrusevych met with various local representatives and he developed a close relationship with a regional Czech priest. ("I Saw, I Saw, A Wounded Comrade...", pp. 1-2).

18. According to Babij, at the conclusion of the training and prior to the soldiers departure from Straseci to the "Wiking" Division, a final mass was held, confessions were heard and a banquet was held. Babij cited that the date of departure was approximately 10 September 1944. (Babij's letter of 21 February 1994).

At this time, Chaplain Gabrusevych by himself, was dispatched to the translators school in Oranienburg, in the vicinity of Berlin. Enlisting into the Division on 17 July 1944, Chaplain Gabrusevych arrived to Heidelager on approximately 20 July to link up with the 1,000 Ukrainians who, on 8 July, had arrived to Heidelager from Gross Kirshbaum for military training. But according to Chaplain Gabrusevych, approximately one week later, he was transferred to a town in the vicinity of Frankfurt-on-the-Oder where he underwent four weeks of training. (Remembering that on 26 July 1944 the Ukrainians departed Heidelager for Frankfurt-on-the-Oder and on 28 July arrived to Kohlow where they trained briefly prior to their departure to Straseci, than Chaplain Gabrusevych's sequence of events in "I Saw, I Saw, A Wounded Comrade..." is correct). Departing Kohlow, Chaplain Gabrusevych arrived to Straseci where he remained with the others until they departed for Modlin. But at this time, the Chaplain was dispatched to the translators school. After five weeks of instruction, Chaplain Gabrusevych was afforded leave. (In his account the chaplain did not cite where he spent his leave). Following his leave, in mid November 1944, Chaplain Gabrusevych reported to the "Wiking" Divisions headquarters only to learn that just several days before, the Ukrainians had already departed. Chaplain Gabrusevych immediately returned to the Division.

19. Babij's letter of 21 February 1994.

20. The "Totenkopf" regiment was actually a panzergrenadier regiment within the 3rd Waffen-SS "Totenkopf" ("Death's Head") Division. In actuality, very few (if any) Ukrainians were selected for the "Totenkopf" unit. The vast majority were selected for the "Wiking" Division. (Personal discussion with Yuriy Krokhmmaliuk).

21. Babij's letter of 21 February 1994. In a personal discussion with Yuriy Krokhmaliuk and veteran survivors of this action, once the Ukrainians were inserted into "Wiking's" infantry regiments, they were further broken down into the various battalions and company's found within the "Germania" and "Westland" panzergrenadier regiments. Although the majority ended up in the infantry, some were posted into the artillery, anti-tank, communications, and support elements found within the "Germania" and "Westland" regiments.

22. Activated in July 1941 in the Transcaucasian Military District around the 28th Mechanized Corps, the 47th Army was subordinated to Stavka's RVGK Reserve. In 1941, 1942, and early 1943, units of the 47th were utilized as a nucleus for the organization of other armies. Committed into combat in 1943, combat activities included Krasnodar, Kursk, Kiev (1943); and Korsun-Cherkassy, Kovel in 1944. In July 1944, the 47th reinforced the Soviet front at Lublin. Replacing the 2nd Tank Army in late August/early September 1944 on the Warsaw bridgehead, the 47th fought with the 1st Belorussian Front.

23. Raised in late 1942 through early 1943 from NKVD border and internal security forces from the Far East, Central Asia, and the Transbaikal Military Districts, the 70th (NKVD) Army was augmented by Asiatic and paratroop personnel. The last army to be raised by the Soviet Union during World War II, the 70th was formed in the Ural Military District, with its headquarters at Sverdlovsk. Deployed to the eastern front in February 1943, it first appeared at Kursk in July 1943, and participated in the July counteroffensive. Assigned again to the RVGK in November 1943, the 70th reappeared in the Kovel region in February 1944. At this time, it was officially posted to the 2nd Belorussian Front. Until its placement into the RVGK reserve once again in late July 1944, the 70th was largely utilized in mopping up activities and as a security force. Combat included operations against the UPA. The 70th did, however, participate in ground operations as evidenced in July 1944 when it fought with other Soviet ground forces to secure Brest. Reappearing in late August/early September 1944 on the Warsaw front, the 70th was again at first held in a reserve position. Augmented that month with additional NKVD, Asiatic and criminal penal personnel, in October 1944, the 70 (NKVD) Army was recommitted into combat at Modlin.

24. Personal discussion with Zakhary Blushko. In Babij's letter of 21 February, Babij cites that Galicia's soldiers battled the 47th Army. Although Babij is correct in his observation, the 70th communist army was also committed by Stavka into the Modlin battles and some of Galicia's soldiers did, in fact, battle the 70th. In a personal discussion with Yuriy Krokhmaliuk, Krokhmaliuk stated that in the vicinity of Modlin such as at Legionowo, the Ukrainians did combat NKVD forces. For additional combat accounts, as well as a study of the personal hardships experienced by Europe's front line volunteers such as SS-Obersturmführer Ola Olin, a Finnish volunteer and tank commander in the "Wiking" Division, see "Defensive Fighting East of Warsaw, 1944" in *Armor Battles of the Waffen-SS, 1943-1945*, pp. 106-120; Finn Wigforss's, *The Face of War: Drawings From the Eastern Front* (Oslo, Norway: 1981), and Hans Scheidies, "Totenkopf Is Not Well Liked. Wiking and Totenkopf SS Divisions in the Narew Bridgehead" in Russ Schneider's *Madness Without End. Tales of Horror From the Russian Wilderness, 1941-1945* (Germany: Neue Paradies Verlag, 1994, pp. 12-29. (Scheidies, a German, served as a tank soldier in the "Wiking" Division and is a veteran of the division's battles in Ukraine, Belorussia and Poland. Finn Wigforss, a Norwegian, served as a war correspondent); and Peter Strassner's, *European Volunteers: 5th SS Panzer Division "Wiking"* (Canada: J.J. Fedorowicz Publishing Co., 1988), pp. 170-190. For a Soviet viewpoint of the fighting, see Soviet Marshal K.K. Rokossovsky's "Varshava" [Warsaw], pp. 286-289; and "V Predel'i Germanii" [In Germany's Bounds], pp. 290-292, in *Voenn'ie*

Notes

Memuar'i: Soldatskii Dolg [War Memoirs: Soldier's Duties] (Moscow: Voenizdat, 1972). In his memoirs, Rokossovsky acknowledged that the 5th Waffen-SS "Wiking" Division, the 3rd Waffen-SS "Death's Head" Division, and the 19th Panzer Division put up a very tough resistance in the area of Modlin. Repeated efforts by Soviet forces to achieve a major penetration north of Warsaw resulted only in failure. Rokossovsky also admitted that both the 47th and 70th Armies suffered heavy losses. (*Ibid.*, p. 290). According to General Shtemenko, both the 47th and 70th Armies suffered heavy losses north of Praga in the area between the Narew and Vistula Rivers. In the very end, however, despite the proposals of General Antonov, Chief of Staff of the Red Army, to maintain the attacks by the 47th and 70th Armies to envelop Warsaw from the north and northwest, Stalin himself finally relented and issued orders to cease operations. General S.M. Shtemenko, *The Last Six Months: The First Authentic Account of Russia's Final Battles With Hitler's Armies In World War II* (N.Y.: Doubleday and Company, Inc., 1977), pp. 101-102.

25. Oleksa Javors'kyi, *Visti*, 1983, No. 4, p. 50; personal discussion with Yuriy Krokhmaliuk. Babij cited 30 October 1944 as the date the Ukrainians were recalled from the "Wiking" Division. In Modlin, the Ukrainians fell into formation and roll call was taken. At this time, roll call revealed heavy losses. Of interest to note is that on 24 October 1944, from Cracow, where the Military Board was now located, Colonel Bisanz sent a letter to the "Wiking" Divisions command informing them that a chaplain, Julian Gabrusevych, is enroute to serve Galicia's soldiers; however, by the time the chaplain arrived, the soldiers were returning to the Division. An das Kommando der 5-ten SS-Division Wiking im Feld. Betr.: Divisionspfarrer Julian Gabrysewycz. Der leiter das Wehrausschusses Galizien, Krakau, den 24.10.1944. This letter is signed by Bisanz.

26. SS Panzer Division Wiking, Kommandeur Div. Gef. St., den 4.11.1944. Division-Sonderbefell anl. der Verabschiedung der gal. Waffen-Willingen am 3.11.44. This order citation was received in Cracow on 8 November 1944. In turn, it was forwarded to Osyp Navrots'kyi, a former captain in the Ukrainian Galician Army who served as an executive manager in the Military Board.

27. In "I Saw, I Saw, A Wounded Comrade..." Chaplain Gabrusevych cited that of approximately 1,000 who deployed to Modlin, around 200 were killed-in-action in the vicinity of the Narew and Buh Rivers. In a personal discussion with Yuriy Krokhmaliuk, Krokhmaliuk cited that around 250 soldiers were killed-in-action. And during the discussion with the author, Krokhmaliuk also emphasized that if one takes into consideration the number of troops which deployed versus the number killed-in-action, than no less than 20 percent were killed. Factually speaking, this loss rate exceeded the percentage rate of those who deployed in late June/early July to the eastern front and were killed-in-action at Brody. Therefore, in the Division's annals, Modlin will always be remembered as the location where the Division incurred its heaviest loss.

28. Personal discussion with Yuriy Krokhmaliuk.

29. Divisional soldiers Dmytro Kit (whose brother, Myhailo, perished at Modlin), and Volodymyr Kaplan compiled an unofficial list of the Divisional soldiers who were killed-in-action. Upon their return to Slovakia, this list was submitted to the Divisions staff which, in turn, forwarded copies to the Military Board.

As for those who were killed-in-action, they were interned in a cemetery established by the 4th SS Panzer Corps located outside of Modlin. The "Wiking" Division's deceased, to include the Ukrainians, were buried at the cemetery's western edge under Lot Numbers 1-24. Every Ukrainian was buried under a cross, and the grave was marked with a name. In addition to receiving the names of those deceased, the Ukrainian Military Board also received the numbers of the Lot locations where the Divisions deceased lay. This was done so that if ever in the future any family would want to exhume the remains for reburial, they would be able to do so. But in violation of the rules of warfare and basic human decency, the cemetery was totally destroyed shortly after the communists reoccupied Modlin.

Notes Chapter 21

1. According to Soviet sources, the Slovakian resistance movement was led by the Slovak National Council, a council organized by the Communist Party of Slovakia. In turn, this council coordinated its activities with the Moscow based Communist Party of Czechoslovakia.

Prior to the August 1944 revolt, certain Czech and Slovak communists were selected to attend special short-term insurgency courses in Russia. Subjects taught included attacking small garrisons, assassination, sabotage, the usage of explosives, urban/rural warfare and propaganda warfare.

To ensure success, Soviet advisors (such as operations and planning officers, communications, intelligence, political and logistical personnel) accompanied the Slovak communists. According to Shtemenko (*The Soviet General Staff at War, Book Two*, p. 323), 53 such groups were specifically formed and inserted into Slovakia by parachute. Once inserted, these groups served as a nucleus for the establishment of partisan groups. In addition to these 53 groups, a number of Soviet guerilla unites, commanded by L.Y. Berenshtein, V.A. Karasyov, V.A. Kvitinsky, and M. L. Shukaev, were ordered into Slovakia. (*Ibid*). The mission of these guerrilla units was to reinforce the parachute inserted communists.

Although Shtemenko cites "the resistance movement was led by the Slovak National Council" in actuality, it was directed by Moscow. As for the "special short-term courses [conducted] in the Soviet Union" to produce "partisan leaders," in actuality these courses produced nothing but terrorists. As for the so-called "partisan leaders" in reality, many of the "leader's" were nothing but former national criminals who, under the guise of high sounding exclamations such as "national liberation," "revolutionary warfare," "Marxist liberation," etc. were afforded the opportunity to rob, pillage, murder and rape. Perhaps this explains why in Slovakia Divisional soldiers (especially those from Kampfgruppe "Wildner"), frequently encountered innocent Slovak's who were victimized by Moscow's "liberator's." In conclusion, Shtemenko is correct that "Soviet specialists – staff officers, mine-layers, radio operators, and so on – were assigned to help them." (*Ibid*, p. 323). What Shtemenko failed to portray, however, is that the so-called "Soviet specialists" were primarily NKVD combat policemen whose mission was to maintain command and control over the Czech and Slovak insurgents, and ensure that in the aftermath of the communist revolt, Czechoslovakia would become nothing but a puppet state under Moscow's control.

2. *Bender and Taylor*, Vol. 4, p. 48.

3. Veryha, "And Again Newhammer," *Visti*, 1978, No. 4, pp. 72-73; *Bender and Taylor*, Vol. 4, p. 38. According to Ren, *My Life's Mosaic*, p. 187, the Soviets parachuted in two airborne brigades. *Bender and Taylor*, Vol. 4, p. 38, substantiates Ren's observation that two communist airborne brigades were inserted.

4. SS-FHA Amt II Org.Abt. Ia/II, Tgb. Nr. 3411/44 g.Kdos. v. 28.9.44. 14. Waffen-Gen. Div. der SS ist zur Fortsetzung ihrer Neuaufstellung sofort vom Tr.Ub.Pl. Newhammer in die Slowakei zu verlegen. (The order specified: "14 Waffen-Grenadier Division of SS is to be transferred immediately from the troop training area of Neuhammer to Slovakia to continue its new reformation."). According to John Keegan, "in addition to the security troops which were experienced in anti-partisan operations, two SS divisions formed from ethnic minorities, the 18th Horst Wessel (racial German) and the 14th Galizian (Ukrainian) were concentrated for a counter-offensive, together with five German army divisions." In John Keegan, *The Second World War* (N.Y.: Viking Press, 1990), p. 507, Keegan also cites that the murderous Dirlewanter and Kaminsky brigades were soon redirected from Warsaw to Slovakia. (*Ibid*).

5. In Ren's memoirs, *My Life's Mosaic*, p. 185, the Division received its orders in the first days of October, 1944. Heike, *English ed.*, p. 73, substantiates Ren's version but according to Heike, the battlegroup was to be separated from the Division prior to the Division's departure from Newhammer to Slovakia.

6. Myhailo Matchak, "Z Boiv Kurenia "Wildner" [From Battlegroup Wildner's Battles], *Visti*, 1951, No. 9, p. 3; and *Visti*, 1951, No. 10, p. 3; Heike, *English ed.*, p. 73; *Bender and Taylor*, Vol. 4, pp. 38-39.

7. Heike, *English ed.*, p. 73; and *German ed.*, p. 141. Ren, *My Life's Mosaic*, p. 186, cites that within a battalion composed of three infantry line companies, such elements were found: one heavy (4th) company with its artillery and mortars, one infantry artillery battery, one engineer platoon, one anti-tank platoon, one scout platoon and one support platoon. Its total strength consisted of 900 soldiers. (*Ibid*). In a personal discussion with Yuriy Krokhmaliuk, the former officer stated the battlegroup was composed round a reinforced infantry battalion. In an unpublished document written by Yuriy Krokhmaliuk, Kampfgruppe "Wildner" was built around one battalion composed of three infantry line companies and the battalions 4th "heavy" company. To this a staff headquarters, two platoons of engineers, two communication sections and one battery of field artillery were added.

8. Matchak, *Visti*, 1951, No. 9, p. 3; Ren, My Life's Mosaic, p. 186; personal discussion with Yuriy Krokhmaliuk.

9. The perpetrators of these crimes were especially the communist inserted agents, guerrillas, and troops.

10. Heike, *English ed.*, p. 74. A personal discussion with Yuriy Krokhmaliuk substantiates Heike's observation that Slovakia's insurgents were not very interested in engaging Wildner's battlegroup and even, the Division itself.

11. Heike does not specify as to whom Hoffle had submitted the warnings but undoubtedly, it was to Berlin and Germany's consul in Bratislava, headed by Hans Eland Ludin.

12. The date is approximate.

13. Heike, *English ed.*, p. 75.

14. *Ibid.* p. 76; *Ukrainian ed.*, p. 124. The Training and Replacement Regiment registered a strength of no less that 6,000-7,000.

15. By the end of September 1944, the Training and Replacement Regiment had once again grown to a sizable strength. To maintain better order, an additional battalion was established. Exactly when this (4th) battalion arose is not known, but it appears that it was formed sometime in late August or early September 1944. Its mission was to screen, clothe, equip and maintain civilian personnel prior to their entry into one of the three Training and Replacement Regiments battalions. This battalion was also subordinated to the Training and Replacement Regimental commander, SS-Standartenführer Karl Marks. At this time, Ren was the assistant commander of the Training and Replacement Regiment.

16. Heike, *English ed.*, p. 78; *Ukrainian ed.*, p. 128, identifies the 30th Regiment's 3rd Battalion under the command of Wittenmeyer.

Notes

17. Heike does not provide a personnel strength figure for the battlegroup's strength.

18. Personal discussion with Yuriy Krokhmaliuk.

19. *Ibid.*

20. Heike, *English ed.*, p. 78, cites the final assault on Banska Bystrica took place in November 1944. For a study of the various phases of the revolt in map format, to include the "Galicia" Division's movements, see Simon Goodenough's, "Czechoslovakia: The End of German Arms" in *War Maps: World War II. From September 1939 to August 1945, Air, Sea, and Land, Battle By Battle* (N.Y.: St. Martin's Press, 1982), Map No's. 1-3, p. 118.

21. According to Roman Kolisnyk, the so-called Soviet inserted "advisors" were, in actuality, communist commanders. Kolisnyk's observation is substantiated by many others, to include those such as Shtemenko.

22. To cite an example of the unwillingness of the insurgents to resist, no less than 60,000 insurgents were dispersed in Banska Bystrica and its vicinity. See also Heike, *English ed.*, p. 78.

23. Ren estimated that Kampfgruppe "Wilder" engaged approximately 2,000 insurgents. See, *My Life's Mosaic*, p. 187.

24. According to Heike, Wildner's unit distinguished itself commendably. Many of its soldiers won decorations, including the standard awards issued to the German army. (Heike, *English ed.,* p. 78.). According to Yuriy Krokhmaliuk, Wildner was a soldier who always led by example. To cite just one example: although the Division did provide the battlegroup two automobiles and a couple of light trucks, Wildner's driver and car were always in the rear following the column as Wildner, with a rucksack and shouldered rifle on his back and walking stick in hand, led the way on foot. (Personal discussion with Yuriy Krokhmaliuk). See also Ren, *My Life's Mosaic,* pp. 186-188.

25. Angered that the insurgents escaped, Freitag dismissed one of Wittenmeyer's company commanders and recommended a court martial. According to Heike, the encirclement was thorough with even a reserve force standing by; yet, the insurgents escaped. An evaluation of the day's action revealed that a Ukrainian company commander (who, until that incident was, as attested by Heike, a "competent and exemplary leader"), disregarded an order for all officers to remain at their posts. Deciding to do otherwise, the commander spent the night in a local farmhouse. Meanwhile, the insurgent scouts found a gap and successfully (undoubtedly in single file), escaped the encirclement. According to Roman Kolisnyk, the trial never took place. The commander was simply found guilty and demoted to the rank of a lowly soldier. Kolisnyk also cites the incident occurred within the 29th Regiment's 1st Battalion and not within Wittenmeyer's 3rd Battalion found within the 30th Regiment. According to Heike, there were occasions when Ukrainians "failed to follow orders, neglected basic military principles, and failed to pay attention to detail." (See Heike, *English ed.*, p. 82). It appears that such was the case in this incident.

26. Matchak, *Visti,* 1951, No. 9, p. 3.

27. Heike, *English ed.*, p. 87; personal discussion with Yuriy Krokhmaliuk.

28. *Ibid.* Once the Division withdrew from Czechoslovakia, its personnel never re-entered that nation. But shortly after their departure, Czechoslovak army units entered Slovakia. Among its soldiers, Ukrainian personnel were found. From Slovakia's citizen, they learned of the Division. But most importantly, they heard stories of kindness, how the Division's soldiers behaved accordingly and protected Slovakia's citizens from Moscow's inserted communist guerrillas. (See Pavlo Babets' "U Chehkho-Slovats'komu Korpussi" [In the Czechoslokavian Corps], *Visti,* 1972, No. 4, p. 51).

29. In the area which the Division occupied in Slovakia from 25 October 1944 until 31 January 1945, its soldiers lived well with the local and regional populace. So cordial was the relationship that many soldiers spent a friendly afternoon and evening in the home of a Slovak family. In some cases, Divisional soldiers even married Slovakia's women.
   In its operations outside of its perimeters, Kampfgruppe's "Wildner," "Wittenmeyer," and "Dern" behaved cordially and sympathetically toward Slovakia's people. This arose out of the knowledge that the Division's personnel remembered the cordial and proper treatment Czechoslovakia's government and its people displayed towards Ukrainian's in the interwar period, and because Slovakia's populace, adjacent to the Ukrainian border, were regarded as "kinfolk." Because some of the Division's Volksdeutsche officers (such as Wildner), and NCOs hailed from Czechoslovakia and some were even related to the Czechs and Slovaks, this factor also played a role in maintaining a harmonious relationship with the civilian population. Perhaps this explains why in the aftermath of World War II, Czechoslovakia's government never implicated the Division of any war crimes, not has it ever demanded that any of its personnel be extradited to that nation to face any criminal charges. And when in 1985 OSI Director Ryan dispatched to Prague a memorandum (Subject: Judicial Assistance: War Crimes Investigation, OSI No. P-6. 85 State 082929), seeking information on war crimes supposedly committed by the Division in that nation, Prague never responded favorably to OSI's inquiry.

Galicia Division

30. For a study on how the award was issued, see Jost W. Schneider's, *Their Honor Was Loyalty!*, pp. 457-462.

31. Heike, *English ed.*, p. 84, cites a figure of "about 200 men deserted from the Division during its stay in Slovakia."

32. *Ibid.*, p. 83. Heike who cites a figure of about 20), states that the possibility exists that these soldiers could have defected to the partisans. Although Heike does not cite as to what partisans these 20 defected to, Heike does concede that virtually all of the deserters strove to enter the UPA. (See pp. 83-84).

33. *Ibid*, p. 83. To cite another example: just before the Division marched to Slovenia Waffen-Untersturmführer Sviatoslav "Koko" Petriv led his entire platoon to the UPA. (Personal discussion with Roman Kolisnyk; see also "Sviatoslav "Koko" Petriv," *Visti*, 1988, No. 5-6, p. 110). Upon the completion of recruit training at Heidelager, Petriv was sent to an NCO academy at Radolfzell. Upon the completion of the NCO academy, he was sent to an officer's school in the vicinity of Prague, Czechoslovakia. Shortly after his return to the Division, he was promoted to an officer. In January 1945, Petriv and his entire platoon crossed through the German-Soviet front and after entering UPA territory, joined the UPA. Captured in 1946, Petriv was deported to a slave labor camp in central Asia; there, under very adverse conditions, he lost his eye sight. Released in 1964, he returned to the Western Ukraine and resided in Truskavtsi and later in Drohobych. Born 30 May 1925, he passed away on 10 August 1988.

34. Possibly, a small number did defect to the communist side. (See also Heike, *English ed.*, p. 83). To counter the communist Slovak and Soviet propaganda leaflets, the Division's Ic Section issued, on 6 November 1944, a decree titled "Enemy Propaganda Employed as Informational Material." The decree warned the Division's personnel about the way communist agents have been distributing false leaflets. The decree read: "Neither communism nor the USSR are mentioned in the flyers. The Bolsheviks speak neither of Bolshevism or about the Bolshevik Army, instead, they write about Russia and the Russian Army. This is their way of disguising themselves to other people by suppressing their own communism. This [propaganda] is also directed to the local Slovak citizens who have strong family and religious ties. With community leaders predominantly clerical, there are no large cities and no proletariat in the Bolshevik sense. The Bolsheviks have also placed their communist propaganda in the background and thus claim their emphasis is on the concept of Pan-Slavism. But the real goal remains as such: establish Bolshevik rule over the land of Slovakia, over the dead bodies of its people and once accomplished, push further into the rest of Europe."

35. Personal discussion with a laughing Yuriy Krokhmaliuk.

36. Personal discussion with Yuriy Korkhmaliuk.

37. On 24 March 1945, General Goehler reported to Hitler that the Ukrainian Division had a total of sixty-five MP-43 assault rifles. In actuality, the weapon the Division possessed was the MP44 and Stg44 Sturm Gewehr Assault Rifle. Goehler's report, however, was not totally incorrect because in actuality the MP43, MP43/1, MP44, Stg44 and Stg45 was virtually the same weapon with very minor differences among the five models. Of interest to note is that in the post-war period, a number of UPA troops were armed with this weapon, and it was regarded as one of the finest weapons in UPA's arsenal. Because the weapon was first issued to German forces on the eastern front months after their withdrawal from Ukraine and Galicia, and it is known that the Division's troops retained their MP44 and Stg44 Assault Rifles until the very end, undoubtedly, the UPA obtained their MP44's and Stg44's from the Ukrainian Division just days before its surrender in Austria in May, 1945.

38. Oberkommando des Heeres, Generalstab des-Heeres, Abt. Fremde Heere OST (B/P) den 1.11.1944. "Die National-Ukrainische Widerstands bewegung UPA." Stand: 1.Nov. 1944.

39. Personal discussion with Yuriy Krokhmaliuk.

40. Also knows as Army Group 'South.' See also Goerlitz, *History of the German General Staff*, p. 487.

41. This army group was also within Army Group 'South.' The army groups were named after their respective commanders – Generals Otto Woehler and Maximillian Freitter-Pico.

42. On 1 October 1944, the eastern front's manpower strength was registered at 1,790,138. Of these, approximately 150,000 were Soviet "Hiwis." Of this total strength, Army Group 'South' recorded a strength of 216,000. This was one of the lowest strengths ever registered on the eastern front. OKH, Gen StdH, Org. Abt. (1) Nr. I/II854/44, an OKW w. Ag., I. 12.I.45, H I/562.

43. From August until the end of November 1944, the entire Division was placed under the command of the Replacement Army. In December 1944, it was transferred to the SS-FHA. The reason for the change was because it was determined that the Division was once again combat ready.

44. Actually, the battle group could have rolled even sooner. In a personal discussion with Yuriy Krokhamliuk, the former Divisional staff officer stated that the battlegroup's troops had to wait for the regional German command to provide the extra needed trucks. According to Veryn (who participated in this action), Veryn stated that he and the

others waited at least half a day before the trucks and their drivers from a truck transport battalion finally appeared. Simultaneously, as the 29th Regiment deployed, the 30th Regiment was immediately placed on reinforcement status for possible deployment. See also Heike, *English ed.,* p. 89; Bohdan Stasiv, "Tragediia Pid Brodamy" [Tragedy at Brody], *Visti,* 1992, No. 3, p. 53; "Druhe Stanovlennia Dyvizii Dii Na Slovachyni, Slovenii i Na Fronti v Avstrii" [The Second Reconstituted Division. Its Role in Slovakia, Slovenia and the Front in Austria], in *1943-1993. The 1st Ukrainian Division,* p. 24.

45. With a strength of no less than 325 tanks and self-propelled guns recorded in its November 1944 strength listings, the 6th Guards Tank (previously the 6th Tank) Army, was utilized as a reserve guard tank army in the Soviet RVGK reserve. It contained the 5th Guards Tank Corps and the 5th Mechanized Corps. First committed into combat at Korsun-Cherkassy in March 1944, the army was incorporated into the 2nd Ukrainian front and was designated as a "Guards" army on 12 September 1944.

46. The 53rd was formed in August 1941 in the North Caucasian Military District. Its mission was border defense and the training of active army forces in regimental and divisional strength. Deactivated in December 1941, the 53rd was reactivated in April 1942 when the 34th Army was disbanded and its personnel were utilized for the 11th and 53rd Armies. Committed into Northern Iran in 1942, that same year the 53rd returned and saw action in northern Russia's Demyansk region. Committed to the Battle of Kursk in July 1943, the army afterwards fought throughout Ukraine. Committed to the Budapest front in late 1944, the 53rd fought north of Budapest in the Sahy/Banska-Bystrica area of Czechoslovakia. After suffering heavy losses, the 53rd was withdrawn from the line and posted to Zvolen (approximately 12 miles northeast of its combat area), for reconstituting purposes. It appears it remained there until the conclusion of the war.

47. Heike, *English ed.,* p. 89; Ren, *My Life's Mosaic,* pp. 189-190; *1943-1993. The 1st Ukrainian Division,* p. 24; Tragedy at Brody, *Visti,* 1992, No.3, p. 53.

48. Personal discussion with Yuriy Krokhmaliuk. Years later, the former staff officer would laugh about it.

49. Heike, *English ed.,* p. 91; and "Ochyma Suchasnyka-Chuzhyntsia. Ukrains'ka Dyviziia "Halychyna." Istoriia Formuvannia i boiovykh dii u 1943-45 rokakh. Uryvky" [In the Eyes of a Foreign Participant. The History of the Forming and Combat Activities In the Years 1943-45. Fragments] in *Poryv: Pravda Pro Pershu Ukrains'ku Dyviziiu "Halychyna" (UNA). Statti, Narysy, Spohady* [Impulse: The Truth About the First Ukrainian Division "Halychyna" (UNA). Articles, Accounts, Remembrances] (Lviv: 1994), p. 27; Ren, *My Life's Mosaic,* pp. 190-191, substantiates Heike's date of order. But *Bender and Taylor,* Vol. 4, p. 41, cite the Division received the order on 26 January 1945.

50. A part of the communications battalion was attached to March Group B.

51. One engineer company was attached to March group A.

52. Personal discussion with Veryha.

53. Personal discussion with Yuriy Krokhmaliuk.

54. The figure of 22,000 also included the 7,000-8,000 soldiers found in the Training and Replacement Regiment.

55. Heike, *English ed.,* p. 92. In Heike's German edition, p. 168, Heike uses the word "Bespannfahrzeuge." Roughly translated, this word means "horse-drawn transport" or, simply, it indicates a cart or wagon of some type. On the following page, Heike breaks the word in half and just cites the word "fahrzeuge." While in the German language "fahrzeuge" denotes vehicle, vessel or a craft of some type, in Heike's writing it still indicates a cart or wagon. In the *Ukrainian edition,* pp. 145-146, the Ukrainian word "voziv" – wagons – is used. But in the *English ed.,* pp. 91- 92, the word "trucks" is used. Regarding the translations, it must be pointed out that a correct translation was made from the German to the Ukrainian edition. However, when Heike's work was translated into the English language, the word "truck" was incorrectly inserted. The correct (and in this case the best) word to use is "wagon." In a personal discussion with Roman Kolisnyk, Kolisnyk stated that Heike's original writing referred to wagons and not trucks. Remembering that in Slovakia the Division replenished most of its artillery, and that four to six horses were required to pull a very heavy artillery piece and its ammunition or a heavy piece of equipment, and that many (if not most) of the wagons would be heavily loaded, a ratio of four horses per artillery piece or heavy wagon was not unusual. This explains why the Divisions staff estimated that approximately 800-900 additional horses were urgently needed along with extra wagons.

56. Personal discussion with Yuriy Krokhmaliuk and various other ex-Divisional soldiers.

57. Heike, *English ed.,* p. 92.

58. *Ibid.*

59. Personal discussion with Yuriy Krokhmaliuk.

60. Heike, *English ed.*, p. 92

61. Personal discussion with Yuriy Krokhmaliuk.

62. Heike, *English ed.*, p. 92.

63. *Ibid.*

64. In a personal discussion with Vashchenko, the former UPA intelligence officer acknowledged that the UPA had also infiltrated the Division's supply system. Indeed, some of UPA's personnel were infiltrated into the Division specifically to: a) learn how a military supply system is established, managed and operated; and b) once within the supply system, to establish a way to funnel arms, ammunition, military equipment, communications equipment, medical supplies, and intelligence information into the ranks of the UPA.

Of course, this was not an easy task. Generally speaking, the best time to rush military materiel into the hands of the UPA was during combat or when a lull occurred in the fighting, during a withdrawal, military displacement to another base or region of operation, or during a period of intense training. "Lost" arms, ammunition, and material could be written off to "combat activities," "training," "accidents," "partisan/guerrilla theft," and even "allied air strikes." UPA's personnel also developed various smuggling techniques and they mastered the art of juggling supply records. And as more and more Ukrainian officers and non-commissioned officers attained leadership positions and replaced the German personnel, it became easier for the UPA to operate within the Division.

Notes Chapter 22

1. According to Heike, "The route the Division was to follow to reach its new district was about one thousand kilometers long," (Heike, *English ed.*, p. 91. See also *Ukrainian ed.*, pp. 147-154). Ren, *My life's Mosaic*, p. 191 and 195, cites each march route was over 500 kilometers. But Ren also stated that if one takes into consideration the terrain and winding roads and trails, such factors increased the marching distance. Ren believes that at the end of the march each soldier (with weapon, rucksack and personal equipment) marched about 700 kilometers. (Approximately 435 miles). (See p. 195. See also pp. 190-195). Ren also cites the march was difficult and unpleasant. Yet, the Division's soldiers successfully accomplished the trek. Heike's, Yuriy Krokhmaliuk's, and Ren's observations are also substantiated by Ready who described the Division's soldiers as "good soldiers" who "trudged over muddy roads, frozen ruts, up steep narrow snow-covered mountain passes, through rain and snowstorms, in bitterly cold conditions, for a distance of 600 miles!" (Ready, p. 467).

2. Because of a shortage of fuel, freight cars and flat beds, the Division's heavy equipment and most of its truck transport was held up in Zilina. Eventually, the materiel reached Maribor by rail.

3. Heike, *English ed.*, p. 94; personal discussion with Yuriy Krokhmaliuk and various members of the Division. According to *1943-1993. The 1st Ukrainian Division*, p. 24, the Division commenced its march on 31 January 1945 and arrived to its new area-of-operation on 28 February 1945.

4. Heike, *English ed.*, pp. 91 and 97; *Ukrainian ed.*, pp. 153-156. Styria, the northern region of Slovenia, was also known as Stajerska.

5. Personal discussion with Yuriy Krokhmaliuk. For further information on Austria's and Yugoslavia's mountains, as well as a further understanding of the difficulties mountainous terrain and weather poses to any type of military unit and its operations, see FM 90-6, *Mountain Operations* (Department of the Army, Washington, D.C., 30 June 1980). See especially Appendix G, pp. G-12 and G-20.

6. Heike, *English ed.*, pp. 95-96.

7. Heike, *English ed.*, pp. 96-97; *Ukrainian ed.*, pp. 153-156. See p. 97 (English ed.) and p. 155 (Ukrainian ed.) for a detailed posting of the Division's various units. In a personal discussion with Yuriy Krokhmaliuk, the former Divisional staff officer substantiated these locations.

8. Established in 1943 by the Yugoslavian communist high command, the Fourth Partisan Operational Zone was commanded by a commander named Joze Borstnar, a former communist commissar. (Borstnar's rank has also been cited as that of a "colonel" or "general" but in most cases his title was "commander."). Mentally unstable, Borstnar also harbored a strong anti-American and anti-British sentiment. Allied inserted officers who met Borstnar found the communist commander to be unresponsive, highly suspicious and even, rude. Prior to Borstnar's entry into the communist movement, he was a petty criminal and pornographer.

Borstnar's assistant was Alois Kolman, alias Commander "Marok." A seasoned fighter and die-hard communist who prior to the Second World War had served with the French Foreign Legion in Morocco (and whose nickname derived from a variation of the word Morocco), "Marok" undoubtedly was selected because of Borstnar's weak military skills. Sometime in February or March 1945, "Marok" was killed in combat.

Notes

But the real brain behind both Borstnar and Kolman was Captain Franc Primozic. A highly skilled operations officer, Primozic was also one of the most capable leaders found within the Fourth Partisan Operational Zone. A Slovene by birth, Primozic was a soldier who hailed from a professional family and prior to the war, had served as an operations officer in the Yugoslavian Army and as an exchange officer in the Greek Army. Proficient in a number of languages, Primozic was not a fanatical communist; indeed, it appears that he even loathed communism. Undoubtedly, his sole motive for serving in the Yugoslavian communist guerrilla movement was based on personal survival.

9. Appearing in 1942, the 14th Partisan Division was initially utilized in Western Yugoslavia in the Dolenjska Region, an area west/southwest of the city of Zagreb. In March 1944, the 14th Partisan was ordered by Tito's headquarters to reposition itself north of the Sava River into Styria. The immediate objective was one of a military nature - to reinforce the weak communist force operating in Styria, and to expand operations into the Karawanken Alps and Pohorje Mountains in order to cripple the critical road, railway and communications network utilized by Nazi Germany's occupational forces in the area of Maribor and Dravograd; the long term was political - in the aftermath of World War II and the German defeat, the 14th Partisan would be utilized to secure certain disputed areas of Southern Austria and Eastern Italy.

Although classified as a "division," initially the 14th Partisan possessed a combat strength of no more than 600-650 fighters. The division was, however, organized into three brigades and plans were undertaken to expand the 14th Partisan into a strength of approximately 4,500-5000 fighters. In late February 1945, as a result of an intensive German anti-guerrilla operation, the 14th Partisan was ordered to withdraw south of the Sava River. But in the following month (March 1945), with a strength of no less than 5,000 fighters, the 14th Partisan Division (now also classified as the "14th Shock Division" by Tito's headquarters), suddenly reappeared north of the Sava River into an area adjacent to where the Ukrainian ("Galicia") Division was stationed. Of interest to note is that in mid-August 1944, German military intelligence correctly identified that a partisan division was inserted north of the Sava River in the vicinity of the Drava River south/southeast of Austria. See "German estimate of guerrilla strength and dispositions in Yugoslavia and Albania as of mid-August 1944" in German Anti-Guerrilla Operations In the Balkans (1941-1944) (Washington, D.C.: U.S. Army, Center of Military History, 1989), CMH Pub 104-18, Map No. 6. (This publication replaces DA Pamphlet 20-243, August 1954). For a highly detailed and extensive study of the war in Yugoslavia from 1941-1945, see Colonel Zdravko Klanjscek, ed., *Narodnoosvobodilna Vojna Na Slovenskem 1941-1945* [The National Liberation War In Slovenia, 1941-1945] (Ljubljana, 1977).

10. Both the 6th "Slander" and 11th "Zidansek" Partisan Brigades were established in 1943 from two small existing battalions in Styria. In addition to these two brigades and the three brigades contained in the 14th Partisan Division, such forces also existed in the Fourth Zone: a political agitation and propaganda section headed by a communist commissar named Dragomir Bencic; an independent Fourth Zone "Guard" Company which provided direct protection to the zone commander, his assistant, operations staff, intelligence, supply, propaganda, commissar, courier and communication sections which basically stayed intact and travelled together; the teams which monitored the Allied drop zones and whose primary mission was to gather and distribute the allied supplies inserted via parachute or landed by aircraft; and within every sizable town and city, there existed the intelligence, courier, assassination, and sabotage sections.

11. Personal discussion with Yuriy Krokhmaliuk. Of importance to note is that although Wiesenthal, Littman, Fleishmann, Vasylenko, Styrkul, Terlytsia, Beliaiev, Rydnyts'kyi, Szczesniak, Aaron, Babich and more recently Morley Safer and Jeffrey Fager of CBS's "60 Minutes" have raised various so-called "war crimes" charges against the Division, not once have any of these Ukrainian bashing propagandists, dupes and "war crimes experts" ever raise the issue about the verified and documented war crimes committed against the Division's personnel.

This included: the torture and murder of members of Kampfgruppe "Beyersdorff;" the murder of captured wounded Divisional soldiers at Brody; the deliberate destruction of medical facilities, orderlies, doctors and nurses (frequently after capture such as at Brody) by Soviet ground forces and NKVD personnel; the cruel incarceration of captured soldiers as slave laborers for many years in the aftermath of World War II deep in Russia and Siberia; the deliberate emplacement of bombs and mines to cripple Divisional soldiers; the deliberate usage of sniper warfare to wound (as later experienced by American, French, and other United Nations troops in Korea, Indochina, and Vietnam); the murder of Doctor Anatoli Puposhynskiy as he walked totally disarmed and without an armed military escort in clear view under a white flag displaying a red cross arm band and clutching a medical bag toward a wounded soldier; and abuse of children, young women and senior citizens, under the guise of a medical emergency or accident, to lure soldiers and medical personnel into places of ambush where, once the unwary arrived, a terrorist execution team killed unscrupulously. Divisional chaplains were also fired upon and instances arose were poison was inserted into food and water supplies to sicken, and kill soldiers. And by no means were Divisional soldiers the exception. In the aftermath of the communist reoccupation of Galicia, family members who remained behind experienced arrests, torture, murder or banishment to communist slave labor camps. In the event they survived the harsh conditions of a slave labor camp, upon their return to Ukraine it was not uncommon for them to be deprived of proper employment, medical care, and other basic necessities. In the years following World War II, many Divisional soldiers had no knowledge of what had happened to particular family members and loved ones.

Of course, the above criminal acts were banned by a series of international agreements formulated before, and in the aftermath of, World War I. But despite these agreements (among some of which, one of the signataries was Soviet Russia), when it came to terrorist warfare, Moscow totally disregarded the rules of warfare and continued to wage an indiscriminate campaign of terror.

507

Galicia Division

12. But as always is the case in any heavily infested mine and booby-trapped region, casualties will occur. In one case, Waffen-Untersturmführer Terleckyi was torn apart by an explosive device while examining a road sign.

13 A close examination of the various titles and unit identifications of Tito's various brigades reveal that no unit existed under the title of "Bachern." It appears the name was conceived by the Germans. (However, it could have been conceived by the Ukrainians). It must be remembered that Bachern is the German name for the Pohorje Plateau, a plateau which borders the Austrian frontier and the Drava River. Hence, any insurgents operating in the area would have been dubbed as "Bachern."

According to Heike, there were two types of insurgents: Tito's partisans and the Chetniks. Tito's partisans operated in the territory controlled by the Division (this primarily encompassed the area immediately to the west and southwest of Maribor), whereas the Chetnik's operated east of Maribor. (Heike, English ed., p. 100). Generally speaking, Tito's partisans were on the move. (Ibid). Heike also stated: "they [the Titoists] were supplied by airdrops and assembled in impenetrable mountain regions in formations that grew to twenty thousand or thirty thousand and more. However, regardless of their numbers, they were poorly armed and showed little willingness to fight. Given their numerical strength, they should have enjoyed far greater successes. Nevertheless, they were still a force to be reckoned with." (Ibid.).

Regarding Heike's observations, in general Heike is correct. It is a generally accepted historical fact that Tito's partisans did avoid combat with well-armed and equipped German forces. (Simultaneously, however, a number of German police, army, and units composed of foreign personnel also demonstrated a tremendous reluctance to engage Tito's partisans. Shutting themselves up in strong garrisons usually located in sizable towns and cities, these units seldom ventured out of their safe domains. In the event they were ordered to conduct an operation against the insurgents, these units kept their activities to a minimum. During an operation, they restricted themselves solely to or adjacent any main roads and they seldom ventured into the high hills and mountains to engage the partisans. Tito's harshest opponents were the elite German and Italian mountain troops, and the Waffen-SS soldiers. Unlike the brunt of the axis forces occupying Yugoslavia, mountain and Waffen-SS troops were known to pursue the partisans very aggressively. No terrain was off limits. Cases actually occurred where mountain and Waffen-SS troops were known to pursue an insurgent group for days on end, until the insurgents were either destroyed or captured).

Heike was more than correct that Tito's partisans received allied air drops, especially from the British. According to Heike, the guerrillas also maintained a strength of "20,000 or 30,000 and more." (English ed., p. 100. Heike's figure is also substantiated by Ready, p. 467). Regarding this figure, if one takes into consideration the combined strength of the 14th Partisan (Shock) Division, the 6th and 11th Partisan Brigades, as well the independent guard companies, various staff and support sections, airdrop recovery teams, saboteur units, and the numerous agents, spies, and propagandists, the possibility exists that Heike's estimate of at least 20,000 insurgents is correct. Needless to say, this is a substantial figure and on more than one occasion the insurgents "were still a force to be reckoned with." (Heike, English ed., p. 100).

14. Heike, English ed., p. 101-103. According to Yugoslavian sources, the "14. SS prostovoljska pehota divizija "Galizien" (the 14th SS volunteer infantry "Galicia" Division), along with the 13th SS Police Regiment, commenced operation "Fruhlingsanfang," an anti-guerrilla offensive against the insurgents in the Menina Mountains. The 18th Infantry and the Wehrmacht's "Untersteiermark" regiments also joined the operation. (See Narodnoosvobodilna Vojna, p. 927). This combat activity appears to be the one that Heike is referring to.

15. Heike, English ed., p. 102.

16. Heike, English ed., p. 102. Yugoslavian sources do acknowledge that the "14. SS divizije" (along with other German forces), did commence an offensive against partisans in the area stated by Heike. Yugoslavia's writers and historians have also correctly noted that the surrounded insurgents were successful in extraditing themselves from encirclement. However, the sources also reveal that the 14th SS Division continued to vigorously pursue the insurgents, especially in the area of Mozirja. (Mozirje). According to current sources, two regiments from the "14. SS prostovoljske [volunteer] divizije "Galizien" commenced, on 9 March 1945, an operation against the 6th and 11th Partisan Brigades which did not cease until mid-March. The fighting and pursuit also occurred in high elevations." For additional information about the Divisions action against the insurgents from current Yugoslavian sources, see Colonel Klanjscek's, Narodnoosvobodilna Vojna, pp. 924-925. According to Heike, the area of Boskovec rose to an elevation of 1,590 meters. (Nearly 5,000 feet in height). In a personal discussion with Yuriy Krokhmaliuk, Krokhmaliuk acknowledged that during some of the operations undertaken by the Division's troops, its personnel had to clamber up to heights thousands of feet. Narodnoosvobodilna Vojna, p. 924, also substantiates that much of the combat activities took place in very high mountainous terrain.

17. Remembering that within the Division's area-of-operations a sizable civilian population was found undoubtedly, some of the civilians constantly informed the insurgents of the Division's whereabouts and activities. Even the train attack by allied aircraft could possibly have resulted from underground civilian informants.

18. Personal discussion with Myhailo Lobach. After graduating from the Bad Tolz Officers School (being one of the few from the Division to attend what was regarded as the finest officer school), Lobach returned to the Division in late January 1945. Posted into an intelligence/reconnaissance platoon, that day Lobach linked up with the engineer troops and for the brunt of the day, pursued the insurgents. Until the end of his life, Lobach humorously recalled the Christmas party he and his friends had with the Titoists.

Notes

19. See also Dr. Roman Turko's, "Spomyn Pro Likariv Dyvizii" [Remembrances About the Division's Doctors], Vi*sti*, 1983, No. 3, pp. 59-60.

20. *Bender and Taylor*, Vol. 4, p. 48.

21. Heike, *English ed*, p. 104. For a fairly detailed account of the battalion see Orest Horodys'kyi's "Dva Dni v Partyzantsi" [Two Days In the Insurgency], in *Samostiyna Ukraina*, 1962, July, No. 7;, Iulii Holovats'kyi's, "Do Istorii Postannia Ukrains'koho Legionu Samooborony Na Volyni" [To the Historical Rise of the Ukrainian Self-Defense Legion in Volyn], in Pavlo Dorozynsky, ed., *The New Pathway. Almanac for 1994* (Ontario, Canada: New Pathway Publishers, Ltd., 1994), pp. 121-136; and Heike's *Ukrainian ed.*, pp. 165-166). In February 1945, this Ukrainian battalion was transported by rail to the vicinity of Maribor, where it was incorporated into a security role within such villages: Spilfeld, Obershwartz, and Untershwartz.

22. Heike, *English ed*, p. 104; *Ukrainian ed.*, p. 165. It was also at this time that the Ukrainian Legion (battalion) was retitled into the Ukrainian Self-Defense unit. (*Ukrainian ed.*, p. 165). However, many continued to refer to it as the "Volyn Battalion."

23. *Ukrainian ed.*, p. 165. No official rank is cited on Medvets'kyi. He was described as being a "khorunzhyi" - ensign-bearer.

24. Heike, *English ed.*, p. 10; *Ukrainian ed.*, p. 165.

25. *Ibid.*

26. Krokhmaliuk, *The Glow*, p. 141. Horodys'kyi also identifies Harasymenko as being a commander. See *Ukrainian ed.*, p. 165.

27. Heike, *English ed.*, pp. 104-105. Although Heike does not provide a name, Horodys'kyi (*Ukrainian ed.*, p. 165), cites that at the time the Ukrainian Self-Defense Legion entered an allegiance with the Germans in June 1943, the battalion (legion) fell under the command of Lutsk's SD commander, SS-Sturmbannführer Asmus. But when in July 1944 Soviet forces entered Volyn, the battalion crossed over to Poland. Shortly afterwards, Asmus was killed in an ambush. Replacing Asmus' command position was SS-Sturmbannführer Bigelmaier, also one of Volyn's former SD commanders. (*Ibid.*).

Possibly, Heike is referring to Bigelmaier. In Horodys'kyi's account, one reads how Asmus commanded the Ukrainian Self-Defense Legion before Bigelmaier. Although Horodys'kyi is correct in identifying Asmus as being associated with the Ukrainian legion, Horodys'kyi erred when he cited Asmus as being the Ukrainian legion's commander. According to Holovats'kyi (*The New Pathway*, p. 133), Asmus was one of Volyn's SD commanders. But Holovats'kyi does not identify Asmus as being the Legion's commander. And on p. 135, Holovats'kyi cites Asmus (along with another German by the name of Rawling), as being attached to the Ukrainian Self-Defense Legion to co-ordinate activities and to resolve any misunderstandings and conflicts between the Ukrainians and Germans.

During this same time, various Ukrainian commanders are also identified as being in command. It appears that in June 1943, Asmus either assumed nominal command of the Ukrainian Self-Defense Legion or (as presented by Holovats'kyi in *The New Pathway*, p. 135), was posted to the Ukrainian legion to co-ordinate and assist in maintaining a control over the Ukrainian battalion. Remembering that Asmus was more of a regional administrator rather than a "commander" who, simultaneously, was also overlooking other affairs, regarding Asmus' "command," it appears he was more of a supervisor who dictated from his SD headquarters rather than being a field commander. And this explains why Ukrainian commanders (who, unlike Asmus, served directly in the battalion) are identified as being the battalion's commanders by other sources. Regardless, Asmus never commanded the Ukrainian Self-Defense Legion.

28. Krokhmaliuk, *The Glow*, p. 141. In *Ukrainian ed.*, p. 166, Horodys'kyi cites a strength of almost 600 men organized into four companies.

29. Krokhmaliuk, *The Glow*, p. 141. According to Roman Kolisnyk, Skakal's'kyi was a monk. Kolisnyk cites Reverend Palladi Dudyts'kyi as being the battalion's chaplain. Both the monk and chaplain were of the Orthodox faith. It appears that Kolisnyk is correct that Dudyts'kyi was the battalion's chaplain. But Dudyts'kyi's service was short-lived because just before the conclusion of the war, General Pavlo Shandruk, who assumed command of the so-called Ukrainian Army, posted Chaplain Dudyts'kyi to the Ukrainian Army's staff. Of interest to note is that neither Chaplain Laba, nor any of the other Ukrainian chaplains who served on the Divisions staff, ever mention Skakal's'kyi or Dudyts'kyi. Perhaps this is attributed to the fact that both the monk and chaplain served very briefly in the Division.

30. Heike, *English ed.*, p. 105. As acknowledged by Heike, the Chetniks had no knowledge of this Ukrainian force and realistically speaking, would not have accepted the Ukrainians into their ranks. Nor were the Chetniks in a position to assist the Ukrainians in their journey back to Ukraine.

31. *Ibid.*

32. *Ibid.* According to Heike, "two-thirds of the battalion had deserted, taking their equipment, weapons, horses, and wagons with them."

33. Of interest to note is that although there was much dissatisfaction in the Volyn battalion, the entire battalion did not defect. As presented by Horodys'kyi, almost 250 soldiers, under the command of Lieutenant Roman Kyveliuk (alias "Voron") and Lieutenant Koval, entered a forested area to establish contact with the Chetniks in order to return to Ukraine. But Horodys'kyi also cited that at this time, the Chetniks were in concert with the Germans and they immediately informed the Germans as to what was occurring. Following some discussions between the Germans and Ukrainians, the defectors returned to the Division. As for the German promise that no one would be punished, Horodys'kyi cites that this promise was violated. According to Horodys'kyi, Lieutenant Kyveliuk, while under escort to Divisional staff, was executed under the guise that "he was escaping."(For Horodys'kyi's account as to what occurred, see Heike's *Ukrainian ed.*, p. 166). Heike substantiates that Lieutenant Kyveliuk was shot but Heike offers a different version as to what occurred. According to Heike: "Unfortunately, the Ukrainian commander of the company, First Lieutenant "Voron" (Roman Kyveliuk), was later executed by General Freitag for theft." (*English ed.*, p. 106). Heike, who described the executed officer as a leader respected for his military bearing, also states that Kyveliuk's execution was brought to his (Heike's) attention by Makarushka. Heike, who leaves no doubt that Freitag had Kyveliuk executed for the desertion incident, also verified that the Volynian's (who by now were integrated into the Divisions various units and "fought well") remained convinced that Kyveliuk was shot for the desertion.

34. Personal discussion with Yuriy Krokhmaliuk. Various former members of the Division also substantiate this.

35 Letter to author from H.P. Taylor, 15 October 1988.

36. In a personal discussion with Yuriy Krokhmaliuk, the former Divisional staff officer presented the various reasons why the Division refused to accept individuals known or suspected of being concentration camp personnel. But on 22 June 1987, during the trial of Ivan Demjanjuk, an Israeli historian, Dr. Spector, testified on behalf of the prosecution. And Spector's words verified what Krokhmaliuk had previously stated.

Under the cross examination of prosecutor Yona Blatman, Dr. Spector spoke at length about eastern front events, Germany's foreign units, and the Division. However, a close examination of his testimony reveals that although Dr. Spector was generally correct, he did make errors regarding dates, units, strengths; what armies and commands the Division was subordinated to; and certain military terminology was erroneously presented. Regardless, in examining the period of February/March 1945, Dr. Spector stated "this division was joined by parts of units, refugees, various other groups and on the basis of available source materiel some Ukrainian groups joined this, but this division included the 600... unit, which was an S.S. self-defense unit as it was called, and amongst others. Also the guards at concentration camps joined the division." (Court transcript of State of Israel vs. Ivan (John) Demjanjuk, 22 June 1987, Criminal Case No. 373/86, p. 6212, Lines 7-8).

Continuing on, Dr. Spector stated how upon the (allied) liberation of the concentration camps, the various guards "became available" [for military service?] and "also apparently units of the guards of the concentration camps composed of non-Germans – these, as they became available, were sent to this area and they came to the training units of this Ukrainian Division." (Ibid., p. 6212, Lines 24-28 and p. 6213, Lines 1-2). Dr. Spector then spoke briefly about the eastern front, how "1,200 German Luftwaffe ground crews were sent to them [the Division]" and how "the division didn't know what to do about them." He also spoke about Hitler's discussion and order to disarm the Division.

But after Dr. Spector mentioned the "Volyn Regiment" which entered the Division, prosecutor Blatman again steered Dr. Spector into the topic of concentration camp personnel by asking "What happened to the guards of the concentration camps? From the concentration camps?" (Ibid., p. 6215, Lines 21-22).

Responding to Blatman, Dr. Spector answered: "First of all these guards were not militarily trained. And secondly the officers of the [Ukrainian] division and... [personnel?] of the division looked at them as [ineligible] and they did not consider them fit to join their division. So most of them joined the ranks of a sort of work battalion without being issued arms. And they were told to build fortifications. Because early in April 1945, in April 1945 this division was moved to the front line itself. At any rate, part of the guards from the concentration camps were sent on. They were told to move up north in the direction of the Soviet army, the liberating Soviet army, under the command of Vlasoff. [Vlasov]. From here northwest, the staging points of Vlasoff's army." (Ibid., p. 6215, Lines 23-28 and p. 6216, Lines 1-11).

An examination of Dr. Spector's testimony reveals two versions: concentration camp personnel did enter the Division, but then they attempted to enter the Division. Regardless, in his latter version, Dr. Spector is more informative. And in this version, Dr. Spector's remark substantiates what former Divisional staff officer Yuriy Krokhmaliuk was always saying – simply put, the Division's personnel opposed the incorporation of concentration camp personnel into their ranks.

But whereas Dr. Spector stated that "part of the guards from the concentration camps were sent on... to the liberating Soviet army..." while others entered "the ranks of a sort of work battalion" and by this appears to imply that some of the former guards remained disarmed within a Divisional construction unit, previous discussions with Krokhmaliuk reveal that concentration camp personnel were not only totally rejected but as well, no construction battalion ever existed within the Division.

So the question remains: what "sort of [disarmed] work battalion" is Dr. Spector talking about? And did it belong to the Division?

Notes

In the two years of the Division's existence, no work or construction battalion was ever found within the Division. No such battalion is identified on any German organizational rosters, in Heike's, or Krokhmaliuk's writings, or in any independent sources. While it is true that a Divisional engineer battalion did exist, under no circumstances should this battalion be interpreted as being a "work battalion."

Dr. Spector failed to mention that within Germany's forces, independent work battalions did exist. Generally, these battalions were subordinated to the command of an army corps, army, or army group. Primarily, they were utilized to construct fortifications and defense positions. Although situations did arise where their personnel were committed to reinforce a front during a critical moment, work battalions were primarily utilized for construction purposes. Since it is common knowledge that many untrained and unreliable (both German and foreign) personnel were found within construction/work battalions, Dr. Spector is more than correct when he states "they [the concentration camp personnel] joined [and undoubtedly by his usage of the word 'joined' Dr. Spector meant they were inserted into] the ranks of a work battalion." And because the Division refused (as verified by Dr. Spector) to accept concentration camp personnel and upon its movement to the front in early April 1945 was not accompanied by any construction/work battalion, Dr. Spector's remark that "the guards from the concentration camp were sent on... up north in the direction of the Soviet army, the liberating Soviet army, under the command of Vlasoff" is correct regarding the events of that era. Krokhmaliuk, however, had no knowledge to which exact units the former concentration camp personnel were dispatched to. Krokhmaliuk stated, however, that the Division refused to provide them arms (as also corroborated by Dr. Spector, they were not armed) and most - if not all - were dispatched north to an area where it was rumored that Vlasov was establishing some of his units.

Notes Chapter 23

1. Volodymyr Motyka, "Starshyns'kyi Vyshkil v Posen-Treskau Lypen'-Hruden' 1944" [Officer Training in Posen-Treskau in July-December 1944], *Visti*, 1992, No 4, p. 93. According to Bohdan Prypkhan, the graduates of the officer school and the Advanced Arms Training Center returned to the Division in the latter part of March 1945. Bohdan Prypkhan, "My Pryziahaly Ukraini" [We Swore Allegiance To Ukraine], *Visti*, 1951, No. 4 (6), p. 4.

2. Heike, *English ed.*, p. 108; *Ukrainian ed.*, p. 169. For an interesting human study of combat in Yugoslavia, as well as the difficulties Divisional soldier's experienced with terrain, weather and the partisans, see Vasyl Bilan's "Smert' Pomyluvala (Spomyn iz Iugoslavii)" [Death's Forgiveness (Remembrances From Yugoslavia)], *Visti*, 1952, No. 8-9, pp. 13-18; and Vasyl Peleshchuk's, "Spohad Pro Dyviziiu" [Remembrances About the Division], *Visti*, 1994, No. 4, p. 93.

3. *Ibid.* Heike does not specify as to why this occurred. But a simple glance of the chronological events on the eastern front reveals that if forced to disperse, the Division would have to retire to a north/northwesterly direction.

4. Yugoslavian sources acknowledge that the Division conducted security operations in the region adjacent to the Austrian border. For a further study of the Division's role on the Austrian-Yugoslavian frontier, see *Narodnoosvobodilna Vojna Na Slovenskem 1941-1945*, pp. 916, 919, 924-925, 927, 1001. For an interesting map depicting the movements and actions of various German and insurgent forces until 9 May 1945, to include the actions of the "Galicia" Division immediately south of the Drava River, see p. 995.

5. Felix Gilbert, *Hitler Directs His War* (NY.: 1950), p. 147. For the entire discussion pertaining to the Galician-Ukrainian Division, see pp. 147-150.

6. *Ibid.* A Table and Organization (T/O), indicates a military units personnel strength, and the number of vehicles, weapons, and pieces of equipment a unit possesses.

7. *Ibid.*

8. A. Hartzwalde, "Decline of the Waffen-SS," in *The Kersten Memoirs, 1940-1945* (N.Y.: The MacMillan Co., 1957), pp. 262-263.

9. Heike, *English ed.*, pp. 108-110; *Ukrainian ed.*, pp. 169-170; Ren, *My Life's Mosaic*, p. 198; *Bender and Taylor*, Vol. 4, pp. 41-42; personal discussion with Yuriy Krokhmaliuk. According to Heike, the order was received on 20 March 1945. If indeed this order had anything to do with the Fuhrer conference of 23 March, then Heike's date is incorrect. A more realistic date would have been 24, 25, or 26 March. But according to a footnote found in the Ukrainian edition (p. 171), the order was probably issued as a result of Hitler's personal insistence that the Division be disarmed following the discussions of 23-24 March. Numerous other Ukrainian (see Ren, *My Life's Mosaic*, p. 200), and non-Ukrainian sources cite 23 March 1945 as the date of the discussion.

10. Heike, *English ed.*, p. 113. According to *1943-1993. The 1st Ukrainian Division*, it was Himmler who ordered the Division to be disarmed. However, the order was rescinded when the Division was committed into combat to assist in halting a Soviet penetration into Eastern Austria. *Bender and Taylor*, Vol. 4, p. 42, also acknowledges that the order was reversed. In the end, the Division was never disarmed.

11. Heike, *English ed.*, p. 113. Heike did not identify the general. But it appears that the paratroop general was von Hoffman who, just days before, was promoted from colonel to general.

12. Heike, *English ed.*, p. 113. German Order-of-Battle charts of 24 March 1945 classify the 10th Paratroop as "forming" within the 1st Cavalry Corps, 2nd Panzer Army.

13. Heike, *English ed.*, p. 113. According to H.P. Taylor, it was Hitler who considered taking the Division's arms for the newly forming 10th Paratroop Division; however (as verified by Taylor), it is not known to what extend this was done. Taylor's letter of 15 October 1988 to author.

14. *Bender and Taylor*, Vol. 4, p. 42, cites the Division was to be incorporated into the 10th Paratroop Division. But Heike, *English ed.*, p. 113, stated the Ukrainian Division "Galicia" was ordered to immediately reform itself into the "10th Paratroop Demolition Division." (*Ibid.*).

15. Heike, *English ed.*, p. 113.

16. Activated in 1939, by 1942 "Special Forces Brandenburg" had reached a level of expertise known only in the Allied world in the decades following the Second World War. Missions included: special assignments behind enemy lines such as the capture and destruction of critical roads, bridges, railways, and oil refineries; the kidnapping of key enemy personnel; operations against partisan/guerrilla strongholds; and sabotage and intelligence gathering. Germany's commandos were the first to develop the so-called "team concept." Within a team, each soldier was cross-trained. (I.e., a medic could be trained to be a communications expert; a demolitions expert was also trained to be a weapons specialist). Within these teams, organized in strengths of 10-15 commandos, a number of linguists were found. Such teams, either dropped by parachute or infiltrated through enemy lines, were to perform a specific mission. Personnel for Brandenburg Special Forces included Germans who had resided abroad and thus, were proficient in various languages, and foreigners from virtually every European nation. Individuals selected for entry were recruited from the Wehrmacht, Luftwaffe, paratroop, and Waffen-SS. To enter, a candidate had to first undergo recruit training, serve within an infantry/fusilier unit, possess a specific military specialty which could be utilized within a team, be proficient in two or more languages, meet certain physical standards, be of sound character, and display exceptional toughness.

17. Incorrectly, some authors have stated that the Division was converted into the 10th Paratroop Division See James Lucas, *Storming Eagles: German Airborne Forces In World War II* (England: 1988), p. 168.

18. Heike, *English ed.*, p. 120; Yuriy Krokhmaliuk, "Ostanni Boi" [The Last Battles], *Visti*, 1965, No. 2, p. 33; and personal discussion. *Bender and Taylor*, Vol. 4, p. 42, cites 3,000-4,000 Luftwaffe ground crewmen were absorbed by the Ukrainian Division. The Division did absorb the 10th Paratroop and as of 24 March 1945, the 10th Paratroop no longer appears on any military unit charts. According to Krokhmaliuk, none of the approximately 2,500 Germans had any infantry training. (*The Last Battles*, p. 33).

19. Heike, *English ed.*, p. 121; personal discussion with Yuriy Krokhmaliuk. See also "The Last Battles," *Visti*, 1965, No. 2, pp. 33-34.

20. *Ibid.*

Notes Chapter 24

1. Initially created in 1939 for the invasion of Poland, Army Group 'South' was redesignated Army Group 'A' for the 1940 invasion of Western Europe. In 1941, in preparation for Operation Barbarossa, it was again redesignated Army Group 'South.' But with the entry of Army Group 'South' into Ukraine, it also became known as Army Group 'Ukraine.' Although in March 1944 a part of Army Group 'South' was converted into Army Group 'North Ukraine,' with the German withdrawal from Ukraine and Galicia, it was again redesignated as Army Group 'South.' Unofficially, this redesignation acknowledged that Germany had lost Ukraine. In the remaining weeks of the war, it was also known as Army Group 'Ostmark.'
From 7 April until 7 May 1945, Army Group 'South' was commanded by Colonel General Lothar Dr. Rendulic; his Chief-of-Staff was Lieutenant General Heinz von Gyldenfeldt. From April until the end of the war, Army Group 'South' consisted of four armies (2nd Panzer, 6th, 6th SS Panzer, and 8th). Facing eastward, its right flank bordered on the Drava River and (from south to north) Army Group 'South's' front line ran adjacent to the towns and cities of Graz, Wiener Neustadt, Vienna and Brno. Its northern flank anchored in the vicinity of Brno. For additional information on Army Group 'South' see Colonel General Lothar Dr. Rendulic's, "Army Group 'South' (7 April-7 May 1945)" in Steven H. Newton's, *German Battle Tactics on the Russian Front 1941-1945* (Pa.: Schiffer Publishing Co., 1994), pp. 219-246.

2. Commanded from July 1944 by General Maximillian de Angelis, the origins of the 2nd Panzer Army lie in the 19th Motorized Corps, first formed in May 1939. This corps fought in the Polish campaign and, in 1940, fought in the western campaign as a part of Panzer Group 'Guderian.' Redesignated as 'Panzergruppe 2' (still under Guderian's

Notes

command), the 2nd Panzergruppe was one of the four panzergruppe's which spearheaded Operation "Barbarossa." In the bitter winter of October-December 1941, the 2nd Panzergruppe also spearheaded Operation "Typhoon," Germany's offensive to capture Moscow. Forced on the defensive by Zhukov's counteroffensive in December 1941, that same month the battered 2nd Panzergruppe was redesignated the 2nd Panzer Army. This army remained on the eastern front's central sector until its transfer to the Balkans in the latter part of 1943. It fought in Croatia but in the latter part of 1944, was defending a sector in Hungary adjacent to the southern part of Lake Balaton. Forced to withdraw from Hungary, the 2nd Panzer Army fought in eastern Austria against the Soviets until the conclusion of the war. It disappeared in May 1945.

3. The 1st Cavalry Corps was formed in Poland in the summer of 1944 from elements of the 78th Infantry Corps and Training and Support personnel from Wehrkreis VIII. From its inception, the Cavalry Corps was commanded by Cavalry General Gustav Hartenack. It fought in East Prussia but in January 1945, was transferred to Hungary. Withdrawing in late March 1945 into Austria, it concluded the war in Austria.

4. Heike, *English ed.*, p. 115. Both Ren, *My Life's Mosaic*, p. 203; and Krokhmaliuk, "The Last Battles," *Visti*, 1965, No. 1, p. 32, substantiate Heike's date. However, in regard to what army the Division entered, there are some differences and some errors are made. Although Krokhmaliuk and Ren correctly cite that the Division was ordered into the 1st Cavalry Corps, Ren cites the Division entered the 2nd Army while Heike, in his memoirs, stated the Division was subordinated into the 2nd Panzer Army. (*English ed.*, p. 115; *Ukrainian ed.*, p. 174). As for Krokhmaliuk, he stated that the 1st Ukrainian Division was ordered to proceed into the area of Gleichenberg and Feldbach to contain a Soviet penetration between the 1st and 6th German Armies. ("The Last Battles," *Visti*, 1965, No. 1, p. 32). According to *1943-1993. The 1st Ukrainian Division*, p. 24, Army Group 'South' ordered, on 31 March 1945, the Ukrainian division to be posted to the 2nd Army. In turn, the Division was posted into the 1st Cavalry Corps. According to author Hugh Page Taylor, German Order-of-Battle charts reveal that on 12 April 1945, the Division was in the 1st Cavalry Corps, 2nd Panzer Army. (Letter to author dated 15 October 1988). See also *Bender and Taylor*, Vol. 4, p. 42.

For historical clarity, the Ukrainian Division was posted to the 2nd Panzer Army, and not the 2nd Army. (The 2nd Panzer Army must not be confused with the 2nd Army. At the same time that the 2nd Panzer Army was battling in Austria in 1945, the remainder of the battered and weak 2nd Army, which previously had fought on the eastern front's central sector and had withdrawn through the Pripyat Marshes into Northern Poland, was so ineffective that on approximately 10 April 1945, Hitler merged the 2nd Army with the battered 4th Army in Prussia to create a new army – Army of East Prussia). As for the 1st Army, by April 1945 this army (which, incidentally, from the beginning was never in the strength of an army) was largely destroyed by the western allies in France and the Saar and by April 1945 (excluding scattered elements in Southern Germany), was no longer in existence. The 1st Army was never a part of Army Group 'South.'

The Division's placement into the 1st Cavalry Corps has also been substantiated by various German authors. According to author Ernst Rebentisch, while describing the final battles in the period of 7 April to 8 May 1945, Rebentisch verifies that the "14. SS-Waffen-Grenadier-Division (ukrainische Nr. 1)," was in the 1st Cavalry Corps. (Rebentisch, however, erroneously titled the Division as a "SS-Waffen-Grenadier Division" when, in actuality, since 27 June 1944, the "SS" preceding the Waffen-Grenadier-Division was no longer utilized. And from 25 April 1945 until the conclusion of the war, the Division was officially titled as the "1. Ukrainische Division der Ukrainischen National-Armee."). See "Letzte Kampf an der Sudostgrenze des Reiches Bis zur Kapitulation 7. April bis 8. May 1945" in Rebentisch's, *Zum Kaukasus und Zu Den Tauern, Die Geschichte der 23. Panzer-Division 1941-1945* (Germany: 1963), p. 506.

5. Heike, *English ed.*, p. 111; *Ukrainian ed.*, pp. 173-174.

6. Heike, *English ed.*, p. 115. According to Ren, *My Life's Mosaic*, p. 203, the Division entered the 1st Cavalry Corps, 2nd Army (Ren did not cite 'panzer'), on 31 March 1945. Ren also cited that on 31 March, General Freitag produced a map and informed him that a communist breakout had occurred between Gleichenberg and Feldbach, and a plan was immediately set into motion for the Division to begin a counteroffensive. This counteroffensive was to commence on the following day, 1 April, at 0630 hours in the morning. But what especially concerned Ren was that the Soviet breakout occurred in favorable terrain for an advance and the Division, minus its fusilier battalion, was without one of its most effective combat elements.

7. Victor Madeja, *The Russo-German War 25 January to 8 May 1945* (Pa.: Valor Publishing Co., 1987), p. 67. At this time the charts also reveal the Division was serving with the 1st Cavalry Corps, 2nd Panzer Army.

8. On 2 October 1943, the Southwest Front was redesignated as the 3rd Ukrainian Front. Incorrectly, in "The Final Battles," *Visti*, 1965, No. 1, p. 34, Yuriy Krokhmaliuk cited the Division engaged enemy formations from the "First Ukrainian Front."

By late October 1944, Stavka had devised a plan for a campaign to end the war. The main concept's of the plan were as such:

- to rout the East Prussian grouping and occupy East Prussia;

- to defeat the enemy in Poland, Czechoslovakia, Hungary, and Austria;

- to move out to the line running through the Vistula mouth, Bromberg (Bydgoszcz), Poznan, Breslau (Wroslaw), Moravska Ostrava, and Vienna.

Galicia Division

Once accomplished, a strategic thrust would be launched against Nazi Germany's capital city of Berlin. (Colonel M. Glantz, "The Third Period of War" in *The Role of Intelligence In Soviet Military Strategy in World War II* (Ca.: Presidio Press, 1990, p. 172). For additional information, as well as a study of the importance of Soviet military operations in the areas of Prussia/the Baltic region and Hungary/Austria in the concluding months of the war, see "The 1945 Campaign, January-May and August 1945," pp. 170-203.

As for air support, the 3rd Ukrainian Front would be supported by Colonel-General V.A. Sudets' 17th Air Army.

9. Formed as an independent army at Stalingrad within the North Caucasian Military District in October 1941, the 57th Army was committed to the Kharkiv front in January 1942. Destroyed in the Kharkiv offensive of May 1942, its shattered elements retreated to its home base at Stalingrad. Reformed east of the Volga River the 57th, now under the command of General F.I. Tolbukhin, played a key role in encircling and destroying the German forces at Stalingrad. Further combat included Kursk and Kharkiv in the summer of 1943; Bulgaria, Southeast Yugoslavia, and Hungary in the fall, winter, and spring months of 1944-45. In April 1945, the 57th was commanded by Lieutenant General N.M. Sharokin and it was regarded as one of the more elite Soviet Armies.

10. Activated in the Baltic Special Military District in May 1941, that same year in December, the 27th Army was transformed into the 4th Shock Army. Reactivated in March 1942, the 27th was subordinated to the RVGK reserve system and served in various regions of the eastern front but notably in Demyansk (Northern Russia), Kharkiv, Kiev, and Zhytomir. The 27th Army also served in Rumania and Hungary, and concluded the war in Austria. In Austria, it was commanded by F.I. Trofimenko.

11. Heike, *English ed.*, p. 114; Krokhmaliuk, "The Last Battles," *Visti*, 1965, No. 1, p. 32 and personal discussion; Ren, *My Life's Mosaic*, p. 203. But Ready, p. 469, cites the Division received its orders on 20 March to "withdraw" to Southeast Austria. In addition to citing an incorrect date, Ready's observation is incorrect because at no time did the Division ever receive orders to "withdraw;" rather, the Division received orders to advance and engage Soviet forces advancing into Eastern Austria.

12. Heike, *English ed.*, p. 116; Krokhmaliuk, "The Last Battles," *Visti*, 1965, No. 1, p. 32; Ren, *My Life's Mosaic*, p. 203; Bohdan Stasiv, "Tragediia Pid Brodamy" [Tragedy At Brody], *Visti*, 1992, No. 3, p. 53. See also Fostun's, "U 50-Richchia Postannia 1-oi UD UNA" [In the 50th Anniversary of the Rise of the 1st Ukrainian Division, Ukrainian National Army], *Visti*, 1993, No. 4, p. 27. In an unpublished account titled "Persha Ukrains'ka Dyviziia UNA Pid Fel'dbakhom" [The 1st Ukrainian Division At Feldbach], 31 March 1945 is also cited as the date the Division was committed into eastern front combat.

13. Although neither Heike, Ren, or any other writers and historians emphasis this point, such a military maneuver is indeed a very difficult – and dangerous – one. See also Volodymyr Vashkovych, "Pid Gliaikhenbergom" [Under Gleichenberg], *Visti*, 1972, No. 1, p. 41. As a liaison officer, Vashkovych participated in the Division's conferences and meetings. And as attested by Vashkovych, one of the problems encountered was a lack of intelligence pertaining to Soviet strengths, whereabouts, and intents.

14. According to Heike, "in Slovenia the Ukrainians maintained the most cordial relations with the local population." (*Ukrainian ed.*, English synopsis, p. 251). In a personal discussion with Yuriy Krokhmaliuk, Veryha, Veryn and a host of former Divisional soldiers, all acknowledge that during the brief period of time the Division served on the Austro-Yugoslavian frontier, the Division's soldiers encountered no serious conflicts with any of Austria's or Yugoslavia's citizens.

15. Heike, *English ed.*, p. 106.

16. *Bender and Taylor*, Vol. 4, p. 48. This figure did not include those serving in the Training and Replacement Regiment.

17. Personal discussion with Yuriy Krokhmaliuk.

18. The Division's Training and Replacement Regiment remained at Deutschlandsberg. Its mission: to continue its training, maintain regional security of Southern Austria in the event any communist guerrillas from Yugoslavia crossed the border into Austria proper, and provide flank and rear security to the Division operating further to the north/northeast. (See also Fostun's "In the 50th-Anniversary of the Rise of the 1st Ukrainian Division Ukrainian National Army," *Visti*, 1993, No. 4, p. 27).

19. For an interesting account of Kozak's experiences, see Volodymyr Kozak's, "Boii za Zamok Gliaikhenberg" [Battles For the Gleichenberg Castle], *Visti*, 1951, No. 4 (6), pp. 2-4.

20. Also spelled as Bliankengor.

21. Initially, the 31st Infantry Regiment was utilized as a reserve. However, as the enemy's situation became clearer, the 31st was committed into combat. (See also Heike *English ed.*, p. 116). According to Volodymyr Kozak, Major Kurtzbach commanded the 31st Regiments 1st Battalion and Major Sholts commanded the regiments 2nd

Notes

Battalion. Kozak did not identify the commander of the regiment's 3rd Battalion, but a winter roster of the Division's command reveals the 3rd Battalion was commanded by a Ukrainian, Waffen-Sturmbannführer (Major) Podlesch. However, some have identified Podlesch as being a German, while others cite his nationality as Ukrainian from German descent. In an account titled "Boiovi Dii v Slovenii, Pid Fel'dbakhom i Vidstup z Frontu" [Combat Actions In Slovenia, At Feldbach and the Withdrawal From the Front], *Visti*, 1994, No. 4, p. 97, author Myhailo Bodnaruk identified Major Podlesch as being the 31st Regiments 3rd Battalion commander during the time the 31st Regiment served in Slovenia and Austria.

22. According to Heike "all units of the Division that had taken part in the advance, including the field reserve battalion, carried out their orders." (*English ed.*, p. 116). Heike also acknowledged that there was heavy fighting for the village of Gleichenberg, and for the lookout points located at Stradner-Kogel, Gleichneberg-Kogel, and the Gleichenberg castle. Consequently, morale rose tremendously. (*Ibid*). And Bohdan Stasiv, "Tragedy At Brody," *Visti*, 1992, No. 3, p. 53, cites: "In the opening stages, Soviet armies conducted a breakthrough of the front against which the Division "Galicia" counterattacked and repulsed the enemy and sealed his penetration."
Both Heike (*English ed.*, p. 116), and Yuriy Krokhmaliuk (personal discussion) acknowledged that the Division successfully executed a very difficult combat mission. Once the Division accomplished its mission, it held had a frontline sector of 25 kilometers. (15.5 miles). "The Final Battles," *Visti*, 1965,No. 1, p. 34. See also pp. 32-33; and *Visti*, 1965, No. 2, pp.33-38.

23. Personal discussion with Yuriy Krokhmaliuk. See also Heike, *English ed.*, pp. 116-117. For additional accounts of combat in Austria see Kozak's, "Battle For the Gleichenberg Castle," *Visti*, 1951, 4 (6), pp. 2-4; Stasiv, "Tragedy At Brody," *Visti*,1992, No. 3, p. 53; Omelian Kul'chyts'kyi, "Odyn Bii v Avstrii. Do Istorii Kurenia Boiovoi Grupy "Vil'dner" [One Battle In Austria. To the History of the Battle Group "Wildner"], *Visti*, 1994, No. 4, pp. 89-91; Vasyl' Peleshchuk, "Spohad Pro Dyviziiu [Remembrances About the Division], *Visti*, 1993, No. 4, p. 93; Ivan Boichak, "Spomyny Radysta" [A Radio Operator's Remembrances], Visti, 1994, No.4, pp. 94-95; and Lev Stetkevych, "Povorot Do Avstrii i Front" [Return To Austria and the Front] in "Yak z Bereshan Do Kadry. Spomyn z Dyvizii – Nekhai Vichna Bude Slava" [From Bereshan To the Cadre. Remembrances From the Division – Let Its Glory Live Forever]. (Self-published text), pp. 155-178.

24. Vasil Kushchelep, "Spohad Pro Dyvisiiu" [Remembrances About the Division], *Visti*, No. 3, 1982, pp. 64-65; Peleshchuk, "Remembrances About the Division], *Visti*, No. 4, p. 93; personal discussion with Veryn.

25. Personal discussion with Yuriy Krokhmaliuk.

26. Personal discussion with Vashchenko.

27. O. Hor, "V Amerikans'komy Poloni" [In American Captivity], *Visti*, No. 4, p. 20. Indeed, this is a shocking figure. And if one takes into consideration that in western allied armies composed of millions of soldiers not one western allied army executed so many of its soldiers, than this is more than enough proof that the Divisions soldiers were exposed to not only a very severe discipline but tragically, a very brutal one.

28. "The Last Battles," *Visti*, 1965, No. 1, p. 34; personal discussion with Yuriy Krokhmaliuk; Heike, *English ed.*, p. 119; Ren, *My Life's Mosaic*, p. 205; Bohdan Pidhainyi, "Kinets' Viiny 1945 r. i Pochatok Taboru Polonenykh v Italii" [The End Of the War In 1945 and the Beginning As a Prisoner-of-War In Italy], *Visti*, 1979, No. 1, p. 66. According to Yuriy Krokhmaliuk, the Soviets even bombarded the Ukrainian Division with a very strong anti-American, anti-British and anti-capitalist propaganda. The communists even urged the Ukrainians to join the Red Army in the upcoming battle against the "American imperialists" which would commence following the defeat of Nazi Germany. But as acknowledged by Krokhmaliuk, the Soviets only wasted their time with their anti-American/anti-western propaganda because the Ukrainian soldiers had no quarrels with the United States or England and some of the Divisions soldiers even had brothers and cousins serving in the American Army. According to General Lothar Dr. Rendulic, Army Group 'South's' last commander, "at various places along the front, especially in the sectors of Sixth Army [where, incidentally, the Ukrainian Division was operating] and the Sixth SS Panzer Army, the Russians made [such] propaganda statements from loudspeakers:
The greatest betrayal in the history of mankind is in preparation. If you do not wish to continue fighting against us side by side with the forces of Capitalism, come over to us." See Steven Newton's, *German Tactics On the Russian Front 1941-1945*, p. 231.

29. According to Myhailo Lobach (who returned to the Division in early March 1945 following his graduation from the Bad Tolz Officer's School and was posted into an intelligence- reconnaissance section), Soviet agents did infiltrate the Division; as well, there were those who succumbed to promises of a good life in a "working man's paradise." According to Vashchenko, UPA's inserted personnel constantly kept a lookout for NKVD inserted agents, communists, and UPA's agents even monitored those who they felt would succumb to Soviet promises.

30. Pidhainyi, "The End Of the War 1945," *Visti*, 1979, No. 1, p. 66.

31. Personal discussion with Yuriy Krokhmaliuk, Veryha, Veryn, Vashchenko, Lobach and a host of former Divisional soldiers. According to *Ready*, p. 515, "all relatives of known osttruppen and hiwis were sent to prison, even though they themselves may have proven their loyalty." Although in due time a number were released, as also ac-

knowledged by Ready, "they were released without work permits, and they were forced to become dependents of their families, or, if they had no one, to turn to prostitution and crime in order to survive." (*Ibid.*).

32. Heike, *English ed.*, p. 119. In a humorous manner, Yuriy Krokhmaliuk recalled how once in Austria, with a bullhorn in his hands, he began to broadcast a message to the Soviet side from a Divisional frontline position. But before Krokhmaliuk could conclude his broadcast, from the other side he heard such a response: "Good morning, Mr. Krokhmaliuk. Listen, we've heard it all before. So either you come up with something new, or just forget it!" Krokhmaliuk never did say what course of action he took afterwards.

33. Ren, *My Life's Mosaic*, p. 205. According to Ren, the Divisions propaganda/anti-propaganda section was actually established the moment the Division arose. This section was headed by a German officer named Kleinhoff. But because Kleinhoff never pursued his task aggressively (and no higher authority from Divisional staff ever raised the issue of Kleinhoff's inefficiency) in the end the Division was denied an effective propaganda/counter-propaganda section. In due time, some of the Divisions soldiers were dispatched for the training. But this occurred in the concluding weeks of the war and by now, it was too late.

34. Pidhainy, "The Last Battles," *Visti*, 1979, No. 1, p. 66.

35. Heike, *English ed.*, p. 119. However, as acknowledged by Heike, "this was a negligible [figure] considering the large number of soldiers in the Division, the critical time of general disintegration, and the incidence of desertion in the German divisions of the corps." (P. 120). Of course, Heike is more than correct in his observation. If one takes into consideration .the difficulties facing the Division in Austria in 1945, and in general the chaotic wartime conditions especially in the months of April-May 1945 which resulted in the collapse of entire units to include some in relatively strong strengths, than the figure of 98 is not only low but is actual proof that until the very end, the Ukrainian Division remained as a strong, well-disciplined and cohesive military force. And of the 98 desertions, not all crossed over to the Soviets.

36. Personal discussion with Yuriy Krokhmaliuk.

37. In a personal discussion with Yuriy Krokhmaliuk, Krokhmaliuk acknowledged that in Austria, the Division began to encounter communist weapon systems never previously encountered. One such weapon was the JS-11 and JS-111 (Joseph Stalin) tank. Although its speed was comparable to that of a German Tiger tank, in firepower it far surpassed the Tiger's. With a 122mm cannon, one 12.7mm Dshk machinegun and three 7.62mm machine guns, the JS was a formidable weapon which, in the concluding months of the war, was unmatched by anything produced by Nazi Germany. Exceptional thick armor afforded the tank excellent protection from handheld anti-armor weaponry. Because the Division lost its 88 weapons system at Brody, various other methods of countering this tank had to be implemented. Flame throwing JS tanks also caused hardships. Possessing the capability to hurl flames hundreds of meters (and well out of the range of hand-fired anti-armor weaponry), the Stalin tank could exert a considerable amount of physical and psychological damage.

38. Raised in Shchelkovo, Moscow Military District from the 8th Airborne Corps in December 1942, the following month the 3rd Guards Airborne Division appeared in Demyansk with the 1st Shock Army. Afterwards, the 3rd Guards Airborne was utilized in various critical sectors with various armies and shock groups such as at Kursk, the Dnieper crossing, Kiev, Debrecen, Budapest, Lake Balaton, Vienna, and Graz. It concluded the war in Austria.

39. Heike, *English ed.*, p. 118; Ren, *My Life's Mosaic*, p. 204; Krokhmaliuk, "The Final Battles," *Visti*, 1965, No. 1, p. 33. At this time, the Ukrainian fusiliers were posted to the 23rd Panzer Division's 126th Panzergrenadier Regiment, and along with the 126th Regiments 1st Battalion, secured the 126th's right (southern) flank positioned south/southwest of Hill 336 on the Weizelbaum-Oberpurkla-Radochen-Hill 332 line. (See Rebentisch, *Zum Kaukasus und Zu Den Tauern*, p. 510).

40. According to Ren, the transfer of the fusiliers to the 23rd Panzer, as well as the engineers to Marburg (undoubtedly to assist in the final construction of defense positions), were strongly felt by the Division during periods of combat. (See *My Life's Mosaic*, p. 204). As for the fusiliers command structure, in the spring of 1945 it stood as such: Commander: SS-Sturmbannführer Karl Bristot; adjutant – Waffen-Untersturmführer Karl Strasser, a Slovakian German; 1st Company: Waffen- Obersturmführer's Hiliarii ("Yasho") Zaryts'kyi and Yaroslav Rybalt; 2nd Co.: Waffen-Obersturmführer's E. Krause, Myroslav Pronchak, S. Dobrians'kyi; 3rd Co.: Waffen-Obersturmführer's Stepan Guliak, Myhailo Nin'ovs'kyi, Kudla; and 4th (Heavy) Co.: Waffen-Obersturmführer Chotovyi Liashevych. The battalion's medical officer was Waffen-Untersturmführer O. Fahrion and the ordnance/supply officer was Waffen-Untersturmführer Kyrylo Hryhorovych. (See K. Hryhorovych, "4-yi Fiuzilers'kyi Kurin' – 14 Fuesilier Batailion) – Komandnyi Sklad 1945 r" [The 4th Fusilier Battalion – 14 Fusilier Battalion – Command Structure], *Visti*, 1992, No. 2, p. 90. Of course, on 27 April 1945, the German rank titles were replaced by Ukrainian rank titles.

41. Ren, *My Life's Mosaic*, p. 204.

42. Heike, *English ed.*, p. 118; Krokhmaliuk, "The Last Battles," *Visti*, 1965, No. 1, p. 33; *Svoboda* (Ukrainian Daily), 28 June 1979, p. 5. In Rebentisch's *Zum Kaukasus und Zu Den Tauern*, no negative thoughts or criticism are

expressed about the Ukrainian fusiliers. And by his writing, Rebentisch makes it understood that the Ukrainian fusilier battalion was undertaking a difficult and critical mission while supporting the 23rd Panzer Division.

43. Formed in October 1939, the 6th Army took part in the western offensive of 1940. In June 1941, under the command of General Walter von Reichenau, the 6th was in Army Group 'South' (Ukraine), and fought in Ukraine. In the summer of 1942, it participated in Operation "Blau" ("Blue"), the German code name for the operation to secure the Caucasian oil fields of Maikop, Grozny, and Baku. Diverted to Stalingrad by Hitler, the 6th Army, now commanded by Friedrich Paulus, was destroyed. Although rebuilt, it never achieved its former effectiveness, and in the lower Dnieper and Dniester River bends the 6th (now operating more as a sizable battlegroup rather than as an army), was repeatedly encircled and largely destroyed. Augmented with Hungarians and Rumanians, it reappeared in Rumania and later in Hungary. Under General Balck's renewed leadership, the 6th Army offered stiff resistance on the Hungarian front, and was responsible for the defense of Budapest. Continuous enemy pressure, however, forced it to withdraw to Eastern Austria. In May 1945, the 6th Army disappeared in Austria.

44. Heike, *English ed.*, p. 122, provides mid-April of 1945 as the period the Division was assigned to the 6th Army and its 4th SS Panzer Corps; Hugh Page Taylor cites that German Order-of-Battle Charts for 30 April 1945 reveal the Division was serving in the 4th SS Panzer Corps, 6th Army (letter of 15 October 1988); Ren, *My Life's Mosaic*, p. 207, does not specify a date but verifies the Ukrainian Division was found within the 4th SS Panzer Corps and 6th Army; Krokhmaliuk, "The Final Battles," *Visti*, 1965, No. 2, p. 35, cites that in mid-April 1945, the Division was posted into the 6th Army and served on its right wing (flank). However, Krokhmaliuk incorrectly cited the Division was posted into the 6th Army's 3rd Corps. Former Army Group 'South' Commander Lothar Dr. Redulic's Army Order of-Battle dated 7 April 1945 reveals the Division was serving within the 6th Army's 4th SS Panzer Corps on 7 April under the command of Brigadeführer Fritz Freitag. (*German Battle Tactics On the Russian Front, 1941-1945*, pp. 235-236). The possibility exists that the Division was posted to the 6th Army on or about 7 April 1945 without the knowledge of the Divisions staff. The last German Army Group charts dated 30 April 1945 reveal the Division was found (along with the 3rd Panzer Division and the 5th SS "Wiking" Division), within the 4th SS Panzer Corps, 6th Army. See also Hans Dollinger, *The Decline and Fall of Nazi Germany and Imperial Japan* (N.Y.: Bonanza Books, 1967), p. 176.

45. Heike does not specify his name, but it appears to be SS-Hauptsturmführer Johannes Kleinow.

46. Born on 28 February 1889 in Volyn, General Pavlo Shandruk entered the Imperial Russian Army in 1911. At the end of 1916, in the rank of captain, he commanded the 232nd Infantry Brigade's 3rd Company, stationed in Tver, Russia. He remained there until the Bolshevik Revolution of 1917. During Ukraine's War of Liberation, Shandruk was a senior officer, and in 1919, was promoted to the rank of brigadier general in the Ukrainian National Army. ("Pamiati Generala Pavla Shandruka" [Remembrances of General Pavlo Shandruk], *Visti*, 1979, No. 2, p. 60). In 1936, he entered the Polish War Academy, and graduated in the spring of 1938. In March 1939, Shandruk was promoted to the rank of Colonel and served as a staff officer in the Polish Army; shortly after, he was assigned to the 18th Cavalry Brigade which on 7 July 1939, was stationed in the vicinity of Poznan in Western Poland. In the 1939 German invasion of Poland, Shandruk commanded the brigade. Devastated by German aircraft and panzers, Shandruk was wounded in the head by shrapnel, and captured. Following a surgical operation by a German Army surgeon, Shandruk was medically discharged by the Germans in April, 1940. During most of the war, Shandruk resided near Warsaw. Although he was medically discharged, Shandruk's activities were constantly monitored and on more than one occasion, he had to explain his whereabouts to the Gestapo.

By an order issued on 15 March 1945 by the exiled Ukrainian National Republic President Andriy Livyts'kyi (Order No. 8), Shandruk was appointed commander of the Ukrainian Army. (*Ready*, p. 469; Roman Drazhn'ovs'kyi, "General Pavlo Shandruk – Voiak" [General Pavlo Shandruk – Soldier], *Visti*, 1979, No. 3, pp. 29-35. Roman Krokhmaliuk cites 12 March 1945 as the date of the appointment. "Zmina Nimets'koi Polityky i Postannia Ukrains'koho Natsional'noho Komitetu" [The Change in German Policy and the Emergence of the Ukrainian National Committee], *Visti*, 1974, No. 1, p. 55]).

At no time did Shandruk ever hold an SS or Waffen-SS officer's rank, as incorrectly implied by certain authors, such as Francois Duprat, *Histoire Des SS* (Les Sept Couleurs, Paris, 1968), p. 357; Edward Prus, *Z Dziejow Wspolpracy Nacjonalistow Ukrainskich z Niemcam i w Okresie II Wotny Swiatowej i Okupacji* (Katowice: Akademia Ekonomiczna Im. Karola Adamirckiego, 1985), p. 324; nor did he ever command the Galician/Ukrainian Division (*Duprat*, p. 181; *Terlytsia*, p. 181) prior, during, or after Brody; nor did Shandruk in the aftermath of Brody "flee to the west and end up in Berlin" as also falsely alleged by the Soviet propagandist Terlytsia (p. 181); nor did Shandruk "actively collaborate with the Nazis since at least 1941" as falsely stated by Simpson, *Blowback*, p. 170. Captured German World War II orders and documents, as well as numerous Ukrainian accounts and Shandruk's own autobiography, *Arms of Valor* (N.Y.: Speller Publishing Co., 1959), reveal no membership in the SS or Waffen-SS.

Following the war, Shandruk emigrated to the United States. He died in New Jersey on 15 February 1979.

47. Livyts'kyi headed the Ukrainian National Republic in exile. At no time did Shandruk ever head the Ukrainian Government-in-Exile as erroneously cited by *Simpson*, p. 170.

48. *Bender and Taylor*, Vol. 4, p. 43; 1943-1945. *The 1st Ukrainian Division. 1943-1993*, p. 92. But Krokhmaliuk, "Zminy Nazv Ukrains'koi Dyvizii Halychyna" [Title Changes of the Ukrainian Division Galicia], *Visti*, 1977, No. 5-6, p. 51, cites 25 April 1945 as the date the Division took on its "Ukrainian" title despite the previous change on 12

Galicia Division

November 1944; Roman Drazhn'ovs'kyi, "General Pavlo Shandruk – Soldier," *Visti*, 1979, No. 3, p. 29, also cited 25 April as the date Shandruk enacted the title change. Although, of course, the change from "Galicia" to "Ukrainian" had been noted by the SS Liaison officer previously on 12 November 1944 (Verbindungsoffizier der SS beim OKH – 11. 12.44. See also *Bender and Taylor*, Vol. 4, pp. 40-41 and fn. 91 on p. 41; Krokhmaliuk, *Visti*, 1977, No. 5-6, p. 51, fn. 7) it appears that nothing had been done about it and this is evidenced by the fact that German Army Battle Order Charts reveal the Division continued to be referred to as "Galician."

49. Bohdan Prypkhan, "My Prysiahaly Ukraini" [We Swore Ukrainian Allegiance], *Visti*, 1951, No. 7 (9), p. 4. According to Prypkhan, the oath was taken in early April, 1945. According to "Vis'kovi Prysiahy" [Military Oath's], the oath was taken on 25 April 1945. *(Visti*, 1993, No. 1, p. 40). Prypkhan's unit, however, could have taken the oath sooner because it is known that some units took it in early April 1945. *1943-1945. The 1st Ukrainian Division*, p. 3; and Volodymyr Trembits'kyi, "Viis'kovi Prysiahy" [Military Oaths], in "Duzhe Znamennyi Akt Viis'kovoi Prysiahy" [A Military Oath Is a Very Significant Act], *Visti*, 1993, No. 1, p. 40, cites 25 April 1945 as the date of the oath; *Bender and Taylor*, Vol. 4, p. 43, cite the Divisions soldiers took a new oath of allegiance to their Ukrainian nation between 25 and 30 April 1945.

50. Born in 1892 in Hadiach, Ukraine, Myhailo Krat graduated from the St. Petersburg Military Academy. This academy was regarded as one of Imperial Russia's oldest – and renowned – military academy's. During World War I, Myhailo Krat served as a captain in the Imperial Russian Army, and was wounded four times. With the rise of the Ukrainian nation in the aftermath of the collapse of Russia and the Austro-Hungarian Empire, Krat first served as a staff officer in Kiev's Military District. With the commencement of hostilities between Bolshevik Russia and Ukraine, Krat served as a staff officer during such years in such places: 1918 – Kiev, Bakhmach, Romen; 1919 – Poltava, Kriukiv, Balta, Tyraspil', Vapniarka, Balanivka, Bershad', Tul'chyn, Zhyvotiv; 1920 – Arseenivka, Oleksiivka, Holta, Nalyvaiky, Dolyns'ka, Voznesens'k, Onapiv, Vapniarka, Trushka, Snitkovo, Sarniv. In 1919, while serving as a staff officer in the 8th "Chornomors'kyi" (Black Sea) Regiment, Colonel Krat assumed command of the regiment at a critical moment when its commander, Colonel Tsarenko, was killed during an engagement with General Denikin's white forces. Quickly restoring order, Colonel Krat overwhelmed the white unit and captured 600 Russian soldiers in the vicinity of Podillia. With the collapse of the Ukrainian nation, Colonel Krat participated in the so-called "Zymovyi Pokhid" (Winter March) into Ukrainian areas occupied by communist Russia's forces. His last service (1920) was with the Zaporozhia Division. As a staff officer, he directed the division's staff section. Following a period of internment in Poland, upon release Krat remained in Poland until World War II. During World War II, he remained inactive. But in the concluding months of the war, Krat was approached by Livyts'kyi to take a command position. From 27 April 1945 until the Ukrainian Division's surrender in May 1945, General Krat commanded the 1st Ukrainian Division. *(Bender and Taylor*, Vol. 4, p. 49. Krat's rank is cited as General-Khorunzhyi. However, during this period of confusion, General Fritz Freitag also remained in command and actually did command the Ukrainian Division). Captured by the British, General Krat commanded the Ukrainian Division during its internment in both Italy and England. (Krokhmaliuk, "Na Sluzhbi Narodu. U Visimdesiatlittia Generala Myhaila Krata" [In Service of a Nation. The 80th Anniversary of General Myhailo Krat], *Visti*, 1972, No. 5-6, pp. 67-70). Emigrating to the United States, General Krat resided in the Detroit, Michigan, area. On 8 August 1979, he passed away. Following funeral services in Detroit, Michigan, General Krat was buried on 13 August in Boundbrook, New Jersey. (See also Ostap Sokol's'kyi's, "Pomer sl. p. Gen. Myhailo Krat" [General Myhailo Krat, a Famous Gentleman-General, Died], *Visti*, 1979, No. 4, pp. 49-50; and Leonid Romaniuk, "General Myhailo Krat" [General Myhailo Krat], *Visti*, 1980, No. 1. pp. 68-73. Romaniuk, a former artillery officer in the 8th Regiment, served under Colonel Krat).

Notes Chapter 25

1. Also known as the Ukrainian Liberation Army (Ukrains'ke Vyzvolne Viys'ko – U.V.V.); and 1st Ukrainian Army

2. The 2nd Ukrainian Division was formed on the basis of the Ukrainian Anti-Brigade, a unit located in the vicinity of Berlin On 25 February 1945, approximately 500 men, under the command of Colonel Petro Tumarenko, were transferred to a military camp at Nimek, approximately 25 miles west of Berlin. ("Polkovnyk Petro Tumarenko" [Colonel Peter Tumarenko], Visti, Nimek, approximately 25 miles west of Berlin. ("Polkovnyk Petro Tumarenko" [Colonel Peter Tumarenko], *Visti*, 1952, No. 6 (9), p. 3). There, at Nimek, the 2nd Ukrainian Division was to be formed and Nimek served as a collection point for the 2nd Division. Through the inclusion of recently released prisoners-of-war, Schuma personnel and refugees, a strength of approximately 2,000 soldiers were assembled and placed under the command of Colonel Petro Dyachenko. (*Arms of Valor*, p. 235). A weak formation of questionable military value, the 2nd Ukrainian Division never established contact with the 1st Ukrainian and, as a matter of fact, disappeared sometime in April 1945. See also *Ready*, p. 469.

3. Shandruk, *Arms of Valor*, p. 255. Ready cites a strength of 50,000. (*Ready*, p. 469). According to Ready, the 14th Waffen-SS "Galicia" Division was immediately redesignated as the 1st Ukrainian Division and was transferred to Shandruk's army. Together with the 2nd Ukrainian Division, the 5,000 Ukrainian infantrymen serving in Denmark in the 281st Ukrainian Reserve Infantry Regiment, the two Ukrainian infantry regiments in the Netherlands, some hiwi, schuma, paramilitary, anti-aircraft and Ukrainian speaking Cossacks, Shandruk possessed a strength of 50,000 troops. (*Ibid.*).

Notes

4. From: *Ukrainian Comm of the Camp 5c.* To: The British Commanding Officer of the Camp POW, 9.8.45. (The letter is presented in its original English version. The letter was not signed by any specific individual, but was concluded with "Colonel and Comm. Ukr. Camp 5c."). A copy of the original letter is found within a portfolio titled in both Ukrainian and English languages: *"Dyviziia "Halychuna" Rimini, Italia (1945-47. Zvernennia, obizhnyky, informatsii,Nakazy, Zariady Taboru Polonenykh u Rimini Ta al'ians'koi viys'kovoi Komandy."* [Division "Galicia" Rimini, Italy (1945-47). Requests, information, orders, circulars from the headquarters of the prisoners' camp in Rimini and the Allied Military Command].

5. Ihor Kamenetsky, *Hitler's Occupation of Ukraine, 1941-44; A Study of Totalitarian Imperialism* (Milwaukee: The Marquette University Press, 1956), p. 61; *Gaucher,* p. 314, cites almost 1,000,000 former Soviet personnel from the end of 1942; and *Thorwald,* pp. 227-228, cites that in October 1944, General Kostring informed Himmler that approximately 900,000 to 1,000,000 Eastern Europeans were in various services. Of this figure, over half were Russian.

6. *Kamenetsky,* p. 61.

7. In a personal discussion with Yuriy Krokhmaliuk, Krokhmaliuk acknowledged that one of the most difficult (if not the most difficult) problems that General Shandruk had was to identify a location where the Ukrainian Army could be organized without any interference of any kind. In his writings, Ready gives the implication that Shandruk was unable to organize his army when he cites that "Shandruk had 50,000 troops, but this mass of Ukrainian manhood would spent the next month in transit across Germany, dodging Allied aircraft and waiting for transportation." (See *Ready,* p. 469). In a letter by Hugh Page Taylor, Taylor states that in actuality, the Ukrainian National Army did exist. But Taylor also concedes that Shandruk had difficulties in assembling his army when he wrote: "No doubt it would have been a tidier solution and pleased Shandruk and the Ukrainians more if they could have all come together in one place but, separate as they were, the 14. SS [Galicia] Division and the Ukrainian Anti-Tank Brigade were briefly the 1st and 2nd Divisions of the U.N.A. [Ukrainian National Army]." (*Letter of 15 October 1988*).

8. For a historic, and tragic, study of this Allied blunder, see Julius Epstein's, *Operation Keelhaul: The Story of Forced Repatriation from 1944 to the Present* (Conn: The Devin-Adair Co., 1973).

Notes Chapter 26

The Final Days of the 1st Ukrainian Division.
1. Heike, *English ed.*, pp. 128-129. It is not known if at this time Balck revealed that Hitler was dead. Possibly, Balck himself did not know. In their writings, neither Heike, or Krokhmaliuk, reveal whether any information was provided on Hitler's death.

2. Heike, *English ed.,* p. 133; personal discussion with Yuriy Krokhmaliuk. According to General Lothar Dr. Rendulic, Army Group 'South's' collapse was largely caused by the American army divisions driving aggressively into its rear. By such an action, the Americans began to overrun Army Group 'South's' supply areas located primarily in upper Austria. The supply transport from central Germany was cut, and the American penetration began to make it impossible for Army Group 'South' to continue its operational mission against the Soviets. See *German Battle Tactics on the Russian Front 1941-1945,* pp. 219 and 227. The former general also identified such American divisions as operating in North and Northwestern Austria: 11th Armored, 65th, 71st and 80 Infantry Divisions. (For a map where these divisions stood on 7 May 1945 in Austria, see p. 230). According to the U.S. Army Order-of-Battle for April-May 1945, the above divisions were from General Patton's 20th Corps. This corps was commanded by Lieutenant-General Walton H. Walker, a highly respected and hard-driving tactician noted for his deep concern for his soldiers. In an effort to avoid casualties, Walker rapidly bypassed all German opposition in Austria as he drove into the rear of Army Group 'South.' For additional information on the histories of these various divisions, as well as their combat and non-combat activities in Austria, see Shelby L. Stanton's, *Order-of-Battle: U.S. Army World War II* (Ca.: Presidio Press, 1984); and "The Last Roundup. Germany on its Last Legs" in George Forty's, *Patton's Third Army At War* (N.Y.: Charles Scribner's & Sons, 1979), pp. 172-174.

3. Certain allied commanders, such as General George Patton, never believed the Nazi's would organize any type of underground resistance. For a further study of Allied suspicions and fears, see Charles Whiting's, *Hitler's Werewolves: A Spellbinding Saga of Secrecy and Sabotage* (N.Y.: Jove Publications, Inc., 1983); and Stephen B. Patrick's, "Werewolves and Redoubts" in *Battle for Germany: The Destruction of the Reich, Dec. 1944-May 1945* (Strategy and Tactics, May/June 1975), p. 13. For an interesting study of the final days of Nazi Germany, see pp. 4-16.

4. Heike, *English ed.*, p. 130; *The Truth About the First Ukrainian Division,* p. 31.

5. *Ibid.* According to former general Lothar Dr. Redulic, on the morning of 6 May 1945, Army Group 'South' dispatched Major-General Gaedcke to meet with General Patton regarding certain requests. Although it appears that Gaedcke never established contact with Patton, Gaedcke did meet with Patton's command. In the evening hours of 6 May, General Gaedcke returned. He reported that the Americans had refused Army Group 'South's' requests and they demanded its surrender. Because it was now determined that further resistance was fruitless and senseless, Army

Galicia Division

Group 'South' issued orders that those forces in Austria facing the American's would cease their resistance effective 0900 hours on 7 May 1945. Simultaneously, orders were issued to the units opposing the Soviets to disengage during the darkness of 7-8 May and retire westward. (*German Battle Tactics on the Russian Front 1941-1945*, pp. 232-233).

6. Heike, *English ed.*, p. 133; 1943-1993. *The 1st Ukrainian Division*, p. 25; personal discussion with Yuriy Krokhmaliuk.

7. In addition to being a first-rate engineer officer, Lieutenant Bohdan Spivak proved to be a true humanitarian. This was first evidenced in Yugoslavia when Spivak's platoon captured a Titoist guerrilla. Realizing that if the insurgent was handed over to the German command he might be shot, Lt. Spivak informed his commander that their company should keep the Titoist for labor purposes. Agreeing to it, the Titoist was issued a uniform to blend in with the others. When Spivak's engineer platoon departed from Yugoslavia, the Titoist came along. Shortly afterwards, at Feldbach, Austria, a small group of Red Army soldiers were also captured by Spivak's troops. As previously he did with the Yugoslavian insurgent, Spivak also incorporated the Red captives into his platoon. At the conclusion of the war and just prior to the Division's surrender, Lt. Spivak released his prisoners.

8. Heike, *English ed.*, p. 132.

The Withdrawal!
1. Personal discussion with Yuriy Krokhmaliuk. See also Heike, *English ed.*, pp. 131-132. According to *1943-1993. The 1st Ukrainian Division*, p. 25, the Division began its withdrawal at 6 a.m. on 8 May 1945. See also Motuk's "The Last Day," *Visti*, 1951, No. 5 (7), p. 2. According to Sviatomyr M. Fostun, "In the 50th Year Of the Rise of the 1st Ukrainian Division, UNA," *Visti*, 1993, No. 4, p. 27, prior to the Divisions withdrawal, a commanders and staff personnel conference was held on 6 May 1945 in the 2nd SS Panzer Corps' headquarters. Regarding the date, Fostun is correct. However, the conference was not held in the headquarters of the 2nd SS Panzer Corps; rather, the conference was held in the 4th SS Panzer Corps headquarters.

2. Emigrating to Canada in the aftermath of World War II, Tyvoniuk joined the Canadian Army. He served in its artillery.

3. Heike, *English ed.*, p. 134. According to Ren, *My Life's Mosaic*, p. 208, the Division's soldiers also withdrew in the face of Tito's guerrillas. For additional information on the withdrawal, see Myhailo Bodnaruk's, "Boyovi Dii v Slovenii, Pid Fel'dbakhom i Vidstup z Frontu" [Battle Events In Slovenia, Feldbach and the Withdrawal From the Front], *Visti*, 1994, No. 4, pp. 96-99. In this personal account, Bodnaruk, a former Divisional soldier, truly depicts the ordeals of combat, the everyday events Divisional soldiers experienced while on the offense and defense in Austria, and Allied captivity.

4. Heike, *English ed.*, p. 134.

5. Personal discussion with Yuriy Krokhmaliuk.

6. Regarding this, there appears to be some confusion as to whether the bridge was blown or not. According to Roman Kolisnyk, the bridge is still standing to this day; according to Oleh Dir, it was blown. So which is it?
From a military point of view, it was only logical to blow the bridge in the face of a Soviet advance. By destroying the bridge, a successful withdrawal was ensured. However, the possibility exists that the engineers could have planned a partial destruction. In warfare, it is not uncommon for combat engineers to destroy a bridge partially. In the event of a counterattack, the destroyed part is quickly repaired. The possibility also exists that the bridge was to be totally blown; however, enough explosive materiel was not on hand (or enough was not placed underneath and/or on the sides of the bridge) to totally destroy the bridge. Following the blast, the bridge's main structure remained undamaged. In the ensuing days, it was repaired by Soviet engineers who, with their departure from Austria, left it intact. Of interest to note is that in his memoirs, General Lothar Dr. Rendulic cited that in April he had received a directive from OKH that all bridges and roads were to be destroyed in front of any advancing Russian and American forces. (*German Battle Tactics on the Russian Front 1941-1945*, p. 227). However, on p. 229, the former commander of Army Group 'South' acknowledged that "in view of the impending cessation of hostilities, Army Group 'South' refrained from destroying bridges and roads in its area."
Of course, the possibility exists that Oleh Dir might have crossed a different bridge. It must be remembered that in the Division's withdrawal, more than one bridge was utilized. To ensure a safe withdrawal, engineers from the Ukrainian Division would have been posted on each site. This explains why Dir exchanged some words with Ukrainian combat engineers as he raced back.

7. Heike, *English ed.*, pp. 135-136. See also Heike's, "Ostanni Frontovi Boii 1-oi Ukrains'koi Dyvizii" [The Last Frontline Battles of the 1st Ukrainian Division], *Visti*, 1952, No. 4-5, April-May, p. 12; and *The Truth About the 1st Ukrainian Division*, pp. 31-32.

8. Heike, *English ed.*, pp. 135-136; Ren, *My Life's Mosaic*, p. 208. According to Ren, 10 May 1945 was the date that the Divisions headquarters ceased to exist. In a personal discussion with Yuriy Krokhmaliuk, Krokhmaliuk also cited 10 May 1945 as officially the last day of the Divisions existence. See also Ostap Sokol's'kyi's, "Dyviziinymy

Notes

Steshkamy" [The Divisions Path], *Visti*, 1991, No. 3, p. 92. Incorrectly, *Bender and Taylor*, Vol. 4, p. 43, cite that the Division surrendered to the British on 8 May 1945. In actuality, on 8 May, the Division began its withdrawal. And Klietmann, *Die Waffen-SS*, p. 195 incorrectly cites the Division capitulated to the Americans in the vicinity of Radstadt.

9. Personal discussion with Yuriy Krokhmaliuk. In Nikolai Tolstoy's, *The Secret Betrayal: 1944-1947* (N.Y.: Charles Scribner's Son's, 1977), p. 256, Tolstoy also cites the Ukrainian Division surrendered to the British 5th Corps. (Incorrectly, however, Tolstoy classified the Division as a "panzer-grenadier" division when in actuality it was a grenadier division).

This would be the first, and only time, that the Division ever made contact with any British (and American), forces. At no time in its existence did the Division ever battle any western Allied forces. Allegations by the Ukrainian-American League (UAL) that the "SS Division 'Halychyna' [Galicia] fought the Americans and British in Italy" are totally untrue. (On 25 June 1946, the Ukrainian American League, a communist Ukrainian organization based in New York City, dispatched a letter of protest to the American State Department. In their letter, the UAL condemned the activities of the various Ukrainian organizations, the emigres, and the Division. Needless to say, UAL's allegations were totally untrue because in addition to the fact that the Division never fought the Americans, British or any other western allied forces, excluding the Divisions post-war internment in Italy, prior to the capitulation of May 1945, neither the Division, nor any of its elements or personnel, ever served in Italy). As well, the implication by authors Aarons and Loftus that some members of the Division "may have fought the west at Monte Casino" (*Unholy Alliance*, p. 189), is not only totally false, but reveals the authors have weak research abilities because numerous texts are available on the Allied and Axis Orders-of-Battle which reveal exactly which combat and combat support units (right down to battalion and even independent company levels), were utilized by both sides at Monte Casino.

10. Veryha, *Along the Roads*, p. 187, cites over 10,000 officers and men surrendered. As for the approximately 10,000 personnel who entered British captivity, the figure would diminish once the German personnel were removed. In the very end, approximately 9,000 Ukrainian soldiers would be interned by the British. In a 1946 lengthy letter submitted to Reverend Peter Jacob Perridon by the Ukrainian prisoners, a figure of 9,000 is cited. (Ukrainian SEP Camp. Rimini-Italy. To: The Right Reverend Peter Jacob Perridon, Greek-Catholic Apostolic Envoy in France, Paris. Rimini Italy, 21 November 1946, p. 1). Incorrectly, Mitcham, *Hitler's Legions*, p. 456, cites the Division was captured by the Soviets and subsequently, most of the Division's soldiers were killed. According to Nikolai Tolstoy, a Soviet Repatriation Committee, headed by General Basilov, cited "10,000 Soviet citizens" when referring to the interned Division. See *Victim's of Yalta* (London: Hoddler and Stoughton, 1977), p. 261. Tolstoy also described the Division as a "disciplined unit" when surrendering to the British. (*Ibid.*, p. 256). In *The Secret Betrayal: 1944-1947*, p. 256, Tolstoy cites how Molotov complained to Winston Churchill that 10,000 Ukrainians were interned in Italy. But Soviet efforts to have the Ukrainian Division repatriated to the Soviet Union failed.

11. The removed German personnel were placed into German prisoner -of-war camps. It is also known that some of the Ukrainians who possessed a fluency in other languages and cited their nationality as being Polish, German or Czech/Slovak, succeeded in having themselves removed and placed into other prisoner-of-war camps. The fear of being repatriated to the Soviet Union is what compelled them to do this.

12. During the time that Heike was a prisoner-of-war, he had no contact with any of the Divisions personnel. This was attributed to the fact that Heike was confined in a non-Divisional POW camp. But following his release, Heike reestablished contact with some of the Divisions personnel. He has also remained a staunch defender of the Division, as evidenced by the letters he submitted to the Canadian Deschennes Committee in the late 1980s.

For the historical record: Major Wolf-Dietrich Heike shall always be known in Ukrainian military history as one of the finest – if not the finest – German officer to serve with the Ukrainian ("Galicia") Division.

13. Ren, *My Life's Mosaic*, pp. 208-209, cites around 700 Divisional soldiers were captured by the Americans. But according to Roman Kolisnyk, approximately 1,000 Divisional soldiers were taken captive by the Americans. In a personal discussion with Yuriy Krokhmaliuk, Krokhmaliuk stated that no less than 700 Divisional soldiers were captured by the Americans. However, he did acknowledge that the figure could be higher because here and there, Divisional soldiers ended up in American captivity individually or, after their capture by other allied troops, were handed over to the Americans. Such was the case with Zenon Goliak*. Captured by a Moroccan patrol in the border region of Southeastern France and Southwestern Germany, within days he was handed over to the French who, in turn, handed him over to the Americans. Regardless of what the true figure is, it may be surmised that no less than 700 but perhaps as many as 1,500 Divisional soldiers ended up in American captivity. For additional information on life as a POW in American captivity, see O. Hor's, "V Amerykans'komu Poloni" [In American Captivity], *Visti*, 1961, No. 4, pp. 17-22. An English synopsis is also provided on p. 79); and Ivan Padyk's, "V Amerykans'komu Poloni" [In American Captivity], *Visti*, 1993, No. 1, pp. 80-84; and *Visti*, 1993, No. 2, pp. 78-88.

In addition to Murnau and Auerbach, Divisional soldiers were also interned in such American P.O.W. camps located within such nations: <u>Austria</u>: Flachau, Wagrain, St. Johann, Bad Ausee, Radstadt, Steyr, Saalfeldon, Hallein, Glasenbach (Salzburg); <u>Germany</u>: Bad Aibling, Murnau, Regensburg, Auerbach, Ludwigsburg (Stuttgart) and Darmstadt. As for those who were initially interned in Austria by the Americans, they were quickly moved to P.O.W. camps in Germany. (For a map of the location of the various American and British camps, see *1943-1993. The 1st Ukrainian Division*, p. 66). Captured by the Americans, Chaplain's Ivan Tomashivs'kyi and Bohdan Levyts'kyi were interned at Murnau. There, the two chaplains organized religious services for the various P.O.W.'s, both Ukrainian and non-Ukrainian. For a further detailed account of life in captivity, see "V Amerykans'komu Poloni v Nimechchyni

Galicia Division

i Avstrii" [In American Captivity in Germany and Austria], in *1943-1993. The 1st Ukrainian Division*, pp. 65-78. According to Roman Kolisnyk, the Ukrainians who were interned in the above camps were, in general, kept together and moved to the various locations as a group. However, at Ludwigsburg and Darmstadt (described by Kolisnyk more as an internment camp versus a POW camp) the only Ukrainian personnel confined in those two locations were the officers and senior NCO's. By now, the remainder of the Ukrainian prisoners-of-war had been released.

As for the Ukrainian officers and senior NCO's who were confined at Darmstadt, prior to their release, they were thoroughly investigated by Polish Army officers serving in the British Army to determine if the Division, or any of its elements or personnel, were utilized in the August/September 1944 suppression of the Warsaw uprising. After extensive discussions, the Polish investigators concluded that the Division was never utilized in the suppression of the revolt. (Personal discussion with Yuriy Krokhmaliuk and various other former Divisional soldiers).

It is also important to note that in the immediate aftermath of World War II, the Polish government conducted a massive study of the numerous reports regarding Nazi war crimes within Poland in the period of 1939-1945. Highly comprehensive, this study was conducted throughout the months of 1946-1947.

In order to determine as factually as possible the key personnel and units involved in committing war crimes, the Polish government's commission studied volumes of German orders, documents, letters; the Polish underground's records, correspondence and combat accounts, as well as numerous Jewish sources. The investigators also conducted extensive interviews with responsible individuals. The Warsaw Ghetto Uprising of 1943 and the Warsaw Uprising of 1944 were thoroughly examined. Areas extensively examined covered the general atrocities, the concentration and extermination camps found within Poland, the Jewish plight, and the experiences of the Allied prisoners-of-war found within Poland. Ultimately, this study encompasses hundreds of pages, and is divided into three volumes. (*Biuletyn Glownej Komisji Niemieckich w Polsce*. Tom 1-3. In 1982, the three volumes were translated into English and for the first time published in the western world. Titled *German Crimes In Poland, 1939-1945*, the three volumes were compiled in entirety into two sizable volumes and published by New York's Fertig Publishers.

Of importance to note is that although the initial 1946-1947 study was conducted by the Polish communist government, in neither the Polish nor English volumes are any references made to the "Galicia" Division, or any of its elements, battlegroups or personnel, as being involved in any war crimes, or committing activities which may be regarded as war crimes, in either Warsaw or any other part of Poland.

Another interesting investigation (conducted decades later) which also totally cleared the Division was the one undertaken in the United States. During the time the former "Galicia" Division was being investigated in Canada for possible war crimes, America's Office of Special Investigations (OSI) began preparations for its own investigation. Established in 1979, the OSI was formed to uncover so-called "war criminals" residing in the United States. In March 1985, the OSI dispatched a formal letter through the United States Department of State to these embassies: Moscow, Prague, Vienna, and Warsaw. Titled: Subject: Judicial Assistance, War Crimes Investigations, America's OSI, headed by Neal Sher, was determined to establish whether the Division was involved in any atrocities. Undoubtedly, Sher was seeking to take action against any former Divisional soldiers residing in the United States.

In the early part of 1985, Mr. David L. Boerigter, America's Counselor General based in Warsaw, Poland, was instructed by the U.S. State Department (via the OSI), to inquire from Poland's "Commission of Investigation of Hitlerite Crimes in Poland-Institute of National Memory," about any atrocities committed by the "Galicia" Division. On 4 April 1985, Boertigter dispatched a letter to Poland's Main Commission. (This is the date that Dr. E. Banasiwski, Deputy Director of Poland's Main Commission, cited as the date of Boertigter's letter in his (Banasiwski's) reply of 12 November 1985). In his letter, Boertigter requested information on various individuals, and information on the Division.

Following a lengthy seven month investigation, Poland's Main Commission responded directly to David Boertigter (on 12 November 1985). Along with a detailed letter signed by Deputy Director Banasiwski, a number of various orders pertaining to the "Galicia" Divisions formation and organization; references to the 4th-7th ordnungspolizei regiments, copies of various welfare and aid letters to Divisional soldiers and their families; Berger's letters, etc., were also submitted. But not one order or document dealt with the Division being utilized in any activity which could be interpreted as being of a "war-crime" nature.

Clearly, this was not the information Sher was seeking. Dissatisfied with the Polish commission's response and determined to implicate the Division in some type of atrocity, Sher proceeded to conduct a wider search. In January 1986, the Department of State (again through OSI's insistence), dispatched a telegram to Warsaw's embassy as well to the embassies of Belgrade, Moscow, Prague, and Vienna. Subject: Judicial Assistance In War Crimes Investigations (OSI No. P-6), January, 1986. Ref: 85 State 082929.

In this telegram (full of incorrect transliterations), five points were made. Points 3 through 5 stated the following:

> 3. For Moscow and Warsaw – the book "We Accuse" (Title of Ukrainian Edition: "Pam' Yatayemo, Zvynuvachyemo, Zasterigayemo") by Valery Styrkul (Kiev: Dnipro Publishers, 1984) has recently come to OSI's attention. This book makes numerous allegations, especially on pp. 134-137, 166-181, 201-11, of atrocities committed in 1943 and 1944 by elements of the Galician Division in occupied Polish and Soviet territory. Places mentioned are Debica, Dolyna, Huta Pieniacka, Iwonicze, Jamna, Jasenice, Kanty, Kokhanivka, Moderowka, Olesko, Ozhetsiv, Osidiv, Pidhirtsi, Ternopol' and Wawrzice. Please request the appropriate authorities for any information relating to atrocities committed by the Galician Division in these or any other localities and any documents connecting specific individuals of any nationality. Whether included in the OSI list or not, with the particular elements of the Division which may have perpetrated these atrocities.

Notes

4. For Warsaw: Please convey to the appropriate Polish authorities OSI's thanks for the documents relating to the Galician Division sent to the embassy by the main commission for the investigation of Hitlerite crimes in Poland on 12 November 1985.

5. Your continuing assistance is appreciated.

On 18 February 1986, the OSI received its first response from Austria. (Ref: State 082929). Basically, this was the same response submitted by Austria previously in March 1985. In regard to the individuals and information sought on the Division by the OSI request of January, 1986, the Austrian Embassy responded under Point No. 2: "There is no general materiel in their [Simon Wiesenthal's Documentation Center] files pertaining to the Galician Division."

As for the other embassies (including that of Moscow) whose assistance was sought, nothing positive was ever concluded. Realizing that no solid information pertaining to any war crimes allegedly committed by the "Galicia" Division could be obtained, the OSI ceased its activities, and decided to await Canada's outcome.

14. In addition to the Ukrainians, other foreign prisoners-of-war were also interned at Auerbach. Estonians, Latvians, and Hungarians numbered among the prisoners. (See *1943-1945. The 1st Ukrainian Division*, p. 66). Possibly, the Ukrainians were relocated to Auerbach because the camp held foreign personnel. For an interesting account of life in a prisoner-of-war camp among the various foreign prisoners-of-war, see Oleksa Gorbach, "Zustrich z Chuzhyntsiamy v Amerykans'komu Poloni" [Meeting Foreigners In American Captivity], *Visti*, 1992, No. 4, pp. 81-83.

15. An das Ober Kommando der 3. U.S. Armee in Bad-Tolz durch 1. P.W. der P.W.E. #24 Auerbach – To the High Command of the 3rd U.S. Army at Bad-Tolz from the Ukrainian Group of War Prisoners, P.W.E. #24, Auerbach.

During this time, the commander of the 3rd American Army was General George Patton. Vehemently anti-communist, Patton had developed a respect for the German army but especially the Waffen-SS when on a number of occasions in France, fighting SS soldiers had succeeded in holding up his advances. To what level this letter reached is not known; however, shortly after its submission, it was returned with a reply that the Ukrainian request is being taken into consideration. (As for the letter, in approximately 1950, it was brought over to the United States and currently, is located – with various other prisoner-of-war documents – at the Ukrainian Taras Shevchenko Institute located in Manhattan, N.Y.). In December 1945, General Patton died as a result of an accident. But in early 1946, in the general prisoner-of-war release, some of the first Ukrainians were released. It is known that within the 3rd Army a number of Ukrainian-Americans (some in officer rank) were serving; possibly, they addressed this matter to 3rd Army Headquarters. Regardless, by the end of November 1946, the remainder of the Ukrainian soldiers held by the Americans were (unlike those held by the British), released and spared the fate of a long internment with uncertainty. See also Ren, *My Life's Mosaic*, pp. 208-209. In a personal discussion with Yuriy Krokhmaliuk, Krokhmaliuk stated that the Divisional soldiers captured by the Americans were released considerably sooner than those held by the British.

16. *Ibid.* According to Ren, *My Life's Mosaic*, p. 208, approximately 700 Divisional prisoners (amongst whom were many officers) were interned at Auerbach. It is known, however, that the Ukrainians were never transferred to the location where the majority of their fellow comrades were kept because shortly after their capture, they were released by their American captors. (*Ibid.* pp. 208-209). O. Hor, "In American Captivity," *Visti*, 1961, No. 4, p. 17), cites a figure of around 700 Divisional soldiers in American captivity. Hor does not identify Auerbach as a prisoner-of-war location but cites the 700 were captured north of Mauterndorf in the vicinity of Radstadt. (P. 18). Hor, however, states that amongst the approximately 700 soldiers, some German personnel, to include cadre personnel, were included. "Misfortune had it, that along with us, the entire German chain [of command] from the Divisions staff (Kleinow, Beyersdorff and so forth) fell along with us into this [captivity] location." (Hor also cited that the Divisions renowned "Papa" Wildner was interned at the location. P. 22. For an English synopsis of "In American Captivity" see p. 79). Although an exact figure is not available on how many of the prisoners were German, it may be assumed that of the 700, approximately 200 were German. But, of course, the possibility exists that some of the German-speaking Ukrainians could have also posed as "Germans" to avoid repatriation and, along with the other Germans, were moved to other camp locations.

17. In Auerbach, Ortyns'kyi was the leader and chief spokesman of the Ukrainian prisoners. Upon release, he returned to Munich and immediately established the first veterans organization. In the ensuing months, efforts were made by this small veteran's organization to assist those still held in British captivity; to provide medical, educational, and spiritual assistance to the families and loved ones of Divisional soldiers missing-in-action or held in captivity, and to provide medical assistance to wounded and injured Divisional soldiers who, in the immediate aftermath of World War II, were unable to obtain assistance from the German government. Born 7 July 1919, Ortyns'kyi succumbed to a massive heart attack on 22 July 1961.

18. Personal discussion with Yuriy Krokhmaliuk. West of Graz (a city approximately 25 miles northwest of Feldbach and Gleichenberg where the Division fought its last battles) the U.S. Army's 80th "Blue Ridge" Infantry Division was advancing deep into Austria; simultaneously, the 1st Ukrainian Division was withdrawing westward. Although the brunt of the Ukrainian Division was captured by a British Army corps advancing eastward, it is known that the 80th Infantry Division did capture a number of Army Group 'South's' personnel. In the historical highlights

of the 80th Division, 8 May 1945 is the date cited when the 80th Division began to formally accept the surrender of the 6th German Army north and west of the Enns River. Remembering that until 8 May 1945 the 1st Ukrainian Division was serving in the 6th Army, surely some of the Ukrainian soldiers must have been captured by the 80th Division. For another interesting account of life as an American captive, see Roman Kolisnyk's, "Polon: Regensburg-Darmstadt-Ludwigsburg" [Captivity: Regensburg-Darmstadt- Ludwigsburg], *Visti*, 1992, No. 4, pp. 72-80.

19. Personal discussion with Yuriy Krokhmaliuk. A small number, however, succeeded in escaping from Soviet captivity. Such was the case with grenadier Vsevolod Diakiv.

Dispatched in mid-December 1944 with 150 other Ukrainians to an NCO school at Lauenburg, Pommern (this group, incidentally, would be one of the last to be dispatched from the Division to any school or training site), Diakov's studies were interrupted with the Soviet winter offensive of January 1945. Dispatched with the other students to the frontline, neither Diakiv nor the others would ever see the Division; most ended up in a grave or a Siberian labor camp.

After several weeks of heavy front-line combat against superior odds, Diakiv and his surviving Divisional friends, along with approximately 3,000 German and foreign soldiers, were captured in early March 1945. (Diakiv cited 6 March as the date of capture). Separated by the NKVD by nationality, Diakiv, who was proficient in the German language, cited his nationality as German and he provided his captors a German name. Diakiv, whose brother Bohdan served with the Division at Brody and was reported as missing-in-action, also had another brother, Oleh, serving in the UPA. Prior to surrendering, Diakiv destroyed his identification, paybook, his brothers pictures, and his mothers final letters. With tremendous sorrow, he also destroyed the picture of the Blessed Mother given to him by his mother on the day he departed for the Division. "Dear Mother of the Lord," prayed Diakiv, "help me with this one."

Regardless of what nationality the soldiers cited, they all experienced a very brutal and harsh treatment. As Diakiv was marched eastward, he passed through towns and villages filled with dead civilians; from surviving civilians who were pressed into the prisoner column, Diakiv heard ugly stories of murder, rape, and abuse at the hands of the communist horde.

Fulling realizing that the chance of a successful escape diminished with each passing mile to the east, Diakiv decided to make a move. Although he was not in the best physical shape, one cold and snowy night, Diakiv bolted into the fog and snow.

In the ensuing days and nights, Diakiv headed westward. It was not an easy journey. During the days, he rested in forests and swamps. Most of his trek took place during the night hours. He especially took advantage of any inclement weather to cover his march. Sometimes, he had to wait for hours to run across a bridge. Diakiv was determined to return.

Upon returning to Southern Germany, Diakiv submitted a report to the Military Board, now established in the vicinity of Munich. Undoubtedly, this was the last Divisional military report submitted by any member of the Division. Learning of his parents whereabouts, on 24 December 1945, Christmas Eve, Diakiv knocked on the door of his parents. For Diakiv's experiences, see "Z Liauenburgu v Peklo!" [From Lauenburg to Hell!], *Visti*, 1951-1952, No. 12 (14) – 1 (15), pp. 4-5.

20. Personal discussion with Lobach. Lobach's experiences and life in the aftermath of World War II, along with the ordeals of various other former Divisional soldiers, will be presented in an upcoming book.

21. Dir survived the war. Emigrating to the west, he worked at various jobs. His last job was as a laborer on a wrecking crew. Dir hated the job, he hated the dust, he hated his way of life, he had no family, and he missed the camaraderie that one can only find in the military.

But all of that changed one mid-afternoon when he entered a delicatessen store to purchase a sandwich. Inside the deli, he spotted a recruiter in a crisp uniform and highly polished shoes. Dir got in a discussion with the recruiter. The next day he was in, and stayed in until he retired. In his initial training, Dir's shooting skills quickly resurfaced; his shooting skills astonished everyone. His room is graced with awards and trophy cups from various service, interservice, international, and civilian competitions. Although Dir has never been a member of any Ukrainian veterans group, and has never officially subscribed to Visti Kombatanta, the Ukrainian military quarterly, he somehow obtains the latest issues; undoubtedly, he possesses a strong interest in the brotherhood.

As of date, Dir is in remarkable shape. At 6 foot and 170 pounds, he weekly runs several times a distance of one to two miles. He holds a black belt in Tae Kwan Do, an oriental martial art, and is convinced that the ancient teachings of Confucianism hold the key to a better world. He hates no one, never has, and lives well with all people. Deeply religious, he attends Mass weekly. Married in the early 1970s, he has also obtained a university degree, as his uncle had desired.

But Dir's happiest moments are out on a firing range. As his steel blue eyes sight in on a target, one can see that Dir's love of shooting, soldiering, and the outdoors has not diminished. After all, he has proven to be an extraordinary individual.

Notes Chapter 27

1. Reitlinger cites the Division "put up an unexpectedly tough resistance at Graz, Austria." (*The SS*, p. 203, fn. 3. See also *Bender and Taylor*, Vol. 4, p. 43). Heike, *Ukrainian ed.*, English synopsis, p. 251, cites that after the Division was "ordered into the front lines, it distinguished itself;" and in *English ed.*, p. 119, Heike cites as such: "The Ukrainian Division defended its sector of the front effectively."

Notes

2. "Pam'iatnyk Ukrains'kym Heroiam" [Memorial to the Ukrainian Heroes], *Visti*, 1961, No. 3, p. 47.

3. Podlesch's nationality has also been cited as being German.

Notes Chapter 28

Die Ordnungspolizei
1. Victor Madej, *Hitler's Elite Guards: Waffen-SS, Parachutists, U-Boats* (Penn.: Game Publishing Co., 1985), p. 11.

2. The 22nd Regiment, formed in Warsaw did, however, dispatch its 1st and 2nd Battalion to assist in the suppression of the Warsaw Ghetto in April-May 1943.

3. *Madej*, p. 11.

The Division's Volunteer Regiments:
1. Der Reichsführer SS, Tgb Nr. 35/88/43g, RF/Bn, Feld-Kommandostelle, den 24 Juni 1943. Geheim! Shortly before, in an undated June 1943 directive issued from Berlin, the directive stipulated that the Reichsführer had ordered the establishment of 5 Galician Free-Volunteer Regiments. Berlin, den (?) Juni 1943. An P, P(Allg.), W, WG, K, N, Ib, IE, Ausb, I – IVa, Kdo. III, VuR. Geb, Vur. III, VuR. Pers. Betr.: Aufstellung von 5 galizischen SS-Freiwilligen-Regimentern. Signed: Flade.
According to a thorough, intensive study of the Ordnungspolizei, four independent "Galizische SS-Freiwilligen Regimenters" were established; they were numbered 4-7. See H.J. Neufeldt, J. Huck, G. Tessin, *Zur Geschichte der Ordnungspolizei, 1936-1945* (Bundesarchiv, Koblenz, 1957). Hereafter referred to as *Tessin*. According to O. Gorbach, "Pikhotni Polky, ch. 4-8" [Infantry Regiments 4-8], *Visti*, 1993, No, 1, p. 89, five independent infantry regiments were temporarily created for training purposes.

2. RF-SS to Wachter, Field Command Post, 28 March 1943, Tgb. Nr. 35/37/43.

3. Der Reichsführer SS, Tgb. Nr. 35/88/43g, RF/Bn, Feld-Kommandostelle, den 24 Juni 1943, Geheim!

4. Despite the initial order that 12,000 were to be transferred to the Ordnungspolizei and placed into the Volunteer Regiments, in actuality this never occurred as will be seen.

5. Himmler's order of 24 June 1943 did not specify which German police regiment was to be disbanded.

6. The figure of 500 cadre personnel per regiment is quite high. Further proof that within the German system, incompetency could be found.

7. This was never carried out.

8. No specific regiment was designated.

9. The reason the Volunteer Regiments were numbered 4-8 is because initially, the Divisions first regiments were numbered 1-3 prior to being redesignated in November 1943 into the 29th, 30th and 31st Infantry Regiments.

10. Shortly after Himmler's guidance to Wachter on 28 March 1943 stipulating that the Division was only to be a front-line combat infantry division and not a police unit, SS-Colonel General Kurt Daluege, the Chief of the Ordnungspolizei, informed SS Police Lt. General Otto Winkelmann on 14 April 1943 that Himmler ordered that the "Galicia" Division was not to be a police division. (*Bender and Taylor*, Vol. 4, p. 17; Yuriy Krokhmaliuk, "Pro Tak Zvanyi 5-yi Politsiinyi Polk CC" [About the So-Called 5th SS Police Regiment], *Visti*, 1977, No. 2, pp. 20-21). Even the word "police" was never found in the Division's various titles. In a personal discussion with former Divisional staff officer Yuriy Krokhmaliuk, the former officer repeatedly emphasized that the "Galicia" Division was never a "police division," nor was the Division ever to be a police force of any kind. Although Krokhmaliuk acknowledged that some personnel were dispatched to four previously disbanded ordnungspolizei regiments for infantry training, this was only conducted because of a lack of training facilities, the urgency to commence some form of training, and to maintain a hold on the Ukrainian manpower. Krokhmaliuk also emphasized that the placement of the volunteers into the ordnungspolizei was strongly protested by Galicia's Military Board and by Wachter. See also Krokhmaliuk's, "About the So-Called 5th Police Regiment SS," *Visti*, No. 2, 1977, p. 20.
Because certain German officials knew from the outset that the Ukrainians who advocated and supported the project of raising the Division would strongly oppose the recruitment of Galicia's manpower into any type of police/security unit, it was hoped that if the word "police" was omitted and replaced with "free-volunteer," such a designation would avoid complications and disputes. Needless to say, such "camouflage" titles did not fool anyone and complications (as will be seen), did indeed arise.

Galicia Division

11. Personal discussion with Yuriy Krokhmaliuk, Vasyl Veryha, and Roman Kolisnyk. Numerous German and Ukrainian documents, military orders, and letters amongst various German and non-German officials substantiate that Volunteer Regiments 4-8 were to be trained as closely as possible to the training standards as conducted by the Wehrmacht. *Bender and Taylor*, Vol. 4, p. 30, cites the German Ordnungspolizei organized the manpower into five infantry regiment's numbered 4-8.

12. At no time was the Division "Galicia" ever a "police" division; nor was it ever referred to as the "Galician Police Division" as falsely stated by author's Aaron and Loftus in *Unholy Trinity*, p. 180; and nor was the Division ever an "anti-partisan police unit" as falsely stated by Sol Littman in his highly distorted and unprofessional article titled "These Aging Men Were Monsters Once" in The Windsor Star, Tuesday, 16 July 1985.

13. Madej, *Hitler's Elite Guard*, p, 11; Tessin, *Zur Geschichte der Ordnungspolizei, 1936-1945*, p. 52; personal discussion with Yuriy Krokhmaliuk. The 2nd directive found in the 24 June 1943 order issued by Berlin's Chief Ordnungspolizei specifically stipulated that each regiment would possess a cadre of German officers and non-commissioned officers.

4th Volunteer Regiment:
1. Der Chef der Ordnungspolizei Kdo, Io (3) I, Nr. 378/43, Berlin, 5. Juli 1943. Betr.: Aufstellung von Gal. SS-Freiw. Regt.

2. Formed initially in France in July 1942, the 4th was soon disbanded. But on 5 July 1943, the 4th was reconstituted by an order telegram from Berlin's Chief of Police (Ordnungspolizei). This order, titled "Organization of the Galician SS Free Volunteer Regiment," specified that the 4th Regiment was to be established by 15 July 1943. The 5 July 1943 order was sent to the various Police Inspectors (Command Staffs) in Danzig, Cracow, Saarbrucken, Stettin-Wiesbadas, and Oranienburg's Police Training Regiment.
Of interest to note is that in early July 1943, the Ordnungspolizei stipulated that the reconstitution of the 4th Regiment was to take place in Poland. But either this was a mistake, or by 5 July 1943, it was decided to base the 4th (which was not yet reformed) to France. See Madej's, *Hitler's Elite Guards: Waffen-SS,Parachutists, U-Boats*, p. 11.

3. Roman Krokhmaliuk, *The Glow*, p. 48. Former Divisional Chaplain Danylo Kovaliuk identified Reverend Osyp Karpinsky as the 4th Regiment's Chaplain and Kovaliuk stated the regiment was posted to Alsace. Reverend Danylo Kovaliuk, "Voenni Spomany 1943-1945" [War Remembrances 1943-1945], p. 47. Kovaliuk's account, which has never been published; was submitted to the author by Yuriy Krokhmaliuk. Gorbach, "Infantry Regiment's 4-8," *Visti*, 1993, No. 1, p. 89, also substantiates that Karpinsky served as the 4th's regimental chaplain.

4. "Deshcho Pro Nazvu "Politsyni Polky," p. 3. Unpublished account submitted by Yuriy Krokhmaliuk to author; and personal discussion. Gorbach cites a strength of 2,000. *Visti*, 1993, No. 1, p. 89.

5. Dokument Ch. 11, "Zvit Sotnyka Liubomyra Makarushky iz Poizdky Po Vyshkil'nykh Taborakh Dobrovol'tsiv Dyvizii "Halychyna" u Poludnevii Frantsii" [Report by Captain Liubomyr Makarushka Regarding Journeys to the Division "Galicia's" Volunteers In the Training Camps in Southern France], in *The Glow*, p. 208. The entire document is seen in pages 205-208. Yet in the same book, on p. 68, a strength of 1,264 soldiers is also cited. In a personal discussion with Yuriy Krokhmaliuk, the former Divisional staff officer placed the 4th Regiment's strength at 1,264 Galician personnel. This figure, however, only refers to the Ukrainian personnel who hailed from Galicia. The reason other (and usually higher) figures are cited is because if cadre, training, and support personnel are included, the figure would rise. Regardless, if one takes into consideration that the 4th Regiment's strength was also approximately the same as that of the other regiments, than Makarushka's figure of 2,000 is too high, and undoubtedly included all of the regiment's non-Ukrainian personnel and possibly, even the personnel of the facilities which supported the 4th Regiment.

6. *The Glow*, p. 68; personal discussion with Roman Krokhmaliuk; Minutes of the Meetings of the Military Board "Galicia." Meeting held 30 October 1943, p. 22.

7. Der Chef der Ordnungspolizei, Kdo. I O (3) 1 Nr. 397/43, Berlin, den 20. Juli 1943.

8. Tessin, *Zur Geschichte der Ordnungspolizei*, p. 52, verifies the 20 July 1943 locations and places the regiments locations under such Field Post Numbers: Staff: 57,316; 1st Bn.: 48,274; 2nd Bn.: 43,315; and 3rd Bn.: 11,853.

9. Der Reichsführer SS und Chef der Deutschen Polizei im Reichsministerium des Innern O-Kdo. I 0 (3) 1 Nr. 543/43, Berlin, den 29. September 1943.

10. *Ibid.*

11. Personal discussion with Yuriy Krokhmaliuk. In an unpublished account written by Krokhmaliuk, "Deshcho Pro Nazvu "Politsiini" Polky" [Some things About the Titles of the "Police" Regiments"] Krokhmaliuk also identified training flaws. (Pp. 1-3).

Notes

12. *Ibid.*

13. Kovaliuk, War Remembrances, p. 50.

14. *The Glow*, p. 48.

15. Der Chef der Ordnungspolizei, den 23. December 1943. Kdo. g I (Org.3) Nr. 2.Betr.: Abgabe von 2,000 Freiwilligen der Gal. SS-Freiw.-Regimenter.

16. Der Chef der Ordnungspolizei, Kdo. g. I-Ia (I) Nr. 983/43 (g.), Berlin, den 25. January 1944, Betr.: Verlegung des III./Galizischen SS-Freiwilligen – Rgt. 4.
Some have also alleged that Ukrainians within the Military Board played a role in having the 4th Regiment transferred to Galicia. This request was made as a result of the intensification of communist guerrilla activities within Galicia proper and a need to counter the threat. Although the records of the Military Board reveal no official requests for any transfers, it is known that some Ukrainians, both within and outside the Military Board, along with certain German officials based in Galicia, requested troops for internal security and frontline reinforcement. In Shankowsky's *UPA and the Division*, p. 73, Shankowsky verified that the 4th Regiment was posted to Galicia for security reasons.

17. An den Chef der Ordnungspolizei in Berlin., Geheim, Kdo. I Org (3) 1 Nr. 78/44, v. 3.2.44 Nr. 552, Betr.: Marsh-und Einsatzfahigkeit des Gal. SS-Freiw. Rgt. 4.

18. *Ibid.*

19. Der Chef der Ordnungspolizei. Abschrift! Berlin, den 9. Februar 1944. Kdo. g I-Ia (1) Nr. 1020 11/43 (g) Betr.: Verlegung der Gal. SS-Freiw. Rgtr. 4 und 5.

20. Der Chef der Ordnungspolizei, Schnellbrief! Berlin, den 12. Februar 1944. Kdo. g I Org. (3) Nr. 317/43 (g.) This directive was issued to the Higher SS and Police Ordnungspolizei leaders in Stuttgart, Paris, Danzig, and Cracow.

21. Geheim-vs. Tgb. Nr. 491/44 geh. – b roem eins tgb. nr. 89/44 geh., 14.2.44.

22. Krokhmaliuk, *The Glow*, pp. 76-77.

23. *Ibid.* It also appears that UPA-West did not agitate the 4th's personnel to defect.

24. In a report personally submitted by Yuriy Krokhmaliuk to the Military Board on 7 March 1944, Krokhmaliuk cited the 3rd Battalion's three company's were situated in such towns: Zaliztsi, Shel'paky, and Dobrovodi. Minutes of the Military Board "Galicia," p. 94. In *UPA and the Division*, Shankowsky cites the 4th Regiment was posted into such locations: 1st Battalion: Radechiv; 2nd Battalion: Brody area; 3rd Battalion: Zbarazh. In *The Glow*, p. 76, Roman Krokhmaliuk substantiates Shankowsky's placement.

25. According to Roman Krokhmaliuk, Zbarazh fell after a brief battle to communist guerrillas. *The Glow*, p. 26. In an interesting unpublished account titled "U Zbarazhi" [In Zbarazh], Yuriy Krokhmaliuk vividly describes the difficulties the Ukrainians experienced – both within the Military Board and those serving on the eastern front in the spring of 1944 – with both the Nazis and the approaching communist force.

26. Krokhmaliuk, *The Glow*, p. 76.

27. In due time, most returned to the Division.

28. "Protokol Spohadiv Stril'tsia Petrovs'koho Vasilia" [The Memoirs of Grenadier Vasil Petrovskyi]. Unpublished account submitted to the author by Yuriy Krokhmaliuk.

29. *Ibid.*, p. 1. Petrovskyi's account substantiates the sequence of events found in various reports and eyewitness accounts submitted by survivors who fought in Ternopil, Zbarazh, and its vicinity. However, regarding the date of 1 March 1944, although Petrovskyi is correct that Zbarazh fell to Red guerrillas in the first week of March 1944, it must also be remembered that Petrovskyi's account was written in January 1945. Hence, he slightly erred when he cited 1 March 1944 as the date of the attack on Zbarazh.
In the aftermath of the 3rd Battalion's defeat at Zbarazh, a number of its survivors were channelized into Ternopil where, with the remnants of the various German infantry, artillery, anti-tank, anti-aircraft, staff personnel, Waffen-SS and Wehrmacht support, administrative, fusilier, technical, supply, and communication soldiers, the 3rd Galician Battalion was incorporated into the defense of Ternopil.
Despite Hitler's orders on 3 and 10 March 1944 designating Ternopil a "fortified place to be held to the fast man!" Hitler soon rescinded his order and ordered the city to be evacuated. But it was to late. By 23/24 March, Ternopil was surrounded. Within a garrison commanded by Generalmajor von Neindorff, approximately 4,600 soldiers were encircled. (Alex Buchner, *Ostfront 1944*, p. 94; T. Kachmarchuk, "Zaborolo – Ternopil', 1944" [Bastion – Ternopil, 1944], *Visti*, 1993, No. 2, p. 91, cites such a strength was encircled at Ternopil: 97 officers, 614 NCOs, and

3,611 riflemen). Regardless of the true strength, Ternopil's battle roster of 23 March 1944 reveals a "Mitscherling Battalion" which comprised the 3rd Battalion of the 4th SS-Volunteer Galizien Regiment. (*Ostfront, 1944*, p. 95). Although a personnel strength for the battalion is not provided, it is known that a number of soldiers from the 3rd Battalion's various companies were utilized in Ternopil's defense.

Yet despite the efforts of various ground and aerial forces to resupply and extradite the encircled garrison to safety, the Soviet's retained their hold. With the death of von Neindorff, Colonel von Schonfeld assumed command. By now, approximately 1,500 defenders remained and they were concentrated in Ternopil's southwestern sector and in the suburb of Zahrobela, located across Ternopil on the western bank of the Seret River. Knowing that further resistance was useless, von Schonfeld ordered the remaining soldiers to either surrender or exfiltrate to the west.

It will never be determined how many attempted to break out. It is known, however, that of those who attempted, no more than 55 (out of an initial 4,600) succeeded in returning to the German line. (*Ostfront, 1944*, p. 94). According to Kachmarchuk, of the 55 soldiers, 2 were from the 4th Regiment. *Visti*, 1993, No. 2, p. 91. According to "The Defensive. Improvised Fortresses," in *Military Improvisations During the Russian Campaign*, chap. 2, p. 37, Ternopil's location was unfavorable for a defense. Despite all protests to turn Ternopil into a fortress, Hitler insisted that it be held. In the end, the garrison held out bravely for one month and succumbed to defeat for lack of rations and ammunition.

30. The Memoirs of Grenadier Petrovskyi, pp. 1-2. Petrovskyi's charges of poor leadership is substantiated by Myhailo Khronoviat who personally visited the 4th Regiment when it was based in Galicia, Yuriy Krokhmaliuk who also visited the 4th Regiment, and Lev Shankowskyi, whose UPA monitored the 4th Regiment. During a Military Board meeting held on 7 March 1944, Khronoviat submitted a report based on his visit to the 4th Regiment's head quarters at Zolochiv. Khronoviat cited that upon his arrival to the 4th Regimental Headquarters, he was first met by Chaplain Karpins'kyi who immediately cried out "Unfortunately, our boys want to shoot the Germans!" (*Minutes of the Military Board "Galicia."* Meeting held on 7 March 1944, p, 91). Accordign to Krokhmaliuk (who also presented a report to the Military Board on 7 March 1944), upon arrival to the 4th Regiments 3rd Battalion's Headquarters, he was greeted with "distrust and reservation" by its German staff. (Ibid., p, 93). The largest complaint, cited Krokhmaliuk, was directed not so much as against the German officers but more so against the German NCOs who were abusing the Galician soldiers. Indeed, claimed Krokhmaliuk, the situation was so volatile that at one point, a German NCO and a Ukrainian rifleman turned their weapon's against one another and threatened to fire. (Ibid., p. 94. For the entire report, and additional information on the disillusionment experienced by the regiments Ukrainian personnel, see pp. 90-95). In *UPA and the Division*, p. 74, Shankowsky cites that at Zbarazh, 600 Ukrainian soldiers were left to their own fate when the 3rd Battalion's German officers suddenly deserted the battalion and departed on a train upon learning that communist ground forces, reinforced with armor, were approaching. As for the Ukrainians left behind, they fled under communist ground fire into the general direction of Ternopil. But those who made it to Ternopil were soon encircled and annihilated. (*Ibid.*, pp. 74-75).

31. The Memoirs of Grenadier Vasil Petrovskyi, p. 2. Needless to say, this resulted in a tremendous amount of backlash and condemnation by various Ukrainians. The anti-Nazi underground Ukrainian journal, "Za Ukrains'ky Dershavy" [For the Ukrainian Nation], which from the outset in 1943 took a strong stand against the creation of the "Galicia" Division and continuously voiced its protests against the Division, was especially critical of what occurred. In Issue No. 3, a publication dated 23 March 1944, under the title of "600 Ukrainian Riflemen Killed As a Result of the Shameful Flight of the Germans!" the Ukrainian journal charged: "On 5 March 1944, an element of the SS Division "Galicia" appeared at Zbarazh to await a train. Communist elements were not far away. The German officers boarded a train and departed, leaving the riflemen leaderless. In the morning, under Bolshevik fire, the riflemen withdrew to Ternopil and later to the village of Dobrovodi. During this same time, another group from the SS Division "Galicia" were constructing bunkers in the vicinity of Zbarazh. They were not informed that the Bolsheviks were in a neighboring village and all fell into Bolshevik captivity. Under the fire of the communist infantry and tanks, many riflemen also perished. The same fate awaited those at Dobrovodi. This is how the German service looks. This is how the German officers regard the Ukrainian riflemen. And, yes, in conclusion, this is how the Division's "politics" are conducted in practice." (For the entire condemnation, see Shankowsky's, *UPA and the Division*, p. 74. See also p. 75.)

32. The Memoirs of Grenadier Petrovskyi, p. 2. According to Vashchenko, UPA's inserted personnel who operated within the "Galicia" Division and the four volunteer regiments frequently submitted to UPA's intelligence the names of Divisional soldiers reported as missing; likewise, UPA's personnel who operated within the NKVD and the various Soviet armies constantly kept a lookout for any Divisional soldiers who somehow ended up in a communist unit and could be marked for death if their true identity was ever discovered. And if a soldier was identified, efforts were made to have him removed.

33. The Memoirs of Grenadier Vasil Petrovskyi, pp. 2-3.(A study of the Soviet Order-of-Battle reveals that the 43rd Rifle Division operated on the Baltic Front. It concluded the war in Latvia). For another interesting account of Petrovskyi's experiences see, "Do istorii 4-oho Politsiinoho Polka" [To the History of the 4th Police Regiment], *Visti*, 1952, No. 6-7 (20-21), p. 8.

34. *War Remembrances*, p. 47.

35. Der Chef der Ordnungspolizei. Berlin, den 22.4.44. Tgb. Nr. Ia/1269/44 geh. Betr.: Galz. SS-Freiw. Regt. 4 und 5. This order also covered the 5th Regiment.

Notes

36. Berlin, den 27. April 1944. An Chef V. Jn K, Jn S, Jn Vet, Jn WO, WE, Ib, Org.5 (This telegram was not titled).

37. Der Chef der Ordnungspolizei, Kdo. g I Org. (3) Nr. 104/44 (g), Berlin, den 9. Juni 1944. Betr.: Uberfuhrung der Gal. SS -Freiw.-Rgt. 4 und 5 in die Waffen-SS. The order also stipulated that further guidance will be provided. *Tessin*, p. 52, cites 9 June 1944 as the date of the regiments disbandment. See also *Bender and Taylor*, Vol. 4, p. 47.

38. Der Chef der Ordnungspolizei, Kdo. g I Org. (3) Nr. 104 II/44, Berlin, den 17. Juni 1944. Betr.: Uberfuhrung der Gal. SS-Freiw.-Regt. 4 und 5 in die Waffen-SS.

39. Personal discussion with Yuriy Krokhmaliuk.

5th Volunteer Regiment:
1. Betr.: Aufstellung von 5 galizischen SS Freiwilligen Regimentern, Berlin, den Juni 1944. This directive was dispatched to various commands.

2. Der Chef der Ordnungspolizei, Kdo, I 0 (3) I Nr. 378/43, Berlin, den 5. Juli 1943.

3. Field Post Staff Numbers: <u>Staff</u>: 57,194; <u>1st Bn</u>.: 42,144; <u>2nd Bn</u>.: 56,334; <u>3rd Bn</u>.: 59,167. (*Tessin*, p. 52).

4. Originally organized in July 1942 in Serbia, the 5th was soon disbanded but exactly one year later in July 1943, the 5th was reconstituted in Poland with Galician volunteers. Disbanded for the last time in June 1944, this ordnungspolizei regiment was never reconstituted.

5. Der Chef der Ordnungspolizei, Kdo. I 0 (3) I. Nr. 397/43. Berlin, den 20. Juli 1943.

6. *Ibid*. According to *Bender and Taylor*, Vol. 4, p. 47, the 3rd Regiment's 1st Battalion provided the cadre for the 5th Regiment.

7. *Ibid*.

8. *Ibid.*, pp. 2-3.

9. Reverend D. Kovaliuk, *War Remembrances*, p. 47; Gorbach, *Visti,* "Infantry Regiments 4-8," 1993, No. 1 , p. 89, also identifies Durbak as the regimental chaplain. In *The Glow*, Roman Krokhmaliuk also cites Leyenberg and Gotenhafen as the 5th Regiment's training area. (P. 48).

10. In actuality, horse transport began to be utilized well before the first Ukrainian recruits arrived.

11. This was the older model World War I Maxim machine gun utilized to an extent by Nazi Germany in World War II.

12. The 98a (Karabiner or Kar 98a) was a popular bolt-action carbine in World War I with limited use in World War II.

13. The 20 July 1944 directive did not specify exactly which model was to be utilized. Although the MP38/40 was utilized, Ordnungspolizei units also utilized the Bergmann 9mm machine pistol (submachine gun), which first appeared in 1918, and was widely utilized in the aftermath of World War I by Germany's civil police and later, by the SS police. This weapon, however, was not utilized by the Wehrmacht and only a few models found their way into the Waffen-SS.

14. Along with the Kar 98 standard infantry rifle, the 20 July directive reveals an "84" model. During World War II, this rifle was not utilized by any German army units; however, it was issued to the so-called "Home Guard" units (especially in places such as Poland) and undoubtedly, a number ended up in the Ordnungspolizei. Perhaps this explains why the 5th Regiment encountered the "84" model.

15. Extra dummy ammunition was issued.

16. "Z Istorii 5-oho Polku Dyvizii "Halychyna." [From the "Galicia" Division's History of the 5th Regiment]. Unpublished account submitted to the author by Yuriy Krokhmaliuk.

17. According to Roman Krokhmaliuk, the 5th was stationed in Lyenberg and Gotenhafen.

18. No dates are provided as to when this occurred, nor are any specific time frames provided as to when the other companies were dispatched. But according to the sequence of events provided it appears this occurred sometime in mid-August. Because I the account also states "the 4th company of our battalion was dispatched for training to Danzig," it appears probably that one company at a time was selected for small-arms weapons training.

Galicia Division

19. *The Glow*, p. 68; Minutes of the Meetings of the Military Board "Galicia." Meeting held on 30 October 1943. See p. 22.

20. The order did not specify as to what unit Chaplain Durbak would be posted to upon returning to the Division. Upon arrival to Neuhammer he undoubtedly entered either the Division's Field Replacement Battalion or its Training and Replacement Regiment prior to his posting into the Division's Field Medical Battalion, a unit with which he deployed to the eastern front in late June 1944.

21. Der Chef der Ordnungspolizei, Kdo. g l-Ia (1) Nr. 1020II/43 (g), Berlin, den 9. Februar 1944. Betr.: Verlegung der Gal. SS-Freiw. Rgtr. 4 und 5.

22. Der Chef der Ordnungspolizei, Kdo. g I Org. (3) Nr. 317/43 (g.), Berlin, den 12. Februar 1944. Betr.: Auflosung des Gal. SS-Freiw. Ers. Bate. Heidenheim.

23. Bdo. Dag. Nr. 154 8/2 0855. An den RFSS und ChdDTPOL. – Chef der Ordnungspolizei – in Berlin NW7, Unter den Linden 74. Betr.: Einsatzbereitschaft des Gal. SS-Freiw. Regt. 5, 3.2.1944.

24. Betr.: Galiz. SS-Freiw. Regt. 4 und 5. Tgb. Nr. Ia/1269/44 geh., 23. April 1944. This 23 April directive was signed by Oberführer Rode.

25. Der Chef der Ordnungspolizei, Kdo. g I Org. (3) Nr. 104/44. Betr.: Uberfuhrung der Gal. SS-Freiw.-Rgt. 4 und 5 in die Waffen- SS, Berlin, den 9. Juni 1944.

26. *Bender and Taylor*, Vol. 4, p. 47.

27. Der Chef der Ordnungspolizei, KDO. G. 1 Org. (3) Nr. 104 II/44, Berlin, den 17. Juni 1944. Betr.: Uberfuhrung der Gal. SS-Freiw.-Rgt. 4 und 5 in die Waffen-SS. Unlike many of the previous directives, this three-page directive was fairly detailed. On page 2, the directive stipulated the transfer of the regiment's foreign (Ukrainian) personnel to Neuhammer. With this directive, the regimental personnel were transferred to Neuhammer. As for the remaining German leaders, cadre and administrative personnel, they were informed to await further orders regarding their future status.

28. Personal discussion with Yuriy Krokhmaliuk. Of interest to note is that in March 1944, when elements of the 5th Regiment were based in Zamosc, a sizable number of its personnel deserted to the UPA. After crossing the Buh River, they reported to UPA Commander Ivan Bogun, whose unit was operating in the region's forest. Because the soldiers brought as much arms, equipment and ammunition as they could carry, their desertion to the UPA was highly welcomed. See Shankowsky's, *UPA and the Division*, p. 75.

6th Volunteer Regiment:
1. Der Reichsführer-SS Feld-Kommandostelle, den 24 Juni 1943, Tgb. Nr. 35/88/43g; Berlin, den Juni 1943. Betr.: Aufstellung von 5 galizischen SS-Freiwilligen-Regimentern; Der Chef der Ordnungspolizei, Kdo. IO (3) 1 Nr. 378/43 Berlin, den. 5 July 1943. Initially raised in August 1943 in Southern Russia, after a short period of eastern front combat, the 6th was disbanded. But in August 1943, it was reconstituted in Southern France with Ukrainian volunteers destined for the "Galicia" Division. See also Gorbach, *Visti*, 1993, No. 1, p. 89.

2. Der Chef der Ordnungspolizei, Kdo. I 0 (3) 1 Nr. 469/43. Betr.: Aufstellung des Gal. SS-Freiw.-Rgt. 6., Berlin, den 6. August 1943; *Tessin*, p. 52.

3. Field Post Numbers: Staff: 04,686; 1st Bn.: 05479; 2nd Bn.: 06,602; 3rd Bn.: 07,023.

4. This strength matches the "strength of approximately 500", cited by Myhailo Protsakevych, a former Divisional soldier who, after volunteering for the Division, was posted into the 6th Regiment and dispatched from Peremysl to Grajewo. According to Protsakevych, the bulk of the 6th was composed of volunteers who hailed from Peremysl and Peremyshchyny, 80% hailed from Yaroslavshchyna, and the remainder from the vicinity of Lviv. Needless to say, as already presented, there was much dissatisfaction with being posted into the 6th Regiment. (M. Protsakevych, "Politsiyni Polky" [The Police Regiments], *Visti*, 1970, No. 3-4, pp. 33-36). For a breakdown of where the volunteers hailed from, as well as an account of the dissatisfaction experienced upon entry into the police regiments, see p. 33.

5. According to Roman Rrokhmaliuk, the 6th Regiment had a strength of 1,293 volunteers. (*The Glow*, p. 68. This figure is also cited at a meeting held on 30 October 1943, by the Military Board. See *Minutes of the Meetings of the Military Board "Galicia."* Meeting held on 30 October 1943, p. 22). But according to Liubomyr Makarevych, during a meeting held with Galicia's Military Board (Makarevych did not cite a date), the 6th Regiment's strength was cited at almost 2,000. (*The Glow*, p. 208) . Yet in an unpublished report titled "Vidvidyny t. zv. Politsiynykh Polkiv Chlenamy Viis'kovoi Upravy u Frantsii, 14 Sichnia 1944" [Visiting the So-Called Police Regiments in France by Representatives of the Military Board, 14 January 1944], the report stated that during a visit by Governor wachter, Colonel Bisanz and Captain Makarushka in the period of 25-30 November 1943, a total of 14 companies within the 6th Regiment were visited. In this report, a strength figure of 2,000 is cited. This figure was provided to the visiting

Notes

dignitaries by Chaplain Ivan Holoida. However, neither the chaplain, nor anyone else, ever revealed how many of these 2,000 were Ukrainian, and how many were cadre and support personnel. (The unpublished three-page report of 14 January 1944 was submitted by Yurly Krokhmaliuk to the author). German sources cite a strength figure of 1,800. But the German figure of 1,800 was based on troop-quartering facilities. And the German figure not only included those who were brought in for training, but it also included the German training cadre and the regiment's support personnel. (Personal discussion with Yuriy Krokhmaliuk).

6. Der Reichsführer SS und Chef der Deutschen Polizei im Reichsministerium des Innern O-Kdo. I 0 (3) Nr. 543/43, Berlin, den 29. September 1943.

7. Der Chef der Ordnungspolizei, 23 December 1943. Kdo. gI (Org.3) Nr.2 Betr.: Abgale von 2.000 Freiwilligen der Gpl. SS-Freiw.Regimenter.

8. *Bender and Taylor*, Vol. 4, pp. 30, 47; personal discussion with Yuriy Krokhmaliuk; Gorbach, *Visti*, 1993, No. 1, p. 89. According to Gorbach, the Galician Military Board was deeply concerned that Nazi officials in France would possibly utilize the 6th and 7th Volunteer Regiments against the western allies. Therefore, they pressed Galicia's governor, otto wachter, to withdraw the two Ukrainian regiments from France as soon as possible.
In a letter dated 25 January 1944 to the Military Board, Chaplain Holoida reported that both the 6th and 7th Regiments were disbanded. However, from the remaining riflemen, a Reserve Battalion was organized, and it was posted to Tarbes. Chaplain Holoida estimated its strength at approximately 900 and stated that Chaplain Kovaliuk was appointed as the battalion's chaplain. As for the remaining soldiers, they were dispatched to the Division at Heidelager. Chaplain Holoida wrote that despite the disbandment, the regiments headquarters have remained intact and are awaiting further orders. Chaplain Holoida also wrote that when the regiments were disbanded, the soldiers were scattered into different directions. As a result, troop morale plummeted. As for the Christmas packages, they arrived on 16 January and because many of the soldiers had already departed, enough packages were available to provide each soldier one extra package. Regarding mail, Chaplain Holoida wrote that it arrives late and often brings bad news. To the Military Board in Lviv, from Chaplain Ivan Holoida, 6th Regimental Chaplain. Reference: Report. 25.1.1944. Seal no. 2.244/Letter no. 04686 A. (A copy of this letter was provided to the author by Yuriy Krokhmaliuk). Hereafter referred to as Holoida's letter of 25 January 1944.

9. Visiting the So-Called Police Regiments in France." Report of 14 January 1944, p. 1. Although the 6th Regiment was officially disbanded on 31 January 1944, a report published by the Military Board pertaining to their 14 January 1944 meeting revealed that as of 14 January, the brunt of the 6th Regiment's personnel were already in Heidelager. (See: "Meeting. 14 January 1944" in *Minutes of the Meetings of the Military Board "Galicia,"* pp. 61-63. During this meeting, it was reported that a strength of 2,000 soldiers arrived from France). Remembering that Berlin's directive of 23 December 1943 specified that the 6th Regiment would immediately dispatch 1,200 of its soldiers to the troop training area of Heidelager, this explains why when the Military Board met several weeks later on 14 January 1944, it was able to record that the brunt of the 6th Regiments personnel were already in Heidelager.

10. *Tessin*, p. 52; *Bender and Taylor*, Vol. 4, pp. 30 and 47; personal discussion with Yuriy Krokhmaliuk.

11. Holoida's letter of 25 January 1944.

12. *Ibid.* Chaplain Holoida's figure is substantiated by Gorbach. See *Visti*, 1993, No. 1, p. 89.

13. Regarding this, Chaplain Holoida was referring to the 6th and 7th Regiment's non-Ukrainian personnel. When the 6th and 7th Regiments were officially disbanded in January 1944 and its Ukrainian soldiers (excluding those temporarily posted to Tarbes) were dispatched to the Division, the Ordnungspolizei did not immediately disband the regiment's cadre as was previously done on occasion; rather, the regiment's cadre was kept relatively intact in the event that fresh personnel would be organized for a "new" 6th Regiment or 7th Regiment. But in the very end, neither the 6th or 7th was reconstituted.

14. Abschrift. BdO. Par. Nr. 810 19/2 1700. Chef der Ordnungspolizei Berlin, Betr.: Aufstellung des Gal.SS-Freiw.Ers.Batl. in Tarbes. Bezug: Erl. v. 31.1.44 Chef d.OP. – O-Kdo. g. I Org (3) Nr. 305/43 (g) -. Berlin, den 25. Februar 1944. Signed: Scheer.

15. As for Chaplain Holoida, shortly after his last letter of 25 January 1944, he returned to Heidelager. In March 1944, he relocated with the Division to Neuhammer.
In the late spring of 1944, Chaplain Holoida was granted leave and he returned to his home located in the Carpathian Lemko region. There the chaplain visited family and friends and on Sunday, assisted the local clergy with services. But one night, his home was attacked by communist Polish guerrillas. After gaining entry, the chaplain was taken outside where, in front of various family members and local citizens, a public announcement was made as to why the chaplain would be executed. Within days of his murder, leaflets also appeared throughout the region proclaiming the killing of Chaplain Holoida and how others would suffer a similar fate if they supported the Division.
Needless to say, the murder of this unarmed military chaplain not only violated the international rules and laws pertaining to clergy and religious institutions, but actually violated the basic rules pertaining to human decency. As well, to this day, the Division's critics have remained silent about this brutal murder and the many other atrocities and war crimes committed against members of the Division.

531

Galicia Division

7th Volunteer Regiment:
1. Der Reichsführer SS und Chef der Deutschen Polizei im Reichsministerium des Innern O-Kdo. I 0 (3) 1 Nr. 543/43 Berlin, den 29. September 1943.

2. *Tessin*, p. 52, cites 29 September 1943 as the date the 7th Regiment was reorganized once again.

3. "Vidvidyny t. zv. Politsiinykh Polkiv," p. 1.

4. *Ibid.* This figure, also provided by a Dr. Shultz to the Military Board, is substantiated in the unpublished report "Deshcho Pro Nazvu "Politsiini Polky," pp. 2 and 3; in Krokhmaliuk's book *The Glow*, p. 68; and in a report submitted on 30 October 1943 to the Military Board. *Minutes of the Military Board "Galicia."* Meeting held on 30 October 1943, p. 22. Of interest to note is that in Roman Krokhmaliuk's book, *The Glow,* p. 208, former Divisional officer Liubomyr Makarushka cites the 7th Regiment possessed a strength of approximately 1,500. Makarushka's figure, however, appears to be incorrect.

5. *The Glow,* p. 69; Kovaliuk, *War Remembrances,* p. 47.

6. M. Protsakevych, "Politsiini Polky" [The Police Regiments], *Visti,* 1970, No. 3-4, p. 33.

7. Kovaliuk, *War Remembrances,* p. 46.

8. *Tessin*, p. 52; *Kovaliuk*, p. 47; *The Glow*, p. 48; Gorbach, *Visti,* 1993, No. 1, p. 89. According to Protsakevych, the 7th Regiment was formed in the latter part of 1943 in Tarbes, in the Pyrenees Mountains in France. See "The Police Regiments," *Visti,* 1970, No. 3-4, p. 33.

9. Field post numbers were as such: <u>Staff</u>: 13,823; <u>1st Bn</u>.: 11,064; <u>2nd Bn</u>.: 14,173; <u>3rd Bn</u>.: 12,704. See also *Tessin*, p. 52.

10. Kovaliuk, *War Remembrances,* p. 48.

11. Der Chef der Ordnungspolizei, 23. December 1943. Kdo. g I (Org.3) Nr. 2. Betr.: Abgabe von 2.000 Freiwilligen der Gal.SS-Freiw.Regimenter.

12. "Vidvidyny t. zv. Politsiynykh Polkiv," p. 1. See also Gorbach, *Visti,* 1993, No. 1, p. 89. *Bender and Taylor,* Vol. 4, pp. 30, 48, cite the 7th Infantry Regiment was disbanded on 31 January 1944 and 745 men were provided to the "Galicia" Division.

8th Volunteer Regiment:
1. In Roman Krokhmaliuk's book, *The Glow,* (p. 69), Roman Krokhmaliuk mentions an 8th Regiment with a strength of 1,573 soldiers, and that it was trained in Germany.
But in a personal discussion with him, Roman acknowledged that this was an error and that the 8th was initially confused with the Division's Training and Replacement Regiment, first based at Wandern, later at Neuhammer and then wherever else the Division went. (It must be remembered, however, that the Divisional Training and Replacement Regiment was never under the numerical designation of "8" but until virtually the end of the war, was always under "14." Under no circumstances should the Division's Training and Replacement Regiment ever be confused with the "8th" which never existed).
According to Roman's brother, Yuriy, the 8th never existed. Yuriy's words are substantiated by his writings, as well as by the points of the 14 January 1944 meeting held by the Galician Military Board which reveals no 8th Regiment; likewise, a thorough examination of various Ukrainian documents, personal memoirs (such as those provided by the various regimental chaplains), German World War II orders and documents, and Tessin's highly detailed and voluminous work all reveal that the 8th Galician Volunteer Regiment never existed. See also Gorbach, *Visti,* 1993, No. 1, p. 89. According to *Bender and Taylor*, Vol. 4, p. 48, the 8th Infantry Regiment was to have been formed in November 1944, but it is not known if the 8th was ever established.

Police-Regiment "Galizien:"
1. According to UPA intelligence officer Vashchenko, the UPA always referred to the Division as the "Halyts'ka" Division, or as the "Ukrains'ka Dyvizia." Post-war UPA accounts and personal memoirs substantiate Vashchenko's words.

Tarbes Reserve Battalion:
1. Chef der Ordnungspolizei, Erl. v. 31.I.44 Chef d. OP.-O-Kdo. g I Org (3) Nr. 305/43 (g)-. Betr.: Aufstellung des Gal. SS-Freiw. Ers. Batl. in Tarbes. This directive was signed by Scheer. See also *Bender and Taylor*, Vol. 4, p. 48.

2. "Vidvidyny t. Zv. Politsiinykh Polkiv Chlenamy Viis'kovoi Upravy u Frantsii. Iz Zvitu na zasidanni Viis'kovoi Upravy 14 Sichnia 1944" [Visiting the So-Called Police Regiments by Members of the Military Board in France. From a Report On a Meeting Held by the Military Board on 14 January 1944], p. 1; Report of 14 January 1944. However, in a letter to the Military Board dated 25 January 1944, Chaplain Holoida revealed a strength of approxi-

Notes

mately 900 by the third week of January 1944. (Holoida's letter of 25 January 1944). Although Chaplain Holoida strongly implies that the greater percentage of these 900 are Ukrainian, neither Holoida, nor any other observer, has ever cited a breakdown as to how many of the 900 were Ukrainian, and how many were German cadre and support personnel. Remembering that until the Reserve Battalion was finally disbanded German personnel were included in its ranks, it may be surmised that of the approximately 900, 740 were Ukrainian.

3. *Tessin*, p. 52.

4. Kovaliuk, *War Remembrances*, p. 53.

5. *Ibid.*, p. 53.

6. *Ibid.*, p. 50.

7. Der Chef der Ordnungspolizei, Kdo. g I Org. (3) Nr. 317/43 (g.)., Berlin, den 12 Februar 1944. Betr.: Auflousung des Gal. SS-Freiw. Ers. Batl. Heidenheim.

8. Chef der Ordnungspolizei, Bdo. Par. Nr. 810, 19/2, 1700, Berlin, den 25. Februar 1944. Betr.: Aufstellung des Gal. SS-Freiw. Ers. Batl. in Tarbes. Bezug: Erl. v. 31.1.44 Chef d.OP. – O-Kdo. g I Org (3) Nr. 305/43 (g) -. Although officially addressed to the Reserve Battalion, the second part of this directive also specified that when the 6th and 7th Regiments would be disbanded, its veterinarian officers would also be removed and posted to the Reserve Battalion.

9. For the historical record, this minor engagement was the only combat activity ever experienced between the French underground and the French-based Ukrainian personnel.

10. Kovaliuk, *War Remembrances*, p. 56.

11. *Ibid.*

12. Der Chef der Ordnungspolizei, Kdo. g I Org. (3) Nr. 49 II/44 (g.)., Berlin, den 8. Mai 1944. Abschrift! Fernschreiben! Betr.: Abgabe von galizischen Freiwilligen.

13. Der Chef der Ordnungspolizei, Kdo. g I Org. (3) Nr. 36 II/44 (g), Berlin, den 9. Juni .1944, Betr.: Auflosung des Gal. SS-Frw.Ers.Batl. Tarbes. This was the last directive issued in regard to the reserve battalion.

14. Personal discussion with Yuriy Rrokhmaliuk.

15. Following the war and a period as a prisoner-of-war, the former chaplain became a civilian clergy in Stryi and Corinthia, Austria. On 14 February 1970, following a serious illness, Reverend Kovaliuk passed away in Gratz, Austria. He was 74 years old.

The "Galicia" Division's Volunteers Within France's Maquis:

1. "Ukrains'kyi Partyzans'kyi Viddil Poruchnyka Osypa Krukovs'koho, 1944" [Lt. Osyp Krukovsky's Ukrainian Partisan Unit] in Myroslav Nebeliuk's, *Pid Chuzhymy Praporamy* [Under Foreign Flags], (Paris-Lyon: 1951), p. 197.

2. For further details on the exploits of Lt. Krukovsky, a "Galicia" Divisional soldier turned resistance and regular French Army soldier, see Nebeliuk's *Pid Chuzhymy Praporamy*, pp. 195-201. A photograph of Krukovsky, in a full French Army uniform, is seen on page 200. See also Gorbach's, "Infantry Regiments 4-8," *Visti*, 1993, No. 1, p. 89. According to Gorbach, Krukovsky commanded the Ukrainians who deserted to the Maquis.

3. Exactly what type of training was afforded is not known. But keeping in mind that the Ukrainians were conscripted to be utilized solely against "terrorists," a security type of training was undoubtedly provided.

4. Nebeliuk's observation that the Ukrainians were posted to the 30th Infantry Division's 1st Infantry Regiment appears to be erroneous. Although the possibility exists that the Germans initially planned to reinforce the 30th Infantry Division (which by 1944 had developed largely into a non-German division composed of Balts, Russians and even, Cossacks) with conscripted Ukrainians, in the end it is unlikely this was done. The 30th Division (a division which, since 1941, had fought on the eastern front), remained on the eastern front while the Ukrainians were dispatched to the west. Hence, the Ukrainians could not have entered the 30th. As well, a regimental study of the 30th reveals that it never contained a "1st" Regiment. Initially formed in 1935 around the German Army's 6th Infantry Regiment, the 30th's infantry was always centered around the divisions 6th, 26th, and 46th Infantry Regiments.

5. *Nebeliuk*, p. 116.

6. *Ibid.*

Galicia Division

7. Nebeliuk cites 18 September 1944, but other sources indicate that the Ukrainians actually arrived earlier.

8. *Nebeliuk*, pp. 116-117.

9. *Ibid.*

10. William Casey, *The Secret War Against Hitler* (Washington: Regnery Gateway, 1988), p. 173; *Nebeliuk*, p. 163; Gorbach, "Infantry Regiments 4-8," *Visti*, 1993, No. 1, p. 89.

11. Casey, *The Secret War Against Hitler*, p. 175. Various Ukrainian sources also substantiate this negotiation.

12. Casey, p. 175, does not cite an exact date, but cites August 1944 as the month of the revolt.

13. *Ibid.*, p. 175.

14. *Ibid.* Casey also stated that the Ukrainians wiped out the entire German cadre which accompanied them. Casey identified the cadre as an SS cadre.

15. Casey cites the Franco-Ukrainian force harassed the Nazis between Dijon and Besancon adjacent to the Confrancon forest for several weeks. (P. 176). Various Ukrainian sources verify this combat activity.

16. *Nebeliuk*, p. 164. As it turned out, Kuzmyk's parents hailed from Kremianen, a town from which a number of the revolting Ukrainians also hailed from. (Casey spells Kuzmyk's name as Kuzmuk).

17. *Casey*, p. 176. In the aftermath of the battle, Lt. Colonel Booth highly praised the Ukrainian heroism. (*Ibid.*).

18. "Franko-Ukrains'ka Manifestatsiia u Versel'" [The Franco-Ukrainian Manifestation in Versailles], *Visti*, 1985, Nr. 4, pp. 52-56. Regarding this manifestation, various articles appeared in French newspapers. For a photograph of the various French civilian and military officials and dignitaries honoring the event with Ukrainian dignitaries, see *Visti*, 1985, No. 4, p. 53.

19. *Casey*, pp. 176-177. According to Casey, it was General Patch's chief intelligence officer, Colonel William "Bill" Quinn, who saved the Ukrainians. He accomplished this by enrolling the Ukrainians into the French Foreign Legion. (P. 177). While Nebeliuk and various other Ukrainian sources acknowledge being incorporated into the French Foreign Legion, none provide details about how this was done. Casey provided the answer.

20. These charges were not only heralded by the Soviets, but as well as by their western sympathizers and supporters.

21 Indeed, the French-based Ukrainian soldiers behavior was so cordial in France that on 17 January 1944, during a meeting held by the Military Board, Yuriy Krokhmaliuk, in submitting a report pertaining to his travels in France, stated how one senior German officer remarked to Krokhmaliuk in France that "your Ukrainian soldiers behave more culturally with the French than us Germans." See *Minutes of the Meetings of the Military Board "Galicia."* Meeting held on 17 January 1944, p. 66.

Bibliography

Christopher Andrew and Oleg Gordievsky, *KGB: The Inside Story* (N.Y.: Harper Collins, 1990).

Mark Arons and John Loftus, *Unholy Trinity: The Vatican, The Nazis, and Soviet Intelligence* (N.Y.: St. Martin's Press, 1991).

John Armstrong, *Ukrainian Nationalism* (N.Y.: Columbia University Press, 1963), 2nd ea.; and (Colorado: Ukrainian Academic Press, 1990), 3rd ed.

Scott Anderson and Jon Lee Anderson, *Inside the League: The Shocking Expose of How Terrorists, Nazis, and Latin American Death Squads Have Infiltrated the World Anti-Communist League* (N.Y.: Dodd, Mead, and Co., 1986).

Army Magazine (May: 1968).

America (Ukrainian Catholic Newspaper), 12 November 1987.

Charles Ashman and Robert J. Wagman, *The Nazis Hunters: The Shocking True Story of the Continuing Search for Nazi Criminals* (N.Y.: Pharos Books, 1988).

Reuben Ainsztein, *The Warsaw Ghetto* (N.Y.: Holocaust Library, 1979).

Colonel Richard N. Armstrong, *Red Army Tank Commanders: The Armored Guards* (Pa.: Schiffer Publishing Co., 1996).

Stepan Baran, *Metropolitan Andrei Sheptytskyi* (Munich: Vernyhora Ukrains'ke Vydavnyche Tovarystvo, 1947).

Josef Buszko, *Historia Polski, 1864-1948* (Warezawa: Panstwowe Wydawnictwo Naukowe, 1984).

Stepan Bonsal, *Suitors and Supplicants: The Little Nations at Versailles* (N.Y.: Prentice-Hall, Inc., 1946).

Laddislav Bittman, *The KGB and Soviet Disinformation: An Insider's View* (International Defense Publishers, 1985).

Roger Bender and Hugh Page Taylor, *Uniforms, Organization and History of the Waffen-SS* (Ca.: Bender Publishing Co., 1975), Vol's 3-5.

Yaroslav Bilinsky, *The Second Soviet Republic: The Ukraine After World War II* (N.J.: Rutger's University Press, 1964).

Brigadier General Ignacy Blum, *Udzial Wojska Polskiego w Walce* o Utrawalenie Wladzy Lubowej: Walki z Bandami UPA (Wojskowy Przegald Historyczny, 1959), Vol. 4.

Athony C. Brown, *Bodyguards of Lies* (N.Y.: Harper and Row, 1975).

Captain John H. Buchsbaum, *German Psychological Warfare On the Russian Front, 1941-1945* (Washington, D.C.: 1953).

Alex Buchner, *Ostfront: The German Defensive Battles On the Russian Front 1944: Cherkasky, Ternopol, Crimea, Vitebsk, Brody, Bobruisk, Kischinev, Jassy* (Pa.: Schiffer Publishing Co., 1991).

Ashley Brown, *Modern Warfare, From 1939 to the Present Day* (N.Y.: Crescent Books, 1986).

A.J. Borkiewicz, *Powstanie Warazawkie 1944* (Warszawa, 1957).

V. Beliaiev and M. Rudnyts'kyi, *Pid Chuzhymy Praporamy* (Kiev: 1956).

Christopher Chant, *Hitler's Generals and Their Battles* (London: Salamander Books, Ltd., 1976).

Matthew Cooper, *The German Army, 1939-1945: Its Political and Military Failure* (N.Y.: Bonanza Books, 1984).

Alan Clark, *Barbarossa: The Russo-German Conflict, 1941-1945* (N.Y.: Quill Publishers, 1985).

Ferdinand Czerin, *Versailles 1919* (N.Y.: 1964).

William Chamberlain, *The Ukraine: A Submerged Nation* (N.Y.: MacMillan Co., 1944).

Joel Colton, *A History of the Modern World* (N.Y.: Alfred A. Knopf, Inc., 1978), 5th ed.

Richard Collier, *The War That Stalin Won* (Great Britain: Hamish Hamilton, Inc., 1983).

Jan M. Ciechanowski, *The Warsaw Rising of 1944* (Cambridge University Press, 1974).

Canadian Jewish News, 8 Octpber 1987.

John Campbell, ea., *The Experience of World War II* (N.Y.: Oxford University Press, 1989).

Duncan Crow, ed. *Armored Fighting Vehicles of Germany* (N.Y.: Arco Publishing Co., 1978).

Bibliography

Court Transcript of state of Israel vs. Ivan (John) Demjanjuk, 22 June 1987, Criminal Case No. 373/86.

Alexander Dallin, *German Rule In Russia* (London: MacMillan and Co., Ltd., 1957).

Dmytro Doroshenko, *A Survey of Ukrainian History* (Winnipeg, Canada: Trident Press, Ltd., 1975).

M.K. Dziewanowski, *Poland In the 20th Century* (N.Y.: Columbia University Press, 1977).

— , *Joseph Pilsudski: A European Federalist, 1918-1922* (Ca.: Hoover Institution Press, 1969).

Roman Dyboski, *Poland In World Civilization* (N.Y.: Barrett Corp., 1950).

O. Dotsenko, *Litopis Ukrains'koi Revoliutsii* (Lviv: 1924).

Ernest Dupuy and Colonel Trevor Dupuy, *The Encyclopedia of Military History* (N.Y: Harper and Row, 1970).

Len Deighton, *Blitzkreig: From the Rise of Hitler to the Fall of Dunkirk* (N.Y.: Ballantine Books, Inc., 1980).

O. Dans'kyi, *Khochu Zhyty! Obrasky z Nimets'kykh Kontsentratsiinykh Taboriv* (Munich: Ukrainian Publishers, 1946).

Colonel Trevor Dupuy, *European Resistance Movements* (N.Y.: Franklin Watts, Inc., 1965).

Marta Dmytrenko, *Mykhailyk* (Canada: Harmony Printing Ltd., 1981).

Myron Dolnyts'kyi, *Geografiia Ukrainu* (Detroit: 1953).

Colonel General David Dragunsky, *Pages From the Story of My Life: A Soldier's Memoirs* (Moscow: Progress Publishers, 1983).

I.F. Dremov, N*astupala Groznaia Bronia* (Kiev: Izdatel'stvo Politicheskoi Literaturi Ukraini, 1981).

Alexander Dallin, *The Kaminsky Brigade, 1941-44* (Cambridge, Mass.: Harvard University Russian Research Center, 1956).

Major Alojzy Dziura-Dziurski, *Freedom Fighter: A Saga of Fighting the Nazi and Communist Oppressions* (Australia: J.A. Dewar Publishers, 1983).

Pavlo Dorozynsky, ea., *The New Pathway. Almanac for 1994* (Ontario, Canada: New Pathway Publishers, Ltd., 1994).

Hans Dollinger, *The Decline and Fall of Nazi Germany and Imperial Japan* (N.Y.: Bonanza Books, 1967).

Francois Duprat, *Histoire Des SS* (Les Sept Couleurs, Paris, 1968).

John Erickson, *The Road to Stalingrad* (N.Y.: Harper and Row, 1975).

— , *The Road to Berlin: Continuing the History of Stalin's War With Germany* (Boulder, Colorado: Westview Press, 1983).

Galicia Division

Encyclopedia of Ukraine (Toronto University Press, 1988).

Ethnic groups of the South-Western Ukraine (Galicia) on the 1st of January, 1939 (London-Munich-Paris-New York Scientific Shevahenko Society, 1953).

Ekran (Ukrainian Magazine for Youth and Adults), January-April, 1978, No. 67-68.

Effects of Climate On Combat In European Russia (Washington, D.C.: U.S. Army Center of Military History, 1952), CMH Pub 1046.

Julius Epstein, *Operation Keelhaul: The Story of Forced Repatriation From 1944 to the Present* (Conn.: The Devin Co., 1973).

M.R.D. Foot, *Resistance: European Resistance to Nazism, 19401945* (N.Y.: McGraw Hill, 1977).

Ladislas Farago, *Burn After Reading* (Ca.: Pinnacle Books, 1978).

FM 22-100, Military Leadership (Washington, D.C.: 1983).

FM 17-95, Cavalry (Washington, D.C.: 1981).

FM 90-6, Mountain Operations (Washington, D.C. 30 i&~E 118°).

D.S.V. Fosten and R.J. Marrion, *Waffen SS. Its Uniforms, Insignia and Equipment, 1938-1945* (London: Altmark Publishing Co., 1972).

Will Fey, *Armor Battles of the Waffen-SS, 1943-45* (J.J. Fedorowicz Publishing Co., 1990).

George Forty, *Patton's Third Army At War* (N.Y.: Charles Scribner's & Sons, 1979).

German Crimes In Poland, 1939-1945 (N.Y.: Fertig Publishers, 1983), Vol. 1-3.

General Heinz Guderian, *Panzer Leader* (N.Y.: Ballantine Books, 1980).

Roland Gaucher, *Opposition In the USSR, 1917-1967* (N.Y.: Funk and Wagnall's, 1969).

Petro Grigorenko, *Grigorenko Memoirs* (N.Y.:-W.W. Norton and Company, 1982).

Josef A. Gierowski, *Historia Polski, 1764-1864* (Warszawa: Panstwowe Wydawnictwo Naukowe, 1984).

Thaddeus V. Gromada, ea., *Essays On Poland's Foreign Policy, 1918-1939* (N.Y.: Pilsudski Institute of America, 1970).

Herbert A. Gibbons, *Europe Since 1918* (London: Jonathan Cape, 1923).

Jan T. Gross, *Revolution From Abroad: The Soviet Conquest of Poland's Western Ukraine and Byelorussia* (N.J.: Princeton University Press, 1988).

Irena and Jan Gross, *War Through Children's Eyes, The Soviet Occupation of Poland and the Deportations, 1939-1941* (Hoover Institution Press, 1981).

General Roman Shukhevych (N.Y.: Published by the OUN, 1966).

Bibliography

Walter Gerlitz, *History of the German General Staff, 1657-1945* (N.Y.: Praeger, 1961).

John A. Garraty, *The American Nation: A History of the United States Since 1865* (N.Y.: Standard Publishing Co., Inc., 1959).

Yaroslav Gallan, *Tvory u Tr'okh Tomakh* (Kiev: Derzhavne Vydavnytstvo Ukrainy, 1960, Vol. 2.

Ian Grey, *Stalin: Man of History* (N.Y.: Doubleday and Company, 1979).

Robert Goralski, *World War II Almanac, 1939-1945* (N.Y.: Putnam's Sons, 1981).

Simon Goodenough, *War Maps: World War II. From September 1939 to August 1945, Air, Sea, and Land, Battle By Battle* (N.Y.: St. Martin's Press, 1982).

German Anti-Guerrilla Operations In the Balkans (1941-1944) (Washington, D.C.: U.S. Army Center of Military History, 1989),
CMH Pub 104-187.

Felix Gilbert, *Hitler Directs His War* (N.Y.: 1950).

Colonel M. Glantz, *The Role of Intelligence In Soviet Strategy in World War II* (Ca.: Presidio Press, 1990).

Heinz Höhne, *The Order of the Death's Head* (N.Y.: Balantine Books, 1971).

Edward House and Charles Seymour, *What Really Happened at Paris:*
The Story of the Peace Conference (N.Y.: Charles Scribner Sons, 1921).

Stepan Horak, *Poland and Her National Minorities, 1919-1939* (N.Y.: Vantage Press, 1961).

Ronald Hingley, *The Russian Secret Police* (N.Y.: Simon and Schuster, 1970).

F.H. Hinsley, *British Intelligence In the Second World War: Its Influence on Strategy and Operations* (Cambridge University Press, 1988), Vol. 3.

Roman Hayetskyj, Yaroslav Zakaliak, Antin Tymkevych, Evhen Shypailo, *1943-1993. The 1st Ukrainian Division, 50 Years* (N.J.: Computorprint, 1993).

Wolf-Dietrich Heike, *Sie Wolten Die Freiheit. Die Geschichte der Ukrainischen Division 1943-45.* (German ed.).

— , *The Ukrainian Division t.Galicial: The History of Its Formation and Military Operations, 1943-1945* (Toronto: Kiev Printers, Ltd., 1970). (Ukrainian ed.).

— , *The Ukrainian Division 'IGalicia,ll 1943-1945, A Memoir* (Toronto-Paris,Munich: The Shevchenko Scientific Society, 1988). (English ed.).

Handbook On German Military Forces, TM-E30-451 (Washington, D.C.: War Department, 15 March 1945).

Volodymyr Hrytsiuk, *Osyni Hnizda. Trydiashchi Tavruiutl Hanlboiu Ukrainslkykh Burzhuaznykh Natsionalistiv.*

Richard Holmes, *Firing Line* (London: Butler and Tanner, Ltd., 1985).

Galicia Division

B.H. Liddell Hart, *History of the Second World War* (N.Y.: Putnam's Sons, 1970).

— , *The Red Army: 1918-1945; The Soviet Army, 1946 to the Present* (N.Y.: Harcourt, Brace and Co., 1956).

Gordon A. Harrison, *Cross-Channel Attack, the United States Army In World War II, the European Theater of Operations* (Washington, D.C.: Center of Military History, U.S. Army, 1951).

Illustrated World War II Encyclopedia (H.S. Struttman, Inc., 1990) .

Myhailo Il'kiv, *Nimets'ki Kontsentratsiini Lagery (Spohad)* (Canada: Harmony Printing Ltd., 1983).

Istoriia Velikoi Otechestvenoi Voine Sovetskogo Soiuza 19411945 (Moscow: 1960-1963), Vol. 4. David Irving, *Hitler's War* (N.Y.: Viking Press, 1977).

Istoriia Mist i Sil' Ukrains'koi RSR, L'vivs'ka Oblast (Kiev Holovna Redaktsiia Ukrains'koi Radians lkoi Entsyklopedii, 1968).

George Iranek-Osmecki, *The Unseen and the Silent: Adventures From the Underground Movement Narrated by Paratroops of the Polish Home Army* (N.Y.: Sheed and Ward, 1954).

Mieczyslaw Juchniewicz, *Polacy w. radzieckim ruchu podziemoym i partyzanckim 1941-1945* (Warsaw: Ministerstwo Obrony Narodowej, 1973).

— , *z dzia alnosci organizacyjnobowej Gwardi Ludowej w Obwodzie lwowskim* (Wojskowy przeglad historyczny, 1968).

John Keegan, *The Waffen-SS* (N.Y.: Ballantine Bppks, Inc., 1970).

Woolodymyr Kozyk, *The Third Reich and the Ukrainian question: 1934-1944* (London, 1991).

Jan Kozik, *The Ukrainian National Movement In Galicia: 18151849* (Canada: University of Alberta, 1986).

Robert Kee, *1939: In the Shadow of War* (Boston: Little, Brown and Co., 1984).

Volodymyr Kubiyovych, *Ukraine: A Concise Encyclopedia* (Toronto: University of Toronto Press, 1963).

John Kolasky, ed. *Ukraine and the Subjugated Nations: Their Struggle for National Liberation (Selected Writings and Speeches by Former Prime Minister of Ukraine)* (N.Y.: Philosophical Library, Inc., 1989).

Nikita Khruschev, *Khruschev Remembers* (Boston: Little, Brown and Co., 1970).

John Kolasky, *The Shattered Illusion: The History of Ukrainian Pro-Communist Organizations in Canada* (Canada: Peter Martin, Ltd., 1979).

Peter Kleist, *Zwischen Hitler und Stalin* (Bonn: 1950).

Roman Kolisnyk, *The Ukrainian Division "Galicia" and Its Military board: Work and Responsibilities of the Military Board I' Galiciall and the German Po-*

Bibliography

litical Attitudes Regarding the Ukrainian armed Forces In 1943-1945 (Canada: Shevehenko Scientific Society, 1990) .

Roman Krokhmaliuk, the Glow In Eastern Europe (Toronto: Kiev Printers Ltd., 1978).

Volodymyr Kubiyovych, Ukraintsi v Henerallnii jubernii, 19391944. Istoriia Ukrainslkoi Tsentralnoi Komitii (Chicago: 1975).

Volodymyr Kubiyovych and Zenon Kuzeli, Entsyklopedia Ukrainoznavstva v Dvokh Tomakh (Munich-New York, 1949), Vol. 1-2.

K.G. Klietman, Die Waffen-SS: Eine Dokumentation (Osnabruck, 1965).

Hans von Krannhals, Der Warschauer Aufstand 1944 (Frankfurt Am Main, 1962).

Anatoly Kuznetzov, Babi Yar: A Documentary Novel (N.Y.: Dell Press, 1967).

I.S. Konev, Zapiski Komanduiushchego Frontom 1943-1945 (Kiev: Izdatellstvo politicheskoi literaturli Ukrainli, 1987).

11 11 I', Year of Victory (Moscow: Progress Publishers, 1969).

Walter Keer, The Secret of Stalingrad (N.Y.: Doubleday and Company, Inc., 1978).

Colonel General G.F. Krivosheev, Grif Sekretnosti Sniat. Poteri Vooruzhennlikh Sil SSSR v Voinakh, Boevlikh Deistviiakh i Voennlikh Konfliktakh (Moscow: Voennoe Izdatellstvo, 1993).

Reverend Stepan Kleparczuk, Dorohamy i Stezhkamy Bridshchyny. Spomyny (Toronto, Canada: Kiev printerls Ltd., 1971).

G. Krivokhizhin, Zvezdli Soldatskoi Slavli (Kiev: Izdatellstvo Tsk Lksmu "Molog'", 1980).

Jersy Kirchmayer, Powstanie Warszawskie (Spoldzielnia Wydawnicza t'Czytelnikll Luty, 1946).

Stefan Korbonski, Fighting Warsaw: The Story of the Polish Underground State, 1939-1945 (Mass.: Harvard University Press, 1956).

General T. Bor-Komorowski, The Secret Army (N.Y.: MacMillan Co., 1951).

John Keegan, The Second World War (N.Y.: Viking Press, 1990).

Colonel Zdravko Klanjscek, ed. Narodnoosvobodilna Vojna Na Slovenskem 1941-1945 (Ljublana, 1977).

Ihor Kamenetsky, Hitlerls Occupation of Ukraine, 1941-44; A Study of Totalitarian Imperialism (Milwaukee: The Marquette University Press, 1956).

James Lucas and Matthew Cooper, Hitler's Elite: Leibstandarte SS (London: MacDonald and Jane's Co., Ltd., 1975).

Hans von Luck, Panzer Commander: The Memoirs of Hans von Luck (N.Y.: Praeger, 1989).

Galicia Division

Raphael Lemkin, *Axis Rule In Occupied Europe. Laws of Occuation/Analysis of Government/Proposals For Redress* (Washington, D.C., 1944).

Kay Lundgreen-Nielsen, *The Polish Problem At the Paris Peace Conference; A Study of the Policies of the Great Poweras and the Poles, 1918-1919* (Odense University Press, 1979).

Jiri Louda, *European Civic Coats of Arms* (London: Paul Hamlyn, Ltd., 1966).

Boris Levytsky, *The Uses of Terror: The Soviet Secret Police, 1917-1970* (N.Y.: Coward, McCann and Geoghegan, Inc., 1972).

Paul Leverkuehn, *German Intelligence* (N.Y.: Weidefeld and Nicholson, 1954).

Lubomyr Y. Luciuk and Bohdan S. Kordan, *Anglo-American Perspectives On the Ukrainian Question, 1938-1951 (A Documentary Collection)* (N.Y.: Limestone Press, 1987).

David Littlejohn, *The Patriotic Traitors: The History of Collaboration In German-Occupied Europe, 1940-45* (N.Y.: Doubleday and Co., Inc., 1972).

James Lucas, *The Last Year of the German Army. May 1944-May 1945* (London: Arms and Armour Press, 1994).

Henri Landemer, *La Waffen-SS* (Ballard Press, 1972).

Francis L. Lowennheim, ed. *Roosevelt and Churchill, Their Secret Wartime Correspondence* (N.Y.: E.P. Dutton and CO., Inc., 1975) .

Graham Lyons, ea., *The Russian Version of the Second World War* (N.Y.: Facts on File, Inc., 1976).

Oleh Lysiak, *Brody, Zbirnyk Stattei i Naryciv* (Munich: 1951). (Reprinted 1974) (N.J: Computorprint).

Sybil Milton, *The Stroop Report: The Jewish Quarter of Warsaw Is No More!* (N.Y.:Pantheon Books, 1979) .

General Walter Lange, *Korpsabteilung* C (Vowinckel, Neckargemund: 1961)

Jerzy Lovell, *Polska jakiej nie znamy i zbior reportazy o miejszosciach narodowych* (Krakow, 1970) .

James Lucas, *Storming Eagles: German Airborne Forces In World War II* (England, 1 988) .

Jeremy Noakes and Geoffrey Pridham, ed's., *Nazism: A History in Documents and Eyewitness Accounts, 1919-1945* (N.Y.: Schocken Books, 1 984) .

Clarence Manning, *Twentieth Century Ukraine* (N.Y.: Bookman Associates, 1951) .

Arnold Margolin, *From A Political Diary: Russia, Ukraine, and America, 1905-1945* (N.Y.: Columbia University Press, 1946).

James Lucas, *War On the Eastern Front, 1941-1945. The German Soldier in Russia* (N.Y.: Bananza Books, 1979).

Bibliography

Petro Mirchuk, *Revoliutsiinyi Zmah Za UCCD* (New York- TorontoLondon, 1981), Vol. II.

— , *Roman Shukhevych: Commander of the Army of Immortals* (London: Ukrainian Publishers, Ltd., 1970).

Military Improvisations During the Russian Campaign, CMH Pub 104-1 (Washington, D.C., 1983. Reprinted 1986).

Roger Manvell and Heinrich Frankel, *Himmler* (N.Y.: Putnam's and Sons, 1965).

Samuel Mitcham, Jr., *Hitler's Legions: The German Army Order of Battle, World War II* (N.Y.: Dorset Press, 1987).

Paul Robert Magocsi, ea., *Morality and Reality: The Life and Times of Andrei Sheptytskyi* (Canadian Institute of Ukrainian Studies, 1989).

Victor Madej, *The German Army Order of Battle: The Replacement Army, 1939-1945* (Penn.: Game Publishing Co., 1984).

— , *German Army Order of Battle: Field Army and Officer Corps, 1939-1945* (Penn.: Game Publishing Co., 1985).

— , *Hitler's Elite Guards: Waffen-SS, Parachutists, U-Boats* (Penn.: Game Publishing Co., 1985).

— , *Russo-German War: Summer 1944 (Destruction of the Eastern Front)* (Pa.: Valor Publishing Co., 1987).

— , *Russo-German War: Autumn 1944-25 January 1945* (Penn.: Valor Publishing Co., 1987).

— , *The Russo-German War: 25 January to 8 May 1945* (Pa.: Valor Publishing Co., 1987).

D. Medvedev, *Sillnye Dukhom* (Kiev: 1963).

Marshall Zhukov: An Outstanding Military Leader (Moscow: Planeta Publishers, 1987).

F.W. von Mellenthin, *Panzer Battles* (University of Oklahoma Press, 1955).

Burkhart Mueller-Hillebrand, *Germany and Its Allies In World War II: A Record of Axis Collaboration Problems* (Maryland: University of Publications of America, 1980).

Alexander McKee, *Last Round Against Rommel; Battle of the Normandy Beachhead* (N.Y.: Signet Books, 1966).

Marshall of the Soviet Union, ZhuXov: Reminiscences and Reflections (Moscow: Progress Publishers, 1985), Vol. 1-2.

Major General V.A. Matsulenko, A.A. Beketov, A.P. Belokon, and S.G. Chermashentsev, *Camouflage, Operational Camouflage of the Troops, Camouflage of Actions by Ground Force Subunits, A Soviet View* (Translated by U.S. Air Force, 1976).

Colonel Vasily P. Morozov and Captain Aleksey V. Basov, *The Soviet Art of War* (N Y Praeger Co , 1982)

Nazi Crimes In Ukraine, 1941-1945: Documents and Materials (Kiev: Naukova Dumka Publishers, 1987).

Helmut Kraus-Nick, Hans Buchheim, Martin Broszat, Hans-Adolf Jacobsen, *Anatomy of the SS State* (N.Y.: Walker and Co., 1965).

Myroslav Sydir Nebeliuk, *Pid Chuzhymy Praporamy* (Paris-Lyon: 1951).

Reverend Sydir Nahayewsky, *A Soldier Priest Remembers* (Toronto: Ukrainian Book Co., 1985).

Steven H. Newton, *German Battle Tactics On the Russian Front, 1941-1945* (Pa.: Schiffer Publishing Co., 1994).

Franklin Mark Osanka, ea., *Modern Guerrilla Warfare* (N.Y.: Glencoe Free Press, 1967).

Order of Battle of the German Army, April 1943 (Washington, D.C.: U.S. Military Intelligence Service, April 1943).

Order of Batle of the German Army, 1944 (Washington, D.C.: U.S. Military Intelligence Service, 1944). Republished by Hippocrene Books, N.Y.: 1975).

Order of Battle of the German Army, 1945 (Washington, D.C.: U.S. Military Intelligence Service, 1945).

Liubomyr Ortyns'kyi, *Brody 1944-1964* (N.Y.: East Side Press, 1964).

Janusz Piekalkiewicz, *Moscow: 1941. The Frozen Offensive* (London, England: Arms and Armour Press, 1985).

Papers Relating to the Foreign Relations of the United States: 1918, Supplement I, The World War (Washington, D.C.: Government Printing Office, 1933).

Anthony Polansky, *Politics In Independent Poland, 1921-1939* (Oxford: Clarendon Press, 1972).

Colonel Evhen Pobihushchyj-Ren, *MY Life's Mosaic* (London: Association of Former Ukrainian Combatants in Great Britain, 1982).

Kost Pankiwsky, *Roky Nimets'koi Okupatsii 1941-44* (East Side Press, 1965).

P.M. Portugal 'skii, *Marshal I,S. Konev* (Moscow: Voyenizdat, 1985).

Robert G. Poirier and Albert Z. Conner, *The Red Army Order of Battle in the Great Patriotic War* (Ca.: Presidio Press, 1985).

Polskie Sily Zbrojne w Druciej Wojnie Swiatowej - Tom II, Armia Krajowa (Komisja Historyczna Polskiego Sztabu Glownego w Londynie) (London: Polish Historical Institute General Sikorsky).

Edward Prus, *Z Dziejow Wspolpracy Nacjonalistow Ukrainskich z Niemcam i w Okresie II Wotny Swiatowej i Okupacji (Katowice: Akademia Ekonomicza Im. Karola Adamirckiego, 1985).*

Bibliography

Poryv: Pravda Pro Pershu Ukrains'ku Dyviziiu "Halychyna" (UNA) (Lviv: 1994).

Bruce Quarrie, *Hitler's Samurai: The Waffen-SS in Action* (England: Patrick Stevens, Ltd., 1986).

— , *Weapons of the Waffen-SS. From small arms to tanks* (Patrick Stevens, Ltd., 1988).

Gerald Reitlinger, *The House Built on Sand: The Conflicts of German Policy in Russia, 1939-1945* (N.Y.: Viking Press, 1960).

— , *The SS: Alibi Of a Nation, 1922-1945* (N.Y.: DaCapo Press, Inc., 1989).

Anthony Reed and David Fischer, *The Deadly Embrace: Hitler, Stalin, and the Nazi-Soviet Pact, 1939-1941* (N.Y.: Norton and Company, 1988).

John S. Reshetar, *The Ukrainian Revolution, 1917-1920* (N.Y.: Arno Press, 1972).

J. Lee Ready, *The Forgotten Axis: Germany's Partners and Foreign Volunteers in World War II* (N.C. McFarland and Co., Inc., 1987).

Russian Combat Methods In World War II (Washington, D.C.: U.S. Army Center of Military History, CMH Pub 104-12, 1950).

Nicholas Riasanovsky, *A History of Russia* (N.Y.: Oxford University Press, 1973).

Milena Rydnytski, ea., *Western Ukraine Under the Bolshevik's 1939-41* (Shevchenko Scientific Society, 1958).

Radians 'ka Entsyklopediia Istorii Ukrainy (Holovna Redakstiia Ukrains'koi Radians 'koi Entsyklopedii, 1970), Vol. II.

Stewart Richardson, *The Secret History of World War II* (N.Y.: Richardson and Steirman, 1986).

Emmanuel Ringelbaum, *Notes From the Warsaw Ghetto: The Journal of Emmanuel Ringelbaum* (N.Y.: McGraw Hill, 1958).

Russian Daily News (Published in New York City, 11 October 1991).

Radians 'ka Entsyklopediia Istorii Ukrainy (Kiev: 1969), Vol. II.

Marshal Konstantin Rokossovsky, *Battle's Hitler Lost and the Soviet Marshals Who Won Them* (N.Y.: Jove Books, 1988).

— , *Voennye Memiaru: Soldatskii Dolg* (Moscow: Voenizdat, 1972).

General Ernst Rebentisch, *Zum Xaukasus und Zu Den Tauern, Die Geschichte der 23. Panzer-Division 1941-1945* (Germany: 1963).

George H. Stein, *The Waffen SS, Hitler's Elite Guard at War, 1939-45* (N.Y.: Cornell University Press, 1966).

Colonel Albert Seaton, *The Battle for Moscow* (N.Y.: Playboy Press, 1980).

Charles Sydnor, Jr., *Soldiers of Destruction: The SS Death's Head Division, 1933-1945* (N.J.: Princeton University Press, 1990) .

Galicia Division

Colonel Albert Seaton, *The Fall of Fortress Europe, 1943-1945* (N.Y.: Holmes and Meier Publishers, Inc., 1981).

William Shirer, *The Rise and Fall of the Third Reich* (N.Y.: Simon and Schuster, 1960).

Svoboda, Ukrainian Daily, 14 November 1979.

Stewart Steven, *The Poles* (N.Y.: MacMillan Publishing Co., Inc., 1982).

Orest Subtelny, *Ukraine: A History* (Toronto: University of Toronto Press, 1988).

Olena Stepaniv, *Suchasnyi Lviv v 700 Littia Zasnovannia Mista L'vova* (Howerla Publishers, 1953).

Raymond J. Sontag, *A Broken World, 1919-1939* (N.Y.: Harper and Row, 1971).

Sherman D. Spector, *Rumanian At the Paris Peace Conference: A Study of the Diplomacy of Ioan I.C. Bratianu* (N.Y.: Bookman Associates, 1962).

Wladyslaw Studnicki, *Das Oestliche Polen* (Gottingen, 1953).

Boris Shub and Bernard Quint, *Since Stalin: A Photo History of Our Time* (N.Y.: Swen Publications, Inc., 1951).

Alexander Solzhenitsyn, *The Gulag Archipelago, 1918-1956* (N.Y.: Harper and Row, Publishers, 1973).

Karlo Stajner, *Seven Thousand Days in Siberia* (N.Y.: Farrar, Strauss and Giroux, Inc., 1988).

V. Styrkul, *The SS Werewolves* (Lviv: Kamenyar Publishers, 1982).

— , *We Accuse* (Kiev: Dnipro Publishers, 1984).

General Sergei M. Shtemenko, *The Soviet General Staff At War* (Moscow: Progress Publishers, 1985).

Major General K.V. Sychev and Colonel M.M. Malakov, *Nastuplenie 15-vo Strelkovogo Korpusa s Pror'ivom Podgotovlennoi Oboronti Protyvnika Strelkovogo s Pror'ivom Podgotovlennoi Oboron'i Protyvnika Ivzhnee Brodi (14-22 iiulia 144 g)* (Moscow: Voyenizdat, 1958).

Jost W. Schneider, *Their Honor Was Loyalty! An Illustrated and Documentary History of the Knight's Cross Holder of the Waffen-SS and Police, 1940-1945* (Ca.: R. James Bender Publishing, 1977).

Stosunki Polsko-Ukrainskie 1917-1947. Od Tragedii Do Wspolpracy (Wydawnictwo "Perturbancii, 1990).

Russ Schneider, *Maddness without End. Tales of Horror From the Russian Wilderness, 1941-1945* (Germany: Neue Paradies Verlag, 1994).

Peter Strassner, *European Volunteers: 5th SS Panzer Division "Wiking"* (Canada: J.J. Fedorowicz Publishing Co., 1988).

General S.M. Shtemenko, *The Last Six Months: The First Authentic Account*

Bibliography

of Russia's Final Battles With Hitler's Armies In World War II (N.Y.: Doubleday and Company, Inc., 1977).

General Pavlo Shandruk, *Arms of Valor* (N.Y.: Speller Publishing Co., 1959).

Shelby L. Stanton's, *Order-of-Battle: U.S. Army World War II* (Ca.: Presidio Press, 1984).

The International Military Tribunal: Trial of the Major War Criminals: Proceedinqs of the International Military Tribunal Sitting at Nuremberg, Germany (Germany, 1948).

H.W.V. Temperley, ea., *A History of the Peace Conference of Paris* (London: 1920).

Arnold Toynbee, *The Eve of War, 1939* (London: Oxford University Press, 1958).

John Toland, *Adolf Hitler* (N.Y.: Doubleday and Co., Inc., 1976).

Danylo Tshaikovsky, *Liudyna, Boret', Providnyk* (N.Y.: 1970).

T.R.V. Toynbee's, ea., *Survey of International Affairs: Hitler's Europe 1939-45* (Oxford University Press, 1954).

Yuriy Tus-Krokhmaliuk, *UPA Warfare IN Ukraine: Strategical, Tactical and Organizational Problems of Ukrainian Resistance in World War II* (N.Y.: Vantage Press, 1972).

Marko Terlytsia, *Pravnyky Pohani. Ukrains'ki Natsionalisty v Kanadi* (Kiev: Radians 'kyi Pys'mennuk, 1960).

Jurgen Thorwald, *The Illusion: Soviet Soldier's In Hitler's Armies* (N.Y.: Harcourt, Brace, and Jovanovich, 1975).

Terrain Factors In the Russian Campaign (Washington, D.C.: Center of Military History, 1982. Reprinted 1986). CMH Publication 104-5.

The German Replacement Army (Ersatzheer) February, 1945 (Washington, D.C.: Military Intelligence Division, War Department, February 1945).

V. Tatars'kyi, *Pid Chotyrma Praporamy* (Munich: Buchdruckerei u. Verlag, 1983).

The Warsaw Insurrection: The Communist Version Versus the Facts (Washington, D.C.: U.S. Government Printing Office, 1969).

The Kersten Memoirs, 1940-1945 (N.Y.: The MacMillan Co., 1957).

Nikolai Tolstoy, *The Secret Betrayal: 1944-1947* (N.Y.: Charles Scribner's Son's, 1977).

— , *Victim's of Yalta* (London: Hoddler and Stoughton, 1977).

U.S. Army Intelligence (G-2) Summary for 28 May 1937 (Unclassified), Washington, D.C.

Ukrains'ka RSR u Velykii Vitchyznianii Viini Radians 'koho Soinzu, 1941-1945 (Kiev: Vydavnytstvo Politychnoi Literatury Ukrainy, 1968), Vol. II.

Galicia Division

Adam B. Ulam *Expansion and Coexistence: The History of Soviet Foreign Policy, 1917-67* (N.Y.: Friedrich A. Praeger, 1968).

Vasyl Veryha, *Along the Roads of World Warr II, Legends of Ukrainian Participation In the Warsaw Uprising of 1944 and the Ukrainian Division "Galicia"* (Toronto: New Pathway Publishers, 1980).

— , *Losses of the Organization of Ukrainian Nationalists During the Second World War* (Canada: New Pathway Publishers, 1991).

Colonel General Dmitri Volkogonov, *Stalin: Triumph and Tragedy. (The First Glasnost Biography)* (N.Y.: Grove Weidenfeld, 1991).

Velikaia Otechestvennaia Voina 19412-1945 v Fotografiiakh i Kinogo Kuteltakh, 1944 (Moscow: Planeta 1979).

I.G. Viktorov, et. al, *SSSR v Velikoi Otechestvennoi Voine 19411945* (Moscow: Voennoe Izdatel'stvo Ministerstva Oboron'i SSSR 1970).

Piotr S. Wandycz, *The [ends of Partioned Poland, 1795-1918* (Seatle and london: University of Washington Press, 1974).

Richard M. Watt, *Bitter Glory: Poland and Its Fate, 1918-1939* (N.Y.: Simon and Schuster, 1982).

Martin Windrow, *The Waffen-SS (Revised Edition)* (England: Osprey Publishing Ltd., 1985).

Alexander Werth, *Russia At War* (N.Y.: E.P. Dutton., 1964).

World War II: A 50th Anniversary History (N.Y.: Holt and Co., 1989).

Robert Wistrich, *Who's Who In Nazi Germany* (N.Y.: Bonanza Books, 1982).

Gordon Williamson, *SS: The Blood-Soaked Soil. The Battles of the Waffen-SS* (Osceola, WI.: Motorbooks International Publishers, 1995).

J.K. Wroniszewski, *Ochota 1944* (Warszawa: Wydanictwo Ministerstwa Obrony narodowej, 1970).

Wielka Encyklopedia Powszechna PWN (Warszawa: Panstwowe Wydawnictwo Naukowe, 1966), No. 7 (Man-Nom)).

Finn Wigforss, *The Face of War: Drawings From the Eastern Front* (Norway, Oslo: 1981).

Charles Whiting's, *Hitler's Werewolves: A Spellbinding Saga of Secrecy and Sabotage* (N.Y.: Jove Publications, 1983).

Michael Yaremko, *Galicia-Halychyna, A Part of Ukraine From Separation to Unity* (Toronto-New York-Paris: Shevchenko Scientific Society, 1967).

Brigadier General Young, ed. *Atlas of the Second World War* (London: Widenfeld and Nicholson, 1973).

Earl F. Ziemke and Magna E. Baur, *Moscow to Stalingrad: Decision In the East* (Washington, D.C.: 1987).

Bibliography

Earl F. Ziemke, *Stalingrad to Berlin: The German Defeat in the East* (Washington, D.C.: Government Printing Office, U.S. Army Historical Series, 1971).

1944 (Ca.: Hoover Institution, 1978).

Periodicals, Magazines, Journals, Newspapers:

Visti Kombatanta (N.J.: New Jersey).

Soviet Military Review (Moscow: Krasnaya Zvesda Publishing House).

Military Historical Journal (Moscow).

Military Review (Ft. Leavenworth, Kansas).

Canadian Jewish News, 8 October, 1987.

YIVO: Annual of Jewish Social Science (N.Y.: 1958-59).

World War II Investigator (London, England: 1989),Vol. 1, No. 10.

Strategy and Tactics Magazine (Wisconsin: Dragon Publishing Co., 1986), Nr. 107, May-June 1986.

Svoboda, Ukrainian Daily (N.J.: Svoboda Press).

Almanac of the Ukrainian National Association (N.J.: Svoboda Press).

The Patriarchate (N.Y.: Meta Publishing Co., January, 1989).

Russian Daily News, 11 October 1991.

Suchasnist (Munich).

The New Pathway. Almanac For 1994 (Canada: New Pathway Publishers, Ltd.: 1994.

Index

Index

Index

Index

Rembalovych, Ivan 145
Remberger, Josef 117
Ren, Evhen 95, 282
Ribbentrop, Joachim von 26
Ritter von Leeb 23
Rodal, Alti 95
Rokossovsky, Konstantin 284
Rommel, Erwin 399
Roosevelt, Franklin 60
Roques, Franz von 27
Rosenberg, Alfred 27
Rudnyk, Vasyl 98
Rudnyts'kyi, M. 274
Rudolf Brandt 53
Rukh, Theodore 255
Rundstedt, Gerd von 23
Rusyk, Stanislav 280
Rydzinski, Alexander 274

S

Sachkivsky, Dmytro 98
Sadovych, Dmytro 280
Salaniak, Omelian 288
Salanyk, Fedir 232
Saprun, Severyn 125
Schimana, Walter 103, 114, 127
Schkira, Mykola 280
Schmitt, Helmut 122
Schneider, Heinrich 152
Schultze, Karl 155
Schutetzenhofer, Alfred 115
Sdydunski, Wladyslaw 274
Seaton, Albert 185
Semen Budenny 36
Semenyk, Bohan 97
Senedeckyi, tanislav 280

Seniv, Bohdan 271
Serkez, Roman 271
Shandruk, Pavlo 350
Shankowsky, Lev 47
Sheptytsky, Andrei 88
Sheptytsky, Clement 89
Shuhan, Stefan 120
Shukhevych, Roman 44, 49, 64, 236
Simon Petliura 36
Sirs'kyi, Vasyl 97, 110
Skakal's'kyi, Job 325
Skobelsky, Petro 268
Skorobohatyi, Roman 171
Skorzeny, Otto 46
Slavutych, Iar 140
Slipak, olodymyr 280
Slozhuk, Ivan 410
Smerenko, Leo 189
Smyl, Yaroslav 209
Sokolovskiy, Vasiliy D. 183
Solomko, Myhailo 98
Soroka, Vasyl 222
Sparsam, Guenther 193
Specht, Maximillian 122
Stetsiuk, Volodymyr
    90, 191, 217, 225
Stetsko, Yaroslav 41
Strasser, Karl 120
Striddle, Gerhard 122
Styrkul, Valery 274
Sulzbach, Otto 123
Sumarokiv, Petro 202
Swarych, Bohdan 280
Sydorenko, Mykola 410
Sylenko, Porfiri 280
Sylenko, Porfirii 231

Index

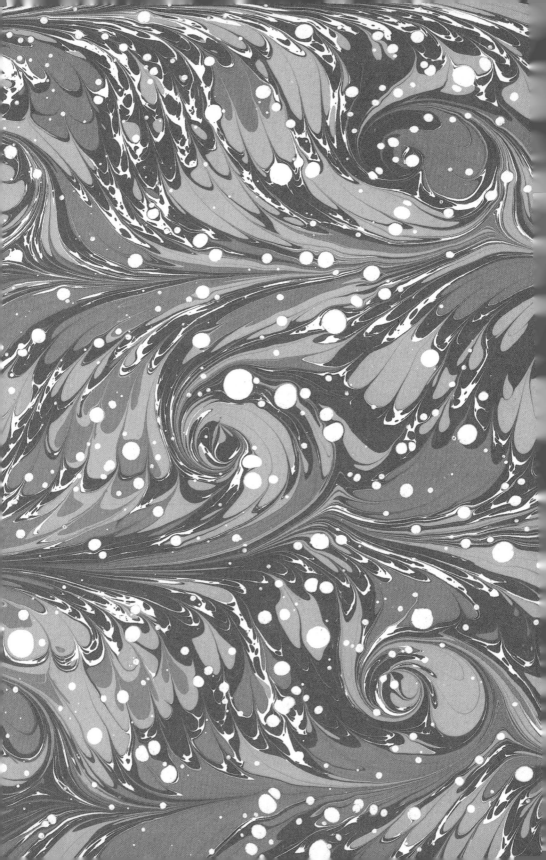